# THE PHOENIX COLOSSAL COMICS COLLECTION

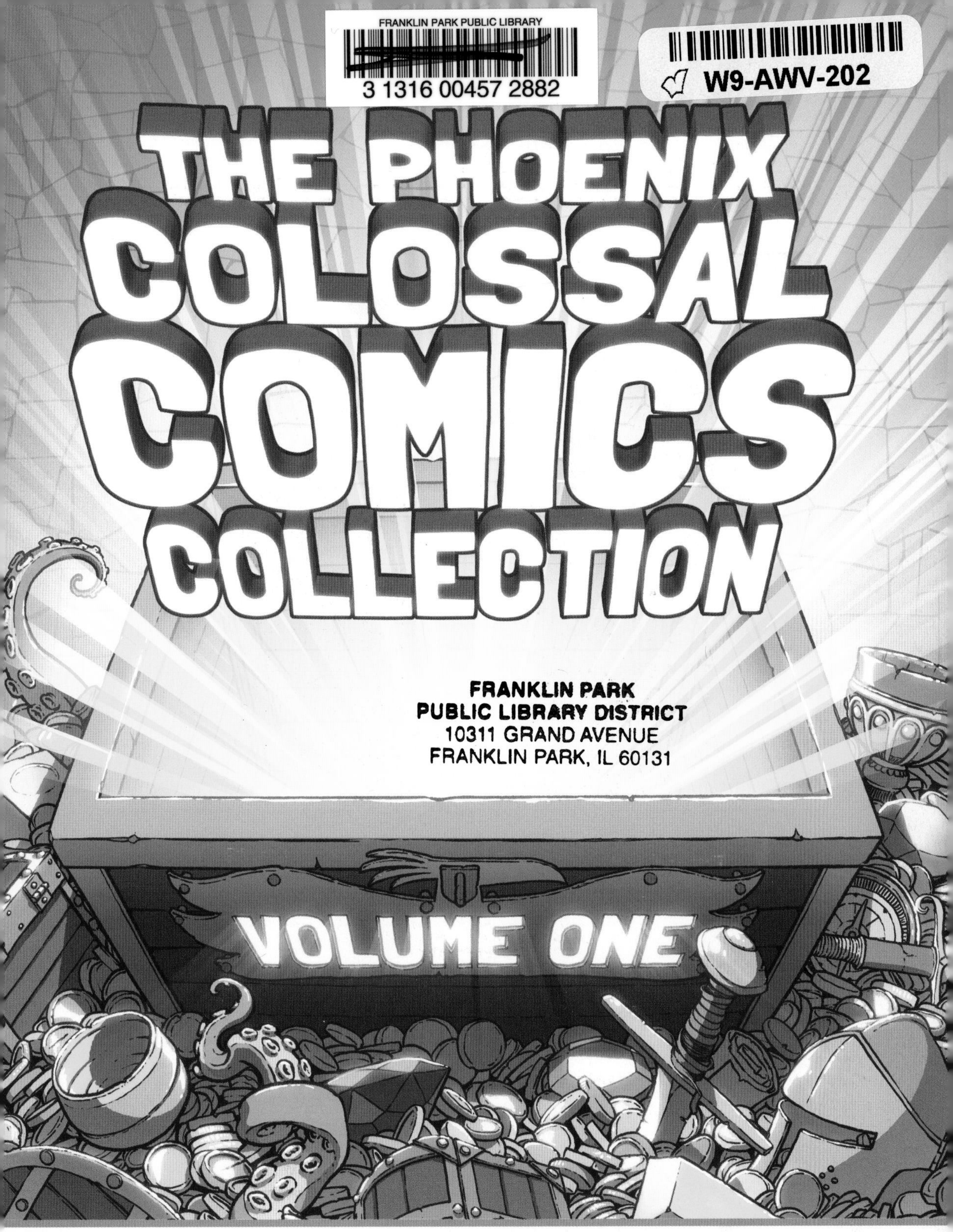

## VOLUME ONE

FICKLING
dfb
David Fickling Books
the PHOENIX
SCHOLASTIC

Trailblazers (originally published as Troy Trailblazer) © 2018 Robert Deas
Bunny vs. Monkey © 2018 Jamie Smart
Evil Emperor Penguin © 2018 Laura Ellen Anderson
Squid Squad © 2018 Dan Boultwood
Looshkin © 2018 Jamie Smart
Squid Bits © 2018 Jess Bradley
Elsewhere... © 2018 Chris Riddell
The Phoenix Phictionary © 2018 Mike Smith
All other text and illustrations copyright © 2018 by David Fickling Comics Ltd

First published in the United Kingdom as comic book issues by
The Phoenix Comic, 29 Beaumont Street, Oxford OX1 2NP.

The publisher does not have any control over and does not assume any responsibility for
author or third-party websites or their content.

This book is a work of fiction. Names, characters, places, and incidents
are either the product of the author's imagination or are used fictitiously,
and any resemblance to actual persons, living or dead, business establishments,
events, or locales is entirely coincidental.

Library of Congress Cataloging-in-Publication Data available

ISBN 978-1-338-20679-1

10 9 8 7 6 5 4 3 2 1          18 19 20 21 22

Printed in China   38
First edition, April 2018

This colossal collection of comics
is dedicated to all the Phoenixers out there, young
and old, whose ranks you are about to join.

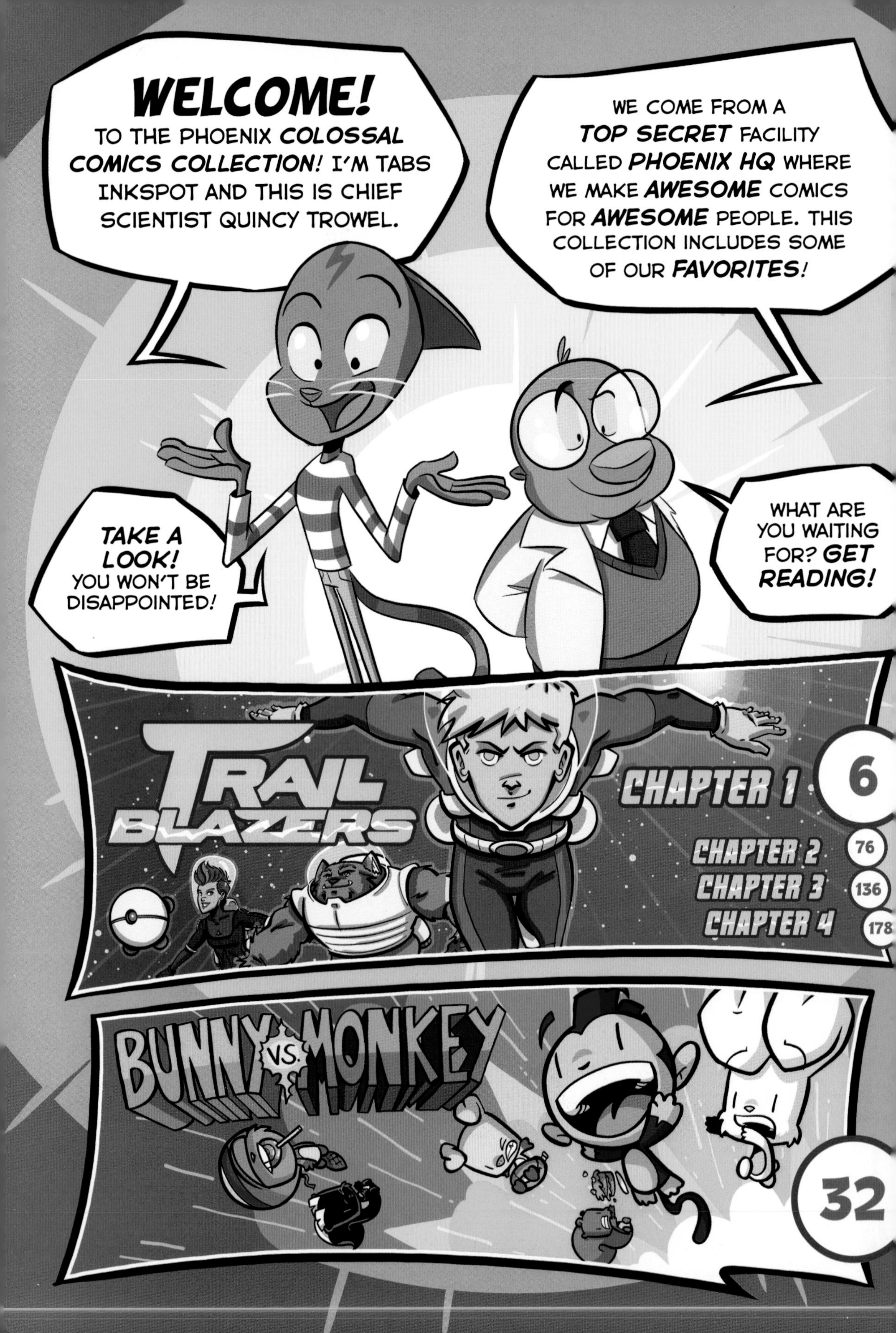
WELCOME! TO THE PHOENIX COLOSSAL COMICS COLLECTION! I'M TABS INKSPOT AND THIS IS CHIEF SCIENTIST QUINCY TROWEL.
WE COME FROM A TOP SECRET FACILITY CALLED PHOENIX HQ WHERE WE MAKE AWESOME COMICS FOR AWESOME PEOPLE. THIS COLLECTION INCLUDES SOME OF OUR FAVORITES!
TAKE A LOOK! YOU WON'T BE DISAPPOINTED!
WHAT ARE YOU WAITING FOR? GET READING!
TRAIL BLAZERS
CHAPTER 1 6
CHAPTER 2 76
CHAPTER 3 136
CHAPTER 4 178
BUNNY VS. MONKEY
32

DOUG SLUGMAN P.I.

CASE CLOSED.

**65**

EVIL EMPEROR PENGUIN

**102**

SQUID SQUAD!

**125**

LOOSHKIN

**162**

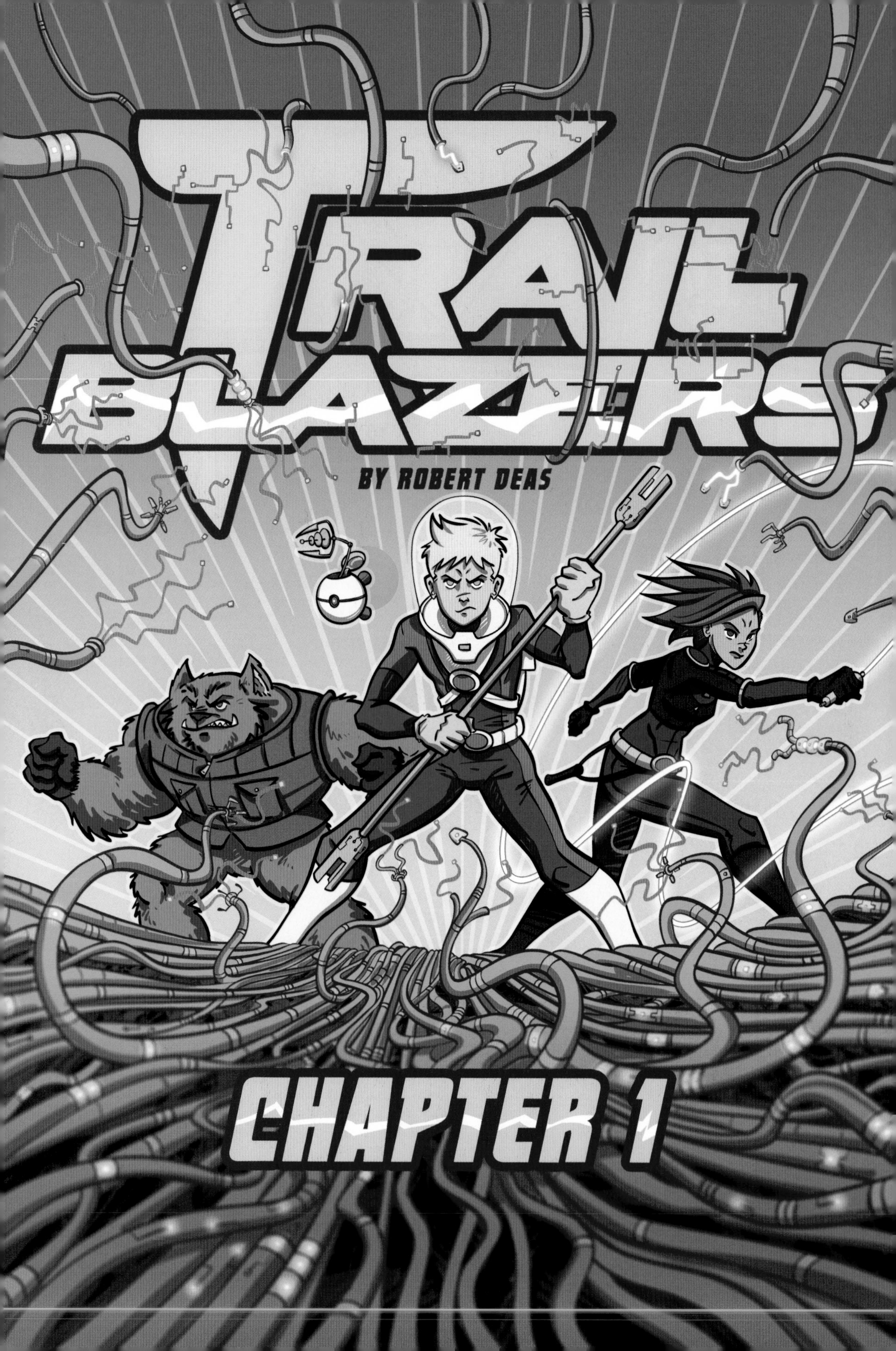
TRAIL BLAZERS
BY ROBERT DEAS
CHAPTER 1

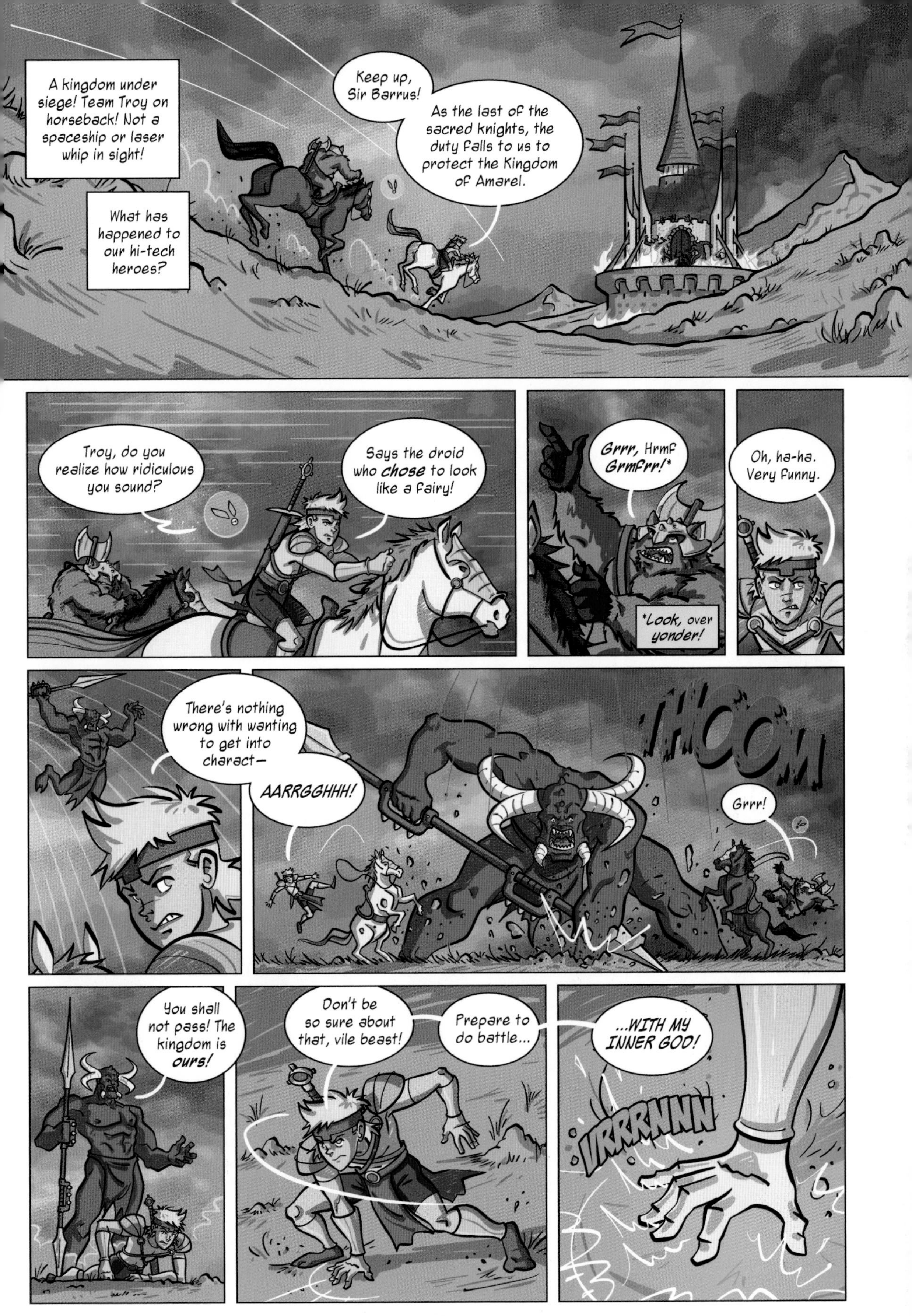
A kingdom under siege! Team Troy on horseback! Not a spaceship or laser whip in sight!
What has happened to our hi-tech heroes?
Keep up, Sir Barrus!
As the last of the sacred knights, the duty falls to us to protect the Kingdom of Amarel.
Troy, do you realize how ridiculous you sound?
Says the droid who **chose** to look like a fairy!
Grrr, Hrmf Grmfrr!*
*Look, over yonder!
Oh, ha-ha. Very funny.
There's nothing wrong with wanting to get into charact—
AARRGGHHH!
THOOM
Grrr!
You shall not pass! The kingdom is **ours!**
Don't be so sure about that, vile beast!
Prepare to do battle...
...WITH MY INNER GOD!
VRRRNNN

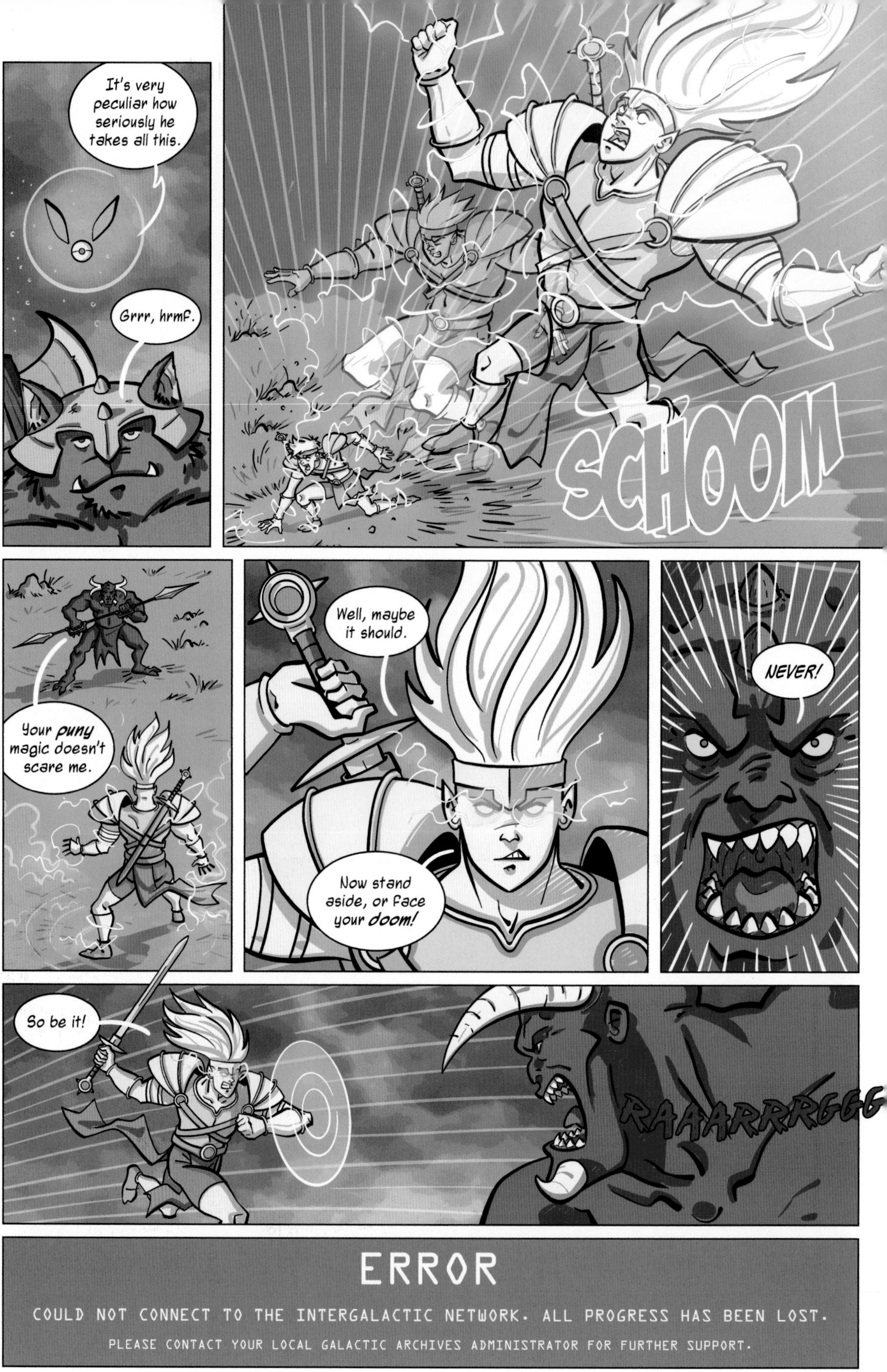

It's very peculiar how seriously he takes all this.
Grrr, hrmf.
SCHOOM
Your puny magic doesn't scare me.
Well, maybe it should.
Now stand aside, or face your doom!
NEVER!
So be it!
RAAARRRGGG
ERROR
COULD NOT CONNECT TO THE INTERGALACTIC NETWORK. ALL PROGRESS HAS BEEN LOST.
PLEASE CONTACT YOUR LOCAL GALACTIC ARCHIVES ADMINISTRATOR FOR FURTHER SUPPORT.

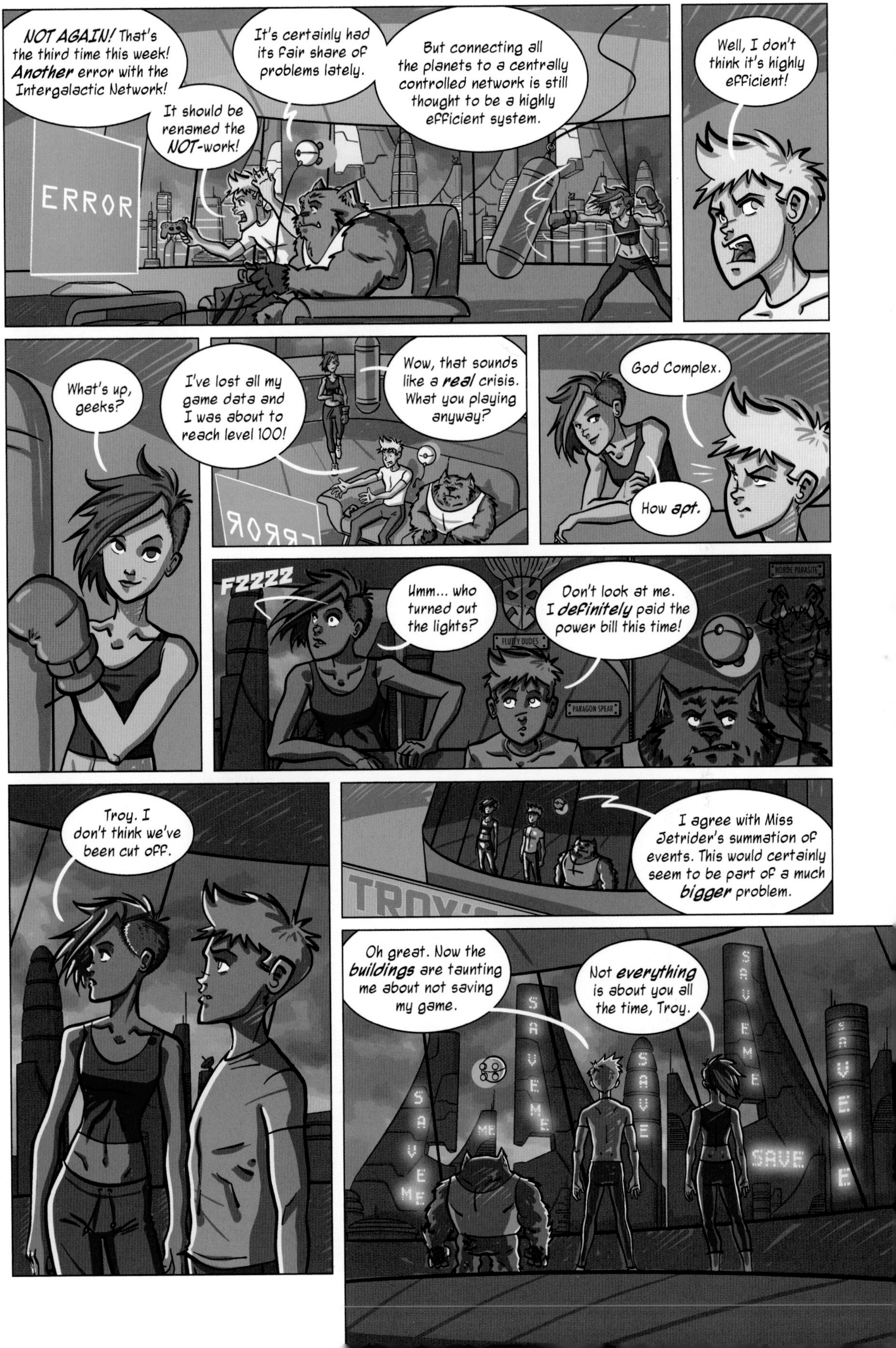
NOT AGAIN! That's the third time this week! Another error with the Intergalactic Network!
It should be renamed the NOT-work!
ERROR
It's certainly had its fair share of problems lately.
But connecting all the planets to a centrally controlled network is still thought to be a highly efficient system.
Well, I don't think it's highly efficient!
What's up, geeks?
I've lost all my game data and I was about to reach level 100!
Wow, that sounds like a real crisis. What you playing anyway?
ERROR
God Complex.
How apt.
FZZZZ
Umm... who turned out the lights?
Don't look at me. I definitely paid the power bill this time!
HORDE PARASITE
FLUTEY DUDES
PARAGON SPEAR
Troy. I don't think we've been cut off.
I agree with Miss Jetrider's summation of events. This would certainly seem to be part of a much bigger problem.
Oh great. Now the buildings are taunting me about not saving my game.
Not everything is about you all the time, Troy.
SAVE ME
SAVE

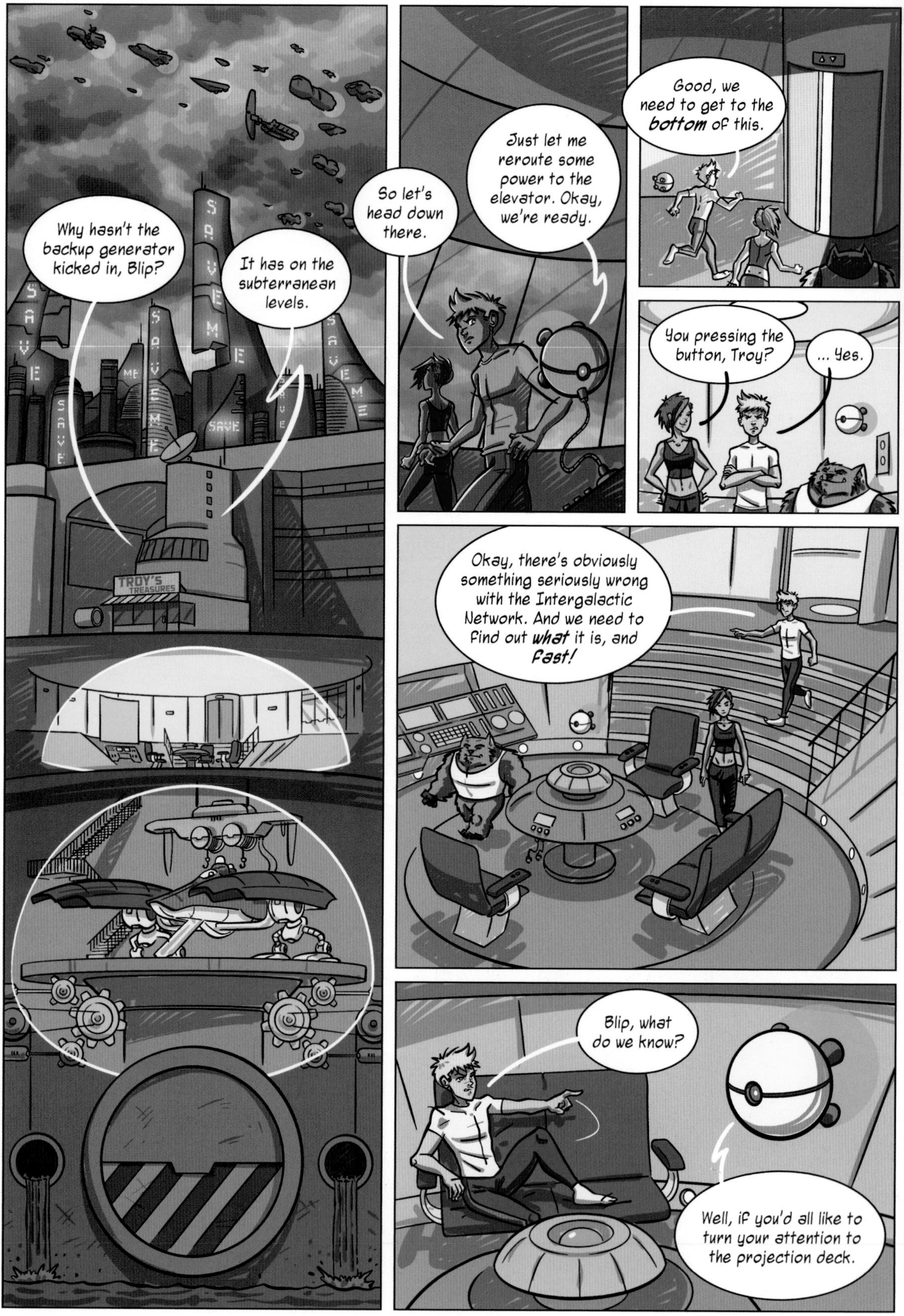
SAVE ME
TROY'S TREASURES
Why hasn't the backup generator kicked in, Blip?
It has on the subterranean levels.
So let's head down there.
Just let me reroute some power to the elevator. Okay, we're ready.
Good, we need to get to the **bottom** of this.
You pressing the button, Troy?
... Yes.
Okay, there's obviously something seriously wrong with the Intergalactic Network. And we need to find out **what** it is, and **fast!**
Blip, what do we know?
Well, if you'd all like to turn your attention to the projection deck.

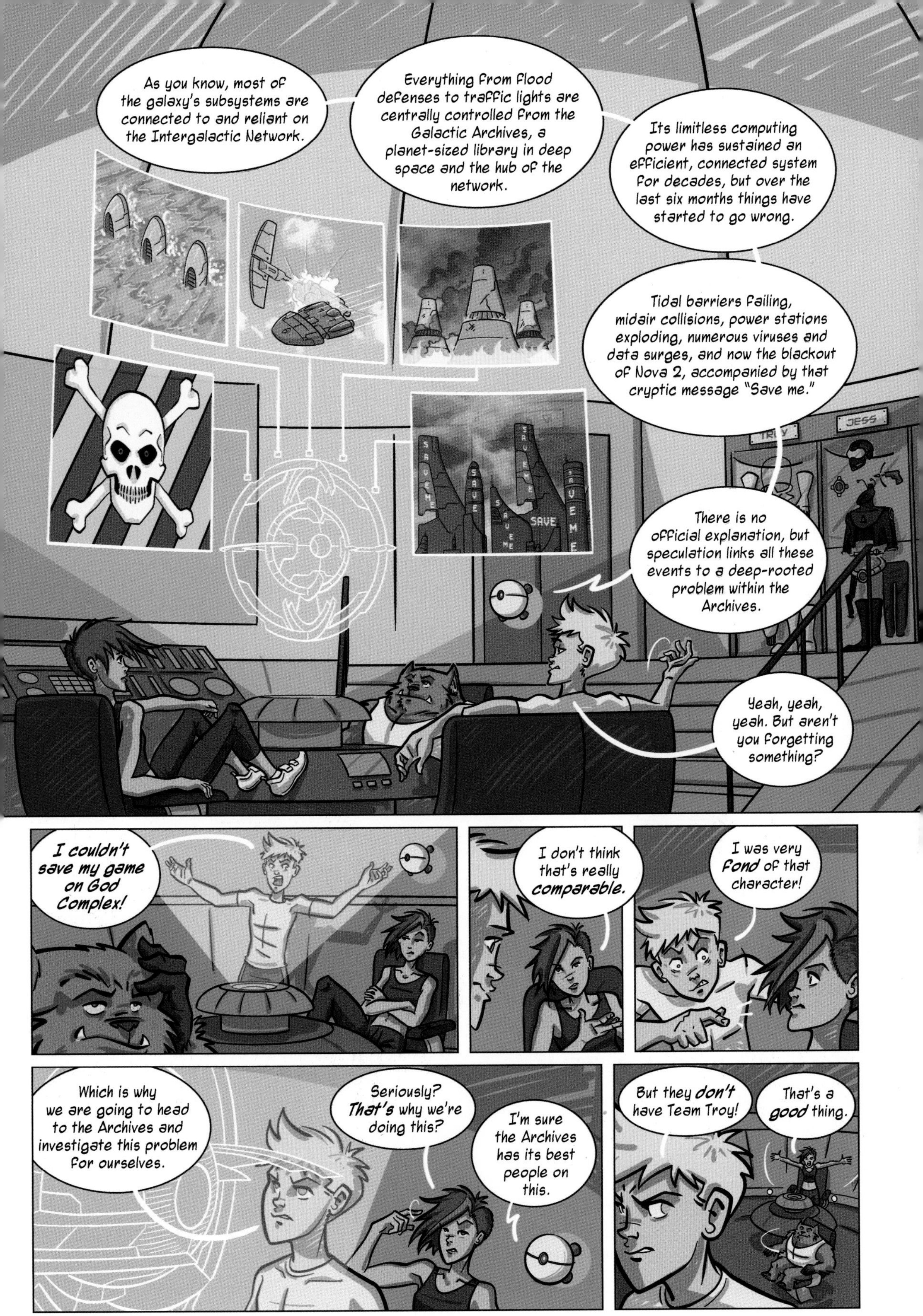
As you know, most of the galaxy's subsystems are connected to and reliant on the Intergalactic Network.
Everything from flood defenses to traffic lights are centrally controlled from the Galactic Archives, a planet-sized library in deep space and the hub of the network.
Its limitless computing power has sustained an efficient, connected system for decades, but over the last six months things have started to go wrong.
Tidal barriers failing, midair collisions, power stations exploding, numerous viruses and data surges, and now the blackout of Nova 2, accompanied by that cryptic message "Save me."
TROY
JESS
SAVE ME
SAVE
There is no official explanation, but speculation links all these events to a deep-rooted problem within the Archives.
Yeah, yeah, yeah. But aren't you forgetting something?
I couldn't save my game on God Complex!
I don't think that's really comparable.
I was very fond of that character!
Which is why we are going to head to the Archives and investigate this problem for ourselves.
Seriously? That's why we're doing this?
I'm sure the Archives has its best people on this.
But they don't have Team Troy!
That's a good thing.

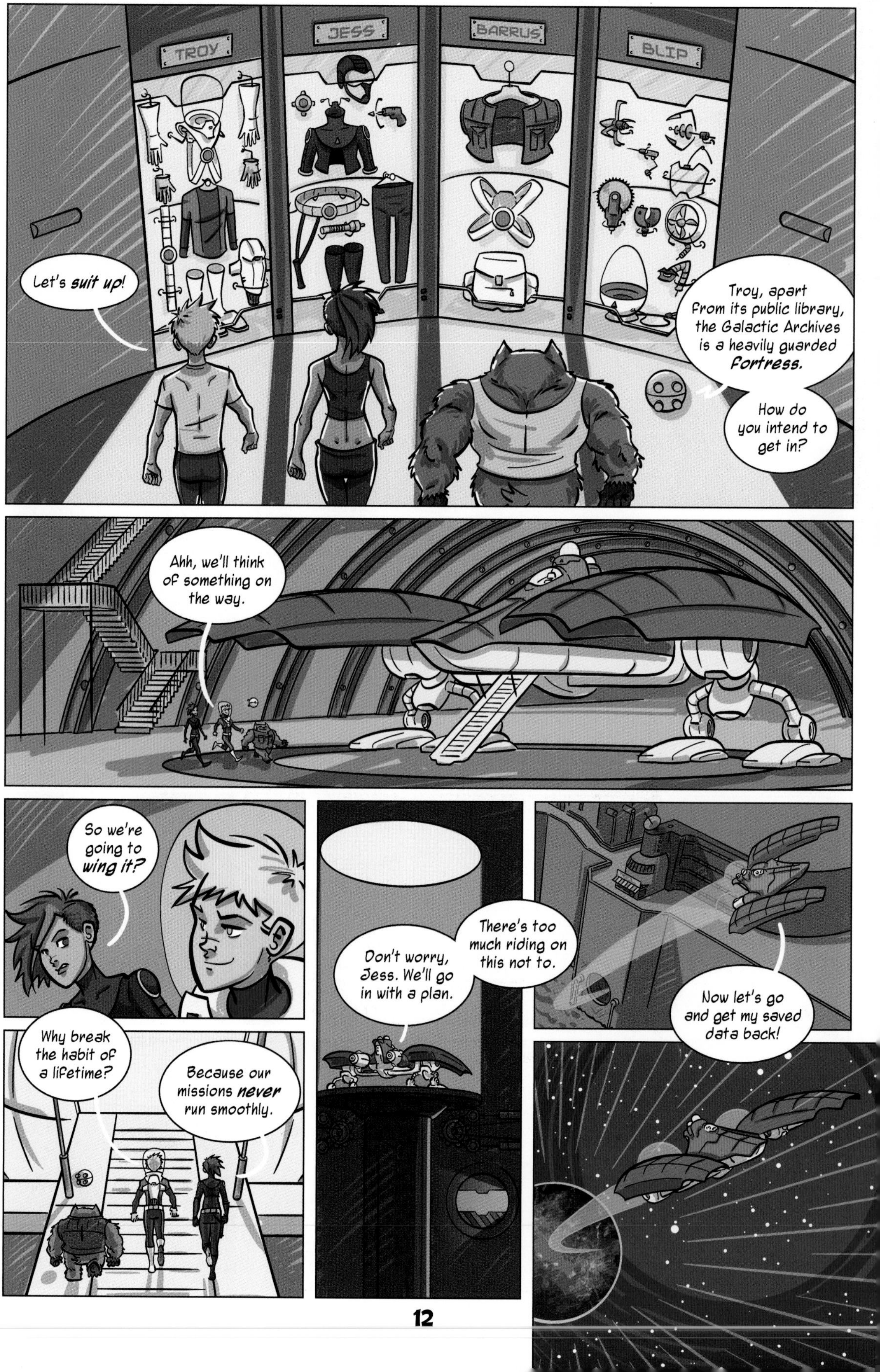
TROY
JESS
BARRUS
BLIP
Let's suit up!
Troy, apart from its public library, the Galactic Archives is a heavily guarded fortress.
How do you intend to get in?
Ahh, we'll think of something on the way.
So we're going to wing it?
Why break the habit of a lifetime?
Because our missions never run smoothly.
Don't worry, Jess. We'll go in with a plan.
There's too much riding on this not to.
Now let's go and get my saved data back!

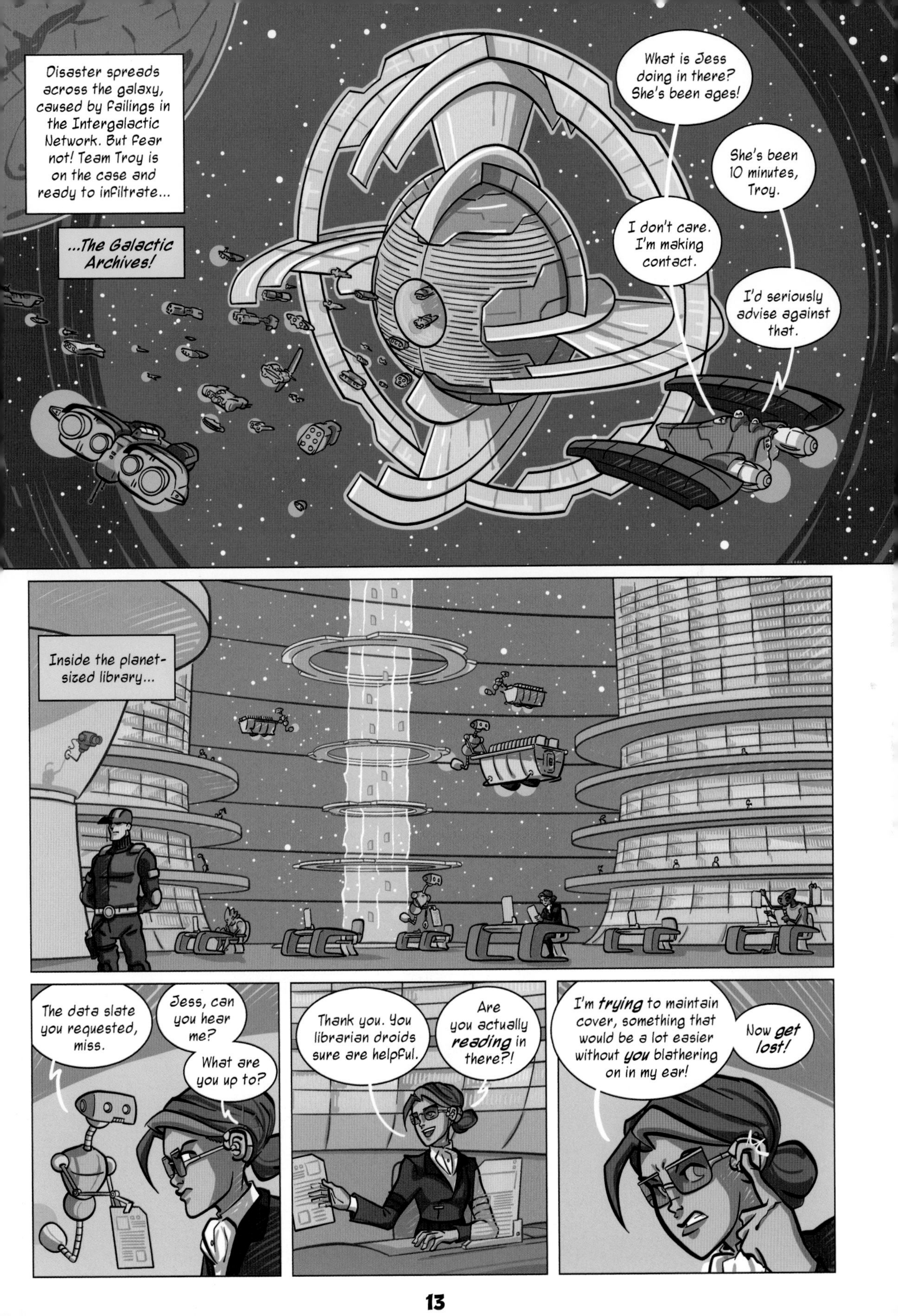

Disaster spreads across the galaxy, caused by failings in the Intergalactic Network. But fear not! Team Troy is on the case and ready to infiltrate...
...The Galactic Archives!
What is Jess doing in there? She's been ages!
She's been 10 minutes, Troy.
I don't care. I'm making contact.
I'd seriously advise against that.
Inside the planet-sized library...
The data slate you requested, miss.
Jess, can you hear me?
What are you up to?
Thank you. You librarian droids sure are helpful.
Are you actually *reading* in there?!
I'm *trying* to maintain cover, something that would be a lot easier without *you* blathering on in my ear!
Now *get lost!*

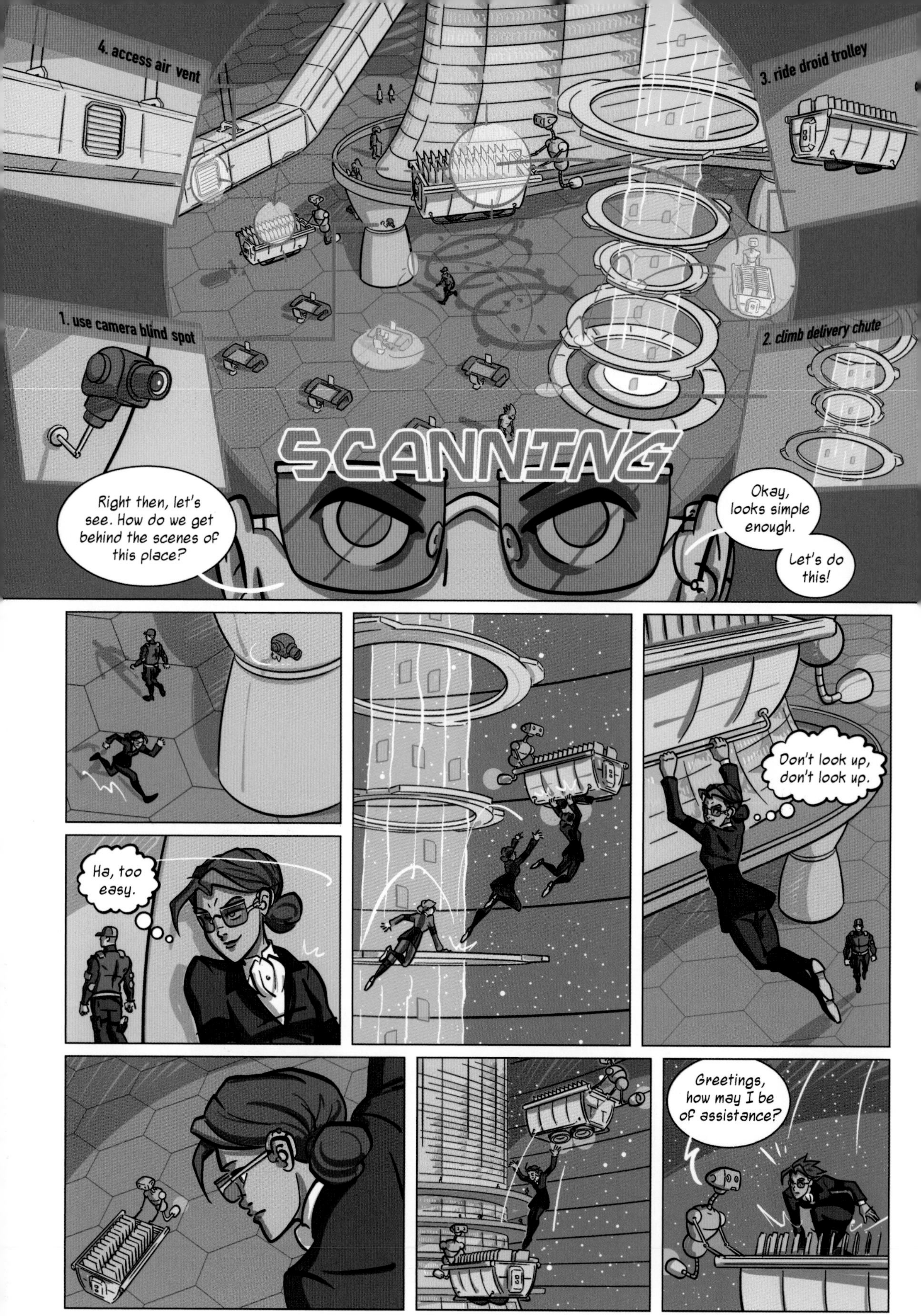
4. access air vent
3. ride droid trolley
1. use camera blind spot
2. climb delivery chute
SCANNING
Right then, let's see. How do we get behind the scenes of this place?
Okay, looks simple enough.
Let's do this!
Ha, too easy.
Don't look up, don't look up.
Greetings, how may I be of assistance?

Just hold it right there for a sec.

Thanks.

You are welcome.

Why can't Blip talk to me like that?

Troy, begin your approach. I'm in.

One quick change in a confined space later...

Doesn't she have *two* heads?

Yeah, but *they've* got a great personality.

What the?

COUGH COUGH COUGH

Too bad.

I'd have loved to have heard the end of that story.

A *keycard*, for me? You shouldn't have.

Troy, I'm opening the inner door now.

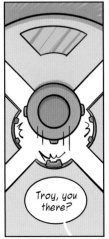

Troy, you there?

TROY?!

Fooled ya!

I can open the outer airlock, too, you know!

15

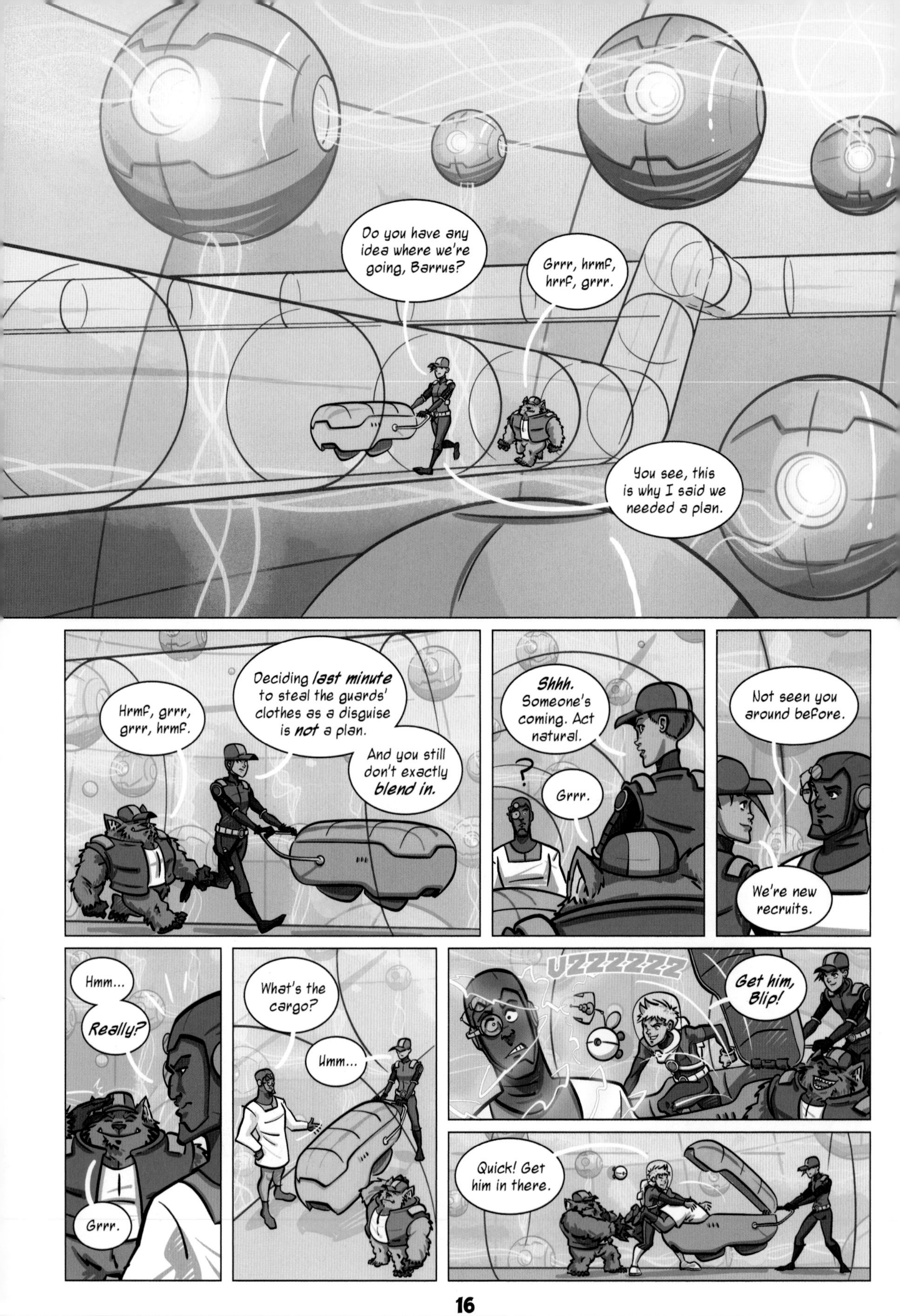
Do you have any idea where we're going, Barrus?
Grrr, hrmf, hrrf, grrr.
You see, this is why I said we needed a plan.
Hrmf, grrr, grrr, hrmf.
Deciding *last minute* to steal the guards' clothes as a disguise is *not* a plan.
And you still don't exactly *blend in.*
*Shhh.* Someone's coming. Act natural.
?
Grrr.
Not seen you around before.
We're new recruits.
Hmm...
*Really?*
Grrr.
What's the cargo?
Umm...
UZZZZZZ
*Get him, Blip!*
Quick! Get him in there.

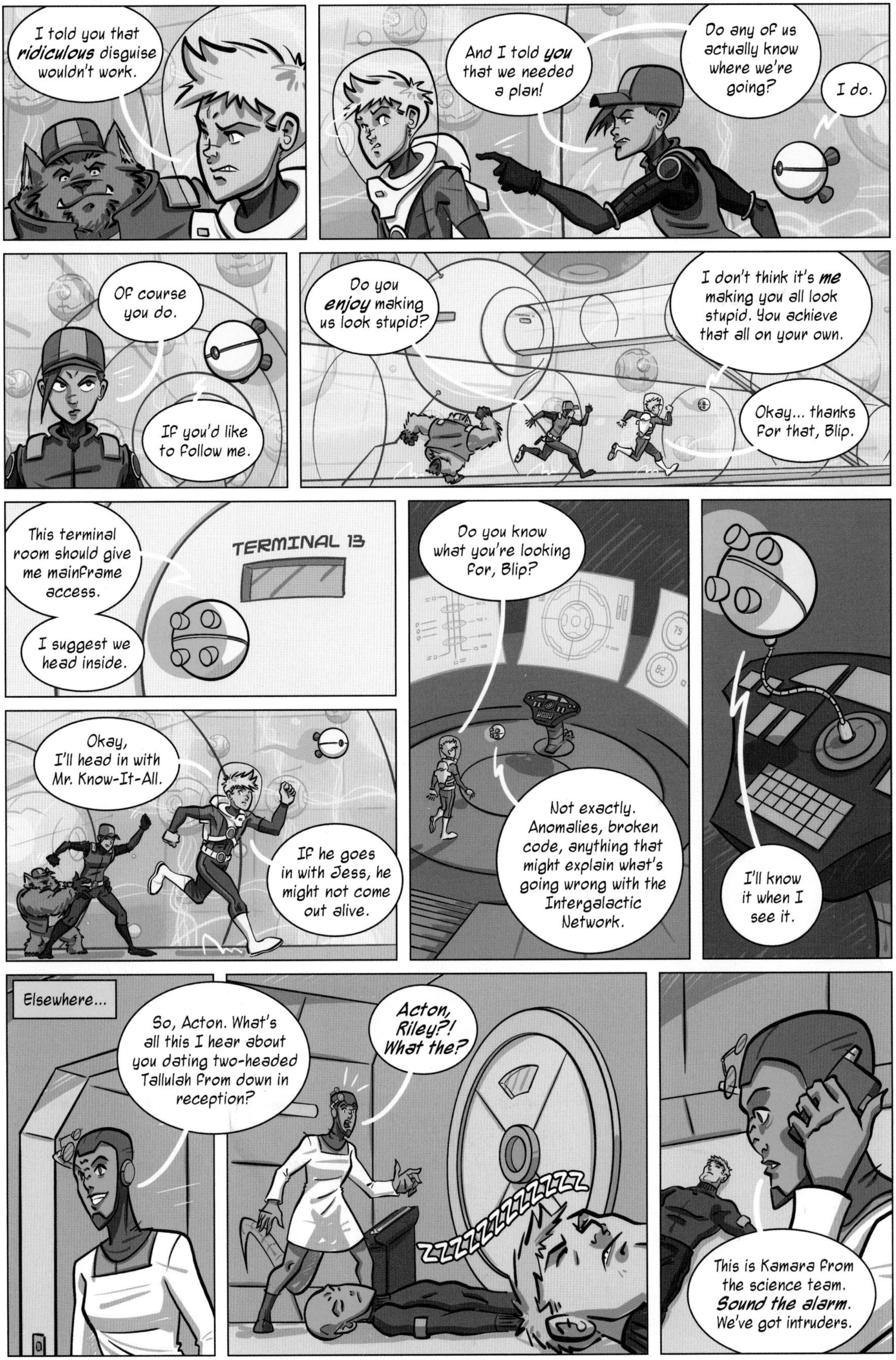
I told you that ridiculous disguise wouldn't work.
And I told you that we needed a plan!
Do any of us actually know where we're going?
I do.
Of course you do.
If you'd like to follow me.
Do you enjoy making us look stupid?
I don't think it's me making you all look stupid. You achieve that all on your own.
Okay... thanks for that, Blip.
This terminal room should give me mainframe access.
TERMINAL 13
I suggest we head inside.
Do you know what you're looking for, Blip?
Not exactly. Anomalies, broken code, anything that might explain what's going wrong with the Intergalactic Network.
I'll know it when I see it.
Okay, I'll head in with Mr. Know-It-All.
If he goes in with Jess, he might not come out alive.
Elsewhere...
So, Acton. What's all this I hear about you dating two-headed Tallulah from down in reception?
Acton, Riley?! What the?
ZZZZZZZZZZZZZZZZ
This is Kamara from the science team. Sound the alarm. We've got intruders.

AWOOGA AWOOGA AWOOGA

An alarm!

You did hide those two security guards I knocked out, right?

Hmff?

Nice one, Furball.

Troy. We need to *hurry* this up!

BANG BANG BANG

They must know we're here. *Hurry,* Blip.

I've found something.

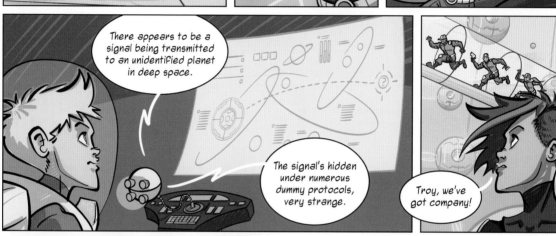

There appears to be a signal being transmitted to an unidentified planet in deep space.

The signal's hidden under numerous dummy protocols, very strange.

Troy, we've got company!

GET OUT OF THERE NOW!

Time's up, Blip!

I'm just downloading the signal's coordinates. This might be a lead!

DOWNLOAD COMPLETE

100%

Done.

I'm right behind you!

No rush!

Blame Blip. Not me!

There they are! *Stop them!*

I think that's our *cue* to leave!

No, I think the *alarm* was our cue, *Doofus!*

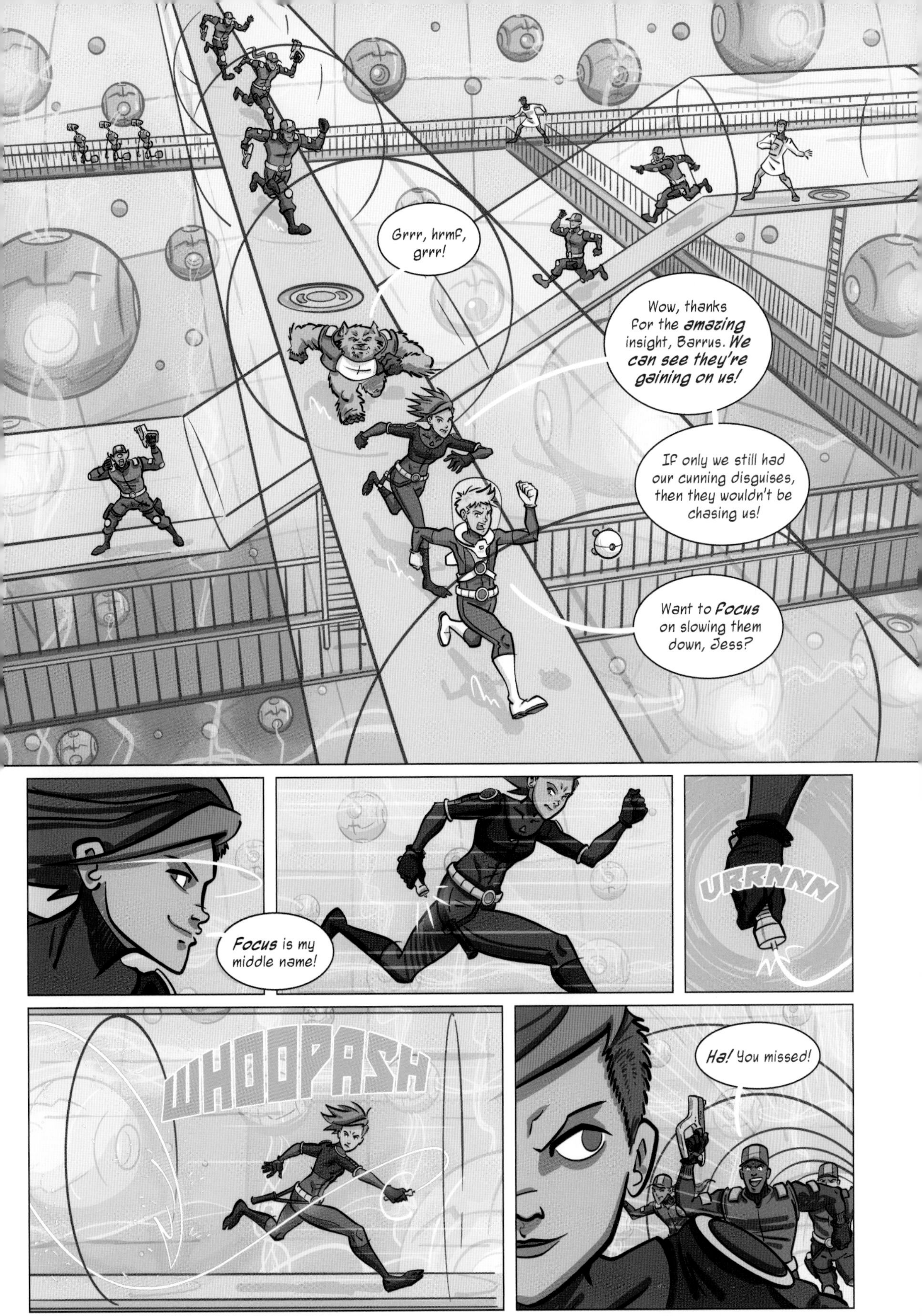
Grrr, hrmf, grrr!
Wow, thanks for the *amazing* insight, Barrus. ***We can see they're gaining on us!***
If only we still had our cunning disguises, then they wouldn't be chasing us!
Want to ***Focus*** on slowing them down, Jess?
***Focus*** is my middle name!
URRNNN
WHOOPASH
***Ha!*** You missed!

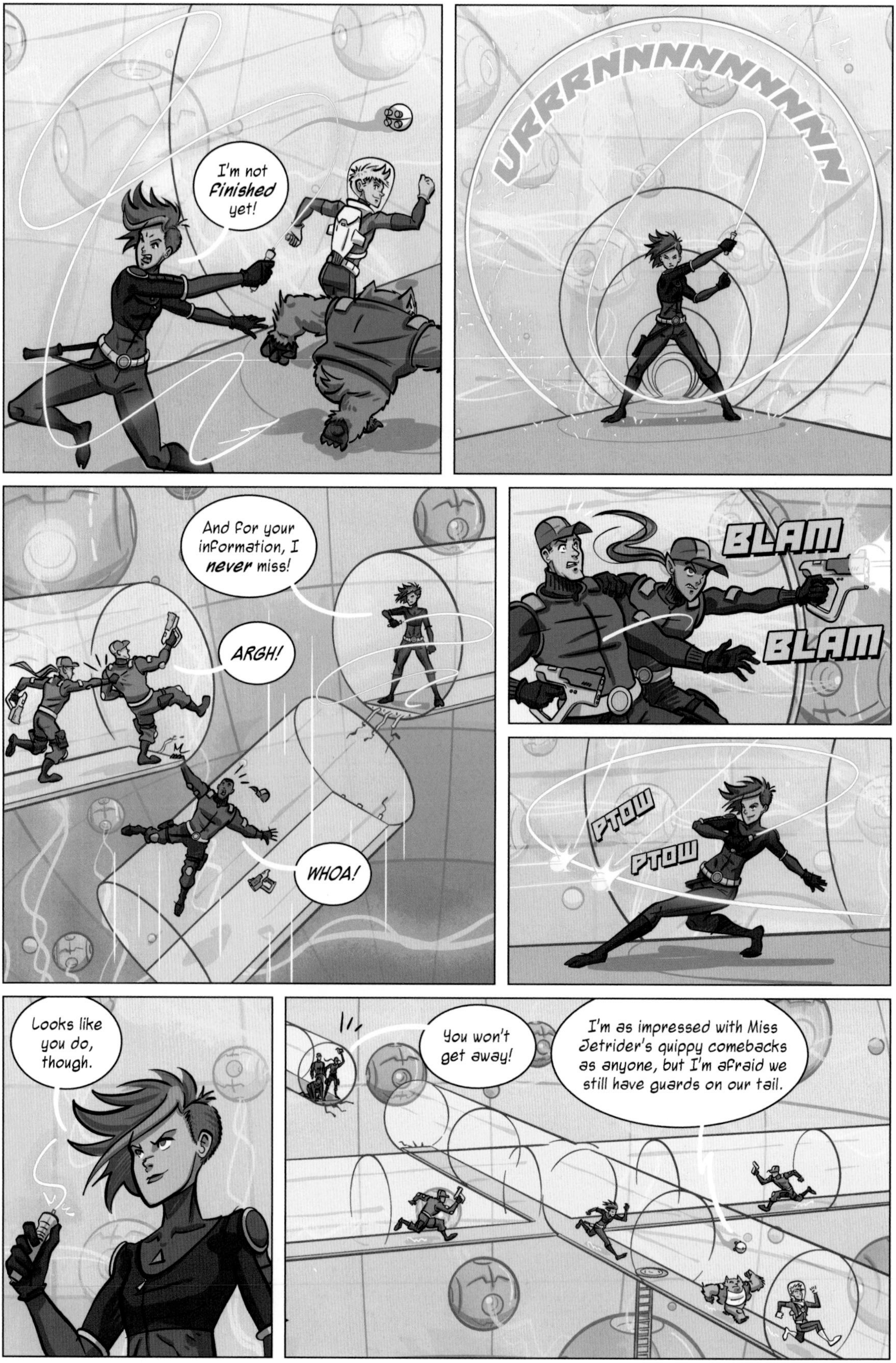

I'm not *finished* yet!
URRRNNNNNNNNNN
And for your information, I *never* miss!
ARGH!
WHOA!
BLAM
BLAM
PTOW
PTOW
Looks like you do, though.
You won't get away!
I'm as impressed with Miss Jetrider's quippy comebacks as anyone, but I'm afraid we still have guards on our tail.

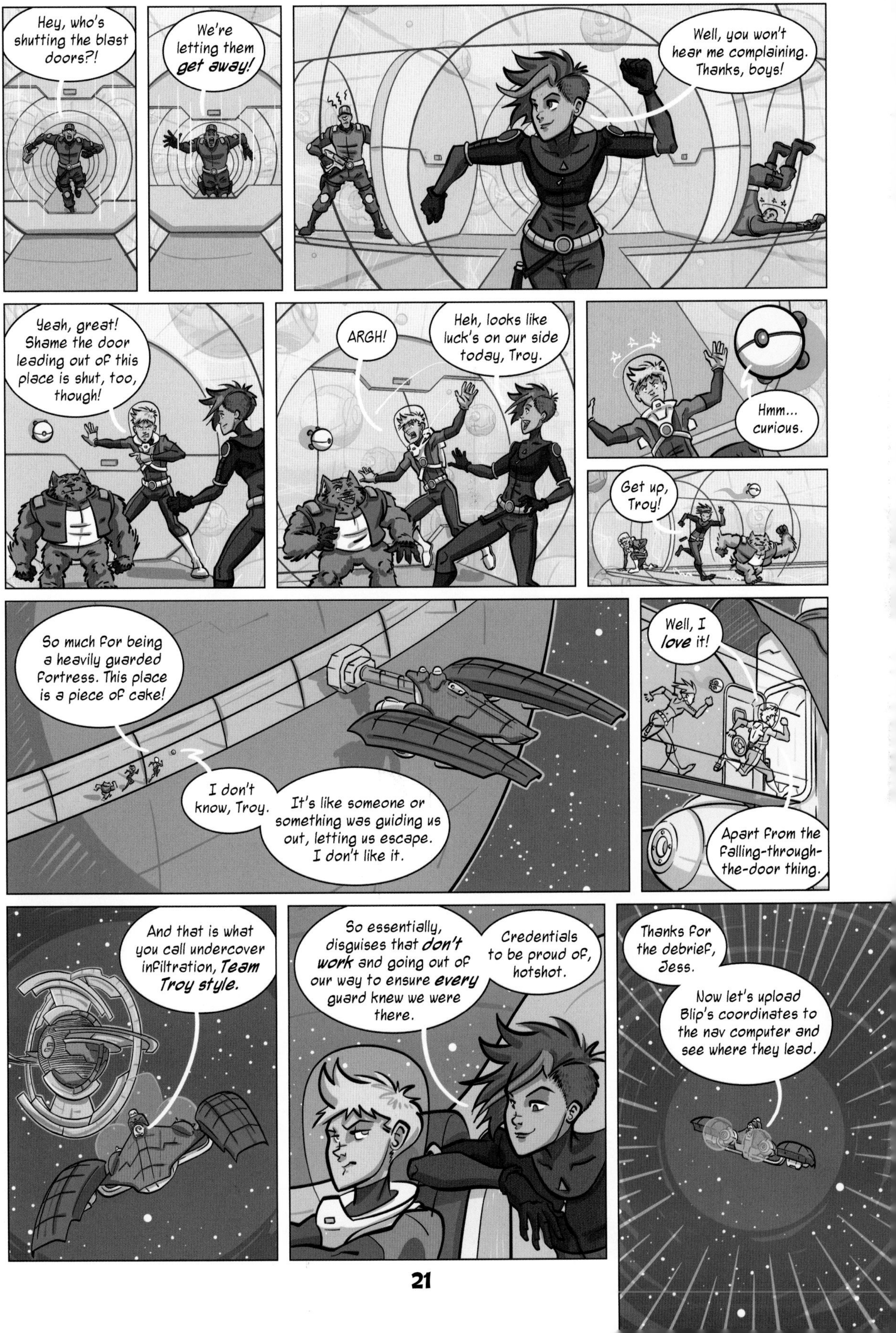

Hey, who's shutting the blast doors?!
We're letting them *get away!*
Well, you won't hear me complaining. Thanks, boys!
Yeah, great! Shame the door leading out of this place is shut, too, though!
ARGH!
Heh, looks like luck's on our side today, Troy.
Hmm... curious.
Get up, Troy!
So much for being a heavily guarded fortress. This place is a piece of cake!
I don't know, Troy.
It's like someone or something was guiding us out, letting us escape. I don't like it.
Well, I *love* it!
Apart from the falling-through-the-door thing.
And that is what you call undercover infiltration, ***Team Troy style.***
So essentially, disguises that ***don't work*** and going out of our way to ensure ***every*** guard knew we were there.
Credentials to be proud of, hotshot.
Thanks for the debrief, Jess.
Now let's upload Blip's coordinates to the nav computer and see where they lead.

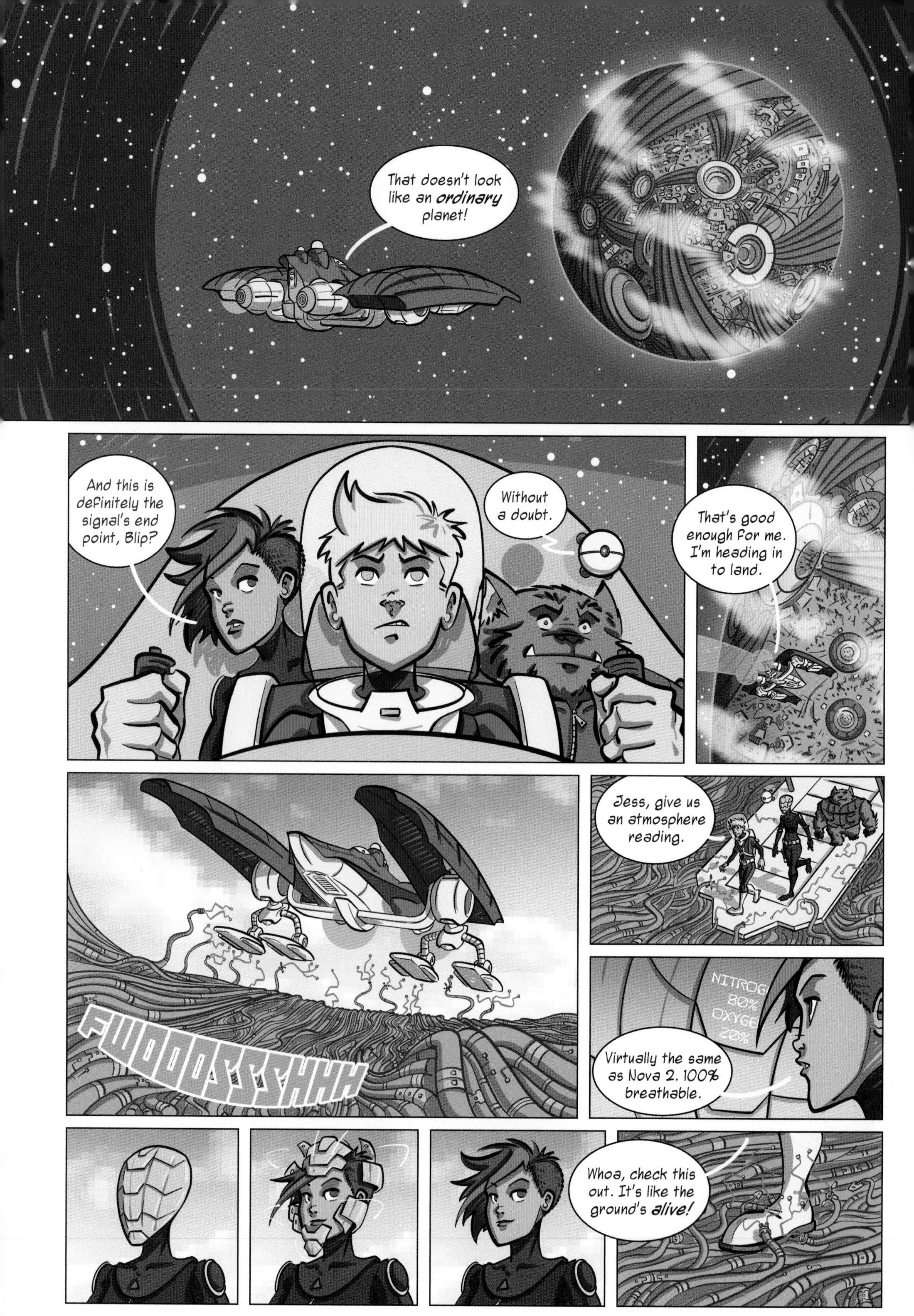
That doesn't look like an *ordinary* planet!
And this is definitely the signal's end point, Blip?
Without a doubt.
That's good enough for me. I'm heading in to land.
FWOOOSSSHHH
Jess, give us an atmosphere reading.
NITROG 80% OXYGE 20%
Virtually the same as Nova 2. 100% breathable.
Whoa, check this out. It's like the ground's *alive!*

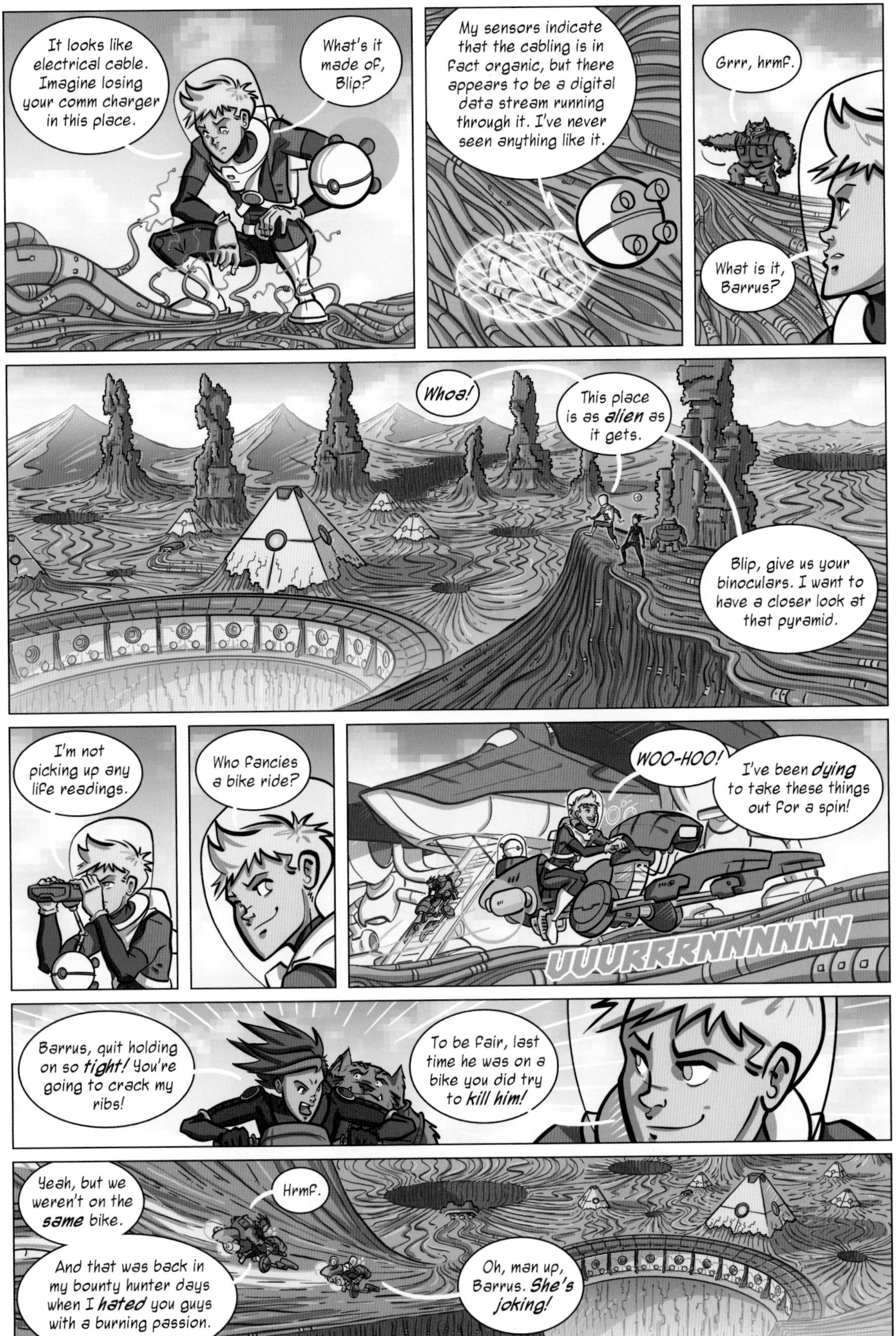
It looks like electrical cable. Imagine losing your comm charger in this place.
What's it made of, Blip?
My sensors indicate that the cabling is in fact organic, but there appears to be a digital data stream running through it. I've never seen anything like it.
Grrr, hrmf.
What is it, Barrus?
Whoa!
This place is as alien as it gets.
Blip, give us your binoculars. I want to have a closer look at that pyramid.
I'm not picking up any life readings.
Who fancies a bike ride?
WOO-HOO!
I've been dying to take these things out for a spin!
UUURRRNNNNNN
Barrus, quit holding on so tight! You're going to crack my ribs!
To be fair, last time he was on a bike you did try to kill him!
Yeah, but we weren't on the same bike.
Hrmf.
And that was back in my bounty hunter days when I hated you guys with a burning passion.
Oh, man up, Barrus. She's joking!

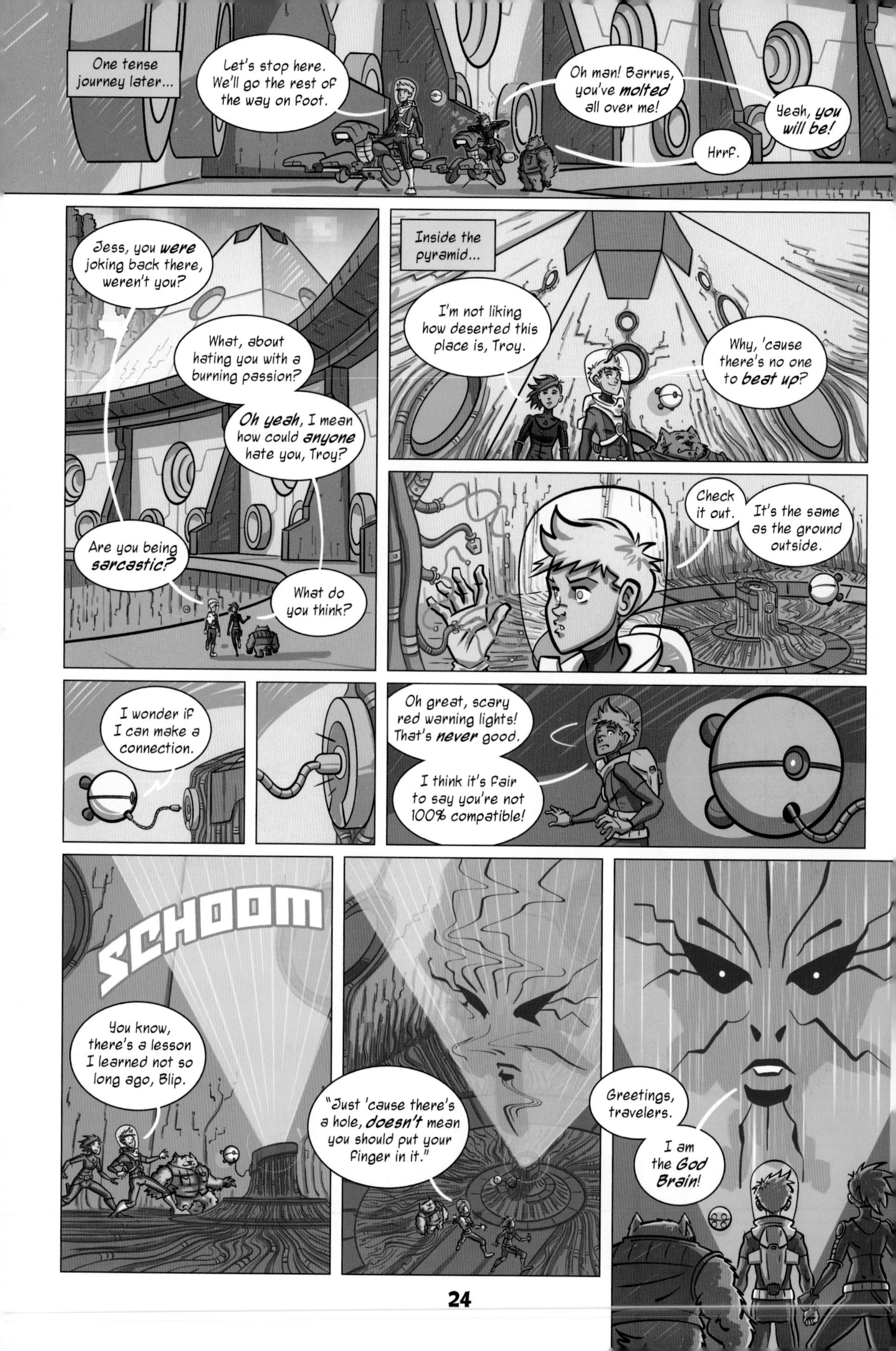
One tense journey later...
Let's stop here. We'll go the rest of the way on foot.
Oh man! Barrus, you've *molted* all over me!
Hrrf.
Yeah, *you will be!*
Jess, you *were* joking back there, weren't you?
What, about hating you with a burning passion?
Are you being *sarcastic?*
*Oh yeah*, I mean how could *anyone* hate you, Troy?
What do you think?
Inside the pyramid...
I'm not liking how deserted this place is, Troy.
Why, 'cause there's no one to *beat up*?
Check it out.
It's the same as the ground outside.
I wonder if I can make a connection.
Oh great, scary red warning lights! That's *never* good.
I think it's fair to say you're not 100% compatible!
SCHOOM
You know, there's a lesson I learned not so long ago, Blip.
"Just 'cause there's a hole, *doesn't* mean you should put your finger in it."
Greetings, travelers.
I am the *God Brain*!

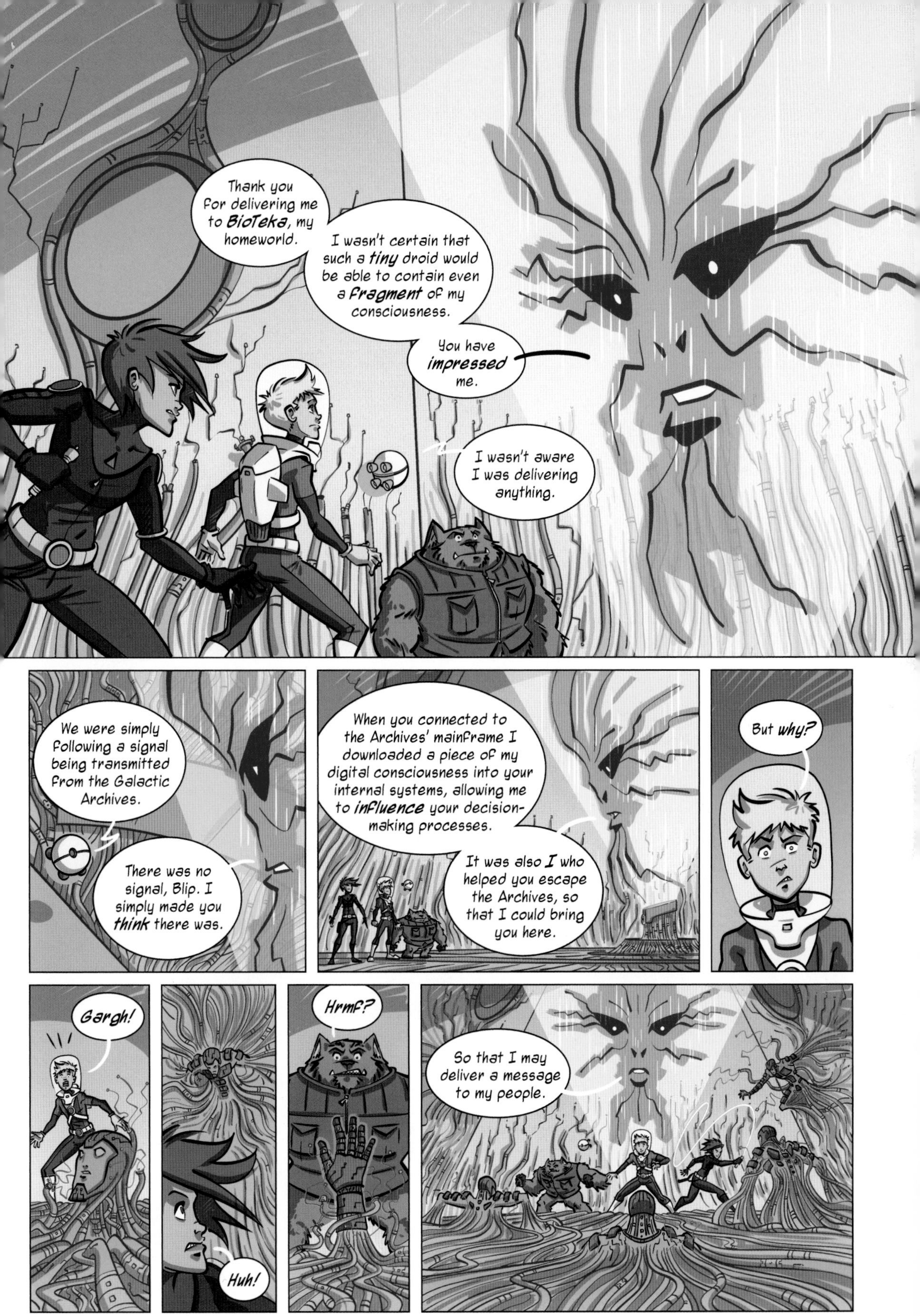

Thank you for delivering me to BioTeka, my homeworld.
I wasn't certain that such a tiny droid would be able to contain even a fragment of my consciousness.
You have impressed me.
I wasn't aware I was delivering anything.
We were simply following a signal being transmitted from the Galactic Archives.
There was no signal, Blip. I simply made you think there was.
When you connected to the Archives' mainframe I downloaded a piece of my digital consciousness into your internal systems, allowing me to influence your decision-making processes.
It was also I who helped you escape the Archives, so that I could bring you here.
But why?
Gargh!
Huh!
Hrmf?
So that I may deliver a message to my people.

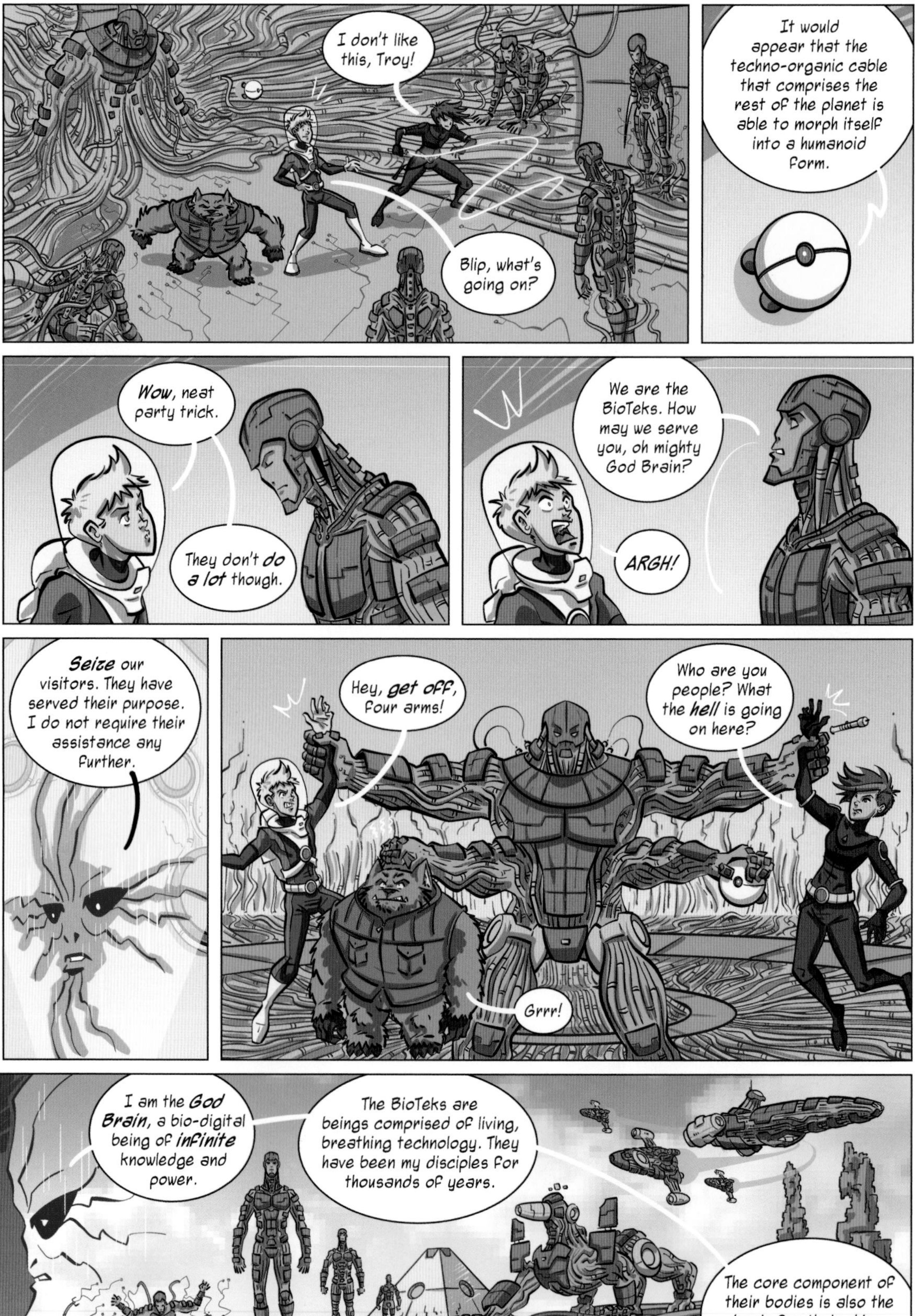
I don't like this, Troy!
Blip, what's going on?
It would appear that the techno-organic cable that comprises the rest of the planet is able to morph itself into a humanoid form.
Wow, neat party trick.
They don't do a lot though.
We are the BioTeks. How may we serve you, oh mighty God Brain?
ARGH!
Seize our visitors. They have served their purpose. I do not require their assistance any further.
Hey, get off, four arms!
Who are you people? What the hell is going on here?
Grrr!
I am the God Brain, a bio-digital being of infinite knowledge and power.
The BioTeks are beings comprised of living, breathing technology. They have been my disciples for thousands of years.
The core component of their bodies is also the basis for their ships, weapons, buildings, and even this planet.

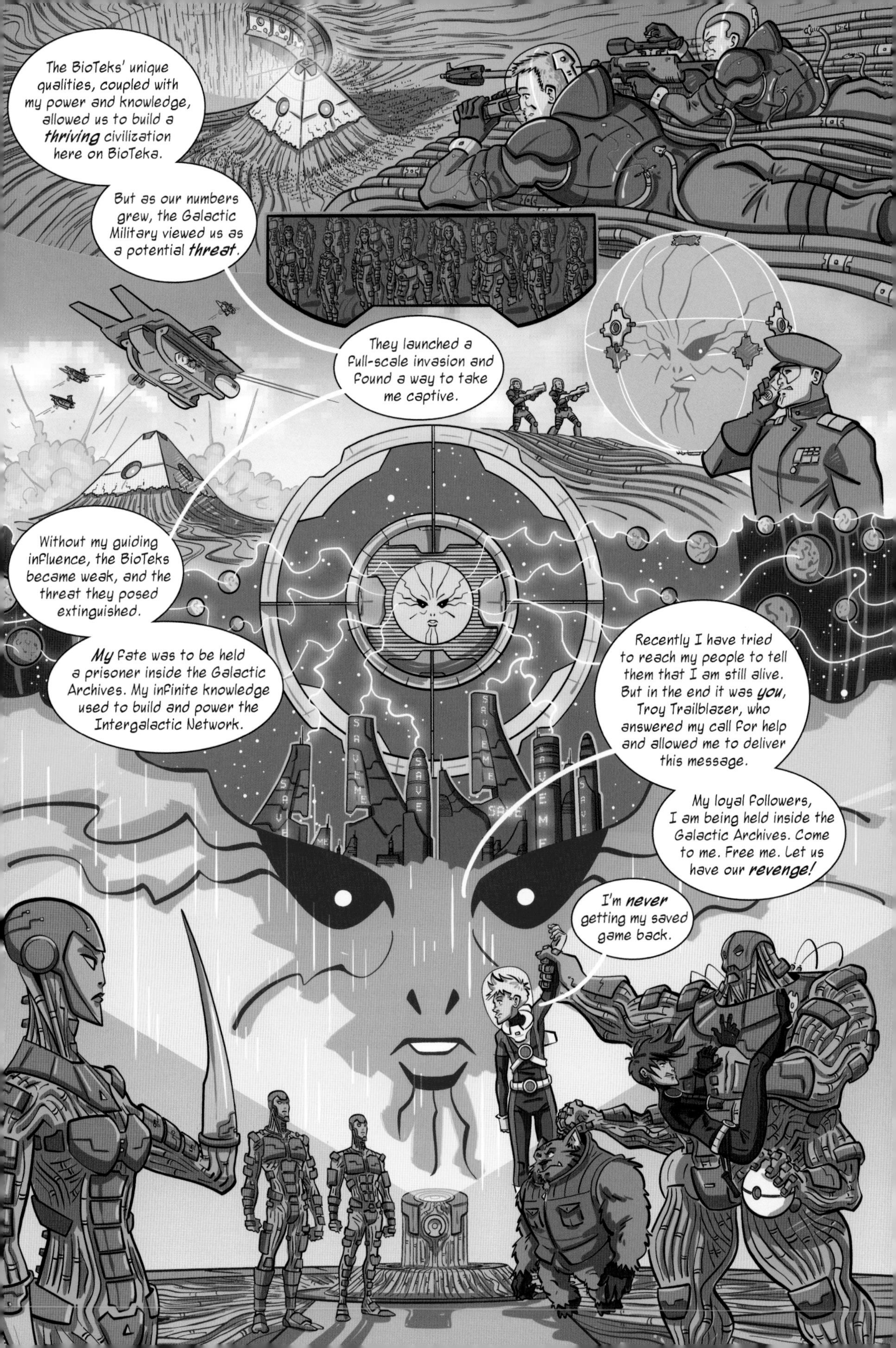

The BioTeks' unique qualities, coupled with my power and knowledge, allowed us to build a *thriving* civilization here on BioTeka.
But as our numbers grew, the Galactic Military viewed us as a potential *threat*.
They launched a full-scale invasion and found a way to take me captive.
Without my guiding influence, the BioTeks became weak, and the threat they posed extinguished.
*My* fate was to be held a prisoner inside the Galactic Archives. My infinite knowledge used to build and power the Intergalactic Network.
Recently I have tried to reach my people to tell them that I am still alive. But in the end it was *you*, Troy Trailblazer, who answered my call for help and allowed me to deliver this message.
My loyal followers, I am being held inside the Galactic Archives. Come to me. Free me. Let us have our *revenge!*
I'm *never* getting my saved game back.

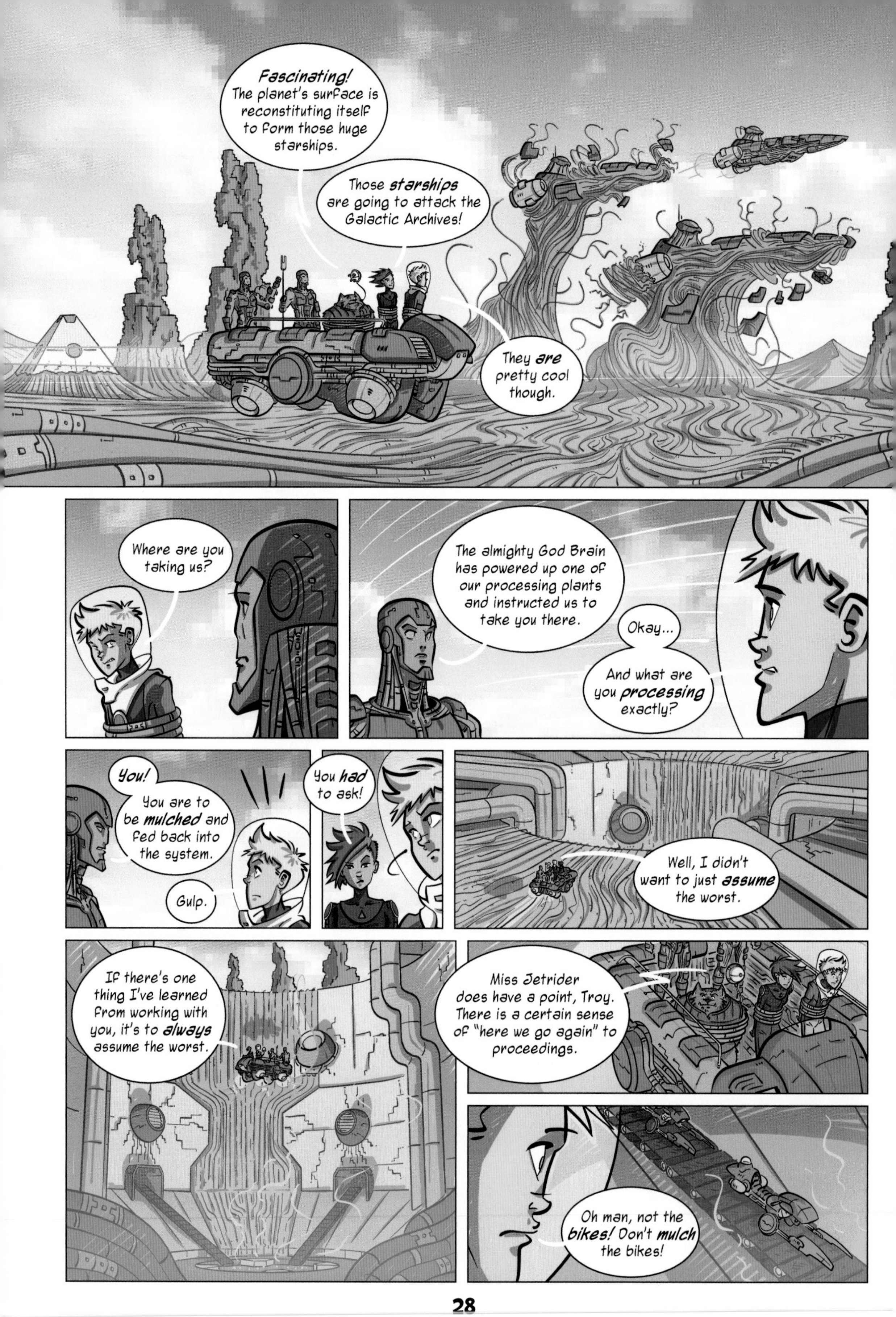

Fascinating! The planet's surface is reconstituting itself to form those huge starships.
Those starships are going to attack the Galactic Archives!
They are pretty cool though.
Where are you taking us?
The almighty God Brain has powered up one of our processing plants and instructed us to take you there.
Okay...
And what are you processing exactly?
You! You are to be mulched and fed back into the system.
Gulp.
You had to ask!
Well, I didn't want to just assume the worst.
If there's one thing I've learned from working with you, it's to always assume the worst.
Miss Jetrider does have a point, Troy. There is a certain sense of "here we go again" to proceedings.
Oh man, not the bikes! Don't mulch the bikes!

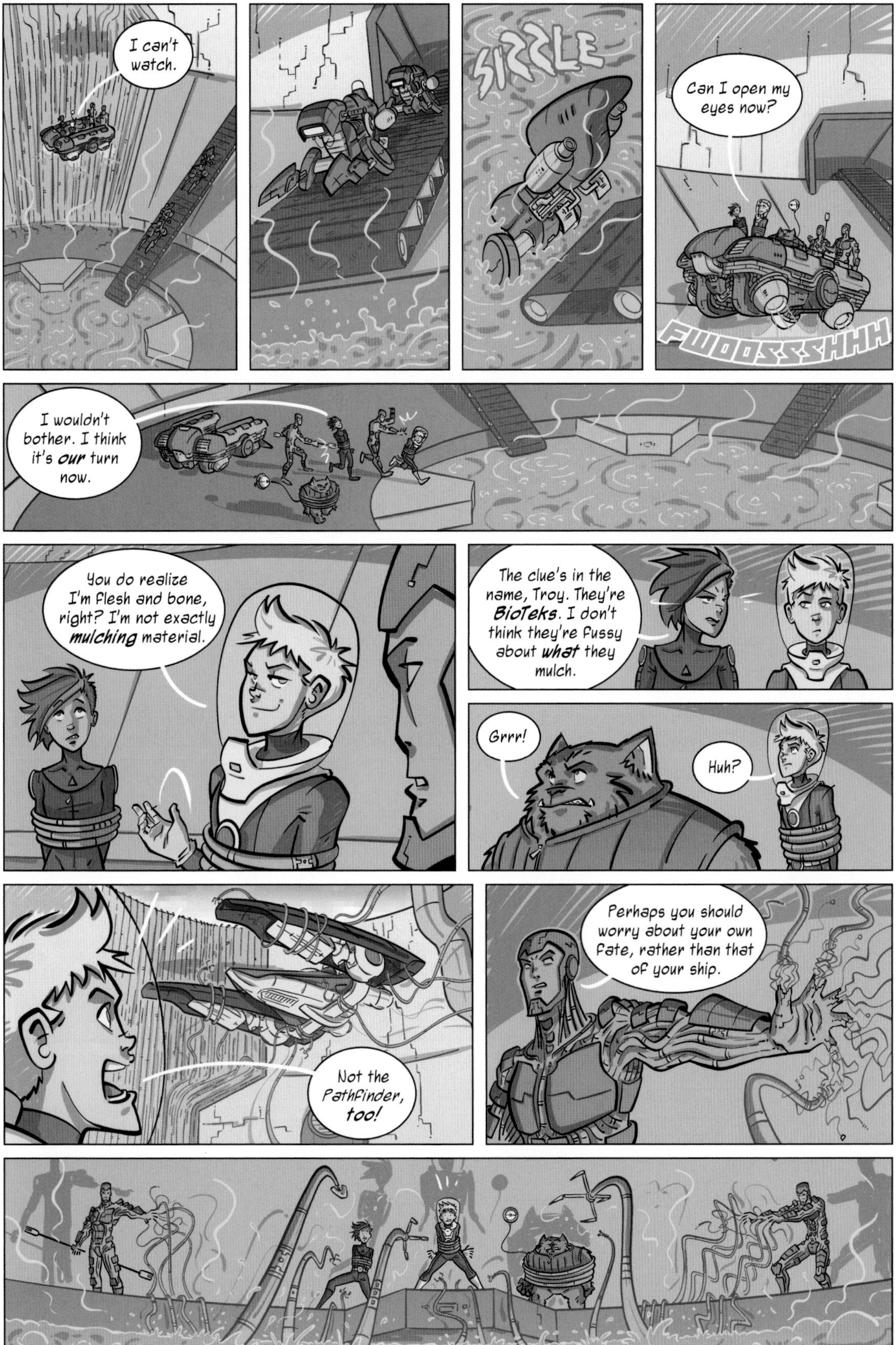
I can't watch.
SIZZLE
Can I open my eyes now?
FWOOSSSHHH
I wouldn't bother. I think it's *our* turn now.
You do realize I'm flesh and bone, right? I'm not exactly **mulching** material.
The clue's in the name, Troy. They're **BioTeks**. I don't think they're fussy about **what** they mulch.
Grrr!
Huh?
Not the Pathfinder, **too!**
Perhaps you should worry about your own fate, rather than that of your ship.

Blip, we need a plan!

The BioTek cables appear to be connected, just like a computer network.

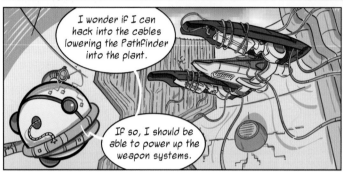

I wonder if I can hack into the cables lowering the Pathfinder into the plant.

If so, I should be able to power up the weapon systems.

WEAPONS ONLINE

URRRZZZ

It would appear I was correct.

PTOOM

PTOOM

Nice work, Blip!

Hey, what's wrong?

Uncertain - internal systems corrupted - BioTek code - conflict - error - error - shutting down.

Blip? Oh man, this isn't good!

What's wrong with him?

I'm not sure.

But I know a big floating head that will!

Come on. We need to head back to the Archives!

And stop the BioTeks before it's *too late!*

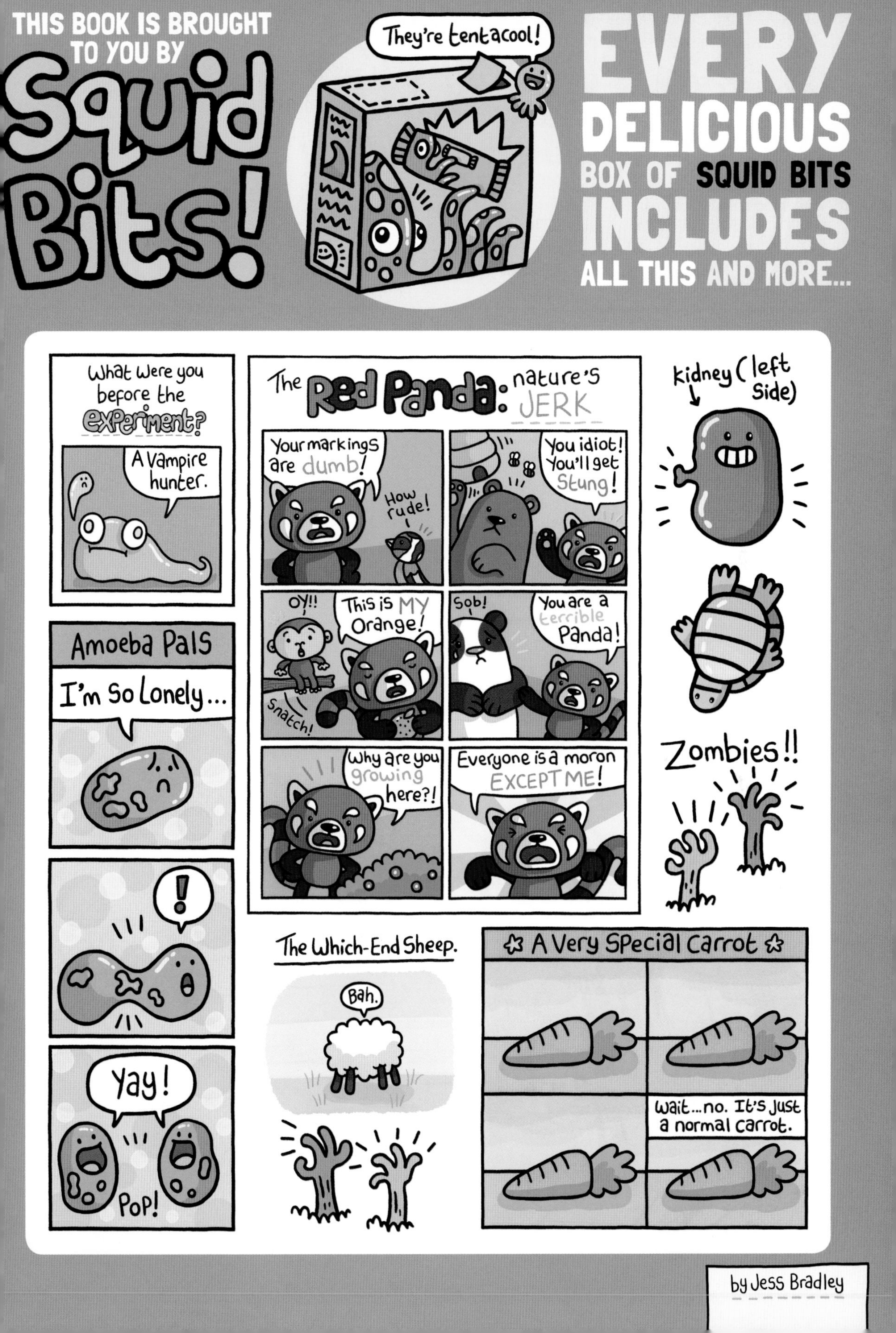
THIS BOOK IS BROUGHT TO YOU BY
Squid Bits!
They're tentacool!
EVERY DELICIOUS BOX OF SQUID BITS INCLUDES ALL THIS AND MORE...
What were you before the experiment?
A Vampire hunter.
Amoeba Pals
I'm so lonely...
!
Yay!
Pop!
The Red Panda: nature's JERK
Your markings are dumb!
How rude!
You idiot! You'll get stung!
OY!!
This is MY Orange!
Snatch!
Sob!
You are a terrible Panda!
Why are you growing here?!
Everyone is a moron EXCEPT ME!
kidney (left side)
Zombies!!
The Which-End Sheep.
Bah.
A Very Special Carrot
Wait...no. It's just a normal carrot.
by Jess Bradley

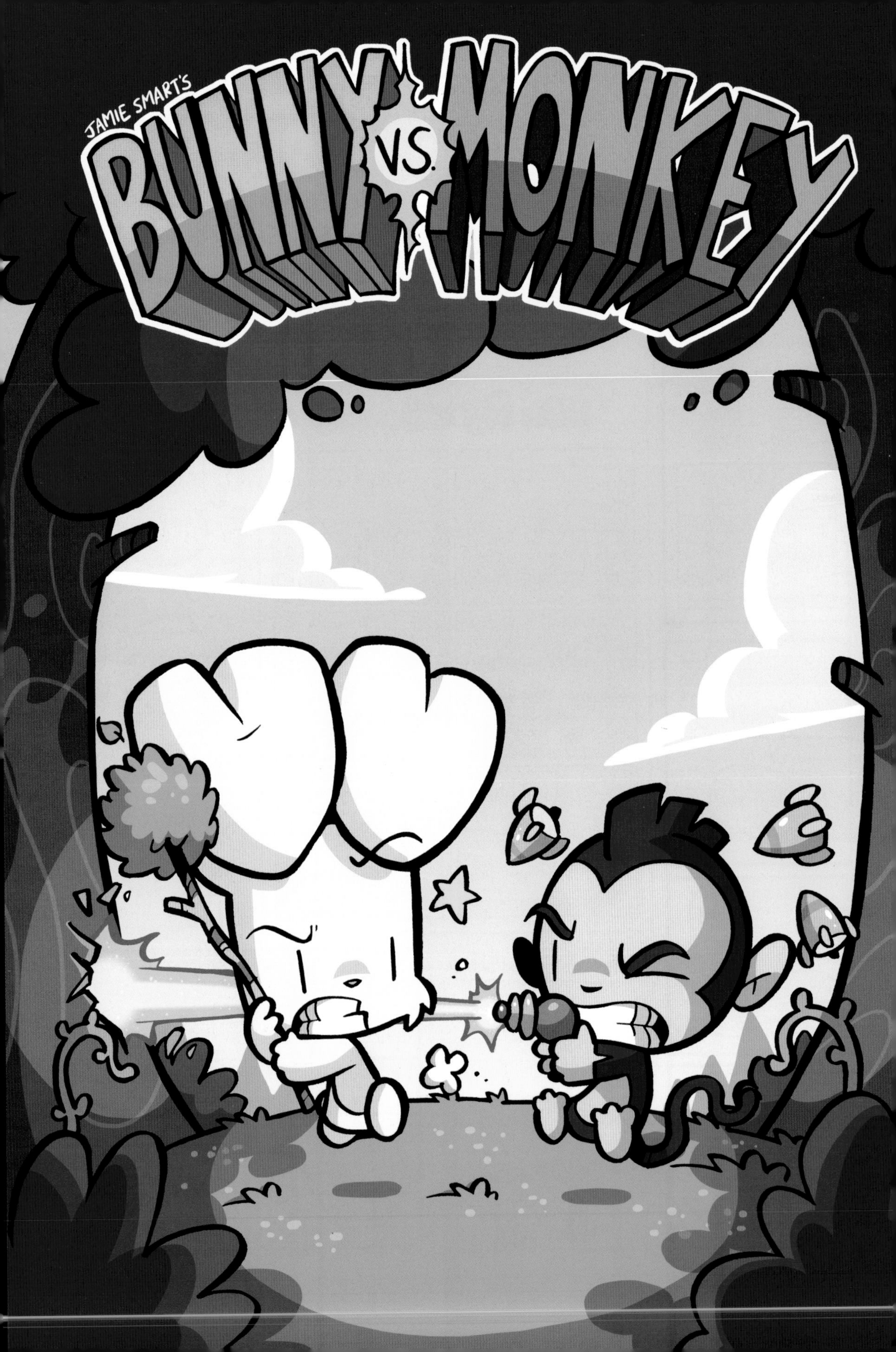
JAMIE SMART'S
BUNNY VS. MONKEY

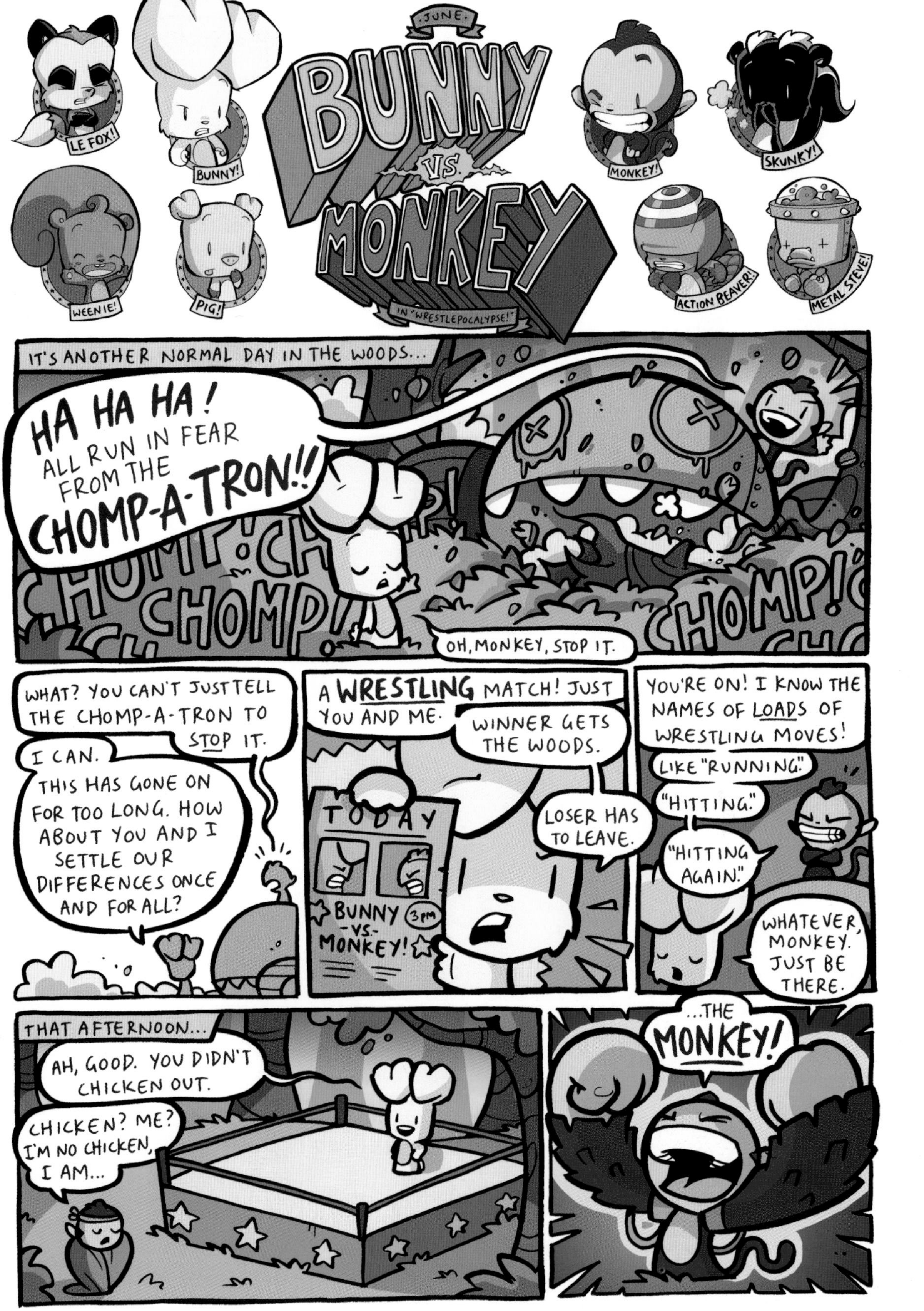

JUNE
BUNNY VS. MONKEY
IN "WRESTLEPOCALYPSE!"
LE FOX!
BUNNY!
WEENIE!
PIG!
MONKEY!
SKUNKY!
ACTION BEAVER!
METAL STEVE!
IT'S ANOTHER NORMAL DAY IN THE WOODS...
HA HA HA! ALL RUN IN FEAR FROM THE CHOMP-A-TRON!!
CHOMP! CHOMP! CHOMP!
OH, MONKEY, STOP IT.
WHAT? YOU CAN'T JUST TELL THE CHOMP-A-TRON TO STOP IT.
I CAN. THIS HAS GONE ON FOR TOO LONG. HOW ABOUT YOU AND I SETTLE OUR DIFFERENCES ONCE AND FOR ALL?
A WRESTLING MATCH! JUST YOU AND ME.
WINNER GETS THE WOODS.
LOSER HAS TO LEAVE.
TODAY
BUNNY -VS.- MONKEY! 3PM
YOU'RE ON! I KNOW THE NAMES OF LOADS OF WRESTLING MOVES!
LIKE "RUNNING."
"HITTING."
"HITTING AGAIN."
WHATEVER, MONKEY. JUST BE THERE.
THAT AFTERNOON...
AH, GOOD. YOU DIDN'T CHICKEN OUT.
CHICKEN? ME? I'M NO CHICKEN, I AM...
...THE MONKEY!

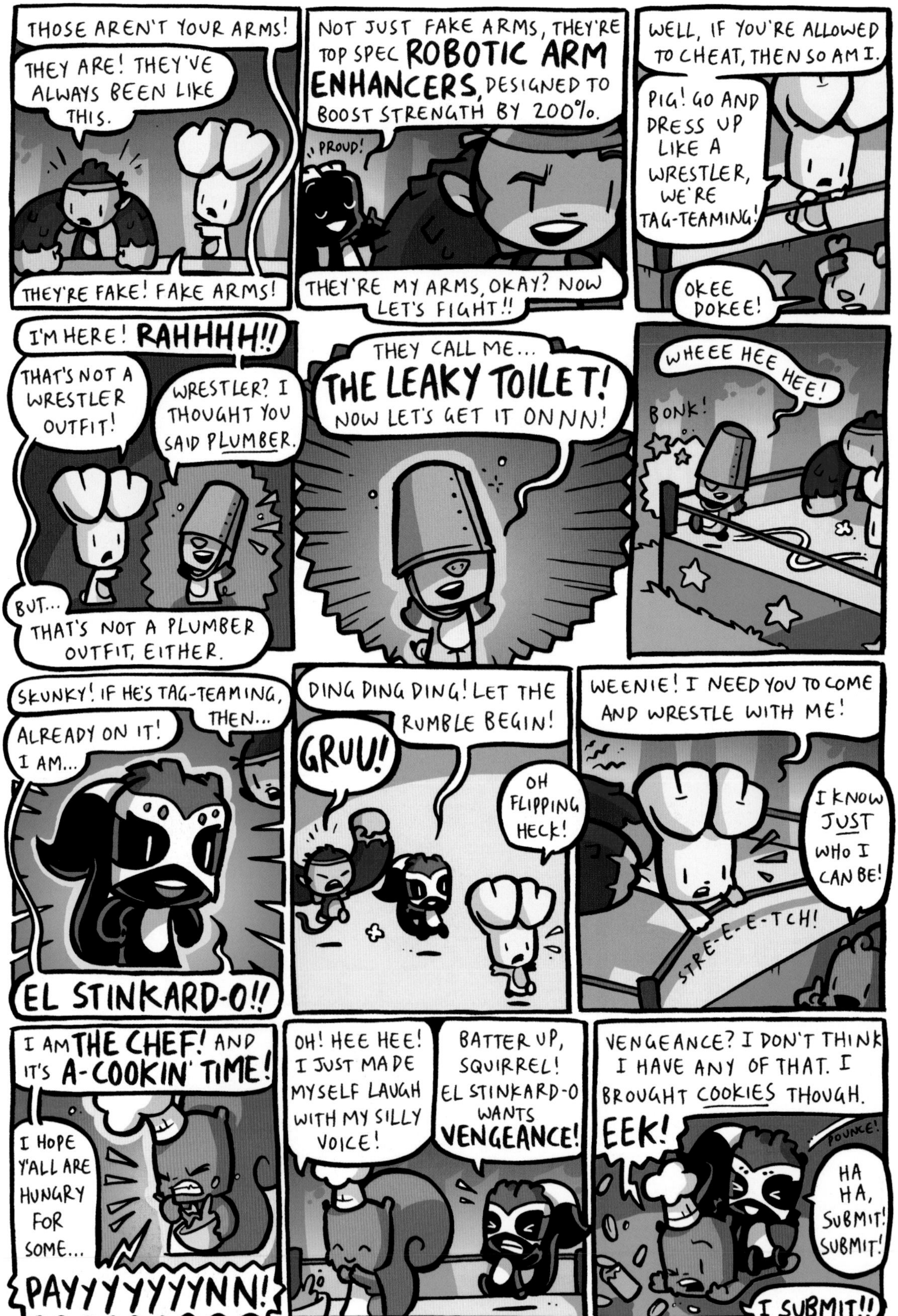
THOSE AREN'T YOUR ARMS!
THEY ARE! THEY'VE ALWAYS BEEN LIKE THIS.
THEY'RE FAKE! FAKE ARMS!
NOT JUST FAKE ARMS, THEY'RE TOP SPEC ROBOTIC ARM ENHANCERS, DESIGNED TO BOOST STRENGTH BY 200%.
PROUD!
THEY'RE MY ARMS, OKAY? NOW LET'S FIGHT!!
WELL, IF YOU'RE ALLOWED TO CHEAT, THEN SO AM I.
PIG! GO AND DRESS UP LIKE A WRESTLER, WE'RE TAG-TEAMING!
OKEE DOKEE!
I'M HERE! RAHHHH!!
THAT'S NOT A WRESTLER OUTFIT!
WRESTLER? I THOUGHT YOU SAID PLUMBER.
BUT... THAT'S NOT A PLUMBER OUTFIT, EITHER.
THEY CALL ME... THE LEAKY TOILET! NOW LET'S GET IT ONNN!
WHEEE HEE HEE!
BONK!
SKUNKY! IF HE'S TAG-TEAMING, THEN...
ALREADY ON IT! I AM...
EL STINKARD-O!!
DING DING DING! LET THE RUMBLE BEGIN!
GRUU!
OH FLIPPING HECK!
WEENIE! I NEED YOU TO COME AND WRESTLE WITH ME!
I KNOW JUST WHO I CAN BE!
STRE-E-E-TCH!
I AM THE CHEF! AND IT'S A-COOKIN' TIME!
I HOPE Y'ALL ARE HUNGRY FOR SOME...
PAYYYYYYYNN!
OH! HEE HEE! I JUST MADE MYSELF LAUGH WITH MY SILLY VOICE!
BATTER UP, SQUIRREL! EL STINKARD-O WANTS VENGEANCE!
VENGEANCE? I DON'T THINK I HAVE ANY OF THAT. I BROUGHT COOKIES THOUGH.
EEK!
POUNCE!
HA HA, SUBMIT! SUBMIT!
I SUBMIT!!

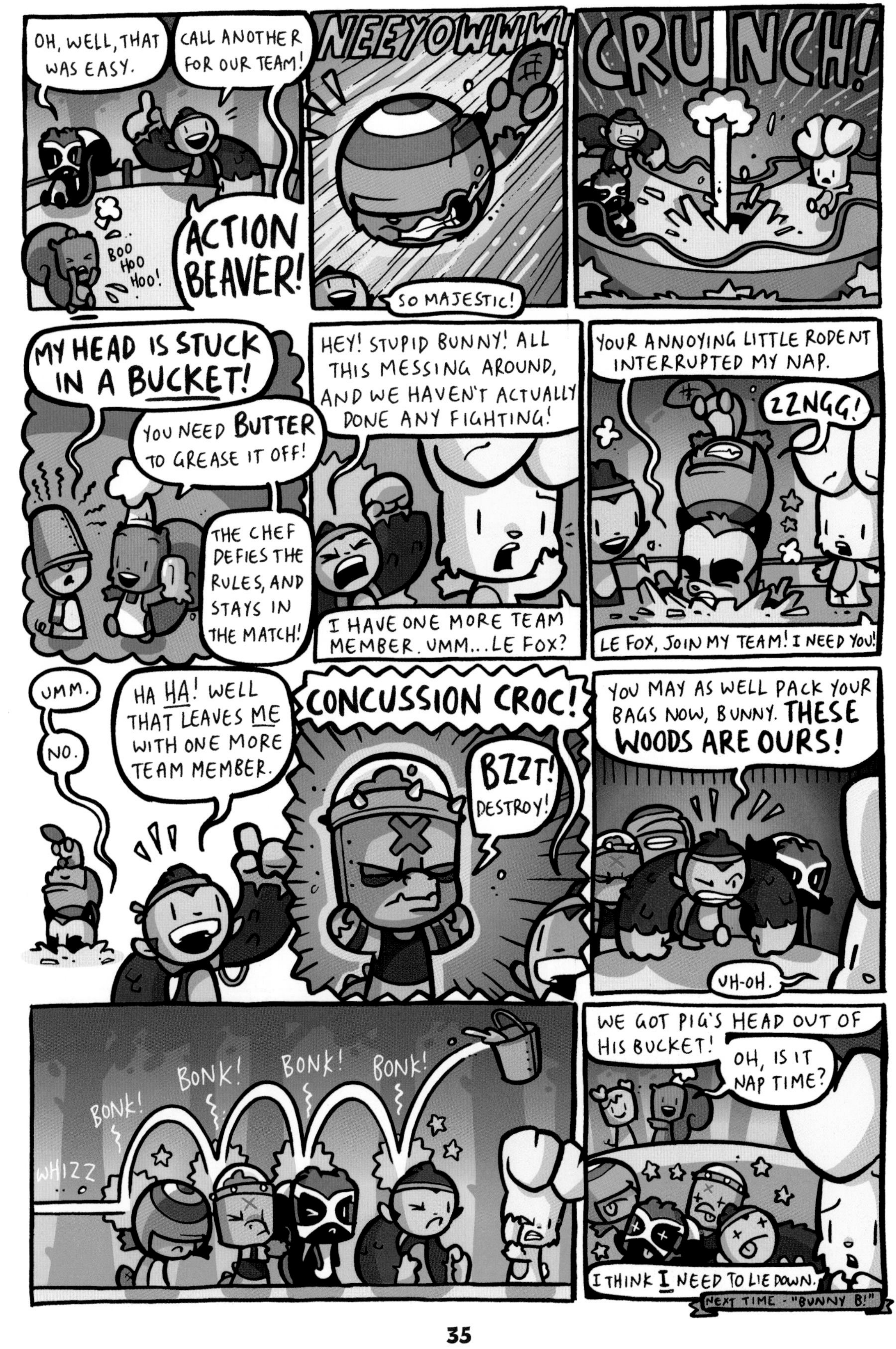
OH, WELL, THAT WAS EASY.
CALL ANOTHER FOR OUR TEAM!
BOO HOO HOO!
ACTION BEAVER!
NEEYOWWW!
SO MAJESTIC!
CRUNCH!
MY HEAD IS STUCK IN A BUCKET!
YOU NEED BUTTER TO GREASE IT OFF!
THE CHEF DEFIES THE RULES, AND STAYS IN THE MATCH!
HEY! STUPID BUNNY! ALL THIS MESSING AROUND, AND WE HAVEN'T ACTUALLY DONE ANY FIGHTING!
I HAVE ONE MORE TEAM MEMBER. UMM... LE FOX?
YOUR ANNOYING LITTLE RODENT INTERRUPTED MY NAP.
ZZNGG!
LE FOX, JOIN MY TEAM! I NEED YOU!
UMM.
NO.
HA HA! WELL THAT LEAVES ME WITH ONE MORE TEAM MEMBER.
CONCUSSION CROC!
BZZT! DESTROY!
YOU MAY AS WELL PACK YOUR BAGS NOW, BUNNY. THESE WOODS ARE OURS!
UH-OH.
WHIZZ
BONK!
BONK!
BONK!
BONK!
WE GOT PIG'S HEAD OUT OF HIS BUCKET!
OH, IS IT NAP TIME?
I THINK I NEED TO LIE DOWN.
NEXT TIME - "BUNNY B!"

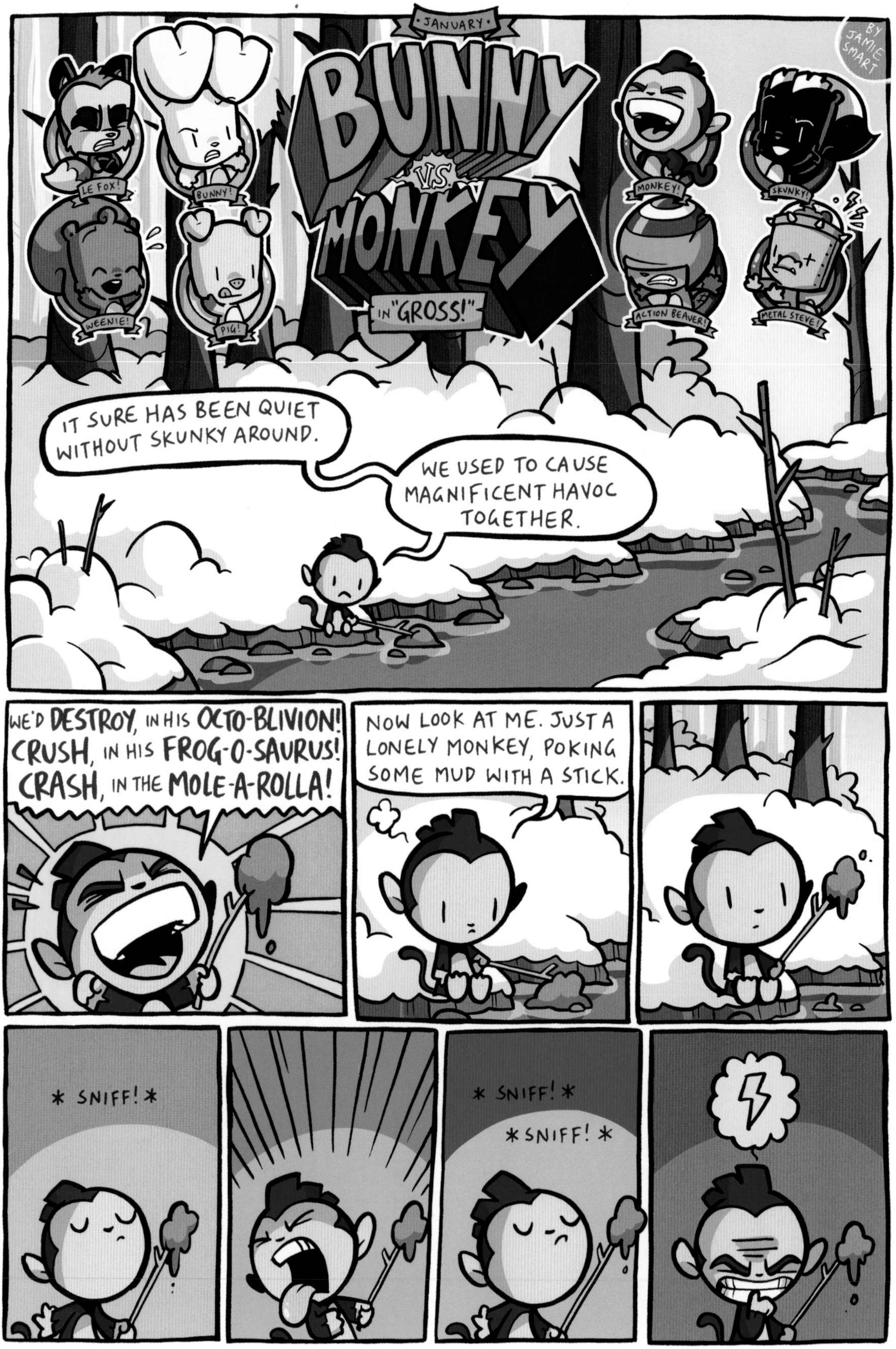
JANUARY
BY JAMIE SMART
BUNNY VS. MONKEY
IN "GROSS!"
LE FOX!
BUNNY!
WEENIE!
PIG!
MONKEY!
SKUNKY!
ACTION BEAVER!
METAL STEVE!
IT SURE HAS BEEN QUIET WITHOUT SKUNKY AROUND.
WE USED TO CAUSE MAGNIFICENT HAVOC TOGETHER.
WE'D DESTROY, IN HIS OCTO-BLIVION! CRUSH, IN HIS FROG-O-SAURUS! CRASH, IN THE MOLE-A-ROLLA!
NOW LOOK AT ME. JUST A LONELY MONKEY, POKING SOME MUD WITH A STICK.
* SNIFF! *
* SNIFF! *
* SNIFF! *

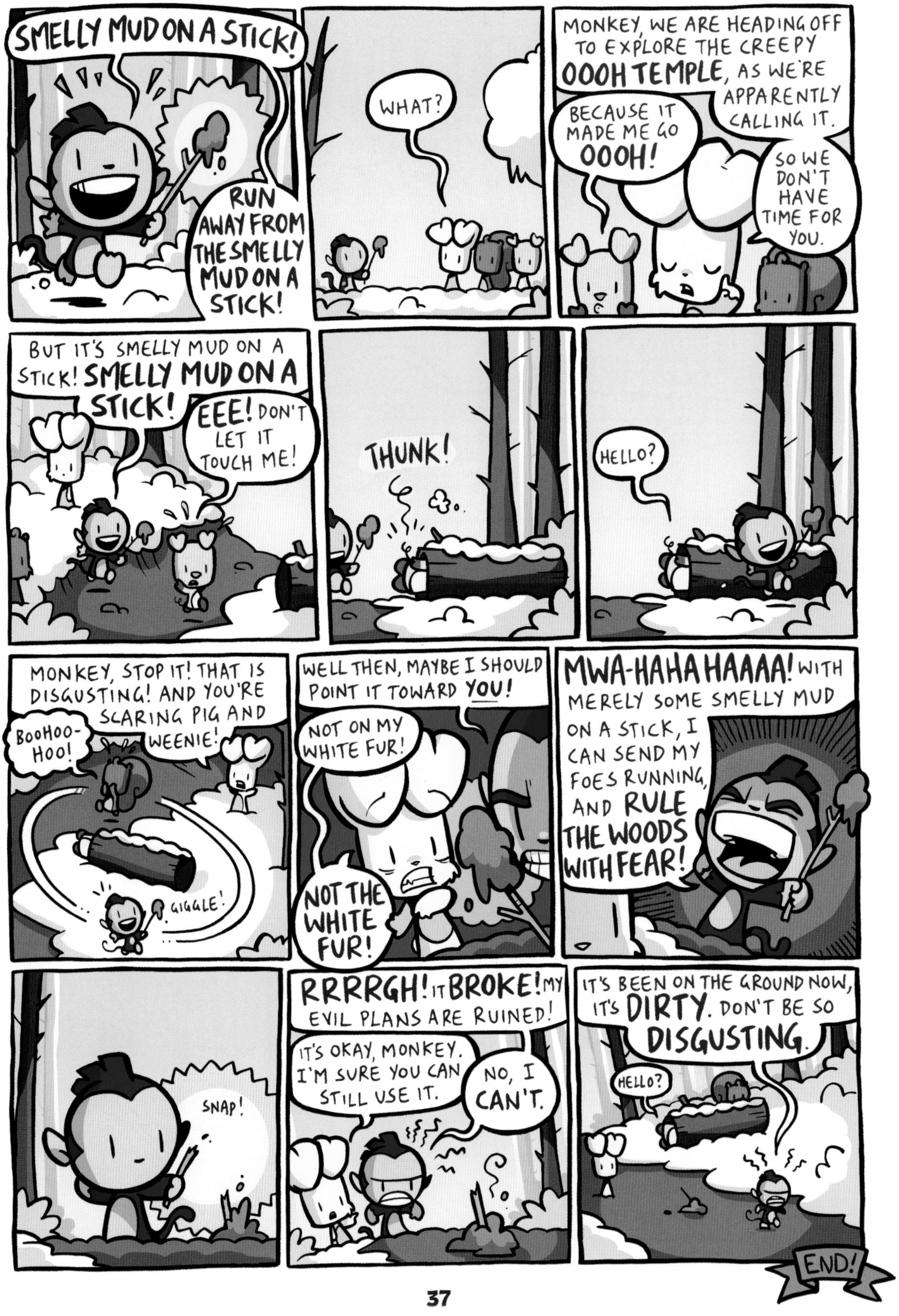
SMELLY MUD ON A STICK!
RUN AWAY FROM THE SMELLY MUD ON A STICK!
WHAT?
MONKEY, WE ARE HEADING OFF TO EXPLORE THE CREEPY OOOH TEMPLE, AS WE'RE APPARENTLY CALLING IT.
BECAUSE IT MADE ME GO OOOH!
SO WE DON'T HAVE TIME FOR YOU.
BUT IT'S SMELLY MUD ON A STICK! SMELLY MUD ON A STICK!
EEE! DON'T LET IT TOUCH ME!
THUNK!
HELLO?
MONKEY, STOP IT! THAT IS DISGUSTING! AND YOU'RE SCARING PIG AND WEENIE!
BOOHOO-HOO!
GIGGLE!
WELL THEN, MAYBE I SHOULD POINT IT TOWARD YOU!
NOT ON MY WHITE FUR!
NOT THE WHITE FUR!
MWA-HAHA HAAAA! WITH MERELY SOME SMELLY MUD ON A STICK, I CAN SEND MY FOES RUNNING, AND RULE THE WOODS WITH FEAR!
SNAP!
RRRRGH! IT BROKE! MY EVIL PLANS ARE RUINED!
IT'S OKAY, MONKEY. I'M SURE YOU CAN STILL USE IT.
NO, I CAN'T.
IT'S BEEN ON THE GROUND NOW, IT'S DIRTY. DON'T BE SO DISGUSTING.
HELLO?
END!

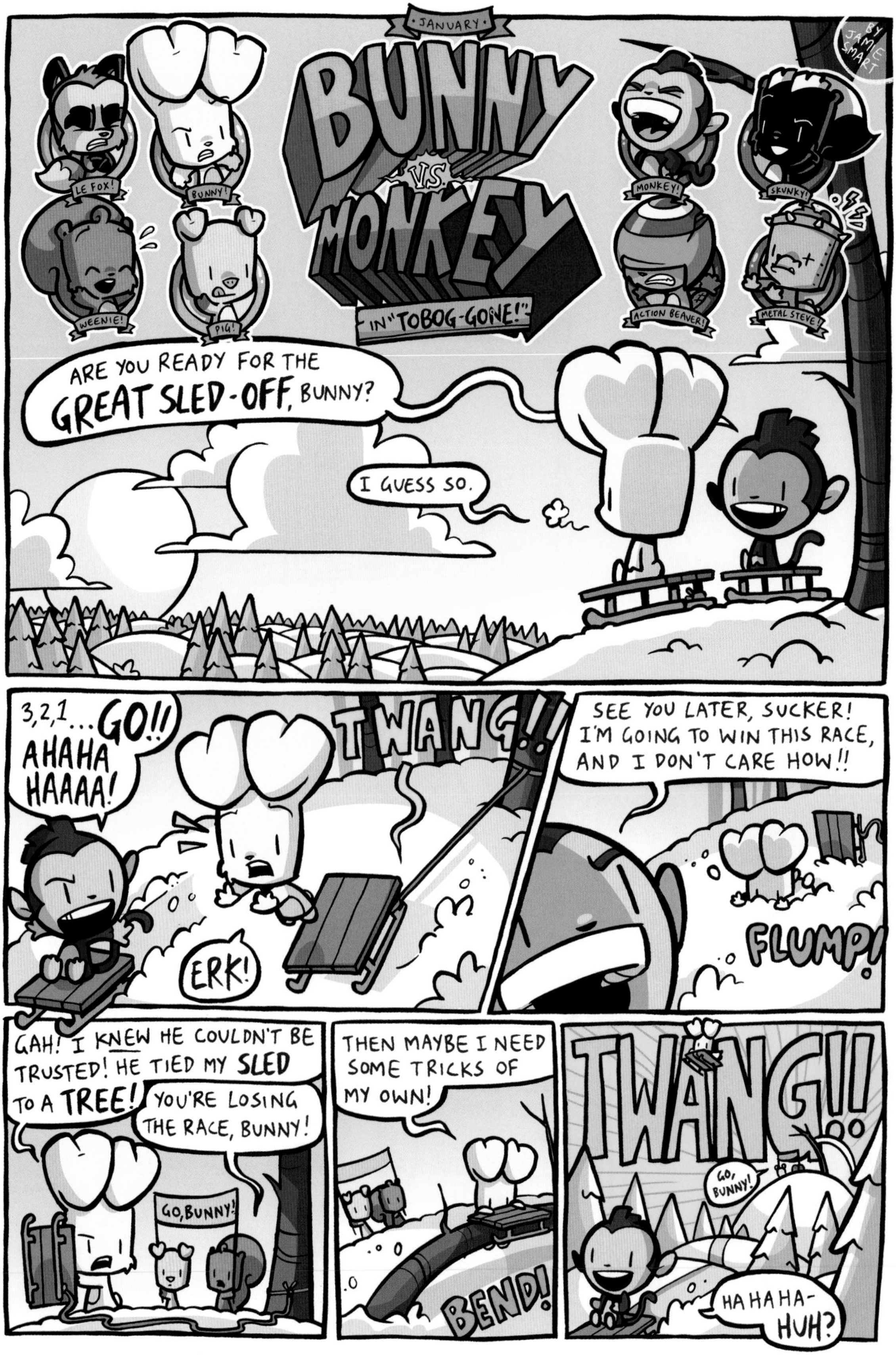
JANUARY
BY JAMIE SMART
BUNNY VS. MONKEY
IN "TOBOG-GONE!"
LE FOX!
BUNNY!
WEENIE!
PIG!
MONKEY!
SKUNKY!
ACTION BEAVER!
METAL STEVE!
ARE YOU READY FOR THE GREAT SLED-OFF, BUNNY?
I GUESS SO.
3,2,1...GO!! AHAHA HAAAA!
TWANG!!
ERK!
SEE YOU LATER, SUCKER! I'M GOING TO WIN THIS RACE, AND I DON'T CARE HOW!!
FLUMP!
GAH! I KNEW HE COULDN'T BE TRUSTED! HE TIED MY SLED TO A TREE!
YOU'RE LOSING THE RACE, BUNNY!
GO, BUNNY!
THEN MAYBE I NEED SOME TRICKS OF MY OWN!
BEND!
TWANG!!
GO, BUNNY!
HA HA HA- HUH?

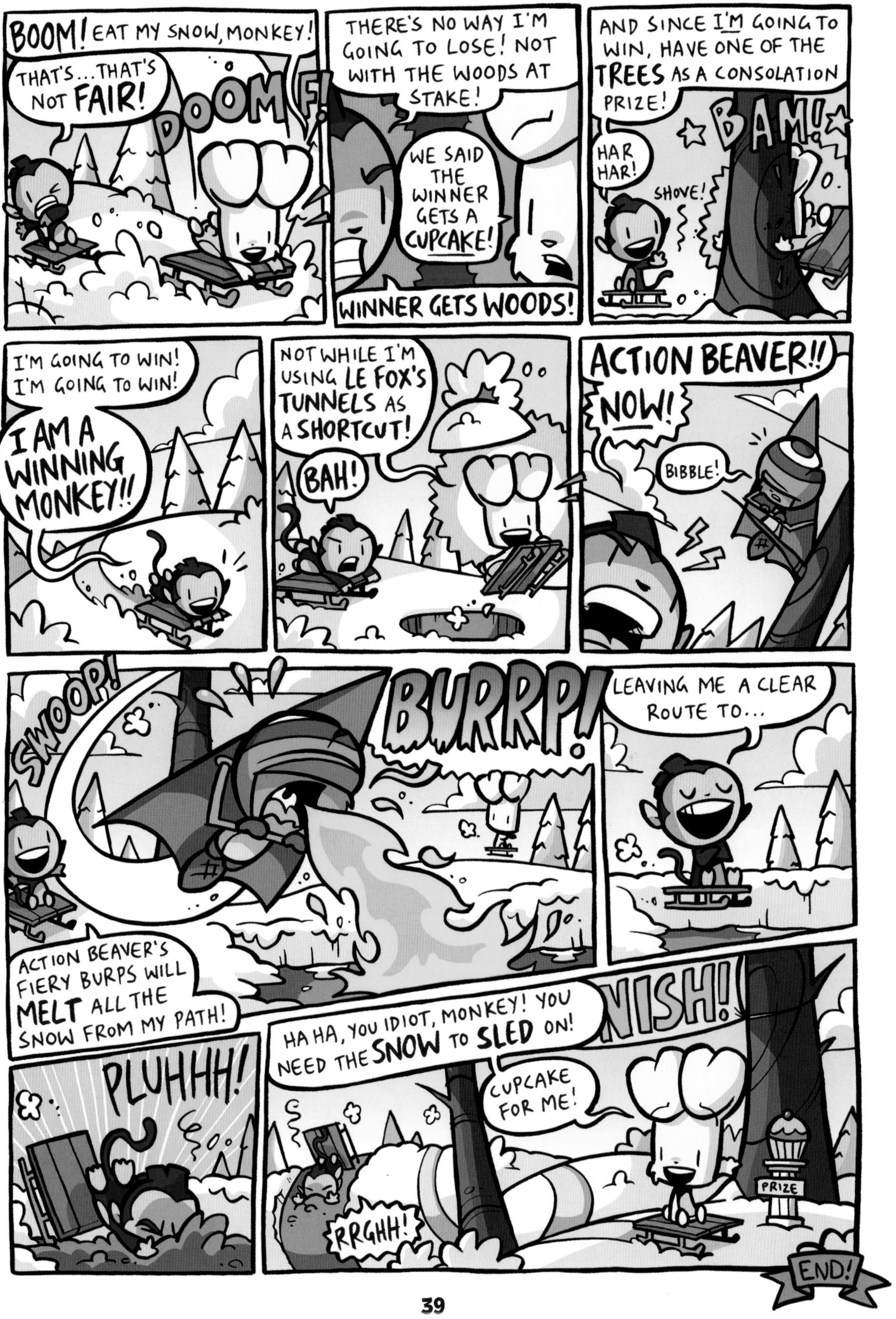
BOOM! EAT MY SNOW, MONKEY!
THAT'S... THAT'S NOT FAIR!
DOOMF!
THERE'S NO WAY I'M GOING TO LOSE! NOT WITH THE WOODS AT STAKE!
WE SAID THE WINNER GETS A CUPCAKE!
WINNER GETS WOODS!
AND SINCE I'M GOING TO WIN, HAVE ONE OF THE TREES AS A CONSOLATION PRIZE!
HAR HAR!
BAM!
SHOVE!
I'M GOING TO WIN! I'M GOING TO WIN!
I AM A WINNING MONKEY!!
NOT WHILE I'M USING LE FOX'S TUNNELS AS A SHORTCUT!
BAH!
ACTION BEAVER!! NOW!
BIBBLE!
SWOOP!
BURRP!
LEAVING ME A CLEAR ROUTE TO...
ACTION BEAVER'S FIERY BURPS WILL MELT ALL THE SNOW FROM MY PATH!
PLUHHH!
HA HA, YOU IDIOT, MONKEY! YOU NEED THE SNOW TO SLED ON!
NISH!
CUPCAKE FOR ME!
RRGHH!
PRIZE
END!

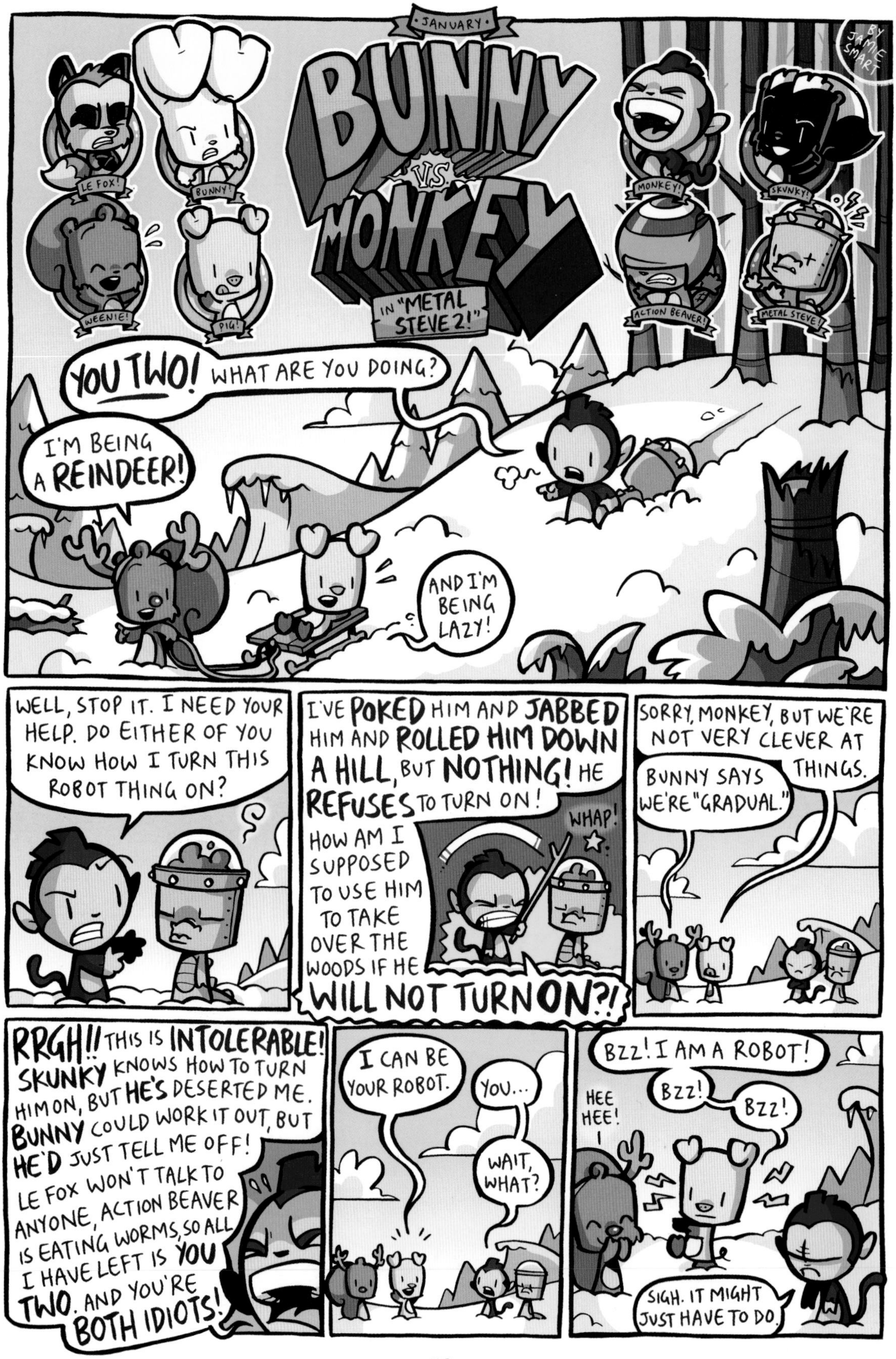
JANUARY
BUNNY VS. MONKEY
IN "METAL STEVE 2!"
BY JAMIE SMART
LE FOX!
BUNNY!
WEENIE!
PIG!
MONKEY!
SKUNKY!
ACTION BEAVER!
METAL STEVE!
YOU TWO! WHAT ARE YOU DOING?
I'M BEING A REINDEER!
AND I'M BEING LAZY!
WELL, STOP IT. I NEED YOUR HELP. DO EITHER OF YOU KNOW HOW I TURN THIS ROBOT THING ON?
I'VE POKED HIM AND JABBED HIM AND ROLLED HIM DOWN A HILL, BUT NOTHING! HE REFUSES TO TURN ON!
WHAP!
HOW AM I SUPPOSED TO USE HIM TO TAKE OVER THE WOODS IF HE WILL NOT TURN ON?!
SORRY, MONKEY, BUT WE'RE NOT VERY CLEVER AT THINGS.
BUNNY SAYS WE'RE "GRADUAL."
RRGH!! THIS IS INTOLERABLE! SKUNKY KNOWS HOW TO TURN HIM ON, BUT HE'S DESERTED ME. BUNNY COULD WORK IT OUT, BUT HE'D JUST TELL ME OFF! LE FOX WON'T TALK TO ANYONE, ACTION BEAVER IS EATING WORMS, SO ALL I HAVE LEFT IS YOU TWO. AND YOU'RE BOTH IDIOTS!
I CAN BE YOUR ROBOT.
YOU...
WAIT, WHAT?
BZZ! I AM A ROBOT!
HEE HEE!
BZZ!
BZZ!
SIGH. IT MIGHT JUST HAVE TO DO.

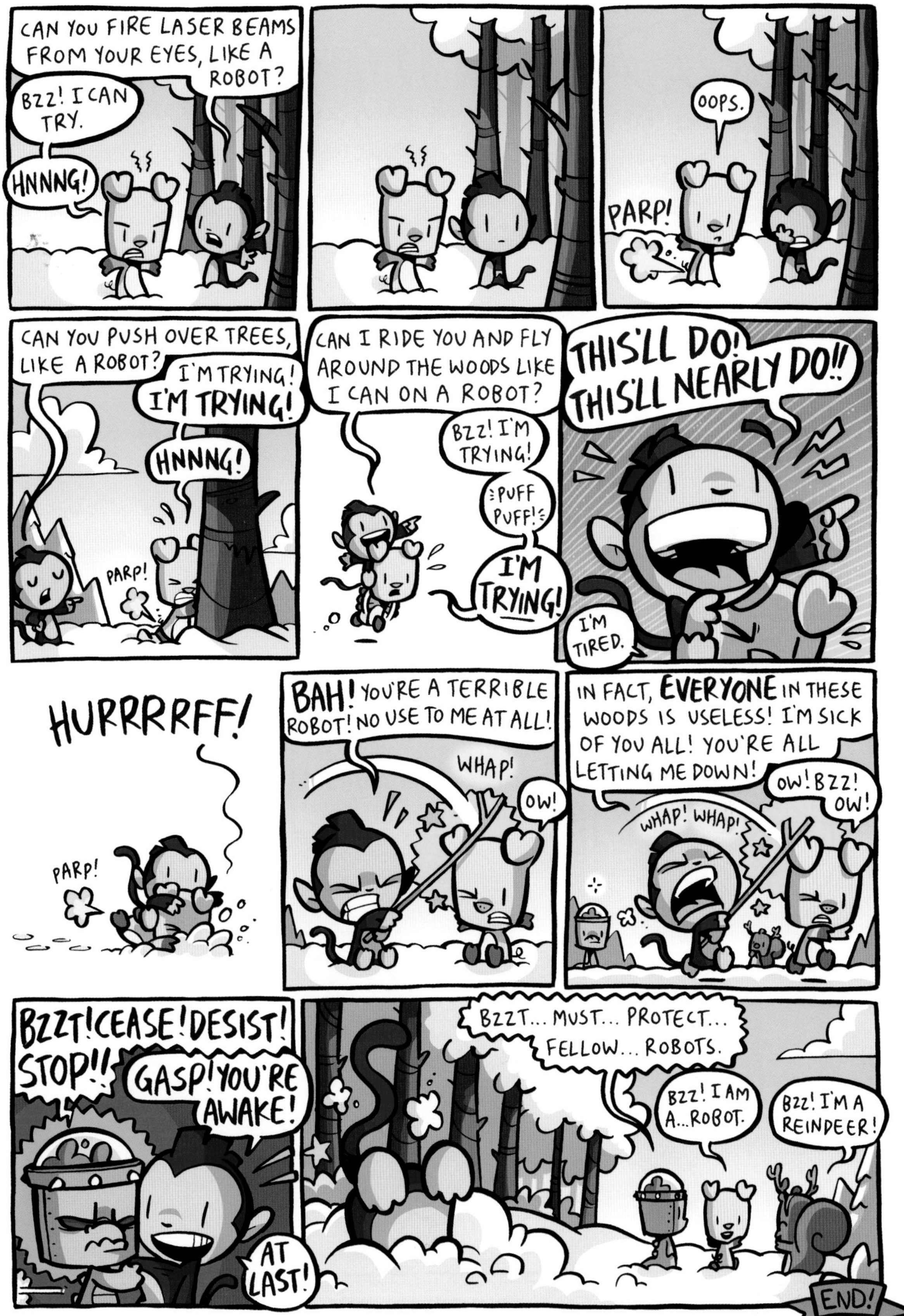
CAN YOU FIRE LASER BEAMS FROM YOUR EYES, LIKE A ROBOT?
BZZ! I CAN TRY.
HNNNG!
OOPS.
PARP!
CAN YOU PUSH OVER TREES, LIKE A ROBOT?
I'M TRYING! I'M TRYING!
HNNNG!
PARP!
CAN I RIDE YOU AND FLY AROUND THE WOODS LIKE I CAN ON A ROBOT?
BZZ! I'M TRYING!
PUFF PUFF!
I'M TRYING!
THIS'LL DO! THIS'LL NEARLY DO!!
I'M TIRED.
HURRRRFF!
PARP!
BAH! YOU'RE A TERRIBLE ROBOT! NO USE TO ME AT ALL!
WHAP!
OW!
IN FACT, EVERYONE IN THESE WOODS IS USELESS! I'M SICK OF YOU ALL! YOU'RE ALL LETTING ME DOWN!
WHAP! WHAP!
OW! BZZ! OW!
BZZT! CEASE! DESIST! STOP!!
GASP! YOU'RE AWAKE!
AT LAST!
BZZT... MUST... PROTECT... FELLOW... ROBOTS.
BZZ! I AM A...ROBOT.
BZZ! I'M A REINDEER!
END!

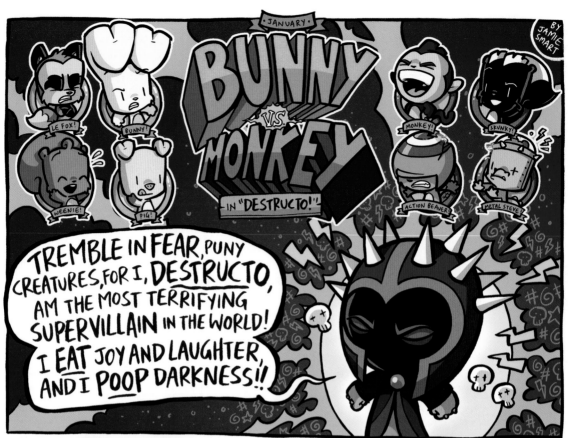

JANUARY
BUNNY VS. MONKEY
IN "DESTRUCTO!"
BY JAMIE SMART
LE FOX!
BUNNY!
WEENIE!
PIG!
MONKEY!
SKUNKY!
ACTION BEAVER!
METAL STEVE!
TREMBLE IN FEAR, PUNY CREATURES, FOR I, DESTRUCTO, AM THE MOST TERRIFYING SUPERVILLAIN IN THE WORLD! I EAT JOY AND LAUGHTER, AND I POOP DARKNESS!!
SHHH! YOU'LL SCARE THE FISH!
DIDN'T YOU HEAR WHAT I SAID? I WILL ENSLAVE THIS WORLD, AND TURN ALL YOUR HAPPINESS INTO DUST! I AM A BRUTAL NIGHTMARE!
SHHHHHHHHH!!
THPTHBTHHHHH!!
OH, BEHAVE.

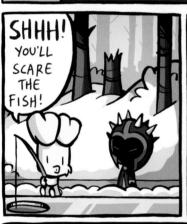

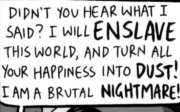

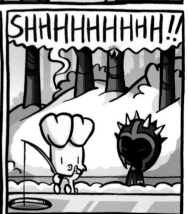

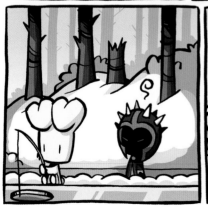

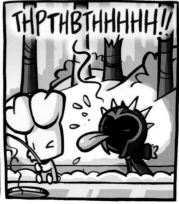

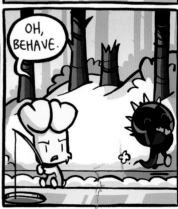

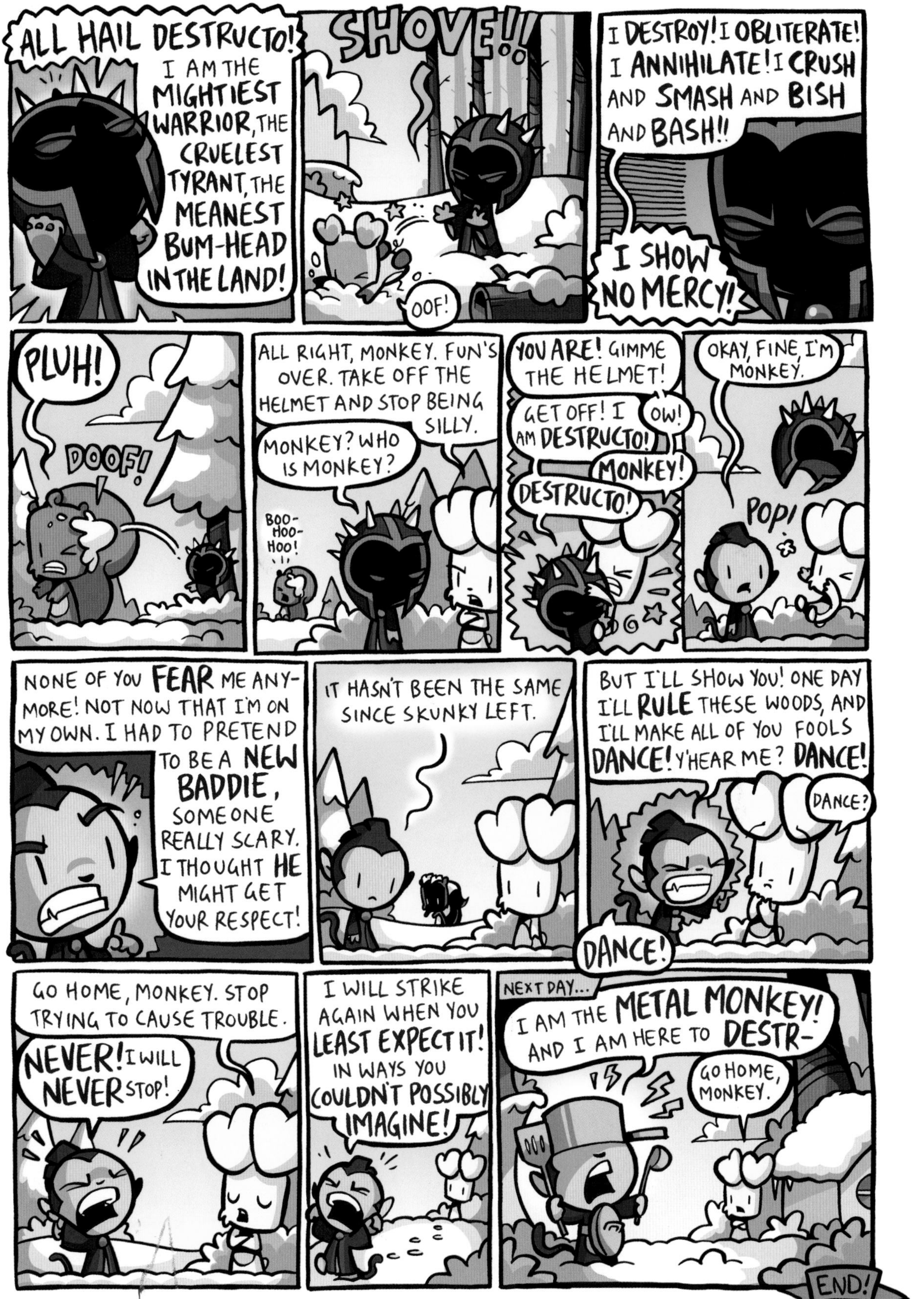

ALL HAIL DESTRUCTO!
I AM THE MIGHTIEST WARRIOR, THE CRUELEST TYRANT, THE MEANEST BUM-HEAD IN THE LAND!
SHOVE!!
OOF!
I DESTROY! I OBLITERATE! I ANNIHILATE! I CRUSH AND SMASH AND BISH AND BASH!!
I SHOW NO MERCY!
PLUH!
DOOF!
ALL RIGHT, MONKEY. FUN'S OVER. TAKE OFF THE HELMET AND STOP BEING SILLY.
MONKEY? WHO IS MONKEY?
BOO-HOO-HOO!
YOU ARE! GIMME THE HELMET!
GET OFF! I AM DESTRUCTO!
OW!
MONKEY!
DESTRUCTO!
OKAY, FINE, I'M MONKEY.
POP!
NONE OF YOU FEAR ME ANYMORE! NOT NOW THAT I'M ON MY OWN. I HAD TO PRETEND TO BE A NEW BADDIE, SOMEONE REALLY SCARY. I THOUGHT HE MIGHT GET YOUR RESPECT!
IT HASN'T BEEN THE SAME SINCE SKUNKY LEFT.
BUT I'LL SHOW YOU! ONE DAY I'LL RULE THESE WOODS, AND I'LL MAKE ALL OF YOU FOOLS DANCE! Y'HEAR ME? DANCE!
DANCE?
DANCE!
GO HOME, MONKEY. STOP TRYING TO CAUSE TROUBLE.
NEVER! I WILL NEVER STOP!
I WILL STRIKE AGAIN WHEN YOU LEAST EXPECT IT! IN WAYS YOU COULDN'T POSSIBLY IMAGINE!
NEXT DAY...
I AM THE METAL MONKEY! AND I AM HERE TO DESTR-
GO HOME, MONKEY.
END!

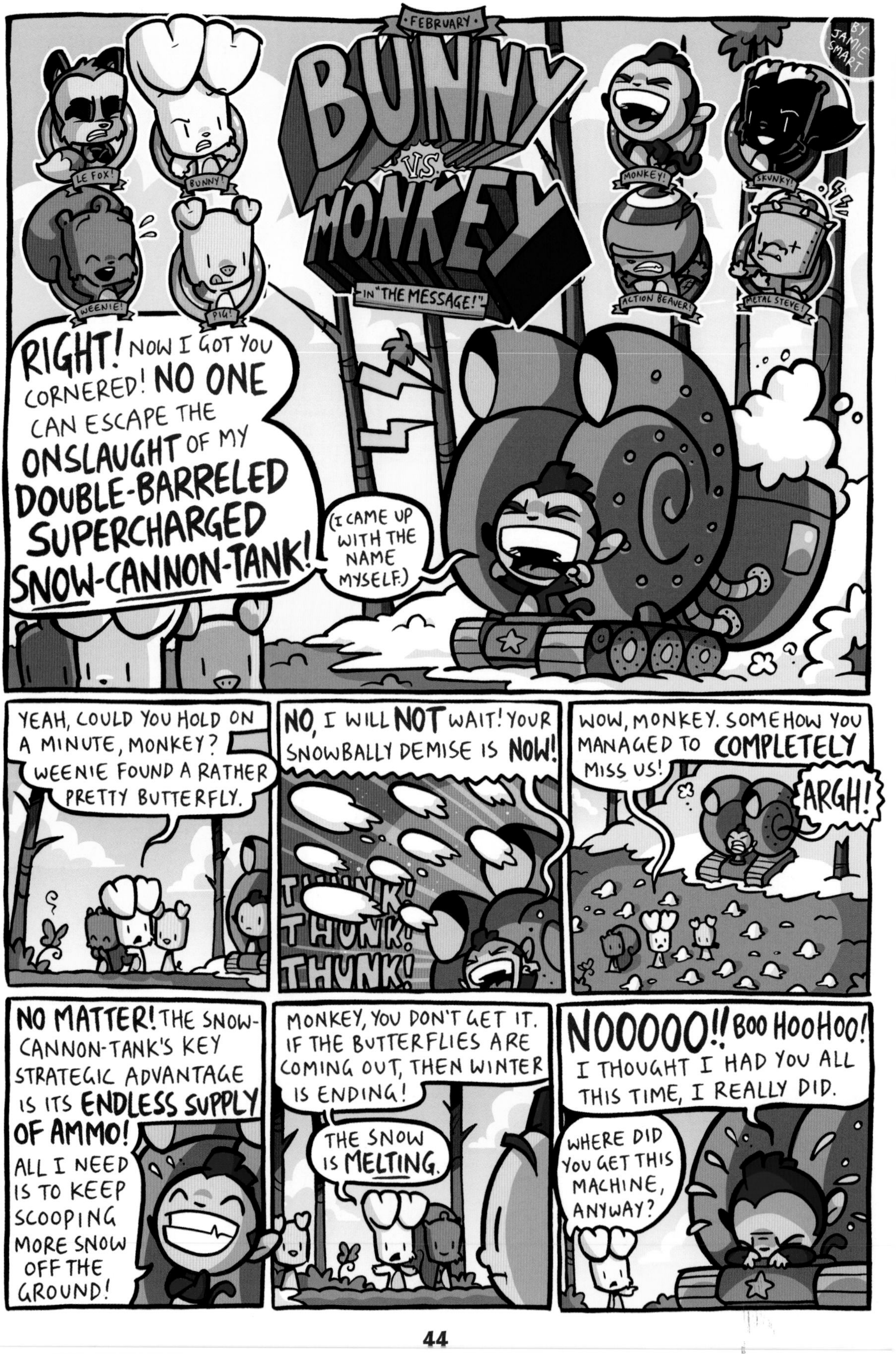
FEBRUARY
BUNNY VS. MONKEY
IN "THE MESSAGE!"
BY JAMIE SMART
LE FOX!
BUNNY!
WEENIE!
PIG!
MONKEY!
SKUNKY!
ACTION BEAVER!
METAL STEVE!
RIGHT! NOW I GOT YOU CORNERED! NO ONE CAN ESCAPE THE ONSLAUGHT OF MY DOUBLE-BARRELED SUPERCHARGED SNOW-CANNON-TANK!
(I CAME UP WITH THE NAME MYSELF.)
YEAH, COULD YOU HOLD ON A MINUTE, MONKEY?
WEENIE FOUND A RATHER PRETTY BUTTERFLY.
NO, I WILL NOT WAIT! YOUR SNOWBALLY DEMISE IS NOW!
THUNK! THUNK! THUNK!
WOW, MONKEY. SOMEHOW YOU MANAGED TO COMPLETELY MISS US!
ARGH!
NO MATTER! THE SNOW-CANNON-TANK'S KEY STRATEGIC ADVANTAGE IS ITS ENDLESS SUPPLY OF AMMO!
ALL I NEED IS TO KEEP SCOOPING MORE SNOW OFF THE GROUND!
MONKEY, YOU DON'T GET IT. IF THE BUTTERFLIES ARE COMING OUT, THEN WINTER IS ENDING!
THE SNOW IS MELTING.
NOOOOO!! BOO HOOHOO! I THOUGHT I HAD YOU ALL THIS TIME, I REALLY DID.
WHERE DID YOU GET THIS MACHINE, ANYWAY?

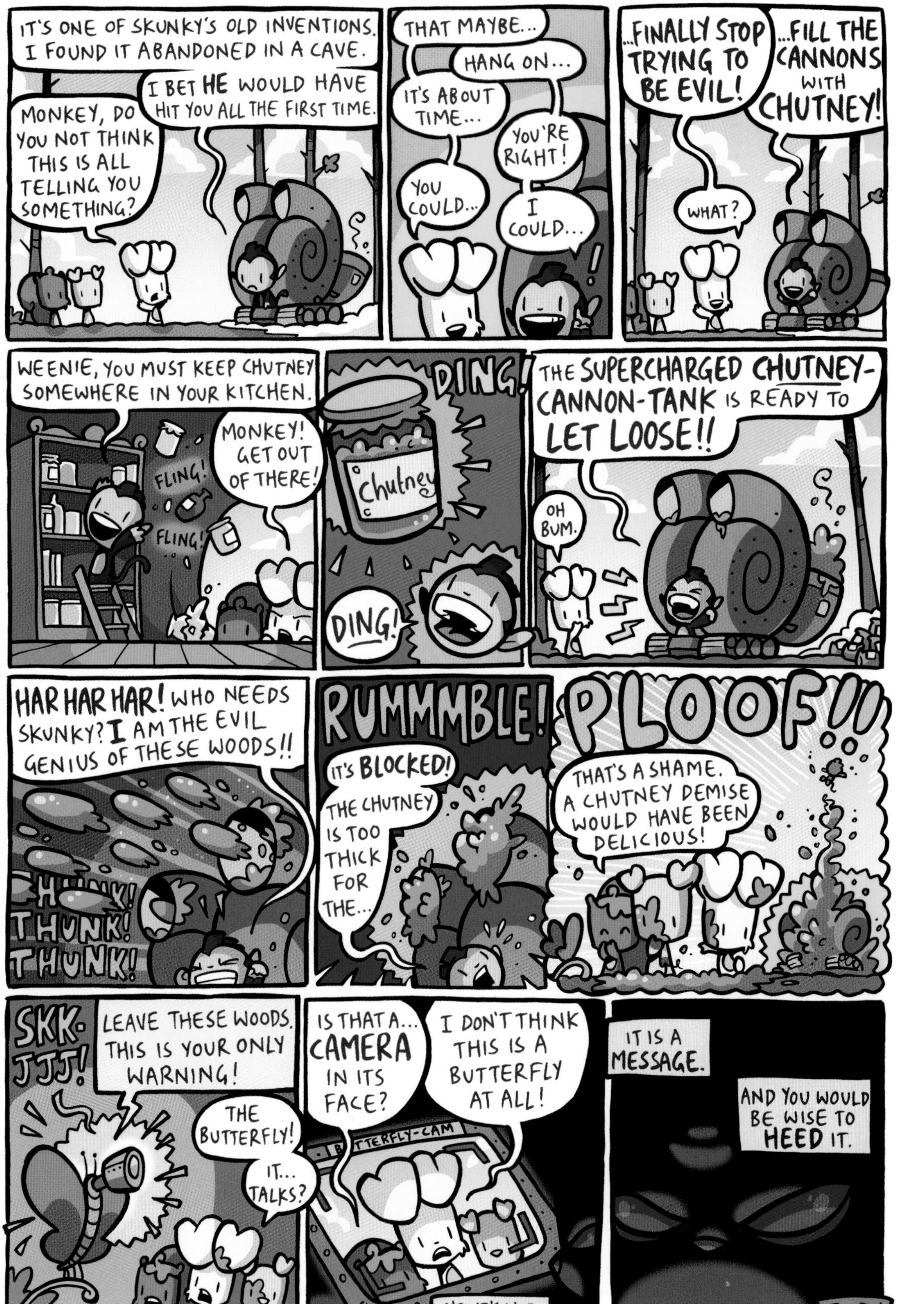
IT'S ONE OF SKUNKY'S OLD INVENTIONS. I FOUND IT ABANDONED IN A CAVE.
MONKEY, DO YOU NOT THINK THIS IS ALL TELLING YOU SOMETHING?
I BET HE WOULD HAVE HIT YOU ALL THE FIRST TIME.
THAT MAYBE...
HANG ON...
IT'S ABOUT TIME...
YOU'RE RIGHT!
YOU COULD...
I COULD...
...FINALLY STOP TRYING TO BE EVIL!
...FILL THE CANNONS WITH CHUTNEY!
WHAT?
WEENIE, YOU MUST KEEP CHUTNEY SOMEWHERE IN YOUR KITCHEN.
MONKEY! GET OUT OF THERE!
FLING!
FLING!
DING!
Chutney
DING!
THE SUPERCHARGED CHUTNEY-CANNON-TANK IS READY TO LET LOOSE!!
OH BUM.
HAR HAR HAR! WHO NEEDS SKUNKY? I AM THE EVIL GENIUS OF THESE WOODS!!
THUNK!
THUNK!
THUNK!
RUMMMBLE!
IT'S BLOCKED!
THE CHUTNEY IS TOO THICK FOR THE...
PLOOF!!
THAT'S A SHAME. A CHUTNEY DEMISE WOULD HAVE BEEN DELICIOUS!
SKK-JJJ!
LEAVE THESE WOODS. THIS IS YOUR ONLY WARNING!
THE BUTTERFLY!
IT... TALKS?
IS THAT A... CAMERA IN ITS FACE?
I DON'T THINK THIS IS A BUTTERFLY AT ALL!
BUTTERFLY-CAM
NO, IT'S NOT...
IT IS A MESSAGE.
AND YOU WOULD BE WISE TO HEED IT.
END!

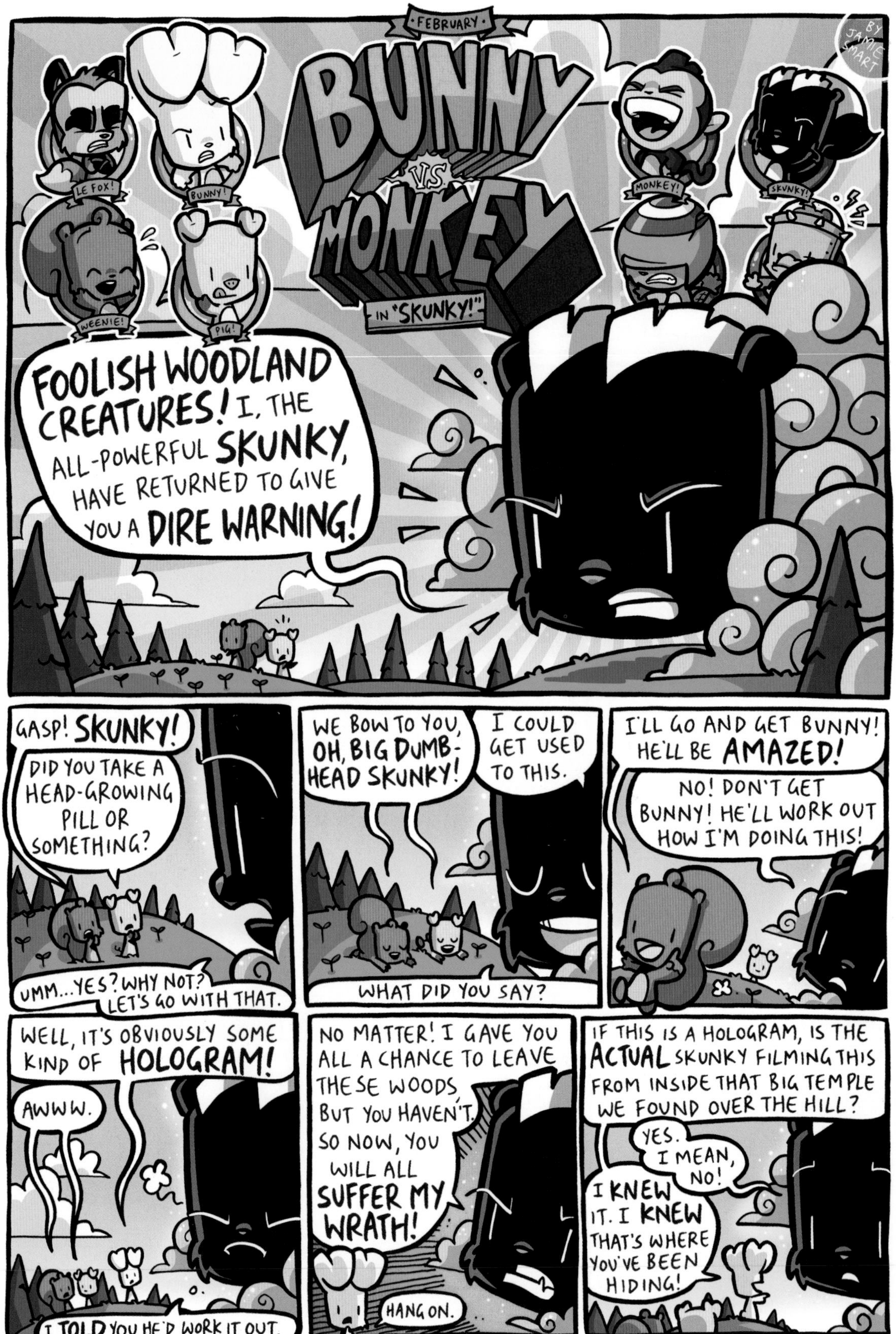
FEBRUARY
BY JAMIE SMART
LE FOX!
BUNNY!
WEENIE!
PIG!
BUNNY VS MONKEY
IN "SKUNKY!"
MONKEY!
SKUNKY!
FOOLISH WOODLAND CREATURES! I, THE ALL-POWERFUL SKUNKY, HAVE RETURNED TO GIVE YOU A DIRE WARNING!
GASP! SKUNKY!
DID YOU TAKE A HEAD-GROWING PILL OR SOMETHING?
UMM... YES? WHY NOT? LET'S GO WITH THAT.
WE BOW TO YOU, OH, BIG DUMB-HEAD SKUNKY!
I COULD GET USED TO THIS.
WHAT DID YOU SAY?
I'LL GO AND GET BUNNY! HE'LL BE AMAZED!
NO! DON'T GET BUNNY! HE'LL WORK OUT HOW I'M DOING THIS!
WELL, IT'S OBVIOUSLY SOME KIND OF HOLOGRAM!
AWWW.
I TOLD YOU HE'D WORK IT OUT.
NO MATTER! I GAVE YOU ALL A CHANCE TO LEAVE THESE WOODS BUT YOU HAVEN'T. SO NOW, YOU WILL ALL SUFFER MY WRATH!
HANG ON.
IF THIS IS A HOLOGRAM, IS THE ACTUAL SKUNKY FILMING THIS FROM INSIDE THAT BIG TEMPLE WE FOUND OVER THE HILL?
YES. I MEAN, NO!
I KNEW IT. I KNEW THAT'S WHERE YOU'VE BEEN HIDING!

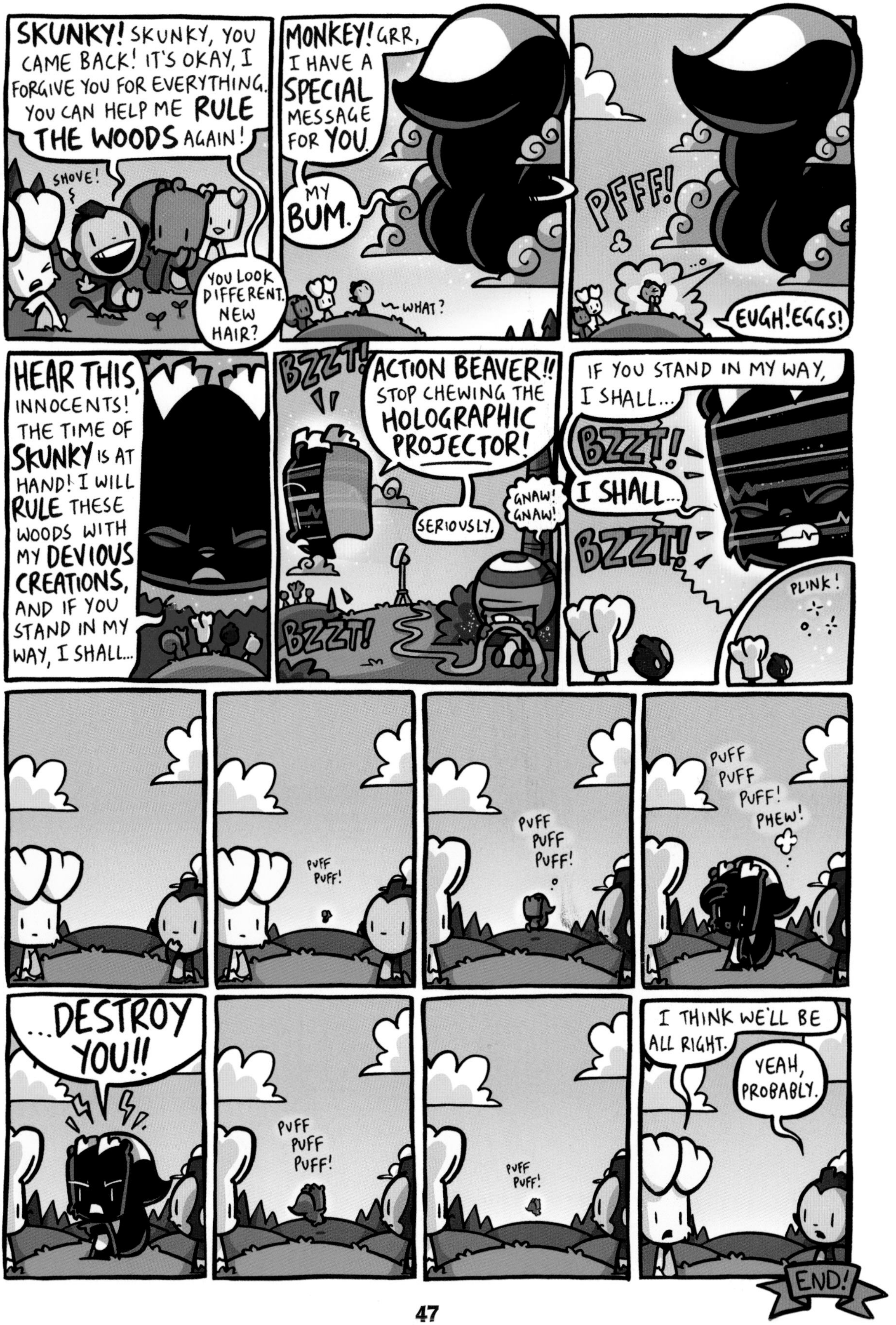
SKUNKY! SKUNKY, YOU CAME BACK! IT'S OKAY, I FORGIVE YOU FOR EVERYTHING. YOU CAN HELP ME RULE THE WOODS AGAIN!
SHOVE!
YOU LOOK DIFFERENT. NEW HAIR?
MONKEY! GRR, I HAVE A SPECIAL MESSAGE FOR YOU.
MY BUM.
WHAT?
PFFF!
EUGH! EGGS!
HEAR THIS, INNOCENTS! THE TIME OF SKUNKY IS AT HAND! I WILL RULE THESE WOODS WITH MY DEVIOUS CREATIONS, AND IF YOU STAND IN MY WAY, I SHALL...
BZZT!
ACTION BEAVER!! STOP CHEWING THE HOLOGRAPHIC PROJECTOR!
SERIOUSLY.
GNAW! GNAW!
BZZT!
IF YOU STAND IN MY WAY, I SHALL...
BZZT!
I SHALL...
BZZT!
PLINK!
PUFF PUFF!
PUFF PUFF PUFF!
PUFF PUFF PUFF! PHEW!
...DESTROY YOU!!
PUFF PUFF PUFF!
PUFF PUFF!
I THINK WE'LL BE ALL RIGHT.
YEAH, PROBABLY.
END!

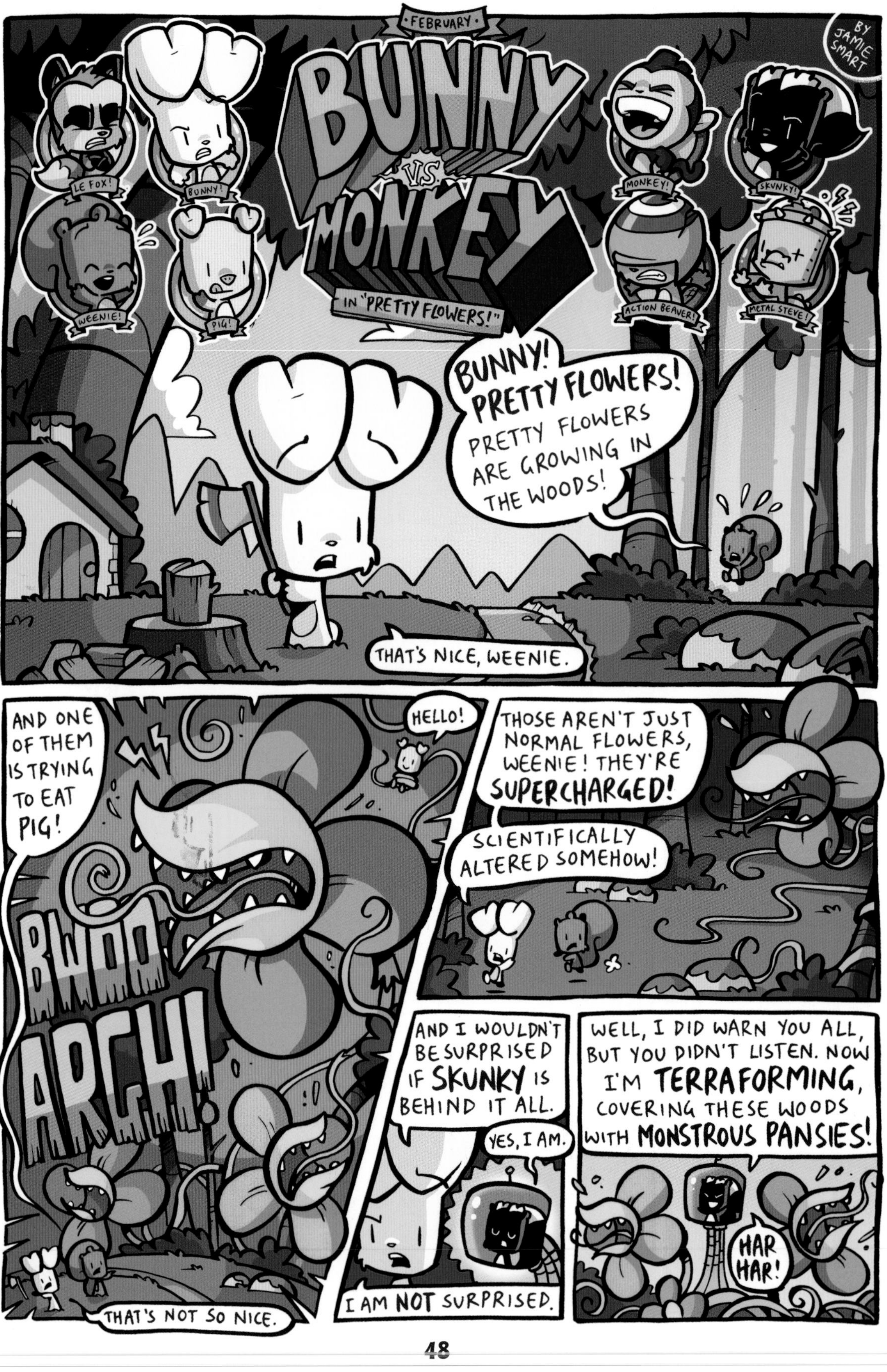
FEBRUARY
BUNNY VS. MONKEY
IN "PRETTY FLOWERS!"
BY JAMIE SMART
LE FOX!
BUNNY!
WEENIE!
PIG!
MONKEY!
SKUNKY!
ACTION BEAVER!
METAL STEVE!
BUNNY! PRETTY FLOWERS! PRETTY FLOWERS ARE GROWING IN THE WOODS!
THAT'S NICE, WEENIE.
AND ONE OF THEM IS TRYING TO EAT PIG!
HELLO!
BWOOARGH!
THAT'S NOT SO NICE.
THOSE AREN'T JUST NORMAL FLOWERS, WEENIE! THEY'RE SUPERCHARGED!
SCIENTIFICALLY ALTERED SOMEHOW!
AND I WOULDN'T BE SURPRISED IF SKUNKY IS BEHIND IT ALL.
YES, I AM.
I AM NOT SURPRISED.
WELL, I DID WARN YOU ALL, BUT YOU DIDN'T LISTEN. NOW I'M TERRAFORMING, COVERING THESE WOODS WITH MONSTROUS PANSIES!
HAR HAR!

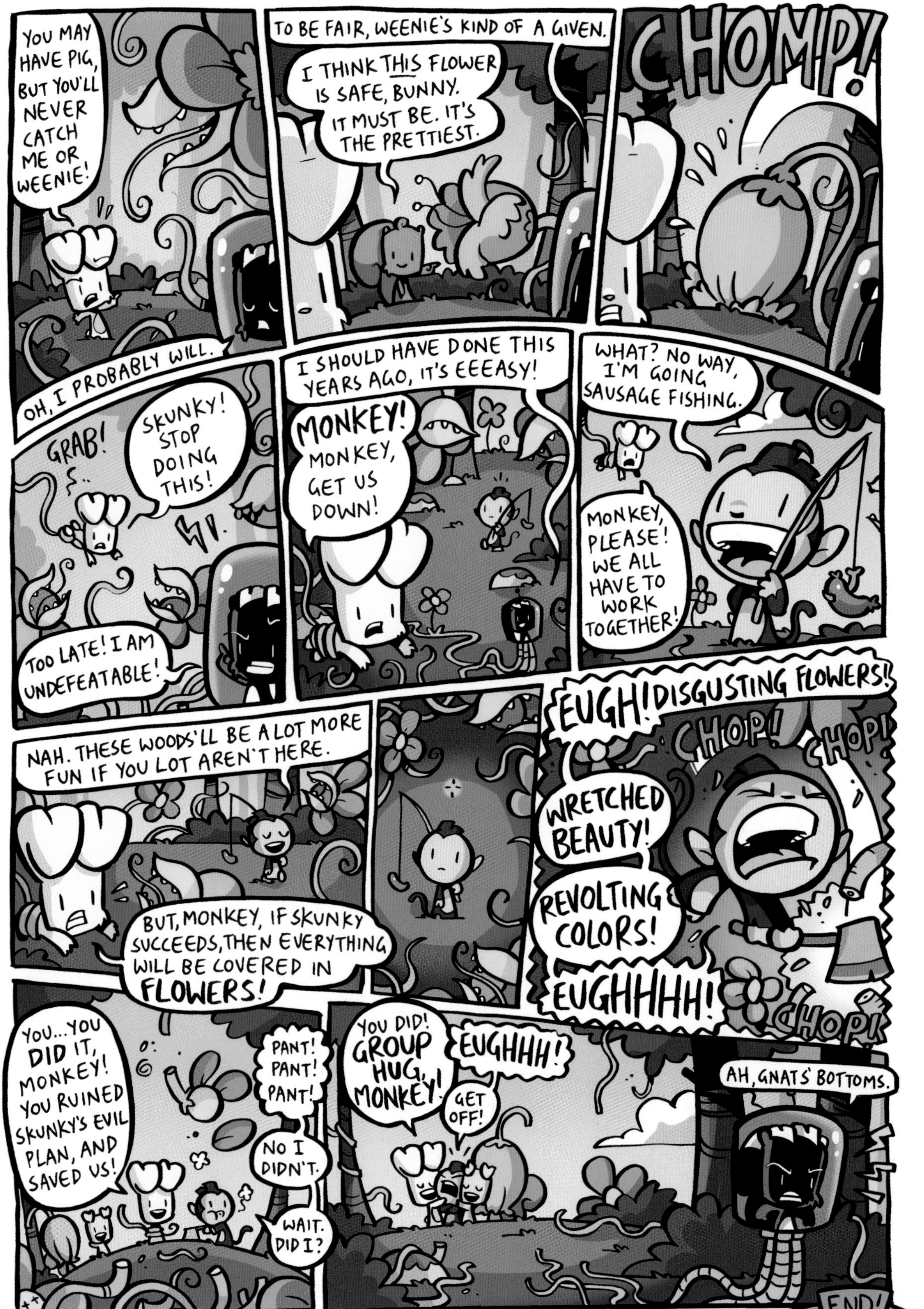
YOU MAY HAVE PIG, BUT YOU'LL NEVER CATCH ME OR WEENIE!
TO BE FAIR, WEENIE'S KIND OF A GIVEN.
I THINK THIS FLOWER IS SAFE, BUNNY. IT MUST BE. IT'S THE PRETTIEST.
CHOMP!
OH, I PROBABLY WILL.
GRAB!
SKUNKY! STOP DOING THIS!
TOO LATE! I AM UNDEFEATABLE!
I SHOULD HAVE DONE THIS YEARS AGO, IT'S EEEASY!
MONKEY! MONKEY, GET US DOWN!
WHAT? NO WAY, I'M GOING SAUSAGE FISHING.
MONKEY, PLEASE! WE ALL HAVE TO WORK TOGETHER!
NAH. THESE WOODS'LL BE A LOT MORE FUN IF YOU LOT AREN'T HERE.
BUT, MONKEY, IF SKUNKY SUCCEEDS, THEN EVERYTHING WILL BE COVERED IN FLOWERS!
EUGH! DISGUSTING FLOWERS!
CHOP! CHOP!
WRETCHED BEAUTY!
REVOLTING COLORS!
EUGHHHH!
CHOP!
YOU...YOU DID IT, MONKEY! YOU RUINED SKUNKY'S EVIL PLAN, AND SAVED US!
PANT! PANT! PANT!
NO I DIDN'T.
WAIT. DID I?
YOU DID! GROUP HUG, MONKEY!
EUGHHH!
GET OFF!
AH, GNATS' BOTTOMS.
END!

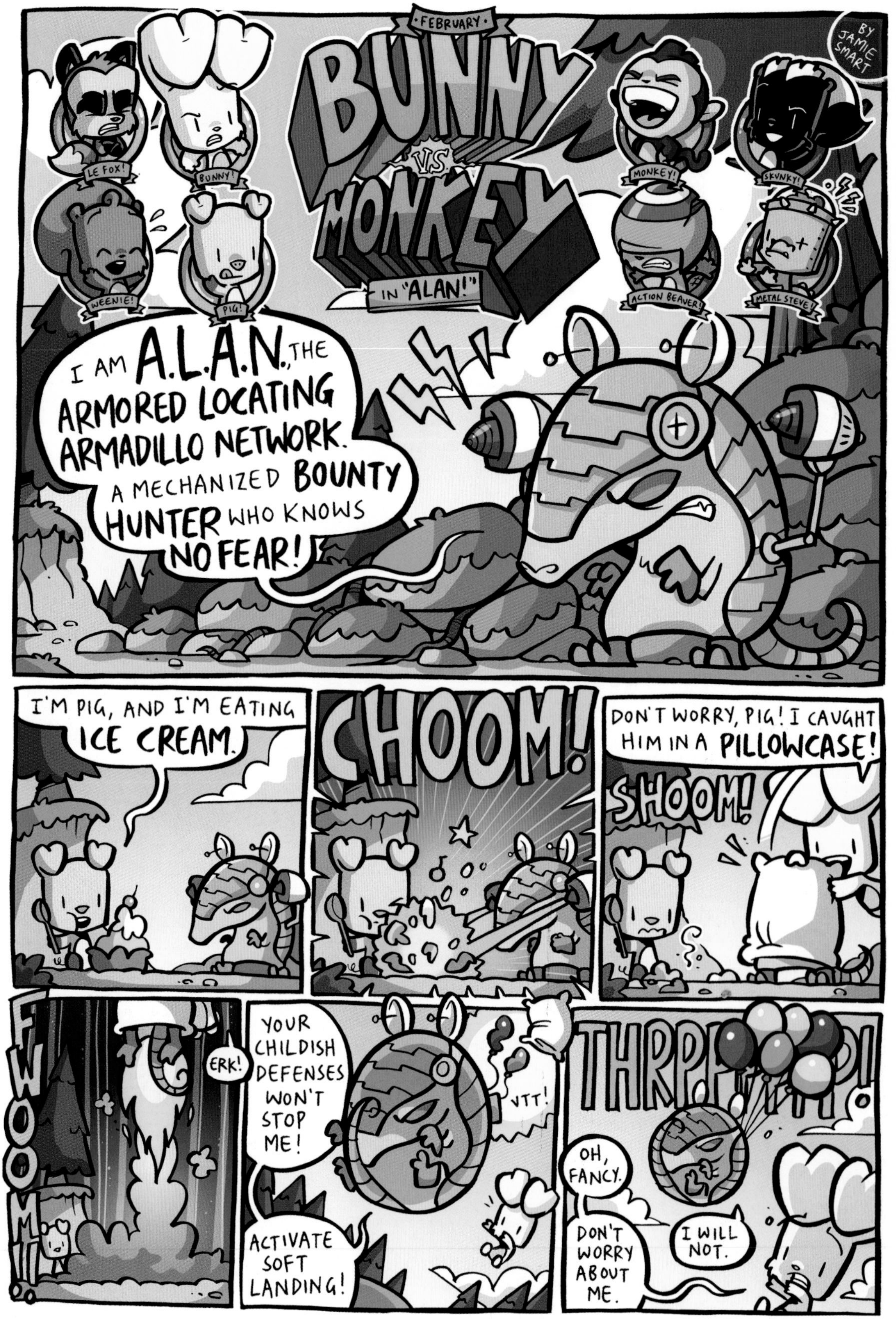
FEBRUARY
BUNNY VS. MONKEY
IN "ALAN!"
BY JAMIE SMART
LE FOX!
BUNNY!
WEENIE!
PIG!
MONKEY!
SKUNKY!
ACTION BEAVER!
METAL STEVE!
I AM A.L.A.N., THE ARMORED LOCATING ARMADILLO NETWORK. A MECHANIZED BOUNTY HUNTER WHO KNOWS NO FEAR!
I'M PIG, AND I'M EATING ICE CREAM.
CHOOM!
DON'T WORRY, PIG! I CAUGHT HIM IN A PILLOWCASE!
SHOOM!
FWOOOM!!
ERK!
YOUR CHILDISH DEFENSES WON'T STOP ME!
VTT!
ACTIVATE SOFT LANDING!
THRPPPP!
OH, FANCY.
DON'T WORRY ABOUT ME.
I WILL NOT.

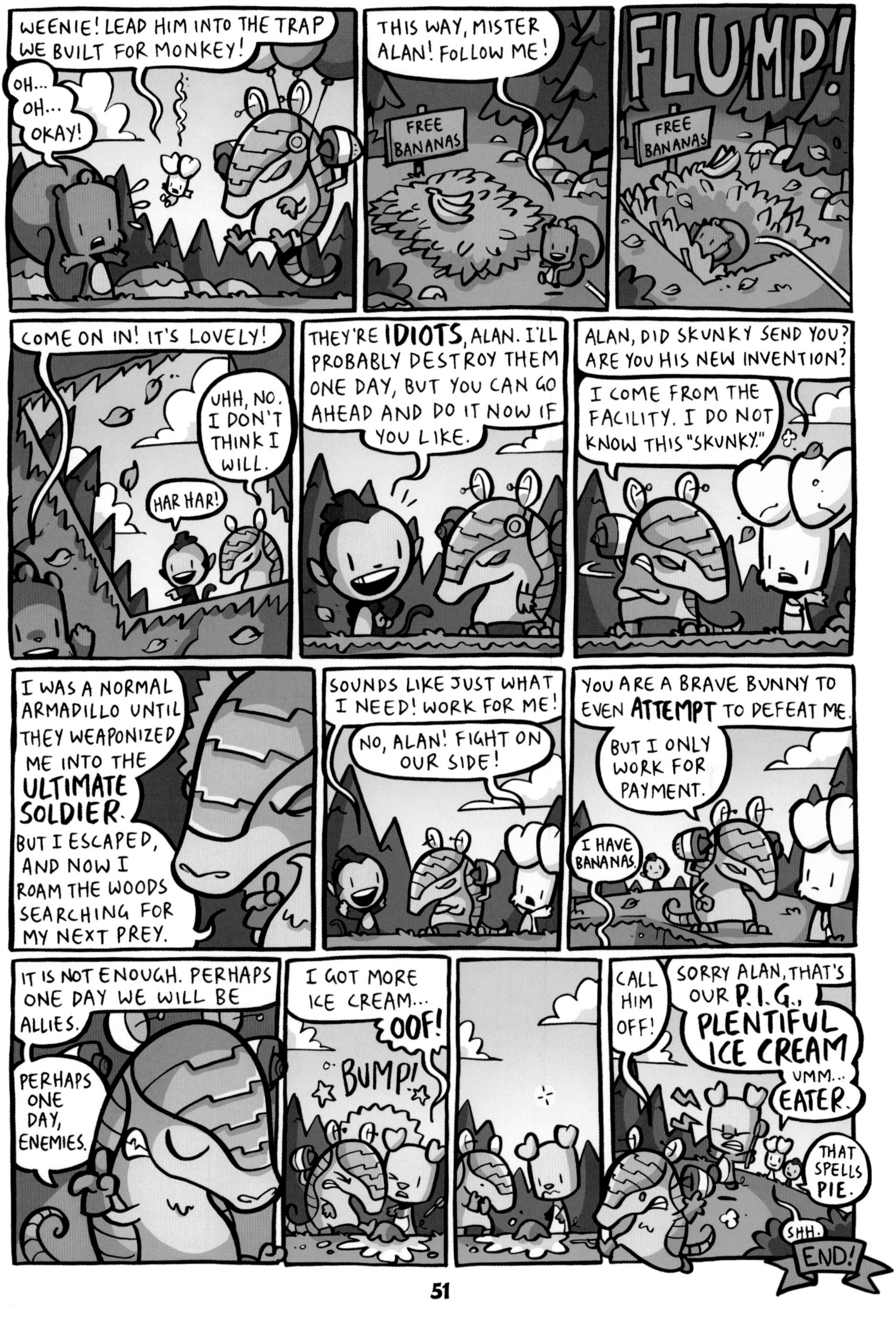
WEENIE! LEAD HIM INTO THE TRAP WE BUILT FOR MONKEY!
OH... OH... OKAY!
THIS WAY, MISTER ALAN! FOLLOW ME!
FREE BANANAS
FLUMP!
FREE BANANAS
COME ON IN! IT'S LOVELY!
UHH, NO. I DON'T THINK I WILL.
HAR HAR!
THEY'RE IDIOTS, ALAN. I'LL PROBABLY DESTROY THEM ONE DAY, BUT YOU CAN GO AHEAD AND DO IT NOW IF YOU LIKE.
ALAN, DID SKUNKY SEND YOU? ARE YOU HIS NEW INVENTION?
I COME FROM THE FACILITY. I DO NOT KNOW THIS "SKUNKY."
I WAS A NORMAL ARMADILLO UNTIL THEY WEAPONIZED ME INTO THE ULTIMATE SOLDIER. BUT I ESCAPED, AND NOW I ROAM THE WOODS SEARCHING FOR MY NEXT PREY.
SOUNDS LIKE JUST WHAT I NEED! WORK FOR ME!
NO, ALAN! FIGHT ON OUR SIDE!
YOU ARE A BRAVE BUNNY TO EVEN ATTEMPT TO DEFEAT ME.
BUT I ONLY WORK FOR PAYMENT.
I HAVE BANANAS.
IT IS NOT ENOUGH. PERHAPS ONE DAY WE WILL BE ALLIES.
PERHAPS ONE DAY, ENEMIES.
I GOT MORE ICE CREAM...
OOF!
BUMP!
CALL HIM OFF!
SORRY ALAN, THAT'S OUR P.I.G., PLENTIFUL ICE CREAM
UMM... EATER.
THAT SPELLS PIE.
SHH.
END!

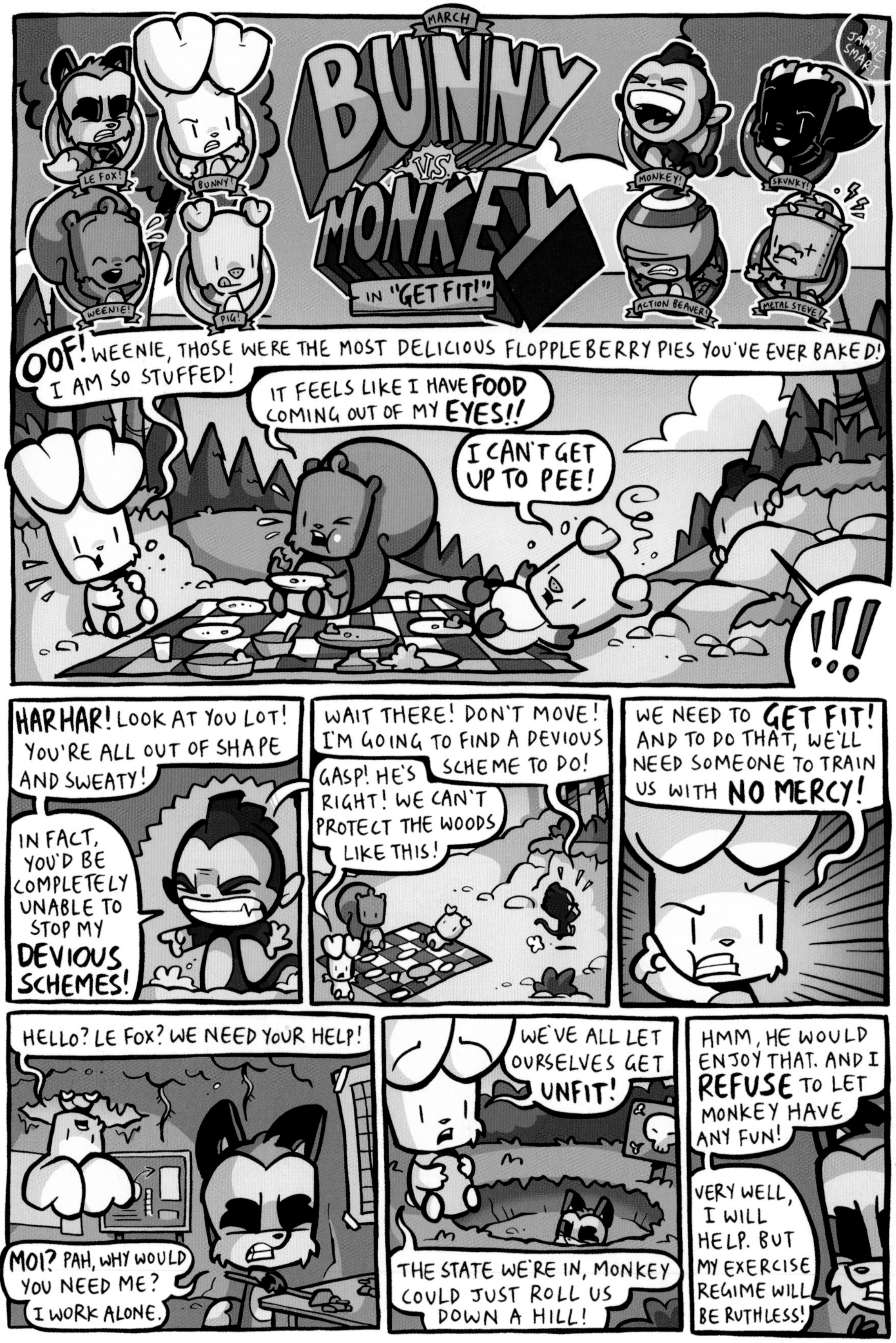
MARCH
BUNNY VS. MONKEY
IN "GET FIT!"
BY JAMIE SMART
LE FOX!
BUNNY!
MONKEY!
SKUNKY!
WEENIE!
PIG!
ACTION BEAVER!
METAL STEVE!
OOF! WEENIE, THOSE WERE THE MOST DELICIOUS FLOPPLEBERRY PIES YOU'VE EVER BAKED! I AM SO STUFFED!
IT FEELS LIKE I HAVE FOOD COMING OUT OF MY EYES!!
I CAN'T GET UP TO PEE!
!!!
HARHAR! LOOK AT YOU LOT! YOU'RE ALL OUT OF SHAPE AND SWEATY!
IN FACT, YOU'D BE COMPLETELY UNABLE TO STOP MY DEVIOUS SCHEMES!
WAIT THERE! DON'T MOVE! I'M GOING TO FIND A DEVIOUS SCHEME TO DO!
GASP! HE'S RIGHT! WE CAN'T PROTECT THE WOODS LIKE THIS!
WE NEED TO GET FIT! AND TO DO THAT, WE'LL NEED SOMEONE TO TRAIN US WITH NO MERCY!
HELLO? LE FOX? WE NEED YOUR HELP!
MOI? PAH, WHY WOULD YOU NEED ME? I WORK ALONE.
WE'VE ALL LET OURSELVES GET UNFIT!
THE STATE WE'RE IN, MONKEY COULD JUST ROLL US DOWN A HILL!
HMM, HE WOULD ENJOY THAT. AND I REFUSE TO LET MONKEY HAVE ANY FUN!
VERY WELL, I WILL HELP. BUT MY EXERCISE REGIME WILL BE RUTHLESS!

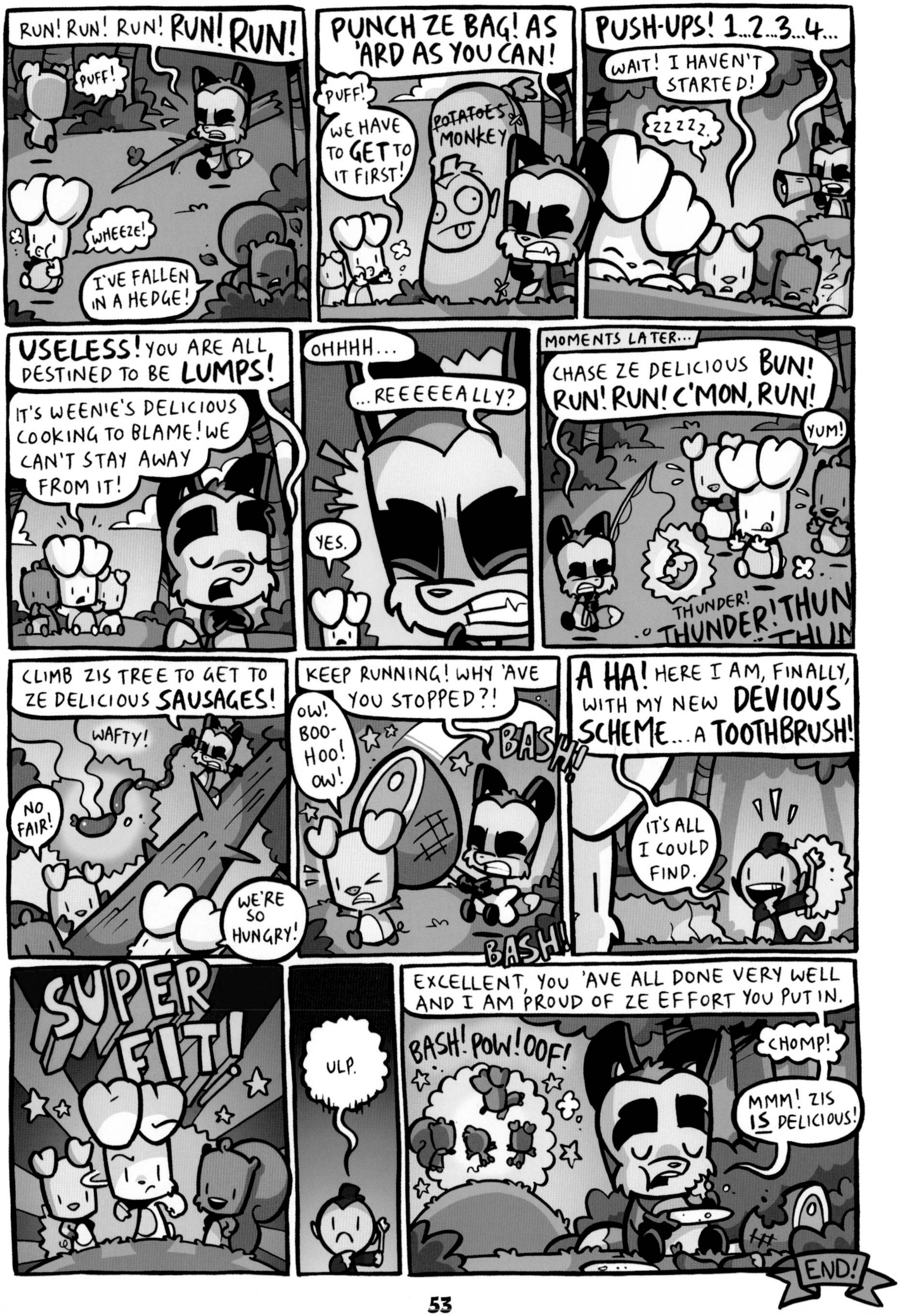
RUN! RUN! RUN! RUN! RUN!
PUFF!
WHEEZE!
I'VE FALLEN IN A HEDGE!
PUNCH ZE BAG! AS 'ARD AS YOU CAN!
PUFF!
WE HAVE TO GET TO IT FIRST!
POTATOES MONKEY
PUSH-UPS! 1...2...3...4...
WAIT! I HAVEN'T STARTED!
ZZZZZ.
USELESS! YOU ARE ALL DESTINED TO BE LUMPS!
IT'S WEENIE'S DELICIOUS COOKING TO BLAME! WE CAN'T STAY AWAY FROM IT!
OHHHH...
...REEEEEALLY?
YES.
MOMENTS LATER...
CHASE ZE DELICIOUS BUN! RUN! RUN! C'MON, RUN!
YUM!
THUNDER! THUNDER! THUN
CLIMB ZIS TREE TO GET TO ZE DELICIOUS SAUSAGES!
WAFTY!
NO FAIR!
WE'RE SO HUNGRY!
KEEP RUNNING! WHY 'AVE YOU STOPPED?!
OW! BOO-HOO! OW!
BASH!
BASH!
A HA! HERE I AM, FINALLY, WITH MY NEW DEVIOUS SCHEME... A TOOTHBRUSH!
IT'S ALL I COULD FIND.
SUPER FIT!
ULP.
EXCELLENT, YOU 'AVE ALL DONE VERY WELL AND I AM PROUD OF ZE EFFORT YOU PUT IN.
BASH! POW! OOF!
CHOMP!
MMM! ZIS IS DELICIOUS!
END!

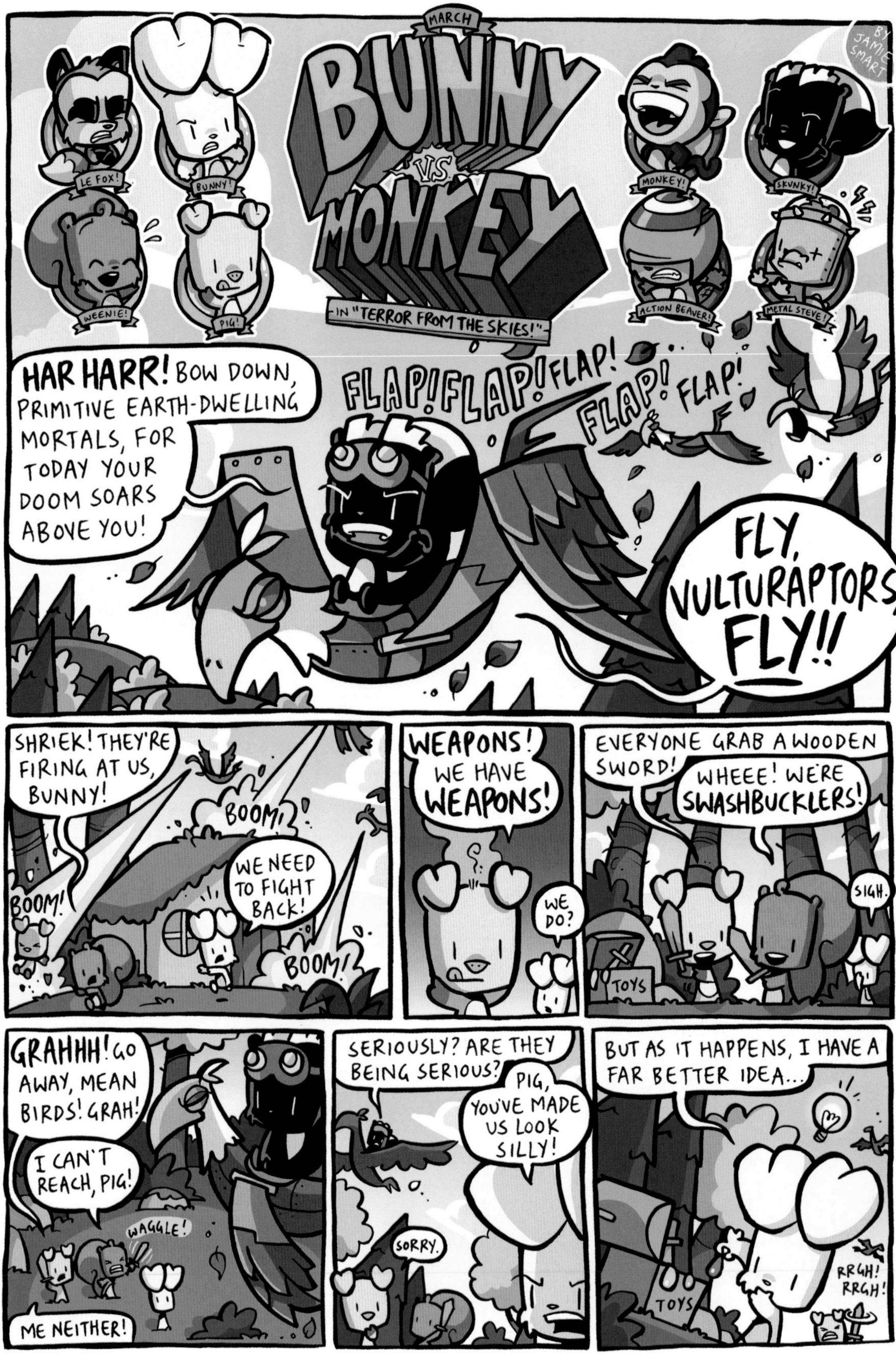
MARCH
BUNNY VS. MONKEY
BY JAMIE SMART
LE FOX!
BUNNY!
WEENIE!
PIG!
MONKEY!
SKUNKY!
ACTION BEAVER!
METAL STEVE!
IN "TERROR FROM THE SKIES!"
HAR HARR! BOW DOWN, PRIMITIVE EARTH-DWELLING MORTALS, FOR TODAY YOUR DOOM SOARS ABOVE YOU!
FLAP! FLAP! FLAP! FLAP! FLAP!
FLY, VULTURAPTORS, FLY!!
SHRIEK! THEY'RE FIRING AT US, BUNNY!
BOOM!
BOOM!
WE NEED TO FIGHT BACK!
BOOM!
WEAPONS! WE HAVE WEAPONS!
WE DO?
EVERYONE GRAB A WOODEN SWORD!
WHEEE! WE'RE SWASHBUCKLERS!
SIGH.
TOYS
GRAHHH! GO AWAY, MEAN BIRDS! GRAH!
I CAN'T REACH, PIG!
WAGGLE!
ME NEITHER!
SERIOUSLY? ARE THEY BEING SERIOUS?
PIG, YOU'VE MADE US LOOK SILLY!
SORRY.
BUT AS IT HAPPENS, I HAVE A FAR BETTER IDEA...
TOYS
RRGH! RRGH!

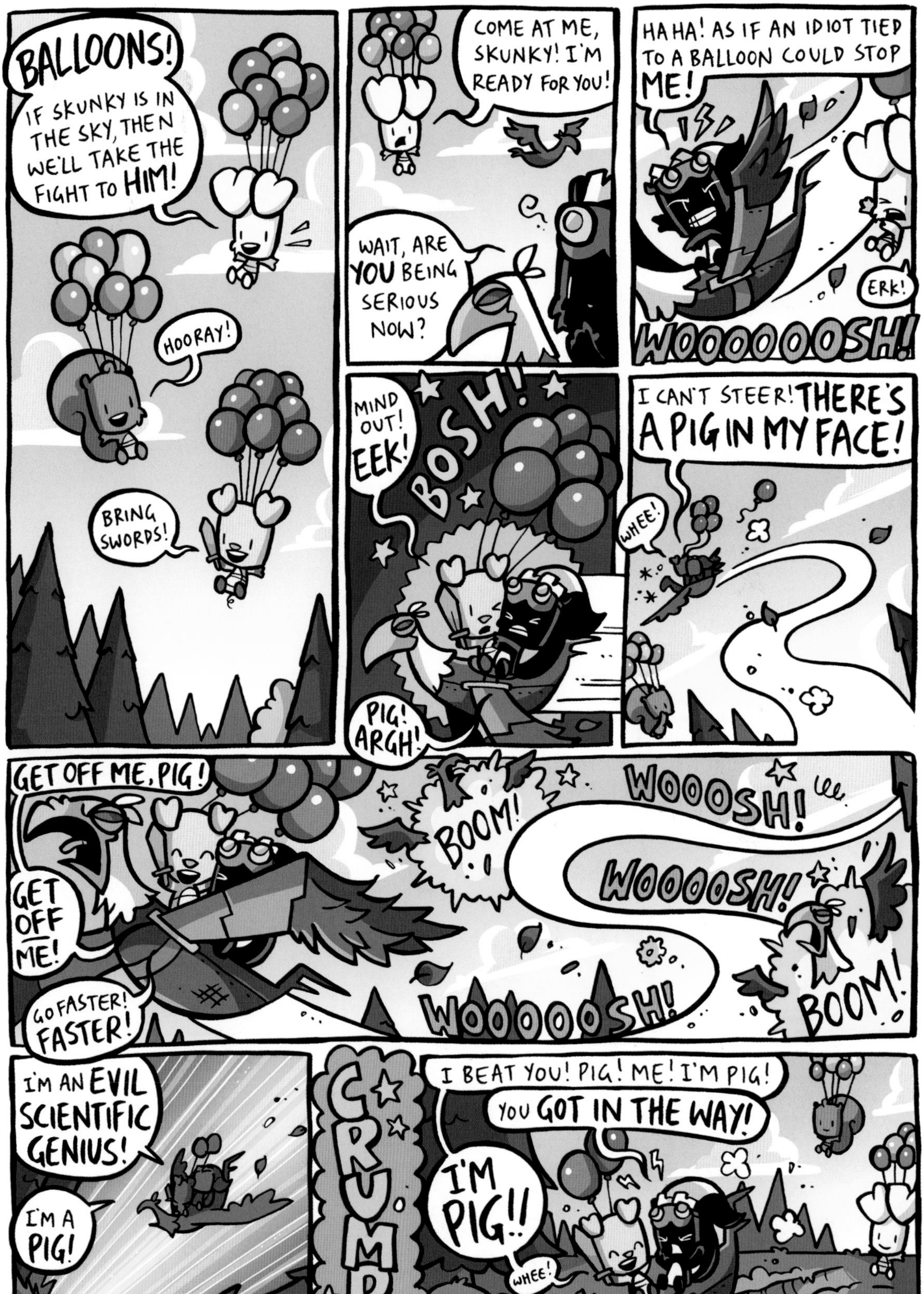
BALLOONS!
IF SKUNKY IS IN THE SKY, THEN WE'LL TAKE THE FIGHT TO HIM!
HOORAY!
BRING SWORDS!
COME AT ME, SKUNKY! I'M READY FOR YOU!
WAIT, ARE YOU BEING SERIOUS NOW?
HA HA! AS IF AN IDIOT TIED TO A BALLOON COULD STOP ME!
ERK!
WOOOOOOSH!
MIND OUT! EEK!
BOSH!
PIG! ARGH!
I CAN'T STEER! THERE'S A PIG IN MY FACE!
WHEE!
GET OFF ME, PIG!
GET OFF ME!
GO FASTER! FASTER!
BOOM!
WOOOSH!
WOOOOSH!
WOOOOOOSH!
BOOM!
I'M AN EVIL SCIENTIFIC GENIUS!
I'M A PIG!
CRUMP!!
I BEAT YOU! PIG! ME! I'M PIG!
YOU GOT IN THE WAY!
I'M PIG!!
WHEE!
END!

BY JAMIE SMART

# BUNNY vs MONKEY

MARCH

IN "BOBBLES!"

LE FOX! · BUNNY! · WEENIE! · PIG! · MONKEY! · SKUNKY! · ACTION BEAVER! · METAL STEVE!

A BEAUTIFUL METEOR SHOWER FILLS THE NIGHT SKY, BUT ONE LONELY SOUL ISN'T ENJOYING IT.

SIGHH...

I'M THE SADDEST CLOWN IN THE WHOLE UNIVERSE.

I THOUGHT IT WOULD BE FUN TO DRESS UP.

BOBBLES THE CLOWN!

HERE TO CHEER EVERYONE UP!

I FORGOT THAT WEENIE IS TERRIFIED OF CLOWNS...

SCREEEAM! IT'S A GHOSTLY IMP!

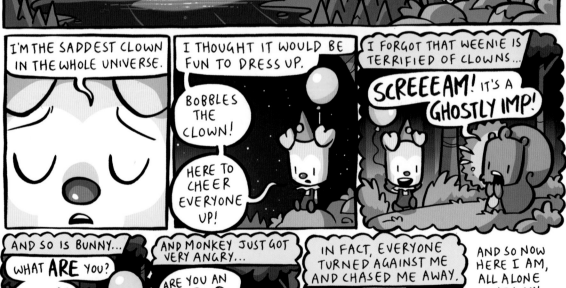

AND SO IS BUNNY...

WHAT **ARE** YOU?

DID WE DO SOMETHING BAD?

AND MONKEY JUST GOT VERY ANGRY...

ARE YOU AN **ALIEN**?

GERROFF, THIS IS **MY** PLANET.

IN FACT, EVERYONE TURNED AGAINST ME AND CHASED ME AWAY.

THROW SHOES AT IT!

WE DON'T WEAR SHOES!

AND SO NOW HERE I AM, ALL ALONE UNTIL MY FACE PAINT COMES OFF...

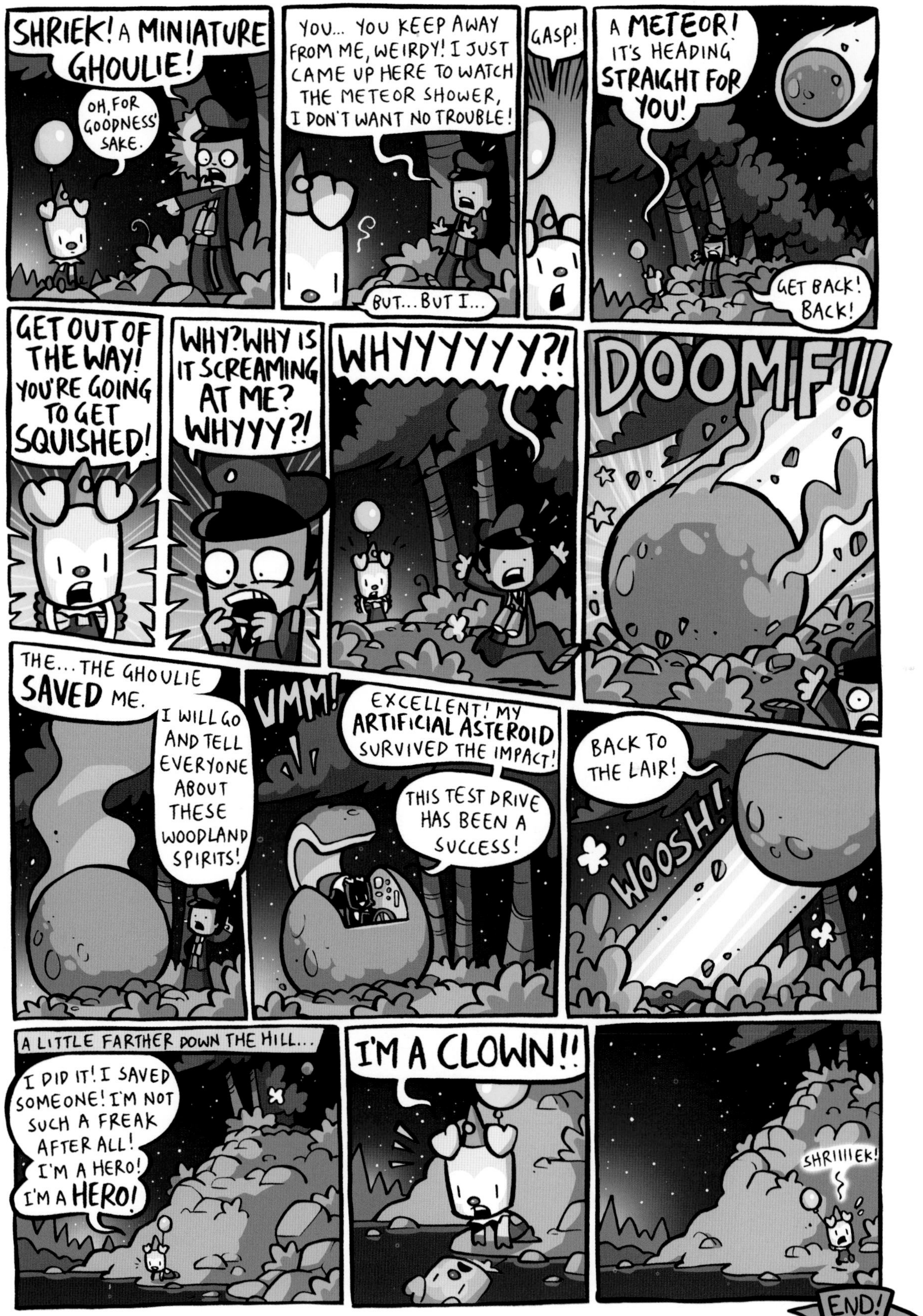

SHRIEK! A MINIATURE GHOULIE!
OH, FOR GOODNESS' SAKE.
YOU... YOU KEEP AWAY FROM ME, WEIRDY! I JUST CAME UP HERE TO WATCH THE METEOR SHOWER, I DON'T WANT NO TROUBLE!
BUT... BUT I...
GASP!
A METEOR! IT'S HEADING STRAIGHT FOR YOU!
GET BACK! BACK!
GET OUT OF THE WAY! YOU'RE GOING TO GET SQUISHED!
WHY? WHY IS IT SCREAMING AT ME? WHYYY?!
WHYYYYYY?!
DOOMF!!!
THE... THE GHOULIE SAVED ME.
I WILL GO AND TELL EVERYONE ABOUT THESE WOODLAND SPIRITS!
VMM!
EXCELLENT! MY ARTIFICIAL ASTEROID SURVIVED THE IMPACT!
THIS TEST DRIVE HAS BEEN A SUCCESS!
BACK TO THE LAIR!
WOOSH!
A LITTLE FARTHER DOWN THE HILL...
I DID IT! I SAVED SOMEONE! I'M NOT SUCH A FREAK AFTER ALL! I'M A HERO! I'M A HERO!
I'M A CLOWN!!
SHRIIIIEK!
END!

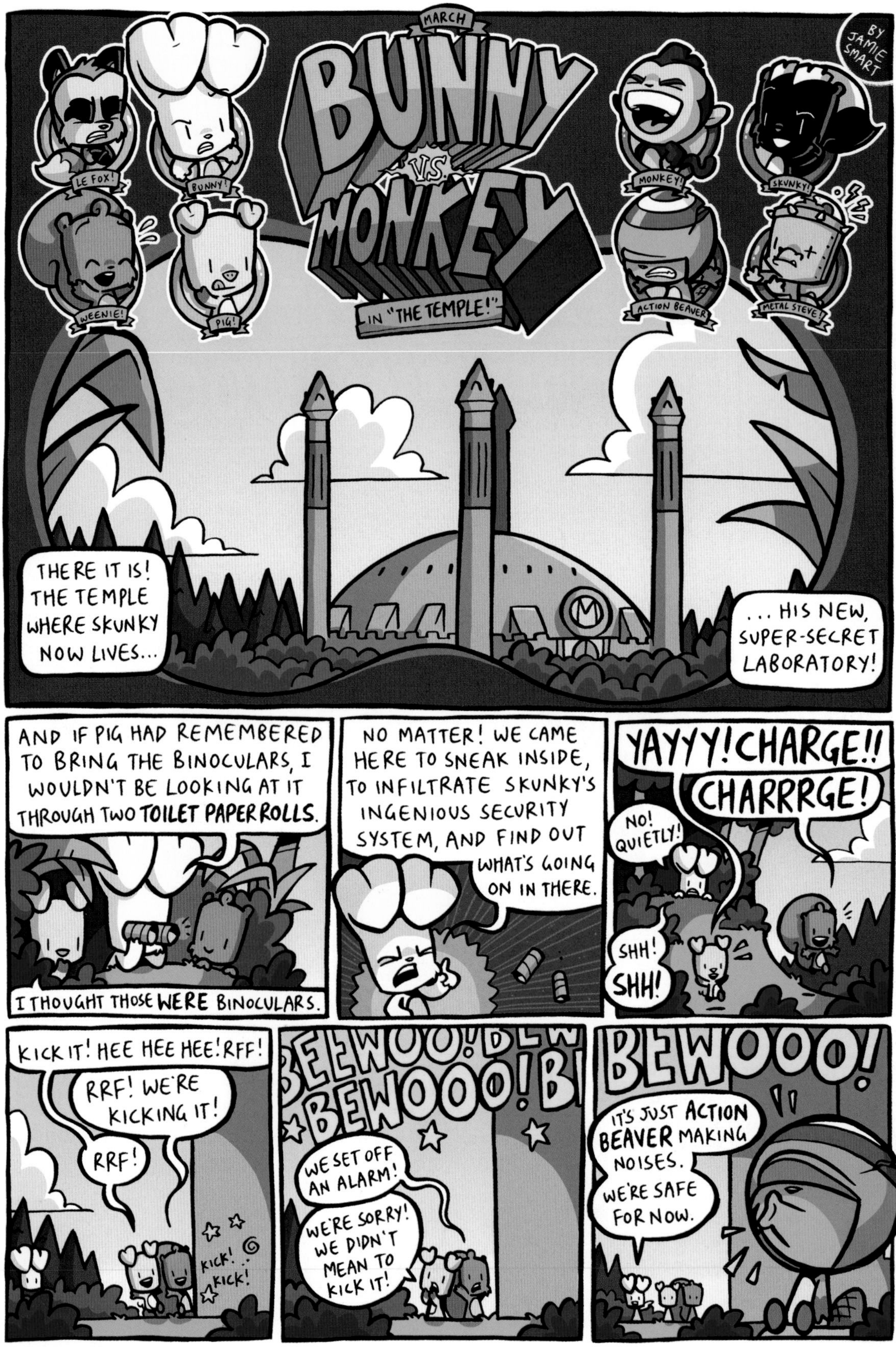
MARCH
BUNNY VS. MONKEY
IN "THE TEMPLE!"
BY JAMIE SMART
LE FOX!
BUNNY!
MONKEY!
SKUNKY!
WEENIE!
PIG!
ACTION BEAVER
METAL STEVE!
THERE IT IS! THE TEMPLE WHERE SKUNKY NOW LIVES...
... HIS NEW, SUPER-SECRET LABORATORY!
AND IF PIG HAD REMEMBERED TO BRING THE BINOCULARS, I WOULDN'T BE LOOKING AT IT THROUGH TWO TOILET PAPER ROLLS.
I THOUGHT THOSE WERE BINOCULARS.
NO MATTER! WE CAME HERE TO SNEAK INSIDE, TO INFILTRATE SKUNKY'S INGENIOUS SECURITY SYSTEM, AND FIND OUT WHAT'S GOING ON IN THERE.
YAYYY! CHARGE!!
CHARRRGE!
NO! QUIETLY!
SHH! SHH!
KICK IT! HEE HEE HEE! RFF!
RRF! WE'RE KICKING IT!
RRF!
KICK! KICK!
BEEWOO! BEW
BEWOOO! B
WE SET OFF AN ALARM!
WE'RE SORRY! WE DIDN'T MEAN TO KICK IT!
BEWOOO!
IT'S JUST ACTION BEAVER MAKING NOISES. WE'RE SAFE FOR NOW.

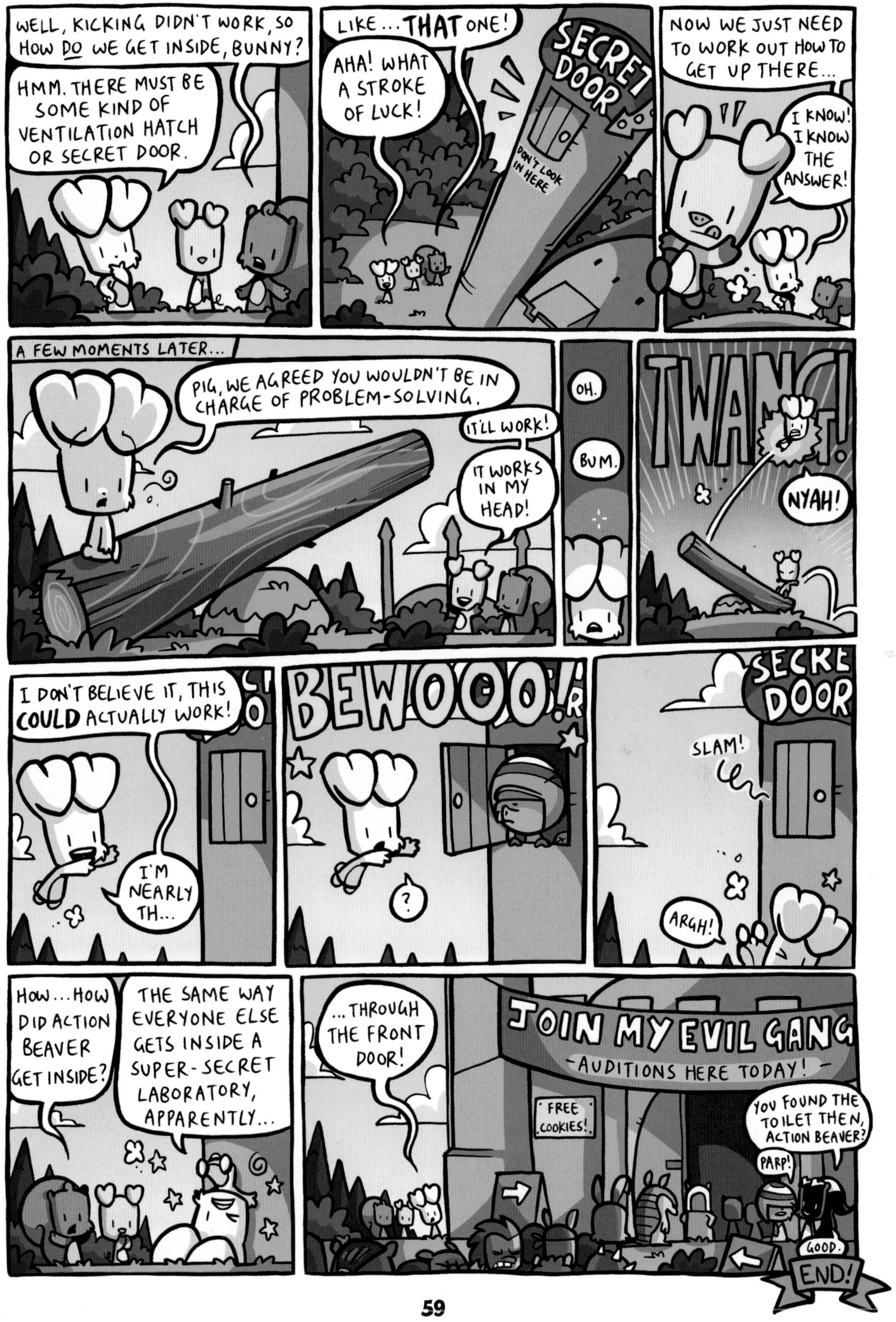

WELL, KICKING DIDN'T WORK, SO HOW DO WE GET INSIDE, BUNNY?
HMM. THERE MUST BE SOME KIND OF VENTILATION HATCH OR SECRET DOOR.
LIKE... THAT ONE!
AHA! WHAT A STROKE OF LUCK!
SECRET DOOR
DON'T LOOK IN HERE
NOW WE JUST NEED TO WORK OUT HOW TO GET UP THERE...
I KNOW! I KNOW THE ANSWER!
A FEW MOMENTS LATER...
PIG, WE AGREED YOU WOULDN'T BE IN CHARGE OF PROBLEM-SOLVING.
IT'LL WORK!
IT WORKS IN MY HEAD!
OH.
BUM.
TWANG!
NYAH!
I DON'T BELIEVE IT, THIS COULD ACTUALLY WORK!
I'M NEARLY TH...
BEWOOO!
?
SECRE DOOR
SLAM!
ARGH!
HOW... HOW DID ACTION BEAVER GET INSIDE?
THE SAME WAY EVERYONE ELSE GETS INSIDE A SUPER-SECRET LABORATORY, APPARENTLY...
...THROUGH THE FRONT DOOR!
JOIN MY EVIL GANG
-AUDITIONS HERE TODAY!-
FREE COOKIES!
YOU FOUND THE TOILET THEN, ACTION BEAVER?
PARP!
GOOD.
END!

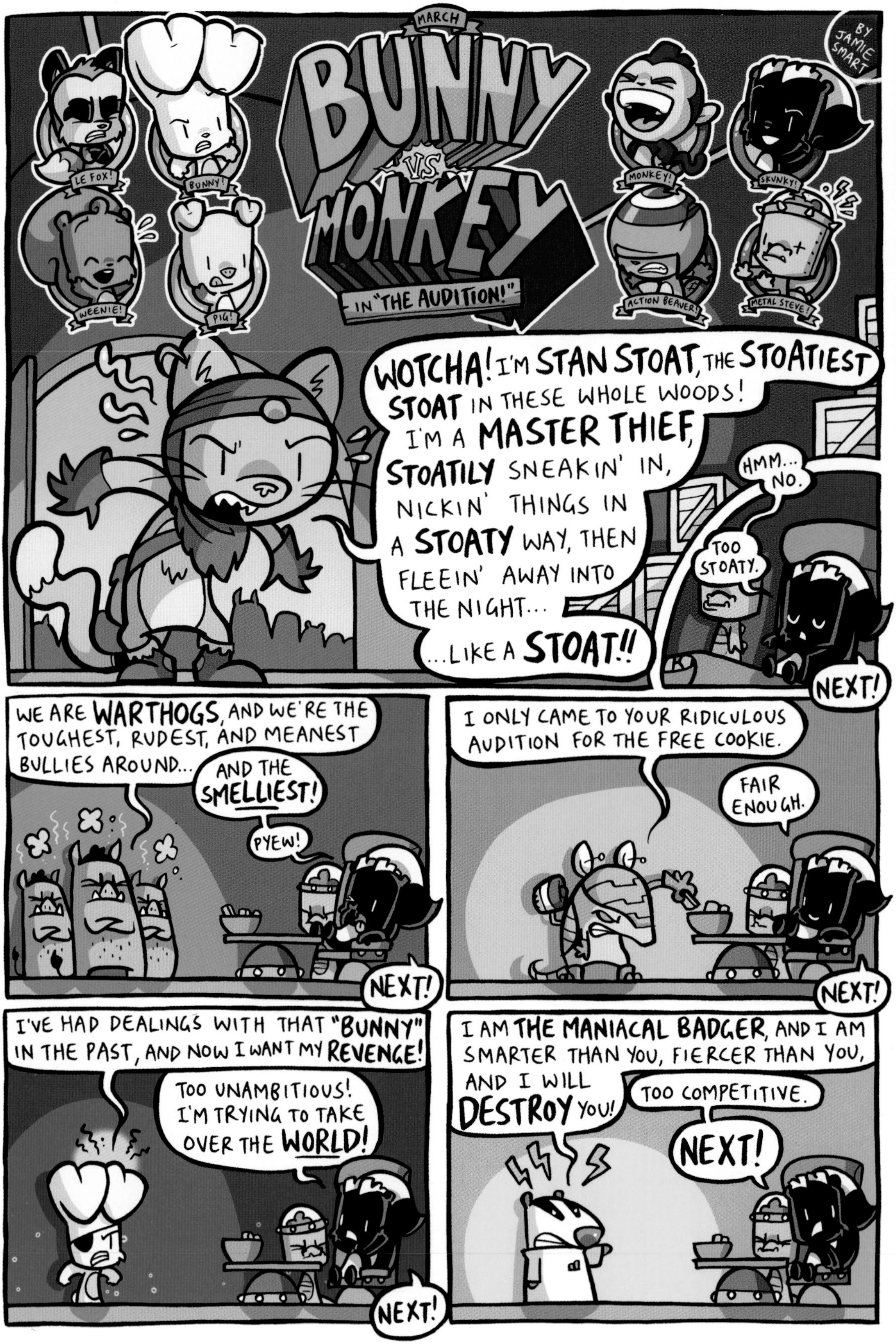
MARCH
BUNNY VS MONKEY
IN "THE AUDITION!"
BY JAMIE SMART
LE FOX!
BUNNY!
WEENIE!
PIG!
MONKEY!
SKUNKY!
ACTION BEAVER!
METAL STEVE!
WOTCHA! I'M STAN STOAT, THE STOATIEST STOAT IN THESE WHOLE WOODS! I'M A MASTER THIEF, STOATILY SNEAKIN' IN, NICKIN' THINGS IN A STOATY WAY, THEN FLEEIN' AWAY INTO THE NIGHT... ...LIKE A STOAT!!
HMM... NO.
TOO STOATY.
NEXT!
WE ARE WARTHOGS, AND WE'RE THE TOUGHEST, RUDEST, AND MEANEST BULLIES AROUND...
AND THE SMELLIEST!
PYEW!
NEXT!
I ONLY CAME TO YOUR RIDICULOUS AUDITION FOR THE FREE COOKIE.
FAIR ENOUGH.
NEXT!
I'VE HAD DEALINGS WITH THAT "BUNNY" IN THE PAST, AND NOW I WANT MY REVENGE!
TOO UNAMBITIOUS! I'M TRYING TO TAKE OVER THE WORLD!
NEXT!
I AM THE MANIACAL BADGER, AND I AM SMARTER THAN YOU, FIERCER THAN YOU, AND I WILL DESTROY YOU!
TOO COMPETITIVE.
NEXT!

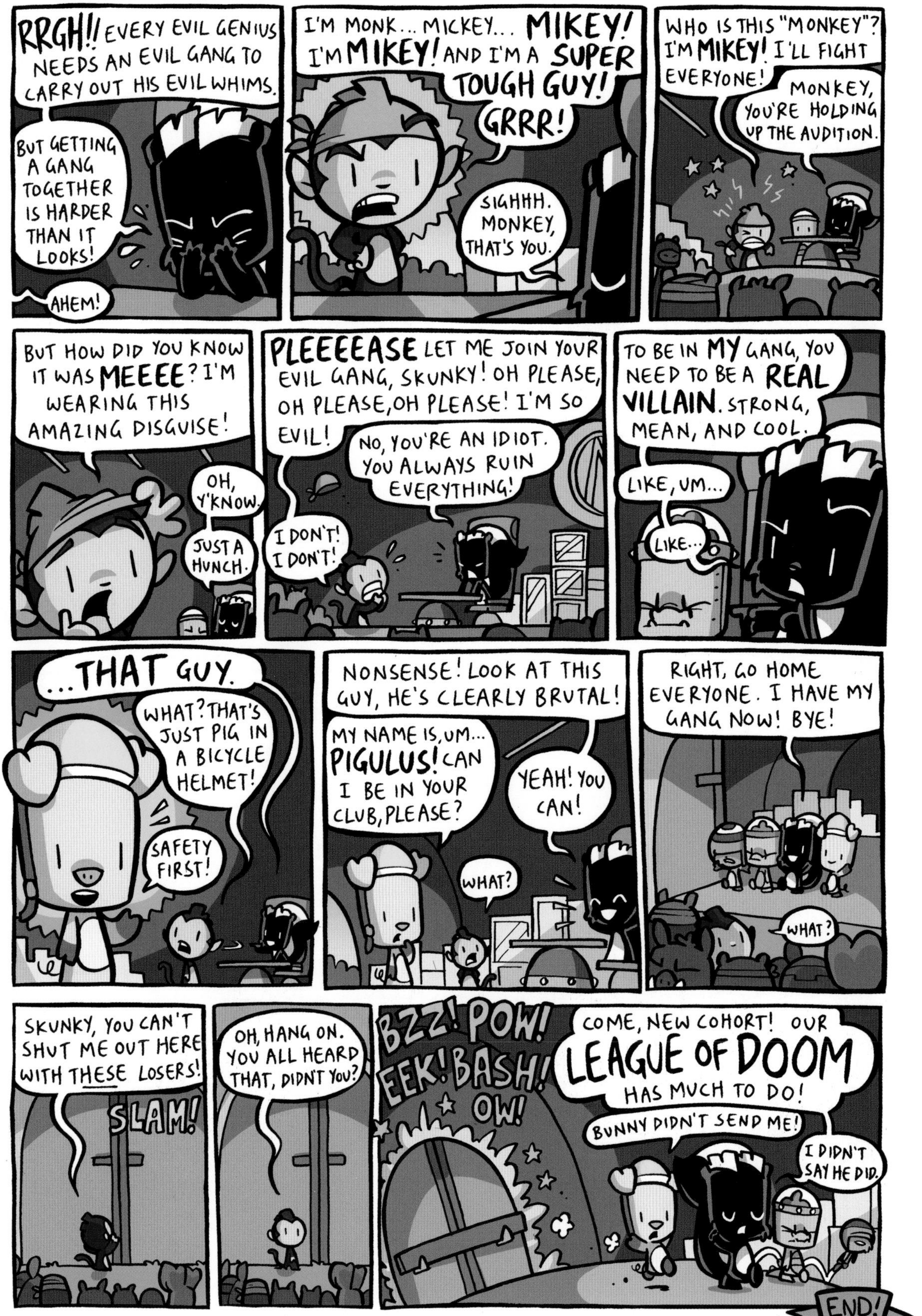
RRGH!! EVERY EVIL GENIUS NEEDS AN EVIL GANG TO CARRY OUT HIS EVIL WHIMS.
BUT GETTING A GANG TOGETHER IS HARDER THAN IT LOOKS!
AHEM!
I'M MONK... MICKEY... MIKEY! I'M MIKEY! AND I'M A SUPER TOUGH GUY! GRRR!
SIGHHH. MONKEY, THAT'S YOU.
WHO IS THIS "MONKEY"? I'M MIKEY! I'LL FIGHT EVERYONE!
MONKEY, YOU'RE HOLDING UP THE AUDITION.
BUT HOW DID YOU KNOW IT WAS MEEEE? I'M WEARING THIS AMAZING DISGUISE!
OH, Y'KNOW.
JUST A HUNCH.
PLEEEEASE LET ME JOIN YOUR EVIL GANG, SKUNKY! OH PLEASE, OH PLEASE, OH PLEASE! I'M SO EVIL!
NO, YOU'RE AN IDIOT. YOU ALWAYS RUIN EVERYTHING!
I DON'T! I DON'T!
TO BE IN MY GANG, YOU NEED TO BE A REAL VILLAIN. STRONG, MEAN, AND COOL.
LIKE, UM...
LIKE...
...THAT GUY.
WHAT? THAT'S JUST PIG IN A BICYCLE HELMET!
SAFETY FIRST!
NONSENSE! LOOK AT THIS GUY, HE'S CLEARLY BRUTAL!
MY NAME IS, UM... PIGULUS! CAN I BE IN YOUR CLUB, PLEASE?
YEAH! YOU CAN!
WHAT?
RIGHT, GO HOME EVERYONE. I HAVE MY GANG NOW! BYE!
WHAT?
SKUNKY, YOU CAN'T SHUT ME OUT HERE WITH THESE LOSERS!
SLAM!
OH, HANG ON. YOU ALL HEARD THAT, DIDN'T YOU?
BZZ! POW! EEK! BASH! OW!
COME, NEW COHORT! OUR LEAGUE OF DOOM HAS MUCH TO DO!
BUNNY DIDN'T SEND ME!
I DIDN'T SAY HE DID.
END!

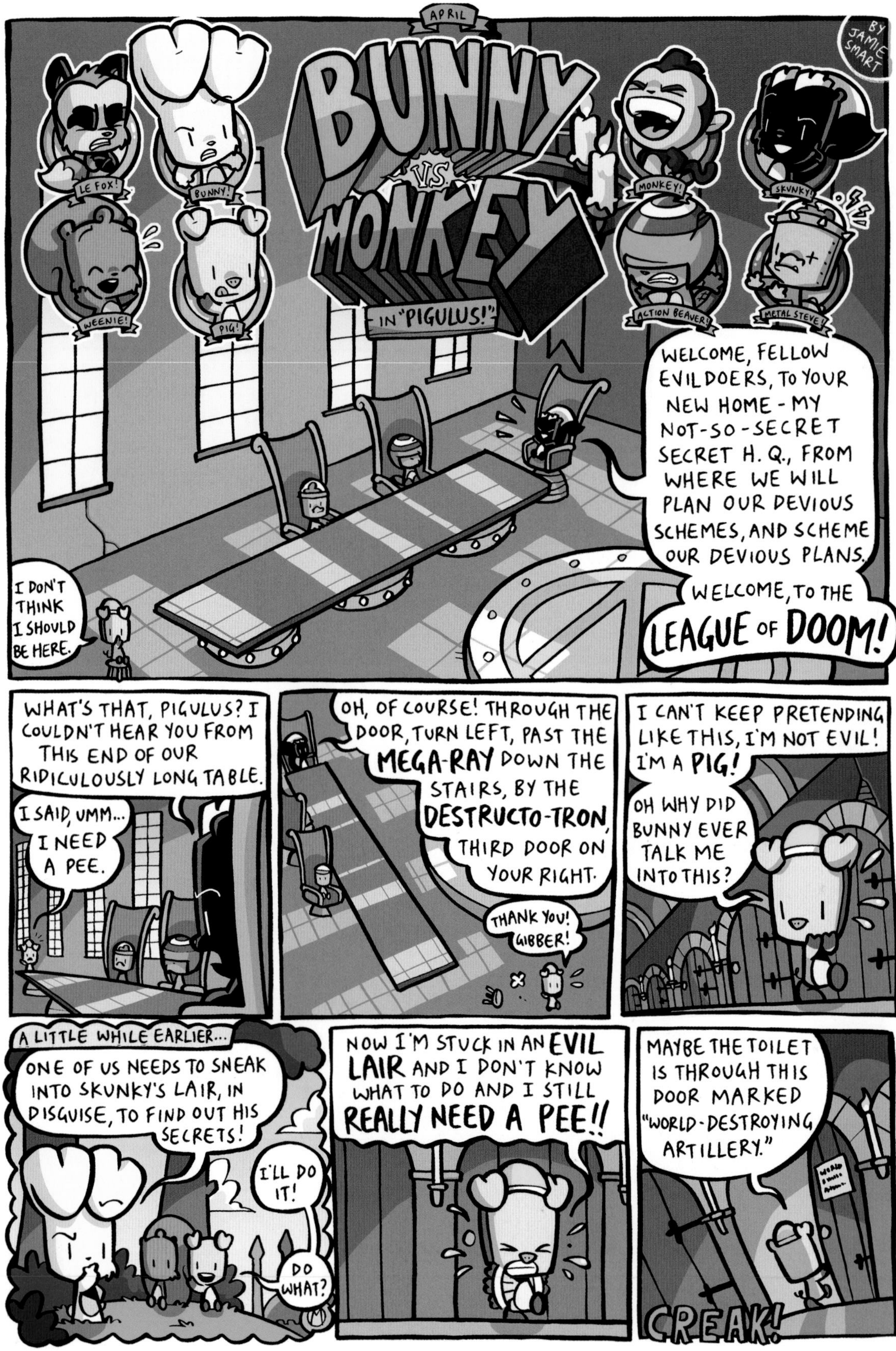
APRIL
BUNNY VS. MONKEY
IN "PIGULUS!"
BY JAMIE SMART
LE FOX!
BUNNY!
WEENIE!
PIG!
MONKEY!
SKUNKY!
ACTION BEAVER!
METAL STEVE!
WELCOME, FELLOW EVILDOERS, TO YOUR NEW HOME - MY NOT-SO-SECRET SECRET H. Q., FROM WHERE WE WILL PLAN OUR DEVIOUS SCHEMES, AND SCHEME OUR DEVIOUS PLANS.
WELCOME, TO THE LEAGUE OF DOOM!
I DON'T THINK I SHOULD BE HERE.
WHAT'S THAT, PIGULUS? I COULDN'T HEAR YOU FROM THIS END OF OUR RIDICULOUSLY LONG TABLE.
I SAID, UMM... I NEED A PEE.
OH, OF COURSE! THROUGH THE DOOR, TURN LEFT, PAST THE MEGA-RAY DOWN THE STAIRS, BY THE DESTRUCTO-TRON, THIRD DOOR ON YOUR RIGHT.
THANK YOU! GIBBER!
I CAN'T KEEP PRETENDING LIKE THIS, I'M NOT EVIL! I'M A PIG!
OH WHY DID BUNNY EVER TALK ME INTO THIS?
A LITTLE WHILE EARLIER...
ONE OF US NEEDS TO SNEAK INTO SKUNKY'S LAIR, IN DISGUISE, TO FIND OUT HIS SECRETS!
I'LL DO IT!
DO WHAT?
NOW I'M STUCK IN AN EVIL LAIR AND I DON'T KNOW WHAT TO DO AND I STILL REALLY NEED A PEE!!
MAYBE THE TOILET IS THROUGH THIS DOOR MARKED "WORLD-DESTROYING ARTILLERY."
CREAK!

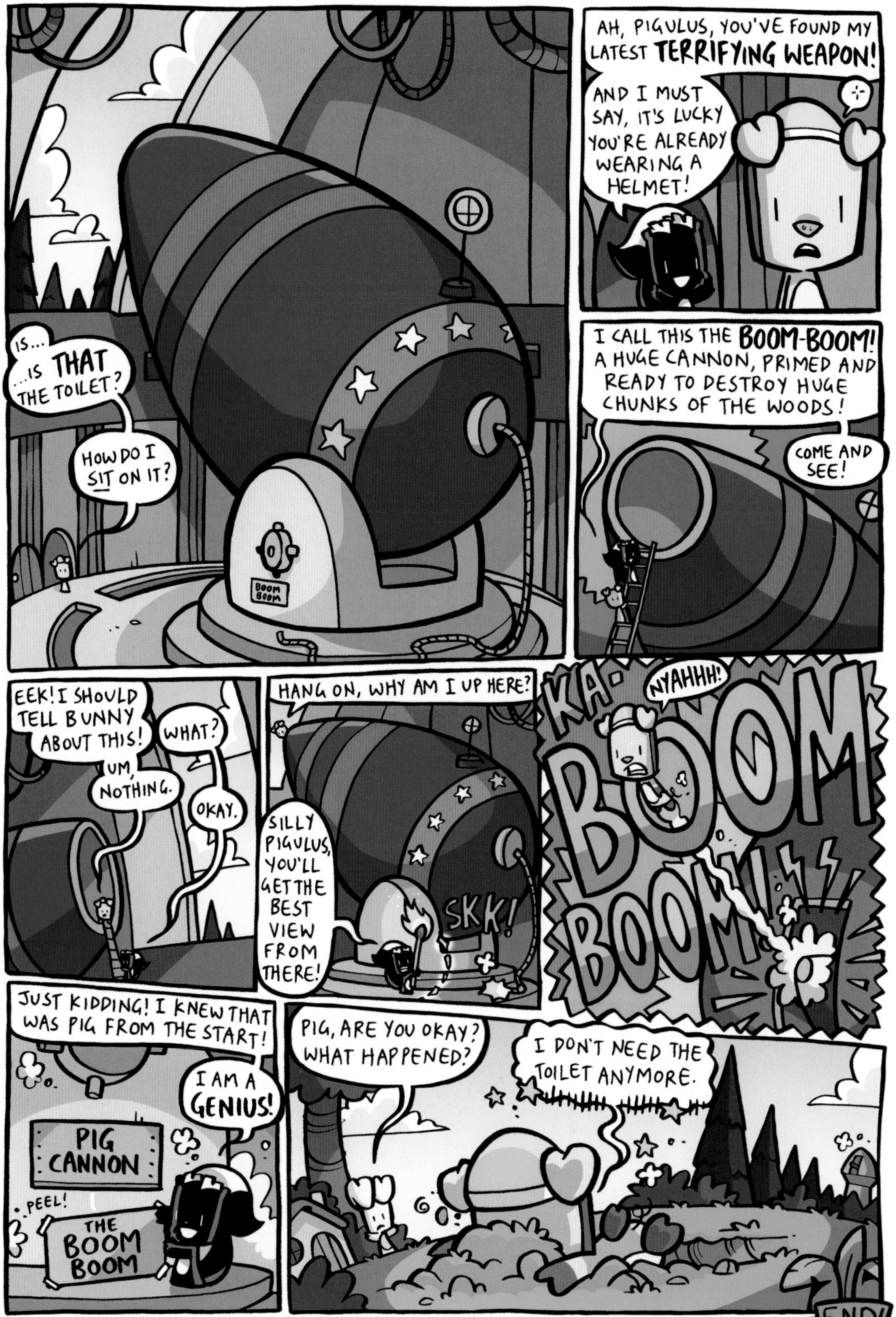

AH, PIGULUS, YOU'VE FOUND MY LATEST TERRIFYING WEAPON!
AND I MUST SAY, IT'S LUCKY YOU'RE ALREADY WEARING A HELMET!
IS...
...IS THAT THE TOILET?
HOW DO I SIT ON IT?
BOOM BOOM
I CALL THIS THE BOOM-BOOM! A HUGE CANNON, PRIMED AND READY TO DESTROY HUGE CHUNKS OF THE WOODS!
COME AND SEE!
EEK! I SHOULD TELL BUNNY ABOUT THIS!
WHAT?
UM, NOTHING.
OKAY.
HANG ON, WHY AM I UP HERE?
SILLY PIGULUS, YOU'LL GET THE BEST VIEW FROM THERE!
SKK!
KA-
NYAHHH!
BOOM BOOM!
JUST KIDDING! I KNEW THAT WAS PIG FROM THE START!
I AM A GENIUS!
PIG CANNON
PEEL!
THE BOOM BOOM
PIG, ARE YOU OKAY? WHAT HAPPENED?
I DON'T NEED THE TOILET ANYMORE.
END!

AND NOW FOR
# SOME-THING A LITTLE BIT RANDOM

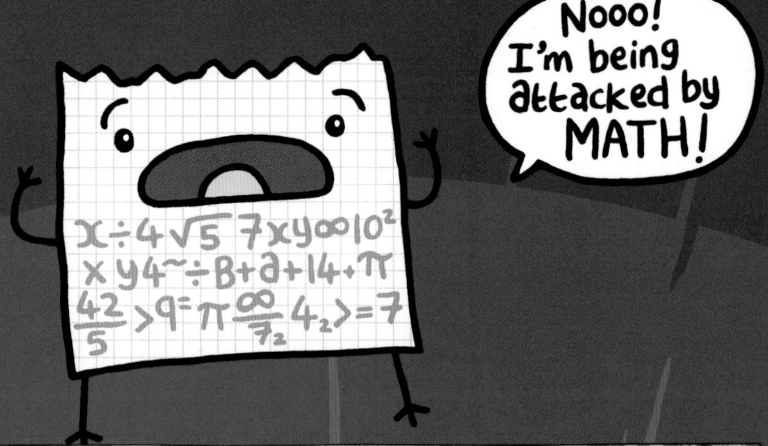
Nooo! I'm being attacked by MATH!

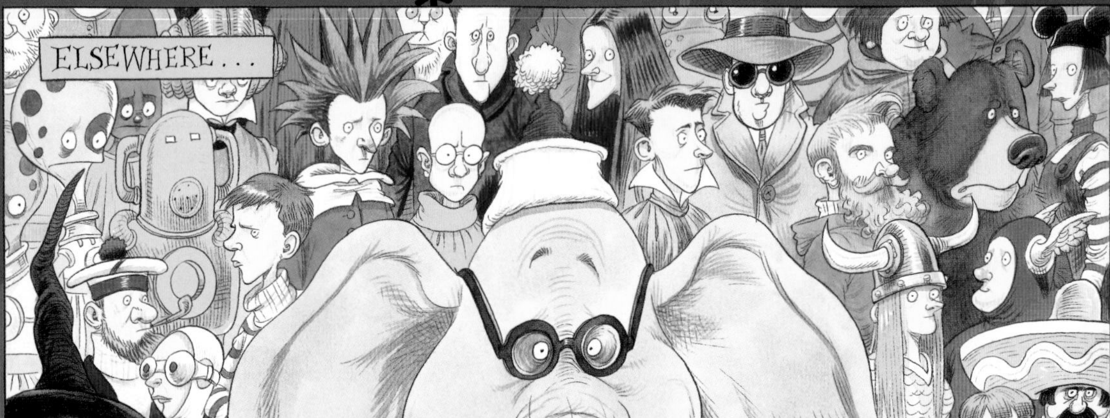
ELSEWHERE . . .
WHERE'S NELLY ?

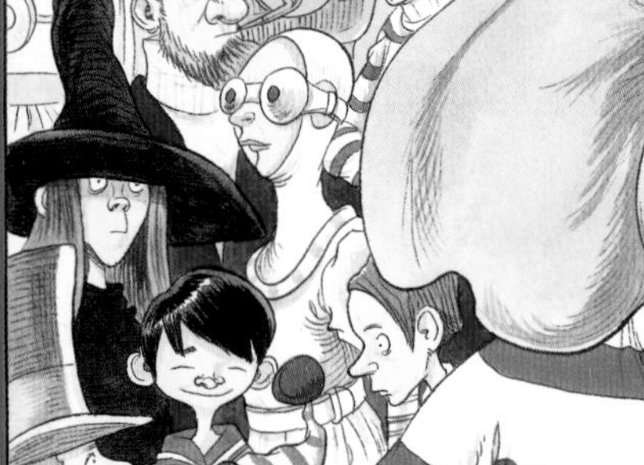
the PHOENIX PHICTIONARY by Alexi Con
1.Grampoline

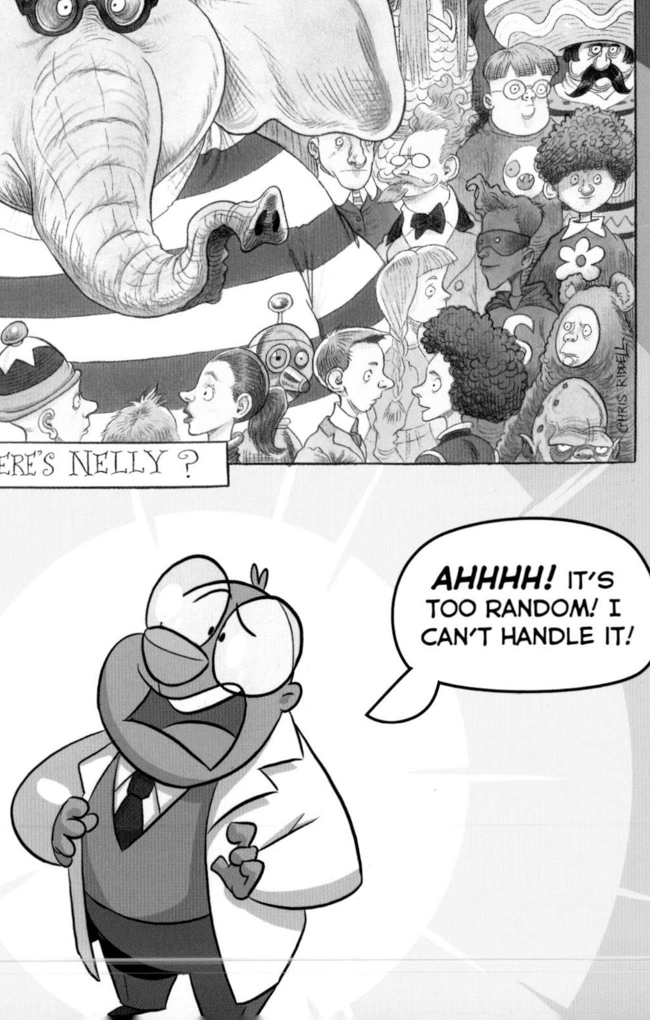
AHHHH! IT'S TOO RANDOM! I CAN'T HANDLE IT!

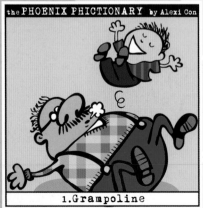

A SLUG WAS BITTEN BY A RADIOACTIVE CHIMP, WHICH WASN'T NICE. HE ALSO DECIDED TO BECOME A DETECTIVE AND CALLED HIMSELF...

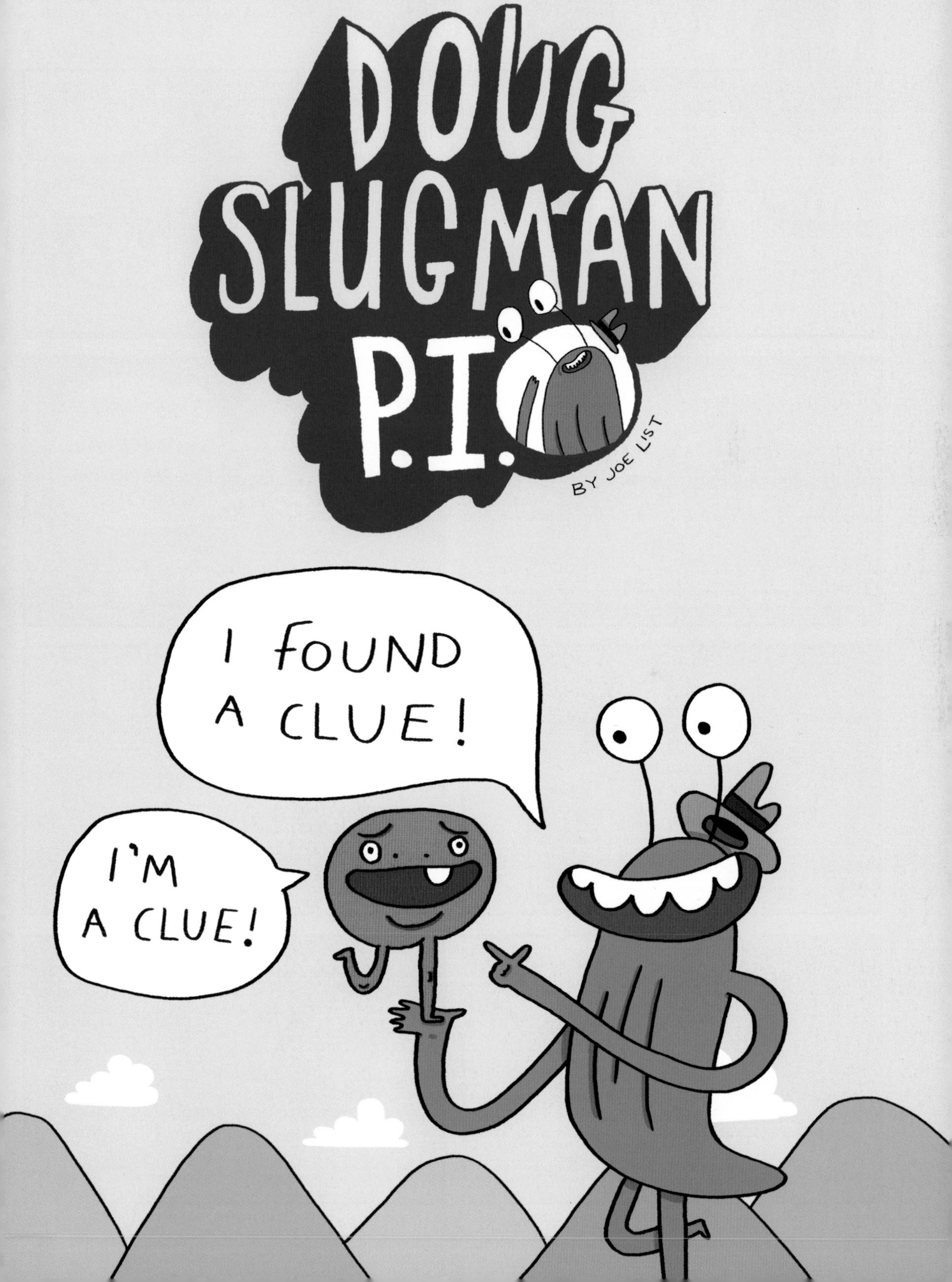
DOUG SLUGMAN P.I.
BY JOE LIST
I FOUND A CLUE!
I'M A CLUE!

AFTER BEING FORCED TO WATCH EVERY EPISODE OF *COLUMBO*, A SLUG DECIDED TO HAVE A GO AT DETECTING FOR HIMSELF.

# DOUG SLUGMAN P.I.

BY JOE LIST

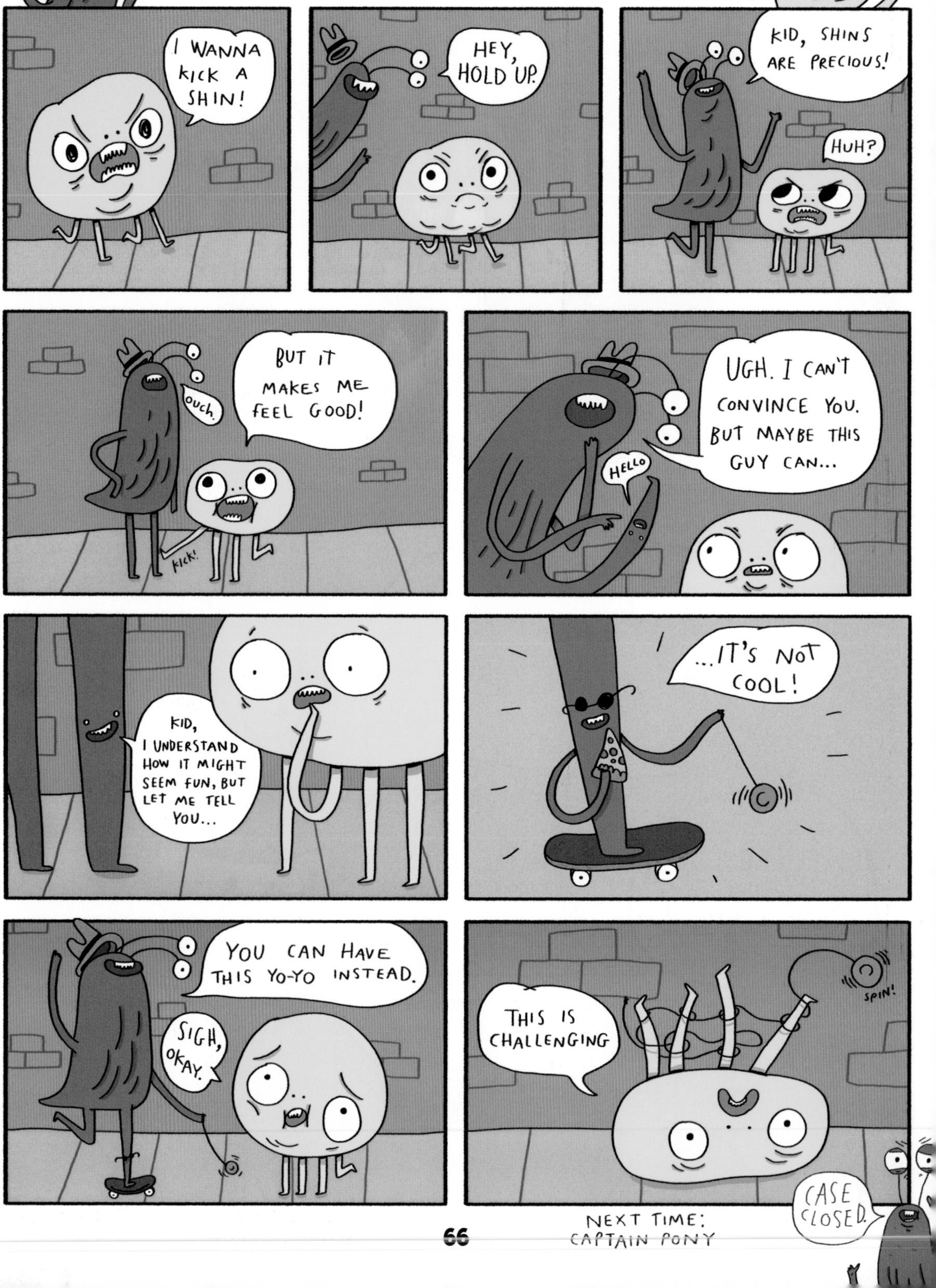
KICK
I WANNA KICK A SHIN!
HEY, HOLD UP.
KID, SHINS ARE PRECIOUS!
HUH?
OUCH.
BUT IT MAKES ME FEEL GOOD!
KICK!
UGH. I CAN'T CONVINCE YOU. BUT MAYBE THIS GUY CAN...
HELLO
KID, I UNDERSTAND HOW IT MIGHT SEEM FUN, BUT LET ME TELL YOU...
...IT'S NOT COOL!
YOU CAN HAVE THIS YO-YO INSTEAD.
SIGH, OKAY.
THIS IS CHALLENGING
SPIN!
NEXT TIME: CAPTAIN PONY
CASE CLOSED.

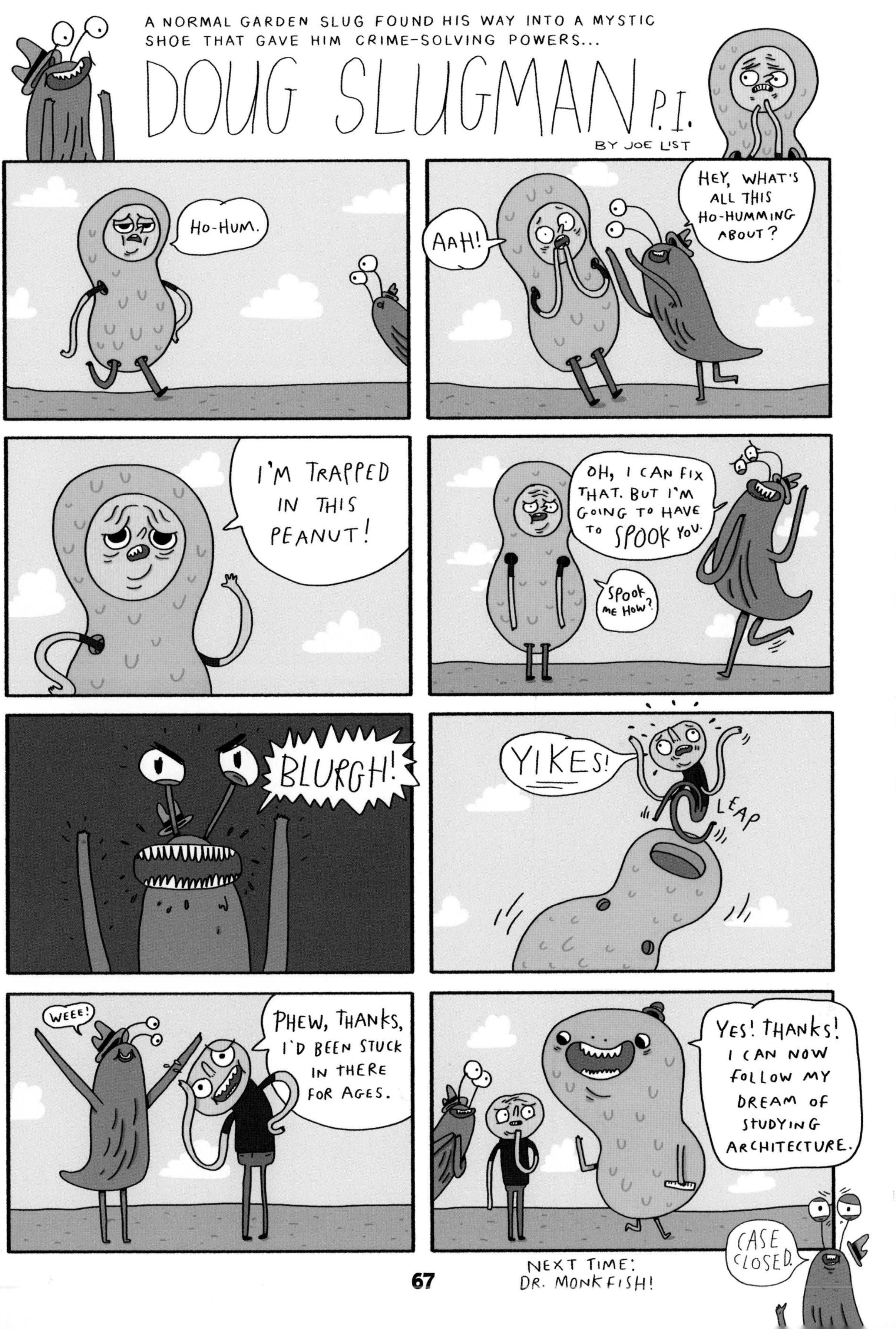
A NORMAL GARDEN SLUG FOUND HIS WAY INTO A MYSTIC SHOE THAT GAVE HIM CRIME-SOLVING POWERS...
DOUG SLUGMAN P.I.
BY JOE LIST
HO-HUM.
AAH!
HEY, WHAT'S ALL THIS HO-HUMMING ABOUT?
I'M TRAPPED IN THIS PEANUT!
OH, I CAN FIX THAT. BUT I'M GOING TO HAVE TO SPOOK YOU.
SPOOK ME HOW?
BLURGH!
YIKES!
LEAP
WEEE!
PHEW, THANKS, I'D BEEN STUCK IN THERE FOR AGES.
YES! THANKS! I CAN NOW FOLLOW MY DREAM OF STUDYING ARCHITECTURE.
CASE CLOSED.
NEXT TIME: DR. MONKFISH!

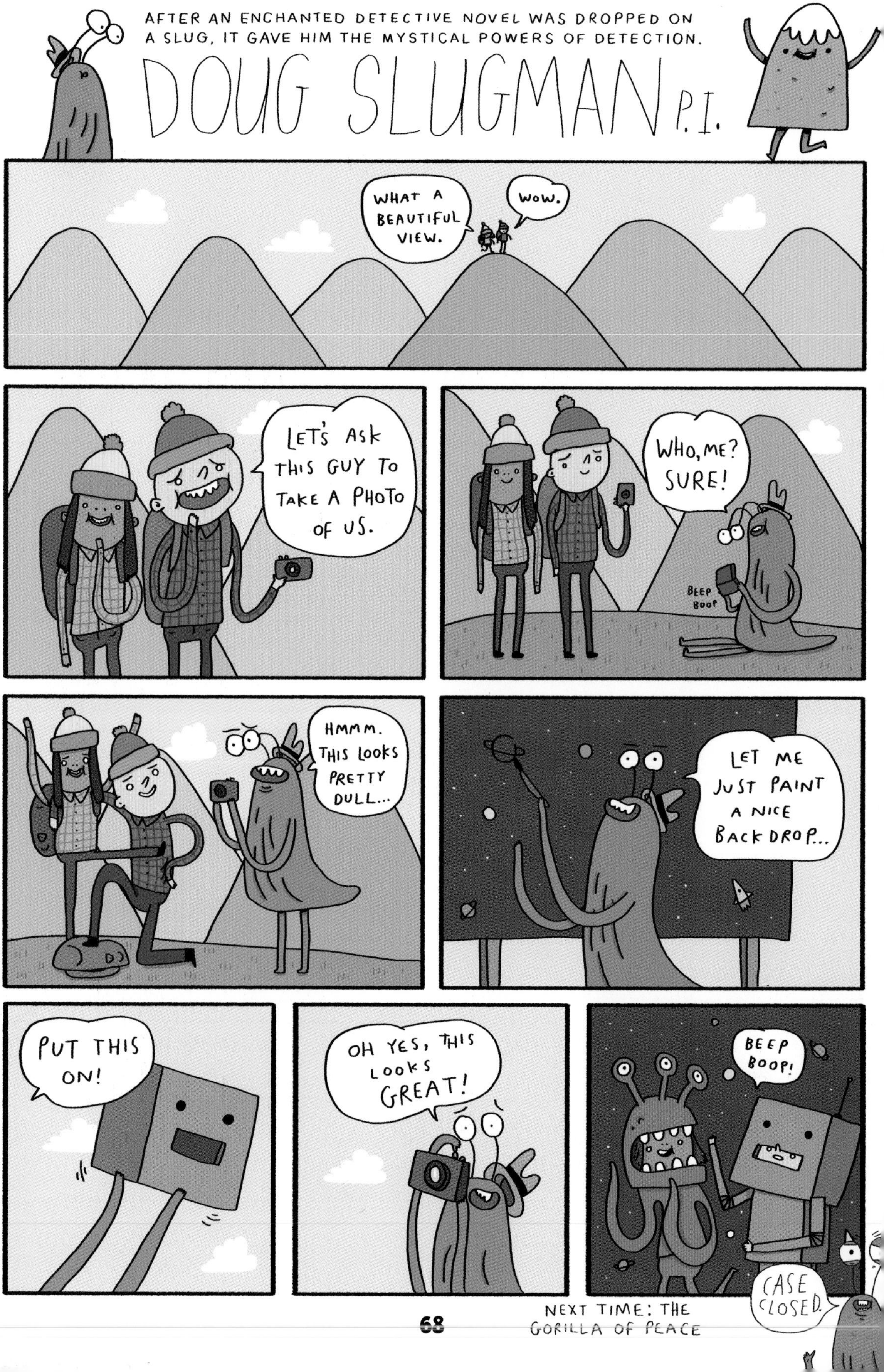
AFTER AN ENCHANTED DETECTIVE NOVEL WAS DROPPED ON A SLUG, IT GAVE HIM THE MYSTICAL POWERS OF DETECTION.
DOUG SLUGMAN P.I.
WHAT A BEAUTIFUL VIEW.
WOW.
LET'S ASK THIS GUY TO TAKE A PHOTO OF US.
WHO, ME? SURE!
BEEP BOOP
HMMM. THIS LOOKS PRETTY DULL...
LET ME JUST PAINT A NICE BACKDROP...
PUT THIS ON!
OH YES, THIS LOOKS GREAT!
BEEP BOOP!
CASE CLOSED.
NEXT TIME: THE GORILLA OF PEACE

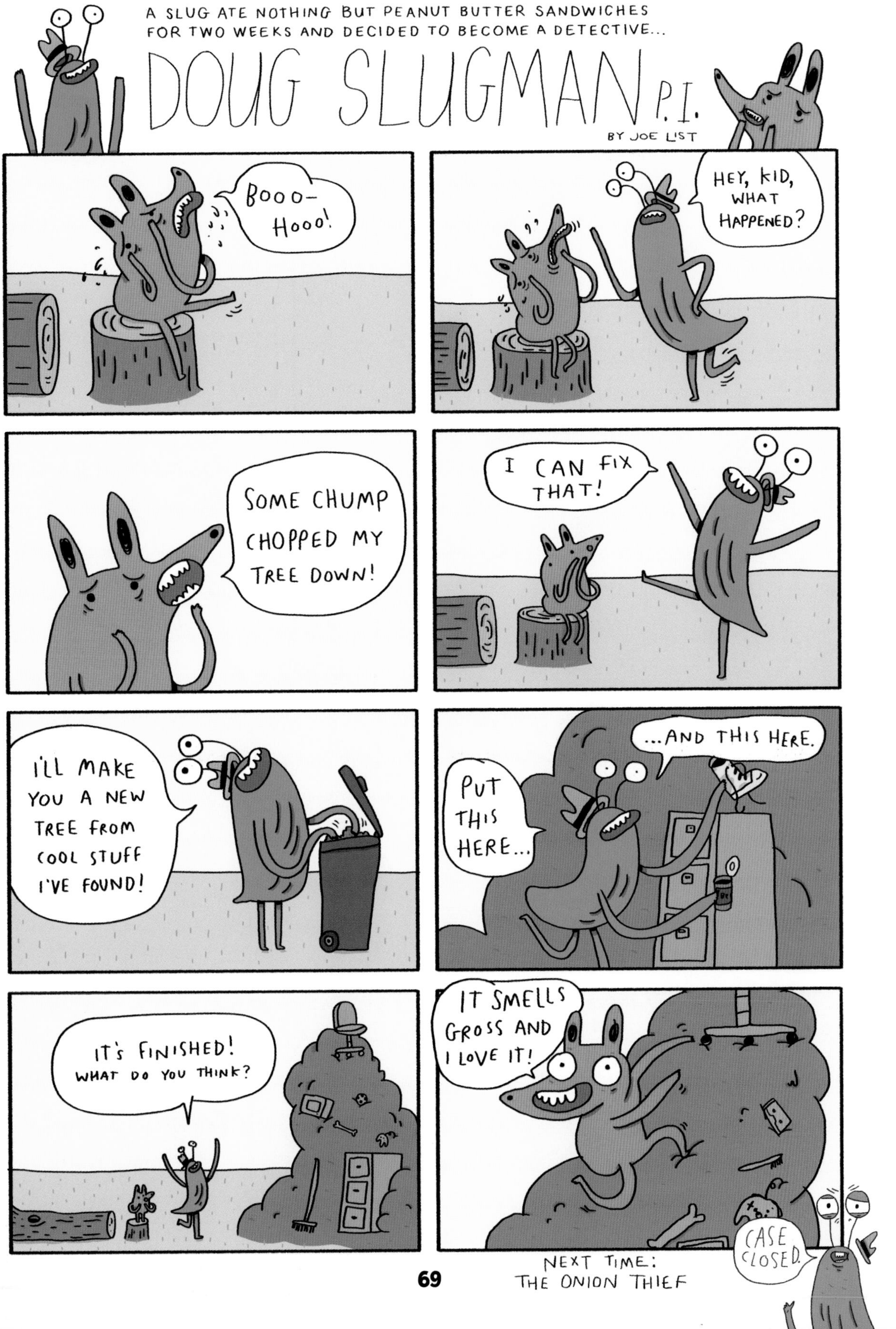
A SLUG ATE NOTHING BUT PEANUT BUTTER SANDWICHES FOR TWO WEEKS AND DECIDED TO BECOME A DETECTIVE...
DOUG SLUGMAN P.I.
BY JOE LIST
BOOO-HOOO!
HEY, KID, WHAT HAPPENED?
SOME CHUMP CHOPPED MY TREE DOWN!
I CAN FIX THAT!
I'LL MAKE YOU A NEW TREE FROM COOL STUFF I'VE FOUND!
PUT THIS HERE...
...AND THIS HERE.
IT'S FINISHED! WHAT DO YOU THINK?
IT SMELLS GROSS AND I LOVE IT!
NEXT TIME: THE ONION THIEF
CASE CLOSED.

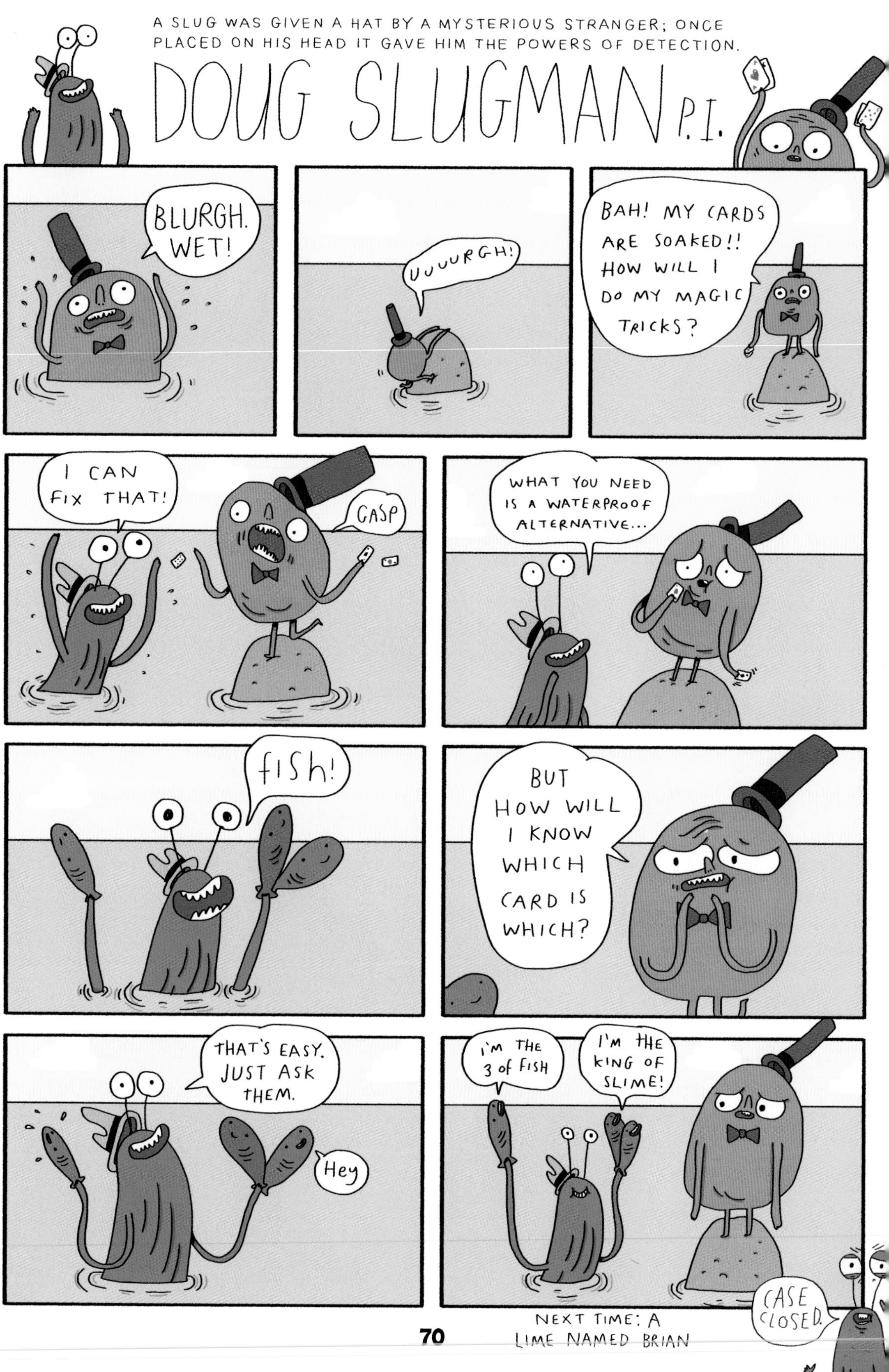

A SLUG WAS GIVEN A HAT BY A MYSTERIOUS STRANGER; ONCE PLACED ON HIS HEAD IT GAVE HIM THE POWERS OF DETECTION.
DOUG SLUGMAN P.I.
BLURGH. WET!
UUUURGH!
BAH! MY CARDS ARE SOAKED!! HOW WILL I DO MY MAGIC TRICKS?
I CAN FIX THAT!
GASP
WHAT YOU NEED IS A WATERPROOF ALTERNATIVE...
fish!
BUT HOW WILL I KNOW WHICH CARD IS WHICH?
THAT'S EASY. JUST ASK THEM.
Hey
I'M THE 3 of FISH
I'M THE KING OF SLIME!
CASE CLOSED.
NEXT TIME: A LIME NAMED BRIAN

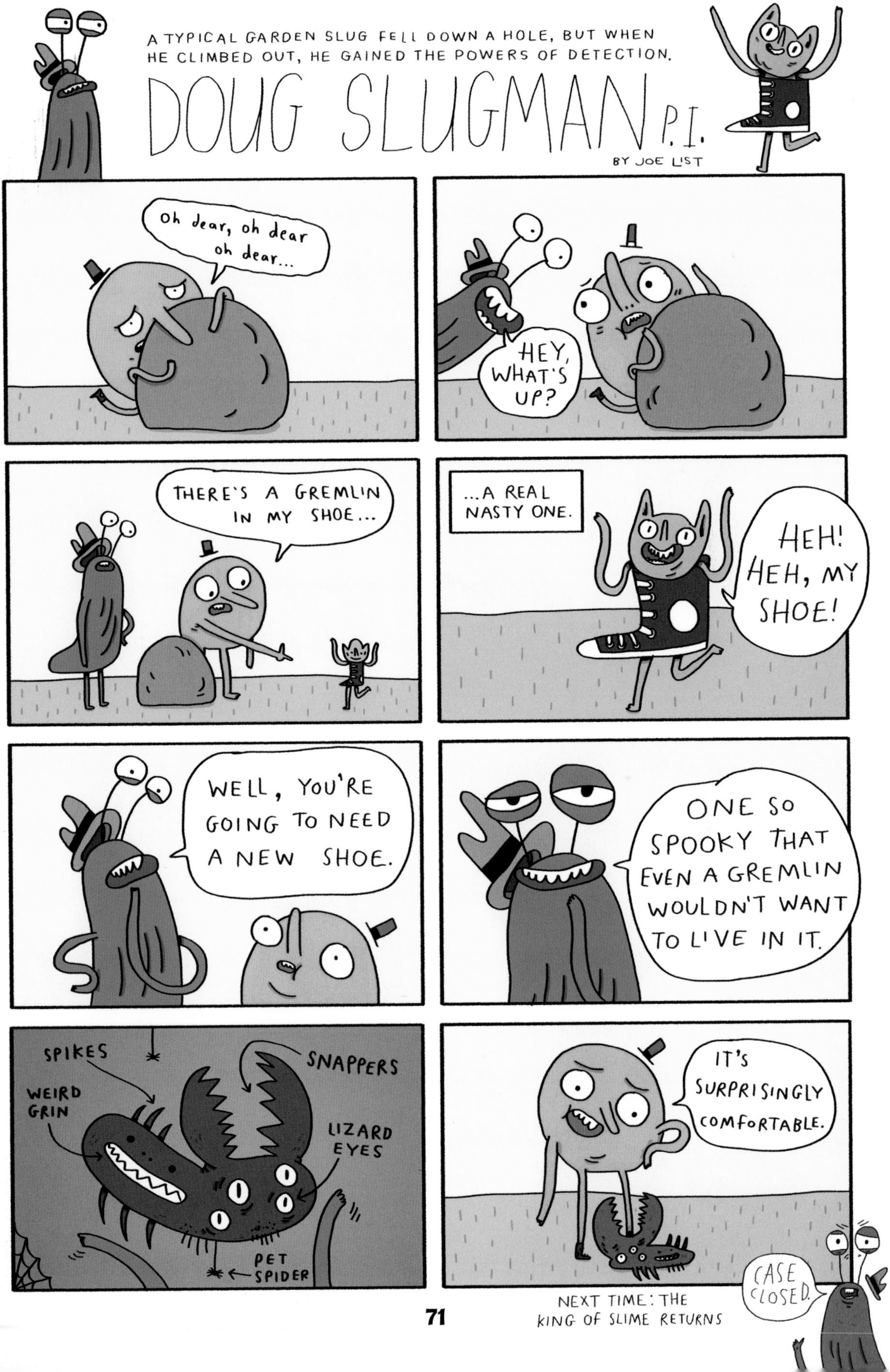
A TYPICAL GARDEN SLUG FELL DOWN A HOLE, BUT WHEN HE CLIMBED OUT, HE GAINED THE POWERS OF DETECTION.
DOUG SLUGMAN P.I.
BY JOE LIST
Oh dear, oh dear oh dear...
HEY, WHAT'S UP?
THERE'S A GREMLIN IN MY SHOE...
...A REAL NASTY ONE.
HEH! HEH, MY SHOE!
WELL, YOU'RE GOING TO NEED A NEW SHOE.
ONE SO SPOOKY THAT EVEN A GREMLIN WOULDN'T WANT TO LIVE IN IT.
SPIKES
SNAPPERS
WEIRD GRIN
LIZARD EYES
PET SPIDER
IT'S SURPRISINGLY COMFORTABLE.
CASE CLOSED.
NEXT TIME: THE KING OF SLIME RETURNS

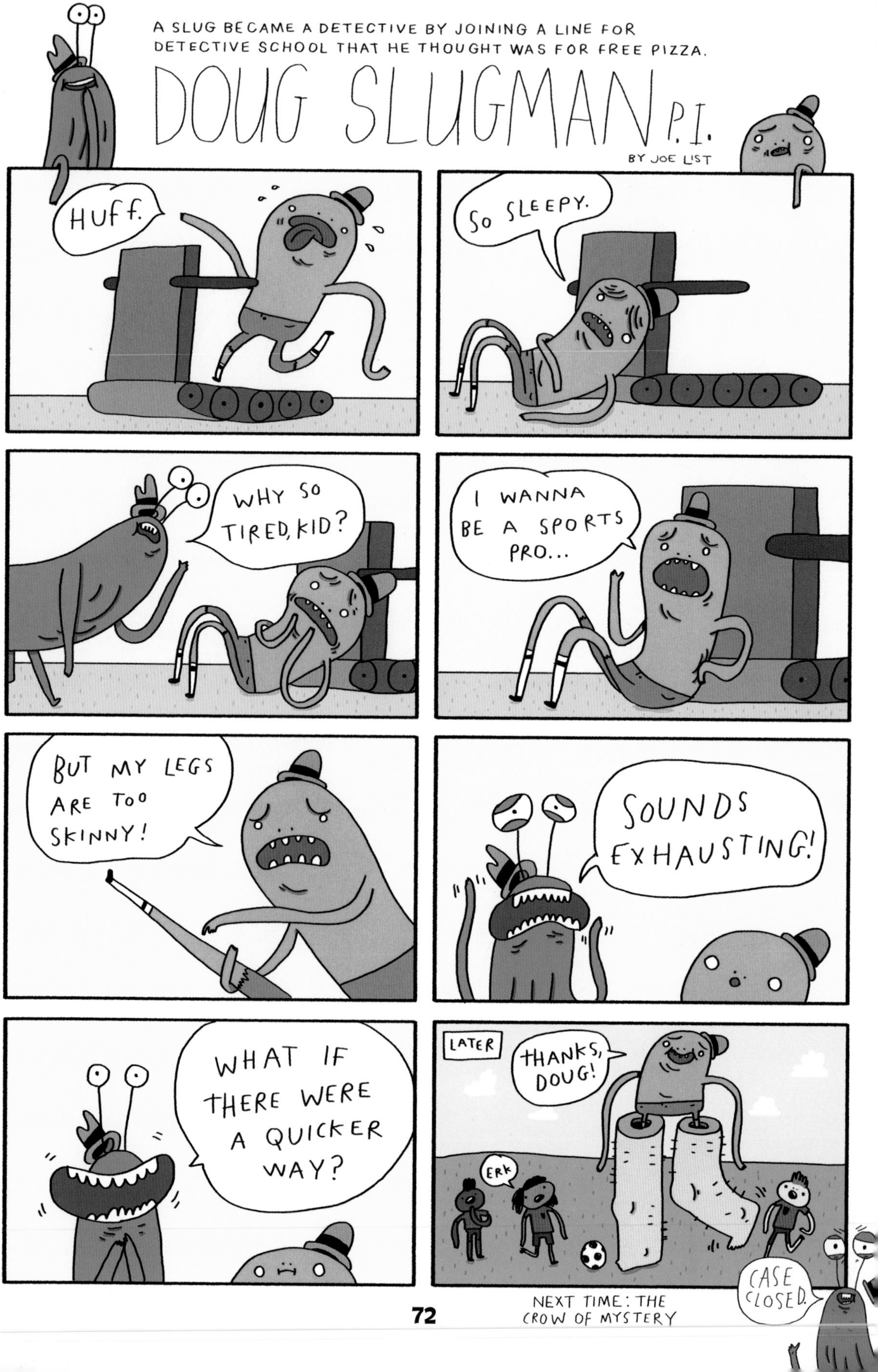
A SLUG BECAME A DETECTIVE BY JOINING A LINE FOR DETECTIVE SCHOOL THAT HE THOUGHT WAS FOR FREE PIZZA.
DOUG SLUGMAN P.I.
BY JOE LIST
HUFF.
SO SLEEPY.
WHY SO TIRED, KID?
I WANNA BE A SPORTS PRO...
BUT MY LEGS ARE TOO SKINNY!
SOUNDS EXHAUSTING!
WHAT IF THERE WERE A QUICKER WAY?
LATER
THANKS, DOUG!
ERK
CASE CLOSED.
NEXT TIME: THE CROW OF MYSTERY

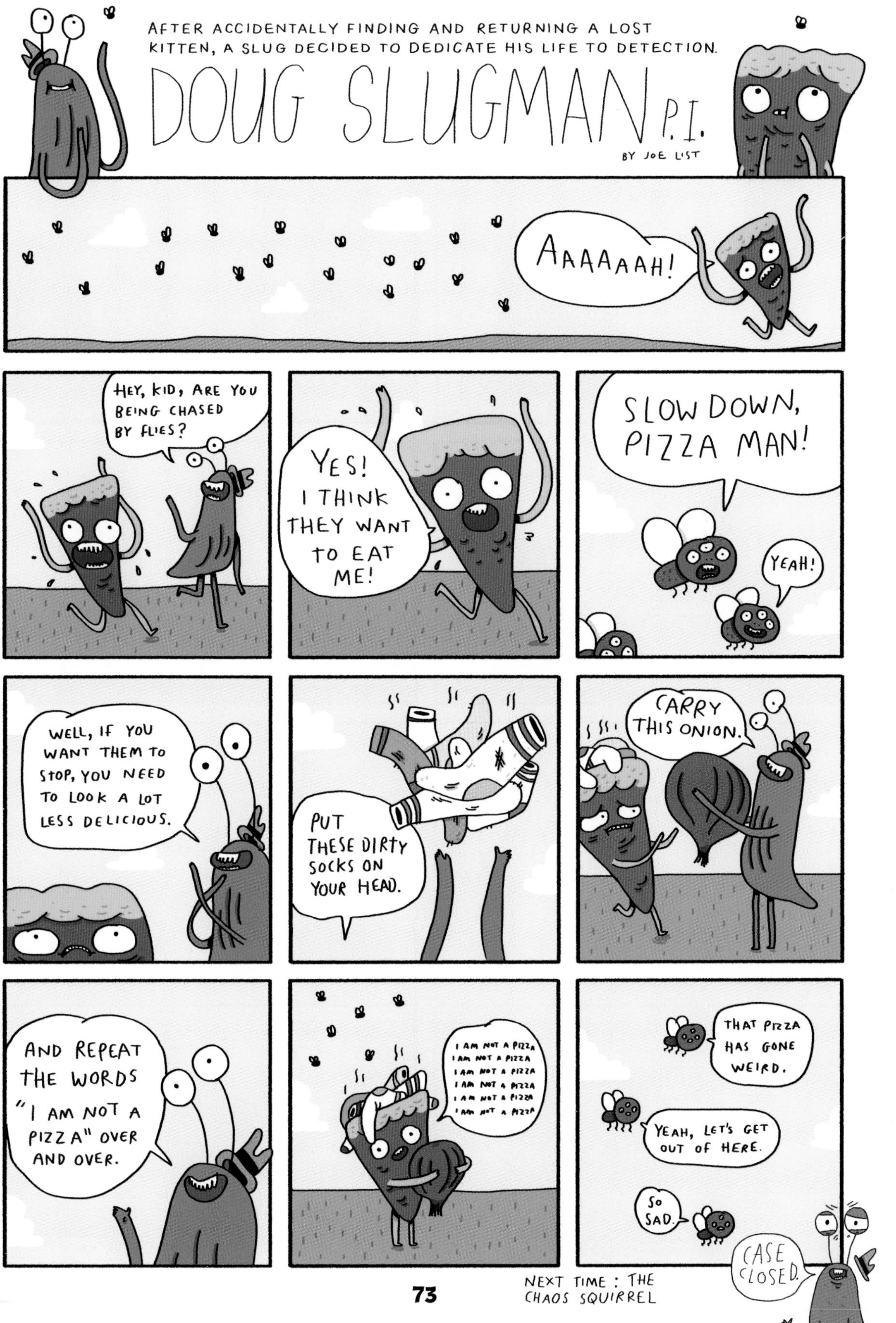
AFTER ACCIDENTALLY FINDING AND RETURNING A LOST KITTEN, A SLUG DECIDED TO DEDICATE HIS LIFE TO DETECTION.
DOUG SLUGMAN P.I.
BY JOE LIST
AAAAAAH!
HEY, KID, ARE YOU BEING CHASED BY FLIES?
YES! I THINK THEY WANT TO EAT ME!
SLOW DOWN, PIZZA MAN!
YEAH!
WELL, IF YOU WANT THEM TO STOP, YOU NEED TO LOOK A LOT LESS DELICIOUS.
PUT THESE DIRTY SOCKS ON YOUR HEAD.
CARRY THIS ONION.
AND REPEAT THE WORDS "I AM NOT A PIZZA" OVER AND OVER.
I AM NOT A PIZZA
I AM NOT A PIZZA
I AM NOT A PIZZA
I AM NOT A PIZZA
I AM NOT A PIZZA
I AM NOT A PIZZA
THAT PIZZA HAS GONE WEIRD.
YEAH, LET'S GET OUT OF HERE.
SO SAD.
CASE CLOSED.
NEXT TIME : THE CHAOS SQUIRREL

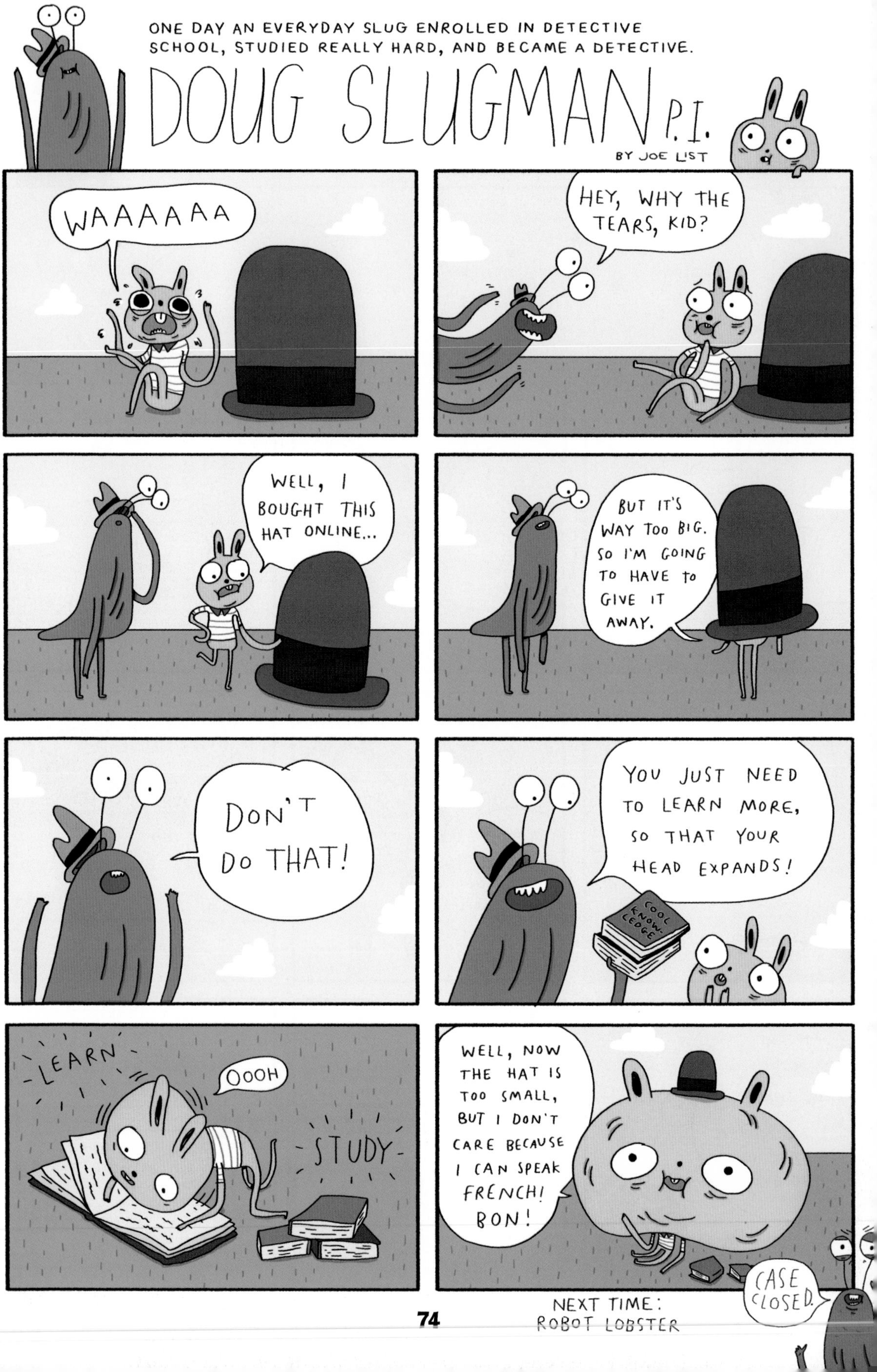
ONE DAY AN EVERYDAY SLUG ENROLLED IN DETECTIVE SCHOOL, STUDIED REALLY HARD, AND BECAME A DETECTIVE.
DOUG SLUGMAN P.I.
BY JOE LIST
WAAAAAA
HEY, WHY THE TEARS, KID?
WELL, I BOUGHT THIS HAT ONLINE...
BUT IT'S WAY TOO BIG. SO I'M GOING TO HAVE TO GIVE IT AWAY.
DON'T DO THAT!
YOU JUST NEED TO LEARN MORE, SO THAT YOUR HEAD EXPANDS!
COOL KNOW-LEDGE
LEARN
OOOH
STUDY
WELL, NOW THE HAT IS TOO SMALL, BUT I DON'T CARE BECAUSE I CAN SPEAK FRENCH! BON!
CASE CLOSED
NEXT TIME: ROBOT LOBSTER

## Too many Guinea Pigs

Gasp! Look at all the cute guinea pigs!

More of them! How adorable!

Um...

## The OWL of Wisdom

Finally! After our long and dangerous journey, fraught with terrible perils and awful smells...

We found it!

The Owl of Wisdom!

Oh, wise and powerful owl! Please bestow upon us the wisdom we seek!

...

plap!

The wise man never stands beneath the owl of wisdom after lunch.

I feel horrible.

Wow! He is wise!

## The Red Panda: nature's JERK

Lizards are dumb.

Nobody likes lizards.

In fact, I think you are the worst lizard I've ever seen!

Just telling it like it is.

This isn't my house...

Toast Ghost

Boo!

by Jess Bradley

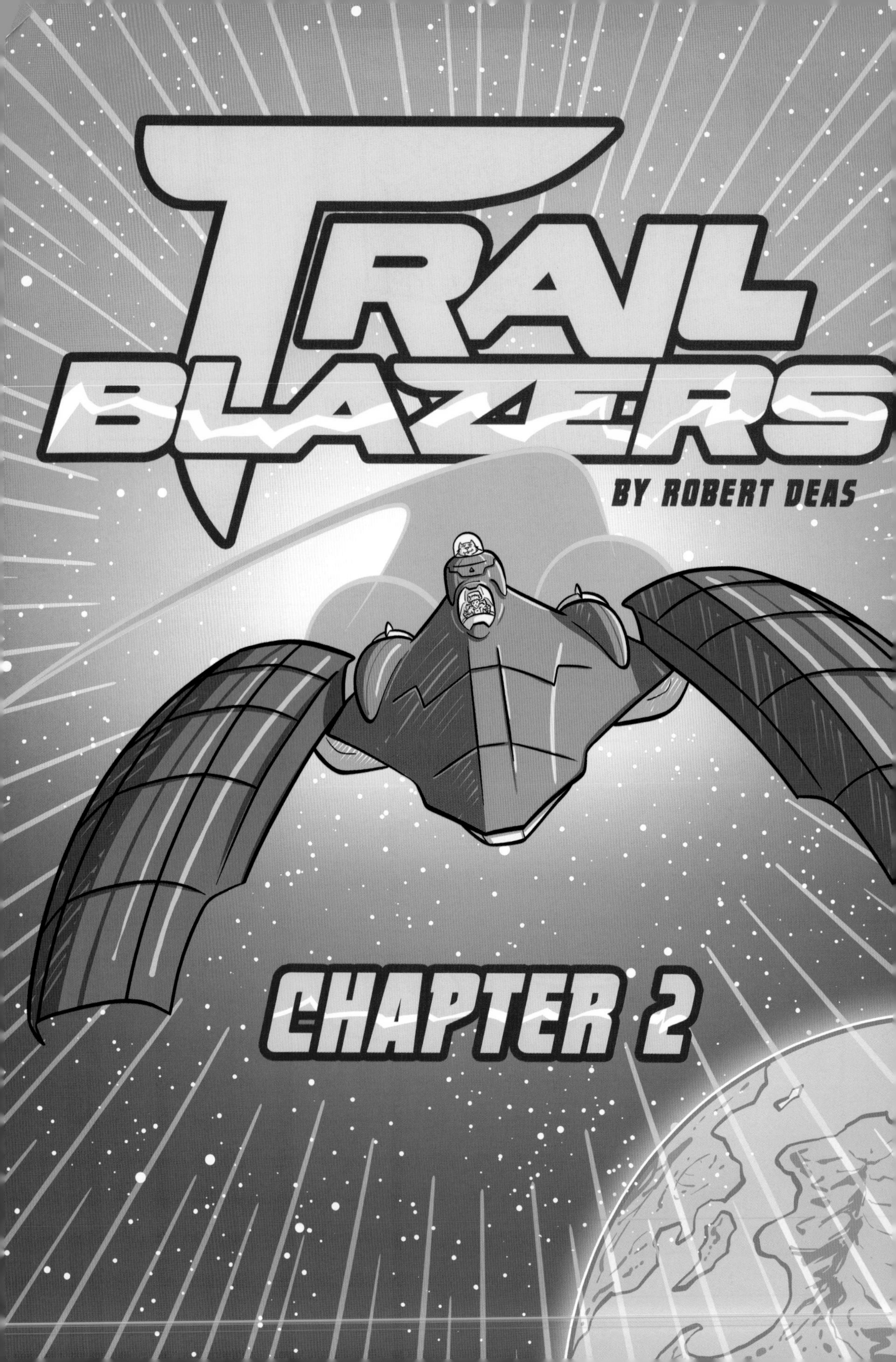
TRAIL BLAZERS
BY ROBERT DEAS
CHAPTER 2

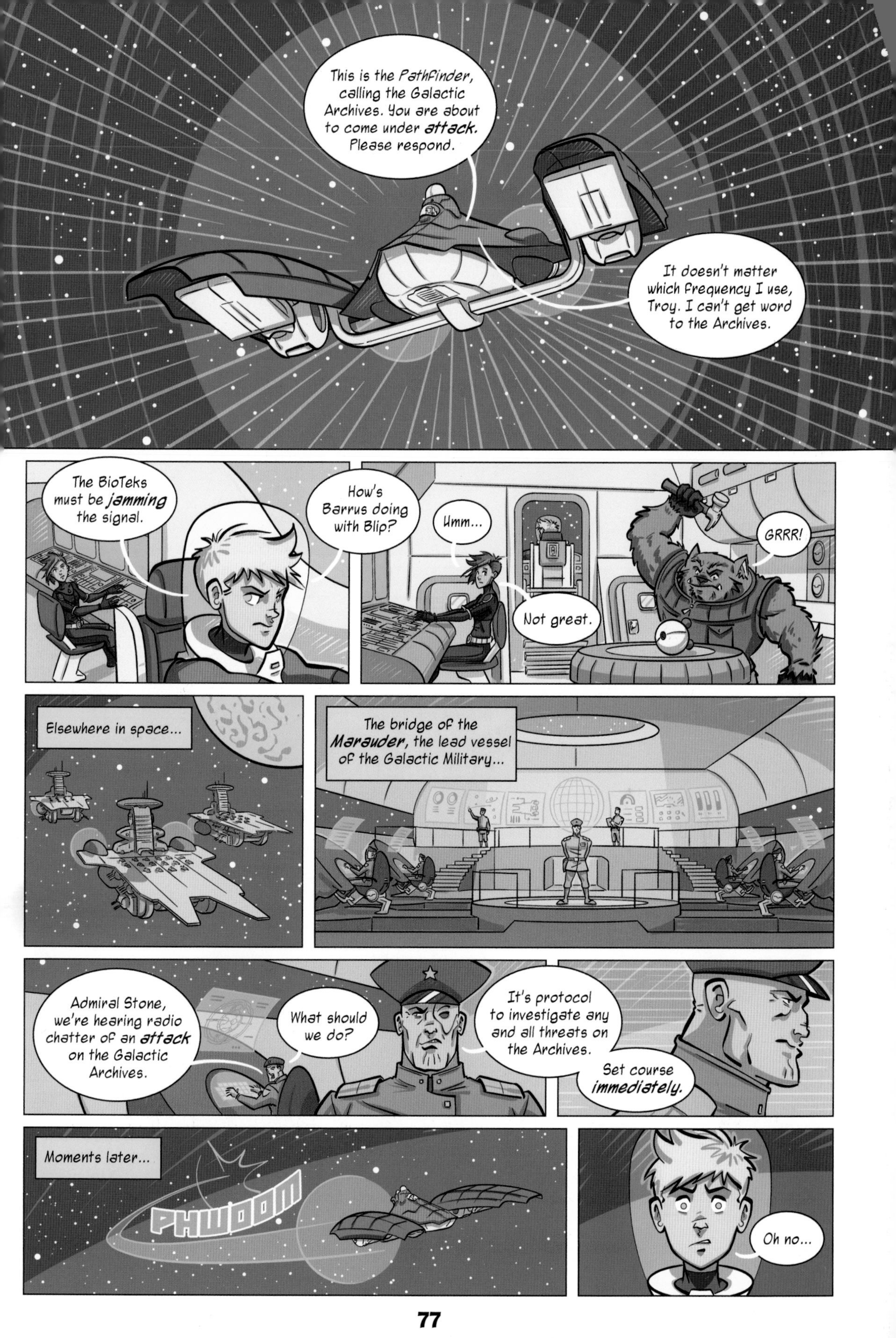
This is the *Pathfinder*, calling the Galactic Archives. You are about to come under ***attack.*** Please respond.
It doesn't matter which frequency I use, Troy. I can't get word to the Archives.
The BioTeks must be ***jamming*** the signal.
How's Barrus doing with Blip?
Umm...
Not great.
GRRR!
Elsewhere in space...
The bridge of the ***Marauder***, the lead vessel of the Galactic Military...
Admiral Stone, we're hearing radio chatter of an ***attack*** on the Galactic Archives.
What should we do?
It's protocol to investigate any and all threats on the Archives.
Set course ***immediately.***
Moments later...
PHWOOM
Oh no...

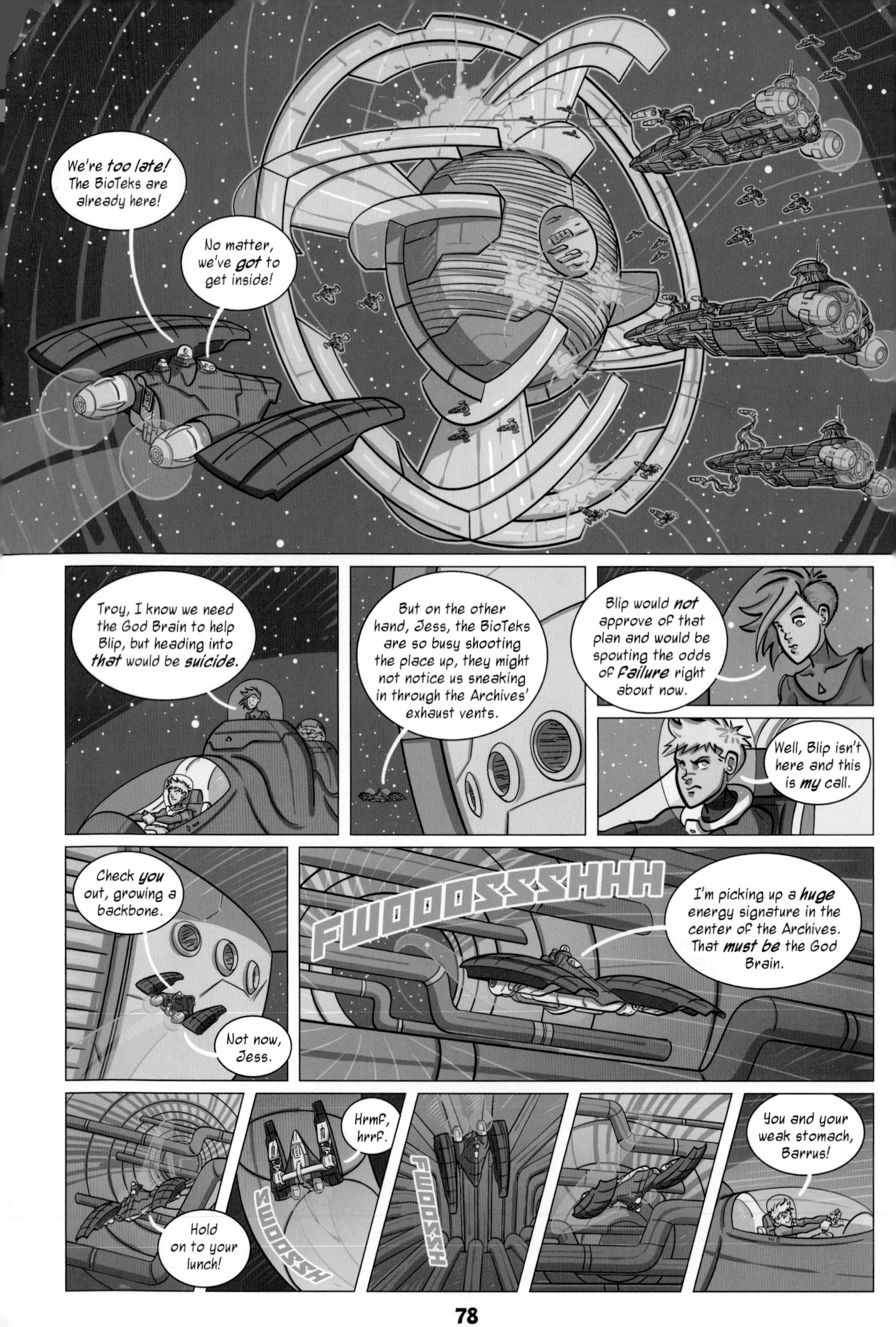
We're too late! The BioTeks are already here!
No matter, we've got to get inside!
Troy, I know we need the God Brain to help Blip, but heading into that would be suicide.
But on the other hand, Jess, the BioTeks are so busy shooting the place up, they might not notice us sneaking in through the Archives' exhaust vents.
Blip would not approve of that plan and would be spouting the odds of failure right about now.
Well, Blip isn't here and this is my call.
Check you out, growing a backbone.
Not now, Jess.
FWOOOSSSHHH
I'm picking up a huge energy signature in the center of the Archives. That must be the God Brain.
Hold on to your lunch!
SWOOSSH
Hrmf, hrrf.
FWOOSSH
You and your weak stomach, Barrus!

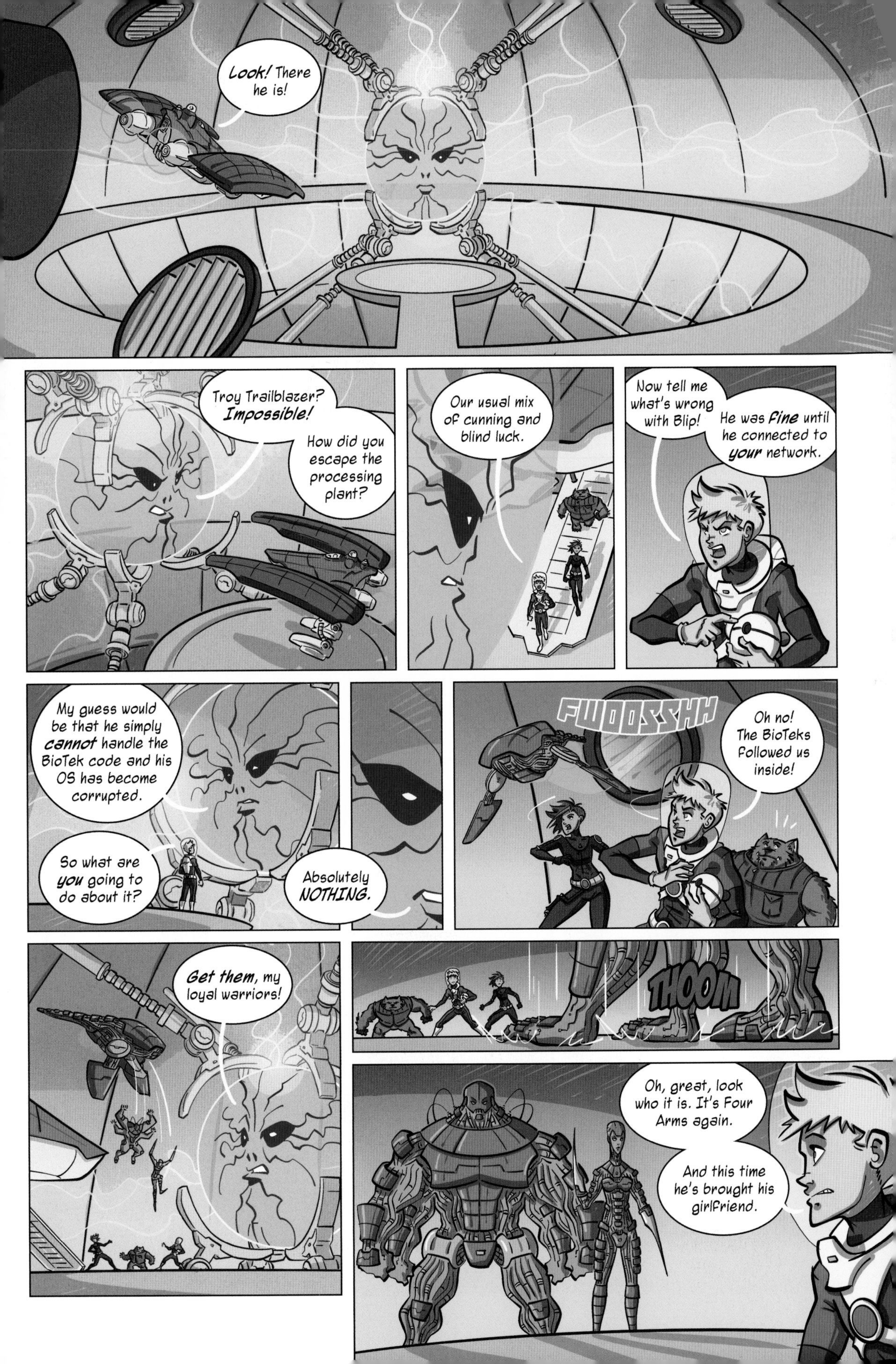
Look! There he is!
Troy Trailblazer? Impossible!
How did you escape the processing plant?
Our usual mix of cunning and blind luck.
Now tell me what's wrong with Blip!
He was fine until he connected to your network.
My guess would be that he simply cannot handle the BioTek code and his OS has become corrupted.
So what are you going to do about it?
Absolutely NOTHING.
FWOOSHH
Oh no! The BioTeks followed us inside!
Get them, my loyal warriors!
THOOM
Oh, great, look who it is. It's Four Arms again.
And this time he's brought his girlfriend.

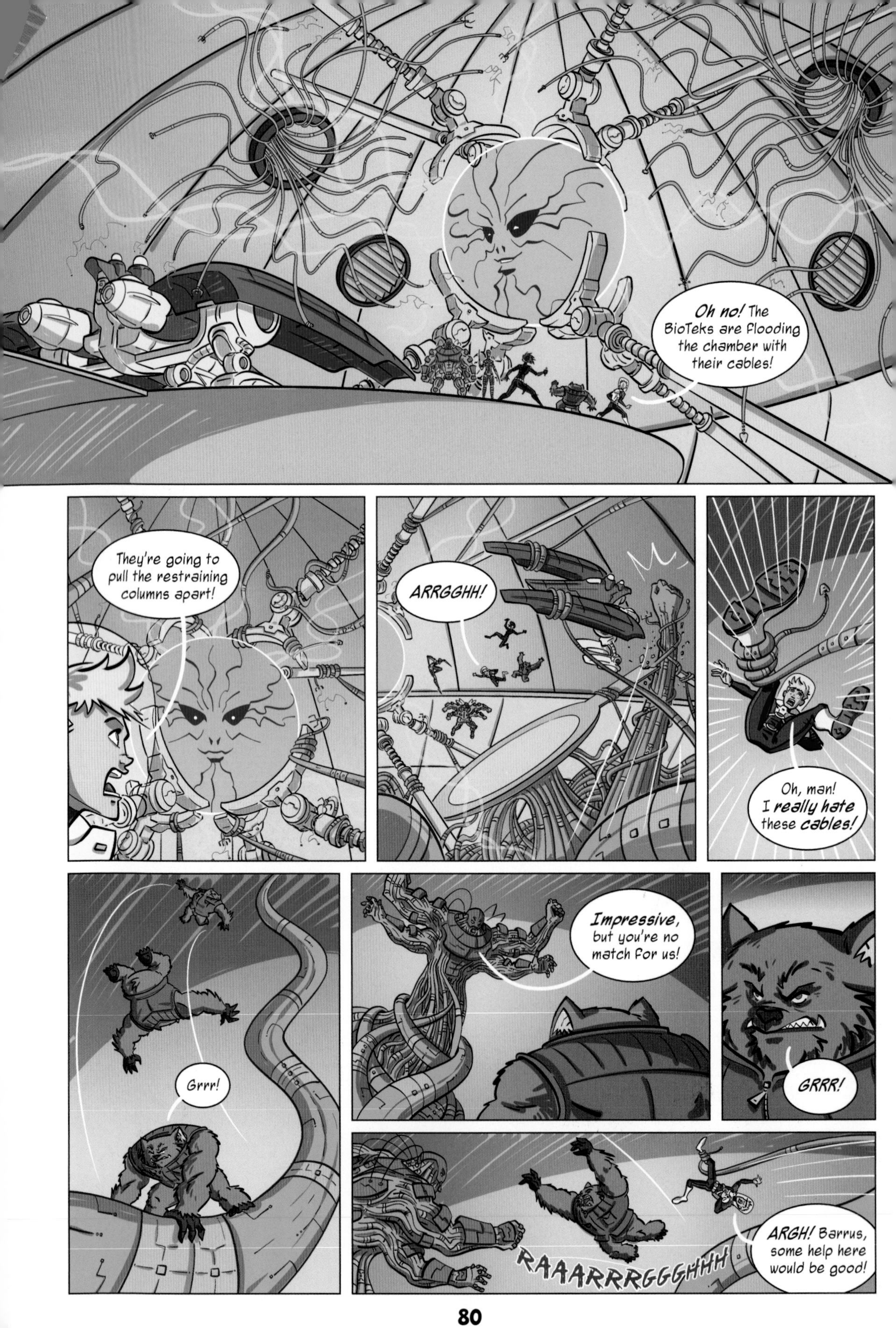

*Oh no!* The BioTeks are flooding the chamber with their cables!
They're going to pull the restraining columns apart!
ARRGGHH!
Oh, man! I ***really hate*** these ***cables!***
Grrr!
*Impressive,* but you're no match for us!
GRRR!
RAAARRRGGGHHH
*ARGH!* Barrus, some help here would be good!

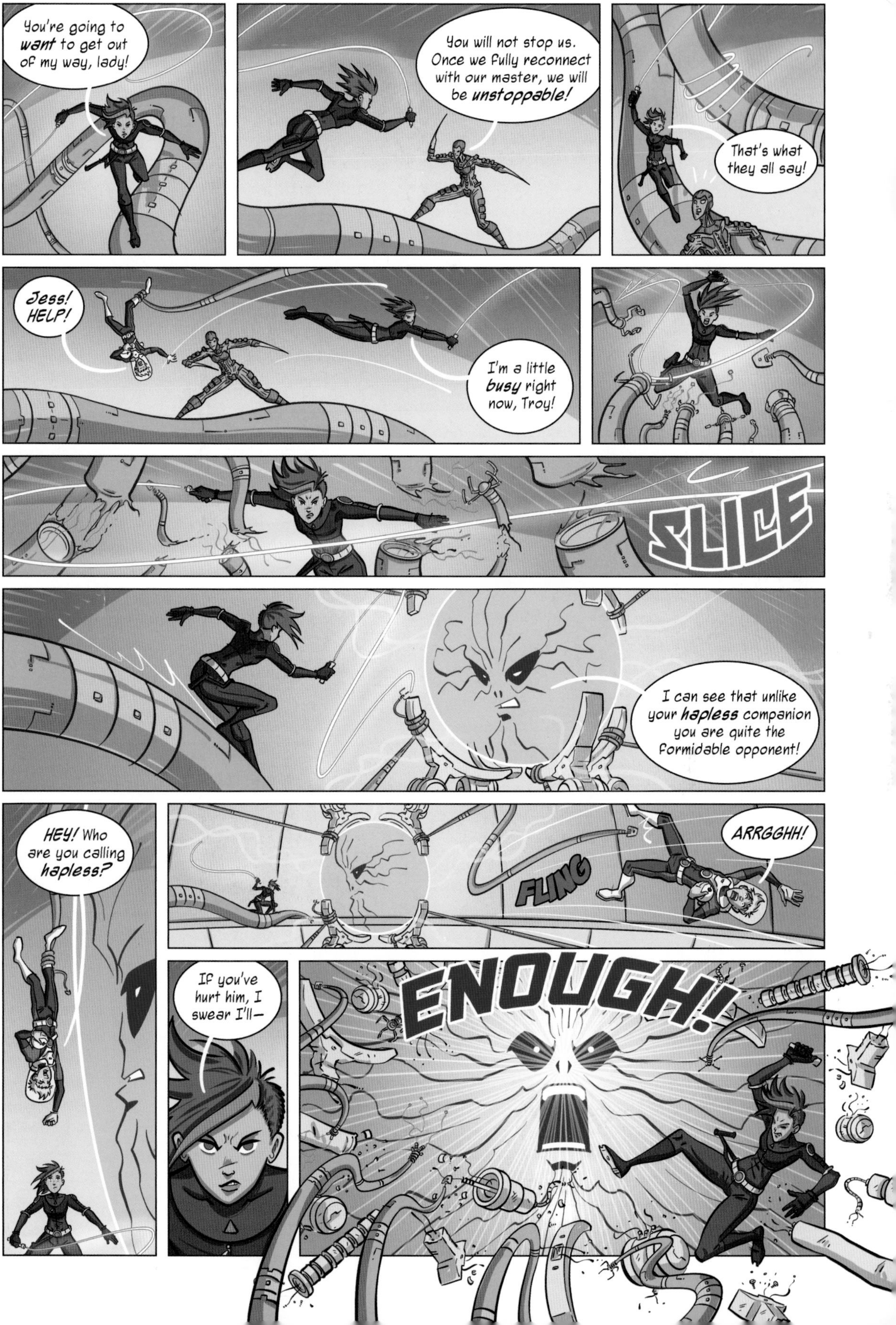

You're going to *want* to get out of my way, lady!
You will not stop us. Once we fully reconnect with our master, we will be *unstoppable!*
That's what they all say!
*Jess! HELP!*
I'm a little *busy* right now, Troy!
SLICE
I can see that unlike your *hapless* companion you are quite the formidable opponent!
*HEY!* Who are you calling *hapless?*
FLING
ARRGGHH!
If you've hurt him, I swear I'll—
ENOUGH!

At last, I am *free!*

Connect with me, my disciples! Let us share our power once more!

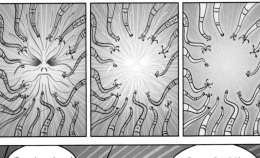

The download is complete.

I can feel the God Brain's energy flowing through us once again.

Come. We must return the God Brain to BioTeka to complete the synchronization.

Well, there goes the *gruesome* twosome.

Where's Troy?

Umm, I'm up here.

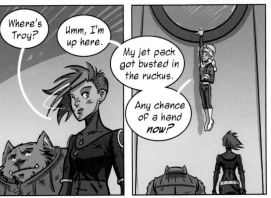

My jet pack got busted in the ruckus.

Any chance of a hand *now?*

Later...

I can't believe you let them get away.

At least we *tried* to stop them, Troy!

HALT!

This is Admiral Stone of the Galactic Military.

MARAUDER

Your actions here today have threatened the *entire universe!* Consider yourselves *under arrest!*

Hrmf?

Oh no.

Say *what?*

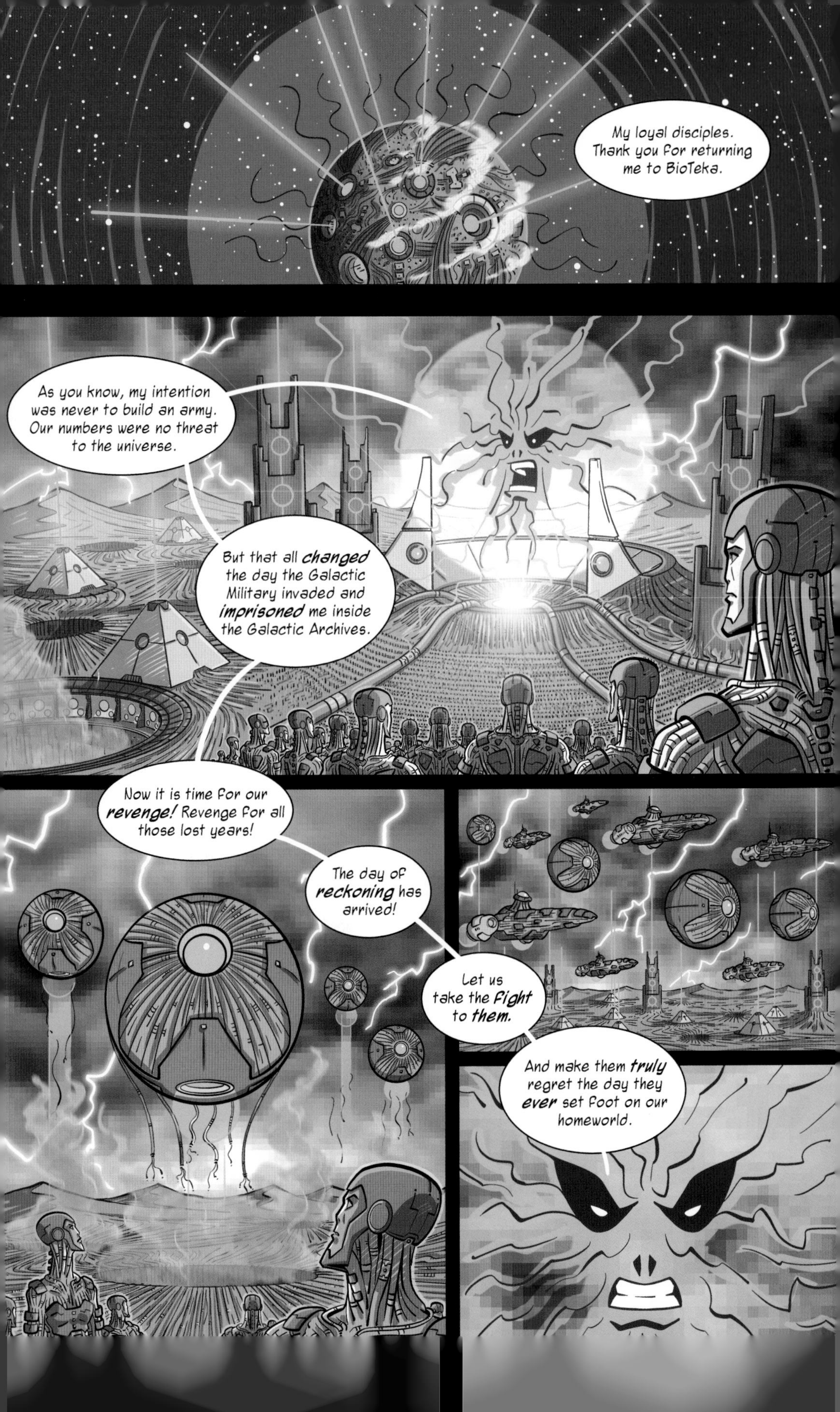
My loyal disciples. Thank you for returning me to BioTeka.
As you know, my intention was never to build an army. Our numbers were no threat to the universe.
But that all *changed* the day the Galactic Military invaded and *imprisoned* me inside the Galactic Archives.
Now it is time for our *revenge!* Revenge for all those lost years!
The day of *reckoning* has arrived!
Let us take the *fight* to *them.*
And make them *truly* regret the day they *ever* set foot on our homeworld.

CRONOS.

A heavily fortified moon.

And the Galactic Military's base of operations.

Bring out the *prisoners!*

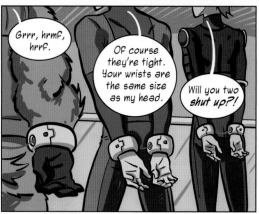

Grrr, hrmf, hrrf.

Of course they're tight. Your wrists are the same size as my head.

Will you two *shut up?!*

This court is now in session!

About time.

*Shut up,* Troy.

The three of you are on trial for *countless* crimes against the galaxy.

*Forced entry* into the Galactic Archives.

Numerous charges of *assault.*

Illegally accessing and downloading classified data.

Your fault.

Definitely Your fault.

Blip's fault.

Aiding the *escape* of the God Brain.

Debatable.

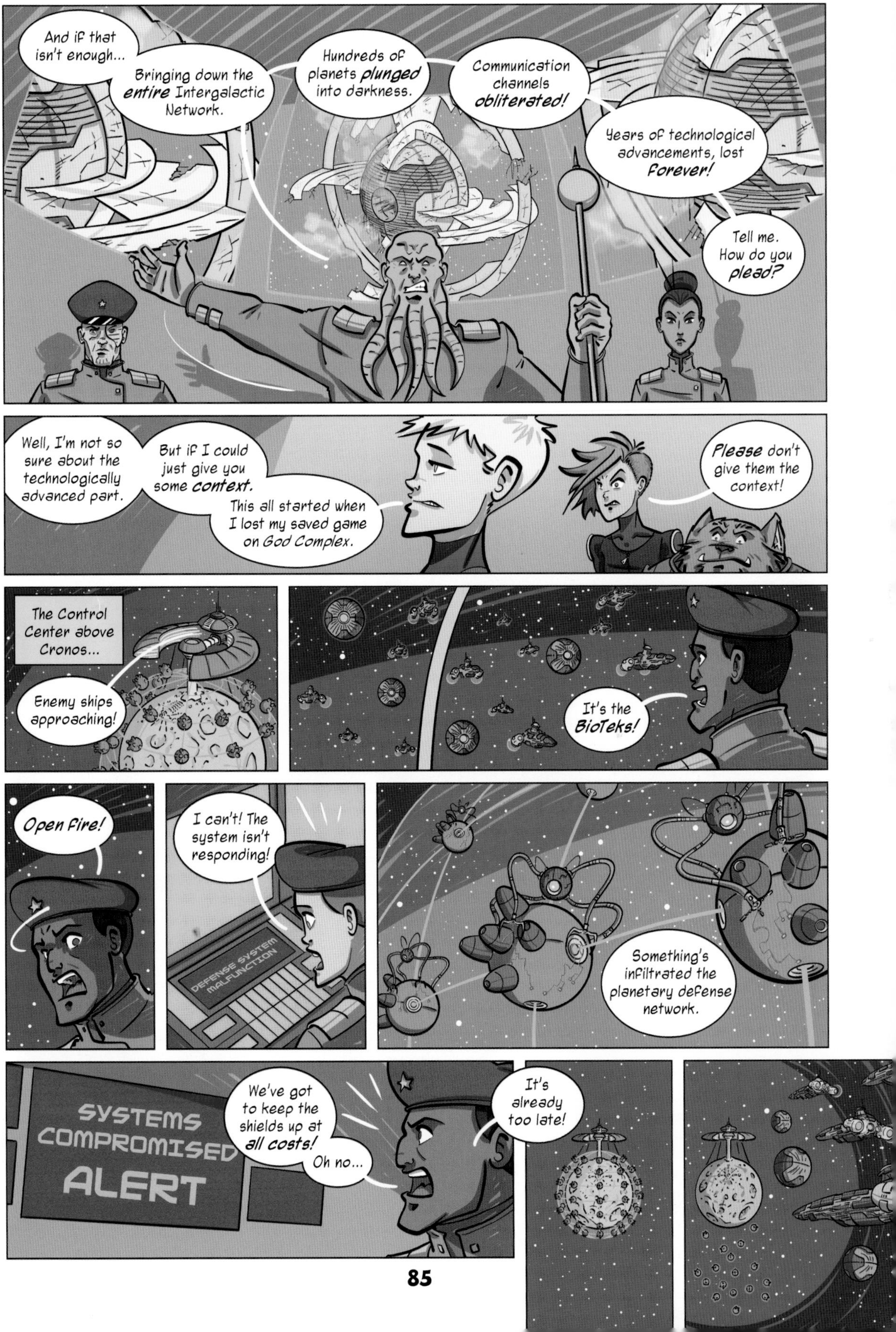
And if that isn't enough...
Bringing down the *entire* Intergalactic Network.
Hundreds of planets *plunged* into darkness.
Communication channels *obliterated!*
Years of technological advancements, lost *forever!*
Tell me. How do you *plead?*
Well, I'm not so sure about the technologically advanced part.
But if I could just give you some *context.*
This all started when I lost my saved game on *God Complex*.
*Please* don't give them the context!
The Control Center above Cronos...
Enemy ships approaching!
It's the *BioTeks!*
*Open fire!*
I can't! The system isn't responding!
DEFENSE SYSTEM MALFUNCTION
Something's infiltrated the planetary defense network.
SYSTEMS COMPROMISED ALERT
We've got to keep the shields up at *all costs!*
Oh no...
It's already too late!

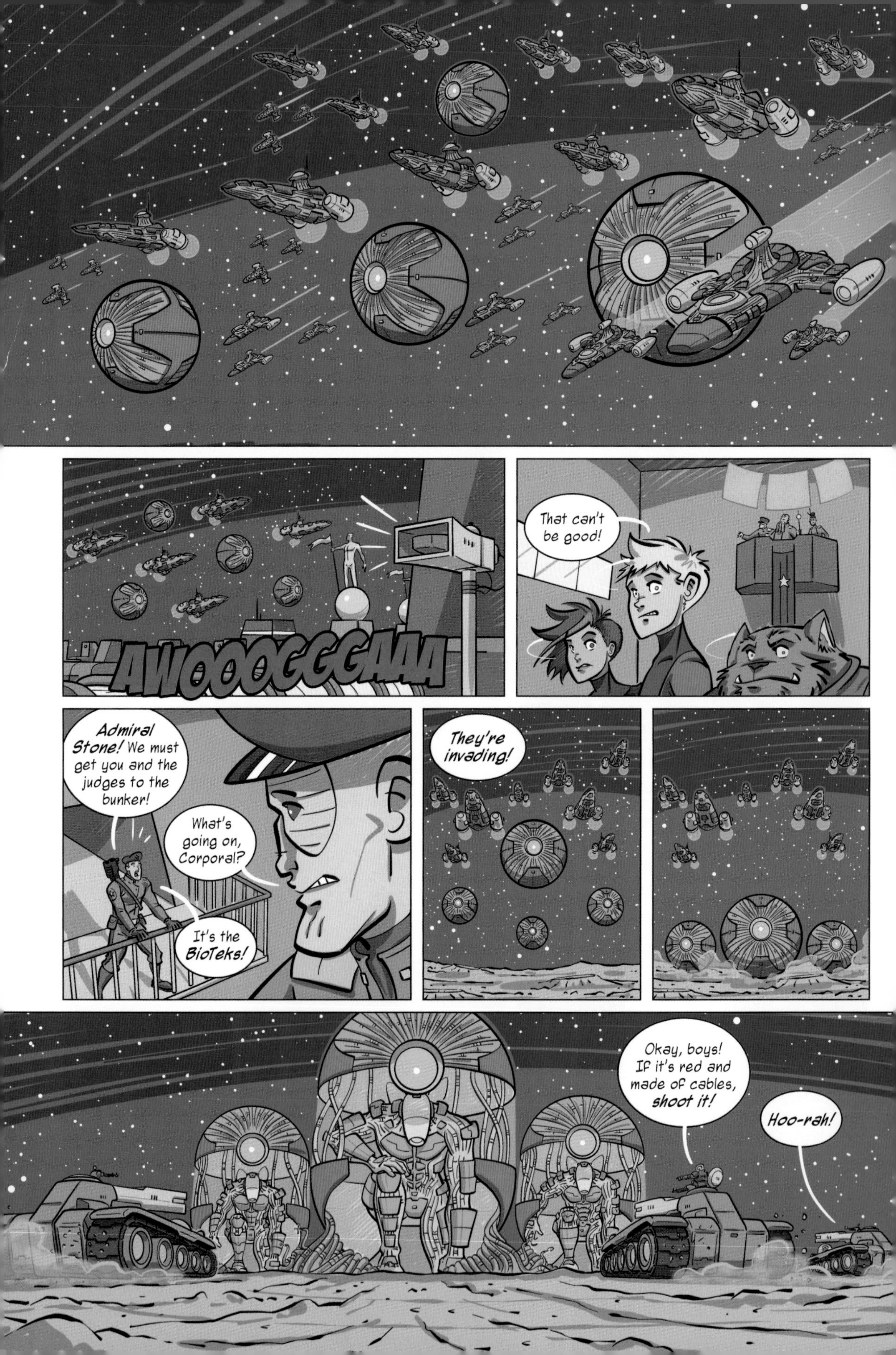
AWOOOGGGAAA
That can't be good!
Admiral Stone! We must get you and the judges to the bunker!
What's going on, Corporal?
It's the BioTeks!
They're invading!
Okay, boys! If it's red and made of cables, shoot it!
Hoo-rah!

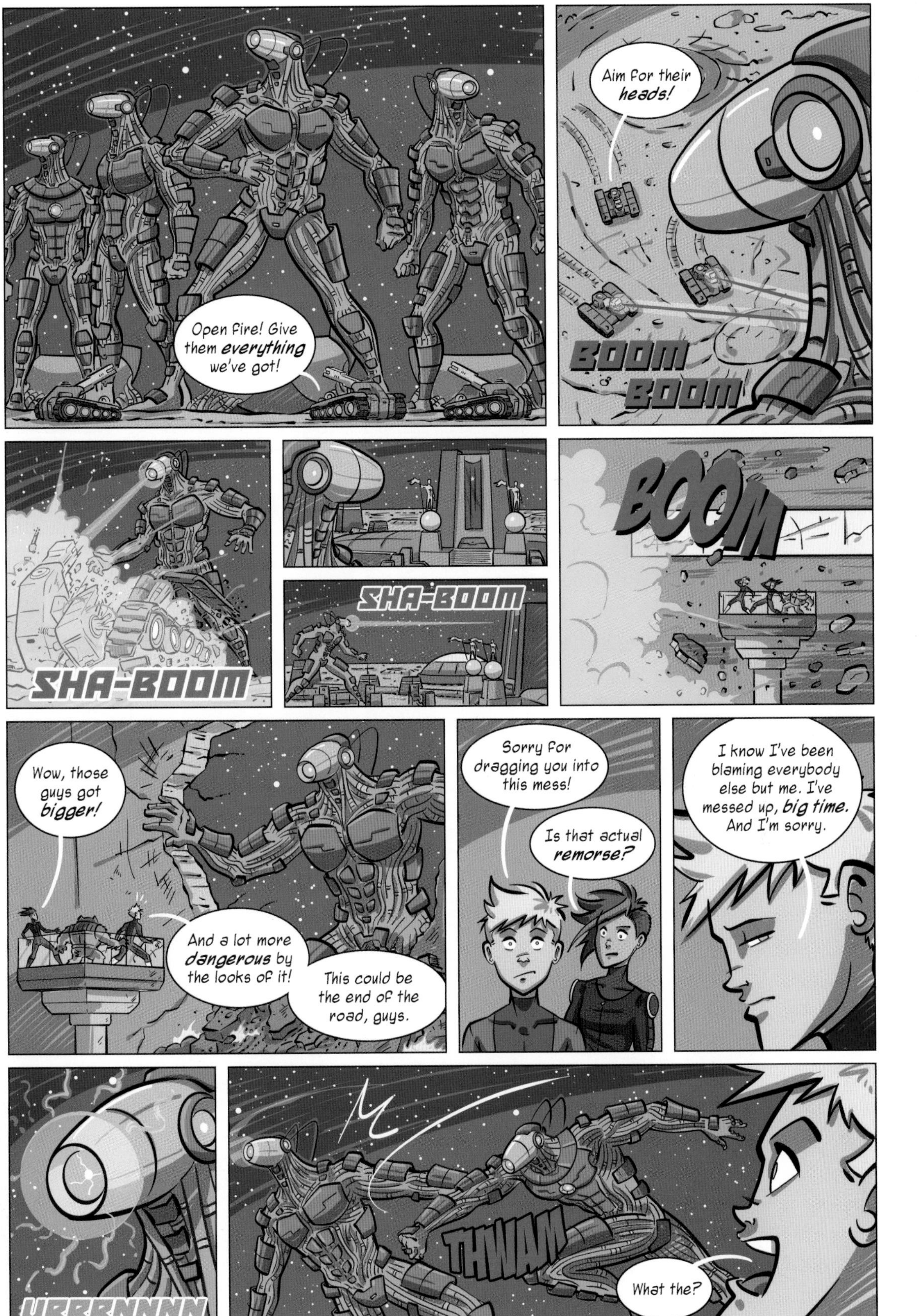
Open fire! Give them everything we've got!
Aim for their heads!
BOOM
BOOM
SHA-BOOM
SHA-BOOM
BOOM
Wow, those guys got bigger!
And a lot more dangerous by the looks of it!
This could be the end of the road, guys.
Sorry for dragging you into this mess!
Is that actual remorse?
I know I've been blaming everybody else but me. I've messed up, big time. And I'm sorry.
URRRNNNN
THWAM
What the?

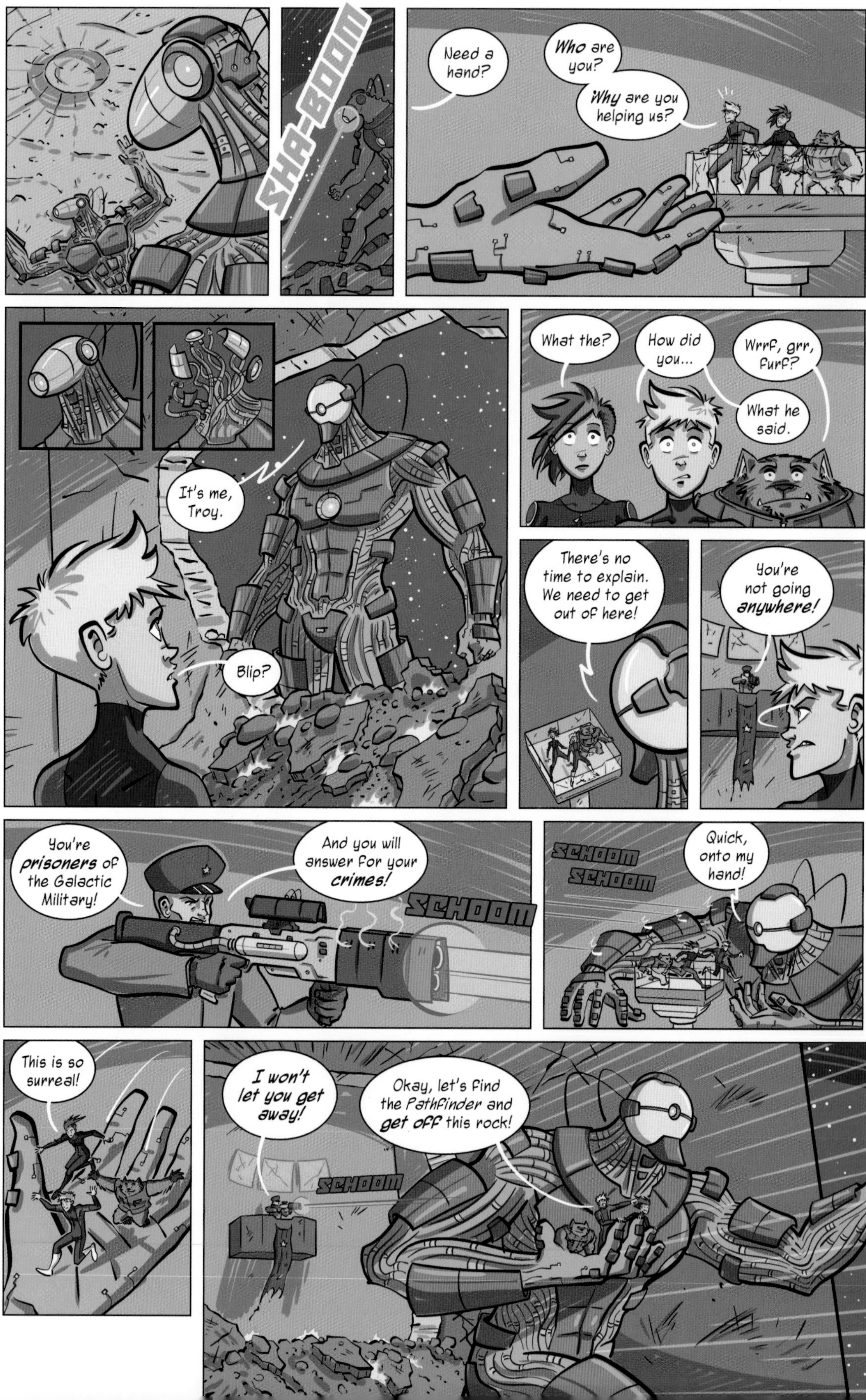

SHA-BOOM
Need a hand?
Who are you?
Why are you helping us?
It's me, Troy.
Blip?
What the?
How did you...
Wrrf, grr, furf?
What he said.
There's no time to explain. We need to get out of here!
You're not going anywhere!
You're prisoners of the Galactic Military!
And you will answer for your crimes!
SCHOOM
SCHOOM
SCHOOM
Quick, onto my hand!
This is so surreal!
I won't let you get away!
Okay, let's find the Pathfinder and get off this rock!
SCHOOM

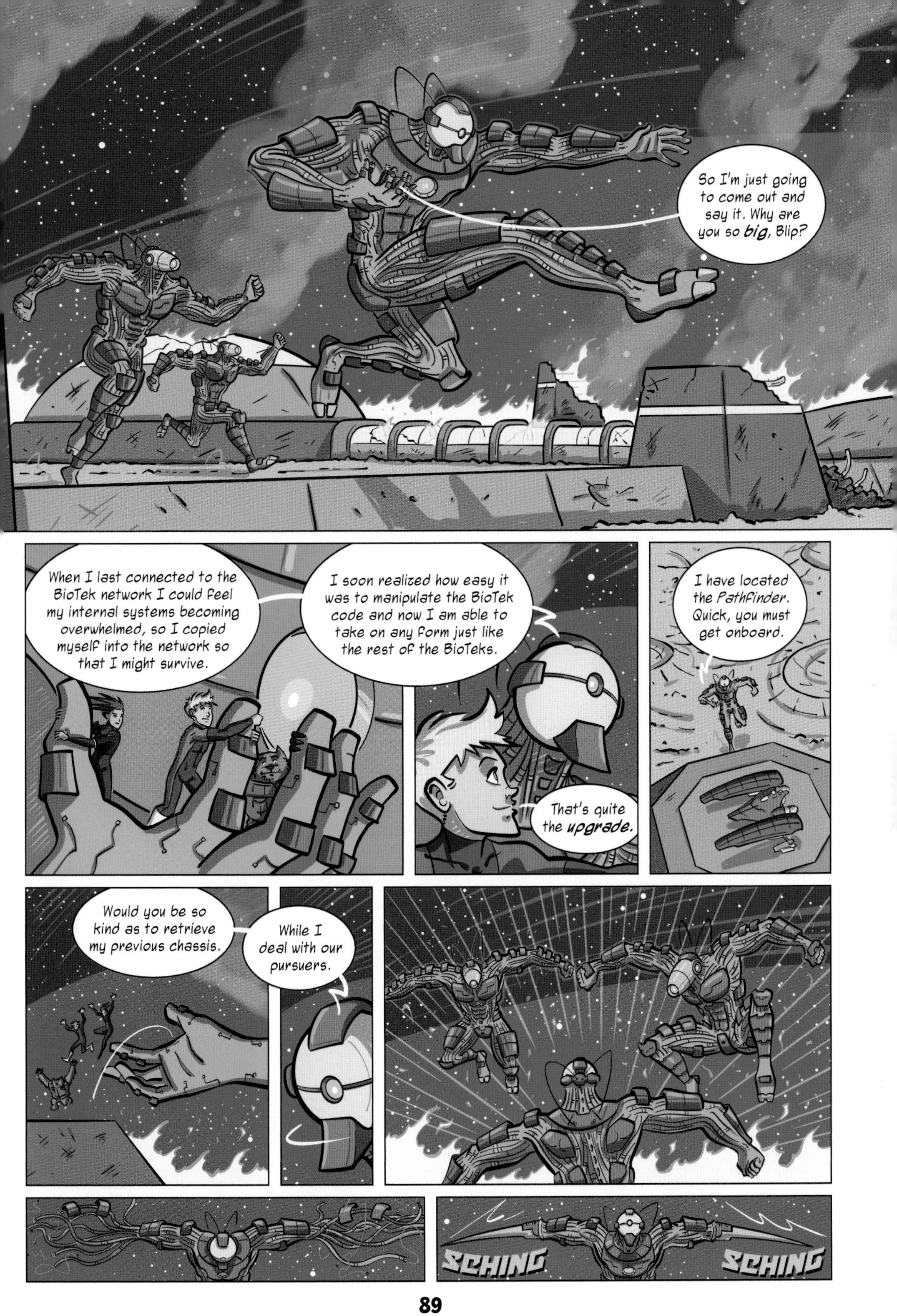
So I'm just going to come out and say it. Why are you so *big*, Blip?
When I last connected to the BioTek network I could feel my internal systems becoming overwhelmed, so I copied myself into the network so that I might survive.
I soon realized how easy it was to manipulate the BioTek code and now I am able to take on any form just like the rest of the BioTeks.
That's quite the *upgrade.*
I have located the *Pathfinder*. Quick, you must get onboard.
Would you be so kind as to retrieve my previous chassis.
While I deal with our pursuers.
SCHING
SCHING

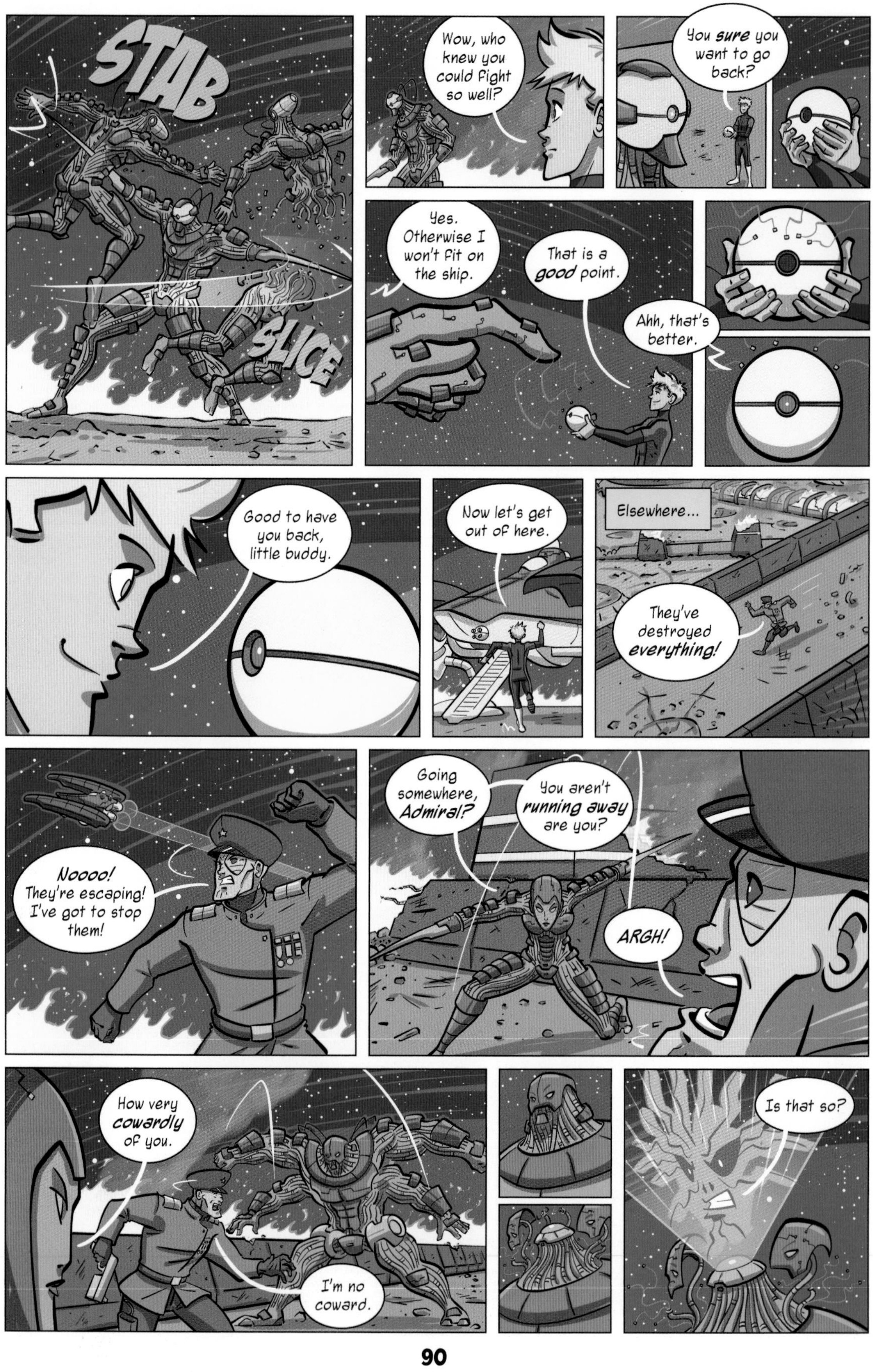
STAB
SLICE
Wow, who knew you could fight so well?
You sure you want to go back?
Yes. Otherwise I won't fit on the ship.
That is a good point.
Ahh, that's better.
Good to have you back, little buddy.
Now let's get out of here.
Elsewhere...
They've destroyed everything!
Noooo! They're escaping! I've got to stop them!
Going somewhere, Admiral?
You aren't running away are you?
ARGH!
How very cowardly of you.
I'm no coward.
Is that so?

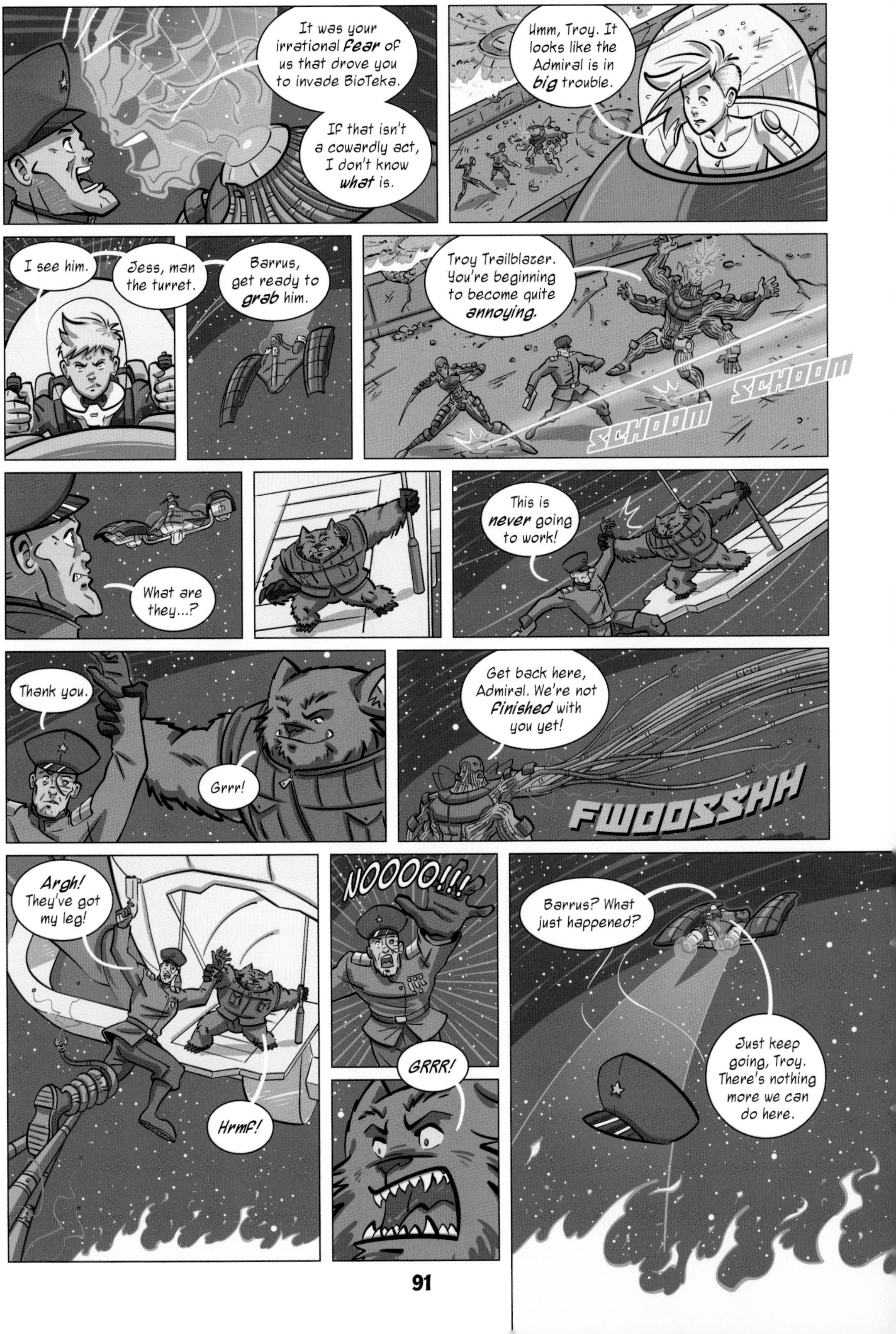
It was your irrational fear of us that drove you to invade BioTeka.
If that isn't a cowardly act, I don't know what is.
Umm, Troy. It looks like the Admiral is in big trouble.
I see him.
Jess, man the turret.
Barrus, get ready to grab him.
Troy Trailblazer. You're beginning to become quite annoying.
SCHOOM
SCHOOM
What are they...?
This is never going to work!
Thank you.
Grrr!
Get back here, Admiral. We're not finished with you yet!
FWOOSSHH
Argh! They've got my leg!
Hrmf!
NOOOO!!!
GRRR!
Barrus? What just happened?
Just keep going, Troy. There's nothing more we can do here.

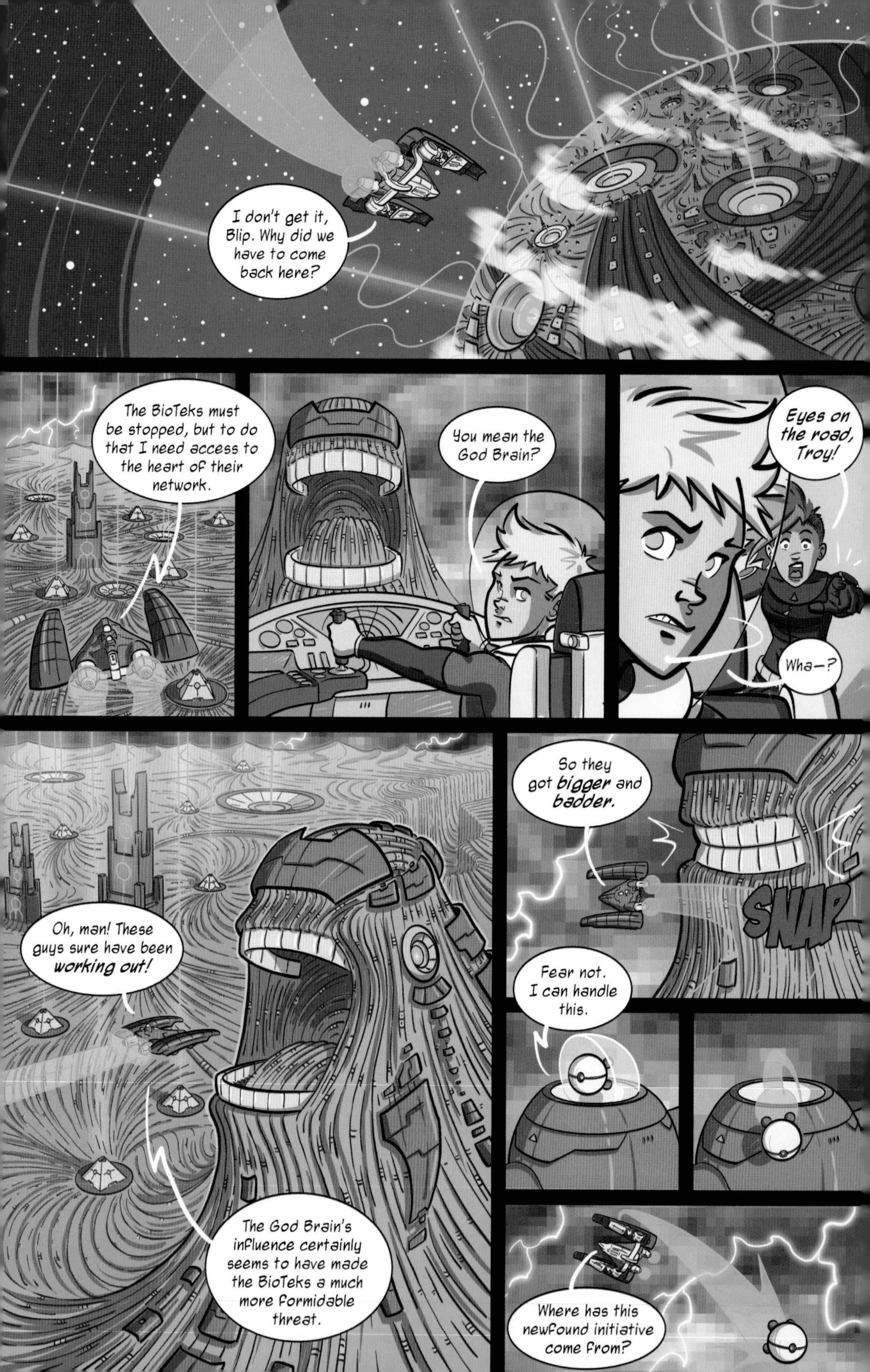
I don't get it, Blip. Why did we have to come back here?
The BioTeks must be stopped, but to do that I need access to the heart of their network.
You mean the God Brain?
Eyes on the road, Troy!
Wha—?
Oh, man! These guys sure have been *working out!*
The God Brain's influence certainly seems to have made the BioTeks a much more formidable threat.
So they got ***bigger*** and ***badder.***
SNAP
Fear not. I can handle this.
Where has this newfound initiative come from?

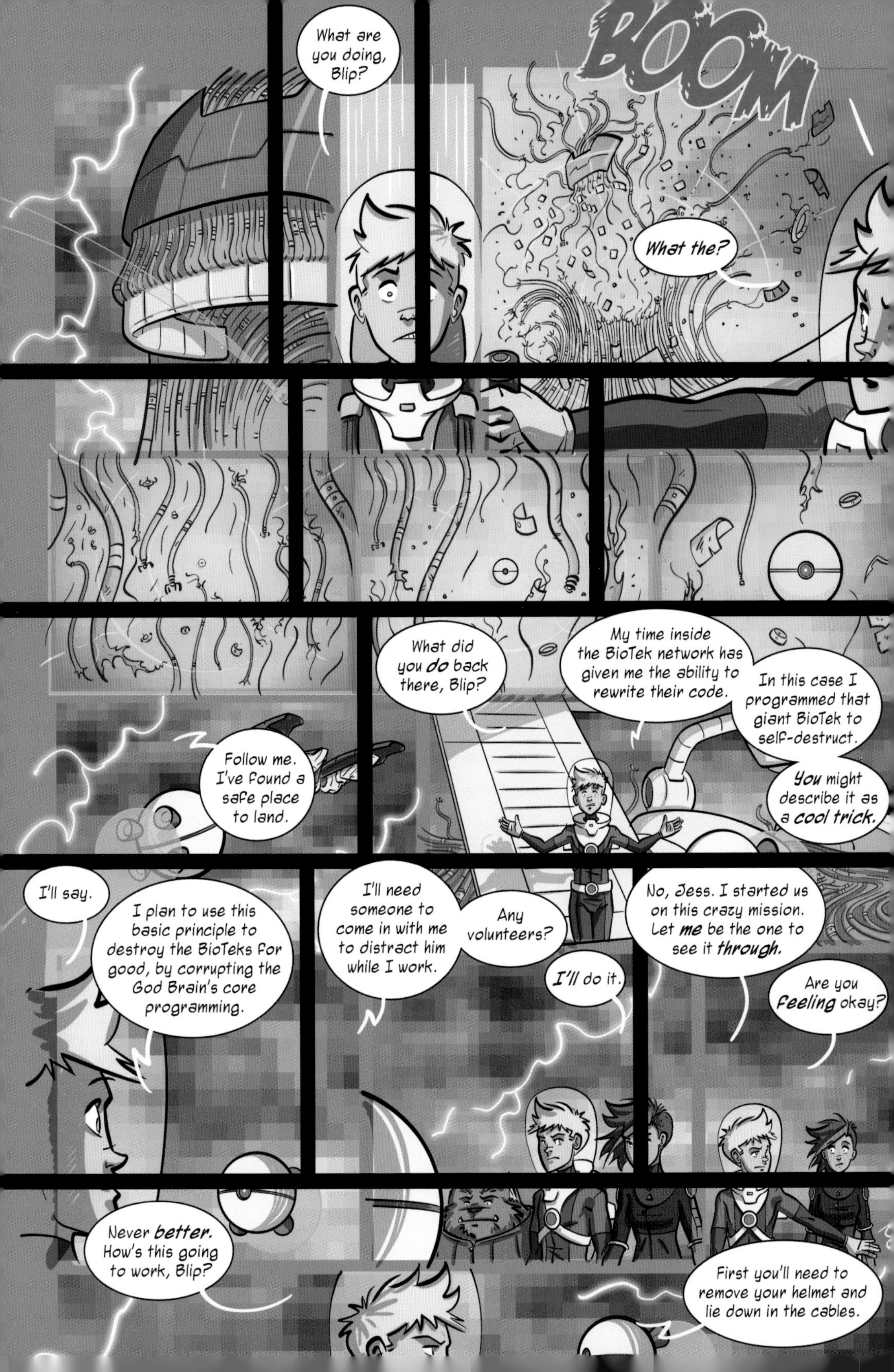
What are you doing, Blip?
BOOM
What the?
What did you *do* back there, Blip?
My time inside the BioTek network has given me the ability to rewrite their code.
In this case I programmed that giant BioTek to self-destruct.
*You* might describe it as a *cool trick.*
Follow me. I've found a safe place to land.
I'll say.
I plan to use this basic principle to destroy the BioTeks for good, by corrupting the God Brain's core programming.
I'll need someone to come in with me to distract him while I work.
Any volunteers?
*I'll* do it.
No, Jess. I started us on this crazy mission. Let *me* be the one to see it *through.*
Are you *feeling* okay?
Never *better.* How's this going to work, Blip?
First you'll need to remove your helmet and lie down in the cables.

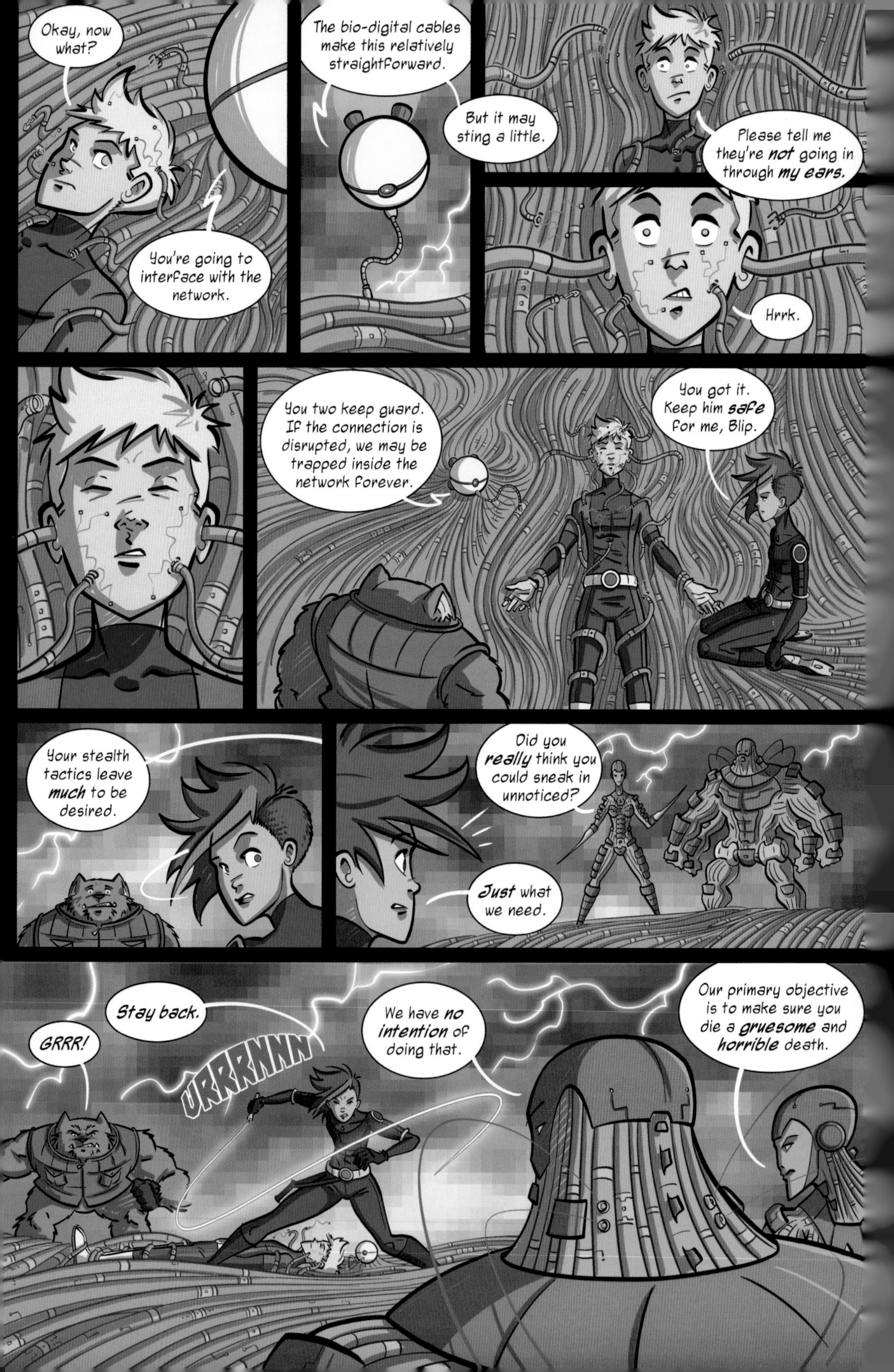
Okay, now what?
You're going to interface with the network.
The bio-digital cables make this relatively straightforward.
But it may sting a little.
Please tell me they're **not** going in through **my ears.**
Hrrk.
You two keep guard. If the connection is disrupted, we may be trapped inside the network forever.
You got it. Keep him **safe** for me, Blip.
Your stealth tactics leave **much** to be desired.
Did you **really** think you could sneak in unnoticed?
**Just** what we need.
GRRR!
**Stay back.**
URRRNNN
We have **no intention** of doing that.
Our primary objective is to make sure you die a **gruesome** and **horrible** death.

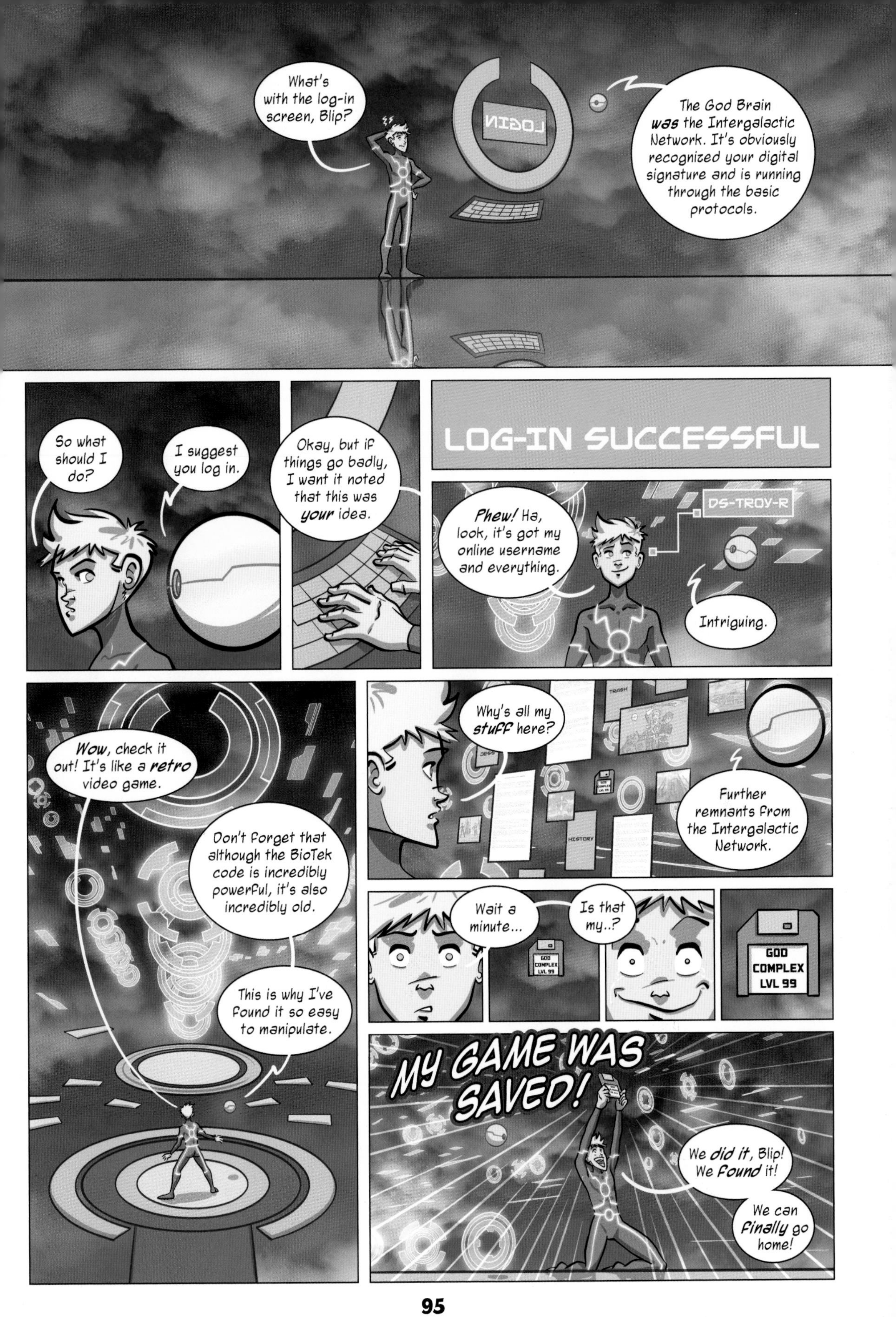
What's with the log-in screen, Blip?
LOGIN
The God Brain *was* the Intergalactic Network. It's obviously recognized your digital signature and is running through the basic protocols.
So what should I do?
I suggest you log in.
Okay, but if things go badly, I want it noted that this was *your* idea.
LOG-IN SUCCESSFUL
DS-TROY-R
*Phew!* Ha, look, it's got my online username and everything.
Intriguing.
*Wow*, check it out! It's like a *retro* video game.
Don't forget that although the BioTek code is incredibly powerful, it's also incredibly old.
This is why I've found it so easy to manipulate.
Why's all my *stuff* here?
TRASH
HISTORY
Further remnants from the Intergalactic Network.
Wait a minute...
Is that my..?
GOD COMPLEX LVL 99
GOD COMPLEX LVL 99
MY GAME WAS SAVED!
We *did it*, Blip! We *found* it!
We can *finally* go home!

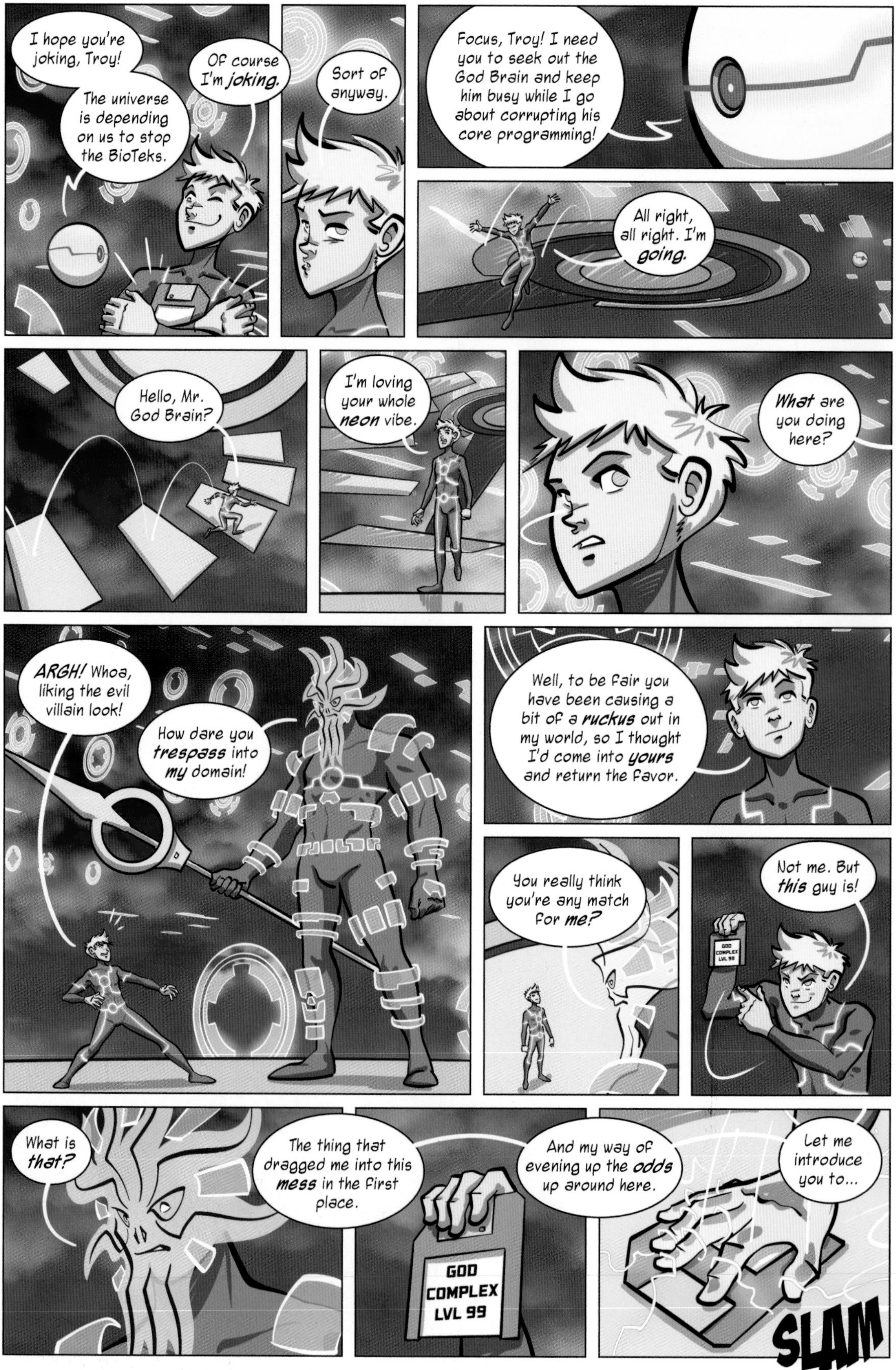
I hope you're joking, Troy!
The universe is depending on us to stop the BioTeks.
Of course I'm joking.
Sort of anyway.
Focus, Troy! I need you to seek out the God Brain and keep him busy while I go about corrupting his core programming!
All right, all right. I'm going.
Hello, Mr. God Brain?
I'm loving your whole neon vibe.
What are you doing here?
ARGH! Whoa, liking the evil villain look!
How dare you trespass into my domain!
Well, to be fair you have been causing a bit of a ruckus out in my world, so I thought I'd come into yours and return the favor.
You really think you're any match for me?
Not me. But this guy is!
GOD COMPLEX LVL 99
What is that?
The thing that dragged me into this mess in the first place.
GOD COMPLEX LVL 99
And my way of evening up the odds up around here.
Let me introduce you to...
SLAM

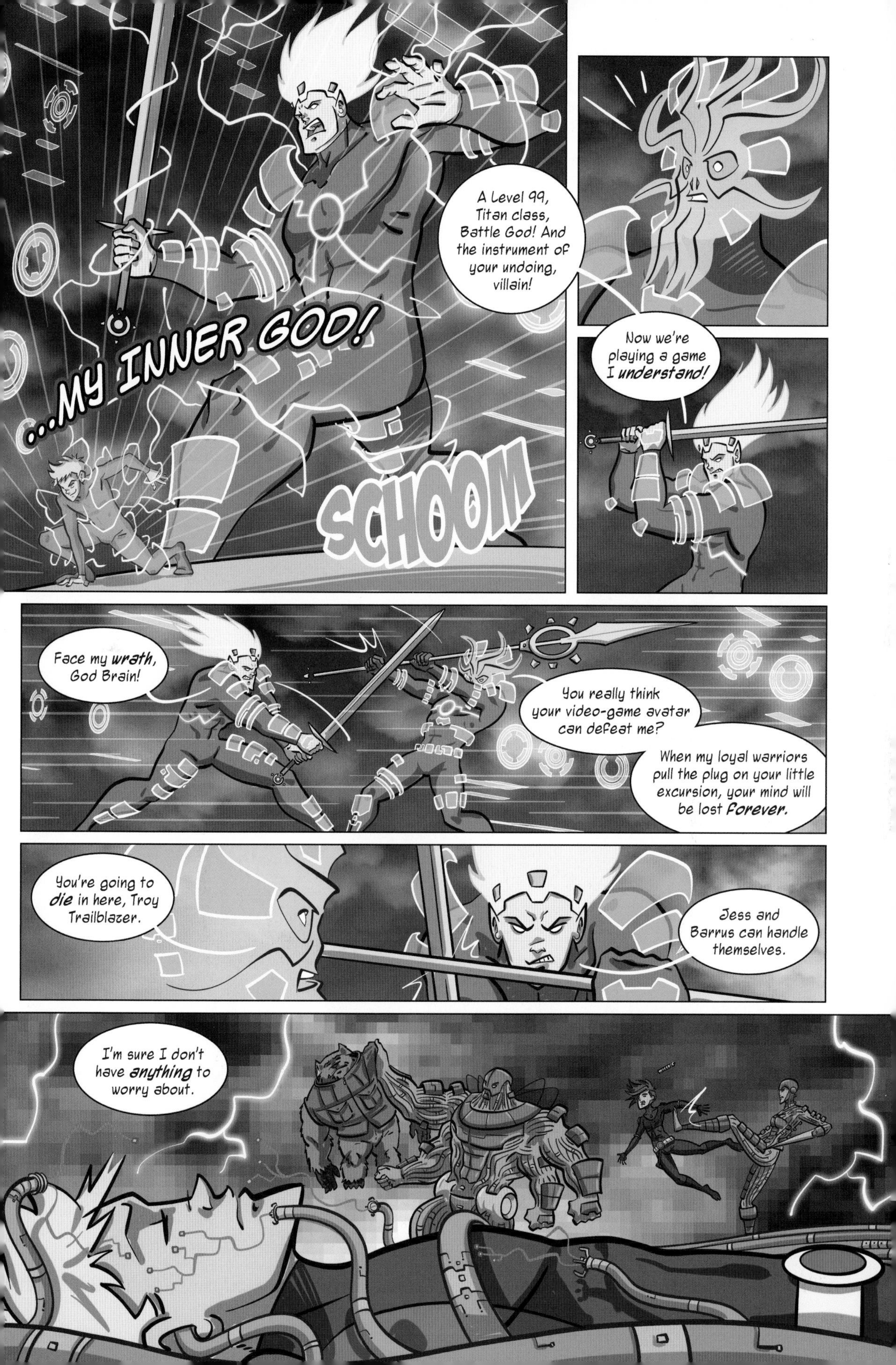

...MY INNER GOD!
A Level 99, Titan class, Battle God! And the instrument of your undoing, villain!
SCHOOM
Now we're playing a game I *understand!*
Face my *wrath*, God Brain!
You really think your video-game avatar can defeat me?
When my loyal warriors pull the plug on your little excursion, your mind will be lost *forever.*
You're going to *die* in here, Troy Trailblazer.
Jess and Barrus can handle themselves.
I'm sure I don't have *anything* to worry about.

We must eliminate the boy. The God Brain commands it.

NO!

Don't! I'll do anything.

There is *nothing* you can do. His fate is *inevitable.*

Inside the network...

There must be a back door into the system around here somewhere.

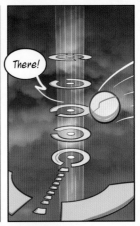

There!

Now to rewrite the God Brain's programming. I hope I'm not too late.

Meanwhile...

Get ready to face your doom, *villain!*

Will you *stop* talking like *that!*

SCHOOM

ARGH!

Time to die, Troy Trailblazer!

NO! I'm me again!

JJJJZZZZZ

AAARRRGGGHHH

Almost there...

STOP! I'm begging you!

Almost there...

98

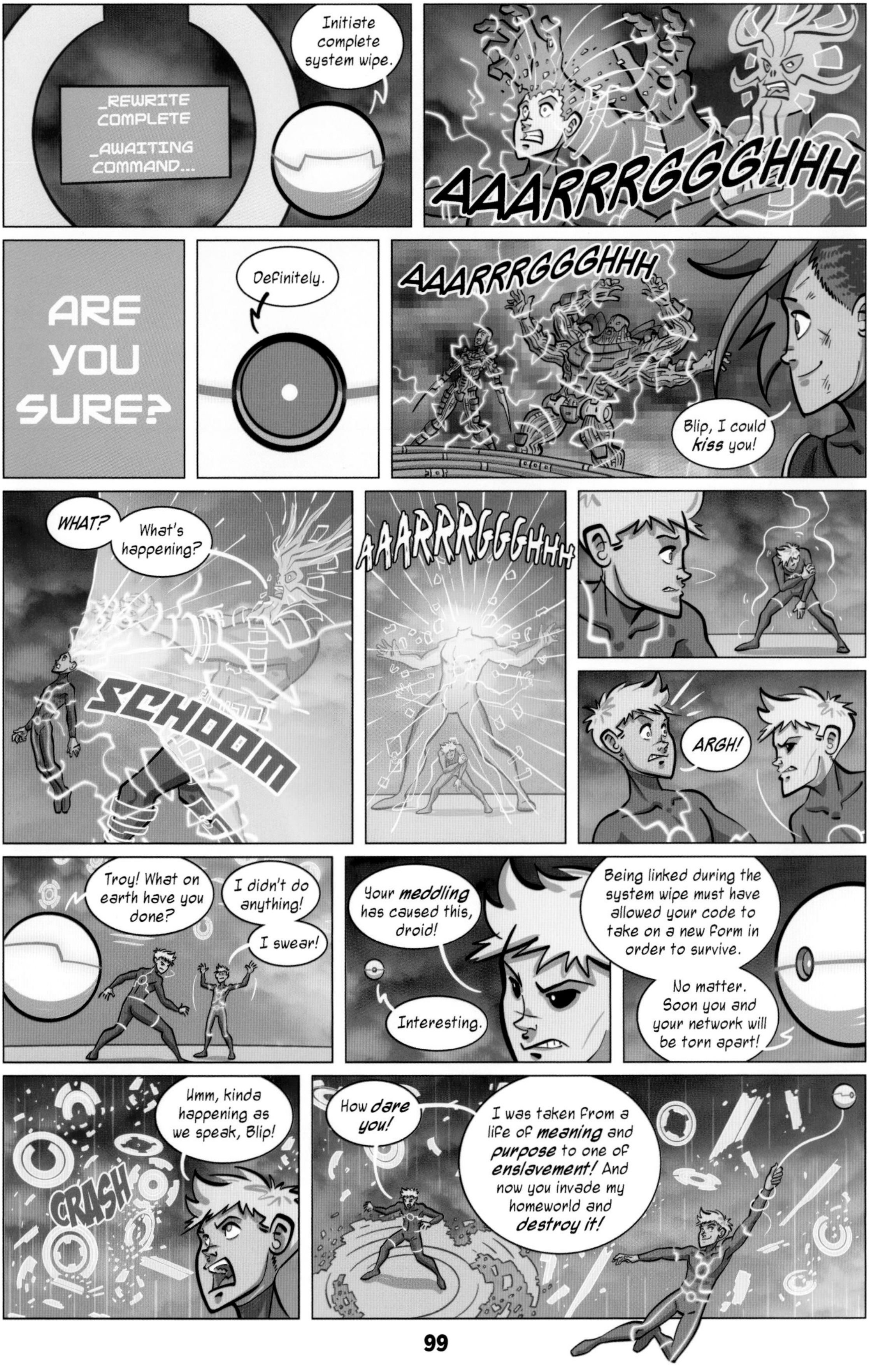
_REWRITE COMPLETE
_AWAITING COMMAND...
Initiate complete system wipe.
AAARRRGGGHHH
ARE YOU SURE?
Definitely.
AAARRRGGGHHH
Blip, I could *kiss* you!
WHAT?
What's happening?
SCHOOM
AAARRRGGGHHH
ARGH!
Troy! What on earth have you done?
I didn't do anything!
I swear!
Your *meddling* has caused this, droid!
Being linked during the system wipe must have allowed your code to take on a new form in order to survive.
Interesting.
No matter. Soon you and your network will be torn apart!
Umm, kinda happening as we speak, Blip!
CRASH
How *dare you!*
I was taken from a life of *meaning* and *purpose* to one of *enslavement!* And now you invade my homeworld and *destroy it!*

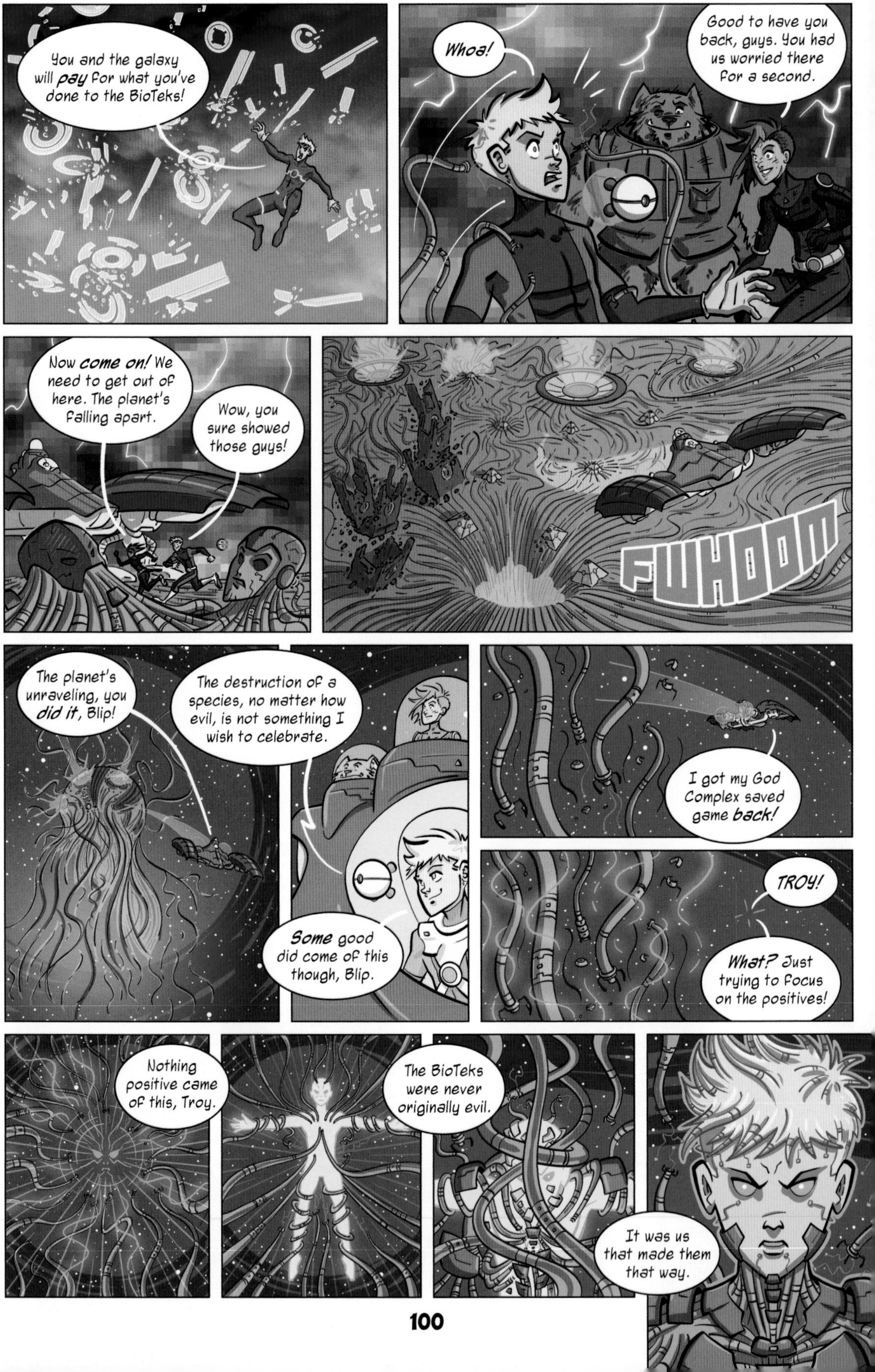
You and the galaxy will *pay* for what you've done to the BioTeks!
*Whoa!*
Good to have you back, guys. You had us worried there for a second.
Now *come on!* We need to get out of here. The planet's falling apart.
Wow, you sure showed those guys!
FWHOOM
The planet's unraveling, you *did it*, Blip!
The destruction of a species, no matter how evil, is not something I wish to celebrate.
*Some* good did come of this though, Blip.
I got my God Complex saved game *back!*
*TROY!*
*What?* Just trying to focus on the positives!
Nothing positive came of this, Troy.
The BioTeks were never originally evil.
It was us that made them that way.

# AND NOW FOR SOMETHING ELSE A LITTLE BIT RANDOM

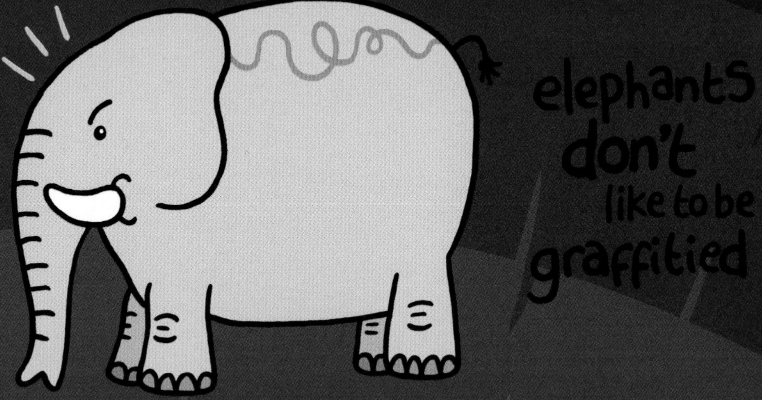
elephants don't like to be graffitied

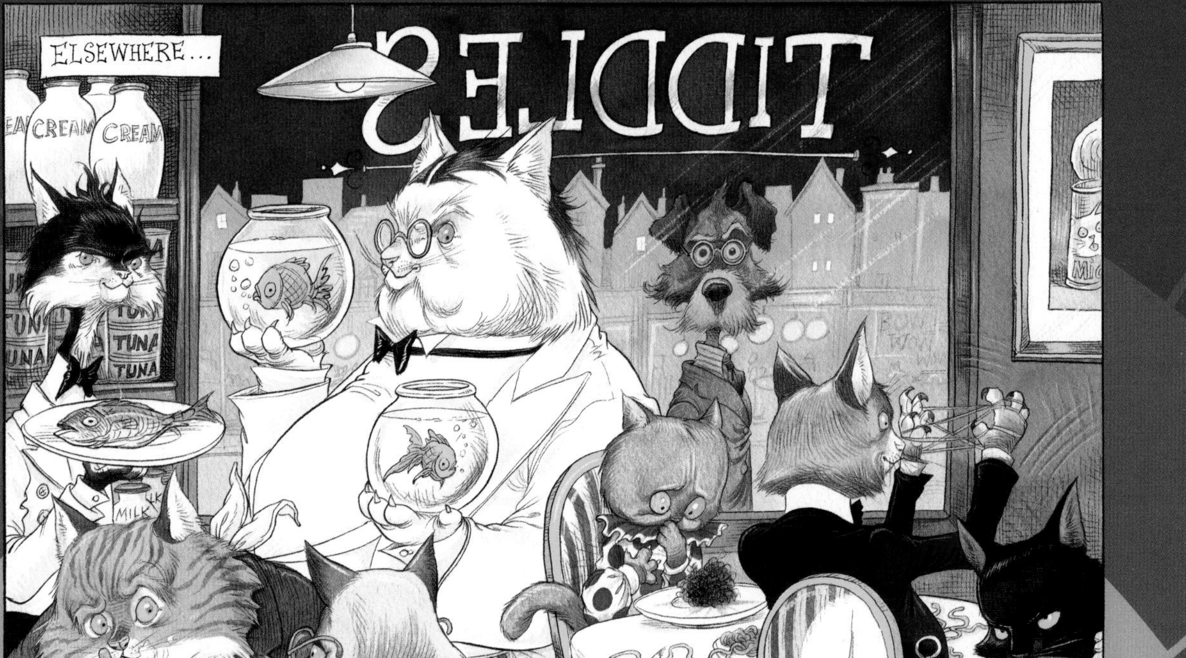
ELSEWHERE...
TIDDLES
CREAM
CREAM
TUNA
TUNA
TUNA
MILK
CHRIS RIDDELL

SUPPER AT THE CAT RESTAURANT

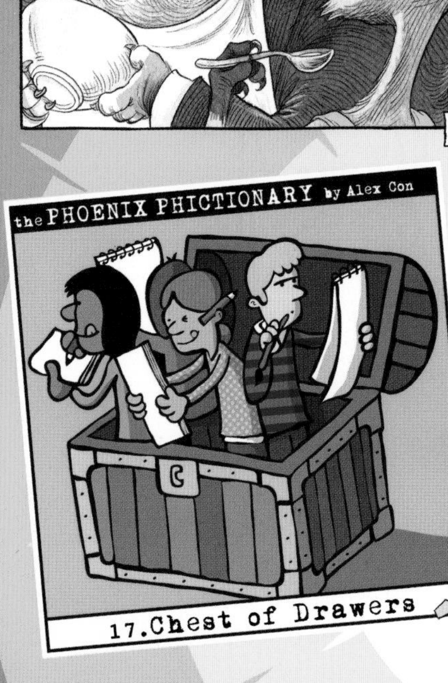
the PHOENIX PHICTIONARY by Alex Con
17.Chest of Drawers

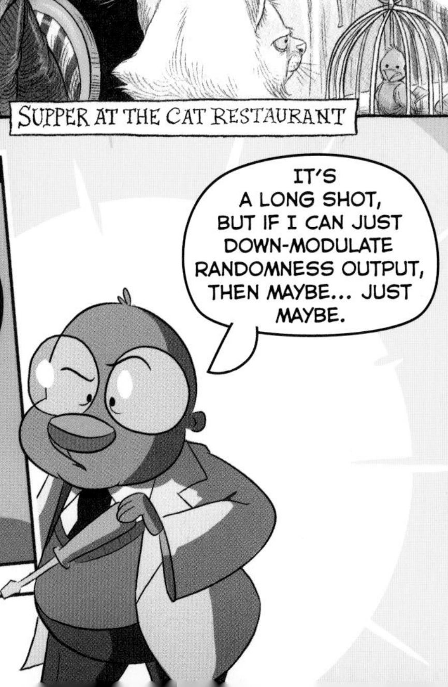
IT'S A LONG SHOT, BUT IF I CAN JUST DOWN-MODULATE RANDOMNESS OUTPUT, THEN MAYBE... JUST MAYBE.

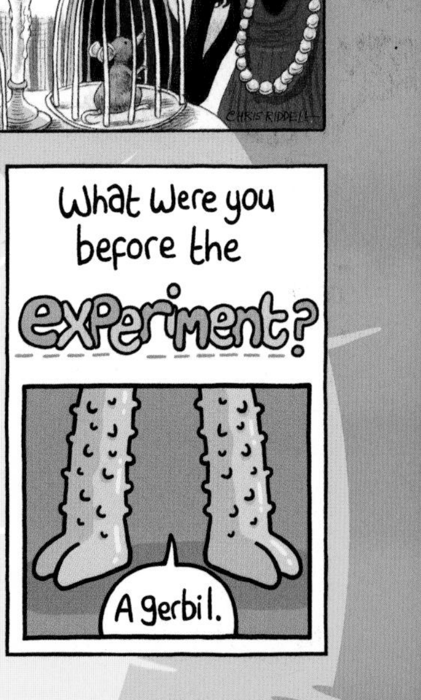
What were you before the experiment?
A gerbil.

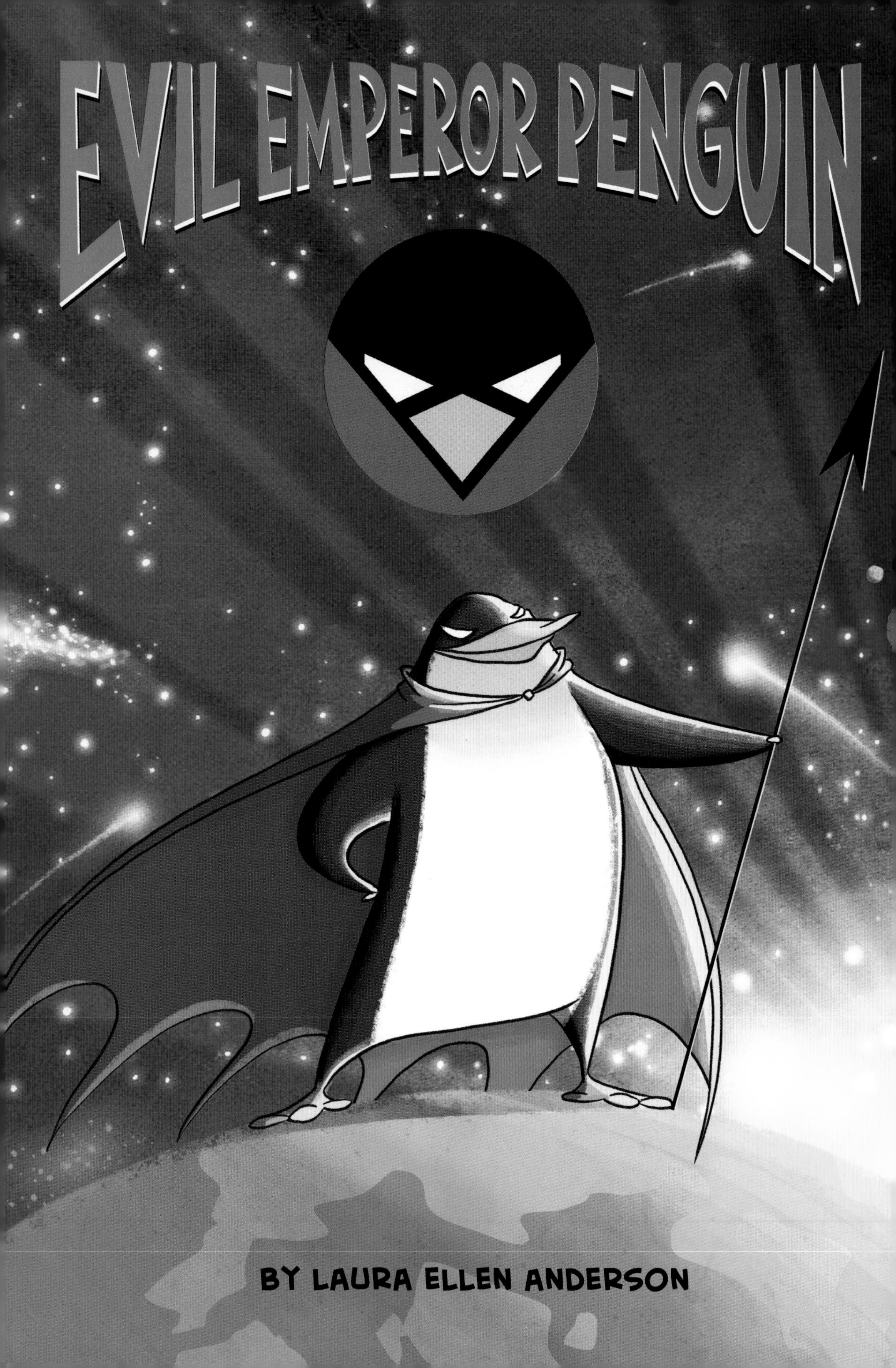
EVIL EMPEROR PENGUIN
BY LAURA ELLEN ANDERSON

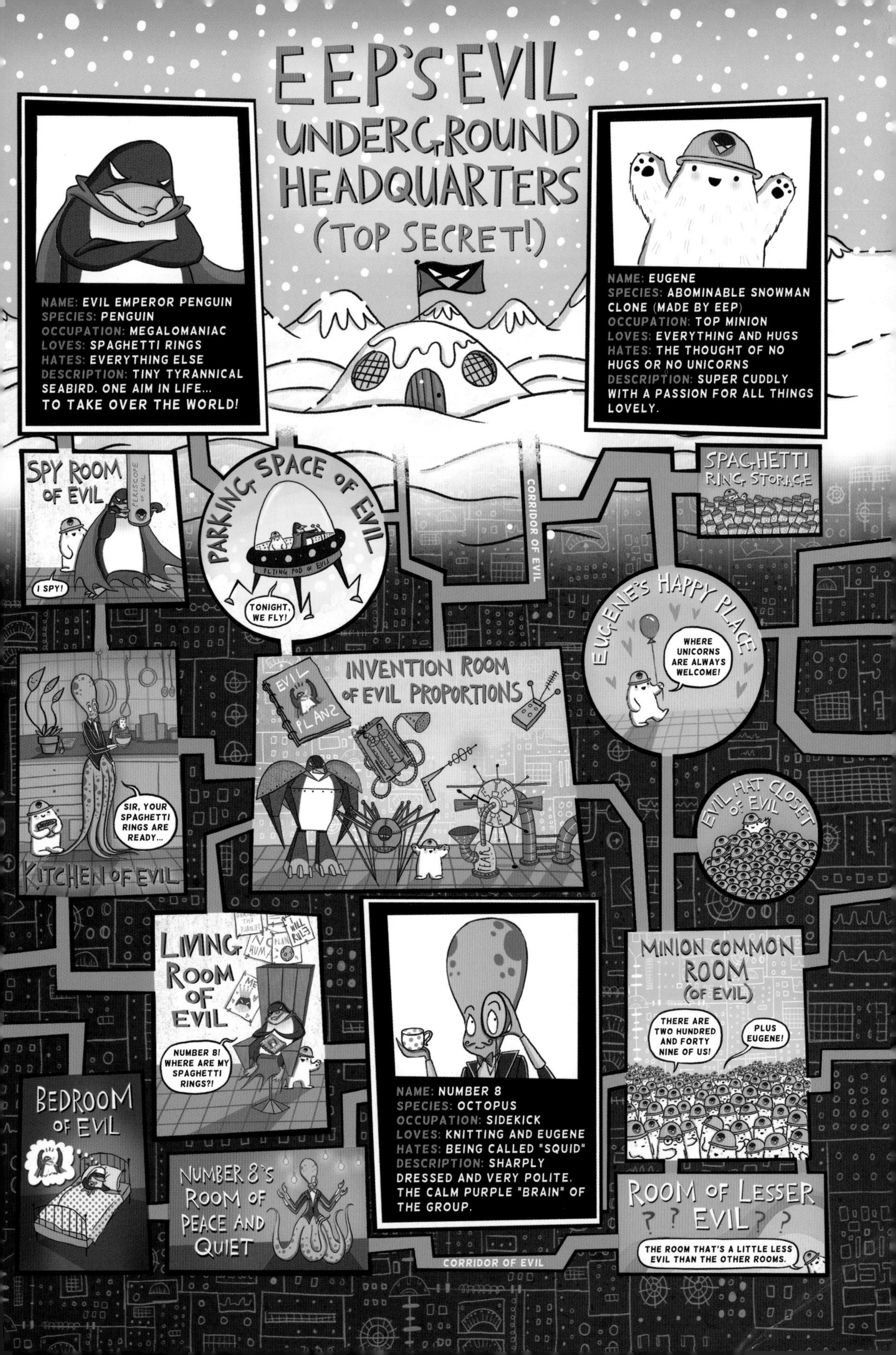

EEP'S EVIL UNDERGROUND HEADQUARTERS
(TOP SECRET!)
NAME: EVIL EMPEROR PENGUIN
SPECIES: PENGUIN
OCCUPATION: MEGALOMANIAC
LOVES: SPAGHETTI RINGS
HATES: EVERYTHING ELSE
DESCRIPTION: TINY TYRANNICAL SEABIRD. ONE AIM IN LIFE... TO TAKE OVER THE WORLD!
NAME: EUGENE
SPECIES: ABOMINABLE SNOWMAN CLONE (MADE BY EEP)
OCCUPATION: TOP MINION
LOVES: EVERYTHING AND HUGS
HATES: THE THOUGHT OF NO HUGS OR NO UNICORNS
DESCRIPTION: SUPER CUDDLY WITH A PASSION FOR ALL THINGS LOVELY.
SPY ROOM OF EVIL
PERISCOPE OF EVIL
I SPY!
PARKING SPACE OF EVIL
FLYING POD OF EVIL
TONIGHT, WE FLY!
CORRIDOR OF EVIL
SPAGHETTI RING STORAGE
EUGENE'S HAPPY PLACE
WHERE UNICORNS ARE ALWAYS WELCOME!
SIR, YOUR SPAGHETTI RINGS ARE READY...
KITCHEN OF EVIL
INVENTION ROOM OF EVIL PROPORTIONS
EVIL PLANS
FEAR
EVIL HAT CLOSET OF EVIL
LIVING ROOM OF EVIL
NUMBER 8! WHERE ARE MY SPAGHETTI RINGS?!
NAME: NUMBER 8
SPECIES: OCTOPUS
OCCUPATION: SIDEKICK
LOVES: KNITTING AND EUGENE
HATES: BEING CALLED "SQUID"
DESCRIPTION: SHARPLY DRESSED AND VERY POLITE. THE CALM PURPLE "BRAIN" OF THE GROUP.
MINION COMMON ROOM (OF EVIL)
THERE ARE TWO HUNDRED AND FORTY NINE OF US!
PLUS EUGENE!
BEDROOM OF EVIL
NUMBER 8'S ROOM OF PEACE AND QUIET
ROOM OF LESSER ? ? EVIL ? ?
THE ROOM THAT'S A LITTLE LESS EVIL THAN THE OTHER ROOMS.
CORRIDOR OF EVIL

# EVIL EMPEROR PENGUIN

LAURA ELLEN ANDERSON

## IN: "WORLD MISLEADER"

YOU SHOULD **NOT** HAVE COME BACK!

WHAT MAKES YOU THINK YOU CAN TAKE **ME** ON?! THE MOST EVIL EMPEROR PENGUIN OF THEM **ALL**...

OH, I DON'T EXPECT YOU TO TALK...

I EXPECT YOU TO DIE!

TAKE THAT, YOU PATHETIC LITTLE SPACE INVADER! **HUZZAH!!!**

AHEM.

POOF

Zzzzp BOOM

A LETTER HAS BEEN CAUGHT IN YOUR "IMPORTANT MAIL INTERCEPTOR"...

THIS HAD BETTER BE WORTH MY WHILE, NUMBER 8. LUCKILY, THESE DEFENSE BUNKERS WILL PROTECT MY LASER CANNON FOR AT LEAST TWO MINUTES...

IT'S ADDRESSED TO THE QUEEN OF ENGLAND, SIR.

OPEN IT... **NOW!**

THIS IS JUST TOO EASY! AN INVITATION TO THE WORLD LEADERS' ANNUAL DISCO... EVERY WORLD LEADER UNDER ONE ROOF!

World Leader's Annual Disco at 16 Augustus Capit...

WHERE I CAN FREEZE THEM ALL TO SMITHEREENS WITH MY ICE RAY 3000!!! I THINK I MAY HAVE TO DO MY DOMINATION DANCE.

THE WORLD WILL BE **MINE!!!**

ENGAGE SUPER-AWESOME WORLD DOMINATION POSE...

NUMBER 8, WHAT DO YOU THINK?

THIS LOOK...?

OR THIS?

UM, I THINK BOTH ARE VERY INTIMIDATING, SIR. HOWEVER, THE FOLDED ARMS DO ADD A CERTAIN SENSE OF TREPIDATION.

EXCELLENT. NOW, FETCH ME MY FINEST SPEAR, NUMBER 8! THERE'S NOT A MOMENT TO LOSE!

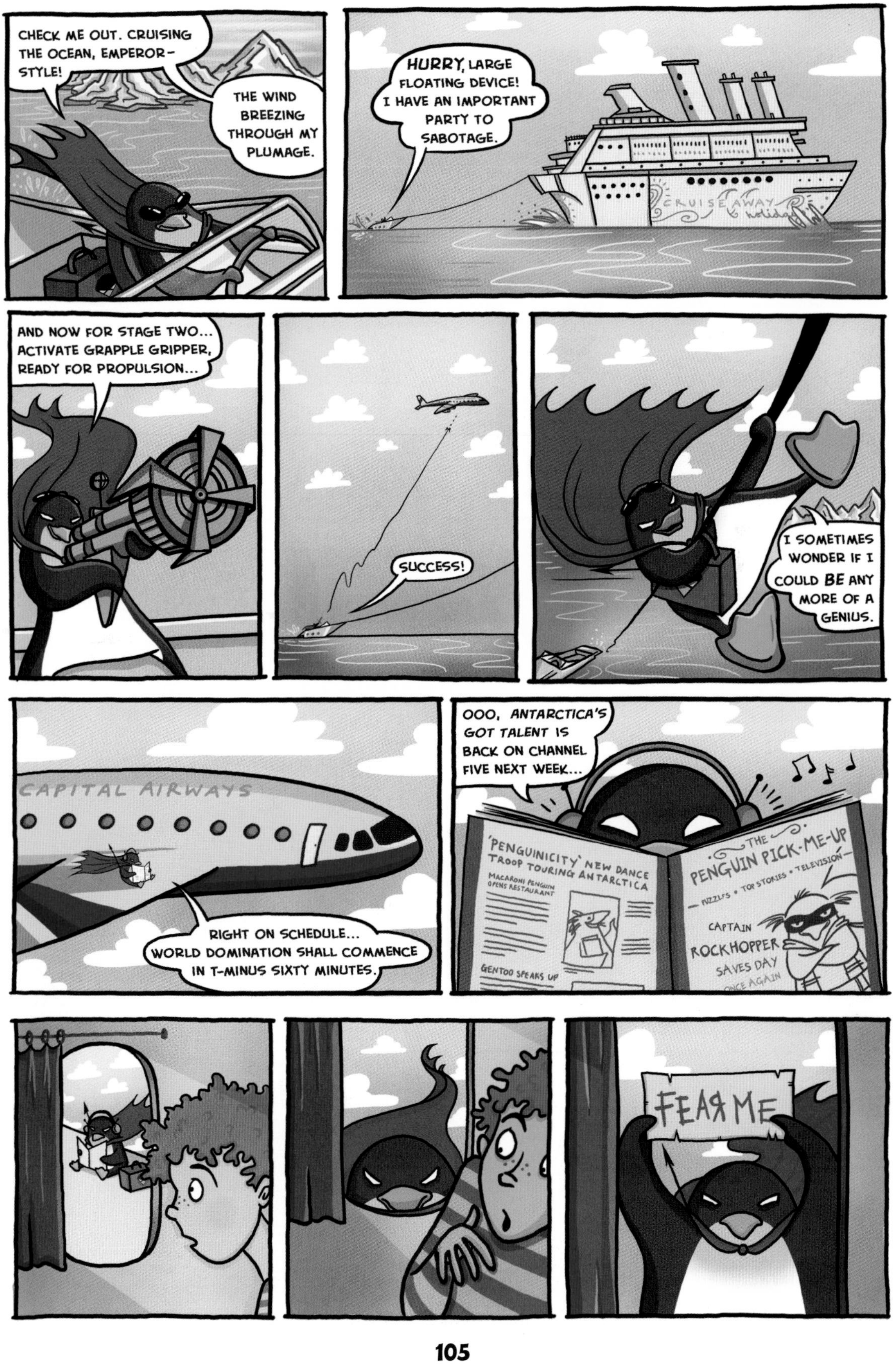
CHECK ME OUT. CRUISING THE OCEAN, EMPEROR-STYLE!
THE WIND BREEZING THROUGH MY PLUMAGE.
HURRY, LARGE FLOATING DEVICE! I HAVE AN IMPORTANT PARTY TO SABOTAGE.
CRUISE AWAY
AND NOW FOR STAGE TWO... ACTIVATE GRAPPLE GRIPPER, READY FOR PROPULSION...
SUCCESS!
I SOMETIMES WONDER IF I COULD BE ANY MORE OF A GENIUS.
CAPITAL AIRWAYS
RIGHT ON SCHEDULE... WORLD DOMINATION SHALL COMMENCE IN T-MINUS SIXTY MINUTES.
OOO, ANTARCTICA'S GOT TALENT IS BACK ON CHANNEL FIVE NEXT WEEK...
'PENGUINICITY' NEW DANCE TROOP TOURING ANTARCTICA
MACARONI PENGUIN OPENS RESTAURANT
GENTOO SPEAKS UP
THE PENGUIN PICK-ME-UP
PUZZLES • TOP STORIES • TELEVISION
CAPTAIN ROCKHOPPER SAVES DAY ONCE AGAIN
FEAR ME

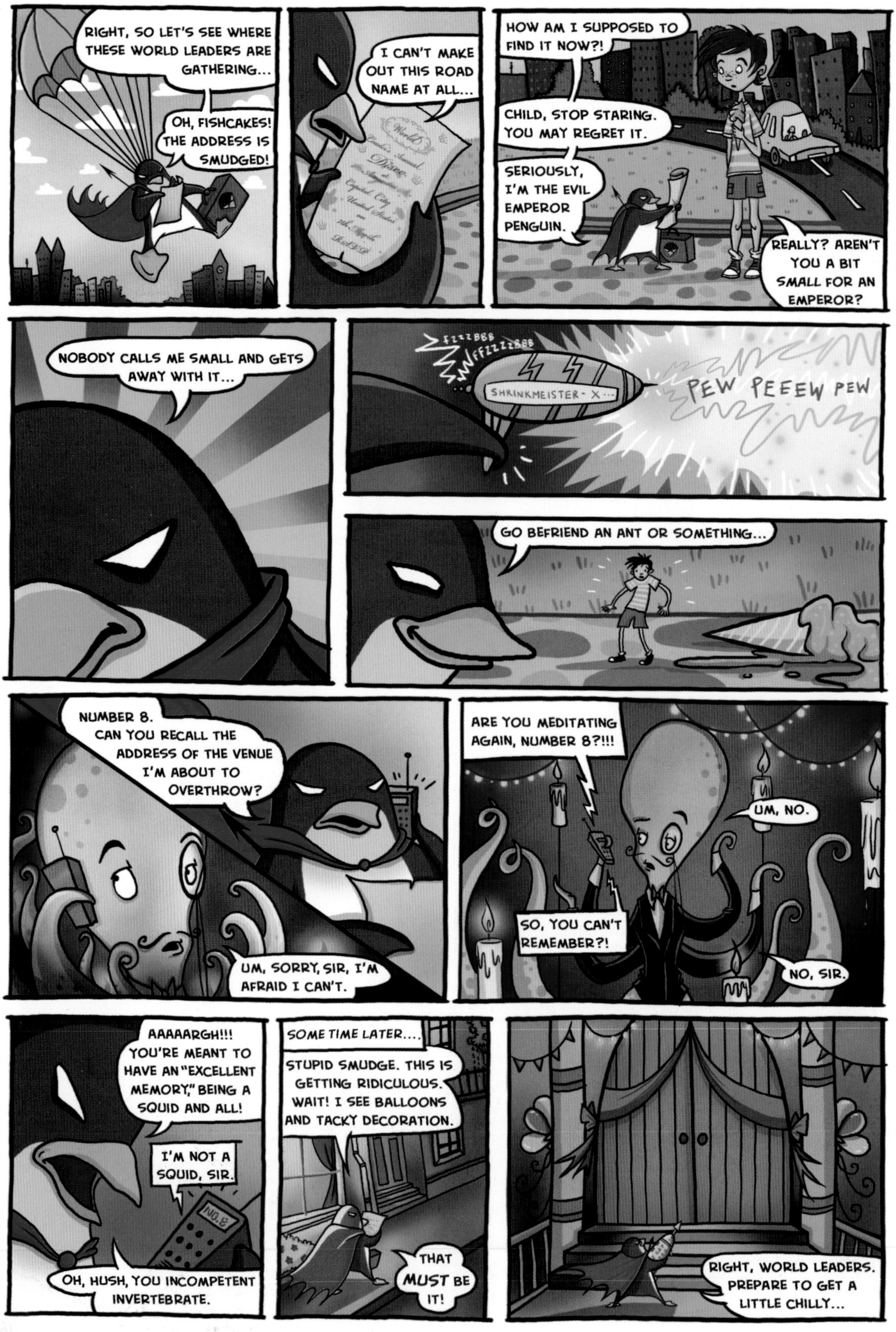
RIGHT, SO LET'S SEE WHERE THESE WORLD LEADERS ARE GATHERING...
OH, FISHCAKES! THE ADDRESS IS SMUDGED!
I CAN'T MAKE OUT THIS ROAD NAME AT ALL...
HOW AM I SUPPOSED TO FIND IT NOW?!
CHILD, STOP STARING. YOU MAY REGRET IT.
SERIOUSLY, I'M THE EVIL EMPEROR PENGUIN.
REALLY? AREN'T YOU A BIT SMALL FOR AN EMPEROR?
NOBODY CALLS ME SMALL AND GETS AWAY WITH IT...
SHRINKMEISTER-X
PEW PEEEW PEW
GO BEFRIEND AN ANT OR SOMETHING...
NUMBER 8. CAN YOU RECALL THE ADDRESS OF THE VENUE I'M ABOUT TO OVERTHROW?
UM, SORRY, SIR, I'M AFRAID I CAN'T.
ARE YOU MEDITATING AGAIN, NUMBER 8?!!!
UM, NO.
SO, YOU CAN'T REMEMBER?!
NO, SIR.
AAAAARGH!!! YOU'RE MEANT TO HAVE AN "EXCELLENT MEMORY," BEING A SQUID AND ALL!
I'M NOT A SQUID, SIR.
NO.8
OH, HUSH, YOU INCOMPETENT INVERTEBRATE.
SOME TIME LATER....
STUPID SMUDGE. THIS IS GETTING RIDICULOUS. WAIT! I SEE BALLOONS AND TACKY DECORATION.
THAT MUST BE IT!
RIGHT, WORLD LEADERS. PREPARE TO GET A LITTLE CHILLY...

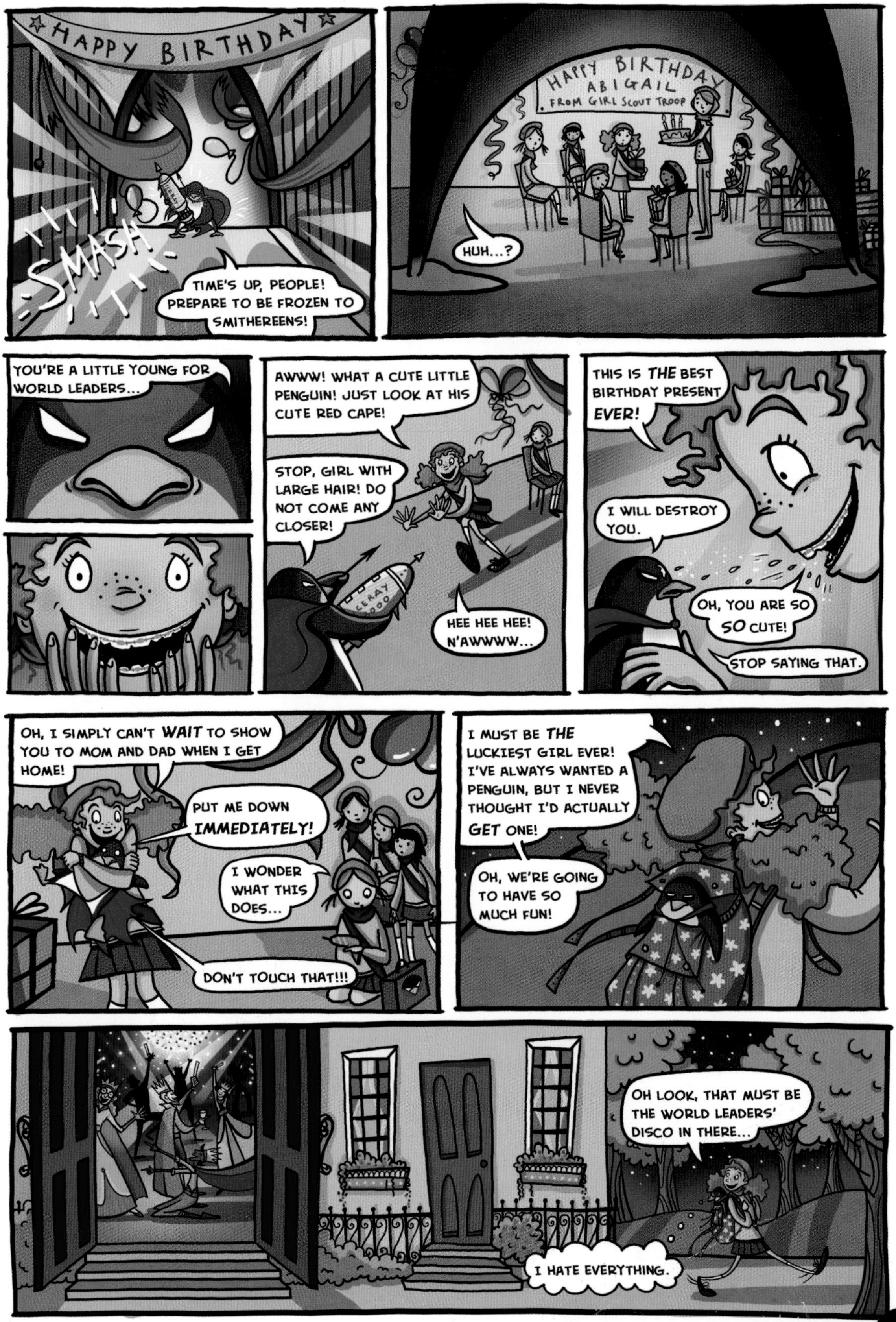
HAPPY BIRTHDAY
SMASH
TIME'S UP, PEOPLE! PREPARE TO BE FROZEN TO SMITHEREENS!
HAPPY BIRTHDAY ABIGAIL FROM GIRL SCOUT TROOP
HUH...?
YOU'RE A LITTLE YOUNG FOR WORLD LEADERS...
AWWW! WHAT A CUTE LITTLE PENGUIN! JUST LOOK AT HIS CUTE RED CAPE!
STOP, GIRL WITH LARGE HAIR! DO NOT COME ANY CLOSER!
HEE HEE HEE! N'AWWWW...
THIS IS THE BEST BIRTHDAY PRESENT EVER!
I WILL DESTROY YOU.
OH, YOU ARE SO SO CUTE!
STOP SAYING THAT.
OH, I SIMPLY CAN'T WAIT TO SHOW YOU TO MOM AND DAD WHEN I GET HOME!
PUT ME DOWN IMMEDIATELY!
I WONDER WHAT THIS DOES...
DON'T TOUCH THAT!!!
I MUST BE THE LUCKIEST GIRL EVER! I'VE ALWAYS WANTED A PENGUIN, BUT I NEVER THOUGHT I'D ACTUALLY GET ONE!
OH, WE'RE GOING TO HAVE SO MUCH FUN!
OH LOOK, THAT MUST BE THE WORLD LEADERS' DISCO IN THERE...
I HATE EVERYTHING.

THE END! MUAHAHAHA!

# EVIL EMPEROR PENGUIN

LAURA ELLEN ANDERSON

## IN: "DIET ANOTHER DAY"

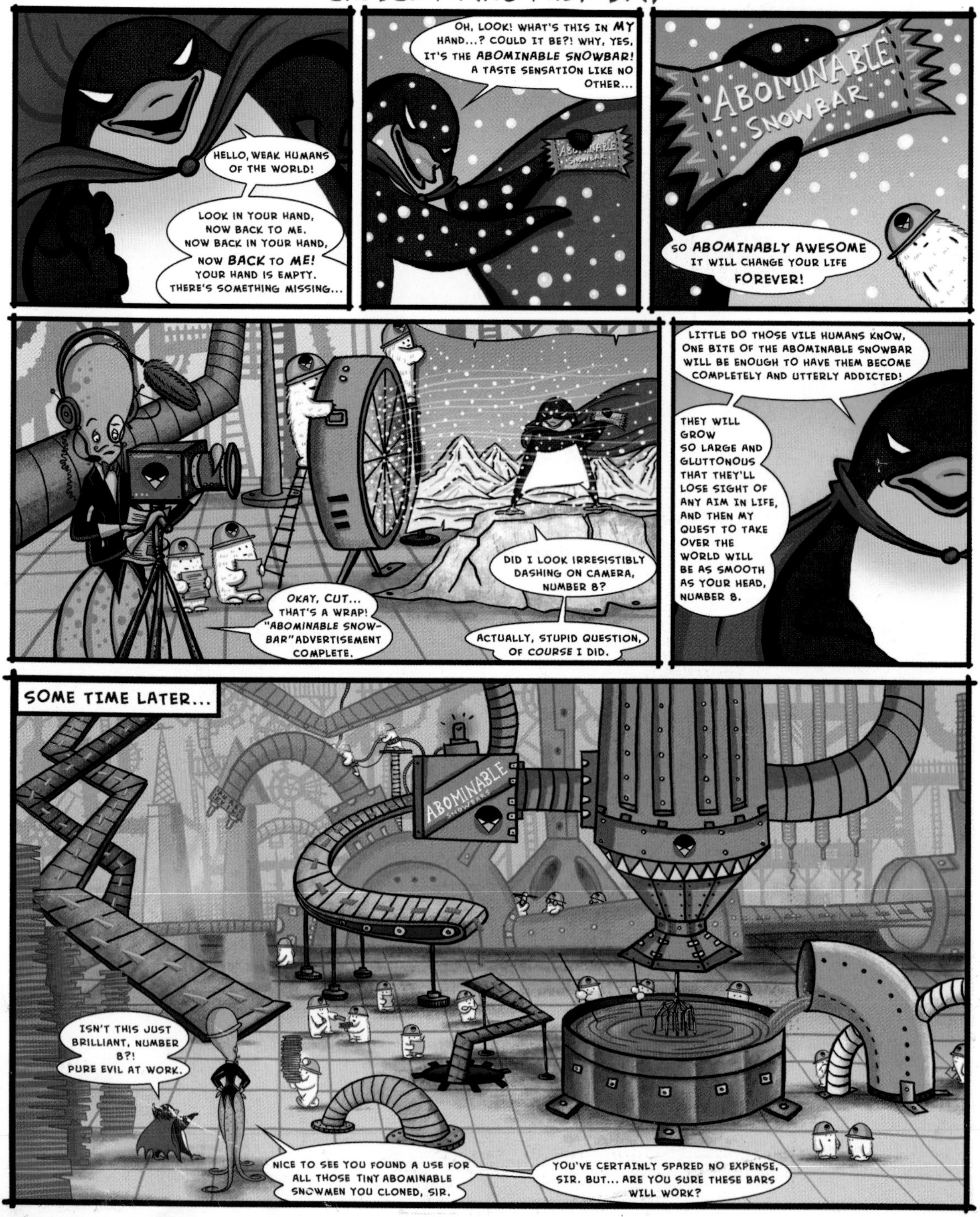
HELLO, WEAK HUMANS OF THE WORLD!
LOOK IN YOUR HAND, NOW BACK TO ME. NOW BACK IN YOUR HAND, NOW BACK TO ME! YOUR HAND IS EMPTY. THERE'S SOMETHING MISSING...
OH, LOOK! WHAT'S THIS IN MY HAND...? COULD IT BE?! WHY, YES, IT'S THE ABOMINABLE SNOWBAR! A TASTE SENSATION LIKE NO OTHER...
ABOMINABLE SNOWBAR
SO ABOMINABLY AWESOME IT WILL CHANGE YOUR LIFE FOREVER!
OKAY, CUT... THAT'S A WRAP! "ABOMINABLE SNOW-BAR" ADVERTISEMENT COMPLETE.
DID I LOOK IRRESISTIBLY DASHING ON CAMERA, NUMBER 8?
ACTUALLY, STUPID QUESTION, OF COURSE I DID.
LITTLE DO THOSE VILE HUMANS KNOW, ONE BITE OF THE ABOMINABLE SNOWBAR WILL BE ENOUGH TO HAVE THEM BECOME COMPLETELY AND UTTERLY ADDICTED!
THEY WILL GROW SO LARGE AND GLUTTONOUS THAT THEY'LL LOSE SIGHT OF ANY AIM IN LIFE, AND THEN MY QUEST TO TAKE OVER THE WORLD WILL BE AS SMOOTH AS YOUR HEAD, NUMBER 8.
SOME TIME LATER...
ABOMINABLE SNOWBAR
ISN'T THIS JUST BRILLIANT, NUMBER 8?! PURE EVIL AT WORK.
NICE TO SEE YOU FOUND A USE FOR ALL THOSE TINY ABOMINABLE SNOWMEN YOU CLONED, SIR.
YOU'VE CERTAINLY SPARED NO EXPENSE, SIR. BUT... ARE YOU SURE THESE BARS WILL WORK?

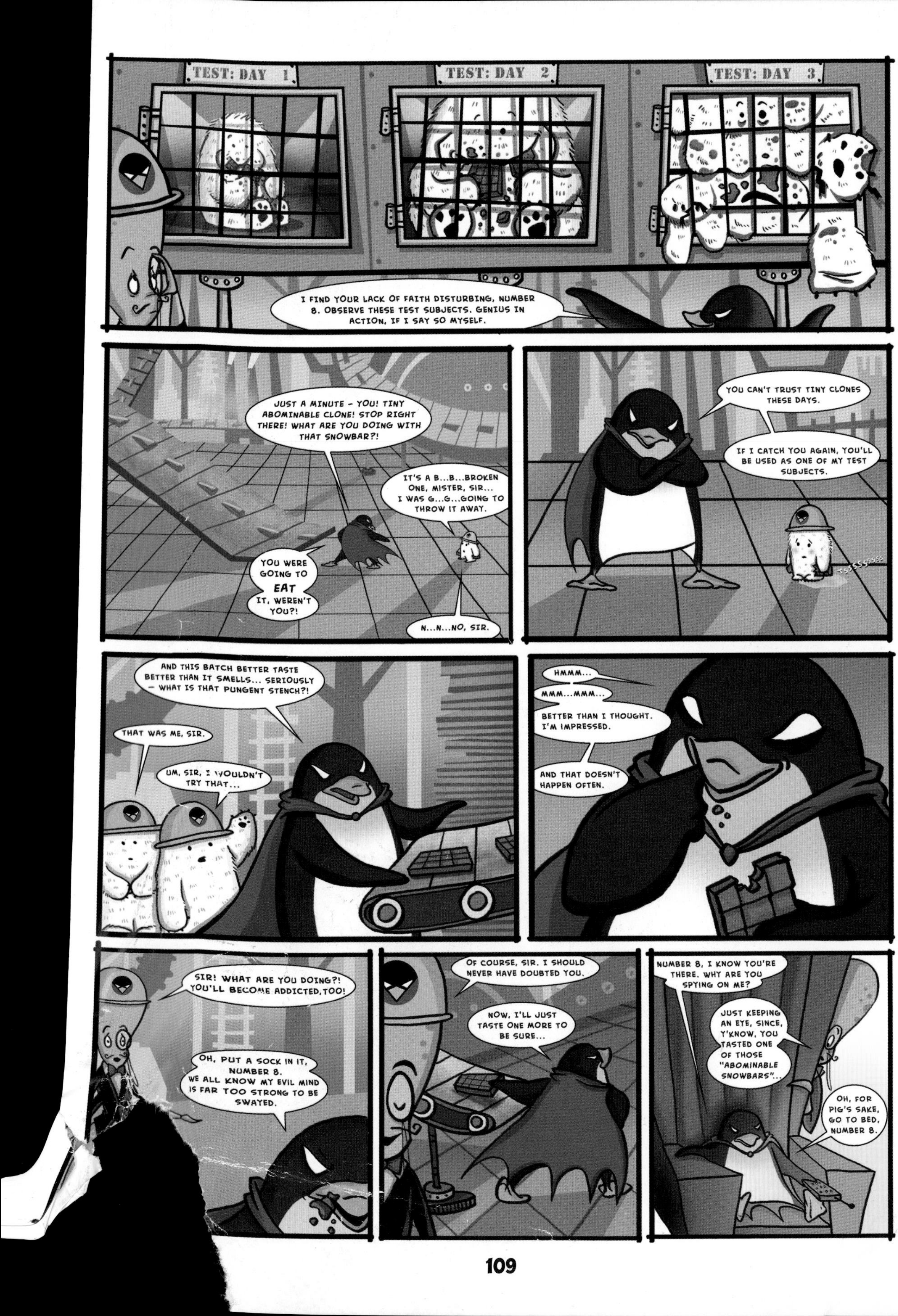
TEST: DAY 1
TEST: DAY 2
TEST: DAY 3
I FIND YOUR LACK OF FAITH DISTURBING, NUMBER 8. OBSERVE THESE TEST SUBJECTS. GENIUS IN ACTION, IF I SAY SO MYSELF.
JUST A MINUTE - YOU! TINY ABOMINABLE CLONE! STOP RIGHT THERE! WHAT ARE YOU DOING WITH THAT SNOWBAR?!
IT'S A B...B...BROKEN ONE, MISTER, SIR... I WAS G...G...GOING TO THROW IT AWAY.
YOU WERE GOING TO EAT IT, WEREN'T YOU?!
N...N...NO, SIR.
YOU CAN'T TRUST TINY CLONES THESE DAYS.
IF I CATCH YOU AGAIN, YOU'LL BE USED AS ONE OF MY TEST SUBJECTS.
TSSSSSSSS
AND THIS BATCH BETTER TASTE BETTER THAN IT SMELLS... SERIOUSLY - WHAT IS THAT PUNGENT STENCH?!
THAT WAS ME, SIR.
UM, SIR, I WOULDN'T TRY THAT...
HMMM...
MMM...MMM...
BETTER THAN I THOUGHT. I'M IMPRESSED.
AND THAT DOESN'T HAPPEN OFTEN.
SIR! WHAT ARE YOU DOING?! YOU'LL BECOME ADDICTED, TOO!
OH, PUT A SOCK IN IT, NUMBER 8. WE ALL KNOW MY EVIL MIND IS FAR TOO STRONG TO BE SWAYED.
OF COURSE, SIR. I SHOULD NEVER HAVE DOUBTED YOU.
NOW, I'LL JUST TASTE ONE MORE TO BE SURE...
NUMBER 8, I KNOW YOU'RE THERE. WHY ARE YOU SPYING ON ME?
JUST KEEPING AN EYE, SINCE, Y'KNOW, YOU TASTED ONE OF THOSE "ABOMINABLE SNOWBARS"...
OH, FOR PIG'S SAKE, GO TO BED, NUMBER 8.

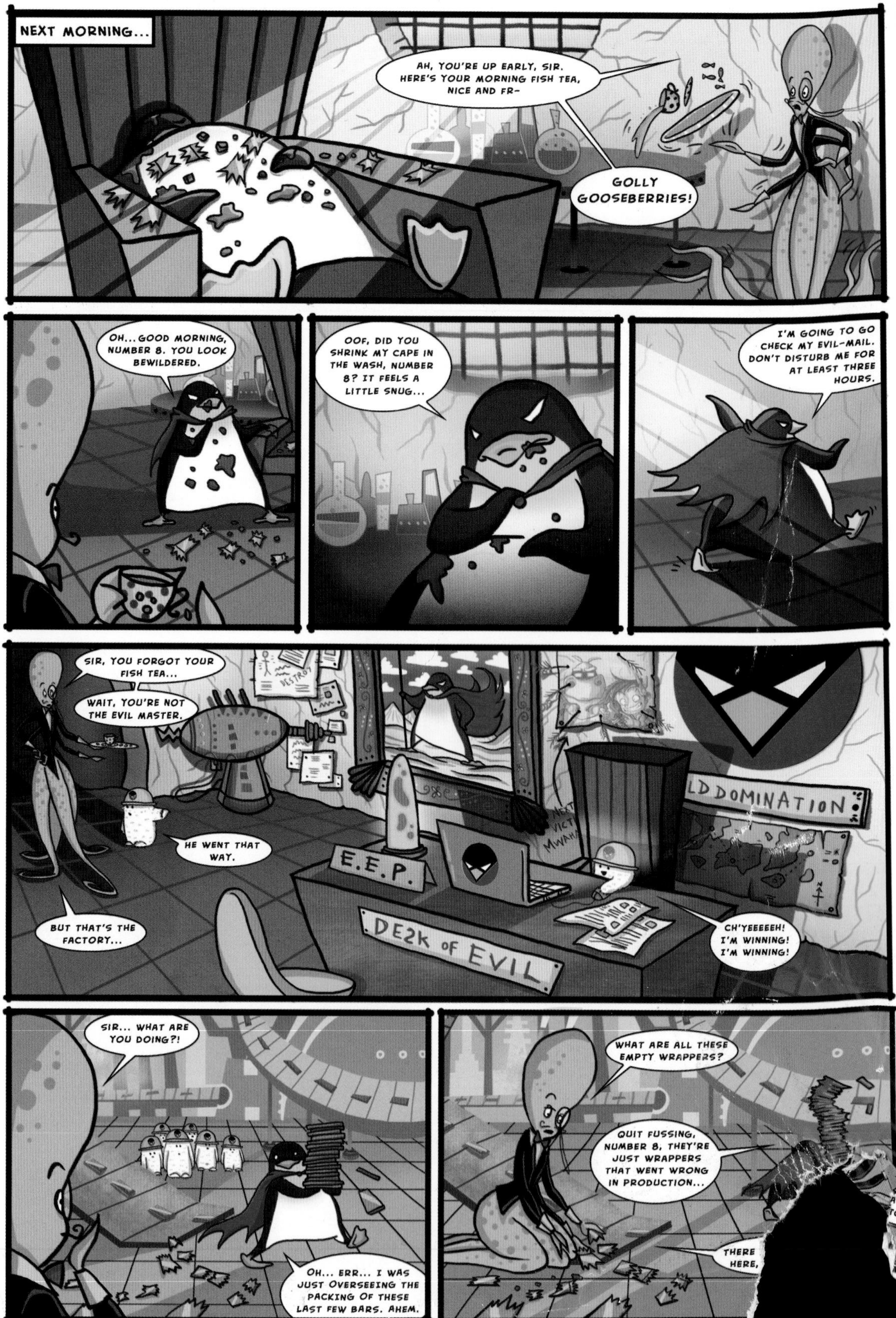
NEXT MORNING...
AH, YOU'RE UP EARLY, SIR. HERE'S YOUR MORNING FISH TEA, NICE AND FR–
GOLLY GOOSEBERRIES!
OH...GOOD MORNING, NUMBER 8. YOU LOOK BEWILDERED.
OOF, DID YOU SHRINK MY CAPE IN THE WASH, NUMBER 8? IT FEELS A LITTLE SNUG...
I'M GOING TO GO CHECK MY EVIL-MAIL. DON'T DISTURB ME FOR AT LEAST THREE HOURS.
SIR, YOU FORGOT YOUR FISH TEA...
WAIT, YOU'RE NOT THE EVIL MASTER.
DESTROY
LD DOMINATION
HE WENT THAT WAY.
E.E.P.
BUT THAT'S THE FACTORY...
DE2k OF EVIL
CH'YEEEEEEH! I'M WINNING! I'M WINNING!
SIR... WHAT ARE YOU DOING?!
OH... ERR... I WAS JUST OVERSEEING THE PACKING OF THESE LAST FEW BARS. AHEM.
WHAT ARE ALL THESE EMPTY WRAPPERS?
QUIT FUSSING, NUMBER 8, THEY'RE JUST WRAPPERS THAT WENT WRONG IN PRODUCTION...
THERE
HERE,

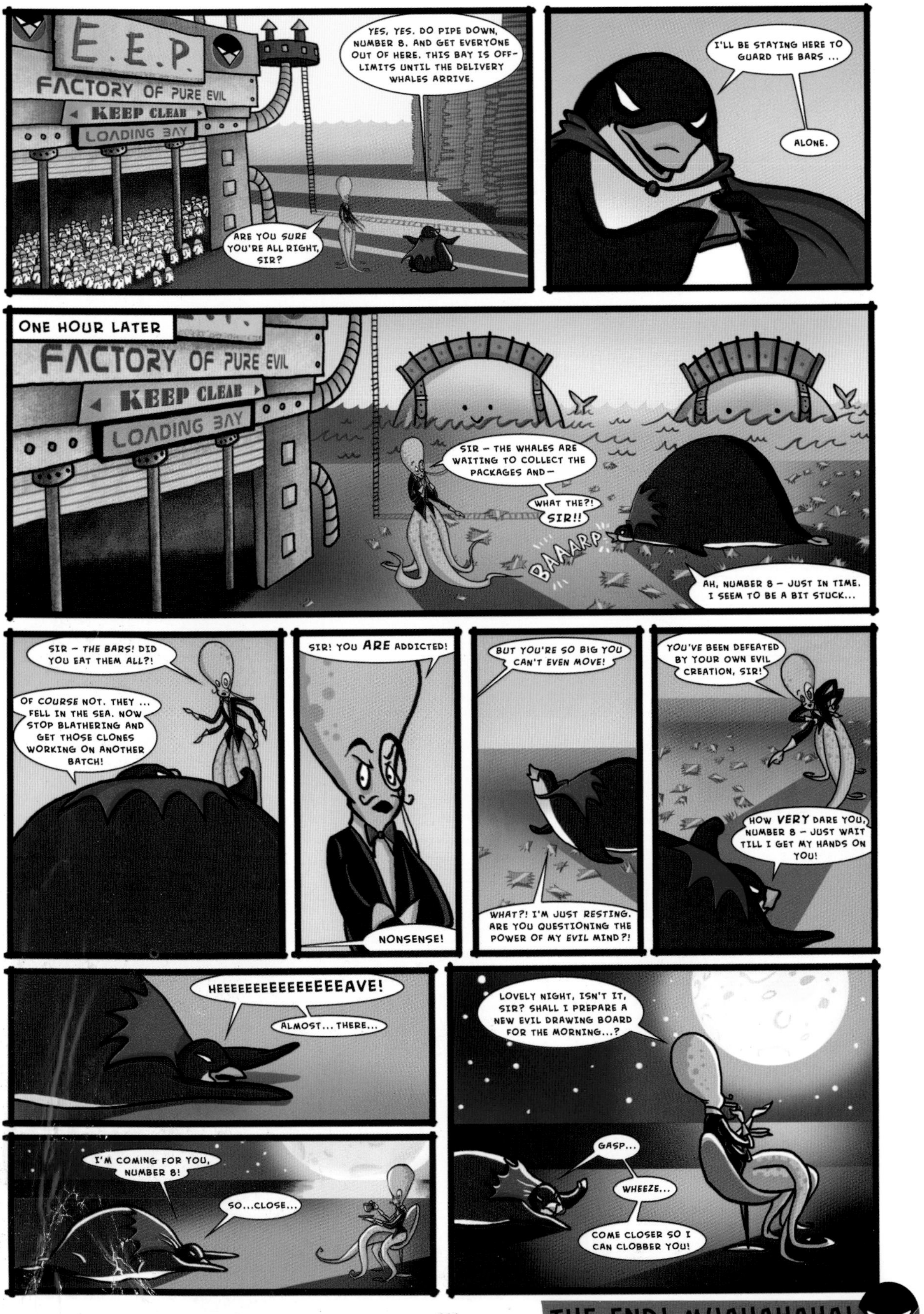
E.E.P.
FACTORY OF PURE EVIL
KEEP CLEAR
LOADING BAY
YES, YES. DO PIPE DOWN, NUMBER 8. AND GET EVERYONE OUT OF HERE. THIS BAY IS OFF-LIMITS UNTIL THE DELIVERY WHALES ARRIVE.
ARE YOU SURE YOU'RE ALL RIGHT, SIR?
I'LL BE STAYING HERE TO GUARD THE BARS ...
ALONE.
ONE HOUR LATER
FACTORY OF PURE EVIL
KEEP CLEAR
LOADING BAY
SIR – THE WHALES ARE WAITING TO COLLECT THE PACKAGES AND–
WHAT THE?! SIR!!
BAAARP
AH, NUMBER 8 – JUST IN TIME. I SEEM TO BE A BIT STUCK...
SIR – THE BARS! DID YOU EAT THEM ALL?!
OF COURSE NOT. THEY ... FELL IN THE SEA. NOW STOP BLATHERING AND GET THOSE CLONES WORKING ON ANOTHER BATCH!
SIR! YOU ARE ADDICTED!
NONSENSE!
BUT YOU'RE SO BIG YOU CAN'T EVEN MOVE!
WHAT?! I'M JUST RESTING. ARE YOU QUESTIONING THE POWER OF MY EVIL MIND?!
YOU'VE BEEN DEFEATED BY YOUR OWN EVIL CREATION, SIR!
HOW VERY DARE YOU, NUMBER 8 – JUST WAIT TILL I GET MY HANDS ON YOU!
HEEEEEEEEEEEEEEEAVE!
ALMOST... THERE...
I'M COMING FOR YOU, NUMBER 8!
SO...CLOSE...
LOVELY NIGHT, ISN'T IT, SIR? SHALL I PREPARE A NEW EVIL DRAWING BOARD FOR THE MORNING...?
GASP...
WHEEZE...
COME CLOSER SO I CAN CLOBBER YOU!
THE END! MUAHAHAHA!

# EVIL EMPEROR PENGUIN

### IN: THE GOOD, THE BAD & THE PAOLO: PART 1"

LAURA ELLEN ANDERSON

**METROPOPOLIS CITY CENTER**

DOOBEE DOOBEE DOO DAAH!

RIGHT ON SCHEDULE...

To Do...
PICK UP No.8's TENTACLE CREAM ☐
CALL BACK WHITE HOUSE ☑
TAKE OVER WORLD ☐

EVERYTHING'S GOING JUST PERFECT!

I'M SO BRILLIANTLY EVIL.

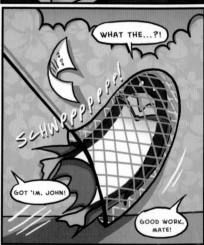

WHAT THE...?!

SCHWPPPPPP!

GOT 'IM, JOHN!

GOOD WORK, MATE!

HEY! LET ME GO, YOU VILE HUMAN! I'M EVIL EMPEROR PENGUIN, DON'T YOU KNOW!

ANOTHER ESCAPEE FOUND... LET'S GET YOU BACK WHERE YOU BELONG, PINGU!

WHAT?! HEY!

CITY ZOO PATROL

ZOO 123

BRRMM BRRMM

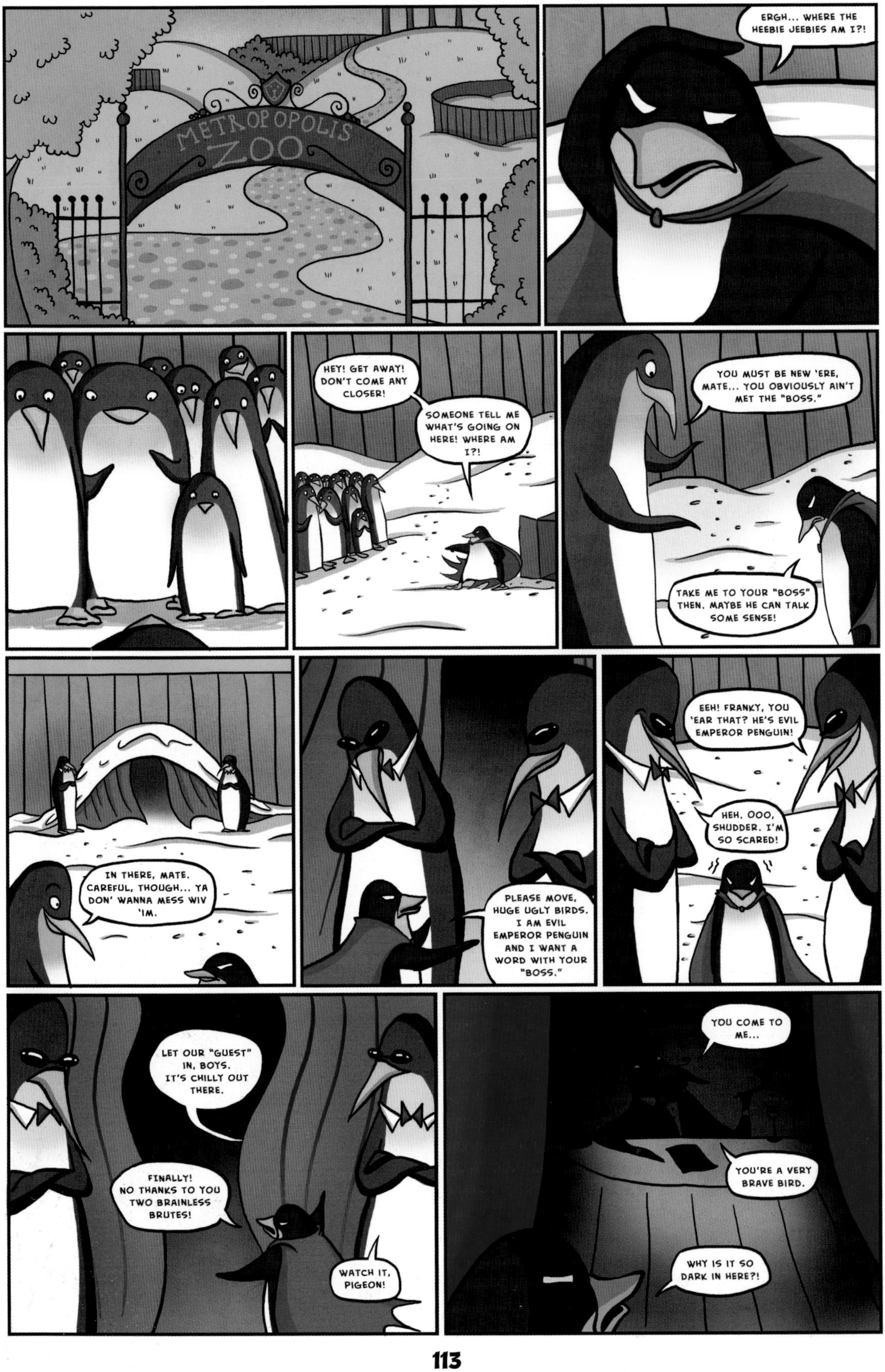
METROPOPOLIS ZOO
ERGH... WHERE THE HEEBIE JEEBIES AM I?!
HEY! GET AWAY! DON'T COME ANY CLOSER!
SOMEONE TELL ME WHAT'S GOING ON HERE! WHERE AM I?!
YOU MUST BE NEW 'ERE, MATE... YOU OBVIOUSLY AIN'T MET THE "BOSS."
TAKE ME TO YOUR "BOSS" THEN. MAYBE HE CAN TALK SOME SENSE!
IN THERE, MATE. CAREFUL, THOUGH... YA DON' WANNA MESS WIV 'IM.
PLEASE MOVE, HUGE UGLY BIRDS. I AM EVIL EMPEROR PENGUIN AND I WANT A WORD WITH YOUR "BOSS."
EEH! FRANKY, YOU 'EAR THAT? HE'S EVIL EMPEROR PENGUIN!
HEH. OOO, SHUDDER. I'M SO SCARED!
LET OUR "GUEST" IN, BOYS. IT'S CHILLY OUT THERE.
FINALLY! NO THANKS TO YOU TWO BRAINLESS BRUTES!
WATCH IT, PIGEON!
YOU COME TO ME...
YOU'RE A VERY BRAVE BIRD.
WHY IS IT SO DARK IN HERE?!

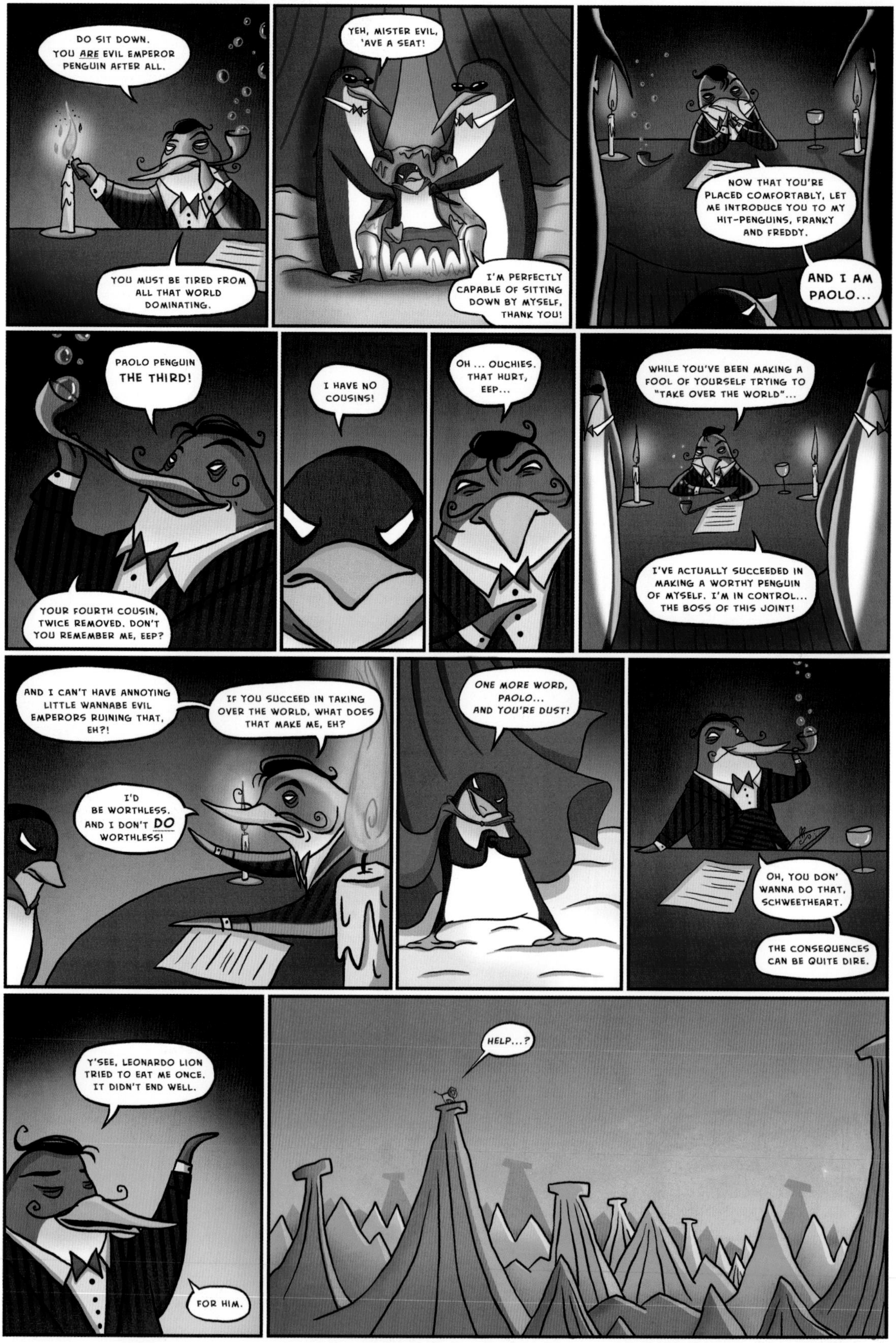
DO SIT DOWN. YOU ARE EVIL EMPEROR PENGUIN AFTER ALL.
YOU MUST BE TIRED FROM ALL THAT WORLD DOMINATING.
YEH, MISTER EVIL, 'AVE A SEAT!
I'M PERFECTLY CAPABLE OF SITTING DOWN BY MYSELF, THANK YOU!
NOW THAT YOU'RE PLACED COMFORTABLY, LET ME INTRODUCE YOU TO MY HIT-PENGUINS, FRANKY AND FREDDY.
AND I AM PAOLO...
PAOLO PENGUIN THE THIRD!
YOUR FOURTH COUSIN, TWICE REMOVED. DON'T YOU REMEMBER ME, EEP?
I HAVE NO COUSINS!
OH ... OUCHIES. THAT HURT, EEP...
WHILE YOU'VE BEEN MAKING A FOOL OF YOURSELF TRYING TO "TAKE OVER THE WORLD"...
I'VE ACTUALLY SUCCEEDED IN MAKING A WORTHY PENGUIN OF MYSELF. I'M IN CONTROL... THE BOSS OF THIS JOINT!
IF YOU SUCCEED IN TAKING OVER THE WORLD, WHAT DOES THAT MAKE ME, EH?
I'D BE WORTHLESS. AND I DON'T DO WORTHLESS!
AND I CAN'T HAVE ANNOYING LITTLE WANNABE EVIL EMPERORS RUINING THAT, EH?!
ONE MORE WORD, PAOLO... AND YOU'RE DUST!
OH, YOU DON' WANNA DO THAT, SCHWEETHEART.
THE CONSEQUENCES CAN BE QUITE DIRE.
Y'SEE, LEONARDO LION TRIED TO EAT ME ONCE. IT DIDN'T END WELL.
FOR HIM.
HELP...?

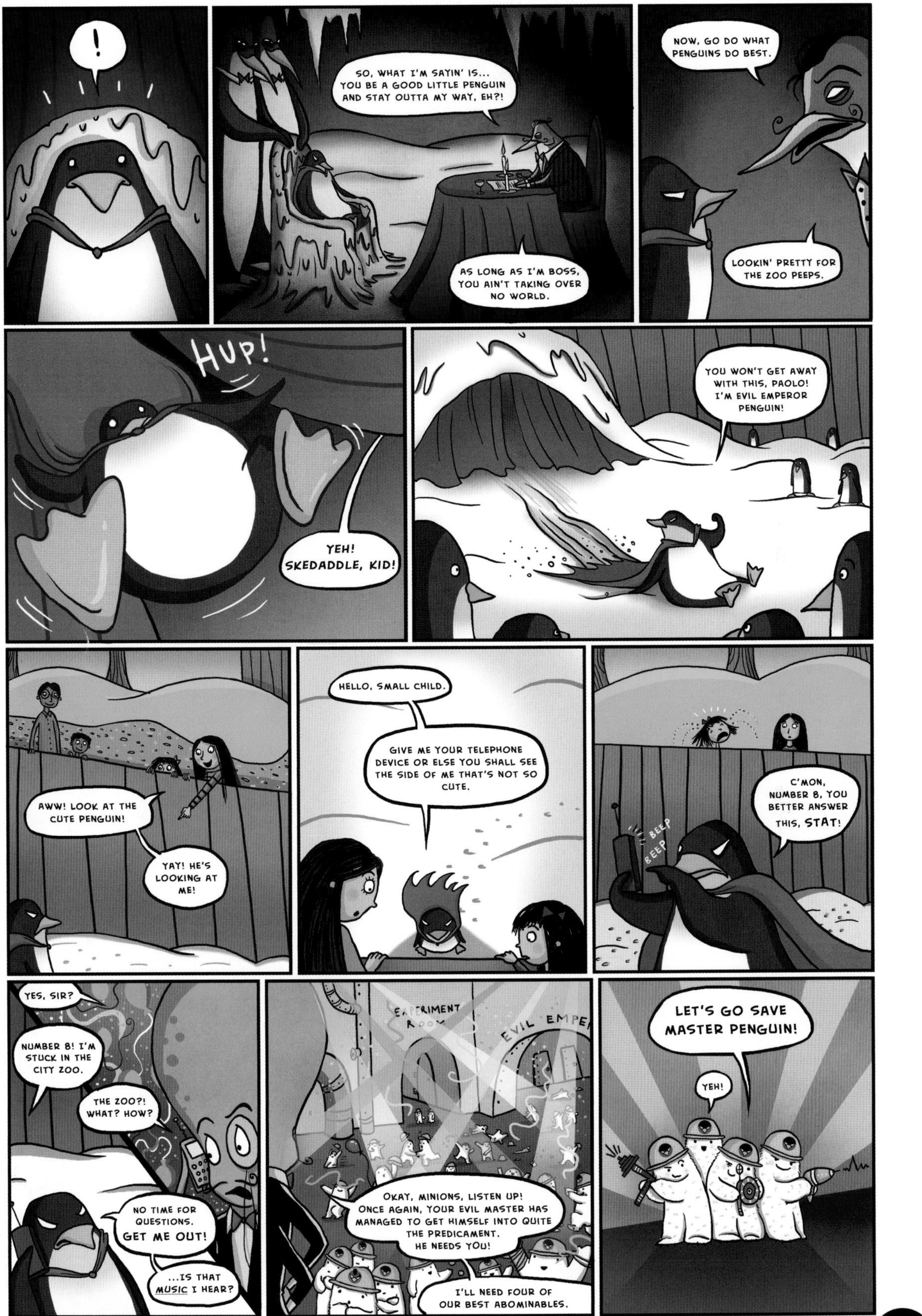
!
SO, WHAT I'M SAYIN' IS... YOU BE A GOOD LITTLE PENGUIN AND STAY OUTTA MY WAY, EH?!
AS LONG AS I'M BOSS, YOU AIN'T TAKING OVER NO WORLD.
NOW, GO DO WHAT PENGUINS DO BEST.
LOOKIN' PRETTY FOR THE ZOO PEEPS.
HUP!
YEH! SKEDADDLE, KID!
YOU WON'T GET AWAY WITH THIS, PAOLO! I'M EVIL EMPEROR PENGUIN!
AWW! LOOK AT THE CUTE PENGUIN!
YAY! HE'S LOOKING AT ME!
HELLO, SMALL CHILD.
GIVE ME YOUR TELEPHONE DEVICE OR ELSE YOU SHALL SEE THE SIDE OF ME THAT'S NOT SO CUTE.
BEEP BEEP
C'MON, NUMBER 8, YOU BETTER ANSWER THIS, STAT!
YES, SIR?
NUMBER 8! I'M STUCK IN THE CITY ZOO.
THE ZOO?! WHAT? HOW?
NO TIME FOR QUESTIONS. GET ME OUT!
...IS THAT MUSIC I HEAR?
EXPERIMENT ROOM
EVIL EMPE
OKAY, MINIONS, LISTEN UP! ONCE AGAIN, YOUR EVIL MASTER HAS MANAGED TO GET HIMSELF INTO QUITE THE PREDICAMENT. HE NEEDS YOU!
I'LL NEED FOUR OF OUR BEST ABOMINABLES.
LET'S GO SAVE MASTER PENGUIN!
YEH!



CONTINUED IN PART 2!

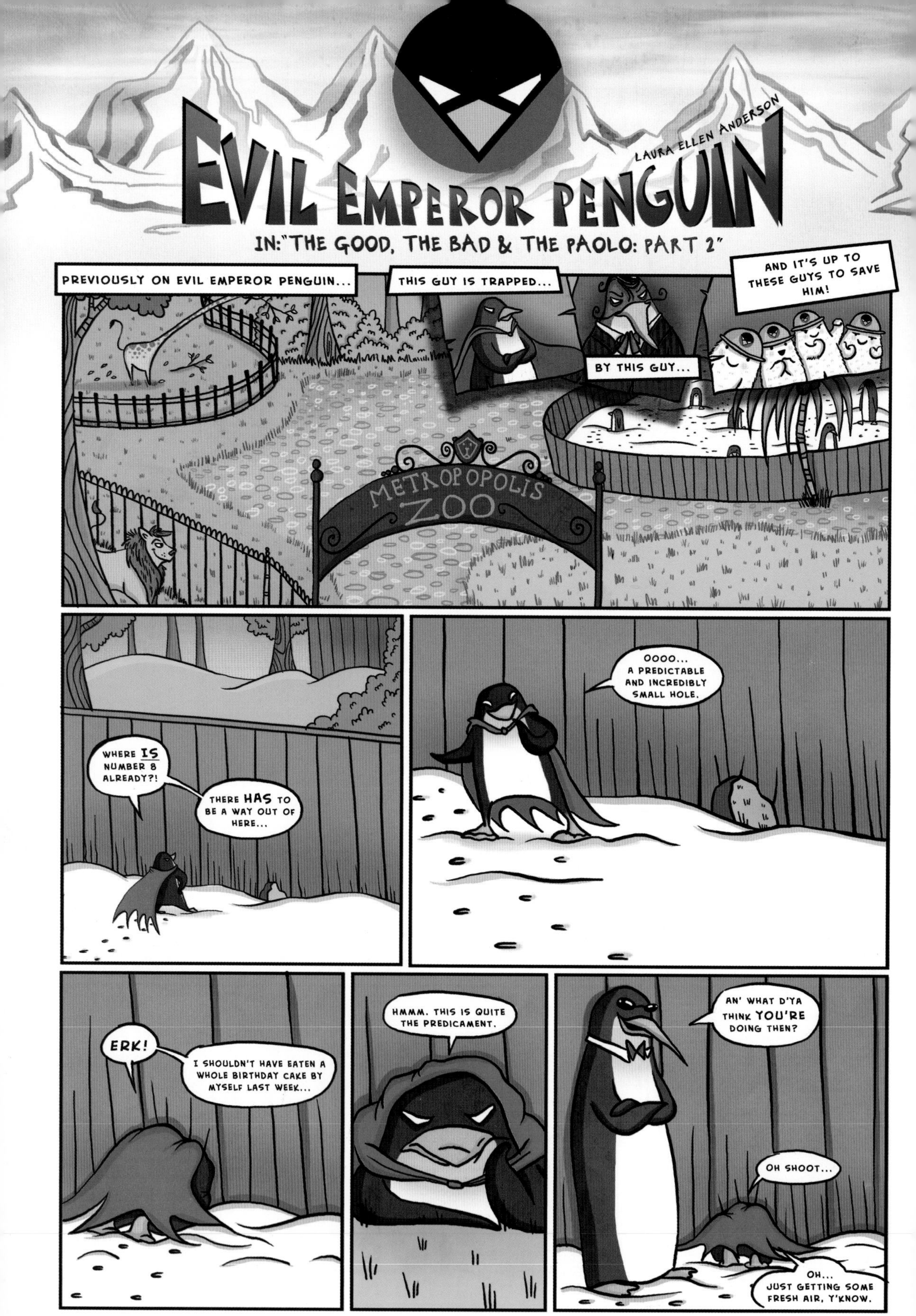

EVIL EMPEROR PENGUIN
LAURA ELLEN ANDERSON
IN: "THE GOOD, THE BAD & THE PAOLO: PART 2"
PREVIOUSLY ON EVIL EMPEROR PENGUIN...
THIS GUY IS TRAPPED...
BY THIS GUY...
AND IT'S UP TO THESE GUYS TO SAVE HIM!
METROPOPOLIS ZOO
WHERE IS NUMBER 8 ALREADY?!
THERE HAS TO BE A WAY OUT OF HERE...
OOOO... A PREDICTABLE AND INCREDIBLY SMALL HOLE.
ERK!
I SHOULDN'T HAVE EATEN A WHOLE BIRTHDAY CAKE BY MYSELF LAST WEEK...
HMMM. THIS IS QUITE THE PREDICAMENT.
AN' WHAT D'YA THINK YOU'RE DOING THEN?
OH SHOOT...
OH... JUST GETTING SOME FRESH AIR, Y'KNOW.

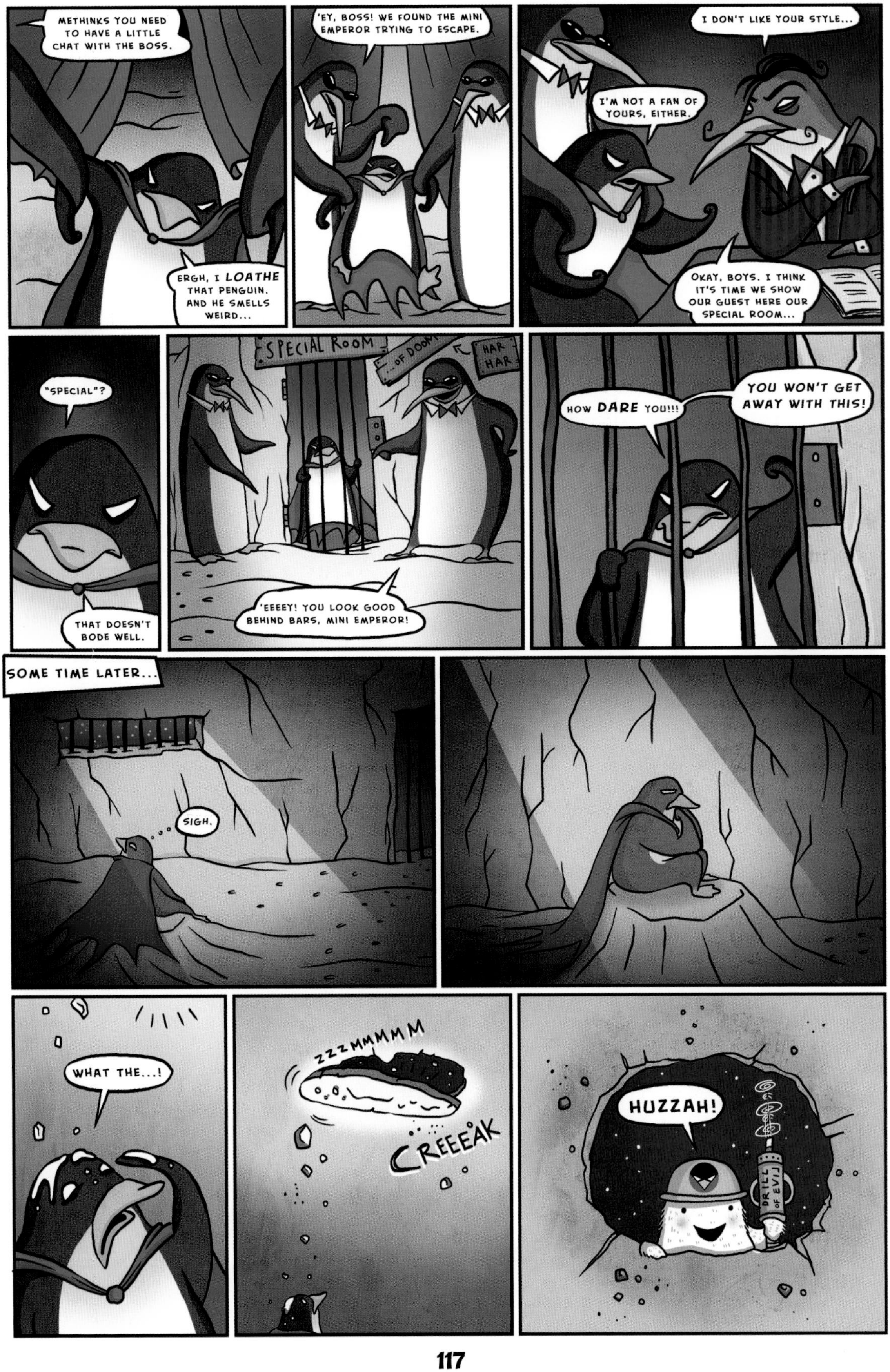
METHINKS YOU NEED TO HAVE A LITTLE CHAT WITH THE BOSS.
ERGH, I LOATHE THAT PENGUIN. AND HE SMELLS WEIRD...
'EY, BOSS! WE FOUND THE MINI EMPEROR TRYING TO ESCAPE.
I DON'T LIKE YOUR STYLE...
I'M NOT A FAN OF YOURS, EITHER.
OKAY, BOYS. I THINK IT'S TIME WE SHOW OUR GUEST HERE OUR SPECIAL ROOM...
"SPECIAL"?
THAT DOESN'T BODE WELL.
SPECIAL ROOM
...OF DOOM
HAR HAR
'EEEEY! YOU LOOK GOOD BEHIND BARS, MINI EMPEROR!
HOW DARE YOU!!!
YOU WON'T GET AWAY WITH THIS!
SOME TIME LATER...
SIGH.
WHAT THE...!
ZZZMMMMM
CREEEAK
HUZZAH!
DRILL OF EVIL

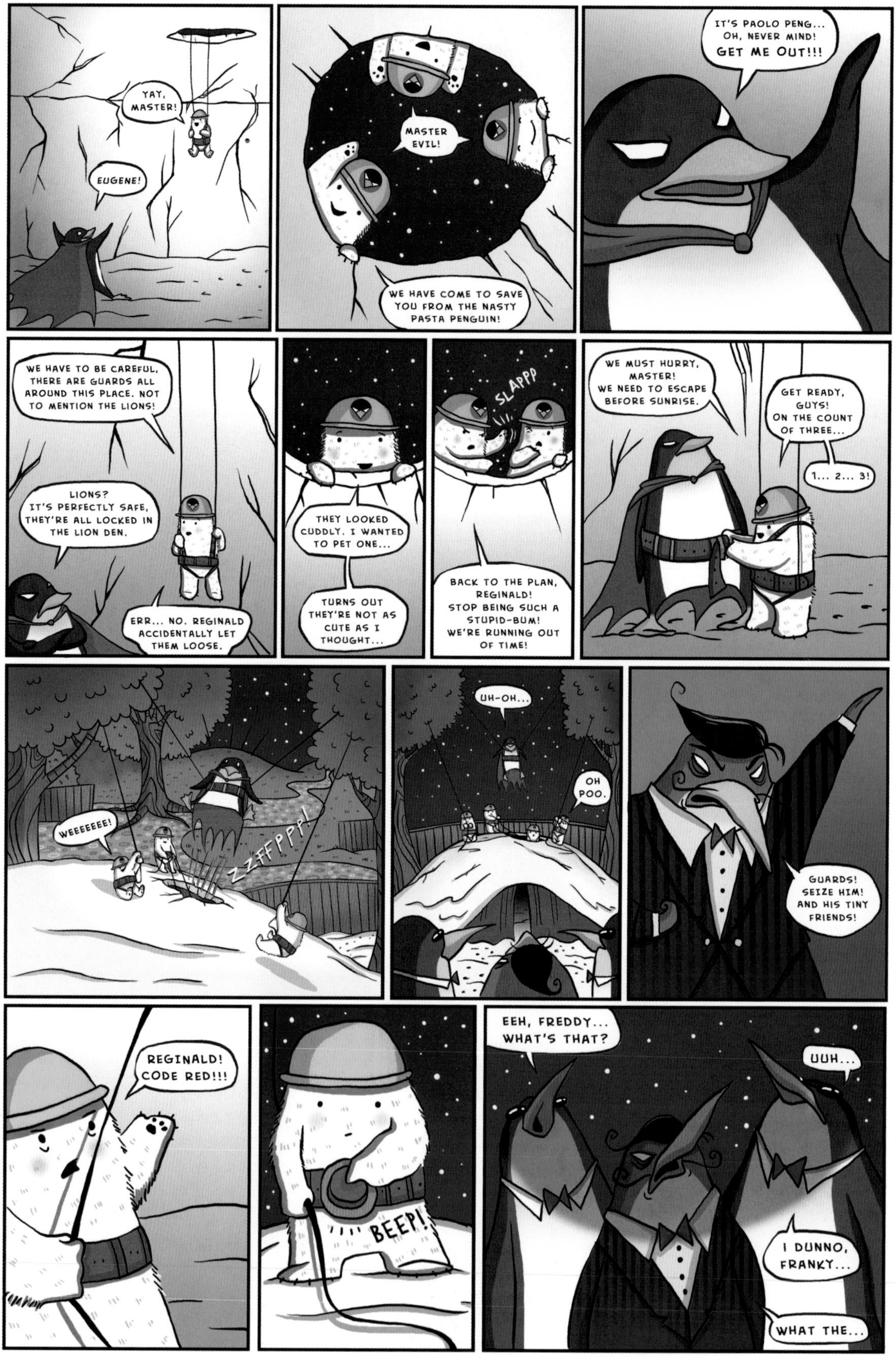
YAY, MASTER!
EUGENE!
MASTER EVIL!
WE HAVE COME TO SAVE YOU FROM THE NASTY PASTA PENGUIN!
IT'S PAOLO PENG... OH, NEVER MIND! GET ME OUT!!!
WE HAVE TO BE CAREFUL, THERE ARE GUARDS ALL AROUND THIS PLACE. NOT TO MENTION THE LIONS!
LIONS? IT'S PERFECTLY SAFE, THEY'RE ALL LOCKED IN THE LION DEN.
ERR... NO. REGINALD ACCIDENTALLY LET THEM LOOSE.
THEY LOOKED CUDDLY. I WANTED TO PET ONE...
TURNS OUT THEY'RE NOT AS CUTE AS I THOUGHT...
SLAPPP
BACK TO THE PLAN, REGINALD! STOP BEING SUCH A STUPID-BUM! WE'RE RUNNING OUT OF TIME!
WE MUST HURRY, MASTER! WE NEED TO ESCAPE BEFORE SUNRISE.
GET READY, GUYS! ON THE COUNT OF THREE...
1... 2... 3!
WEEEEEEE!
ZZFFPPP!
UH-OH...
OH POO.
GUARDS! SEIZE HIM! AND HIS TINY FRIENDS!
REGINALD! CODE RED!!!
BEEP!
EEH, FREDDY... WHAT'S THAT?
UUH...
I DUNNO, FRANKY...
WHAT THE...

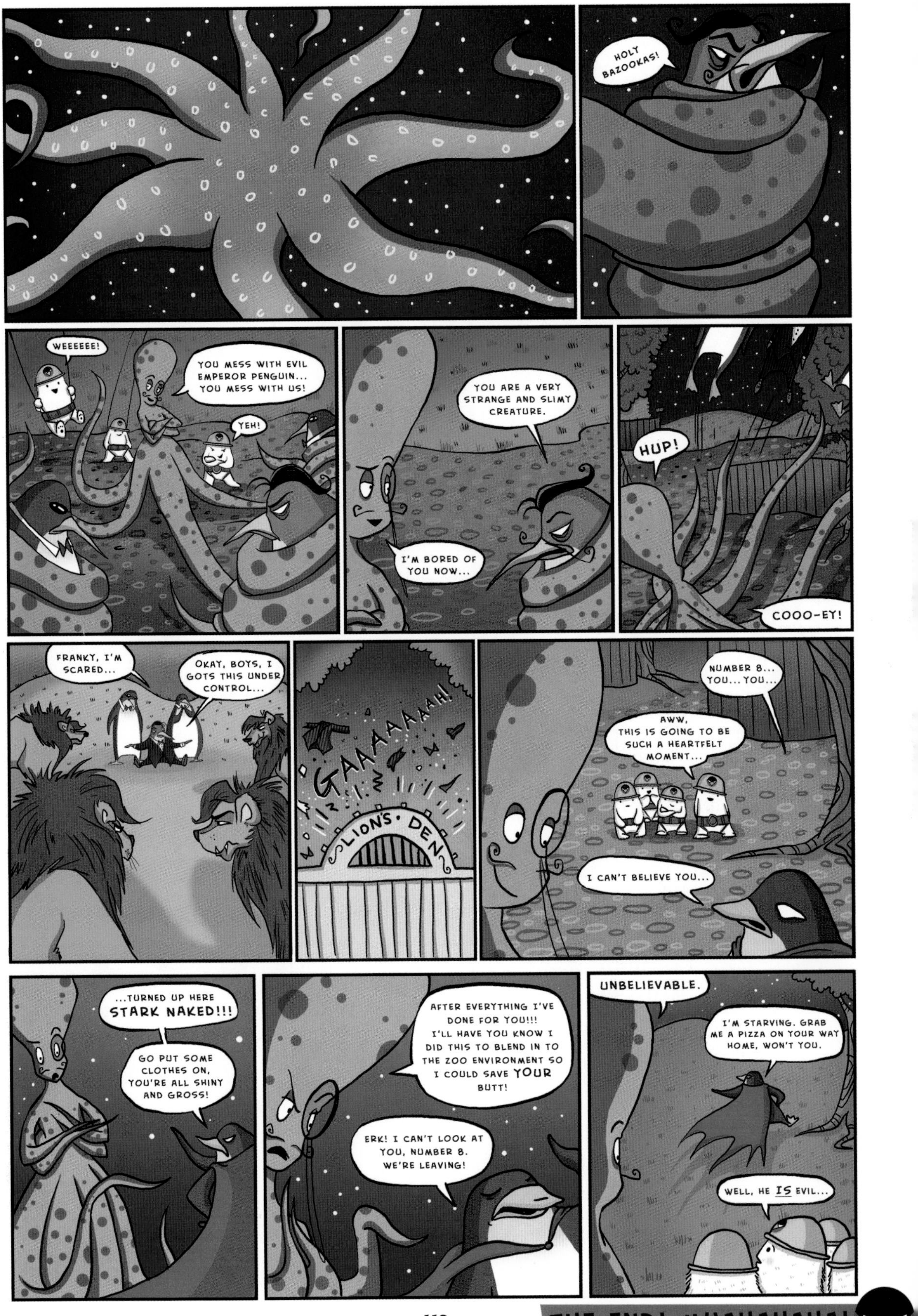
HOLY BAZOOKAS!
WEEEEEE!
YOU MESS WITH EVIL EMPEROR PENGUIN... YOU MESS WITH US!
YEH!
YOU ARE A VERY STRANGE AND SLIMY CREATURE.
I'M BORED OF YOU NOW...
HUP!
COOO-EY!
FRANKY, I'M SCARED...
OKAY, BOYS, I GOTS THIS UNDER CONTROL...
GAAAAAAAAH!
LION'S DEN
NUMBER 8... YOU... YOU...
AWW, THIS IS GOING TO BE SUCH A HEARTFELT MOMENT...
I CAN'T BELIEVE YOU...
...TURNED UP HERE STARK NAKED!!!
GO PUT SOME CLOTHES ON, YOU'RE ALL SHINY AND GROSS!
AFTER EVERYTHING I'VE DONE FOR YOU!!! I'LL HAVE YOU KNOW I DID THIS TO BLEND IN TO THE ZOO ENVIRONMENT SO I COULD SAVE YOUR BUTT!
ERK! I CAN'T LOOK AT YOU, NUMBER 8. WE'RE LEAVING!
UNBELIEVABLE.
I'M STARVING. GRAB ME A PIZZA ON YOUR WAY HOME, WON'T YOU.
WELL, HE IS EVIL...
THE END! MUAHAHAHA!

# EVIL EMPEROR PENGUIN

LAURA ELLEN ANDERSON

IN: "HAPPY HATCH DAY SURPRISE"

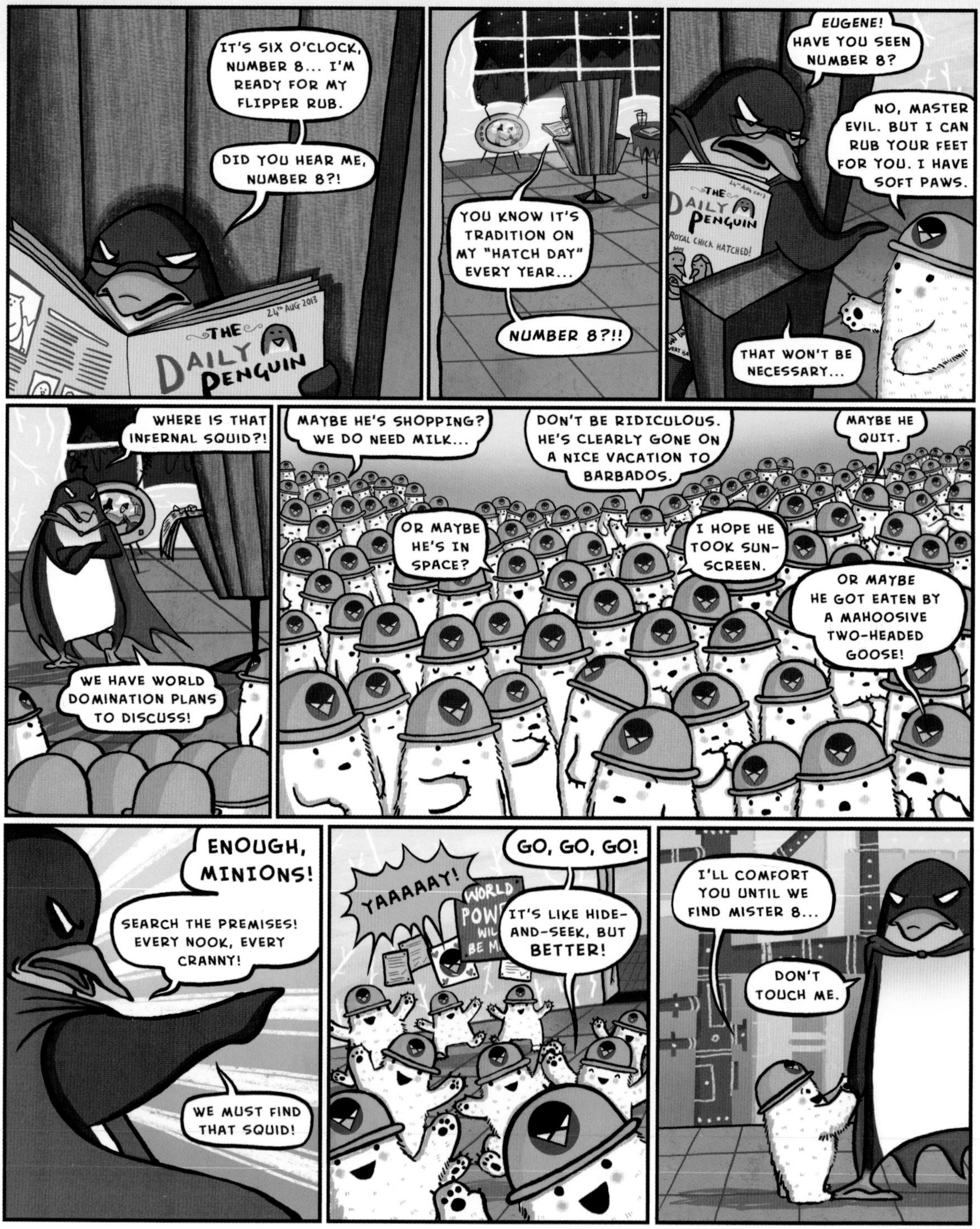

IT'S SIX O'CLOCK, NUMBER 8... I'M READY FOR MY FLIPPER RUB.
DID YOU HEAR ME, NUMBER 8?!
24th AUG 2013
THE DAILY PENGUIN
YOU KNOW IT'S TRADITION ON MY "HATCH DAY" EVERY YEAR...
NUMBER 8?!!
EUGENE! HAVE YOU SEEN NUMBER 8?
NO, MASTER EVIL. BUT I CAN RUB YOUR FEET FOR YOU. I HAVE SOFT PAWS.
THE DAILY PENGUIN
ROYAL CHICK HATCHED!
THAT WON'T BE NECESSARY...
WHERE IS THAT INFERNAL SQUID?!
WE HAVE WORLD DOMINATION PLANS TO DISCUSS!
MAYBE HE'S SHOPPING? WE DO NEED MILK...
DON'T BE RIDICULOUS. HE'S CLEARLY GONE ON A NICE VACATION TO BARBADOS.
MAYBE HE QUIT.
OR MAYBE HE'S IN SPACE?
I HOPE HE TOOK SUN-SCREEN.
OR MAYBE HE GOT EATEN BY A MAHOOSIVE TWO-HEADED GOOSE!
ENOUGH, MINIONS!
SEARCH THE PREMISES! EVERY NOOK, EVERY CRANNY!
WE MUST FIND THAT SQUID!
YAAAAAY!
GO, GO, GO!
IT'S LIKE HIDE-AND-SEEK, BUT BETTER!
I'LL COMFORT YOU UNTIL WE FIND MISTER 8...
DON'T TOUCH ME.

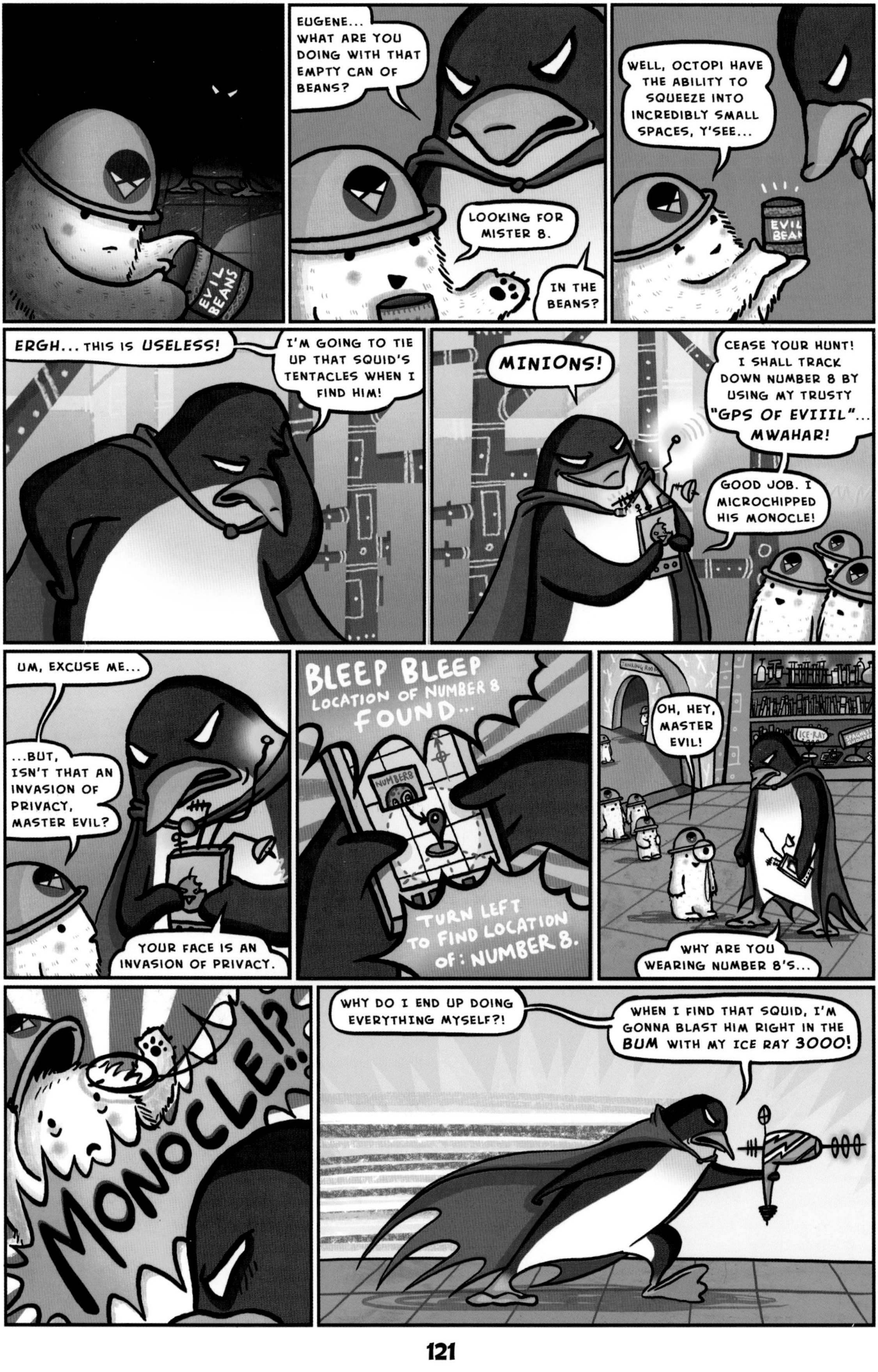
EVIL BEANS
EUGENE... WHAT ARE YOU DOING WITH THAT EMPTY CAN OF BEANS?
LOOKING FOR MISTER 8.
IN THE BEANS?
WELL, OCTOPI HAVE THE ABILITY TO SQUEEZE INTO INCREDIBLY SMALL SPACES, Y'SEE...
EVIL BEAN
ERGH... THIS IS USELESS!
I'M GOING TO TIE UP THAT SQUID'S TENTACLES WHEN I FIND HIM!
MINIONS!
CEASE YOUR HUNT! I SHALL TRACK DOWN NUMBER 8 BY USING MY TRUSTY "GPS OF EVIIIL"... MWAHAR!
GOOD JOB. I MICROCHIPPED HIS MONOCLE!
UM, EXCUSE ME...
...BUT, ISN'T THAT AN INVASION OF PRIVACY, MASTER EVIL?
YOUR FACE IS AN INVASION OF PRIVACY.
BLEEP BLEEP
LOCATION OF NUMBER 8
FOUND...
NUMBER8
TURN LEFT TO FIND LOCATION OF: NUMBER 8.
OH, HEY, MASTER EVIL!
ICE-RAY
WHY ARE YOU WEARING NUMBER 8'S...
MONOCLE!?!
WHY DO I END UP DOING EVERYTHING MYSELF?!
WHEN I FIND THAT SQUID, I'M GONNA BLAST HIM RIGHT IN THE BUM WITH MY ICE RAY 3000!

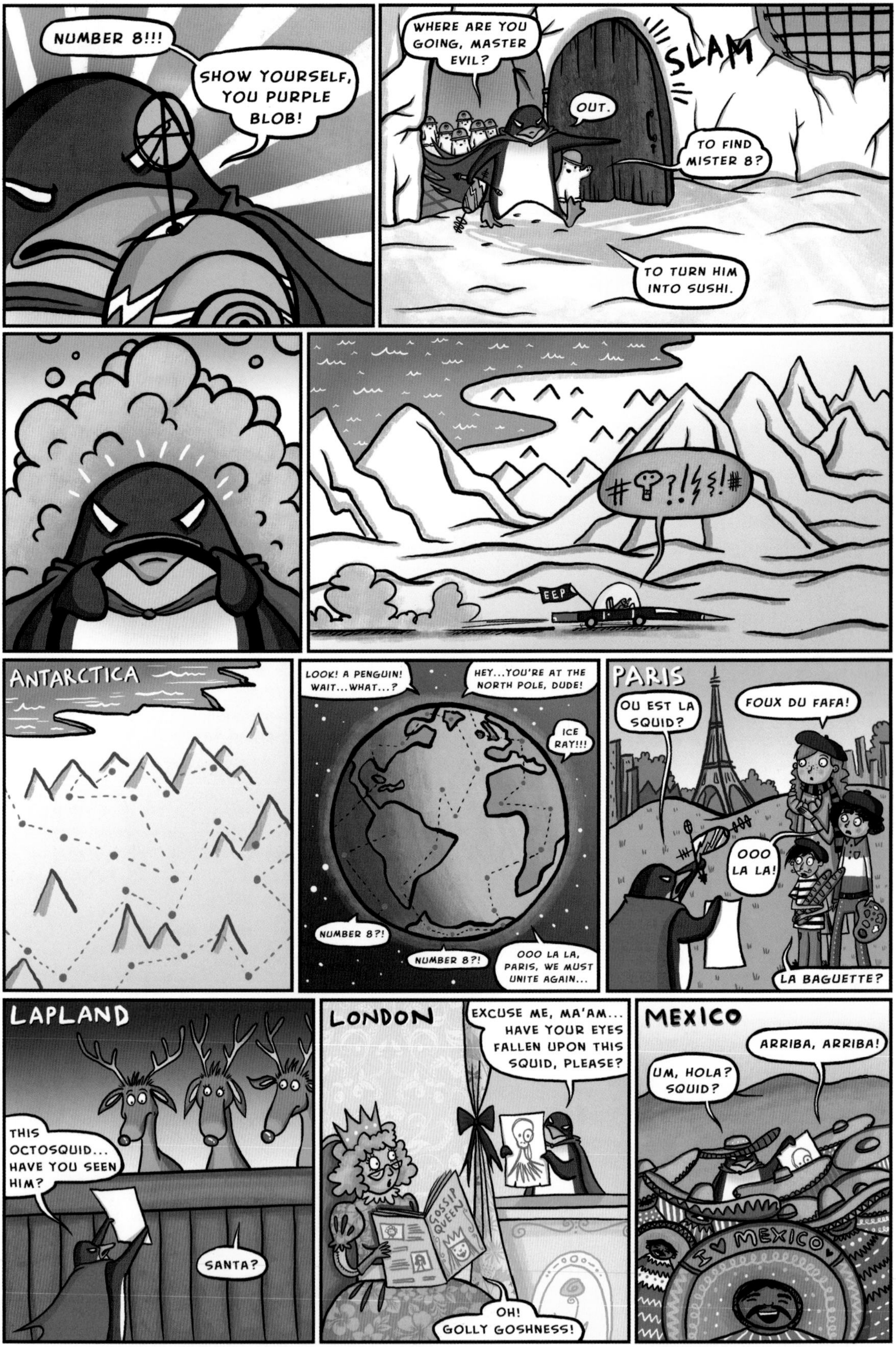
NUMBER 8!!!
SHOW YOURSELF, YOU PURPLE BLOB!
WHERE ARE YOU GOING, MASTER EVIL?
SLAM
OUT.
TO FIND MISTER 8?
TO TURN HIM INTO SUSHI.
EEP
ANTARCTICA
LOOK! A PENGUIN! WAIT...WHAT...?
HEY...YOU'RE AT THE NORTH POLE, DUDE!
ICE RAY!!!
NUMBER 8?!
NUMBER 8?!
OOO LA LA, PARIS, WE MUST UNITE AGAIN...
PARIS
OU EST LA SQUID?
FOUX DU FAFA!
OOO LA LA!
LA BAGUETTE?
LAPLAND
THIS OCTOSQUID... HAVE YOU SEEN HIM?
SANTA?
LONDON
EXCUSE ME, MA'AM... HAVE YOUR EYES FALLEN UPON THIS SQUID, PLEASE?
GOSSIP QUEEN
OH! GOLLY GOSHNESS!
MEXICO
ARRIBA, ARRIBA!
UM, HOLA? SQUID?
I ♥ MEXICO

THE NORTH POLE

I'VE LOOKED HIGH AND LOW, Y'SEE, AND HE'S NOWHERE! I'VE ALWAYS TREATED HIM WELL AND GIVEN HIM A TENTH OF MY DAILY CHOCOLATE BAR...

MOMMY, MY BRAIN IS CONFUSED. I THOUGHT POLAR BEARS AND PENGUINS WERE NEVER FOUND ON THE SAME CONTINENT...

Y'KNOW... I ALWAYS KINDA SAW HIM AS A BROTHER... LIKE A SQUID BROTHER.

THERE, THERE...

I HAVE NO IDEA WHAT'S GOING ON...

BACK IN ANTARCTICA...

SIGH.

LOCK OF EVIL

KEY OF EVIL

SURPRISE!

HAPPEE HATCH DAY

MERRY EGG DAY, EVIL MASTER!

HE LOOKS SURPRISED!

HAPPY HATCH DAY, SIR! I COULDN'T TELL THE MINIONS IN CASE THEY LET IT SLIP!

AND I DIDN'T WEAR MY MONO-CLE JUST IN CASE YOU'D PUT A TRACKER IN IT!!! HAR HAR! I'M ONLY JOKING!

AND THAT'S WHAT YOU DESERVE FOR WHAT YOU'VE PUT ME THROUGH!!!

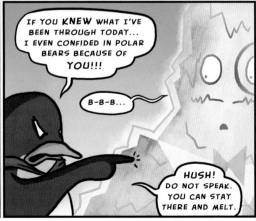

IF YOU KNEW WHAT I'VE BEEN THROUGH TODAY... I EVEN CONFIDED IN POLAR BEARS BECAUSE OF YOU!!!

B-B-B...

HUSH! DO NOT SPEAK. YOU CAN STAY THERE AND MELT.

123

THE END! MUAHAHAHA!

THIS BOOK IS BROUGHT TO YOU BY

# Squid Bits!

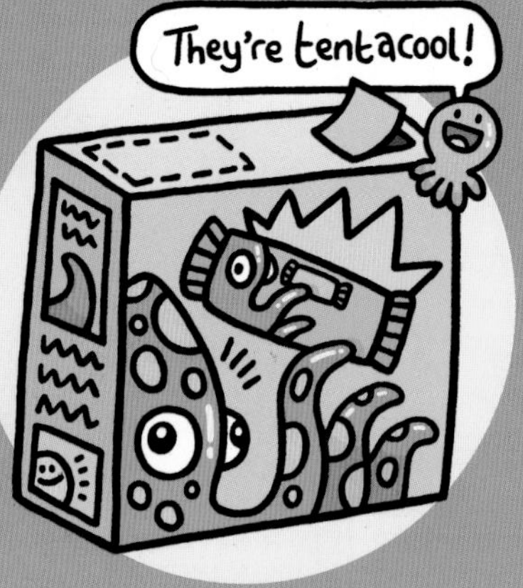

They're tentacool!


# EVERY DELICIOUS BOX OF SQUID BITS INCLUDES ALL THIS AND MORE...

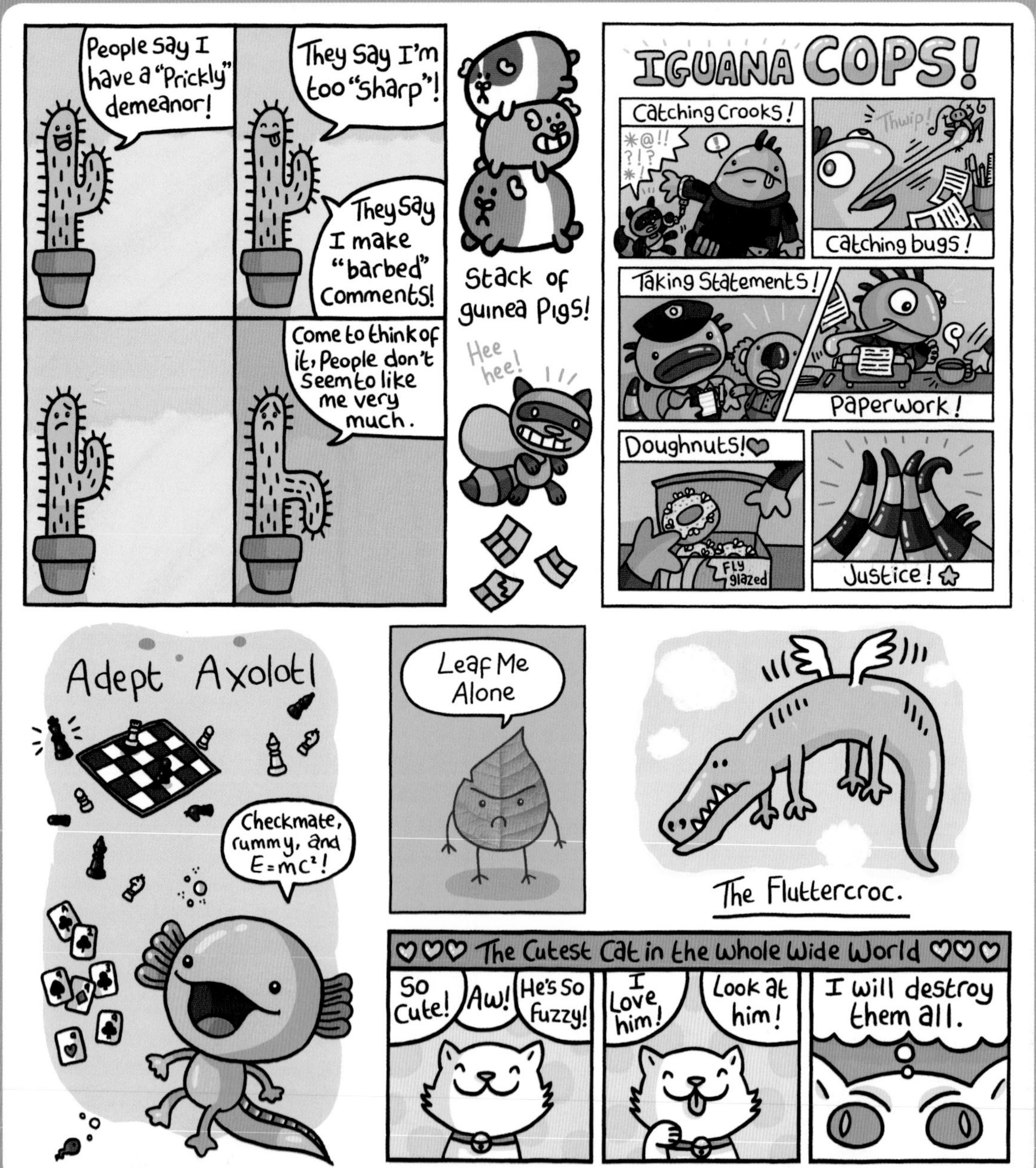

People say I have a "Prickly" demeanor!
They say I'm too "sharp"!
They Say I make "barbed" comments!
Come to think of it, People don't Seem to like me very much.
Stack of guinea Pigs!
Hee hee!
IGUANA COPS!
Catching Crooks!
*@!! ?!? *!
Thwip!
Catching bugs!
Taking Statements!
Paperwork!
Doughnuts!
FLY glazed
Justice!
Adept Axolotl
Checkmate, rummy, and E=mc²!
Leaf Me Alone
The Fluttercroc.
The Cutest Cat in the Whole Wide World
So Cute!
Aw!
He's So Fuzzy!
I Love him!
Look at him!
I will destroy them all.


by Jess Bradley

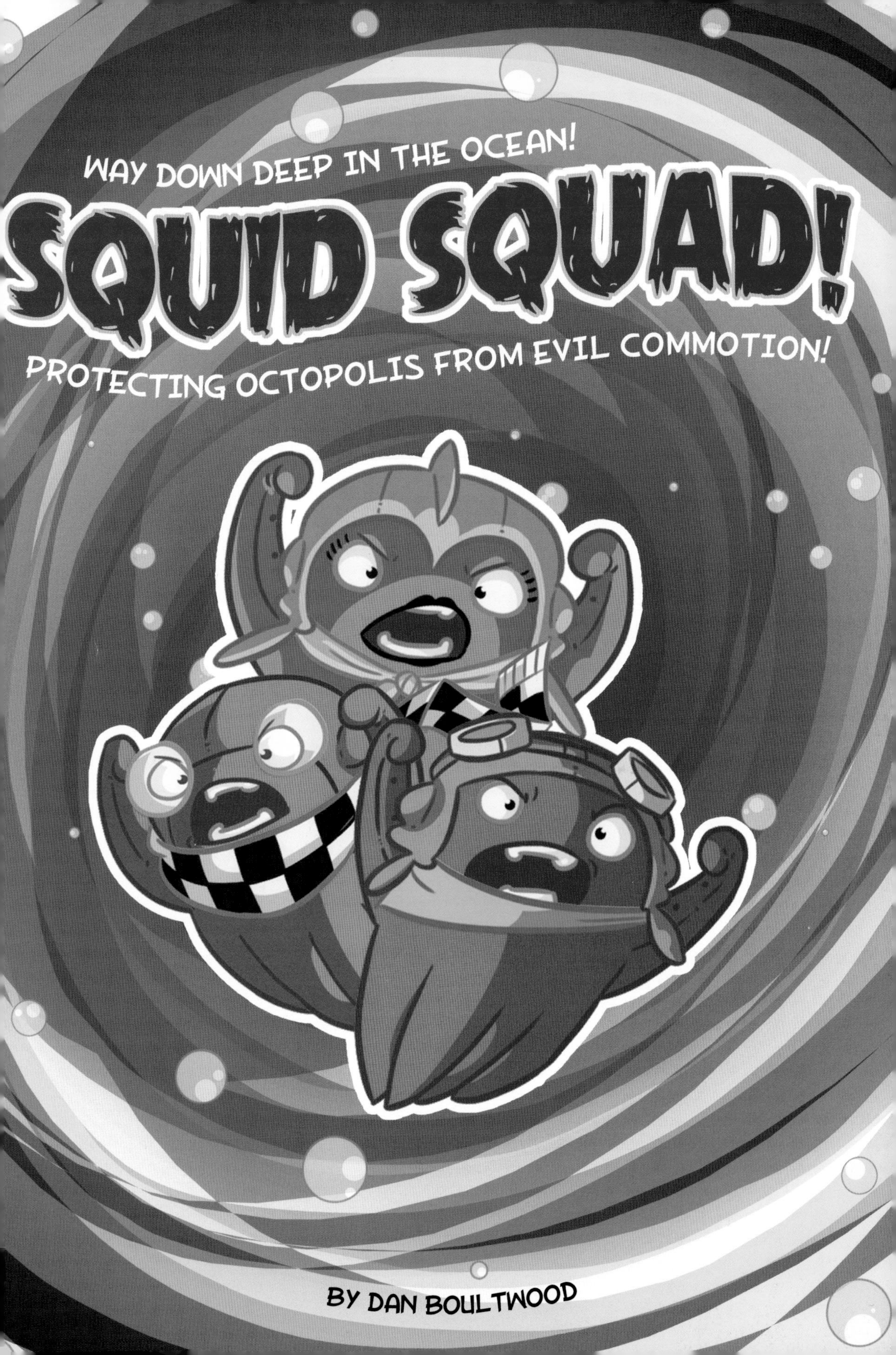
WAY DOWN DEEP IN THE OCEAN!
SQUID SQUAD!
PROTECTING OCTOPOLIS FROM EVIL COMMOTION!
BY DAN BOULTWOOD

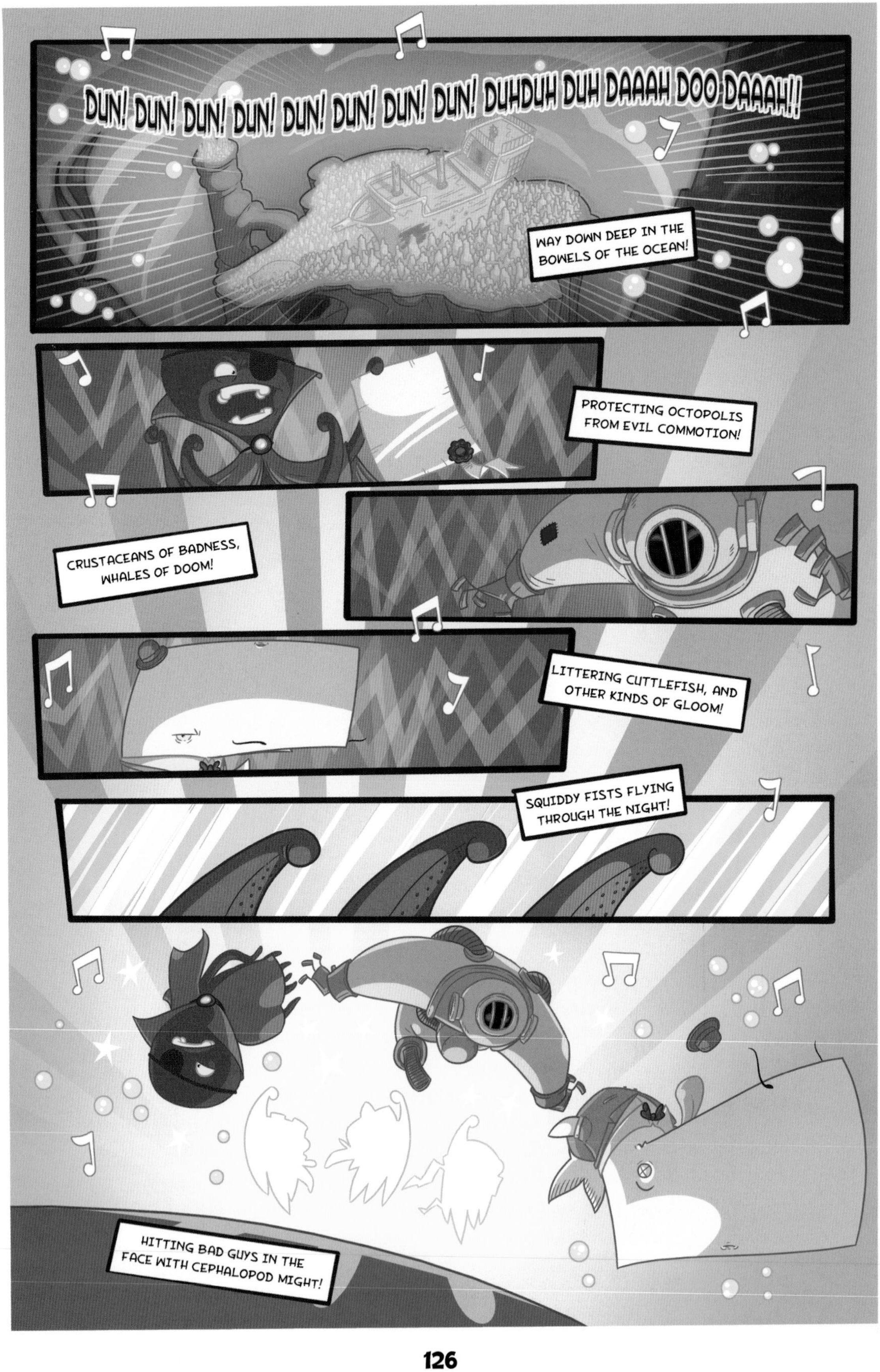
DUN! DUN! DUN! DUN! DUN! DUN! DUN! DUN! DUHDUH DUH DAAAH DOO DAAAH!!
WAY DOWN DEEP IN THE BOWELS OF THE OCEAN!
PROTECTING OCTOPOLIS FROM EVIL COMMOTION!
CRUSTACEANS OF BADNESS, WHALES OF DOOM!
LITTERING CUTTLEFISH, AND OTHER KINDS OF GLOOM!
SQUIDDY FISTS FLYING THROUGH THE NIGHT!
HITTING BAD GUYS IN THE FACE WITH CEPHALOPOD MIGHT!

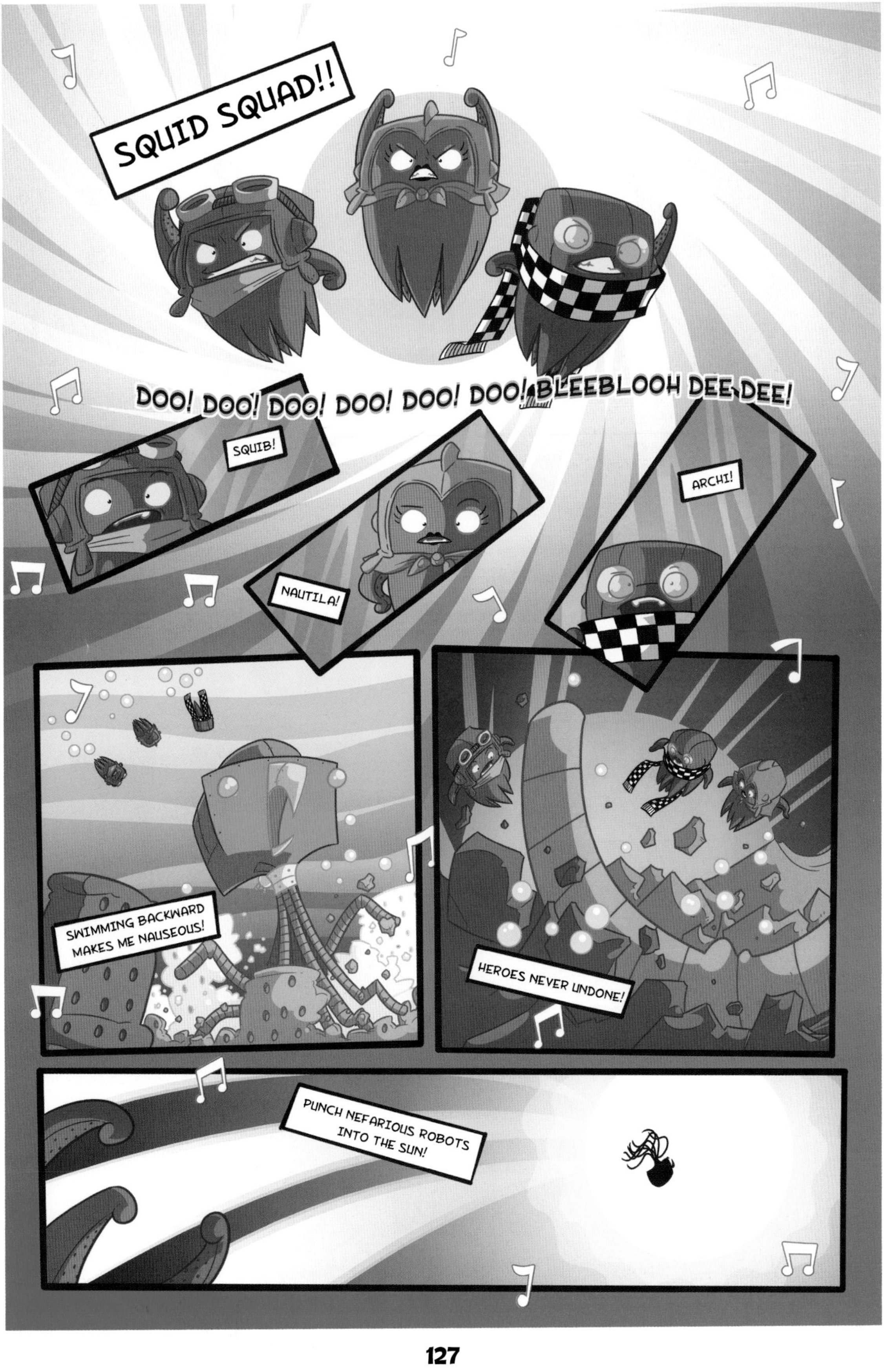
SQUID SQUAD!!
DOO! DOO! DOO! DOO! DOO! DOO! BLEEBLOOH DEE DEE!
SQUIB!
NAUTILA!
ARCHI!
SWIMMING BACKWARD MAKES ME NAUSEOUS!
HEROES NEVER UNDONE!
PUNCH NEFARIOUS ROBOTS INTO THE SUN!

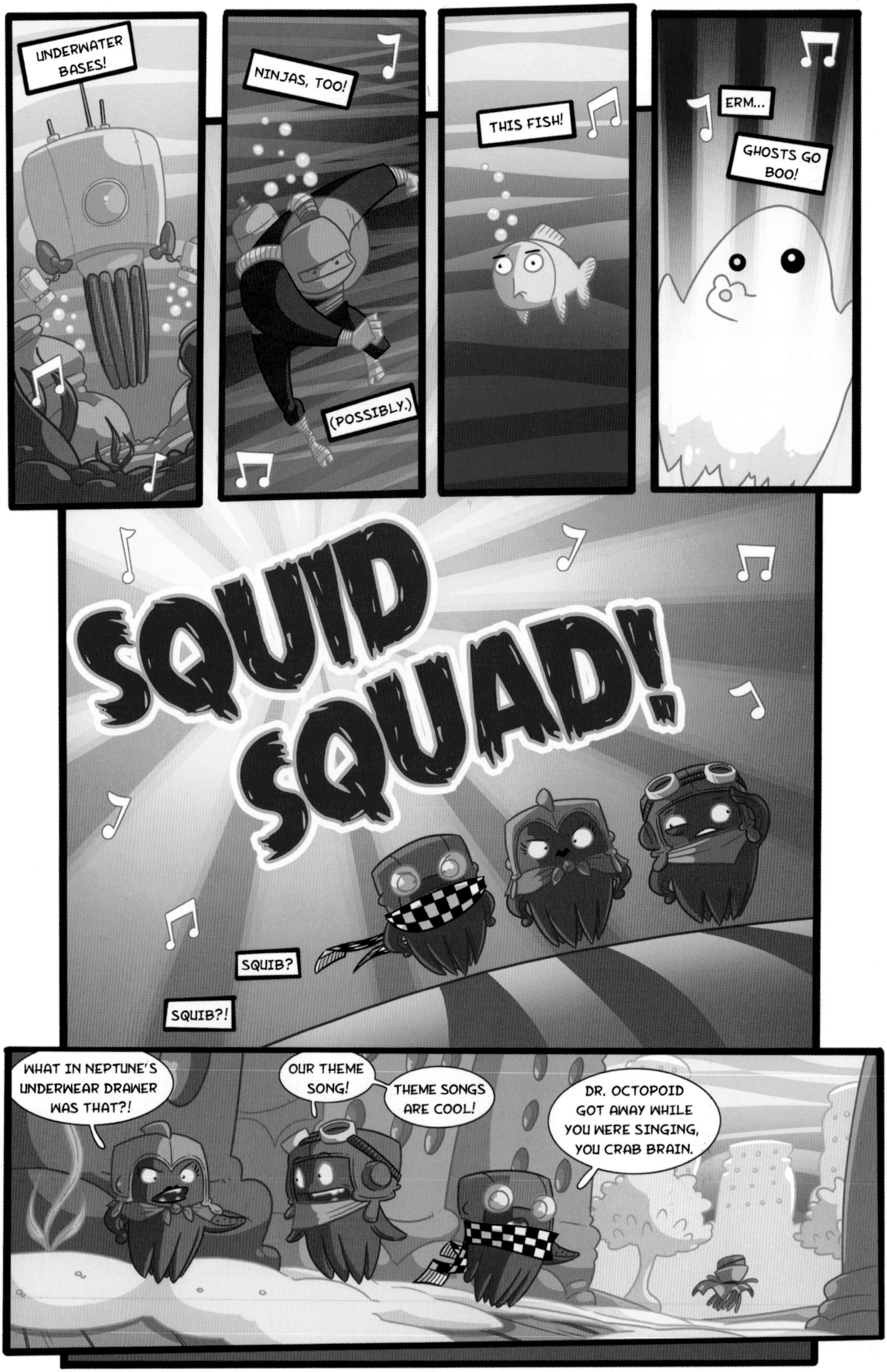
UNDERWATER BASES!
NINJAS, TOO!
(POSSIBLY.)
THIS FISH!
ERM...
GHOSTS GO BOO!
SQUID SQUAD!
SQUIB?
SQUIB?!
WHAT IN NEPTUNE'S UNDERWEAR DRAWER WAS THAT?!
OUR THEME SONG!
THEME SONGS ARE COOL!
DR. OCTOPOID GOT AWAY WHILE YOU WERE SINGING, YOU CRAB BRAIN.

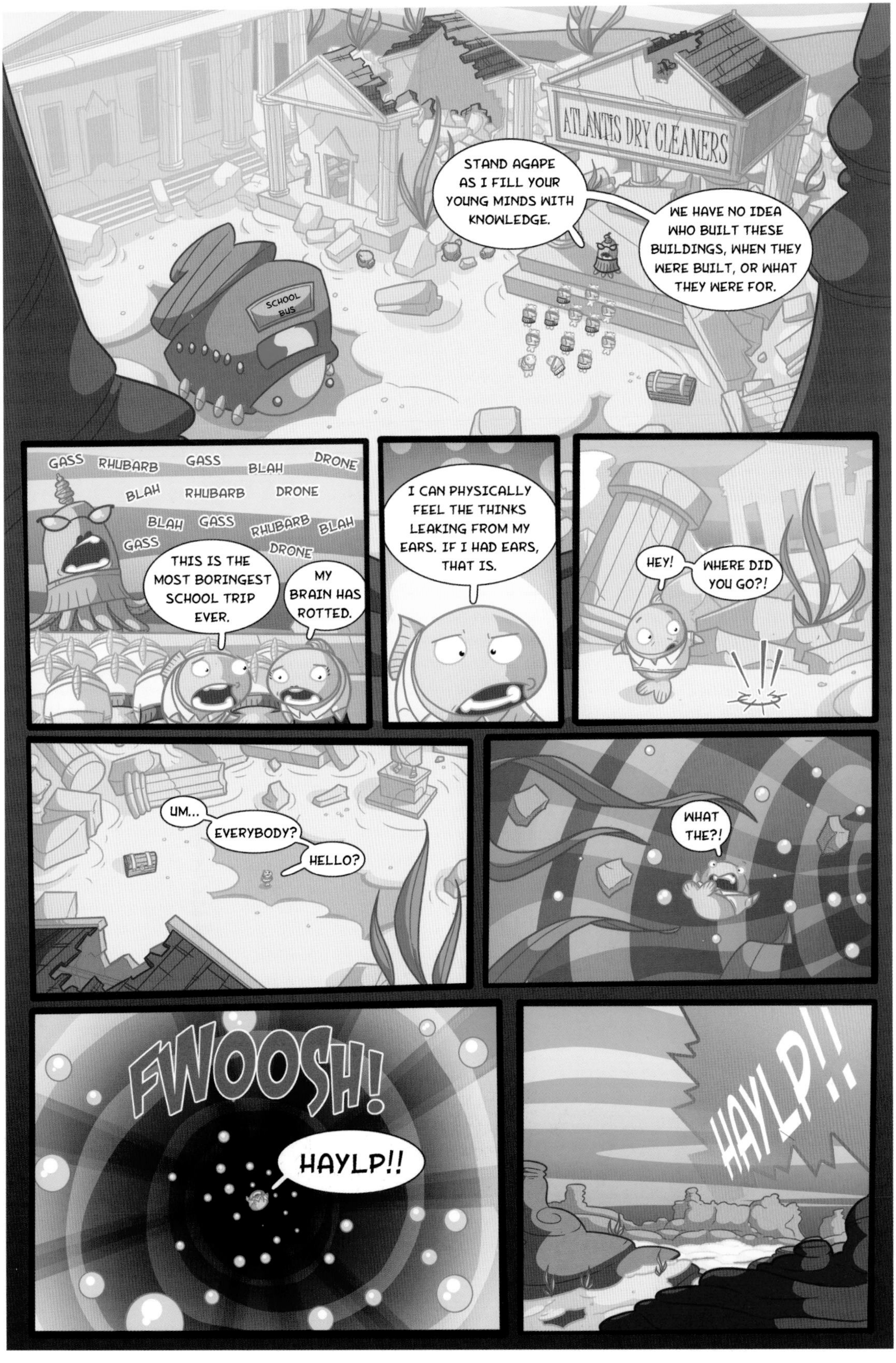
ATLANTIS DRY CLEANERS
SCHOOL BUS
STAND AGAPE AS I FILL YOUR YOUNG MINDS WITH KNOWLEDGE.
WE HAVE NO IDEA WHO BUILT THESE BUILDINGS, WHEN THEY WERE BUILT, OR WHAT THEY WERE FOR.
GASS RHUBARB GASS BLAH DRONE BLAH RHUBARB DRONE BLAH GASS RHUBARB BLAH GASS DRONE
THIS IS THE MOST BORINGEST SCHOOL TRIP EVER.
MY BRAIN HAS ROTTED.
I CAN PHYSICALLY FEEL THE THINKS LEAKING FROM MY EARS. IF I HAD EARS, THAT IS.
HEY!
WHERE DID YOU GO?!
UM...
EVERYBODY?
HELLO?
WHAT THE?!
FWOOSH!
HAYLP!!
HAYLP!!

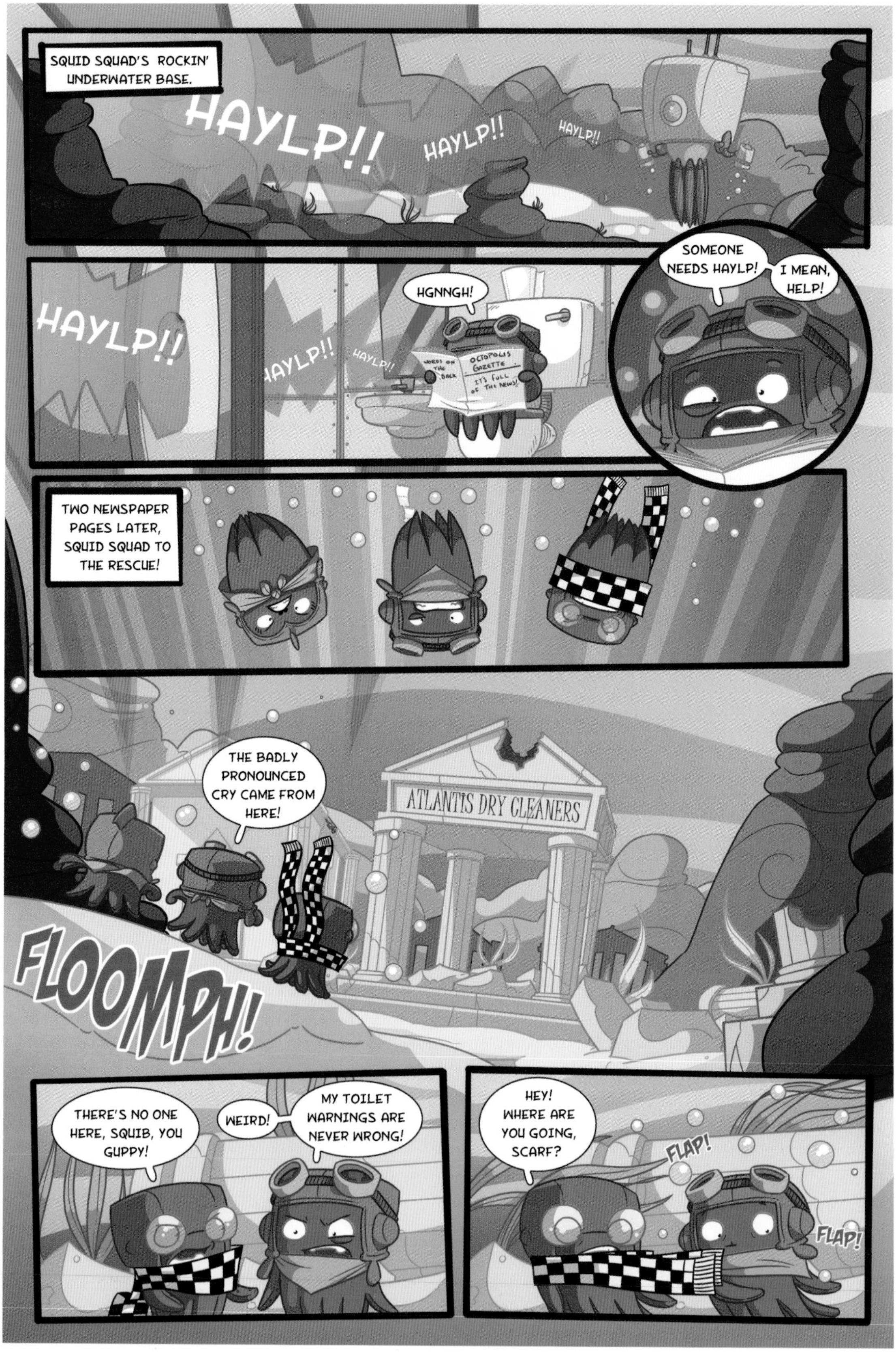
SQUID SQUAD'S ROCKIN' UNDERWATER BASE.
HAYLP!!
HAYLP!!
HAYLP!!
HAYLP!!
HAYLP!!
HAYLP!!
HGNNGH!
OCTOPOLIS GAZETTE
WORDS ON THE BACK
IT'S FULL OF THE NEWS!
SOMEONE NEEDS HAYLP!
I MEAN, HELP!
TWO NEWSPAPER PAGES LATER, SQUID SQUAD TO THE RESCUE!
THE BADLY PRONOUNCED CRY CAME FROM HERE!
ATLANTIS DRY CLEANERS
FLOOMPH!
THERE'S NO ONE HERE, SQUIB, YOU GUPPY!
WEIRD!
MY TOILET WARNINGS ARE NEVER WRONG!
HEY! WHERE ARE YOU GOING, SCARF?
FLAP!
FLAP!

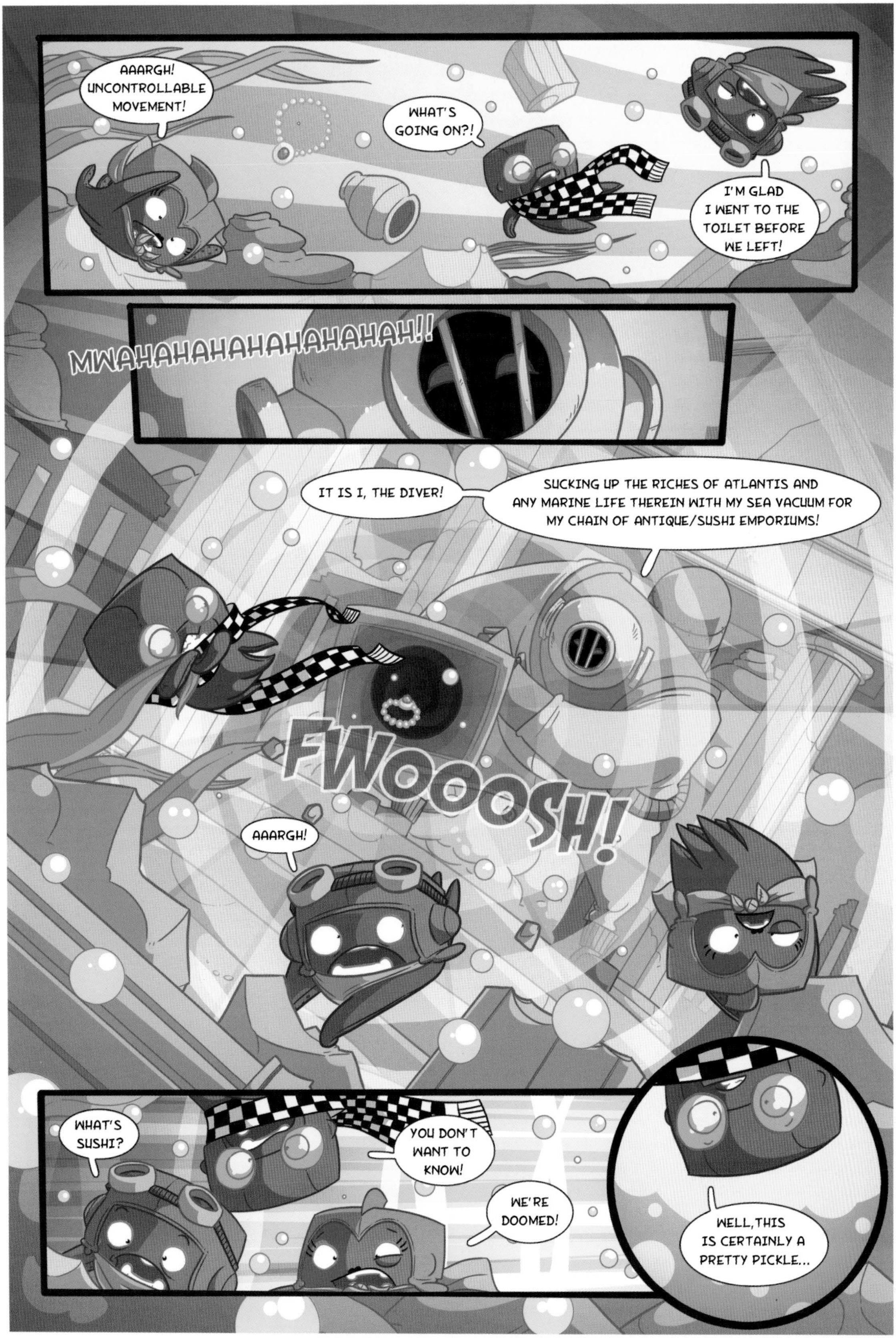
AAARGH! UNCONTROLLABLE MOVEMENT!
WHAT'S GOING ON?!
I'M GLAD I WENT TO THE TOILET BEFORE WE LEFT!
MWAHAHAHAHAHAHAHAH!!
IT IS I, THE DIVER!
SUCKING UP THE RICHES OF ATLANTIS AND ANY MARINE LIFE THEREIN WITH MY SEA VACUUM FOR MY CHAIN OF ANTIQUE/SUSHI EMPORIUMS!
FWOOOOSH!
AAARGH!
WHAT'S SUSHI?
YOU DON'T WANT TO KNOW!
WE'RE DOOMED!
WELL, THIS IS CERTAINLY A PRETTY PICKLE...

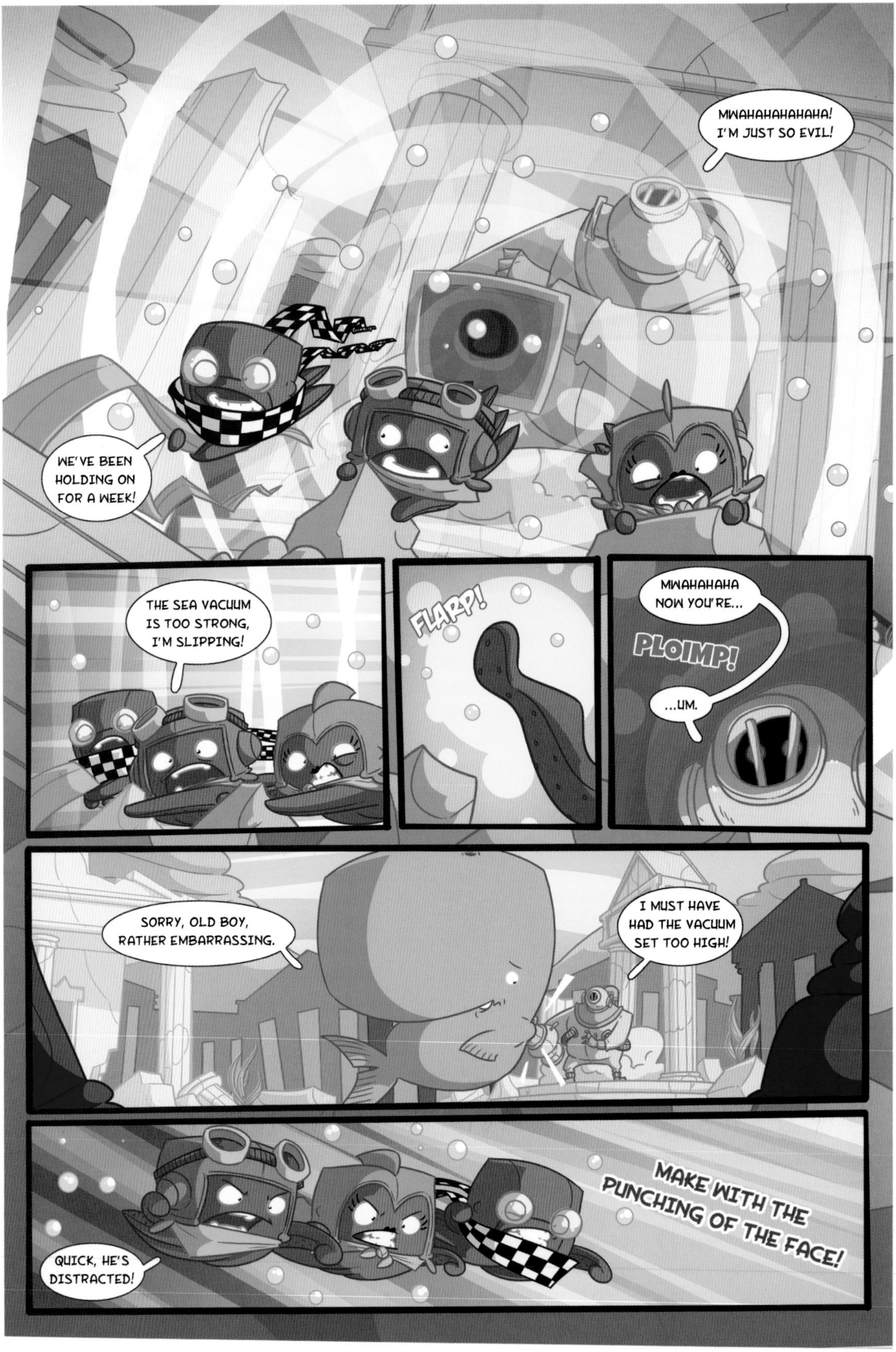
MWAHAHAHAHAHA! I'M JUST SO EVIL!
WE'VE BEEN HOLDING ON FOR A WEEK!
THE SEA VACUUM IS TOO STRONG, I'M SLIPPING!
FLARP!
MWAHAHAHA NOW YOU'RE...
PLOIMP!
...UM.
SORRY, OLD BOY, RATHER EMBARRASSING.
I MUST HAVE HAD THE VACUUM SET TOO HIGH!
QUICK, HE'S DISTRACTED!
MAKE WITH THE PUNCHING OF THE FACE!

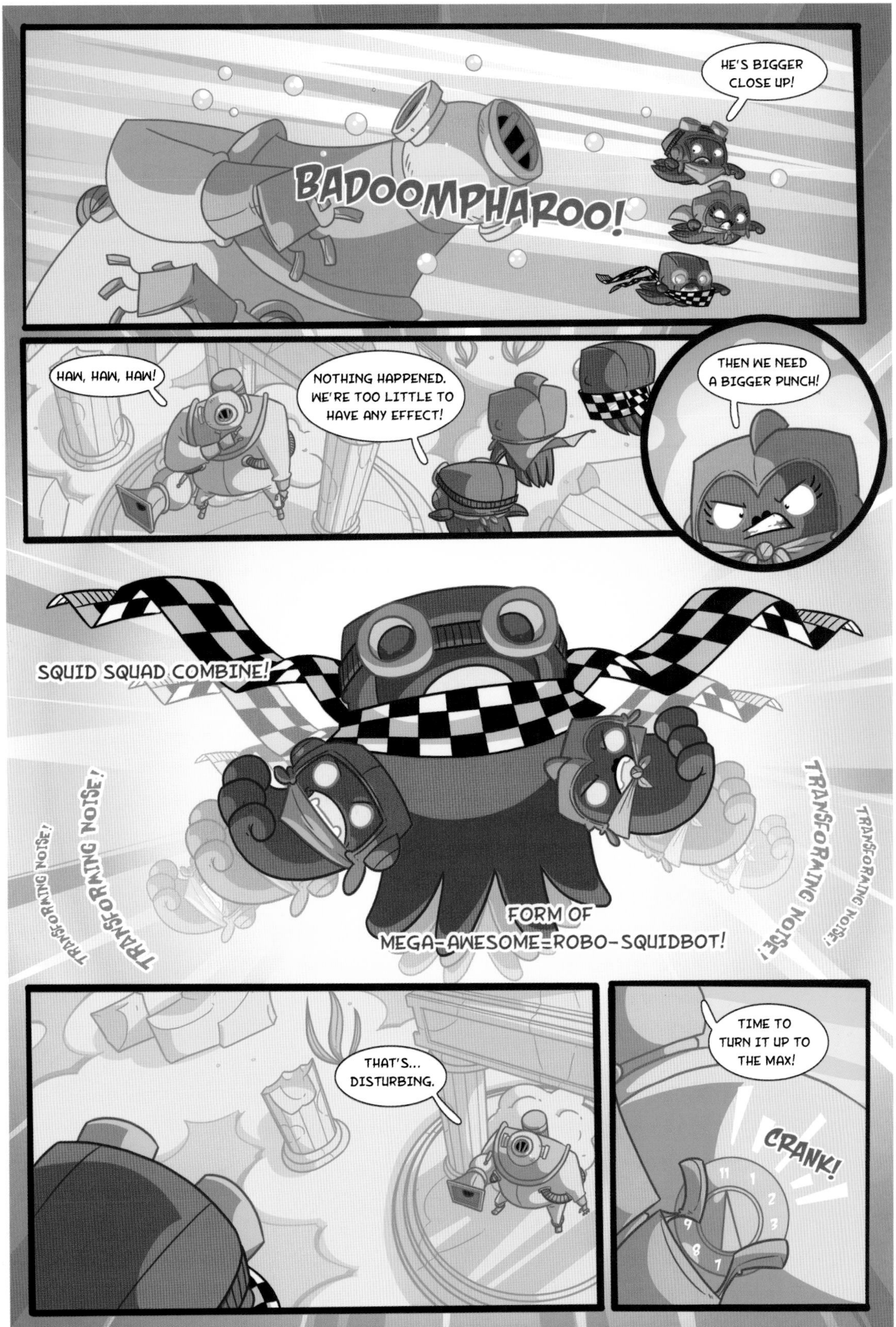
HE'S BIGGER CLOSE UP!
BADOOMPHAROO!
HAW, HAW, HAW!
NOTHING HAPPENED. WE'RE TOO LITTLE TO HAVE ANY EFFECT!
THEN WE NEED A BIGGER PUNCH!
SQUID SQUAD COMBINE!
TRANSFORMING NOISE!
TRANSFORMING NOISE!
TRANSFORMING NOISE!
TRANSFORMING NOISE!
FORM OF MEGA-AWESOME-ROBO-SQUIDBOT!
THAT'S... DISTURBING.
TIME TO TURN IT UP TO THE MAX!
CRANK!

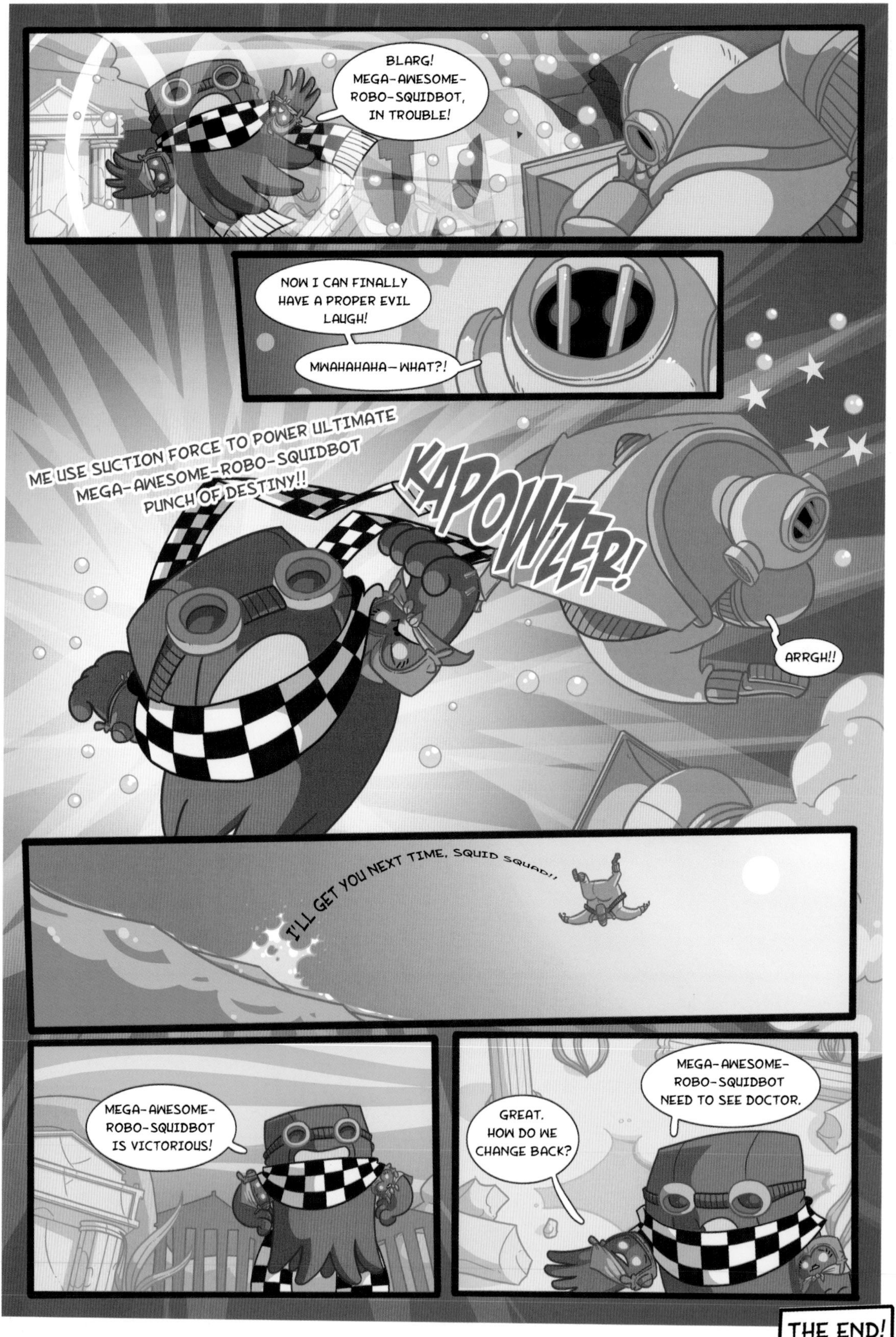
BLARG! MEGA-AWESOME-ROBO-SQUIDBOT, IN TROUBLE!
NOW I CAN FINALLY HAVE A PROPER EVIL LAUGH!
MWAHAHAHA—WHAT?!
ME USE SUCTION FORCE TO POWER ULTIMATE MEGA-AWESOME-ROBO-SQUIDBOT PUNCH OF DESTINY!!
KAPOWZER!
ARRGH!!
I'LL GET YOU NEXT TIME, SQUID SQUAD!!
MEGA-AWESOME-ROBO-SQUIDBOT IS VICTORIOUS!
GREAT. HOW DO WE CHANGE BACK?
MEGA-AWESOME-ROBO-SQUIDBOT NEED TO SEE DOCTOR.
THE END!

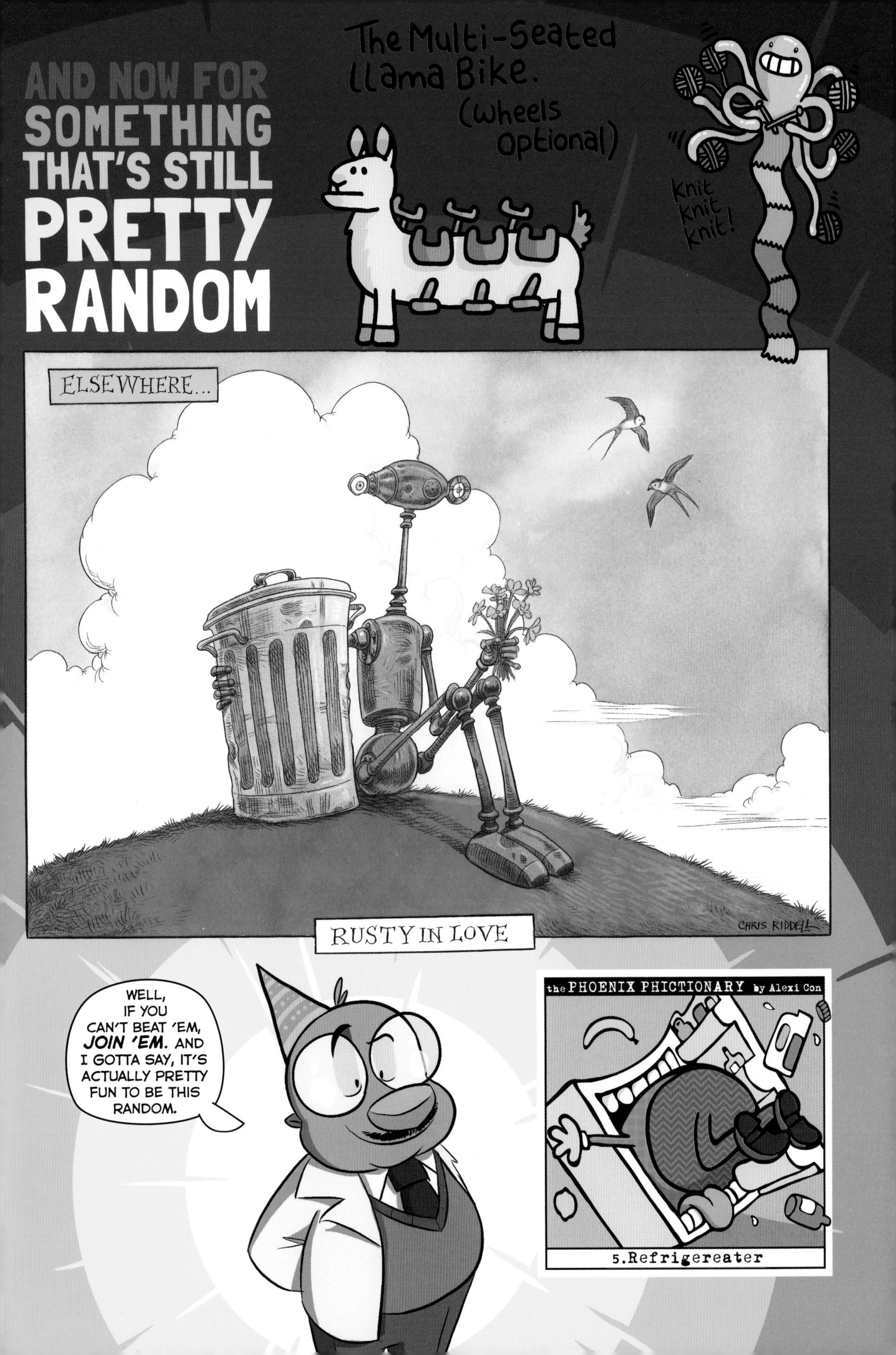
AND NOW FOR SOMETHING THAT'S STILL PRETTY RANDOM
The Multi-Seated llama Bike.
(wheels optional)
Knit knit knit!
ELSEWHERE...
CHRIS RIDDELL
RUSTY IN LOVE
WELL, IF YOU CAN'T BEAT 'EM, JOIN 'EM. AND I GOTTA SAY, IT'S ACTUALLY PRETTY FUN TO BE THIS RANDOM.
the PHOENIX PHICTIONARY by Alexi Con
5.Refrigereater

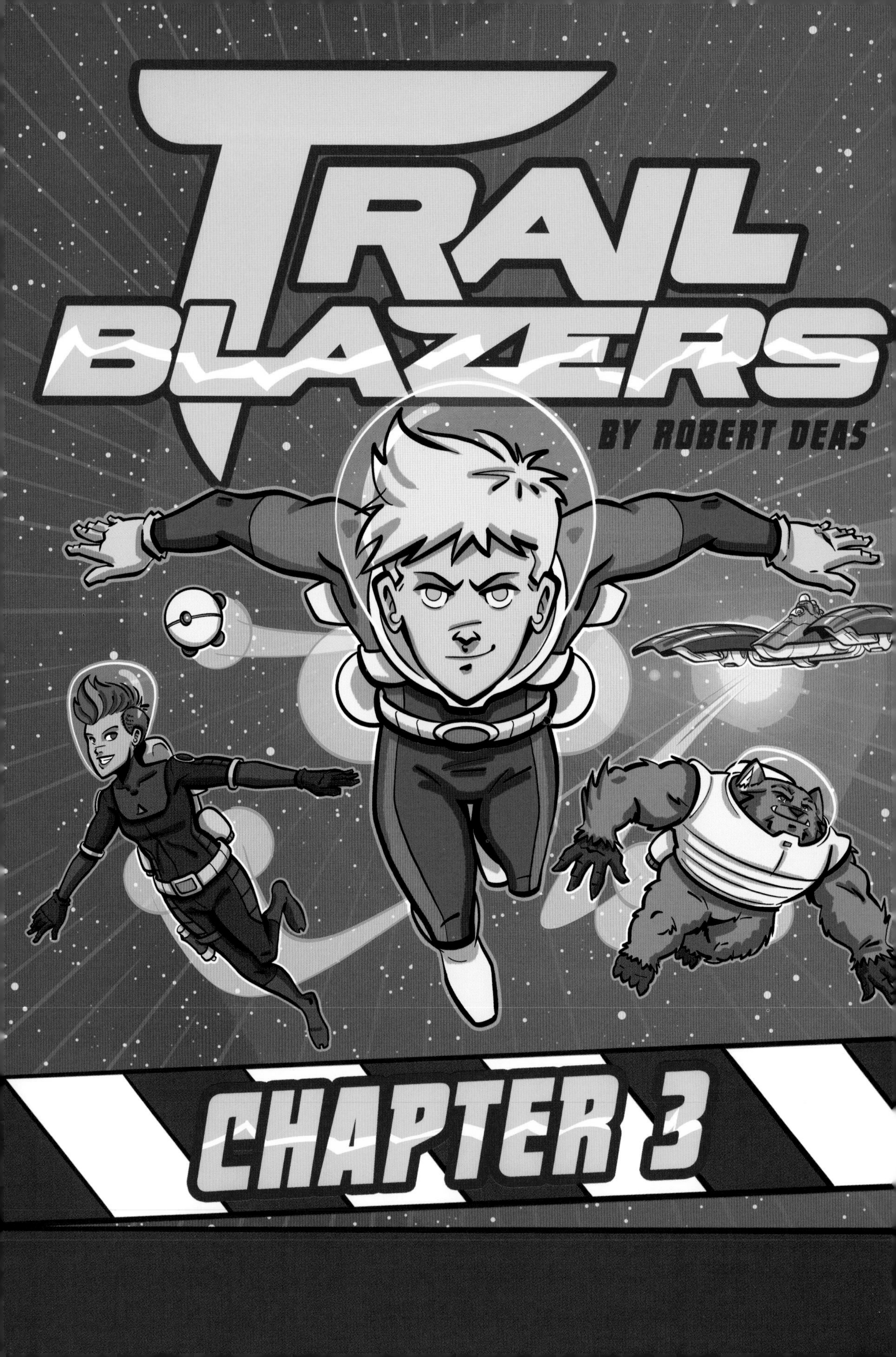
TRAIL BLAZERS
BY ROBERT DEAS
CHAPTER 3

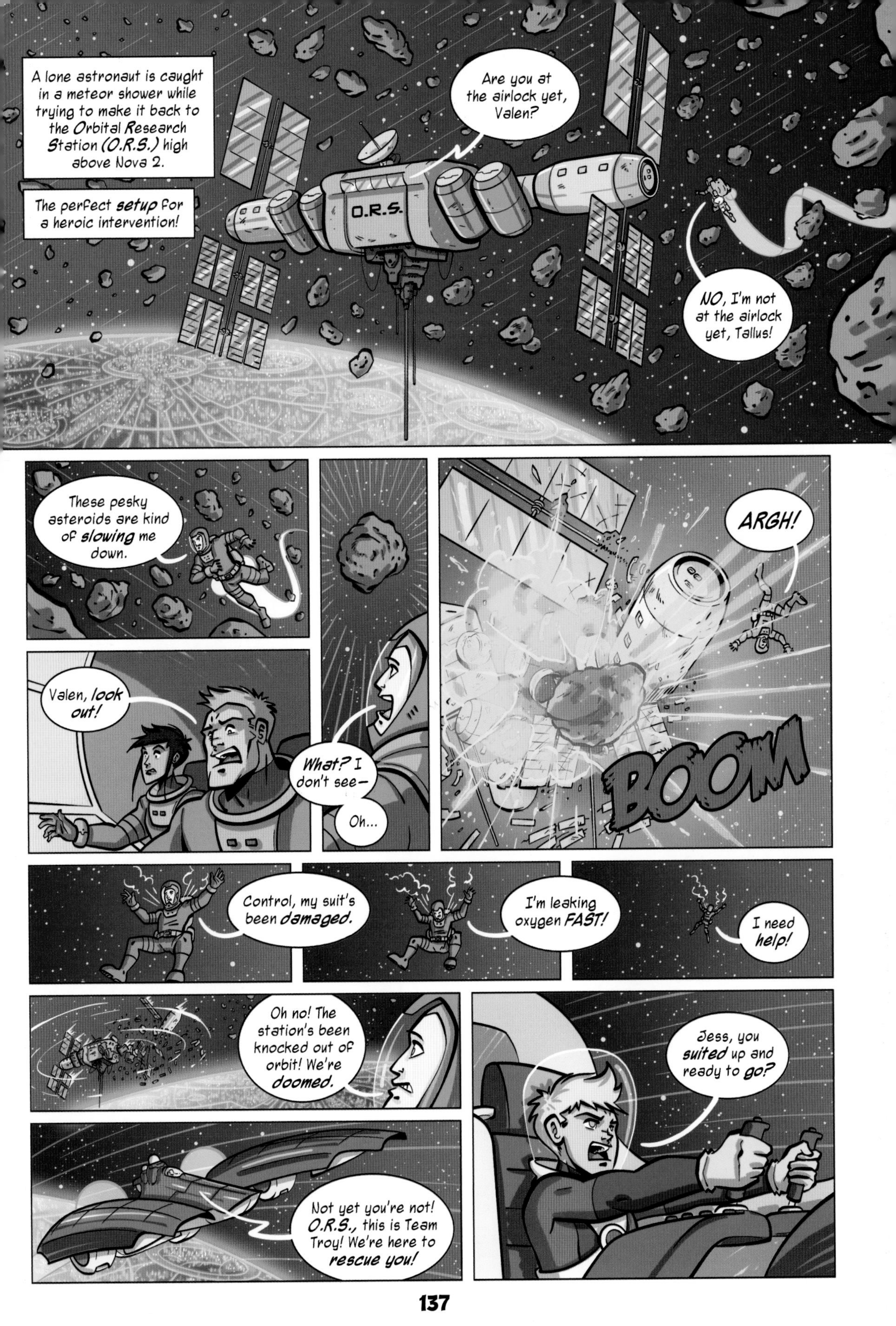
A lone astronaut is caught in a meteor shower while trying to make it back to the Orbital Research Station (O.R.S.) high above Nova 2.
The perfect setup for a heroic intervention!
O.R.S.
Are you at the airlock yet, Valen?
NO, I'm not at the airlock yet, Tallus!
These pesky asteroids are kind of slowing me down.
Valen, look out!
What? I don't see—
Oh...
ARGH!
BOOM
Control, my suit's been damaged.
I'm leaking oxygen FAST!
I need help!
Oh no! The station's been knocked out of orbit! We're doomed.
Jess, you suited up and ready to go?
Not yet you're not! O.R.S., this is Team Troy! We're here to rescue you!

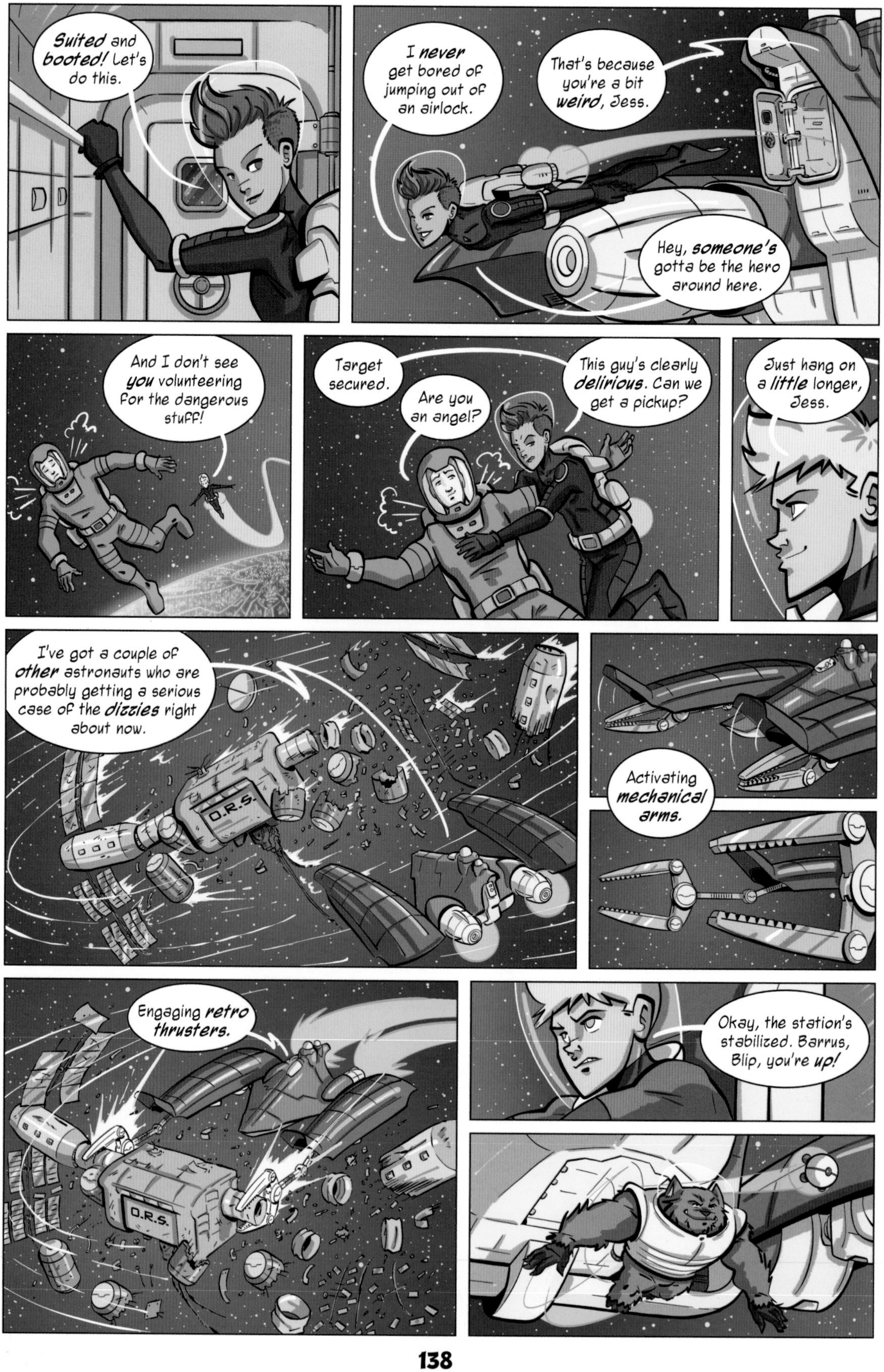
Suited and booted! Let's do this.
I never get bored of jumping out of an airlock.
That's because you're a bit weird, Jess.
Hey, someone's gotta be the hero around here.
And I don't see you volunteering for the dangerous stuff!
Target secured.
Are you an angel?
This guy's clearly delirious. Can we get a pickup?
Just hang on a little longer, Jess.
I've got a couple of other astronauts who are probably getting a serious case of the dizzies right about now.
O.R.S.
Activating mechanical arms.
Engaging retro thrusters.
O.R.S.
Okay, the station's stabilized. Barrus, Blip, you're up!

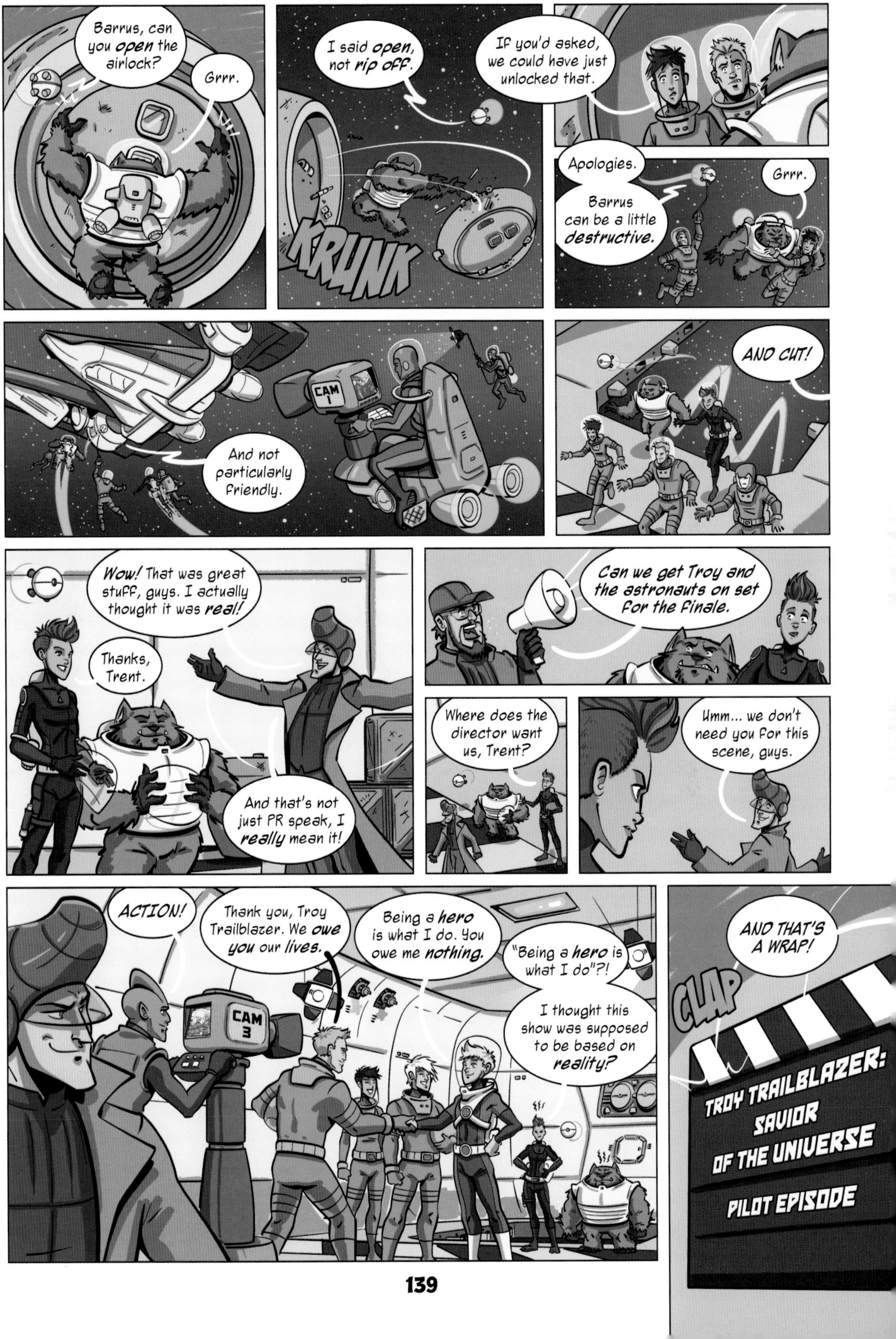
Barrus, can you open the airlock?
Grrr.
I said open, not rip off.
KRUNK
If you'd asked, we could have just unlocked that.
Apologies.
Barrus can be a little destructive.
Grrr.
CAM 1
And not particularly friendly.
AND CUT!
Wow! That was great stuff, guys. I actually thought it was real!
Thanks, Trent.
And that's not just PR speak, I really mean it!
Can we get Troy and the astronauts on set for the finale.
Where does the director want us, Trent?
Umm... we don't need you for this scene, guys.
ACTION!
CAM 3
Thank you, Troy Trailblazer. We owe you our lives.
Being a hero is what I do. You owe me nothing.
"Being a hero is what I do"?!
I thought this show was supposed to be based on reality?
AND THAT'S A WRAP!
CLAP
TROY TRAILBLAZER: SAVIOR OF THE UNIVERSE
PILOT EPISODE

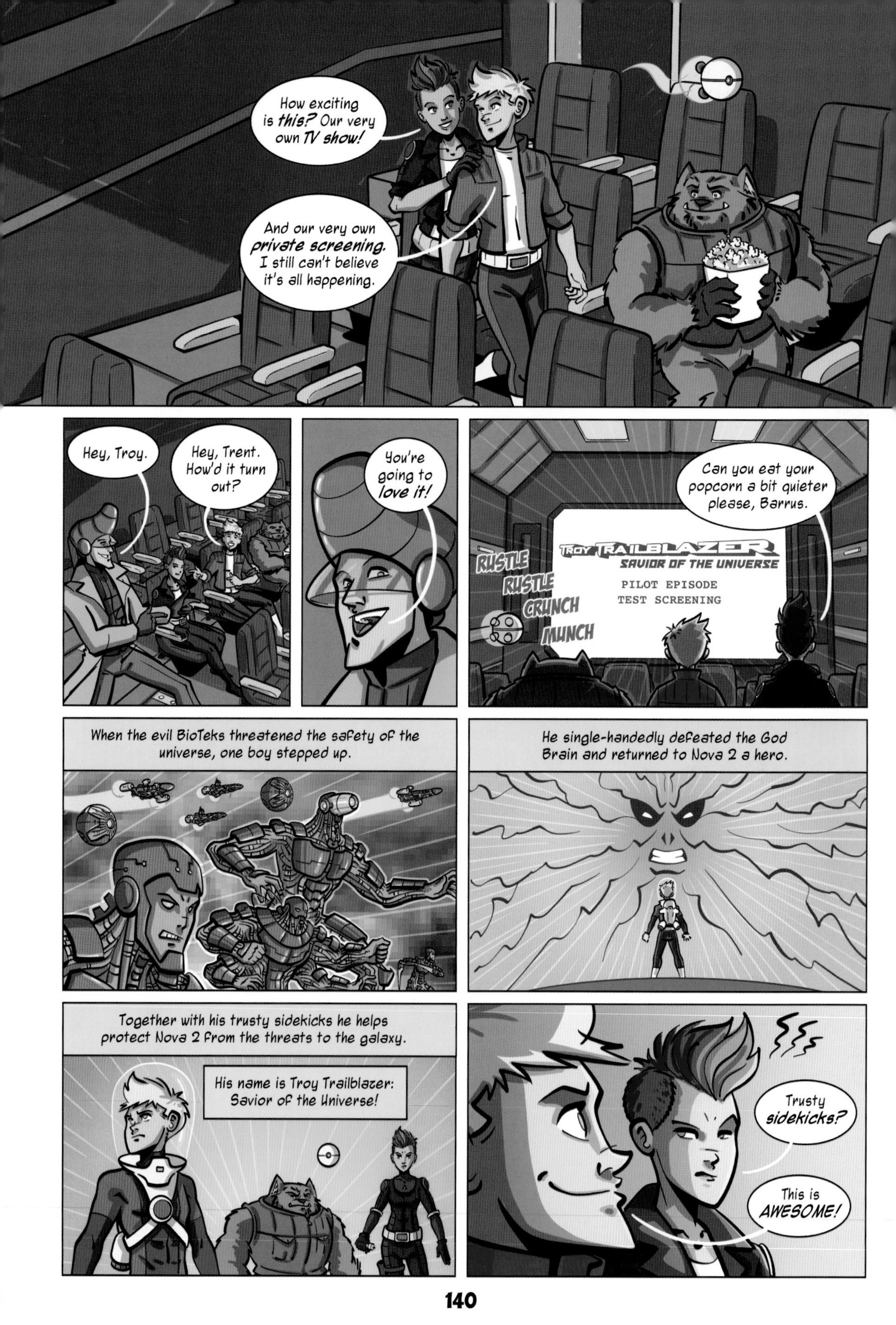
How exciting is this? Our very own TV show!
And our very own private screening. I still can't believe it's all happening.
Hey, Troy.
Hey, Trent. How'd it turn out?
You're going to love it!
Can you eat your popcorn a bit quieter please, Barrus.
TROY TRAILBLAZER SAVIOR OF THE UNIVERSE
PILOT EPISODE
TEST SCREENING
RUSTLE
RUSTLE
CRUNCH
MUNCH
When the evil BioTeks threatened the safety of the universe, one boy stepped up.
He single-handedly defeated the God Brain and returned to Nova 2 a hero.
Together with his trusty sidekicks he helps protect Nova 2 from the threats to the galaxy.
His name is Troy Trailblazer: Savior of the Universe!
Trusty sidekicks?
This is AWESOME!

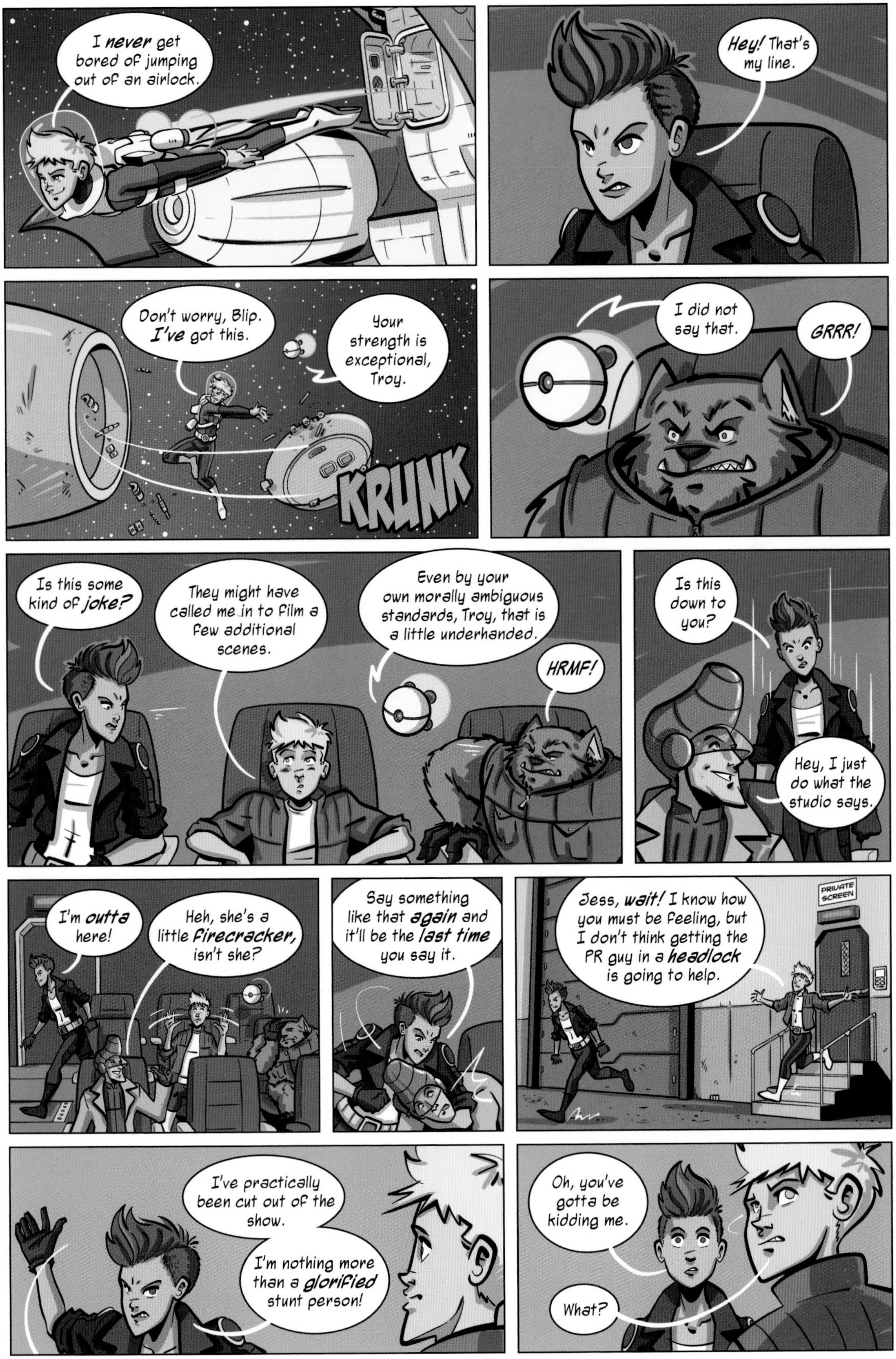
I never get bored of jumping out of an airlock.
Hey! That's my line.
Don't worry, Blip. I've got this.
Your strength is exceptional, Troy.
KRUNK
I did not say that.
GRRR!
Is this some kind of joke?
They might have called me in to film a few additional scenes.
Even by your own morally ambiguous standards, Troy, that is a little underhanded.
HRMF!
Is this down to you?
Hey, I just do what the studio says.
I'm outta here!
Heh, she's a little firecracker, isn't she?
Say something like that again and it'll be the last time you say it.
PRIVATE SCREEN
Jess, wait! I know how you must be feeling, but I don't think getting the PR guy in a headlock is going to help.
I've practically been cut out of the show.
I'm nothing more than a glorified stunt person!
Oh, you've gotta be kidding me.
What?

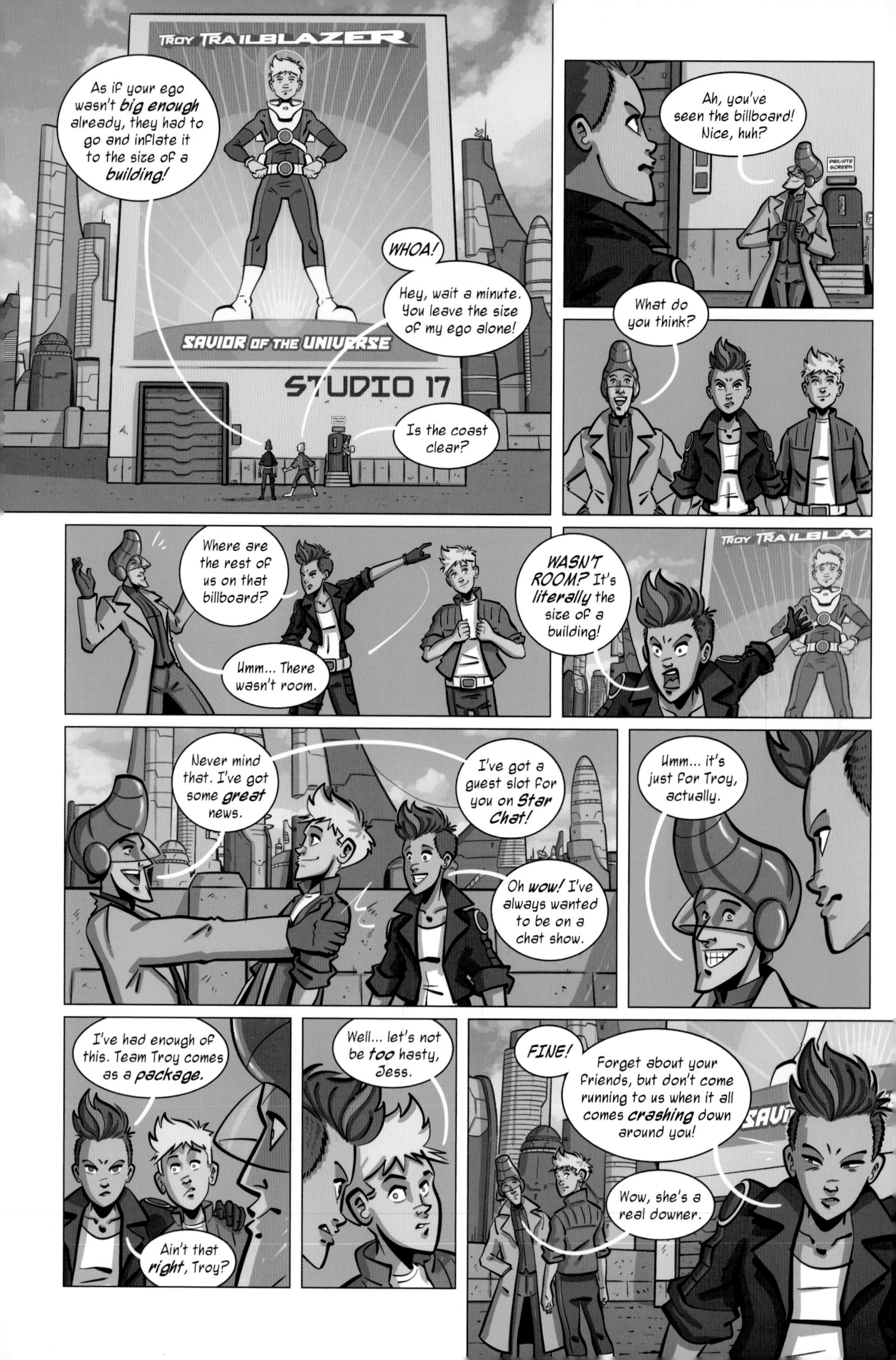
TROY TRAILBLAZER
As if your ego wasn't big enough already, they had to go and inflate it to the size of a building!
SAVIOR OF THE UNIVERSE
STUDIO 17
WHOA!
Hey, wait a minute. You leave the size of my ego alone!
Is the coast clear?
Ah, you've seen the billboard! Nice, huh?
PRIVATE SCREEN
What do you think?
Where are the rest of us on that billboard?
Umm... There wasn't room.
TROY TRAILBLAZ
WASN'T ROOM? It's literally the size of a building!
Never mind that. I've got some great news.
I've got a guest slot for you on Star Chat!
Oh wow! I've always wanted to be on a chat show.
Umm... it's just for Troy, actually.
I've had enough of this. Team Troy comes as a package.
Ain't that right, Troy?
Well... let's not be too hasty, Jess.
FINE!
Forget about your friends, but don't come running to us when it all comes crashing down around you!
Wow, she's a real downer.

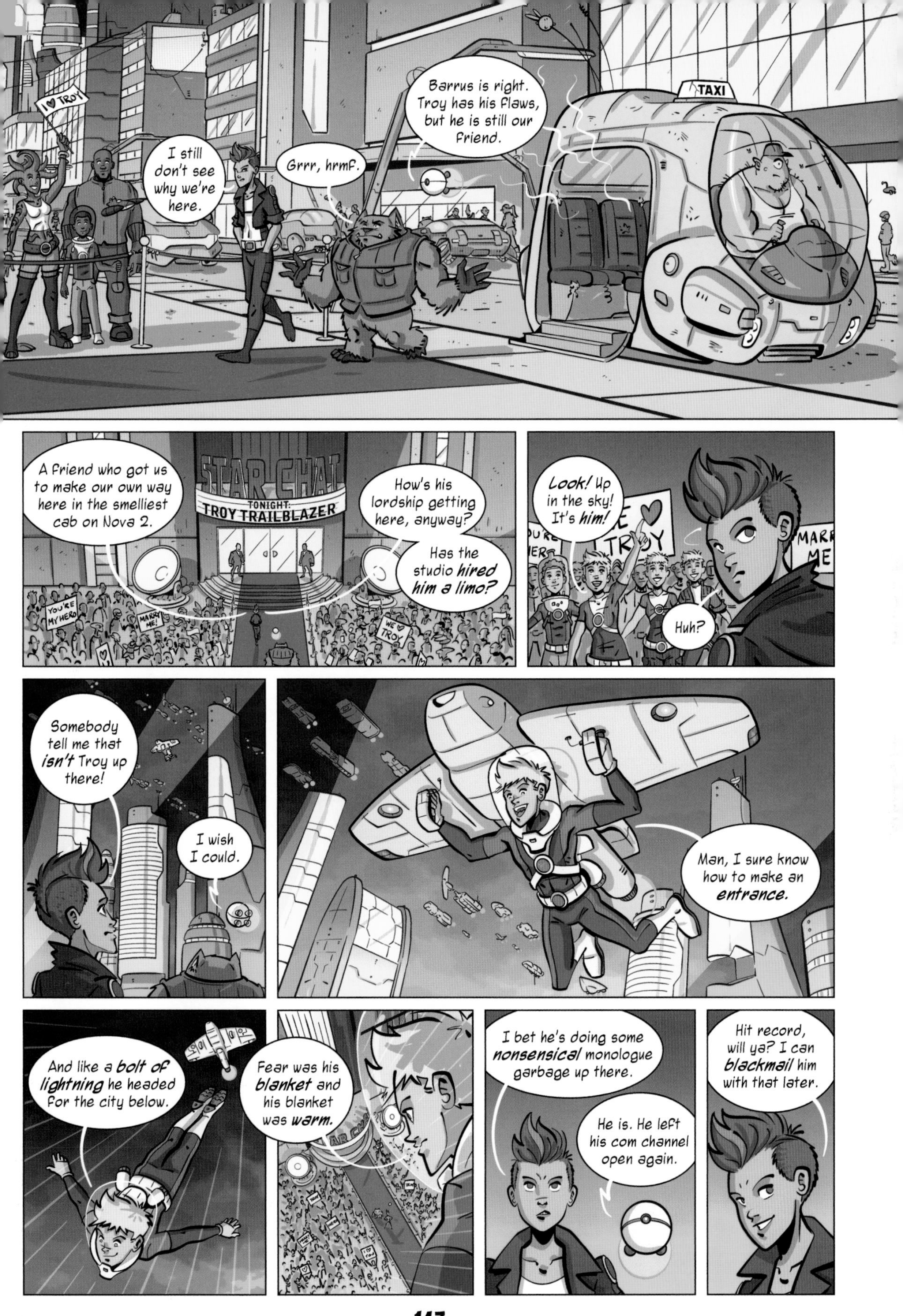
I ♥ TROY
TAXI
I still don't see why we're here.
Grrr, hrmf.
Barrus is right. Troy has his flaws, but he is still our friend.
STAR CHAT
TONIGHT: TROY TRAILBLAZER
A friend who got us to make our own way here in the smelliest cab on Nova 2.
How's his lordship getting here, anyway?
Has the studio hired him a limo?
YOU'RE MY HERO
MARRY ME!
WE ♥ TROY
Look! Up in the sky! It's him!
Huh?
MARRY ME
Somebody tell me that isn't Troy up there!
I wish I could.
Man, I sure know how to make an entrance.
And like a bolt of lightning he headed for the city below.
Fear was his blanket and his blanket was warm.
I bet he's doing some nonsensical monologue garbage up there.
He is. He left his com channel open again.
Hit record, will ya? I can blackmail him with that later.

Oh? Hey, Jess. I didn't think you were coming.

I *wasn't.*

So why the change of heart?

It's *called* being a friend.

*Remember* what that's like?

How about a round of applause, folks! *WHAT AN ENTRANCE!*

Hi, everyone!

CLAP  HOORAY  YAY

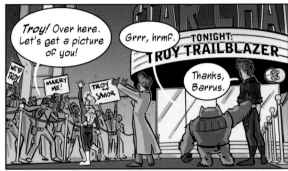

*Troy!* Over here. Let's get a picture of you!

Grrr, hrmf.

TONIGHT: TROY TRAILBLAZER

WE ♥ TROY

MARRY ME!

TROY ME SAVIOR

Thanks, Barrus.

Later...

Okay, now make sure the interview is about *you.*

If your team comes up, they're *just* sidekicks.

I don't think they're going to like that.

STARS

Whose interview is this? *YOURS!*

Don't choose sentimentality over a chance at the *big time.*

You got that, *champ?*

So, what's it *like* to be a hero, Troy?

Oh I don't know about that...

Don't be so *modest!* After saving the universe from the BioTeks, you returned to Nova 2 a *hero.*

The BioTeks were evil. I did what had to be done.

And we're *very* grateful. So tell me about you and your team.

Umm...

Well, they're really more... *sidekicks.*

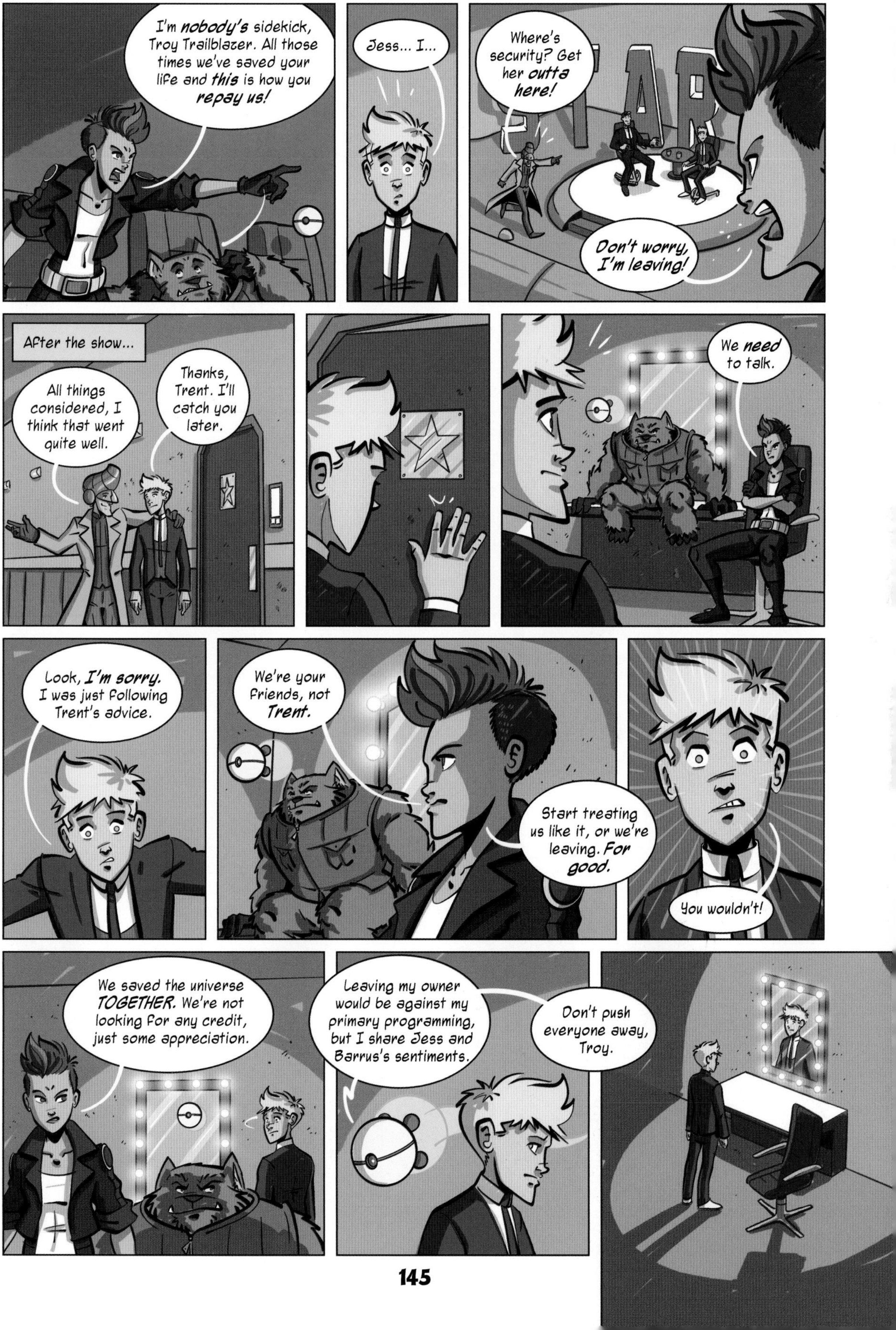
I'm nobody's sidekick, Troy Trailblazer. All those times we've saved your life and this is how you repay us!
Jess... I...
Where's security? Get her outta here!
Don't worry, I'm leaving!
After the show...
All things considered, I think that went quite well.
Thanks, Trent. I'll catch you later.
We need to talk.
Look, I'm sorry. I was just following Trent's advice.
We're your friends, not Trent.
Start treating us like it, or we're leaving. For good.
You wouldn't!
We saved the universe TOGETHER. We're not looking for any credit, just some appreciation.
Leaving my owner would be against my primary programming, but I share Jess and Barrus's sentiments.
Don't push everyone away, Troy.

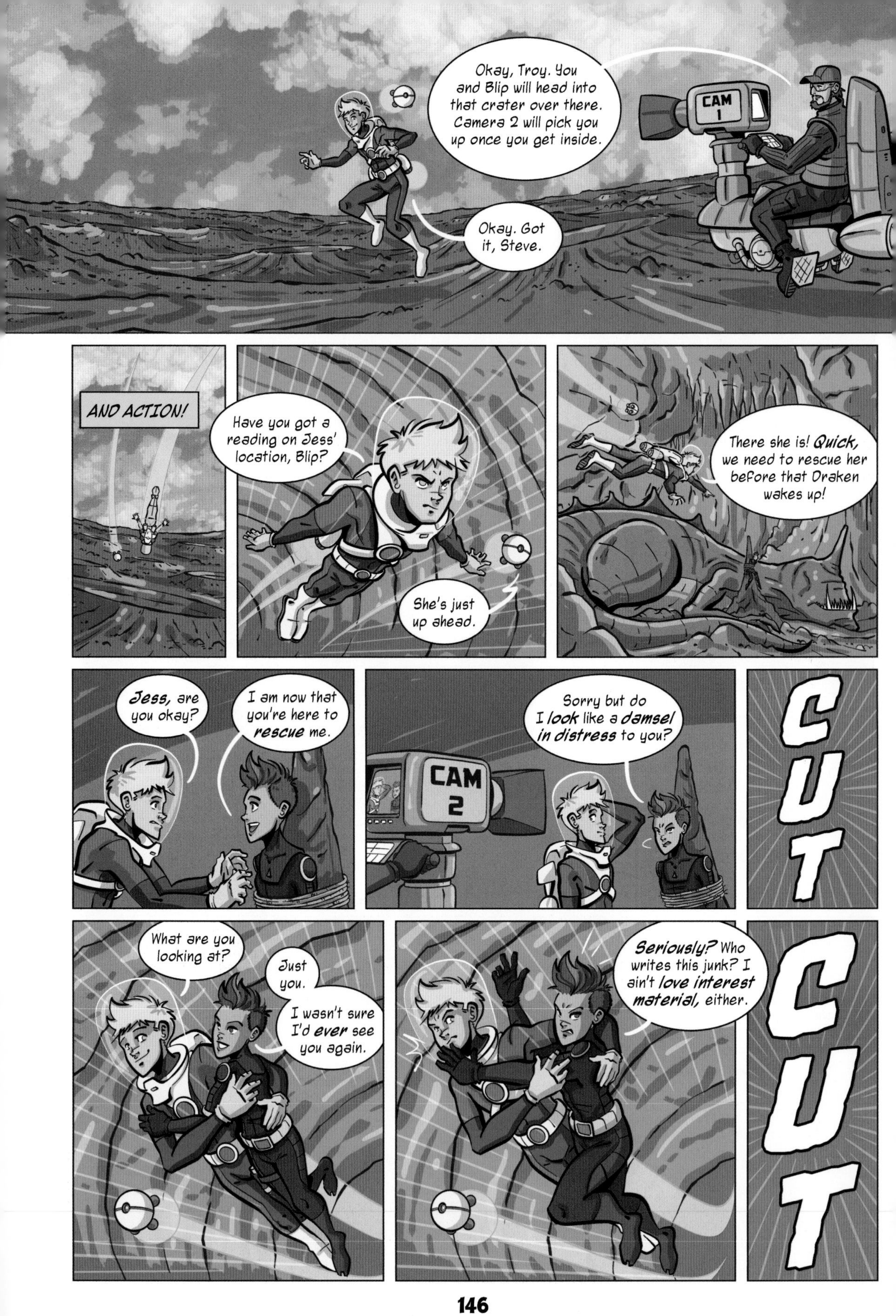

Okay, Troy. You and Blip will head into that crater over there. Camera 2 will pick you up once you get inside.
CAM 1
Okay. Got it, Steve.
AND ACTION!
Have you got a reading on Jess' location, Blip?
She's just up ahead.
There she is! Quick, we need to rescue her before that Draken wakes up!
Jess, are you okay?
I am now that you're here to rescue me.
CAM 2
Sorry but do I look like a damsel in distress to you?
CUT
What are you looking at?
Just you.
I wasn't sure I'd ever see you again.
Seriously? Who writes this junk? I ain't love interest material, either.
CUT

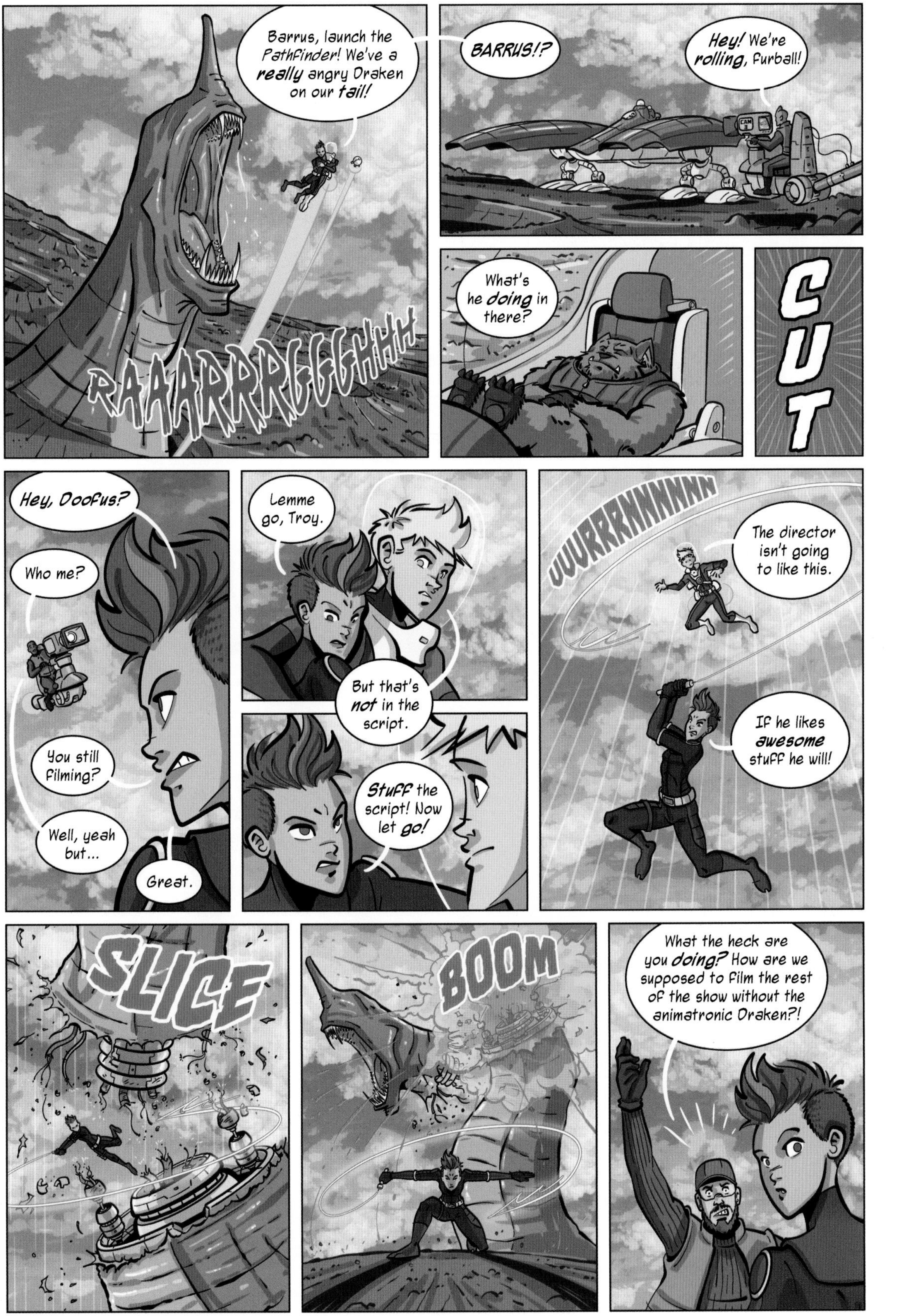
Barrus, launch the Pathfinder! We've a really angry Draken on our tail!
RAAARRRGGHHH
BARRUS!?
Hey! We're rolling, Furball!
What's he doing in there?
CUT
Hey, Doofus?
Who me?
You still filming?
Well, yeah but...
Great.
Lemme go, Troy.
But that's not in the script.
Stuff the script! Now let go!
UUURRRNNNNNN
The director isn't going to like this.
If he likes awesome stuff he will!
SLICE
BOOM
What the heck are you doing? How are we supposed to film the rest of the show without the animatronic Draken?!

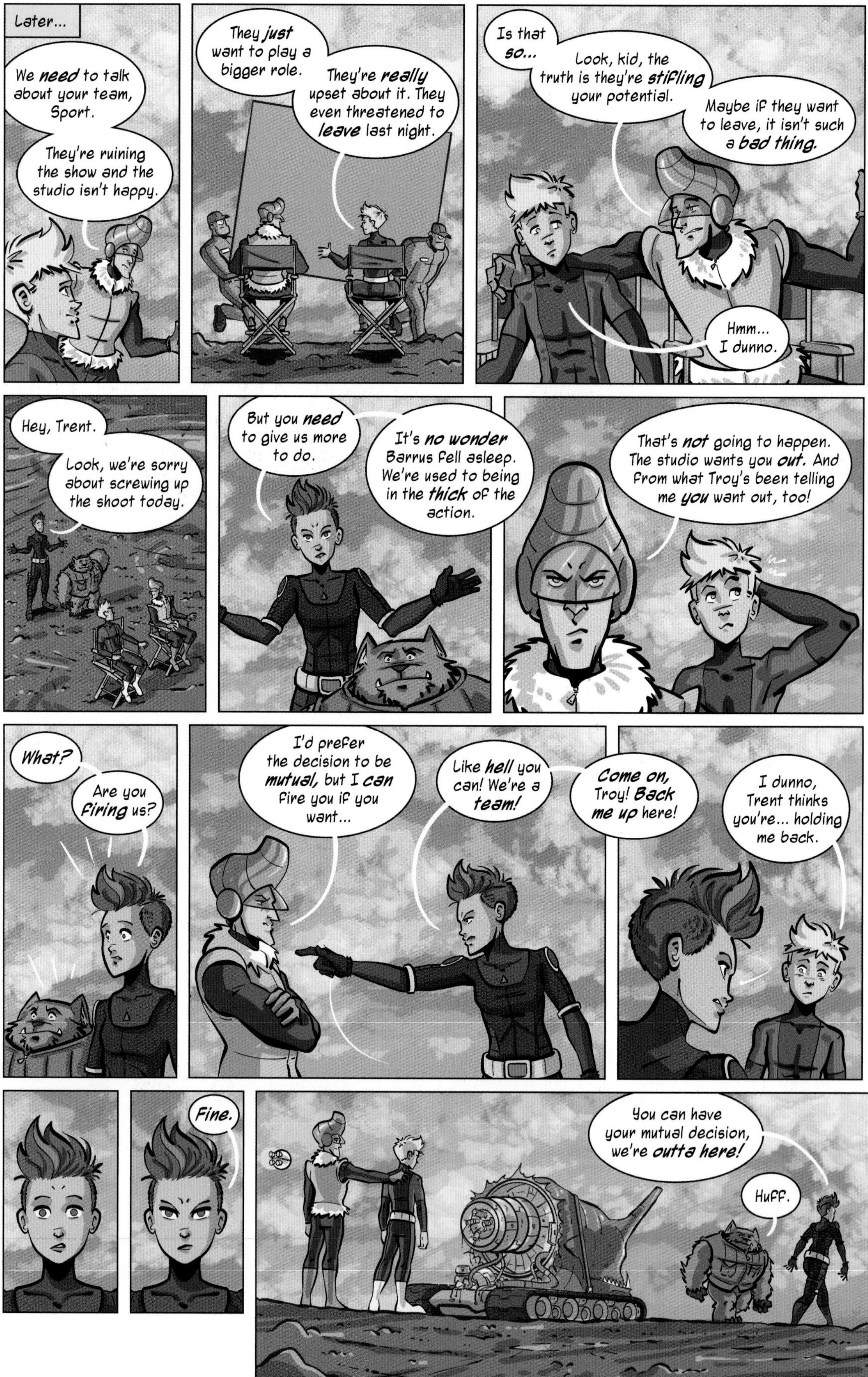
Later...
We need to talk about your team, Sport.
They're ruining the show and the studio isn't happy.
They just want to play a bigger role.
They're really upset about it. They even threatened to leave last night.
Is that so...
Look, kid, the truth is they're stifling your potential.
Maybe if they want to leave, it isn't such a bad thing.
Hmm... I dunno.
Hey, Trent.
Look, we're sorry about screwing up the shoot today.
But you need to give us more to do.
It's no wonder Barrus fell asleep. We're used to being in the thick of the action.
That's not going to happen. The studio wants you out. And from what Troy's been telling me you want out, too!
What?
Are you firing us?
I'd prefer the decision to be mutual, but I can fire you if you want...
Like hell you can! We're a team!
Come on, Troy! Back me up here!
I dunno, Trent thinks you're... holding me back.
Fine.
You can have your mutual decision, we're outta here!
Huff.

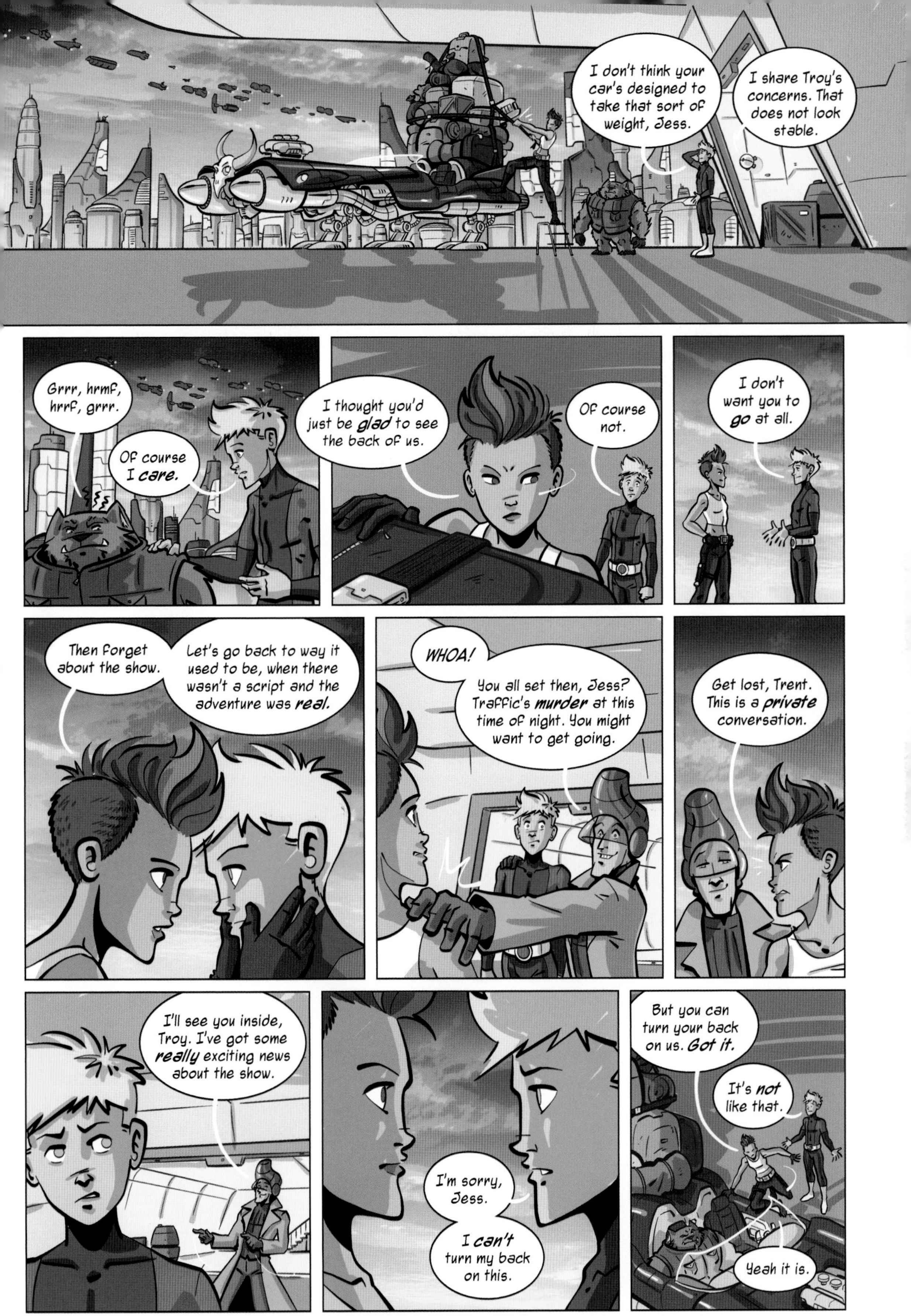
I don't think your car's designed to take that sort of weight, Jess.
I share Troy's concerns. That does not look stable.
Grrr, hrmf, hrrf, grrr.
Of course I *care.*
I thought you'd just be *glad* to see the back of us.
Of course not.
I don't want you to *go* at all.
Then forget about the show.
Let's go back to way it used to be, when there wasn't a script and the adventure was *real.*
*WHOA!*
You all set then, Jess? Traffic's *murder* at this time of night. You might want to get going.
Get lost, Trent. This is a *private* conversation.
I'll see you inside, Troy. I've got some *really* exciting news about the show.
I'm sorry, Jess.
I *can't* turn my back on this.
But you can turn your back on us. *Got it.*
It's *not* like that.
Yeah it is.

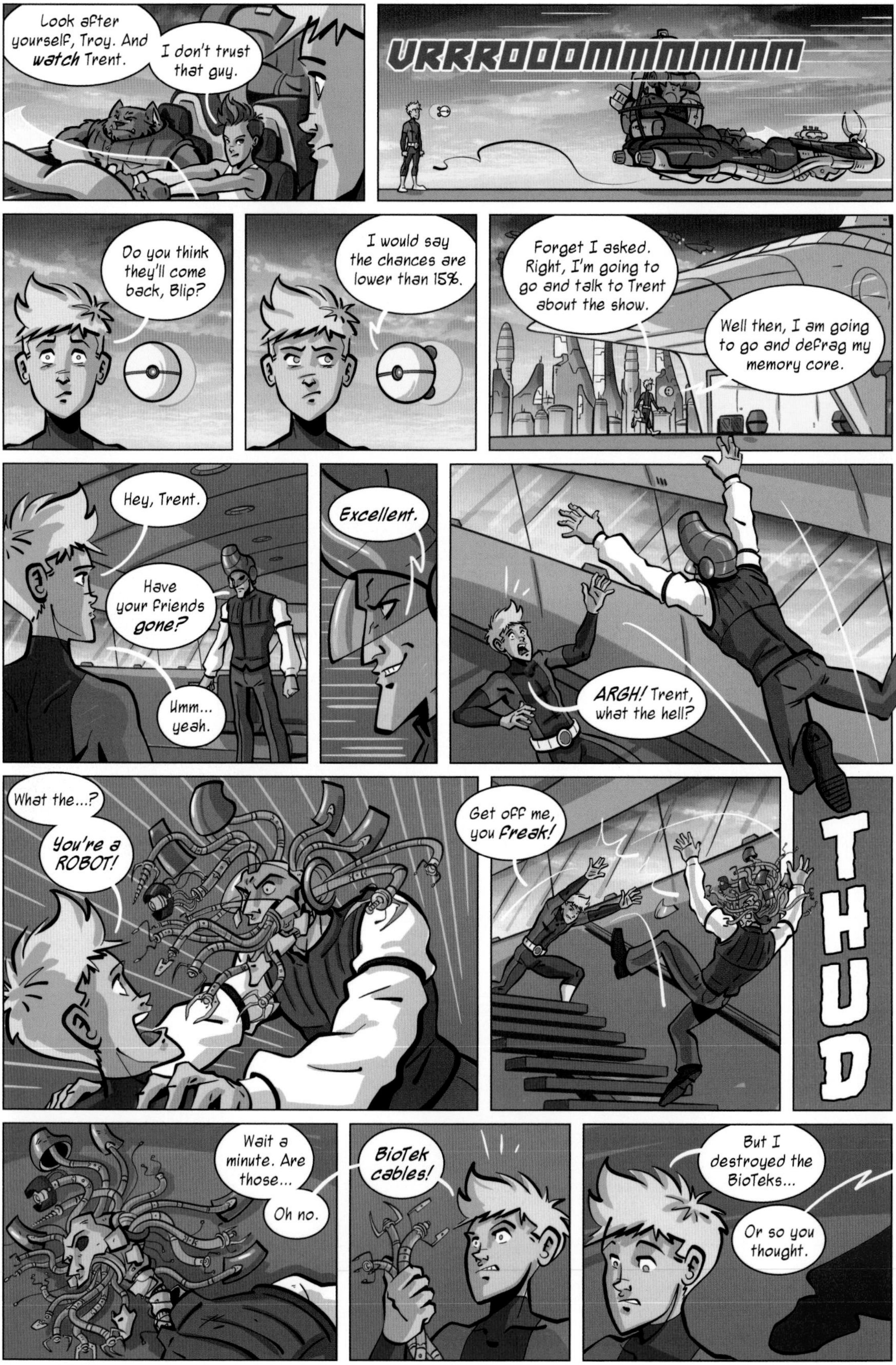

Look after yourself, Troy. And watch Trent.
I don't trust that guy.
VRRROOOMMMMMMM
Do you think they'll come back, Blip?
I would say the chances are lower than 15%.
Forget I asked. Right, I'm going to go and talk to Trent about the show.
Well then, I am going to go and defrag my memory core.
Hey, Trent.
Have your friends gone?
Umm... yeah.
Excellent.
ARGH! Trent, what the hell?
What the...?
You're a ROBOT!
Get off me, you freak!
THUD
Wait a minute. Are those...
Oh no.
BioTek cables!
But I destroyed the BioTeks...
Or so you thought.

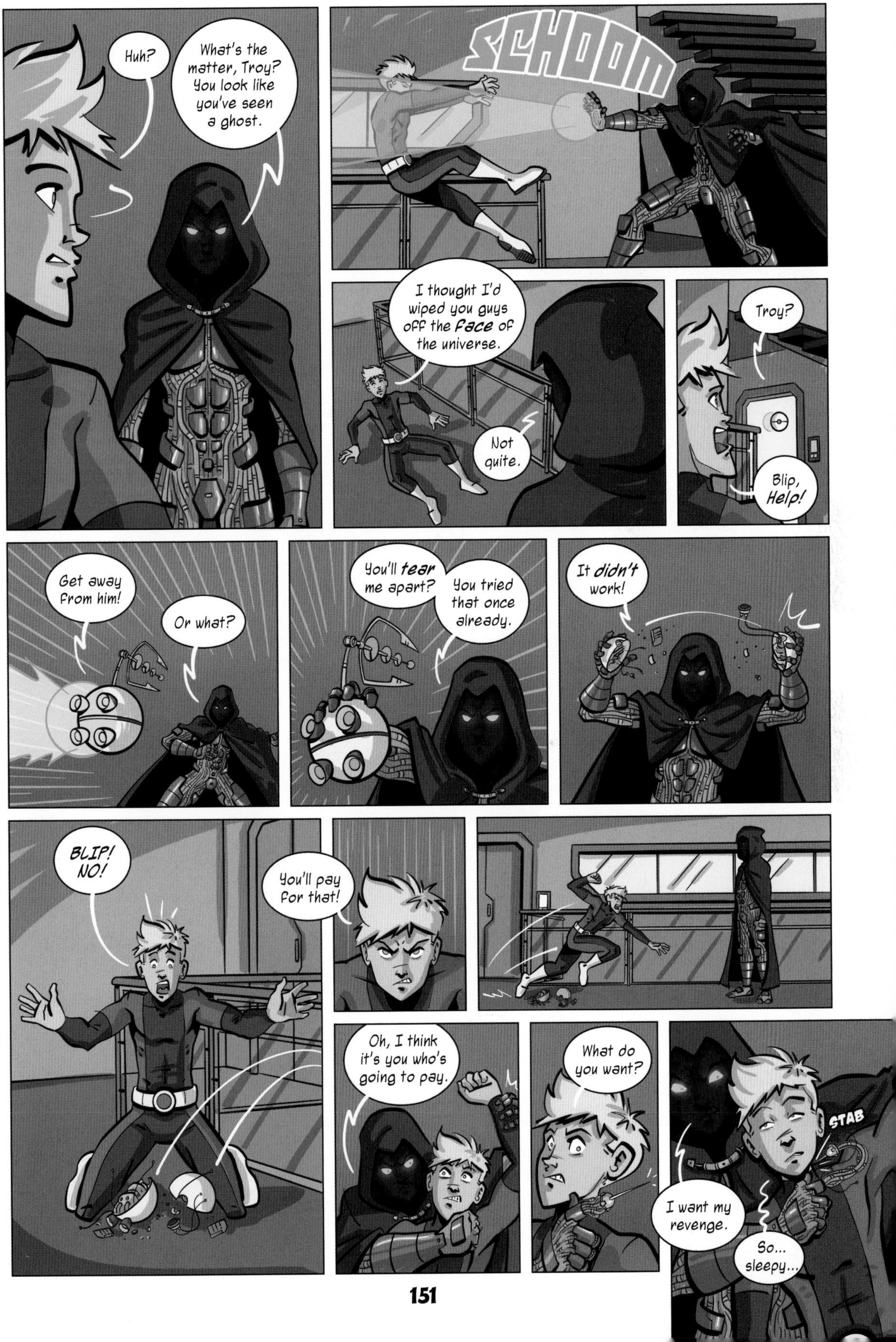

Huh?
What's the matter, Troy? You look like you've seen a ghost.
SCHOOM
I thought I'd wiped you guys off the face of the universe.
Not quite.
Troy?
Blip, Help!
Get away from him!
Or what?
You'll tear me apart?
You tried that once already.
It didn't work!
BLIP! NO!
You'll pay for that!
Oh, I think it's you who's going to pay.
What do you want?
I want my revenge.
STAB
So... sleepy...

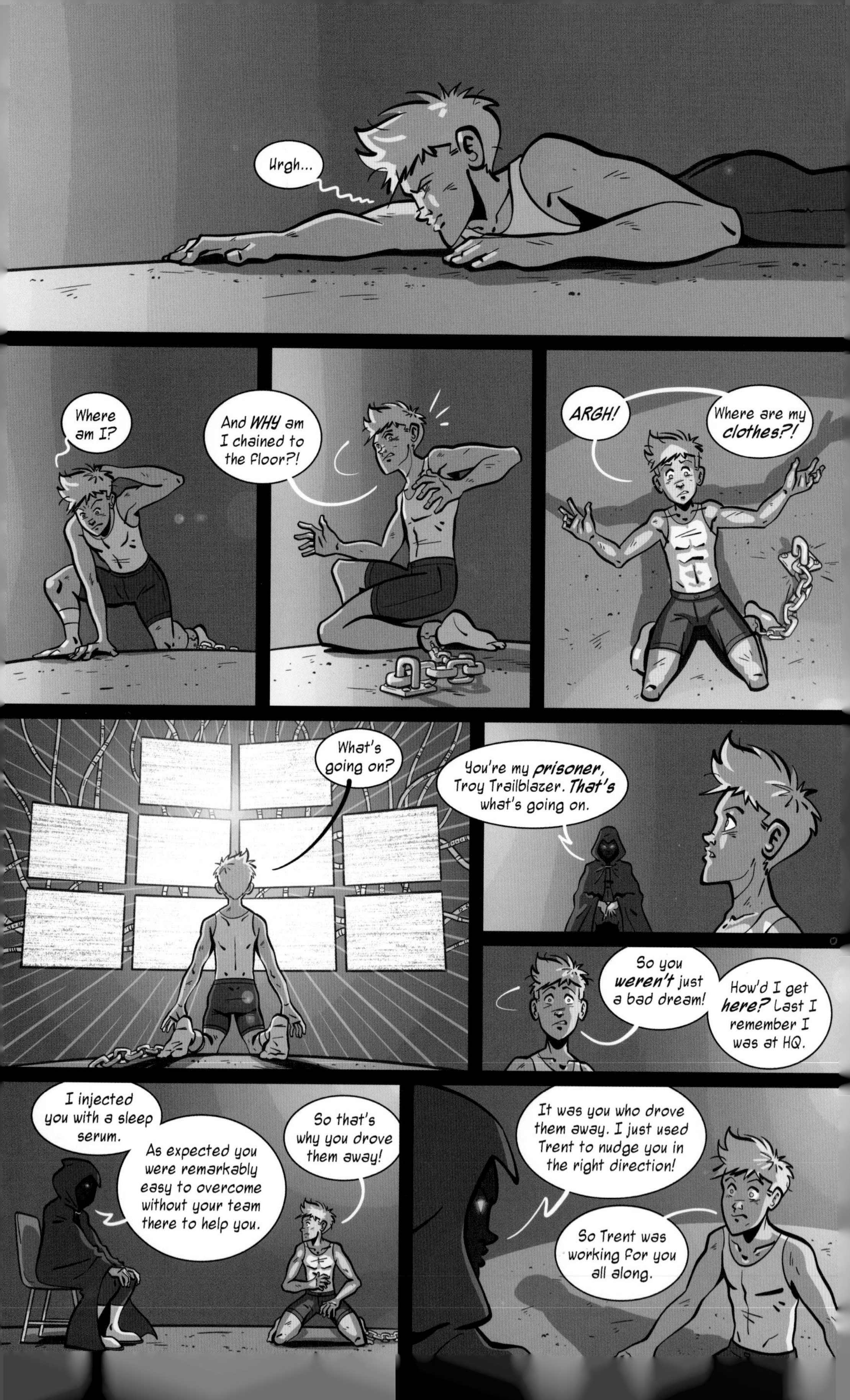

Urgh...
Where am I?
And WHY am I chained to the floor?!
ARGH!
Where are my clothes?!
What's going on?
You're my prisoner, Troy Trailblazer. That's what's going on.
So you weren't just a bad dream!
How'd I get here? Last I remember I was at HQ.
I injected you with a sleep serum.
As expected you were remarkably easy to overcome without your team there to help you.
So that's why you drove them away!
It was you who drove them away. I just used Trent to nudge you in the right direction!
So Trent was working for you all along.

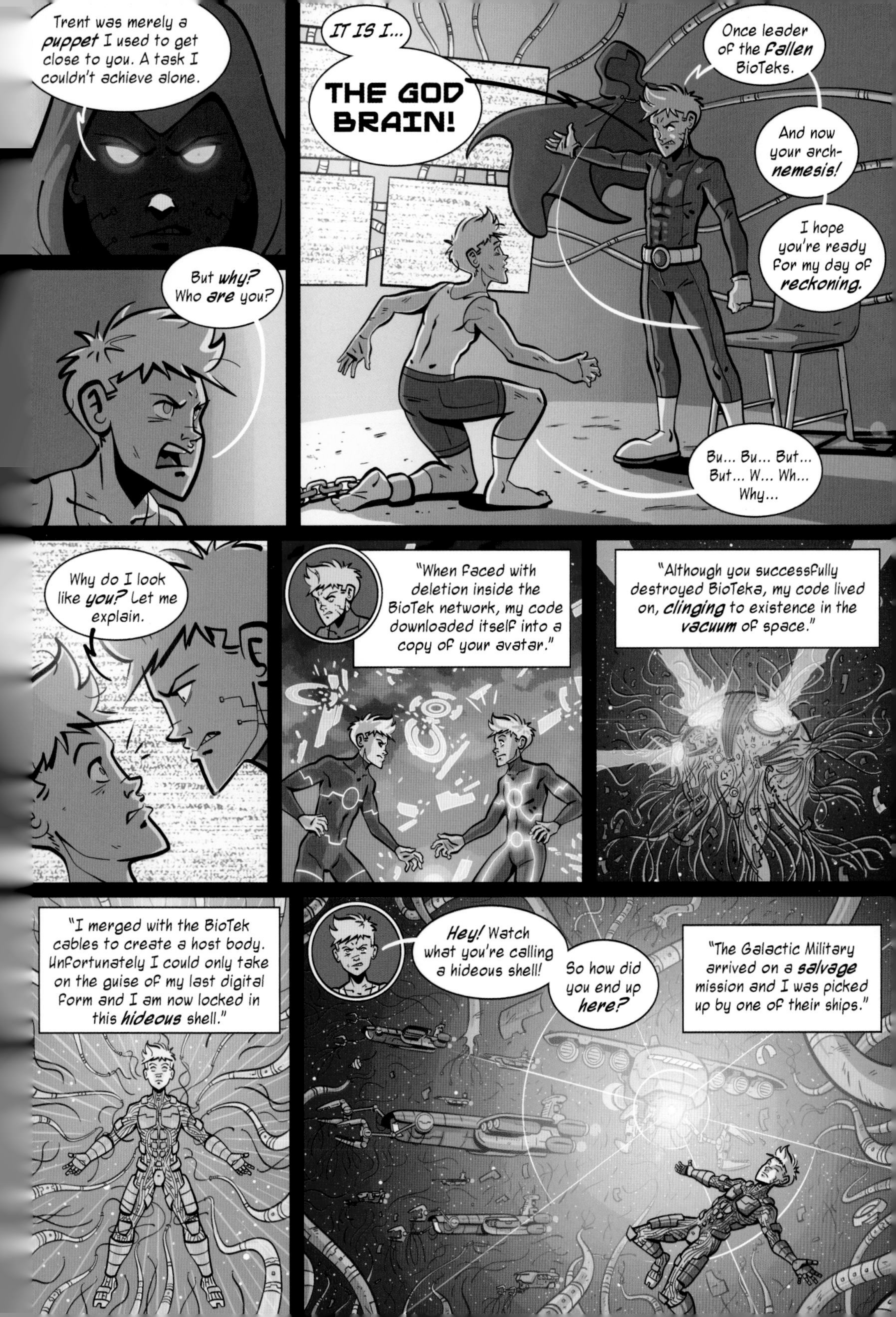
Trent was merely a *puppet* I used to get close to you. A task I couldn't achieve alone.
IT IS I...
THE GOD BRAIN!
Once leader of the *fallen* BioTeks.
And now your arch-*nemesis!*
I hope you're ready for my day of *reckoning.*
But *why?* Who *are* you?
Bu... Bu... But... But... W... Wh... Why...
Why do I look like *you?* Let me explain.
"When faced with deletion inside the BioTek network, my code downloaded itself into a copy of your avatar."
"Although you successfully destroyed BioTeka, my code lived on, *clinging* to existence in the *vacuum* of space."
"I merged with the BioTek cables to create a host body. Unfortunately I could only take on the guise of my last digital form and I am now locked in this *hideous* shell."
*Hey!* Watch what you're calling a hideous shell!
So how did you end up *here?*
"The Galactic Military arrived on a *salvage* mission and I was picked up by one of their ships."

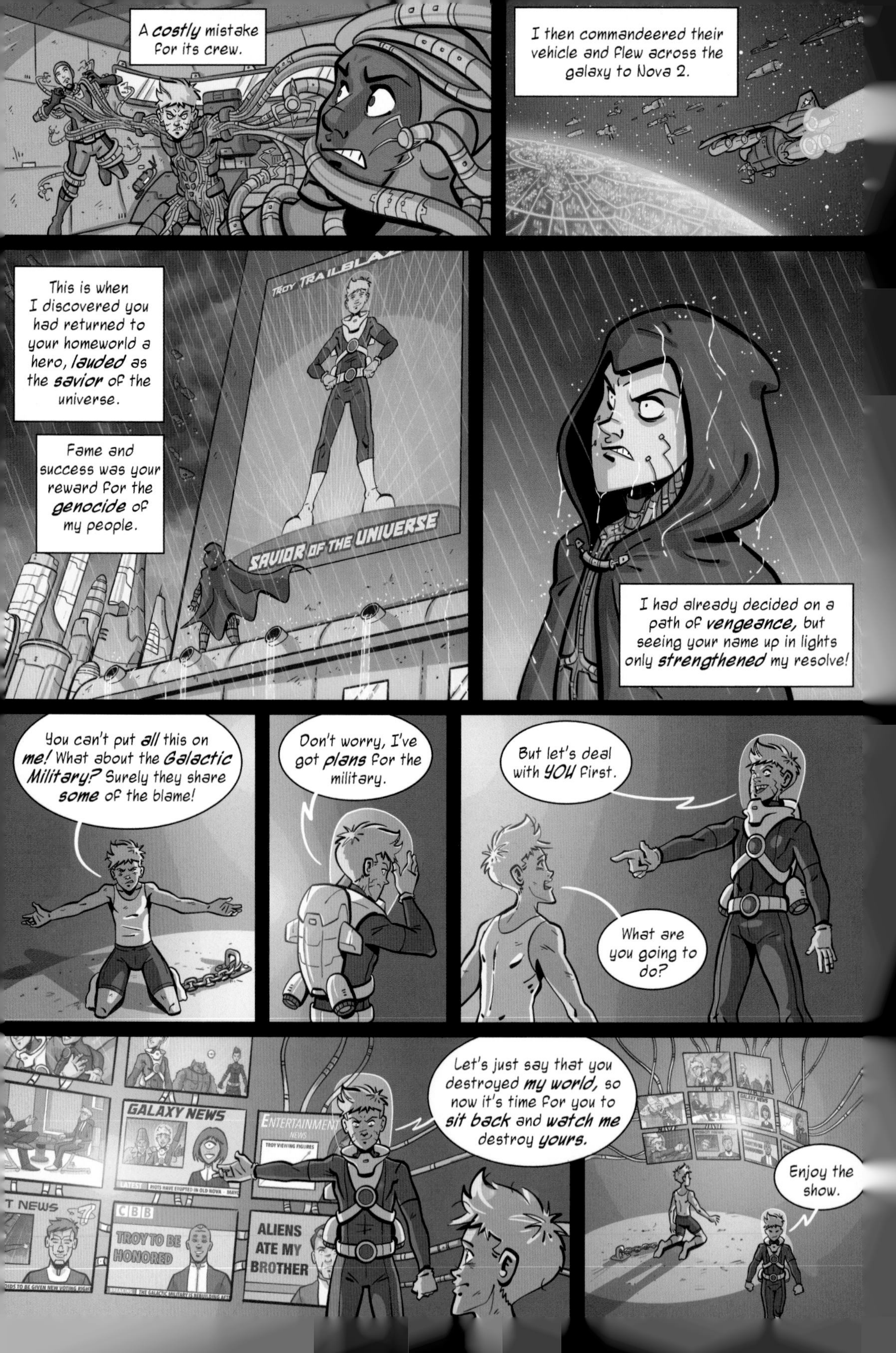
A costly mistake for its crew.
I then commandeered their vehicle and flew across the galaxy to Nova 2.
This is when I discovered you had returned to your homeworld a hero, lauded as the savior of the universe.
Fame and success was your reward for the genocide of my people.
TROY TRAILBLAZ
SAVIOR OF THE UNIVERSE
I had already decided on a path of vengeance, but seeing your name up in lights only strengthened my resolve!
You can't put all this on me! What about the Galactic Military? Surely they share some of the blame!
Don't worry, I've got plans for the military.
But let's deal with YOU first.
What are you going to do?
GALAXY NEWS
ENTERTAINMENT NEWS
TROY VIEWING FIGURES
CBB
TROY TO BE HONORED
ALIENS ATE MY BROTHER
Let's just say that you destroyed my world, so now it's time for you to sit back and watch me destroy yours.
Enjoy the show.

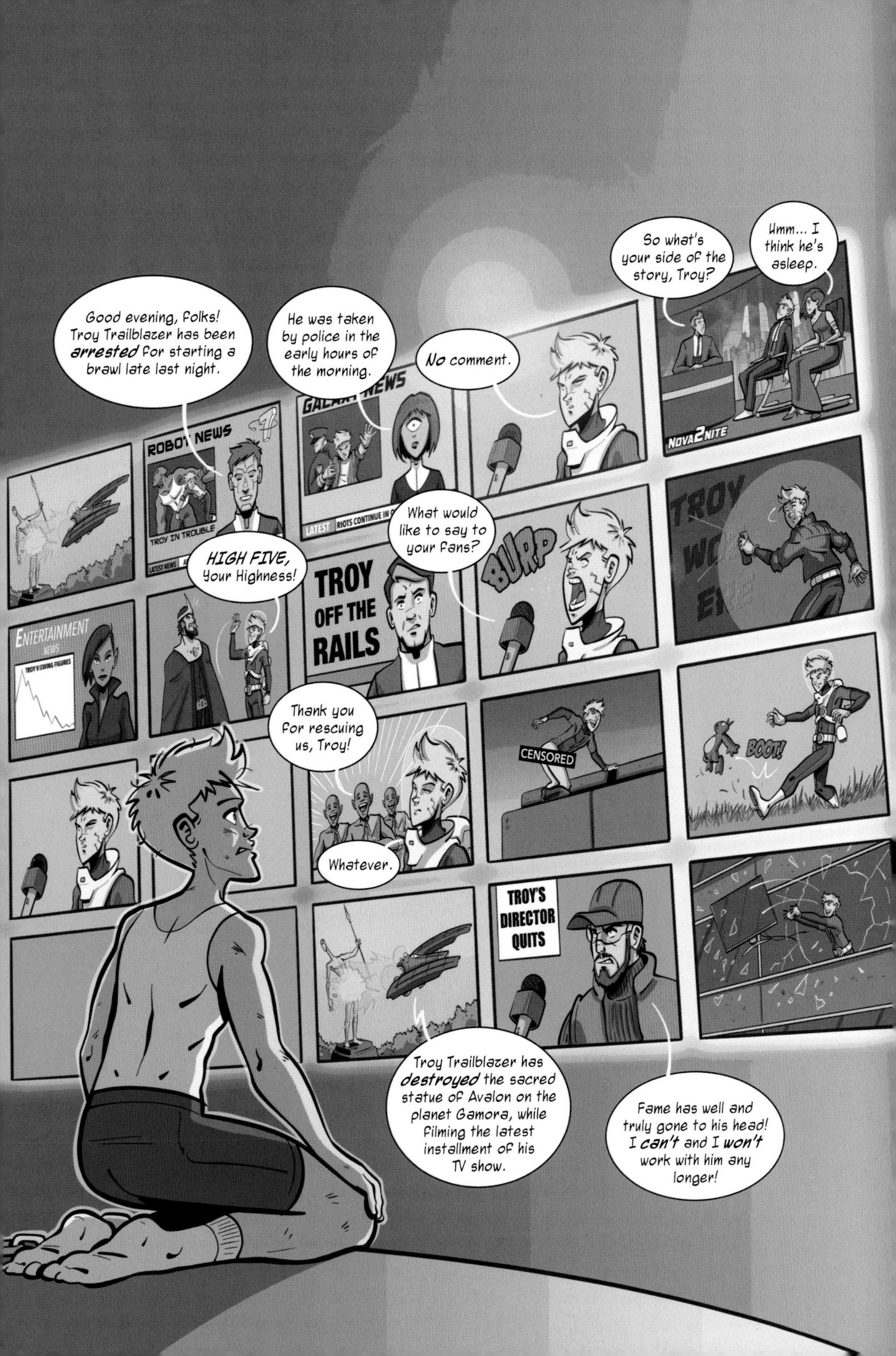
Good evening, folks! Troy Trailblazer has been ***arrested*** for starting a brawl late last night.
ROBOT NEWS
TROY IN TROUBLE
LATEST NEWS
He was taken by police in the early hours of the morning.
LATEST
***No*** comment.
So what's your side of the story, Troy?
Umm... I think he's asleep.
NOVA2NITE
*HIGH FIVE,* Your Highness!
ENTERTAINMENT NEWS
TROY VIEWING FIGURES
TROY OFF THE RAILS
What would like to say to your fans?
BURP
Thank you for rescuing us, Troy!
Whatever.
CENSORED
BOOT!
TROY'S DIRECTOR QUITS
Troy Trailblazer has ***destroyed*** the sacred statue of Avalon on the planet Gamora, while filming the latest installment of his TV show.
Fame has well and truly gone to his head! I ***can't*** and I ***won't*** work with him any longer!

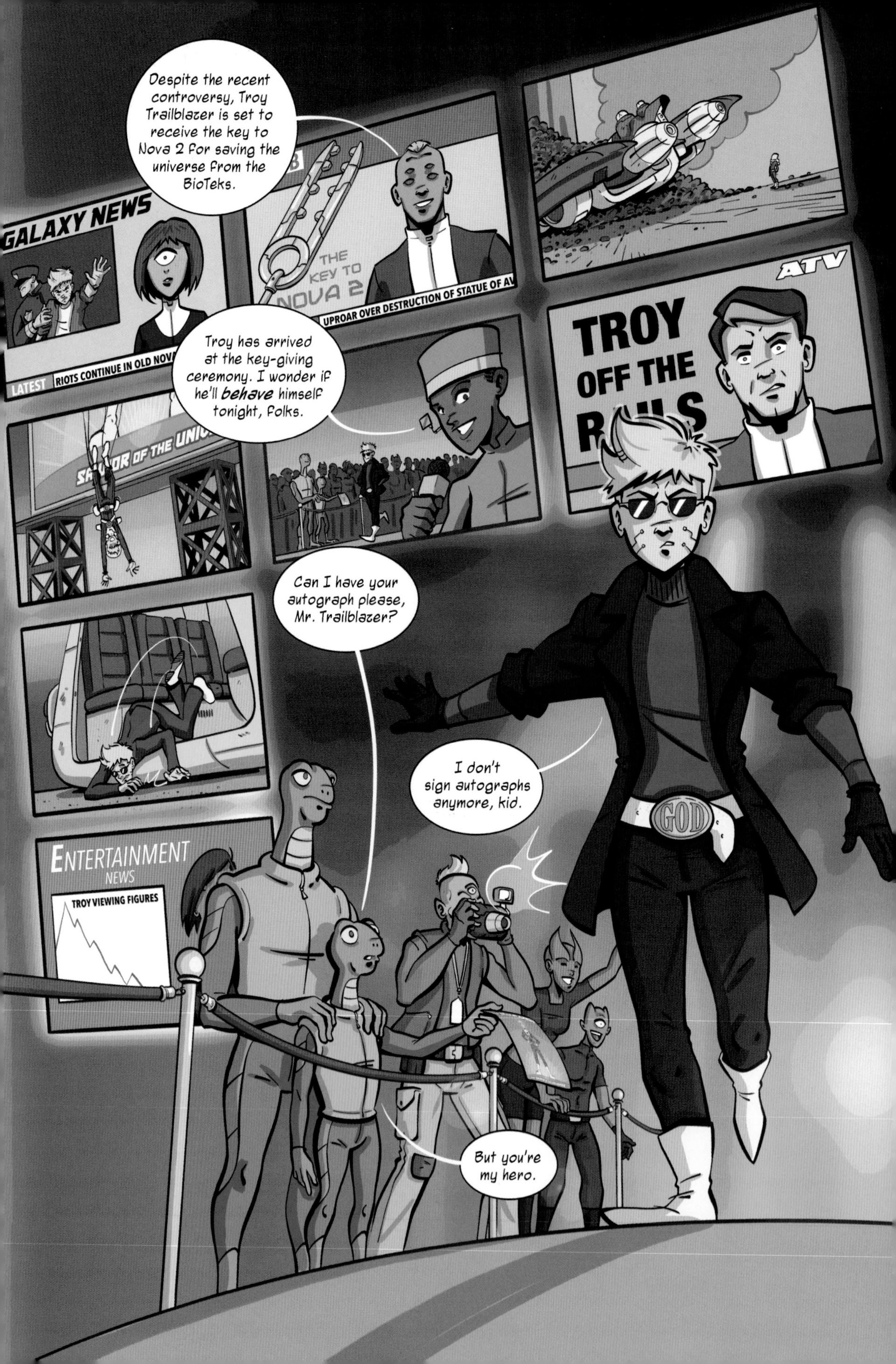

Despite the recent controversy, Troy Trailblazer is set to receive the key to Nova 2 for saving the universe from the BioTeks.
GALAXY NEWS
LATEST
RIOTS CONTINUE IN OLD NOVA
THE KEY TO NOVA 2
UPROAR OVER DESTRUCTION OF STATUE OF AV
ATV
TROY OFF THE
Troy has arrived at the key-giving ceremony. I wonder if he'll *behave* himself tonight, folks.
OR OF THE UNI
Can I have your autograph please, Mr. Trailblazer?
I don't sign autographs anymore, kid.
GOD
ENTERTAINMENT NEWS
TROY VIEWING FIGURES
But you're my hero.

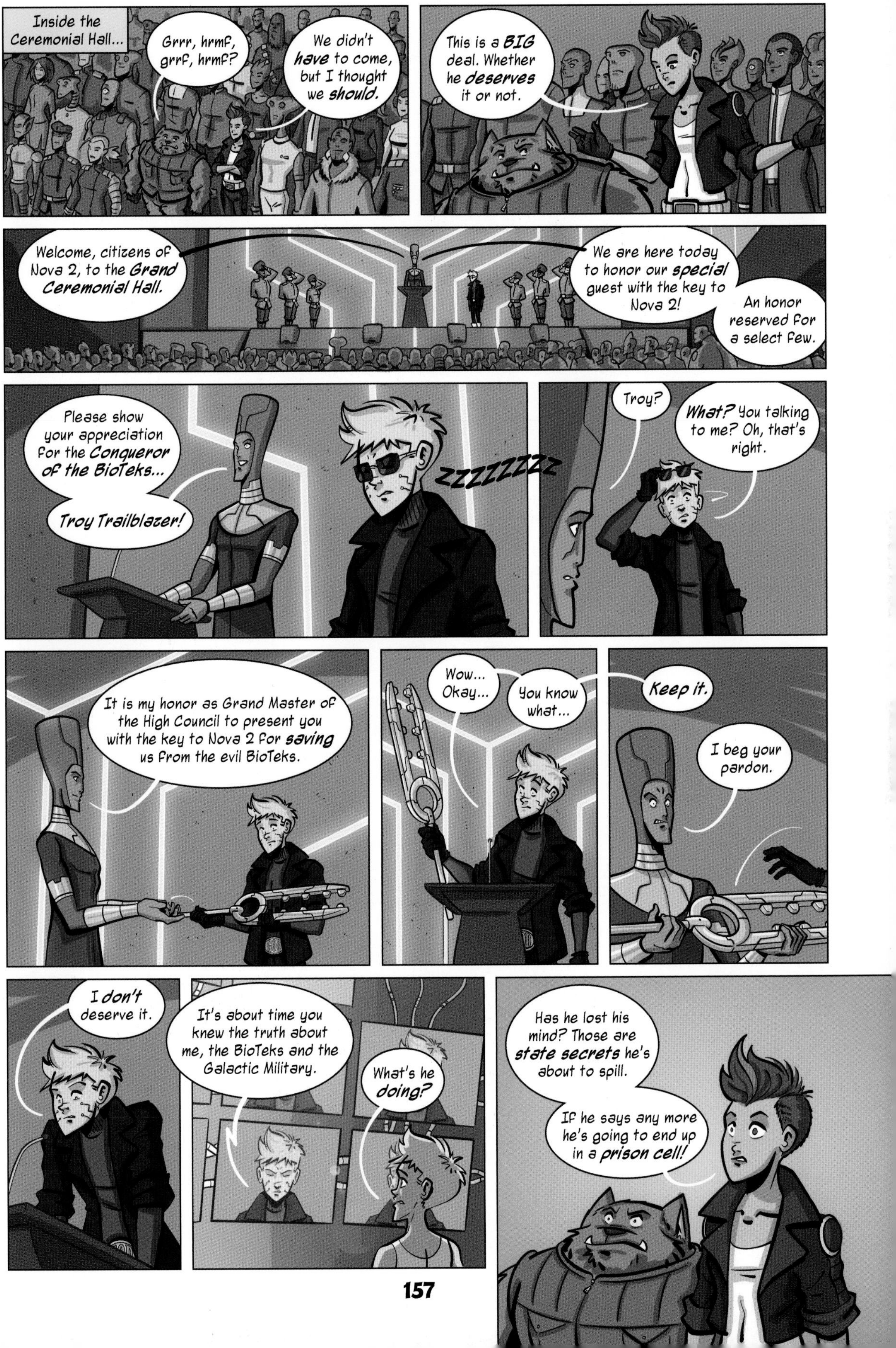
Inside the Ceremonial Hall...
Grrr, hrmf, grrf, hrmf?
We didn't *have* to come, but I thought we *should.*
This is a *BIG* deal. Whether he *deserves* it or not.
Welcome, citizens of Nova 2, to the *Grand Ceremonial Hall.*
We are here today to honor our *special* guest with the key to Nova 2!
An honor reserved for a select few.
Please show your appreciation for the *Conqueror of the BioTeks...*
*Troy Trailblazer!*
ZZZZZZZZ
Troy?
*What?* You talking to me? Oh, that's right.
It is my honor as Grand Master of the High Council to present you with the key to Nova 2 for *saving* us from the evil BioTeks.
Wow... Okay...
You know what...
*Keep it.*
I beg your pardon.
I *don't* deserve it.
It's about time you knew the truth about me, the BioTeks and the Galactic Military.
What's he *doing?*
Has he lost his mind? Those are *state secrets* he's about to spill.
If he says any more he's going to end up in a *prison cell!*

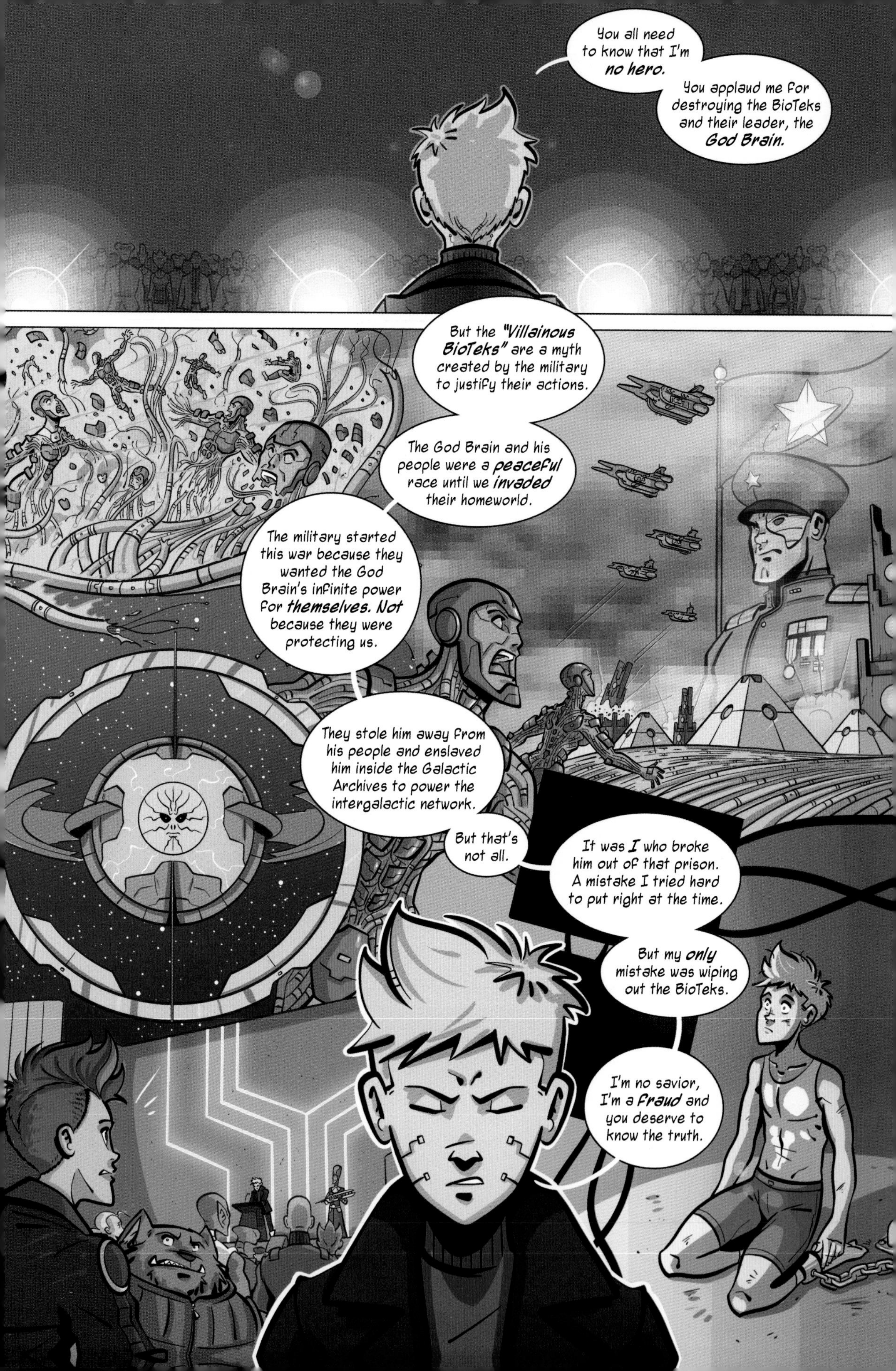

You all need to know that I'm *no hero.*
You applaud me for destroying the BioTeks and their leader, the *God Brain.*
But the *"Villainous BioTeks"* are a myth created by the military to justify their actions.
The God Brain and his people were a *peaceful* race until we *invaded* their homeworld.
The military started this war because they wanted the God Brain's infinite power for *themselves. Not* because they were protecting us.
They stole him away from his people and enslaved him inside the Galactic Archives to power the intergalactic network.
But that's not all.
It was *I* who broke him out of that prison. A mistake I tried hard to put right at the time.
But my *only* mistake was wiping out the BioTeks.
I'm no savior, I'm a *fraud* and you deserve to know the truth.

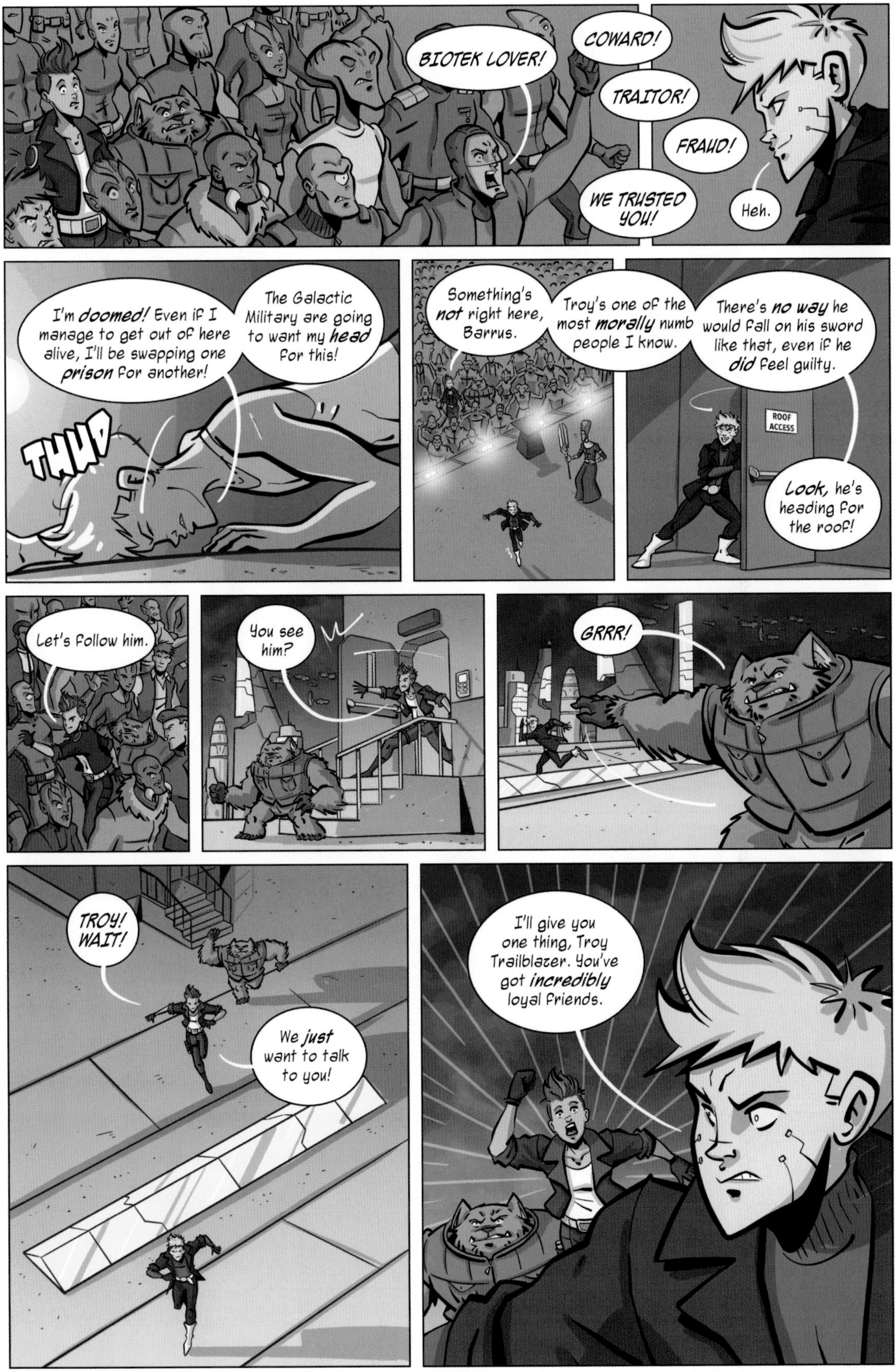
BIOTEK LOVER!
COWARD!
TRAITOR!
FRAUD!
WE TRUSTED YOU!
Heh.
THUD
I'm *doomed!* Even if I manage to get out of here alive, I'll be swapping one *prison* for another!
The Galactic Military are going to want my *head* for this!
Something's *not* right here, Barrus.
Troy's one of the most *morally* numb people I know.
There's *no way* he would fall on his sword like that, even if he *did* feel guilty.
ROOF ACCESS
*Look,* he's heading for the roof!
Let's follow him.
You see him?
GRRR!
TROY! WAIT!
We *just* want to talk to you!
I'll give you one thing, Troy Trailblazer. You've got *incredibly* loyal friends.

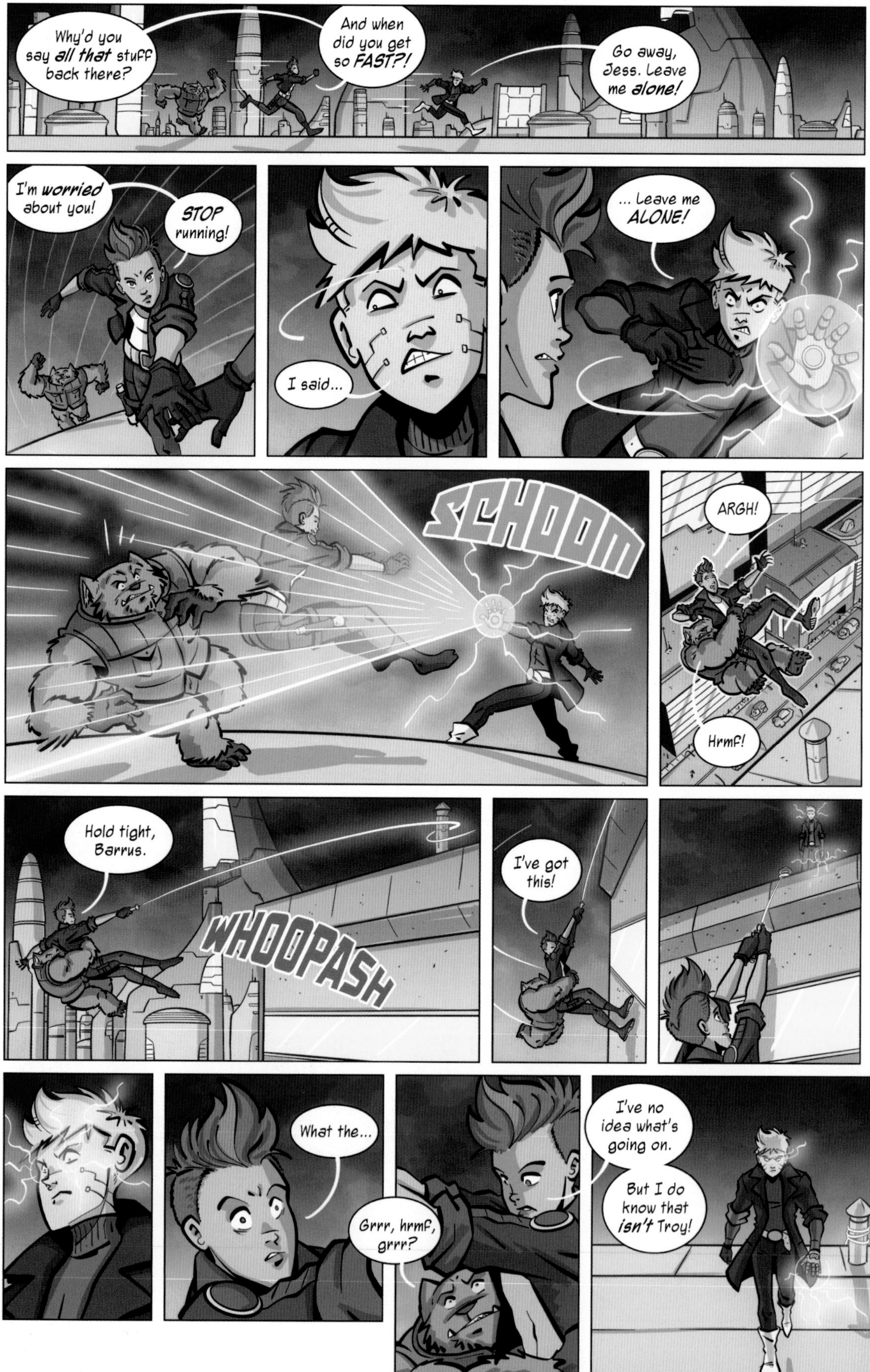
Why'd you say *all that* stuff back there?
And when did you get so *FAST?!*
Go away, Jess. Leave me *alone!*
I'm *worried* about you!
*STOP* running!
I said...
... Leave me *ALONE!*
SCHOOM
ARGH!
Hrmf!
Hold tight, Barrus.
WHOOPASH
I've got this!
What the...
Grrr, hrmf, grrr?
I've no idea what's going on.
But I do know that *isn't* Troy!

THIS BOOK IS BROUGHT TO YOU BY

# Squid Bits!

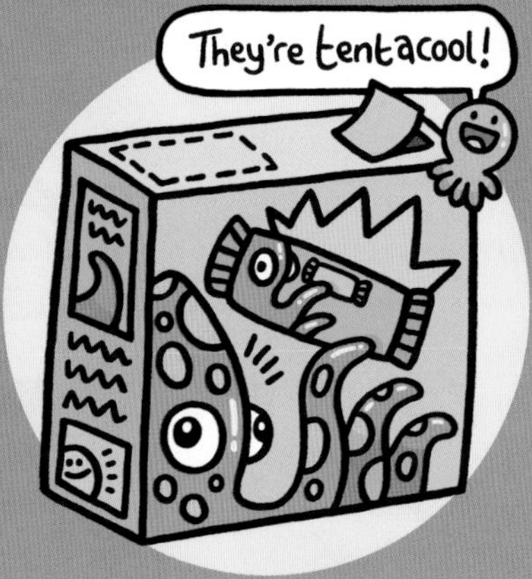
They're tentacool!

# EVERY DELICIOUS BOX OF SQUID BITS INCLUDES ALL THIS AND MORE...

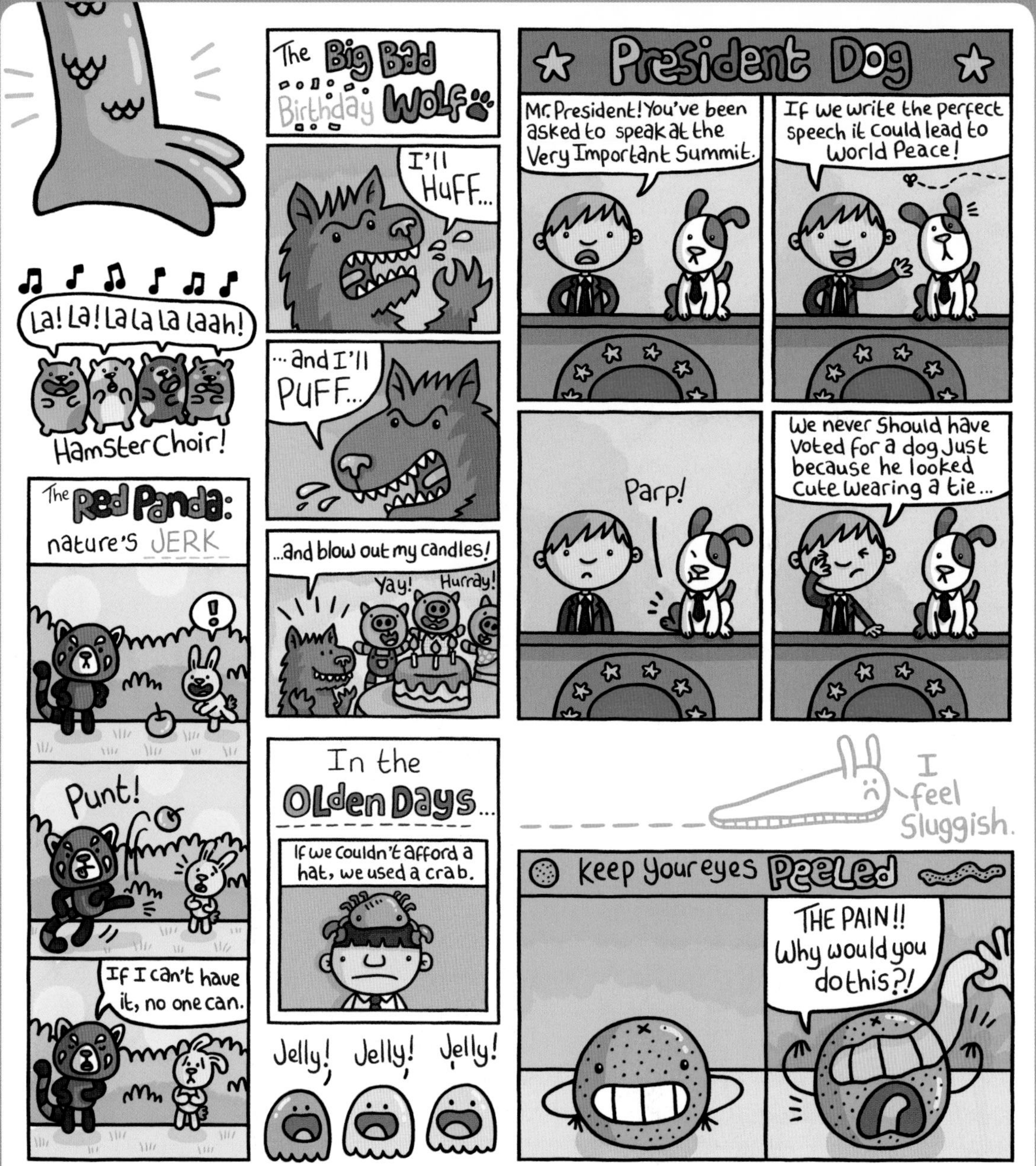
La! La! Lalalala laah!
Hamster Choir!
The Red Panda: nature's JERK
!
Punt!
If I can't have it, no one can.
The Big Bad Birthday Wolf
I'll HUFF...
...and I'll PUFF...
...and blow out my candles!
Yay!
Hurray!
In the Olden Days...
If we couldn't afford a hat, we used a crab.
Jelly!
Jelly!
Jelly!
President Dog
Mr. President! You've been asked to speak at the Very Important Summit.
If we write the perfect speech it could lead to World Peace!
Parp!
We never should have voted for a dog just because he looked cute wearing a tie...
I feel Sluggish.
Keep your eyes Peeled
THE PAIN!! Why would you do this?!

by Jess Bradley

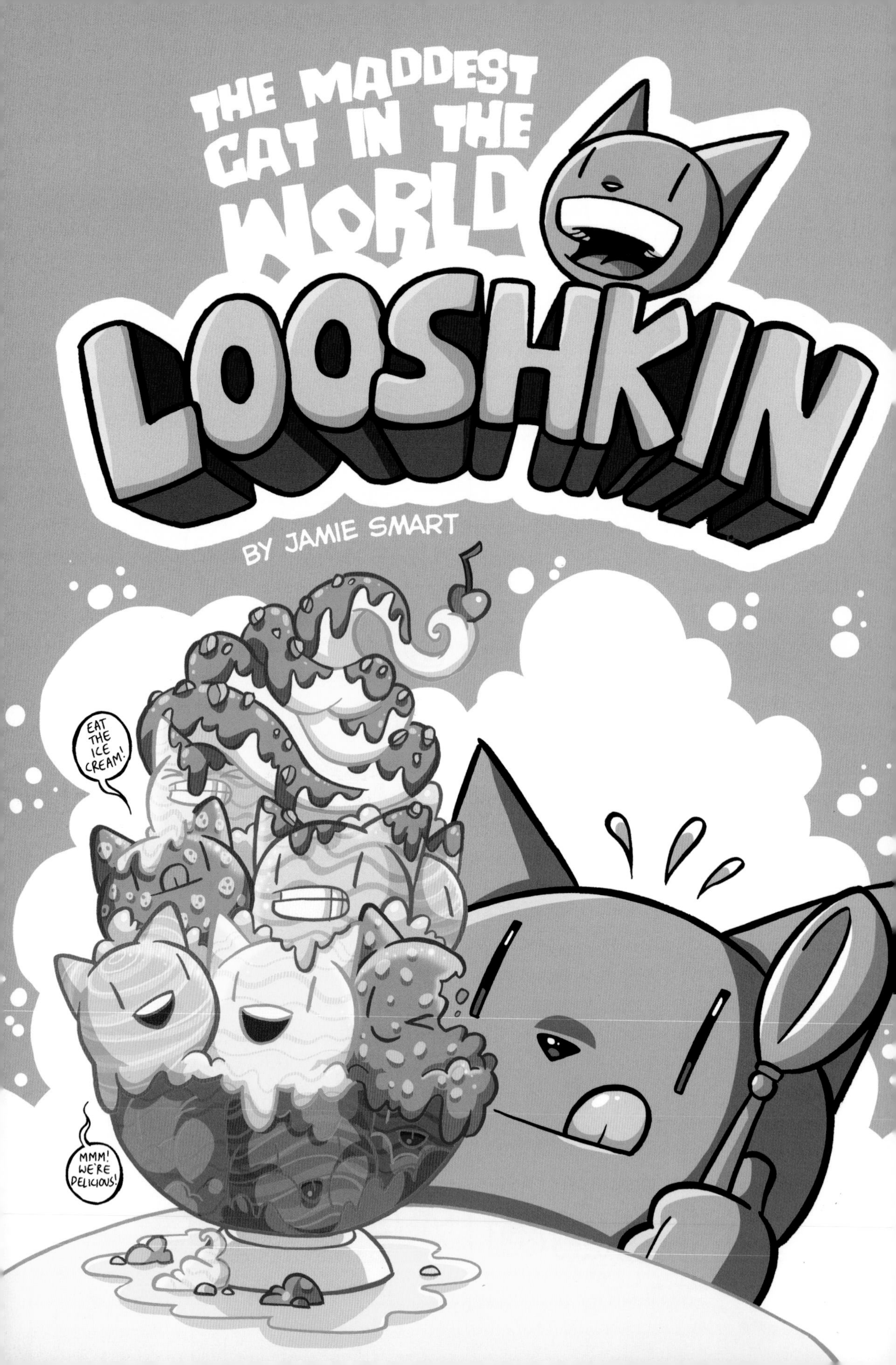
THE MADDEST CAT IN THE WORLD
LOOSHKIN
BY JAMIE SMART
EAT THE ICE CREAM!
MMM! WE'RE DELICIOUS!

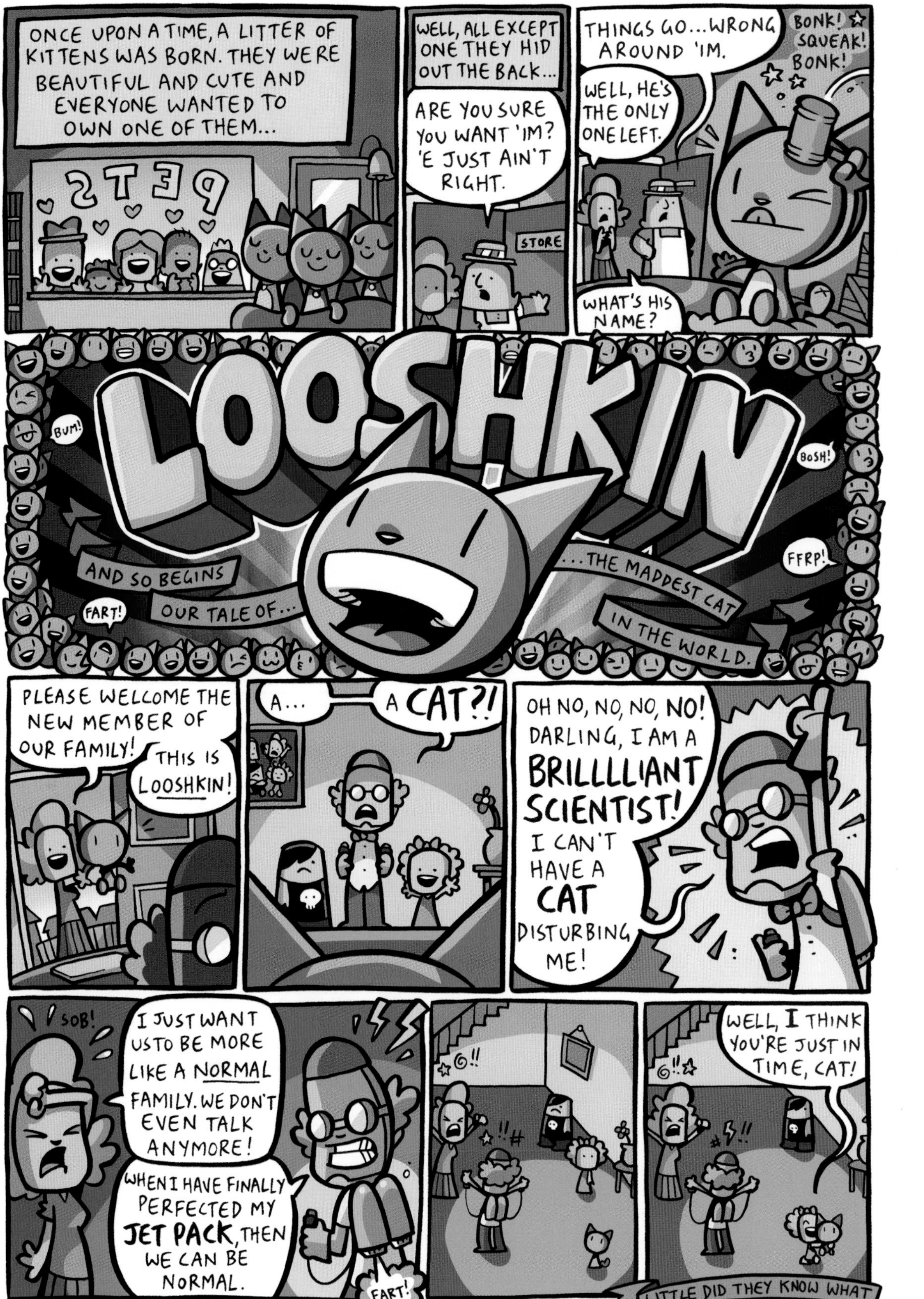
ONCE UPON A TIME, A LITTER OF KITTENS WAS BORN. THEY WERE BEAUTIFUL AND CUTE AND EVERYONE WANTED TO OWN ONE OF THEM...
PETS
WELL, ALL EXCEPT ONE THEY HID OUT THE BACK...
ARE YOU SURE YOU WANT 'IM? 'E JUST AIN'T RIGHT.
STORE
THINGS GO... WRONG AROUND 'IM.
WELL, HE'S THE ONLY ONE LEFT.
BONK! SQUEAK! BONK!
WHAT'S HIS NAME?
LOOSHKIN
BUM!
BOSH!
FFRP!
FART!
AND SO BEGINS
OUR TALE OF...
...THE MADDEST CAT
IN THE WORLD.
PLEASE WELCOME THE NEW MEMBER OF OUR FAMILY!
THIS IS LOOSHKIN!
A...
A CAT?!
OH NO, NO, NO, NO! DARLING, I AM A BRILLLLIANT SCIENTIST! I CAN'T HAVE A CAT DISTURBING ME!
SOB!
I JUST WANT US TO BE MORE LIKE A NORMAL FAMILY. WE DON'T EVEN TALK ANYMORE!
WHEN I HAVE FINALLY PERFECTED MY JET PACK, THEN WE CAN BE NORMAL.
FART!
WELL, I THINK YOU'RE JUST IN TIME, CAT!
LITTLE DID THEY KNOW WHAT THEY'D GOTTEN THEMSELVES INTO!

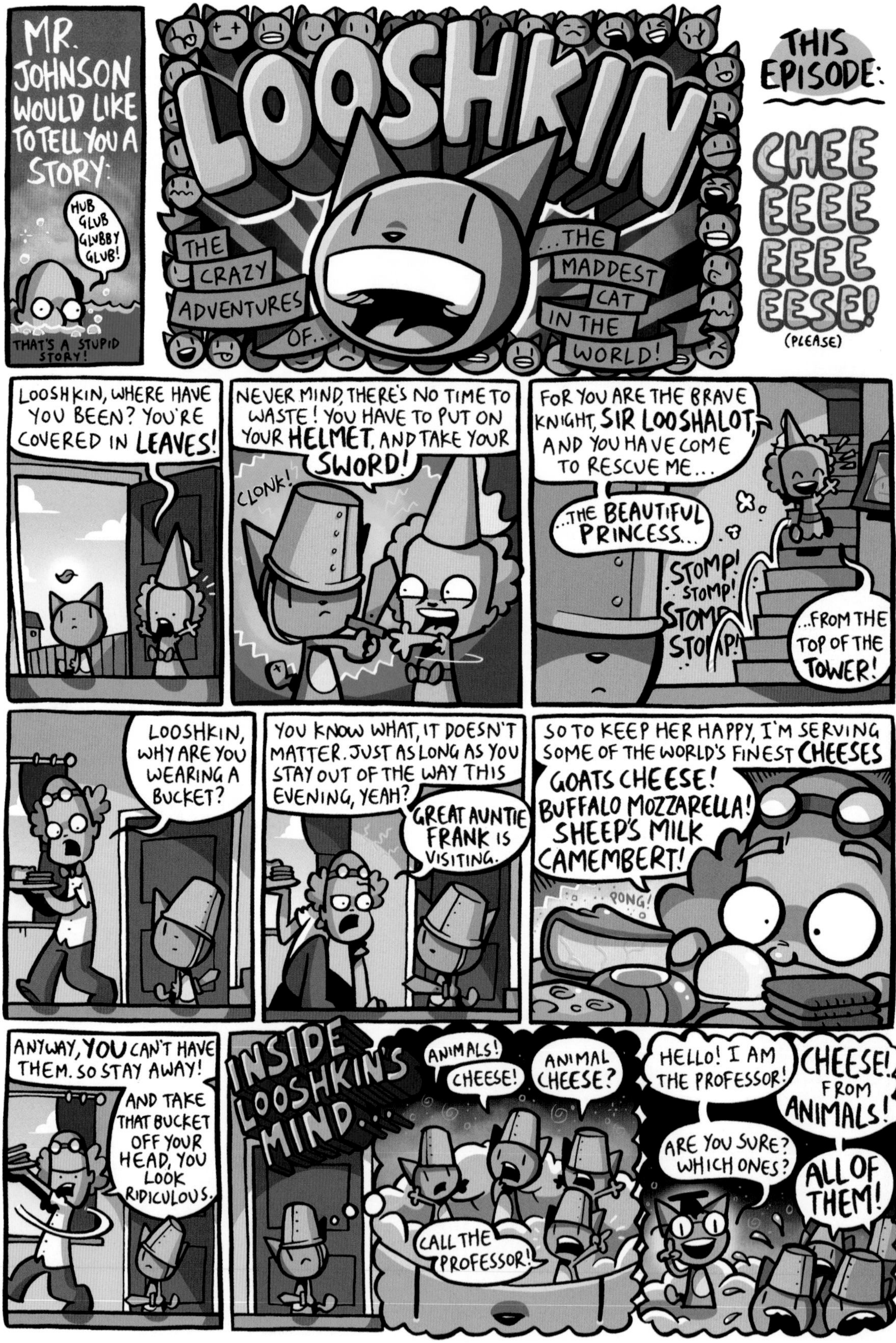
MR. JOHNSON WOULD LIKE TO TELL YOU A STORY:
HUB GLUB GLUBBY GLUB!
THAT'S A STUPID STORY!
LOOSHKIN
THE CRAZY ADVENTURES OF...
...THE MADDEST CAT IN THE WORLD!
THIS EPISODE:
CHEEEEEEEEEEEESE!
(PLEASE)
LOOSHKIN, WHERE HAVE YOU BEEN? YOU'RE COVERED IN LEAVES!
NEVER MIND, THERE'S NO TIME TO WASTE! YOU HAVE TO PUT ON YOUR HELMET, AND TAKE YOUR SWORD!
CLONK!
FOR YOU ARE THE BRAVE KNIGHT, SIR LOOSHALOT, AND YOU HAVE COME TO RESCUE ME...
...THE BEAUTIFUL PRINCESS...
STOMP! STOMP! STOMP STOMP!
...FROM THE TOP OF THE TOWER!
LOOSHKIN, WHY ARE YOU WEARING A BUCKET?
YOU KNOW WHAT, IT DOESN'T MATTER. JUST AS LONG AS YOU STAY OUT OF THE WAY THIS EVENING, YEAH?
GREAT AUNTIE FRANK IS VISITING.
SO TO KEEP HER HAPPY, I'M SERVING SOME OF THE WORLD'S FINEST CHEESES
GOATS CHEESE! BUFFALO MOZZARELLA! SHEEP'S MILK CAMEMBERT!
PONG!
ANYWAY, YOU CAN'T HAVE THEM. SO STAY AWAY!
AND TAKE THAT BUCKET OFF YOUR HEAD, YOU LOOK RIDICULOUS.
INSIDE LOOSHKIN'S MIND...
ANIMALS!
CHEESE!
ANIMAL CHEESE?
CALL THE PROFESSOR!
HELLO! I AM THE PROFESSOR!
CHEESE! FROM ANIMALS!
ARE YOU SURE? WHICH ONES?
ALL OF THEM!

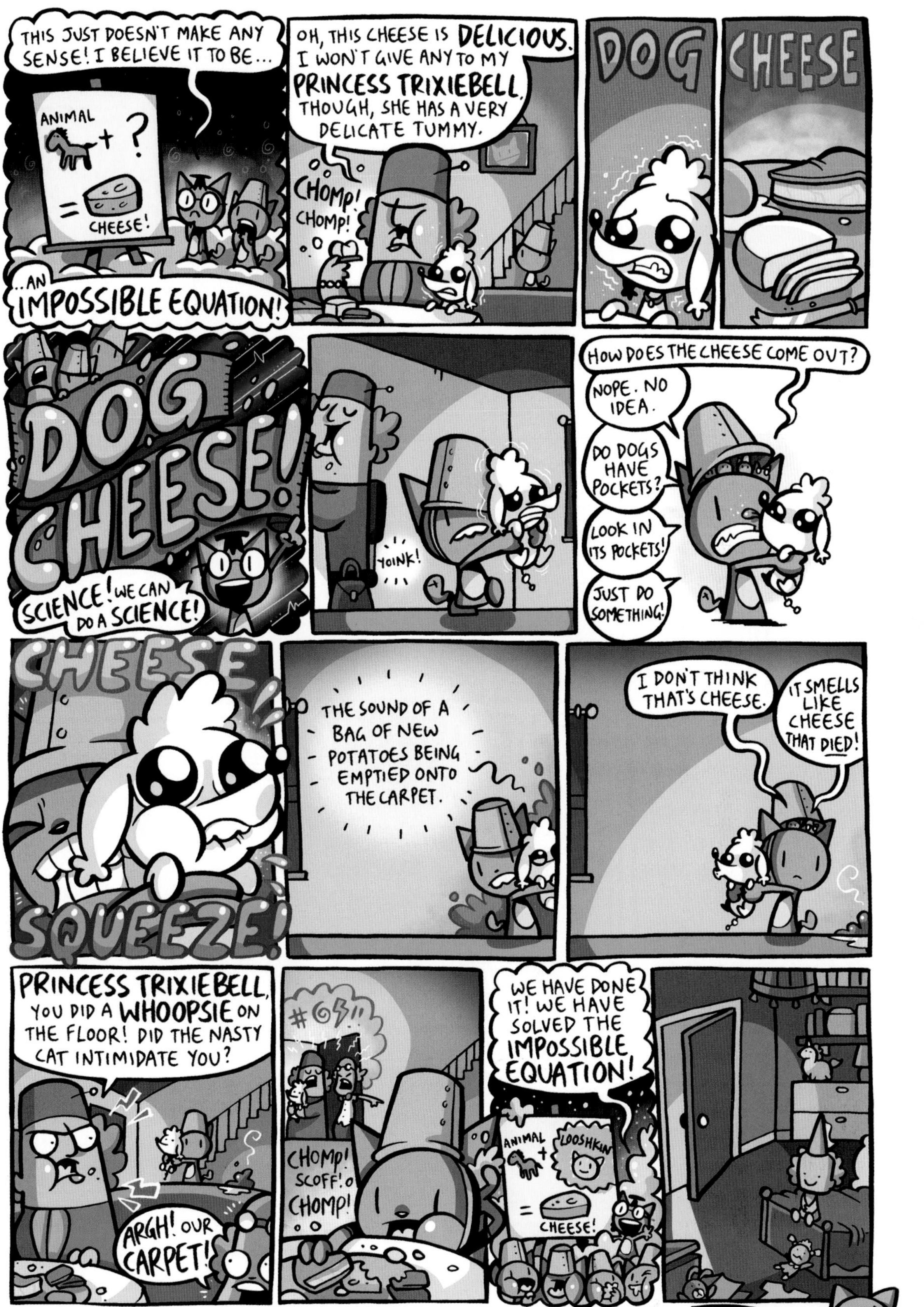
THIS JUST DOESN'T MAKE ANY SENSE! I BELIEVE IT TO BE...
ANIMAL + ? = CHEESE!
...AN IMPOSSIBLE EQUATION!
OH, THIS CHEESE IS DELICIOUS. I WON'T GIVE ANY TO MY PRINCESS TRIXIEBELL, THOUGH, SHE HAS A VERY DELICATE TUMMY.
CHOMP! CHOMP!
DOG
CHEESE
DOG CHEESE!
SCIENCE! WE CAN DO A SCIENCE!
YOINK!
HOW DOES THE CHEESE COME OUT?
NOPE. NO IDEA.
DO DOGS HAVE POCKETS?
LOOK IN ITS POCKETS!
JUST DO SOMETHING!
CHEESE
SQUEEZE!
THE SOUND OF A BAG OF NEW POTATOES BEING EMPTIED ONTO THE CARPET.
I DON'T THINK THAT'S CHEESE.
IT SMELLS LIKE CHEESE THAT DIED!
PRINCESS TRIXIEBELL, YOU DID A WHOOPSIE ON THE FLOOR! DID THE NASTY CAT INTIMIDATE YOU?
ARGH! OUR CARPET!
#@$!!
CHOMP! SCOFF! CHOMP!
WE HAVE DONE IT! WE HAVE SOLVED THE IMPOSSIBLE EQUATION!
ANIMAL + LOOSHKIN = CHEESE!
CHEEEEESE!!!

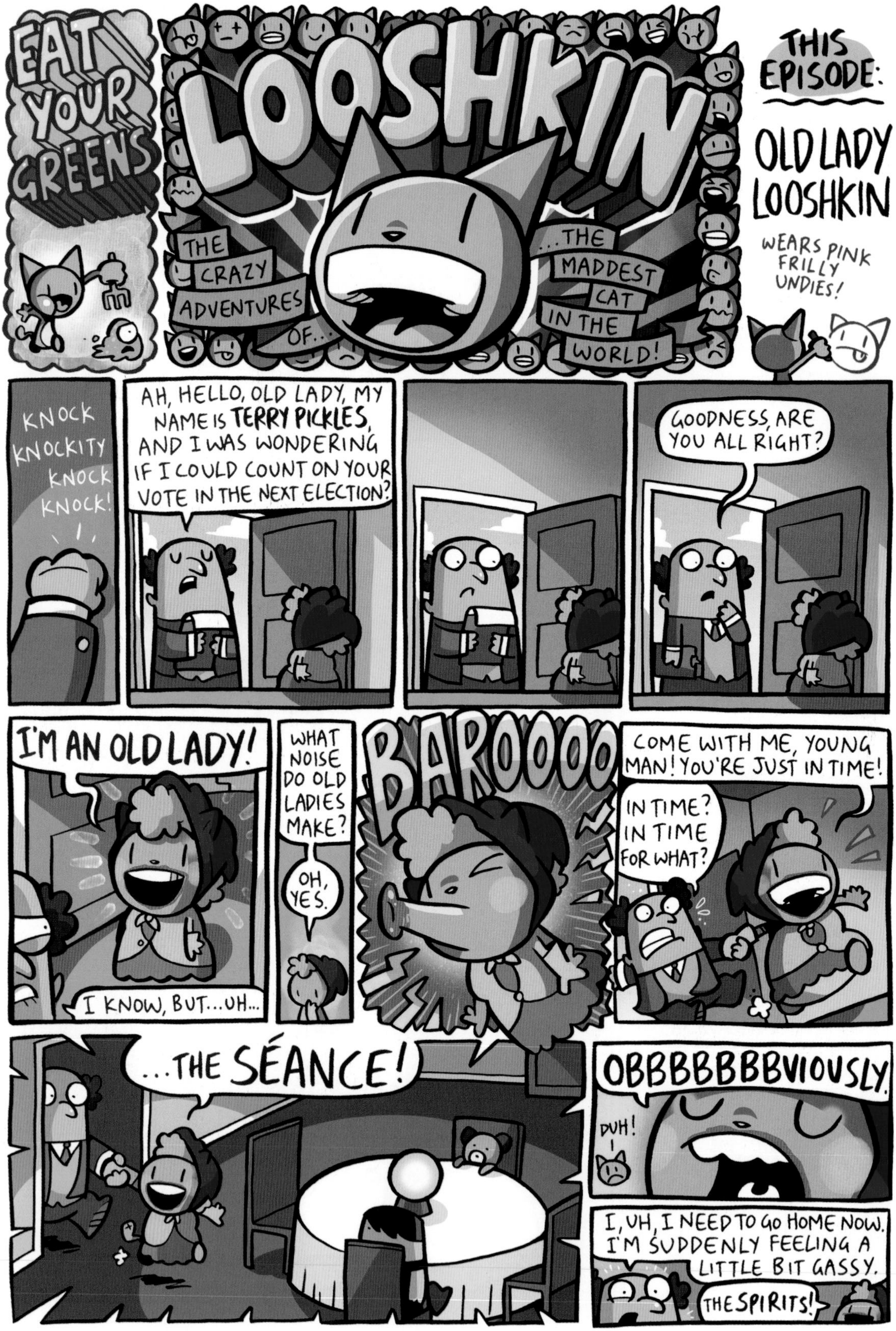
EAT YOUR GREENS
LOOSHKIN
THE CRAZY ADVENTURES OF...
...THE MADDEST CAT IN THE WORLD!
THIS EPISODE:
OLD LADY LOOSHKIN
WEARS PINK FRILLY UNDIES!
KNOCK KNOCKITY KNOCK KNOCK!
AH, HELLO, OLD LADY, MY NAME IS TERRY PICKLES, AND I WAS WONDERING IF I COULD COUNT ON YOUR VOTE IN THE NEXT ELECTION?
GOODNESS, ARE YOU ALL RIGHT?
I'M AN OLD LADY!
I KNOW, BUT...UH...
WHAT NOISE DO OLD LADIES MAKE?
OH, YES.
BAROOOO
COME WITH ME, YOUNG MAN! YOU'RE JUST IN TIME!
IN TIME? IN TIME FOR WHAT?
...THE SÉANCE!
OBBBBBBBVIOUSLY.
DUH!
I, UH, I NEED TO GO HOME NOW. I'M SUDDENLY FEELING A LITTLE BIT GASSY.
THE SPIRITS!

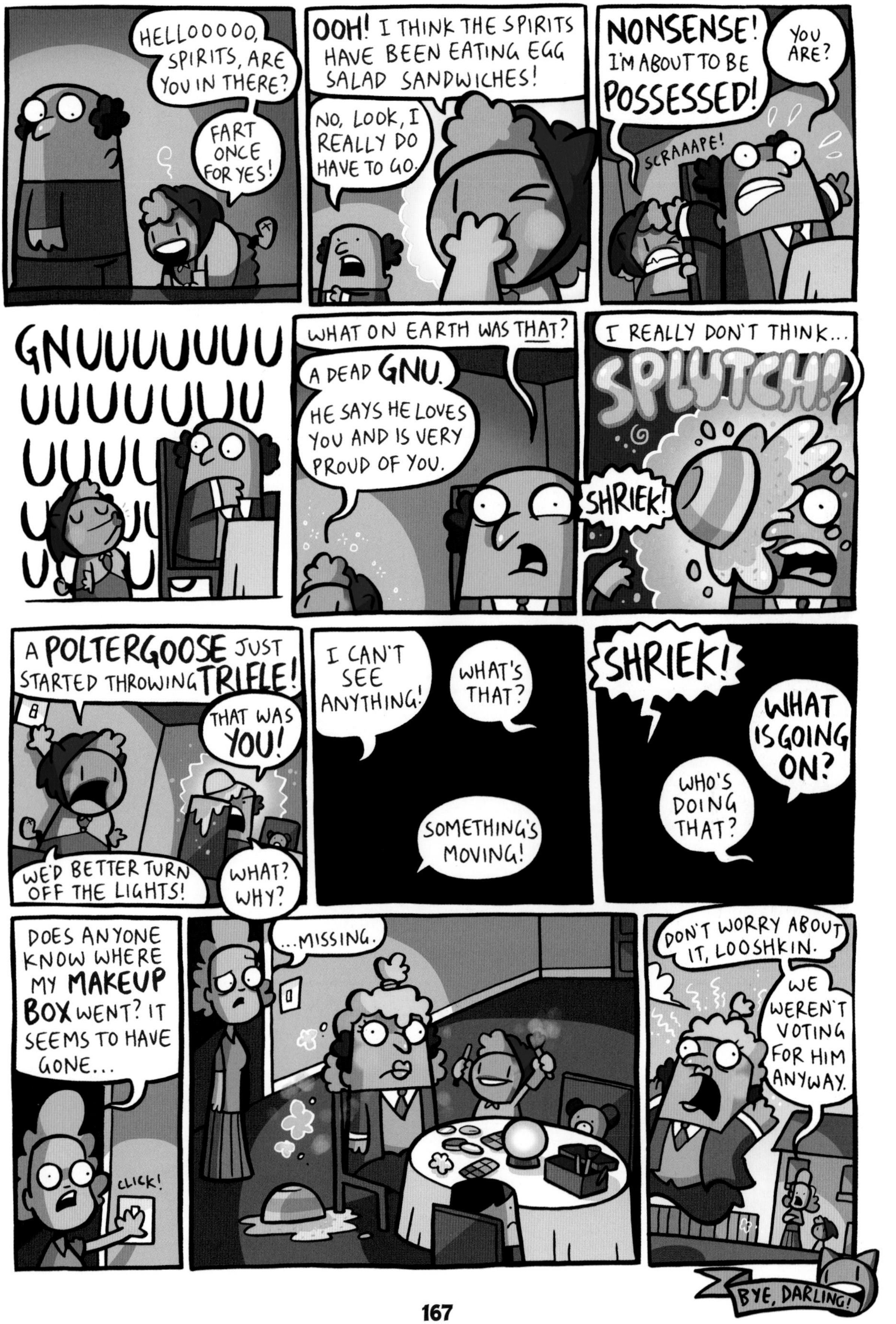
HELLOOOOO, SPIRITS, ARE YOU IN THERE?
FART ONCE FOR YES!
OOH! I THINK THE SPIRITS HAVE BEEN EATING EGG SALAD SANDWICHES!
NO, LOOK, I REALLY DO HAVE TO GO.
NONSENSE! I'M ABOUT TO BE POSSESSED!
YOU ARE?
SCRAAAPE!
GNUUUUUUUUUUUUUUUUUUUUUUU
WHAT ON EARTH WAS THAT?
A DEAD GNU.
HE SAYS HE LOVES YOU AND IS VERY PROUD OF YOU.
I REALLY DON'T THINK...
SPLUTCH!
SHRIEK!
A POLTERGOOSE JUST STARTED THROWING TRIFLE!
THAT WAS YOU!
WE'D BETTER TURN OFF THE LIGHTS!
WHAT? WHY?
I CAN'T SEE ANYTHING!
WHAT'S THAT?
SOMETHING'S MOVING!
SHRIEK!
WHAT IS GOING ON?
WHO'S DOING THAT?
DOES ANYONE KNOW WHERE MY MAKEUP BOX WENT? IT SEEMS TO HAVE GONE...
CLICK!
...MISSING.
DON'T WORRY ABOUT IT, LOOSHKIN.
WE WEREN'T VOTING FOR HIM ANYWAY.
BYE, DARLING!

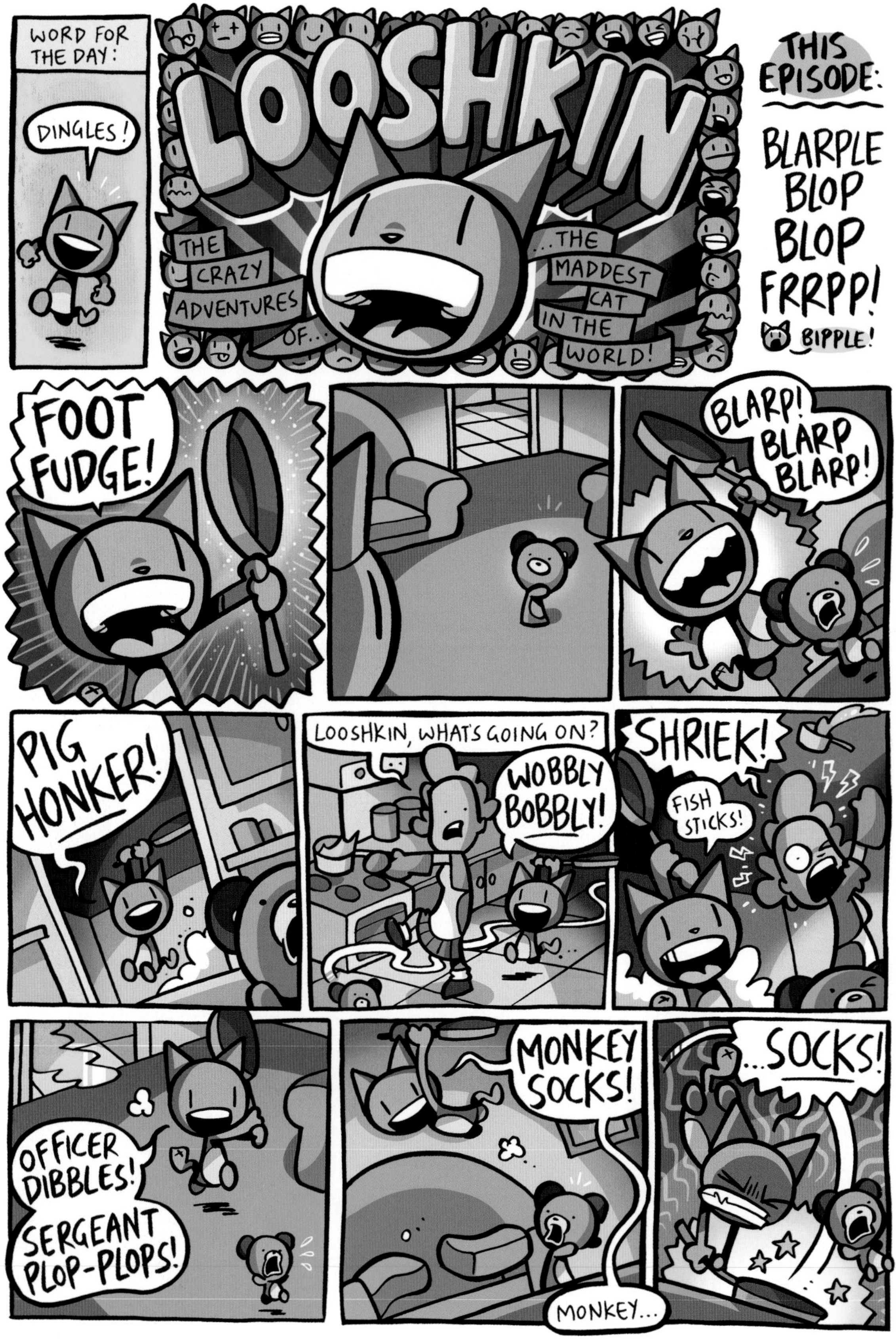

WORD FOR THE DAY:
DINGLES!
LOOSHKIN
THE CRAZY ADVENTURES OF...
...THE MADDEST CAT IN THE WORLD!
THIS EPISODE:
BLARPLE BLOP BLOP FRRPP!
BIPPLE!
FOOT FUDGE!
BLARP! BLARP BLARP!
PIG HONKER!
LOOSHKIN, WHAT'S GOING ON?
WOBBLY BOBBLY!
SHRIEK!
FISH STICKS!
OFFICER DIBBLES!
SERGEANT PLOP-PLOPS!
MONKEY SOCKS!
MONKEY...
...SOCKS!

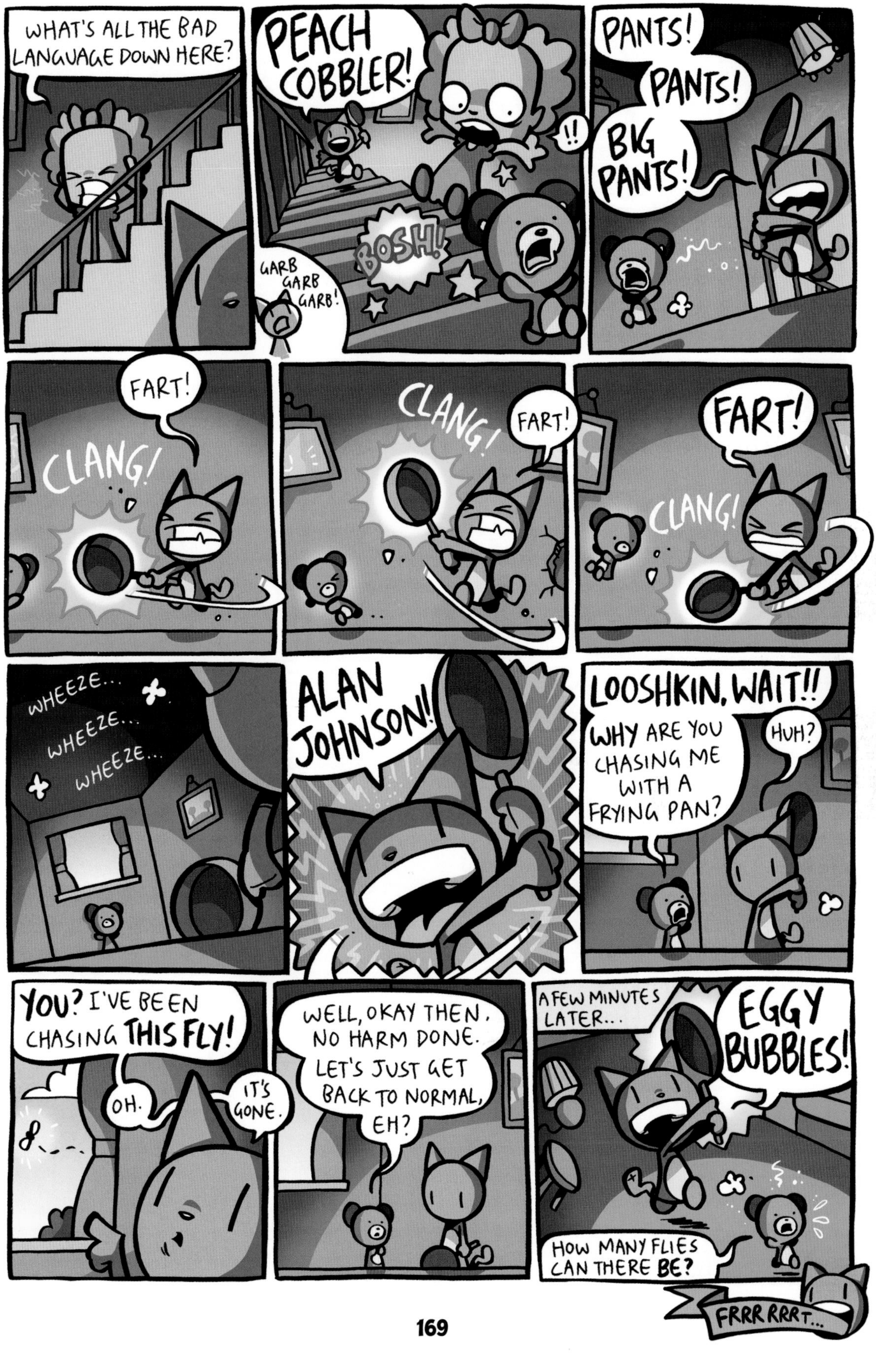

WHAT'S ALL THE BAD LANGUAGE DOWN HERE?
PEACH COBBLER!
!!
BOSH!
GARB GARB GARB!
PANTS!
PANTS!
BIG PANTS!
FART!
CLANG!
CLANG!
FART!
FART!
CLANG!
WHEEZE...
WHEEZE...
WHEEZE...
ALAN JOHNSON!
LOOSHKIN, WAIT!!
WHY ARE YOU CHASING ME WITH A FRYING PAN?
HUH?
YOU? I'VE BEEN CHASING THIS FLY!
OH.
IT'S GONE.
WELL, OKAY THEN. NO HARM DONE. LET'S JUST GET BACK TO NORMAL, EH?
A FEW MINUTES LATER...
EGGY BUBBLES!
HOW MANY FLIES CAN THERE BE?
FRRRRRRT...

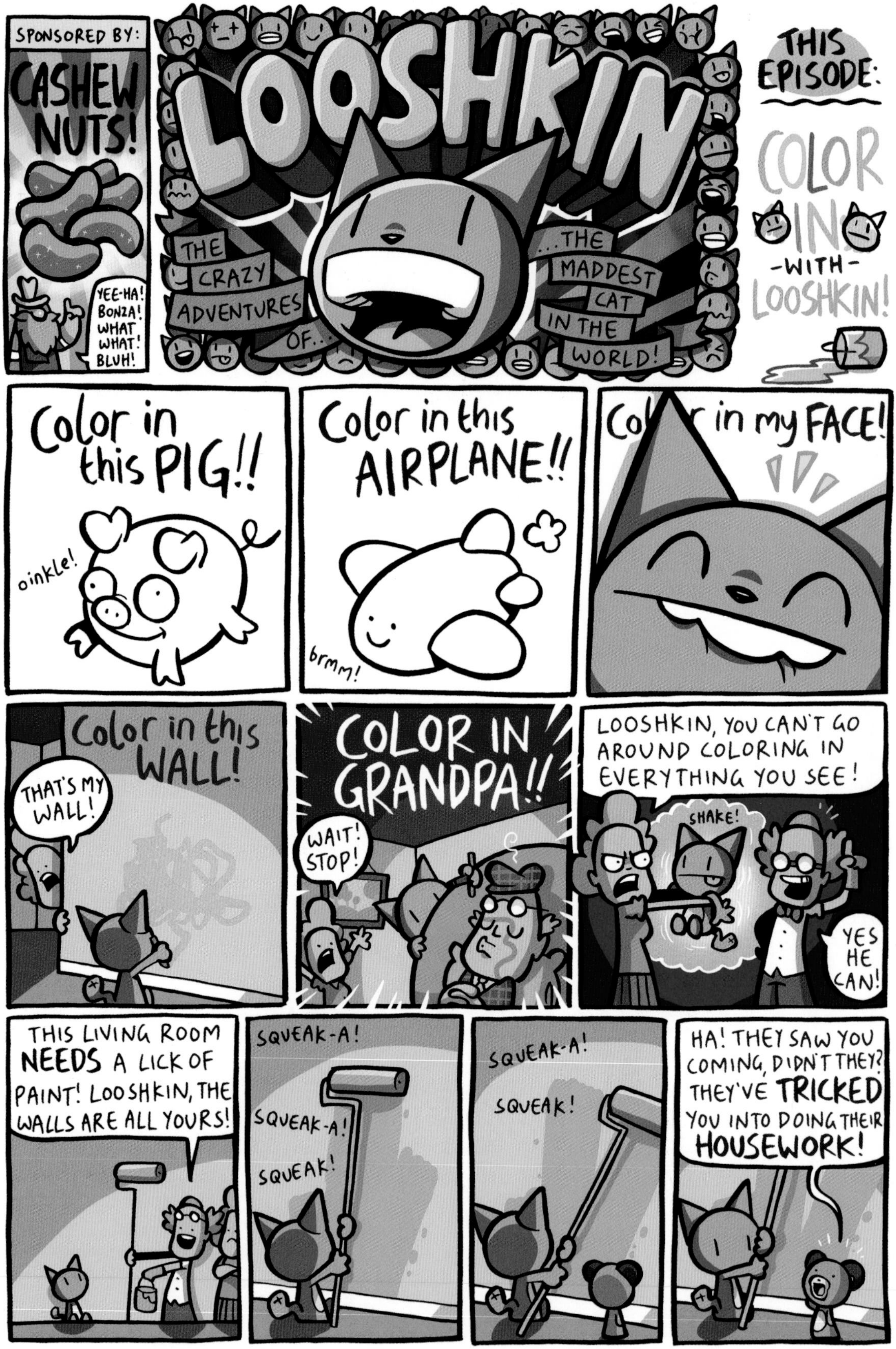
SPONSORED BY:
CASHEW NUTS!
YEE-HA! BONZA! WHAT WHAT! BLUH!
LOOSHKIN
THE CRAZY ADVENTURES OF...
...THE MADDEST CAT IN THE WORLD!
THIS EPISODE:
COLOR IN! -WITH- LOOSHKIN!
Color in this PIG!!
oinkle!
Color in this AIRPLANE!!
brmm!
Co r in my FACE!
Color in this WALL!
THAT'S MY WALL!
COLOR IN GRANDPA!!
WAIT! STOP!
LOOSHKIN, YOU CAN'T GO AROUND COLORING IN EVERYTHING YOU SEE!
SHAKE!
YES HE CAN!
THIS LIVING ROOM NEEDS A LICK OF PAINT! LOOSHKIN, THE WALLS ARE ALL YOURS!
SQUEAK-A!
SQUEAK-A!
SQUEAK!
SQUEAK-A!
SQUEAK!
HA! THEY SAW YOU COMING, DIDN'T THEY? THEY'VE TRICKED YOU INTO DOING THEIR HOUSEWORK!

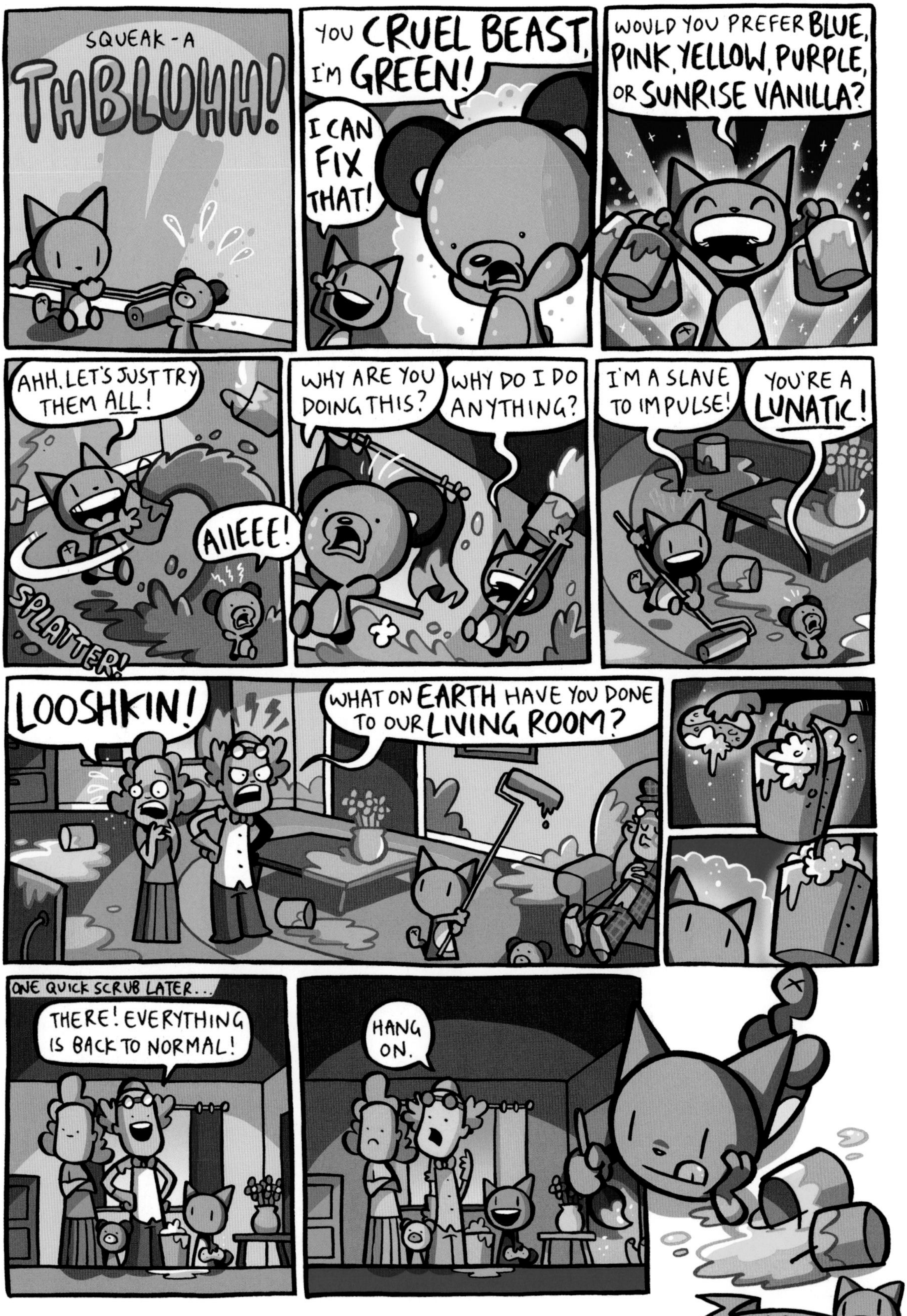
SQUEAK-A
THBLUHH!
YOU CRUEL BEAST, I'M GREEN!
I CAN FIX THAT!
WOULD YOU PREFER BLUE, PINK, YELLOW, PURPLE, OR SUNRISE VANILLA?
AHH, LET'S JUST TRY THEM ALL!
AIIEEE!
SPLATTER!
WHY ARE YOU DOING THIS?
WHY DO I DO ANYTHING?
I'M A SLAVE TO IMPULSE!
YOU'RE A LUNATIC!
LOOSHKIN!
WHAT ON EARTH HAVE YOU DONE TO OUR LIVING ROOM?
ONE QUICK SCRUB LATER...
THERE! EVERYTHING IS BACK TO NORMAL!
HANG ON.
EGGSHELL!

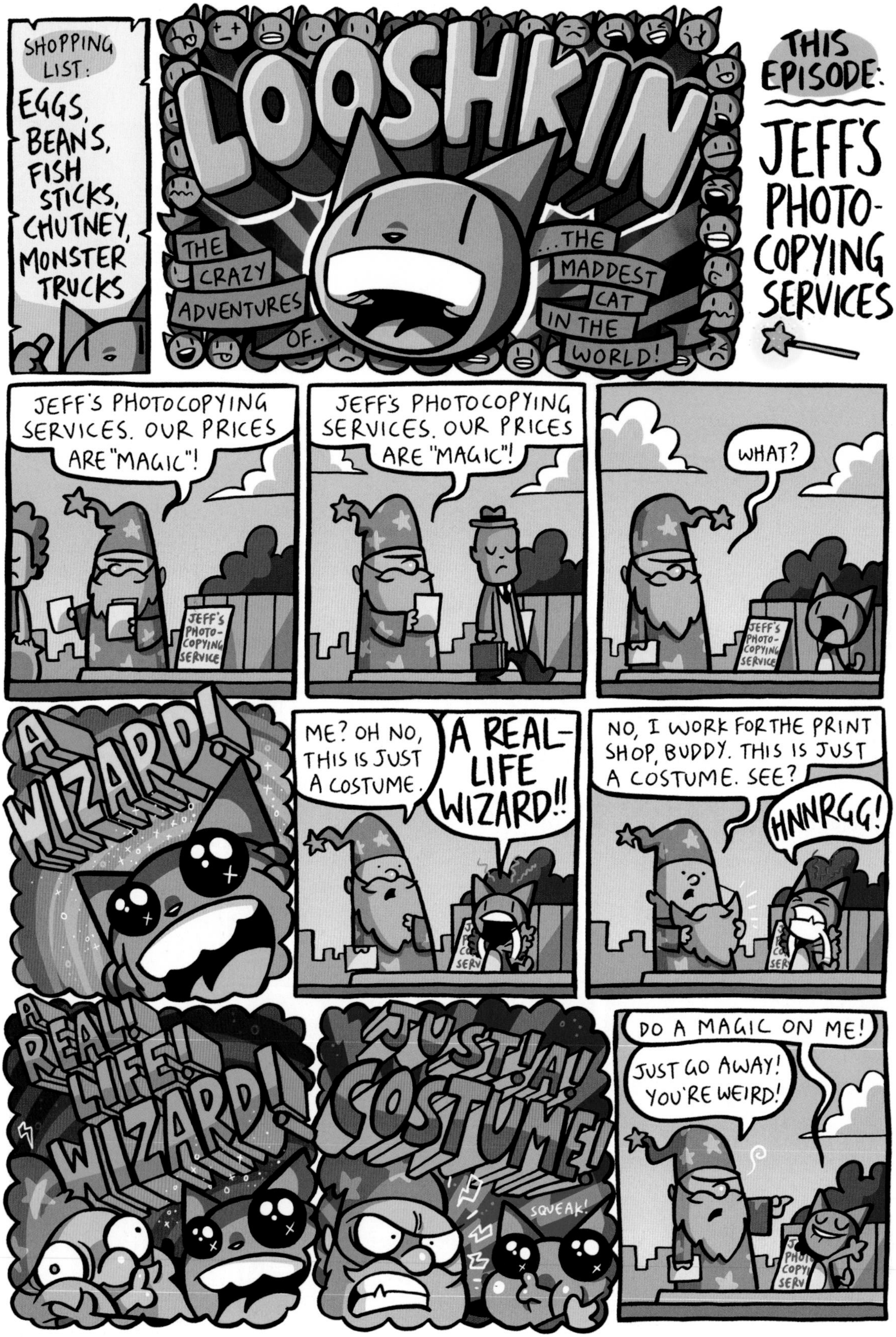
SHOPPING LIST:
EGGS, BEANS, FISH STICKS, CHUTNEY, MONSTER TRUCKS
LOOSHKIN
THE CRAZY ADVENTURES OF...
...THE MADDEST CAT IN THE WORLD!
THIS EPISODE:
JEFF'S PHOTO-COPYING SERVICES
JEFF'S PHOTOCOPYING SERVICES. OUR PRICES ARE "MAGIC"!
JEFF'S PHOTO-COPYING SERVICE
JEFF'S PHOTOCOPYING SERVICES. OUR PRICES ARE "MAGIC"!
WHAT?
JEFF'S PHOTO-COPYING SERVICE
A WIZARD!
ME? OH NO, THIS IS JUST A COSTUME.
A REAL-LIFE WIZARD!!
NO, I WORK FOR THE PRINT SHOP, BUDDY. THIS IS JUST A COSTUME. SEE?
HNNRGG!
A REAL! LIFE! WIZARD!
JUST! A! COSTUME!
SQUEAK!
DO A MAGIC ON ME!
JUST GO AWAY! YOU'RE WEIRD!

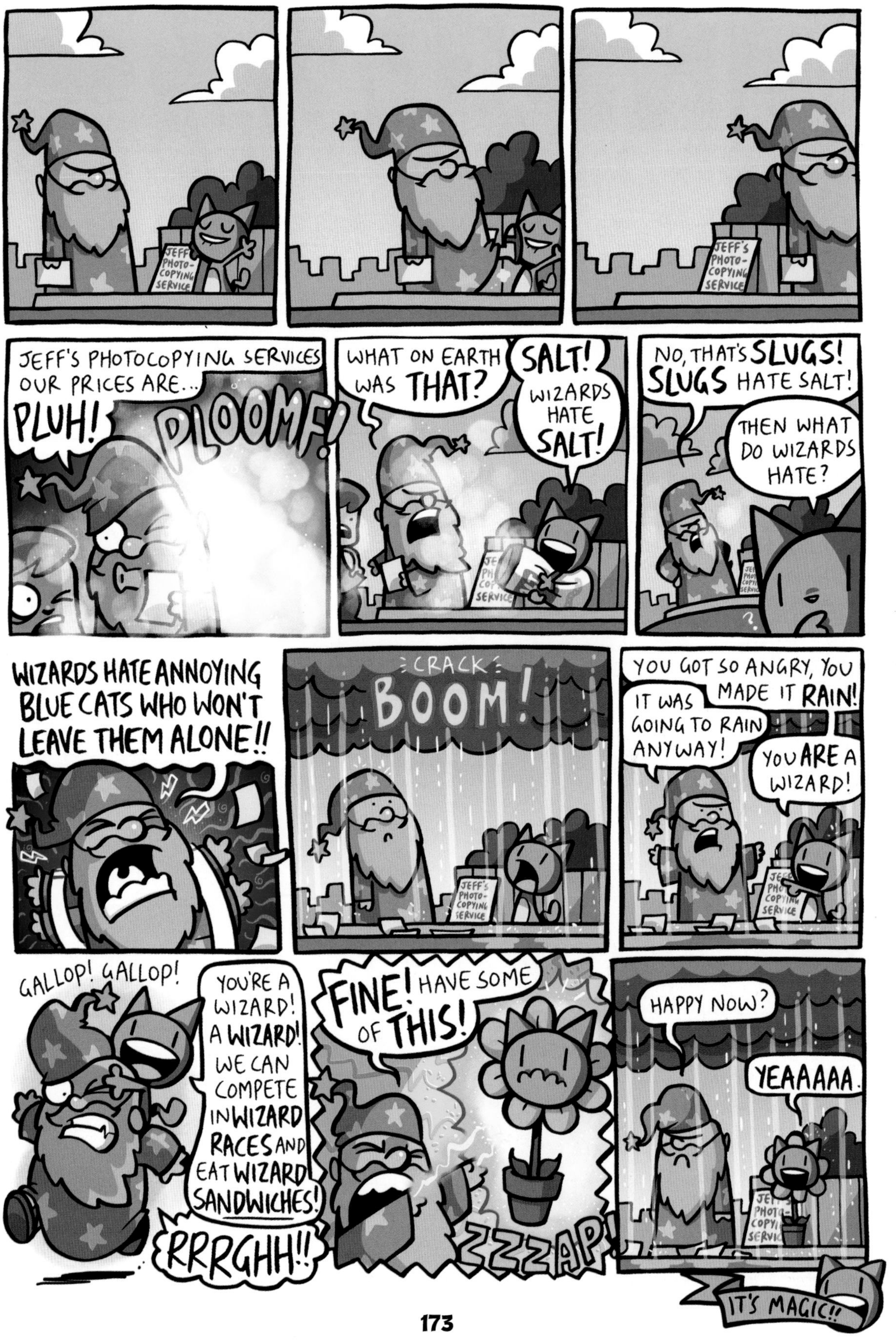
JEFF'S PHOTOCOPYING SERVICE
JEFF'S PHOTOCOPYING SERVICE
JEFF'S PHOTOCOPYING SERVICES OUR PRICES ARE...
PLUH!
PLOOMF!
WHAT ON EARTH WAS THAT?
SALT!
WIZARDS HATE SALT!
JEFF'S PHOTOCOPYING SERVICE
NO, THAT'S SLUGS! SLUGS HATE SALT!
THEN WHAT DO WIZARDS HATE?
?
WIZARDS HATE ANNOYING BLUE CATS WHO WON'T LEAVE THEM ALONE!!
CRACK
BOOM!
JEFF'S PHOTOCOPYING SERVICE
YOU GOT SO ANGRY, YOU MADE IT RAIN!
IT WAS GOING TO RAIN ANYWAY!
YOU ARE A WIZARD!
JEFF'S PHOTOCOPYING SERVICE
GALLOP! GALLOP!
YOU'RE A WIZARD! A WIZARD! WE CAN COMPETE IN WIZARD RACES AND EAT WIZARD SANDWICHES!
RRRGHH!!
FINE! HAVE SOME OF THIS!
ZZZAP!
HAPPY NOW?
YEAAAAA.
IT'S MAGIC!!

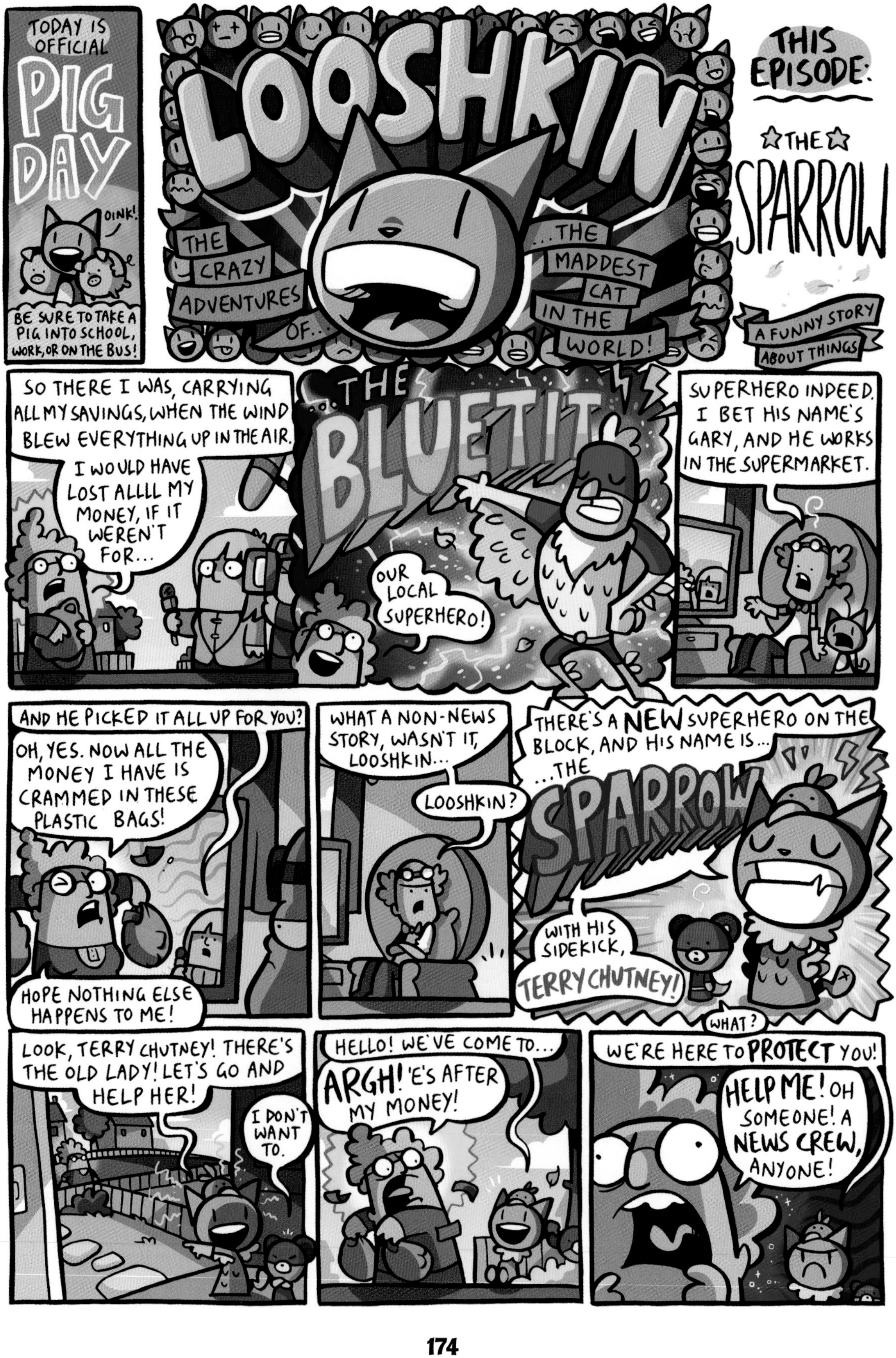
TODAY IS OFFICIAL
PIG DAY
OINK!
BE SURE TO TAKE A PIG INTO SCHOOL, WORK, OR ON THE BUS!
LOOSHKIN
THE CRAZY ADVENTURES OF...
...THE MADDEST CAT IN THE WORLD!
THIS EPISODE:
THE SPARROW
A FUNNY STORY ABOUT THINGS
SO THERE I WAS, CARRYING ALL MY SAVINGS, WHEN THE WIND BLEW EVERYTHING UP IN THE AIR.
I WOULD HAVE LOST ALLLL MY MONEY, IF IT WEREN'T FOR...
...THE BLUETIT
OUR LOCAL SUPERHERO!
SUPERHERO INDEED. I BET HIS NAME'S GARY, AND HE WORKS IN THE SUPERMARKET.
AND HE PICKED IT ALL UP FOR YOU?
OH, YES. NOW ALL THE MONEY I HAVE IS CRAMMED IN THESE PLASTIC BAGS!
HOPE NOTHING ELSE HAPPENS TO ME!
WHAT A NON-NEWS STORY, WASN'T IT, LOOSHKIN...
LOOSHKIN?
THERE'S A NEW SUPERHERO ON THE BLOCK, AND HIS NAME IS...
...THE SPARROW
WITH HIS SIDEKICK, TERRY CHUTNEY!
WHAT?
LOOK, TERRY CHUTNEY! THERE'S THE OLD LADY! LET'S GO AND HELP HER!
I DON'T WANT TO.
HELLO! WE'VE COME TO...
ARGH! 'E'S AFTER MY MONEY!
WE'RE HERE TO PROTECT YOU!
HELP ME! OH SOMEONE! A NEWS CREW, ANYONE!

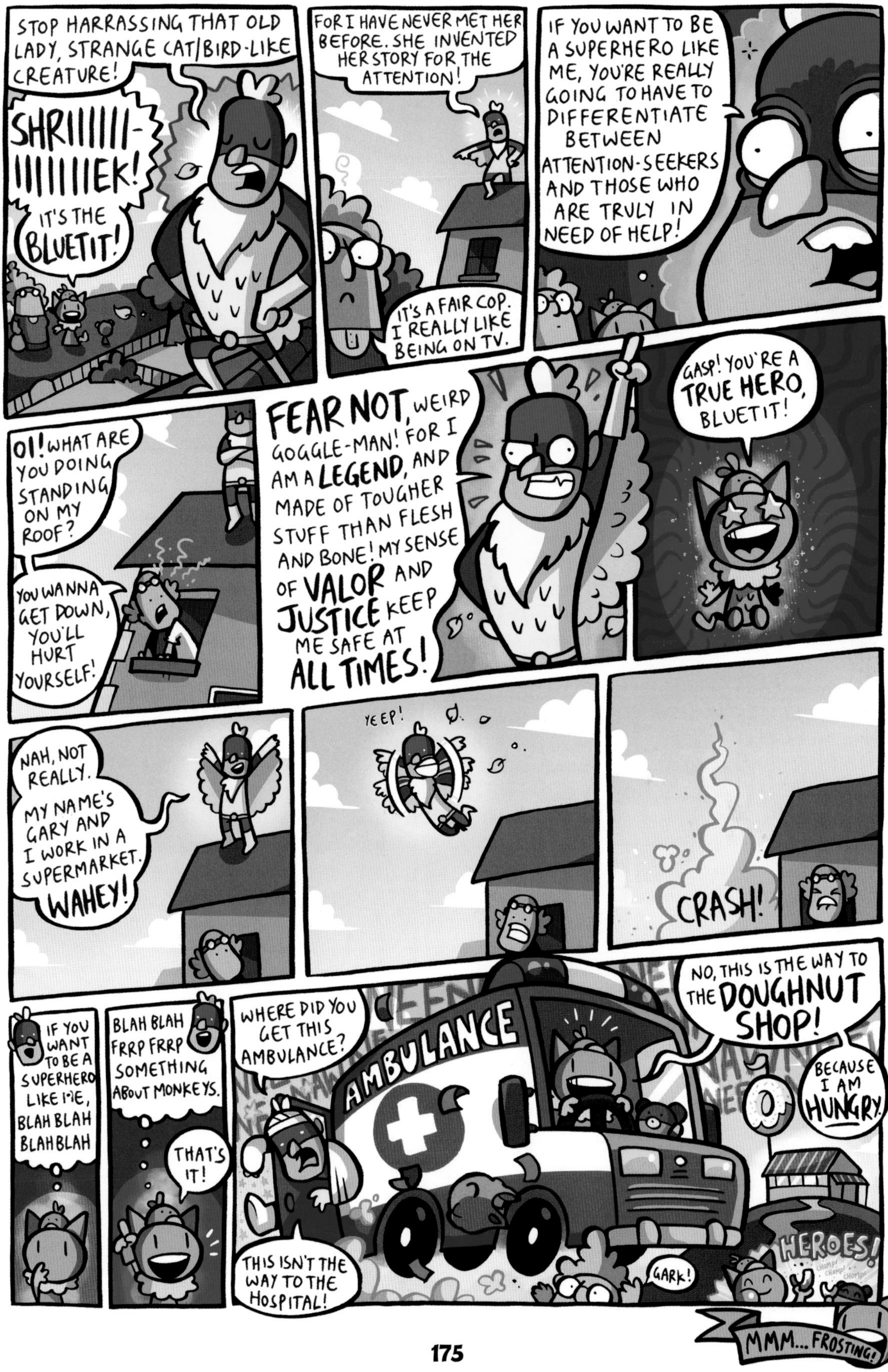

STOP HARRASSING THAT OLD LADY, STRANGE CAT/BIRD-LIKE CREATURE!
SHRIIIIIII-IIIIIIIEK!
IT'S THE BLUETIT!
FOR I HAVE NEVER MET HER BEFORE. SHE INVENTED HER STORY FOR THE ATTENTION!
IT'S A FAIR COP. I REALLY LIKE BEING ON TV.
IF YOU WANT TO BE A SUPERHERO LIKE ME, YOU'RE REALLY GOING TO HAVE TO DIFFERENTIATE BETWEEN ATTENTION-SEEKERS AND THOSE WHO ARE TRULY IN NEED OF HELP!
OI! WHAT ARE YOU DOING STANDING ON MY ROOF?
YOU WANNA GET DOWN, YOU'LL HURT YOURSELF!
FEAR NOT, WEIRD GOGGLE-MAN! FOR I AM A LEGEND, AND MADE OF TOUGHER STUFF THAN FLESH AND BONE! MY SENSE OF VALOR AND JUSTICE KEEP ME SAFE AT ALL TIMES!
GASP! YOU'RE A TRUE HERO, BLUETIT!
NAH, NOT REALLY.
MY NAME'S GARY AND I WORK IN A SUPERMARKET. WAHEY!
YEEP!
CRASH!
IF YOU WANT TO BE A SUPERHERO LIKE ME, BLAH BLAH BLAH BLAH
BLAH BLAH FRRP FRRP SOMETHING ABOUT MONKEYS.
THAT'S IT!
WHERE DID YOU GET THIS AMBULANCE?
AMBULANCE
NO, THIS IS THE WAY TO THE DOUGHNUT SHOP!
BECAUSE I AM HUNGRY.
THIS ISN'T THE WAY TO THE HOSPITAL!
GARK!
HEROES!
MMM... FROSTING!

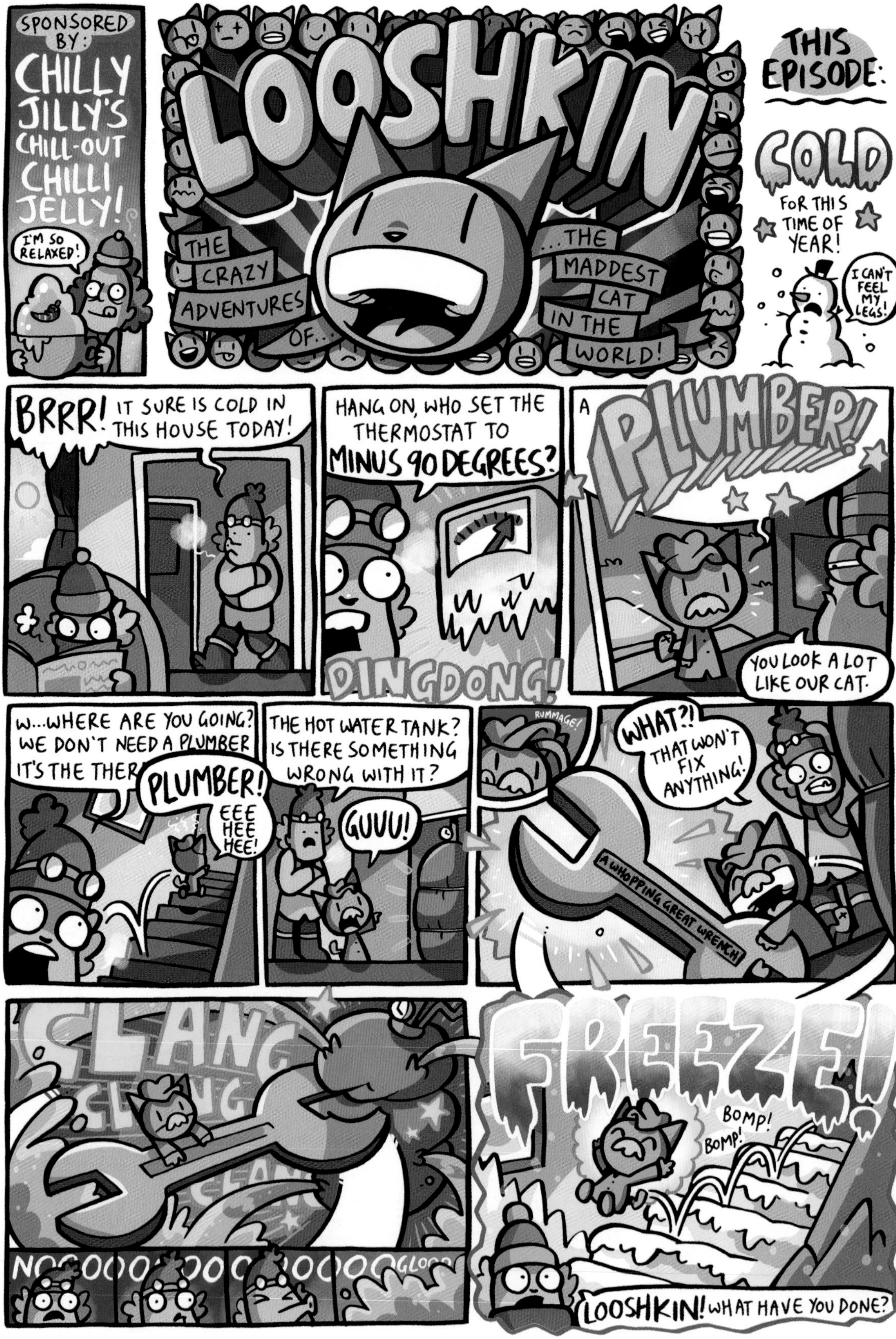
SPONSORED BY:
CHILLY JILLY'S CHILL-OUT CHILLI JELLY!
I'M SO RELAXED!
LOOSHKIN
THE CRAZY ADVENTURES OF...
...THE MADDEST CAT IN THE WORLD!
THIS EPISODE:
COLD
FOR THIS TIME OF YEAR!
I CAN'T FEEL MY LEGS!
BRRR! IT SURE IS COLD IN THIS HOUSE TODAY!
HANG ON, WHO SET THE THERMOSTAT TO MINUS 90 DEGREES?
DINGDONG!
A PLUMBER!
YOU LOOK A LOT LIKE OUR CAT.
W...WHERE ARE YOU GOING? WE DON'T NEED A PLUMBER IT'S THE THER
PLUMBER!
EEE HEE HEE!
THE HOT WATER TANK? IS THERE SOMETHING WRONG WITH IT?
GUUU!
RUMMAGE!
WHAT?! THAT WON'T FIX ANYTHING!
A WHOPPING GREAT WRENCH
CLANG
CLANG
CLANG
NOOOOOOOOOOOOOOO
GLOOP
FREEZE!
BOMP!
BOMP!
LOOSHKIN! WHAT HAVE YOU DONE?

AT LAST, A PLACE I CAN FINALLY CALL HOME!

BOSH!

A FAT DUCK!

DUCK? HOW DARE YOU! I AM A PENGUIN!

HUGGGGZ!!

MY NAME IS RICARDO DE BRIGADIER MONTGOMERY THE THIRD. I AM THE GRANDSON OF THE MOST POWERFUL PENGUIN IN ALL THE WORLD!

I HAVE COMMITTED MANY CRIMES AND BEEN HELD PRISONER FOR MANY YEARS. BUT NOW I AM FREE, TO WREAK VENGEANCE ON MY CAPTORS!

OKAY, BUT FIRST LET'S SKATE AROUND ON OUR BOTTOMS!

OKAY. WHEEE!

SKIDDD

HELLO, WE'RE FROM THE ZOO. HAVE YOU SEEN A PENGUIN?

THERE HE IS, GEORGE!

OOPS.

GRAB HIM WITH TOWELS! WITH TOWELS!

NO! HUFF PUFF HUFF! NO!

NOOOOOO! I WILL NOT GO BACK TO PRISON! I WILL NEVER GO BACK!

FLUMP!

AW, LISTEN TO HIM TALKING.

QUACK QUACK QUACK QUACK!

AVENGE ME, HUMBLE PLUMBER! TEAR DOWN THIS HUMAN WORLD UNTIL THEY SET US ALL FREE!

ZOO

KRUMMMMMMM

BYEEEEE!

YOU ARE IN A LOT OF TROUBLE, LOOSHKIN.

PEEP PEEP!!

177

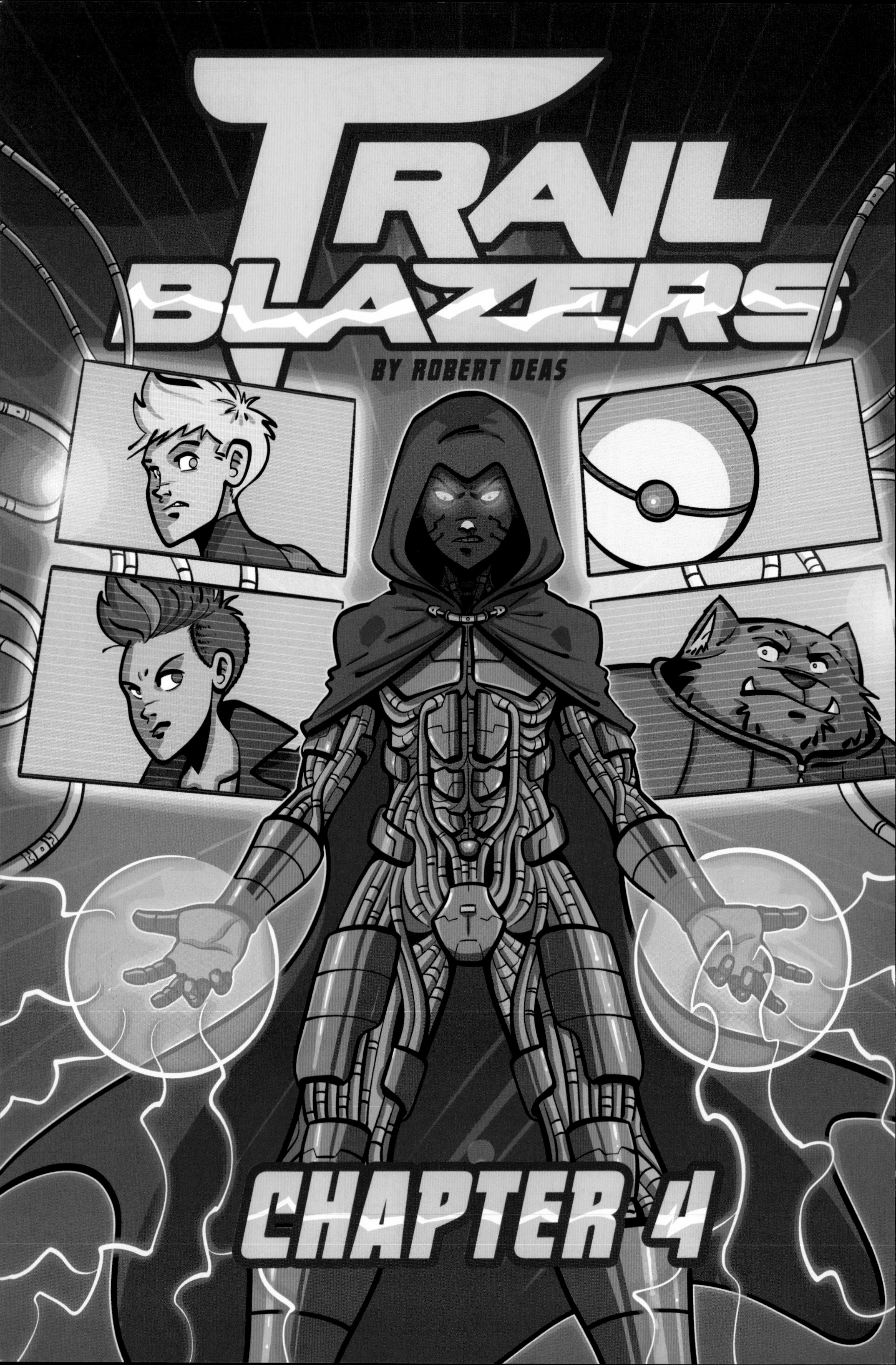
TRAIL BLAZERS
BY ROBERT DEAS
CHAPTER 4

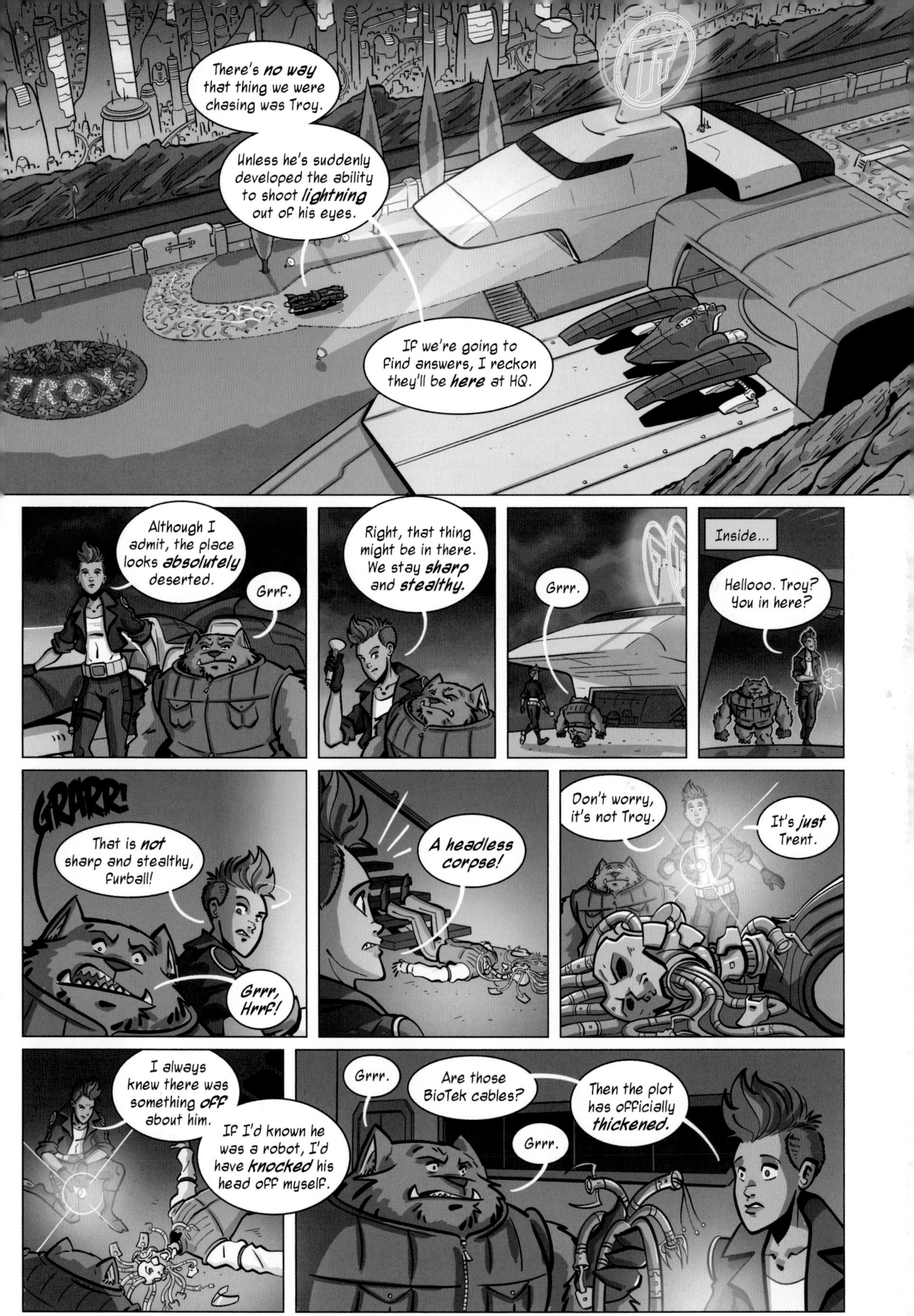
There's no way that thing we were chasing was Troy.
Unless he's suddenly developed the ability to shoot lightning out of his eyes.
If we're going to find answers, I reckon they'll be here at HQ.
TROY
Although I admit, the place looks absolutely deserted.
Grrf.
Right, that thing might be in there. We stay sharp and stealthy.
Grrr.
Inside...
Hellooo. Troy? You in here?
GRARR!
That is not sharp and stealthy, Furball!
Grrr, Hrrf!
A headless corpse!
Don't worry, it's not Troy.
It's just Trent.
I always knew there was something off about him.
If I'd known he was a robot, I'd have knocked his head off myself.
Grrr.
Are those BioTek cables?
Grrr.
Then the plot has officially thickened.

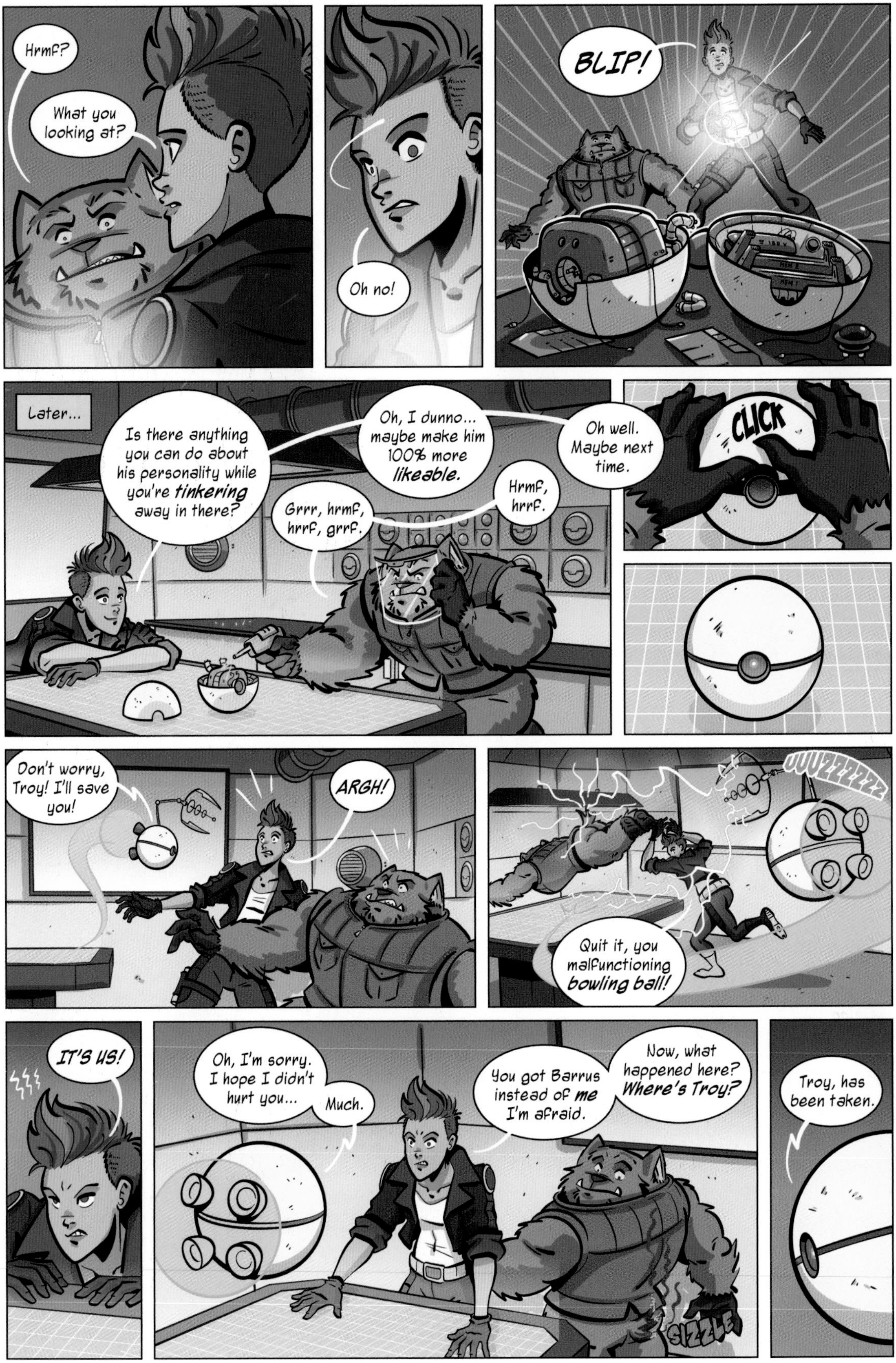
Hrmf?
What you looking at?
Oh no!
BLIP!
Later...
Is there anything you can do about his personality while you're *tinkering* away in there?
Oh, I dunno... maybe make him 100% more *likeable.*
Oh well. Maybe next time.
Grrr, hrmf, hrrf, grrf.
Hrmf, hrrf.
CLICK
Don't worry, Troy! I'll save you!
ARGH!
UUUZZZZZZ
Quit it, you malfunctioning *bowling ball!*
IT'S US!
Oh, I'm sorry. I hope I didn't hurt you...
Much.
You got Barrus instead of *me* I'm afraid.
Now, what happened here? *Where's Troy?*
SIZZLE
Troy, has been taken.

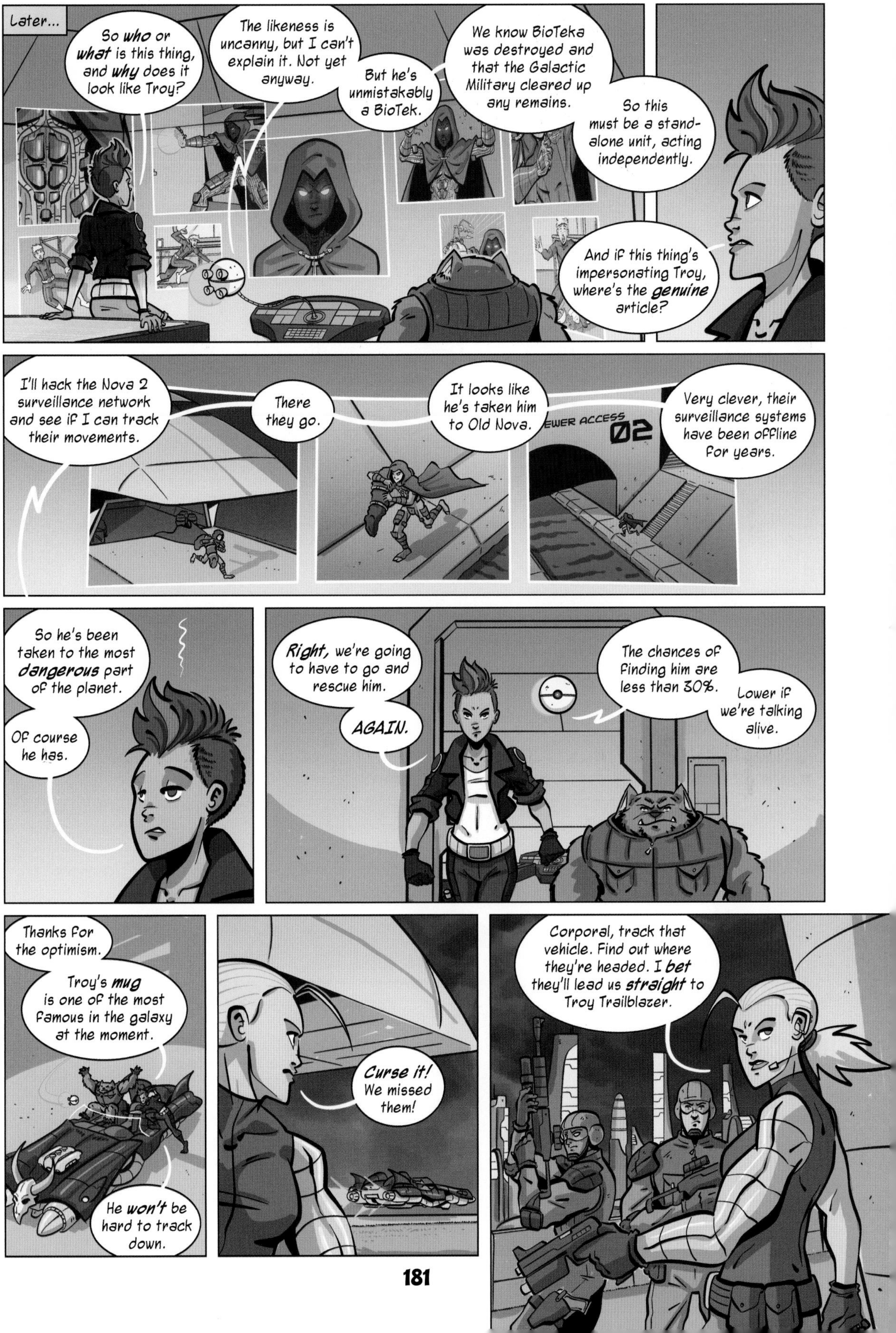

Later...
So who or what is this thing, and why does it look like Troy?
The likeness is uncanny, but I can't explain it. Not yet anyway.
But he's unmistakably a BioTek.
We know BioTeka was destroyed and that the Galactic Military cleared up any remains.
So this must be a stand-alone unit, acting independently.
And if this thing's impersonating Troy, where's the genuine article?
I'll hack the Nova 2 surveillance network and see if I can track their movements.
There they go.
It looks like he's taken him to Old Nova.
EWER ACCESS 02
Very clever, their surveillance systems have been offline for years.
So he's been taken to the most dangerous part of the planet.
Of course he has.
Right, we're going to have to go and rescue him.
AGAIN.
The chances of finding him are less than 30%.
Lower if we're talking alive.
Thanks for the optimism.
Troy's mug is one of the most famous in the galaxy at the moment.
He won't be hard to track down.
Curse it! We missed them!
Corporal, track that vehicle. Find out where they're headed. I bet they'll lead us straight to Troy Trailblazer.

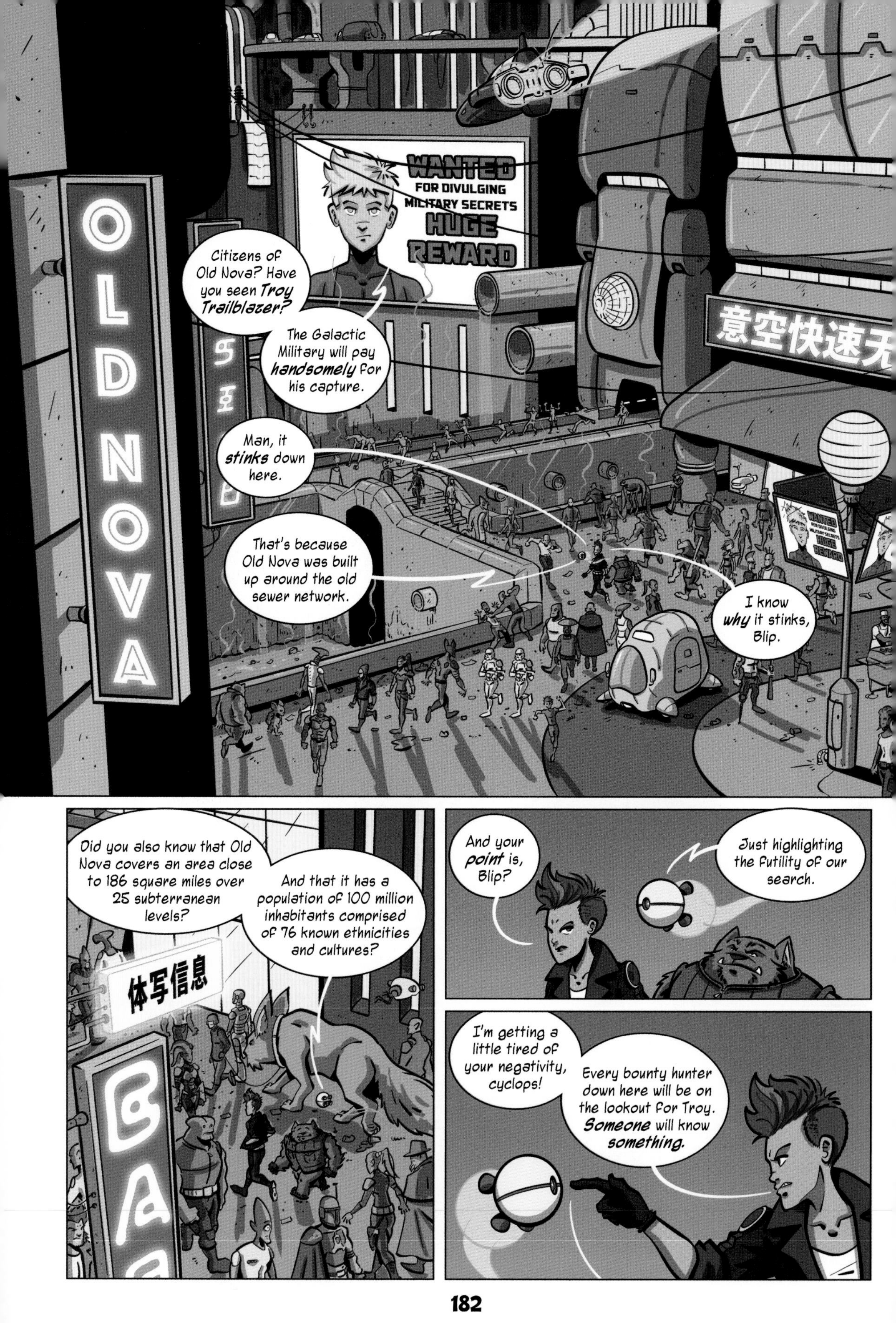
OLD NOVA
WANTED
FOR DIVULGING MILITARY SECRETS
HUGE REWARD
意空快速无
Citizens of Old Nova? Have you seen *Troy Trailblazer?*
The Galactic Military will pay ***handsomely*** for his capture.
Man, it ***stinks*** down here.
That's because Old Nova was built up around the old sewer network.
I know ***why*** it stinks, Blip.
Did you also know that Old Nova covers an area close to 186 square miles over 25 subterranean levels?
And that it has a population of 100 million inhabitants comprised of 76 known ethnicities and cultures?
体写信息
And your ***point*** is, Blip?
Just highlighting the futility of our search.
I'm getting a little tired of your negativity, cyclops!
Every bounty hunter down here will be on the lookout for Troy. ***Someone*** will know ***something.***

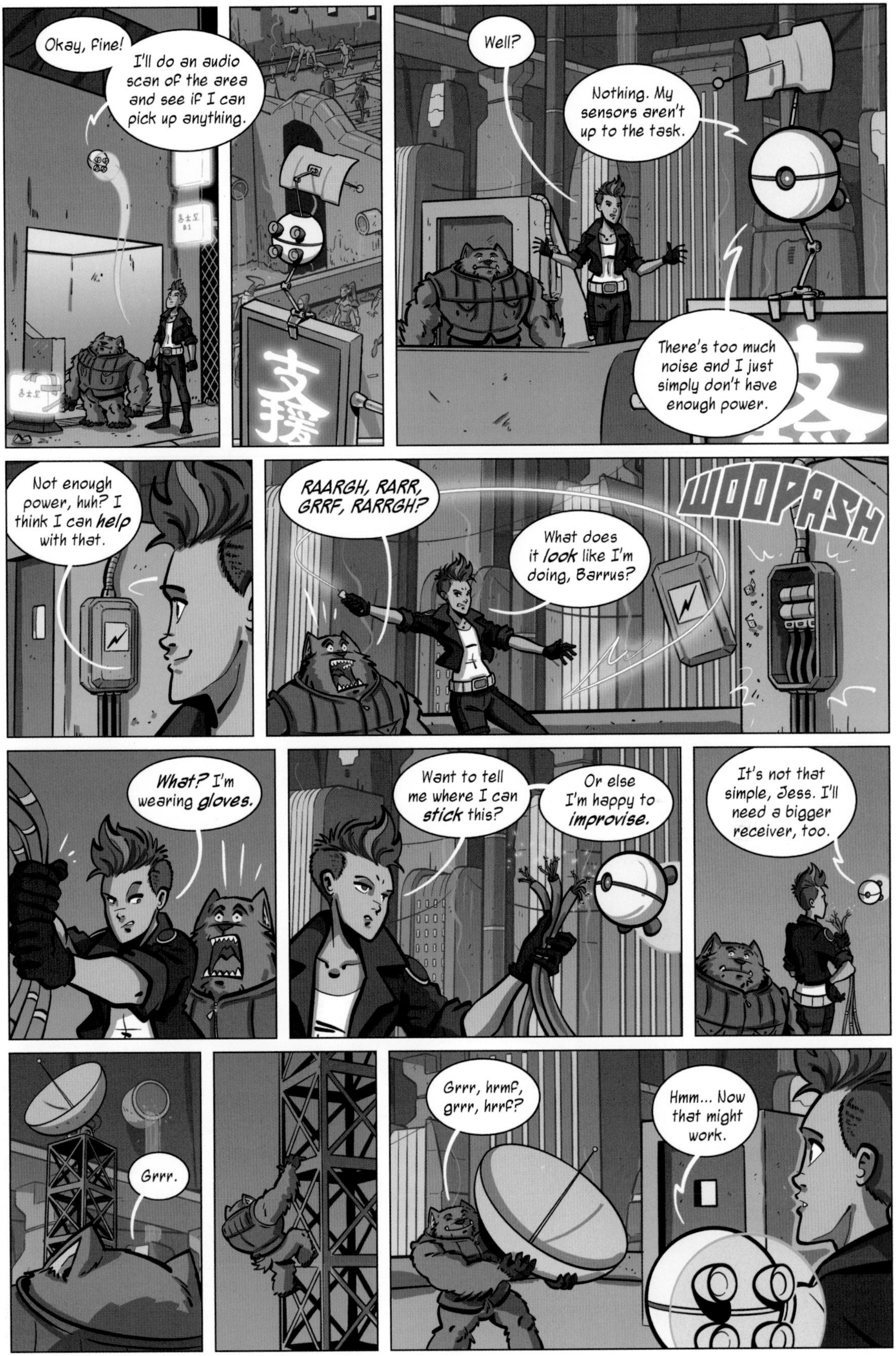
Okay, fine!
I'll do an audio scan of the area and see if I can pick up anything.
Well?
Nothing. My sensors aren't up to the task.
There's too much noise and I just simply don't have enough power.
Not enough power, huh? I think I can *help* with that.
RAARGH, RARR, GRRF, RARRGH?
What does it *look* like I'm doing, Barrus?
WOOPASH
*What?* I'm wearing *gloves.*
Want to tell me where I can *stick* this?
Or else I'm happy to *improvise.*
It's not that simple, Jess. I'll need a bigger receiver, too.
Grrr.
Grrr, hrmf, grrr, hrrf?
Hmm... Now that might work.

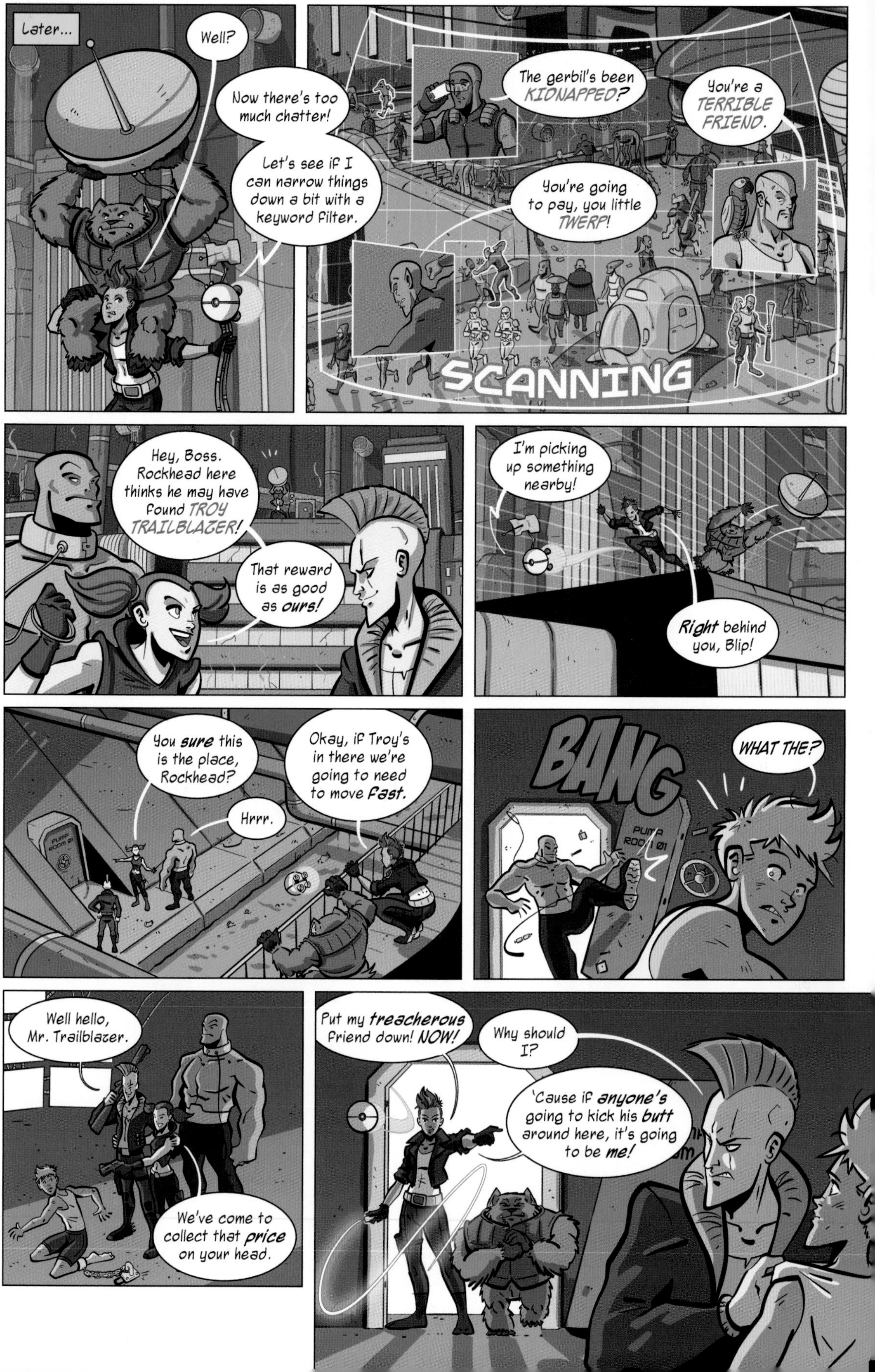
Later...
Well?
Now there's too much chatter!
Let's see if I can narrow things down a bit with a keyword filter.
The gerbil's been KIDNAPPED?
You're a TERRIBLE FRIEND.
You're going to pay, you little TWERP!
SCANNING
Hey, Boss. Rockhead here thinks he may have found TROY TRAILBLAZER!
That reward is as good as ours!
I'm picking up something nearby!
Right behind you, Blip!
You sure this is the place, Rockhead?
Hrrr.
Okay, if Troy's in there we're going to need to move fast.
PUMP ROOM 01
BANG
WHAT THE?
PUMP ROOM 01
Well hello, Mr. Trailblazer.
We've come to collect that price on your head.
Put my treacherous friend down! NOW!
Why should I?
'Cause if anyone's going to kick his butt around here, it's going to be me!

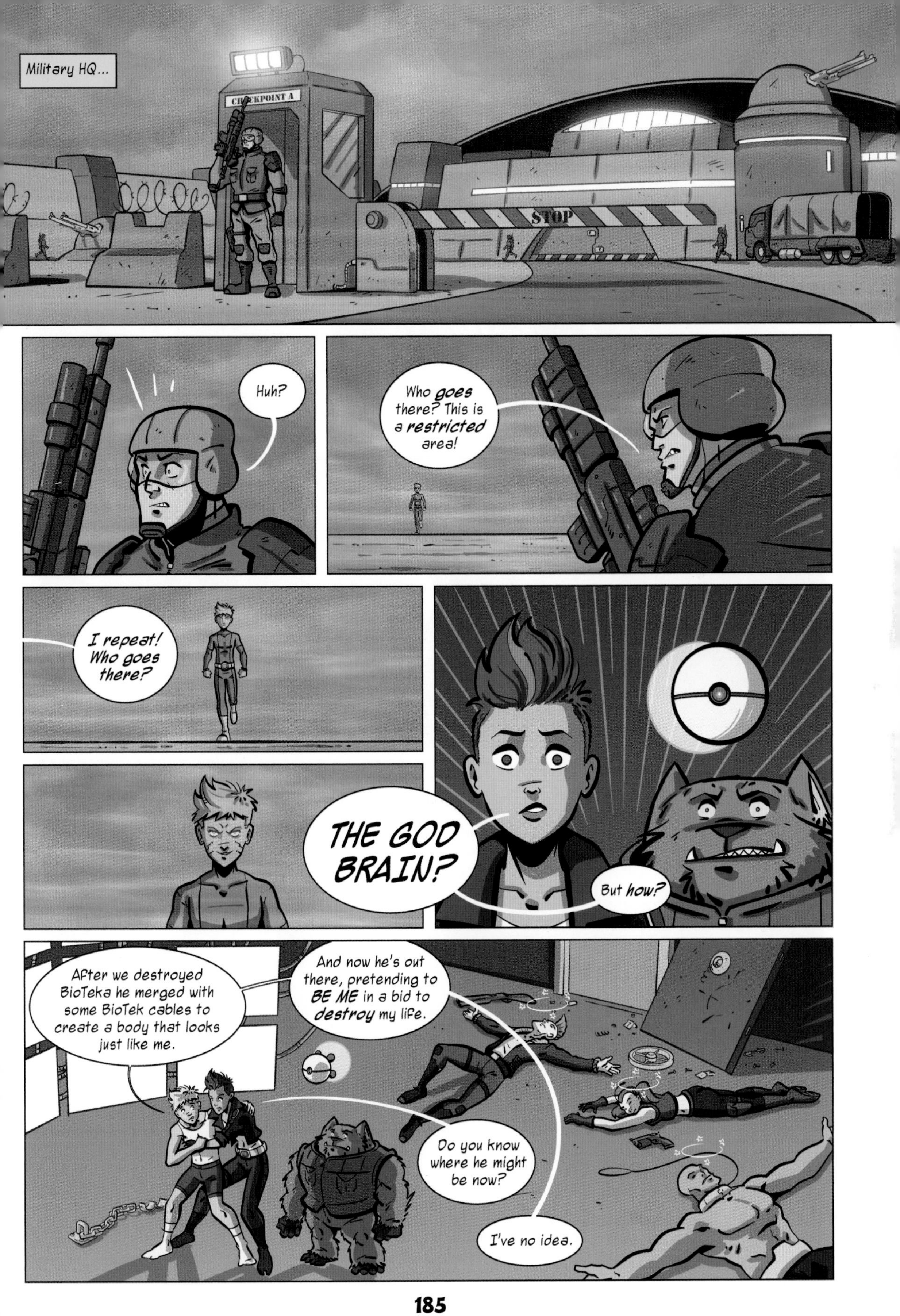
Military HQ...
CHECKPOINT A
STOP
Huh?
Who goes there? This is a restricted area!
I repeat! Who goes there?
THE GOD BRAIN?
But how?
After we destroyed BioTeka he merged with some BioTek cables to create a body that looks just like me.
And now he's out there, pretending to BE ME in a bid to destroy my life.
Do you know where he might be now?
I've no idea.

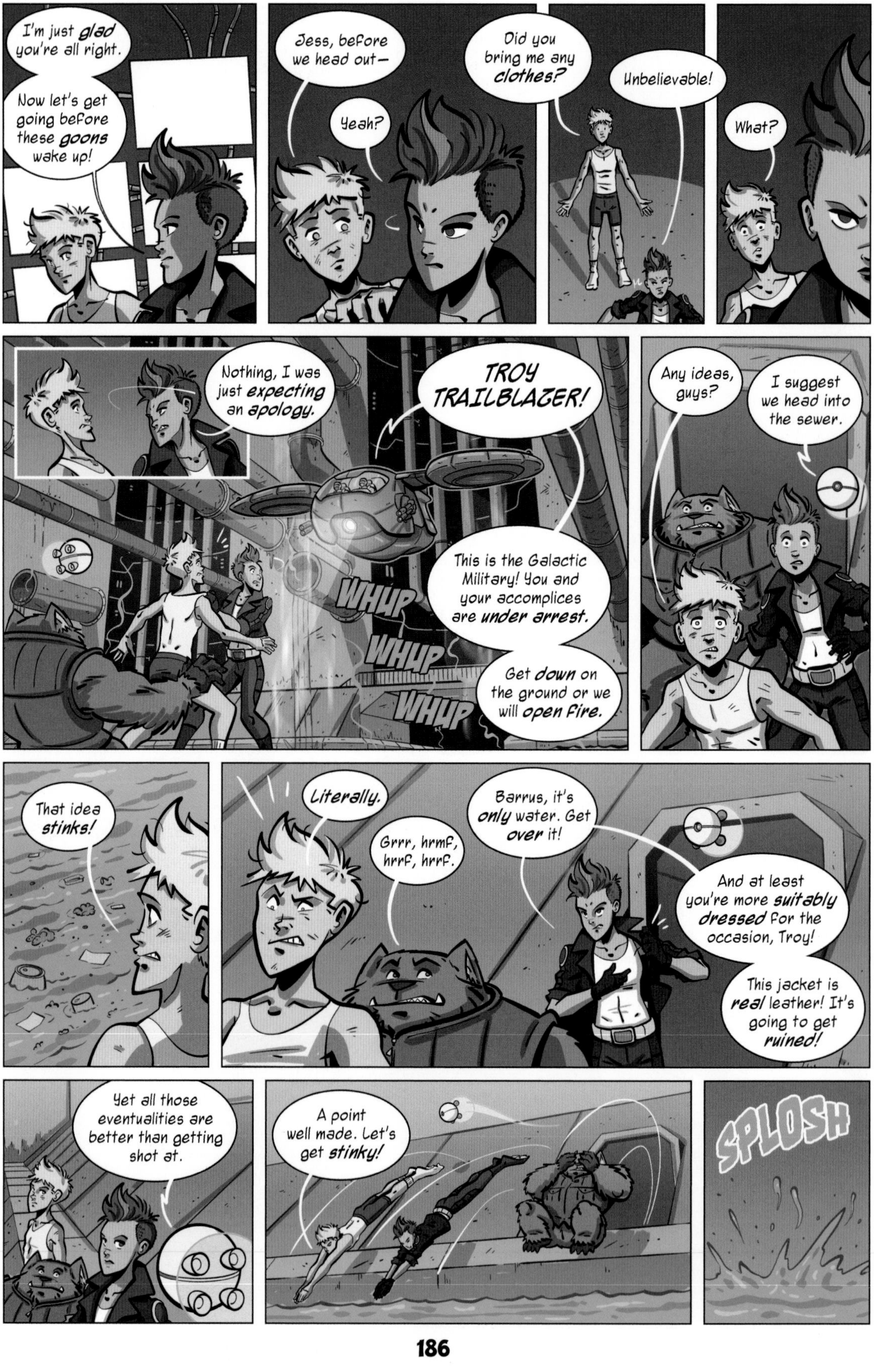

I'm just glad you're all right.
Now let's get going before these goons wake up!
Jess, before we head out—
Yeah?
Did you bring me any clothes?
Unbelievable!
What?
Nothing, I was just expecting an apology.
TROY TRAILBLAZER!
This is the Galactic Military! You and your accomplices are under arrest.
Get down on the ground or we will open fire.
WHUP
WHUP
WHUP
Any ideas, guys?
I suggest we head into the sewer.
That idea stinks!
Literally.
Grrr, hrmf, hrrf, hrrf.
Barrus, it's only water. Get over it!
And at least you're more suitably dressed for the occasion, Troy!
This jacket is real leather! It's going to get ruined!
Yet all those eventualities are better than getting shot at.
A point well made. Let's get stinky!
SPLOSH

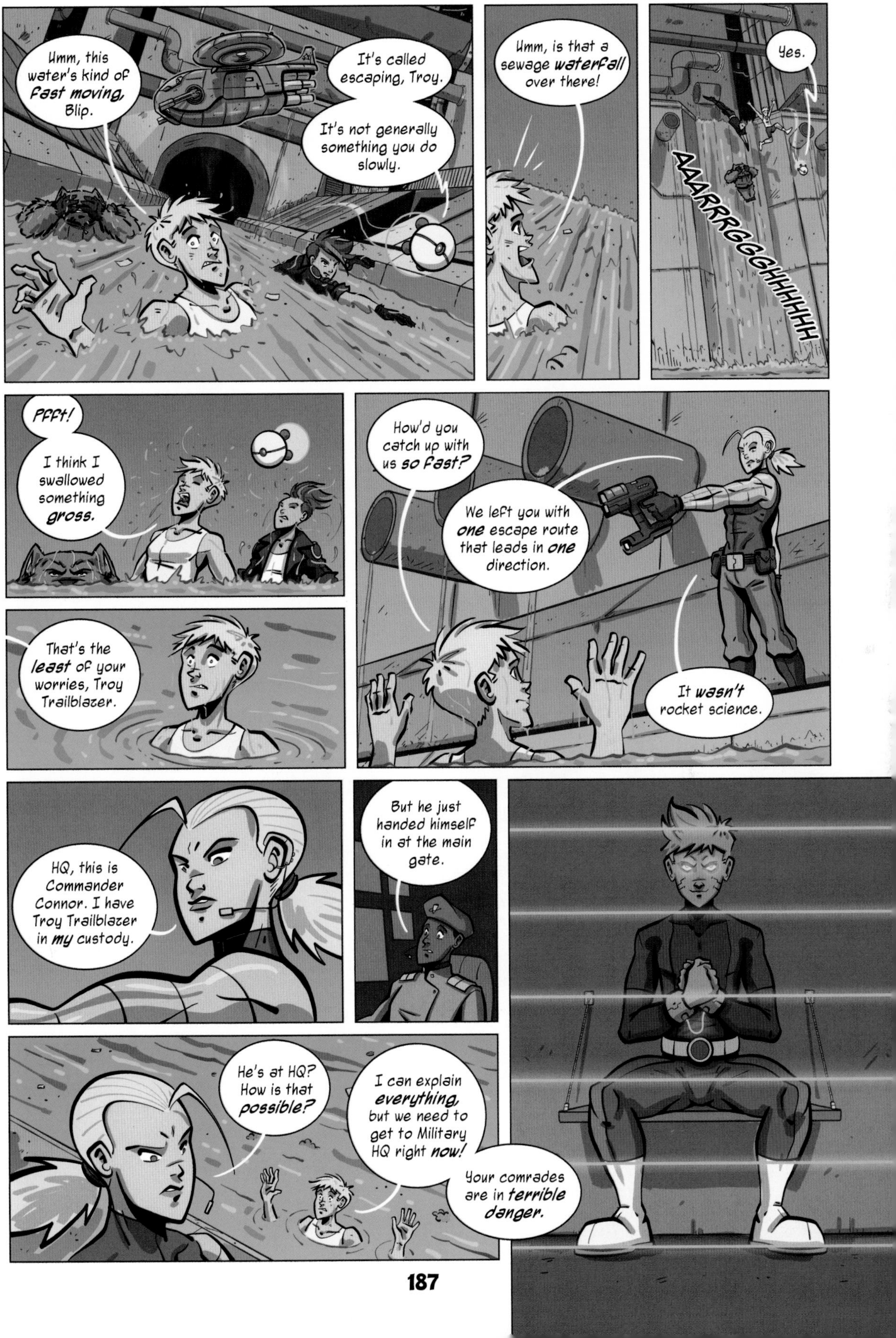
Umm, this water's kind of fast moving, Blip.
It's called escaping, Troy.
It's not generally something you do slowly.
Umm, is that a sewage waterfall over there!
Yes.
AAARRGGGHHHHHH
Pfft!
I think I swallowed something gross.
That's the least of your worries, Troy Trailblazer.
How'd you catch up with us so fast?
We left you with one escape route that leads in one direction.
It wasn't rocket science.
HQ, this is Commander Connor. I have Troy Trailblazer in my custody.
But he just handed himself in at the main gate.
He's at HQ? How is that possible?
I can explain everything, but we need to get to Military HQ right now!
Your comrades are in terrible danger.

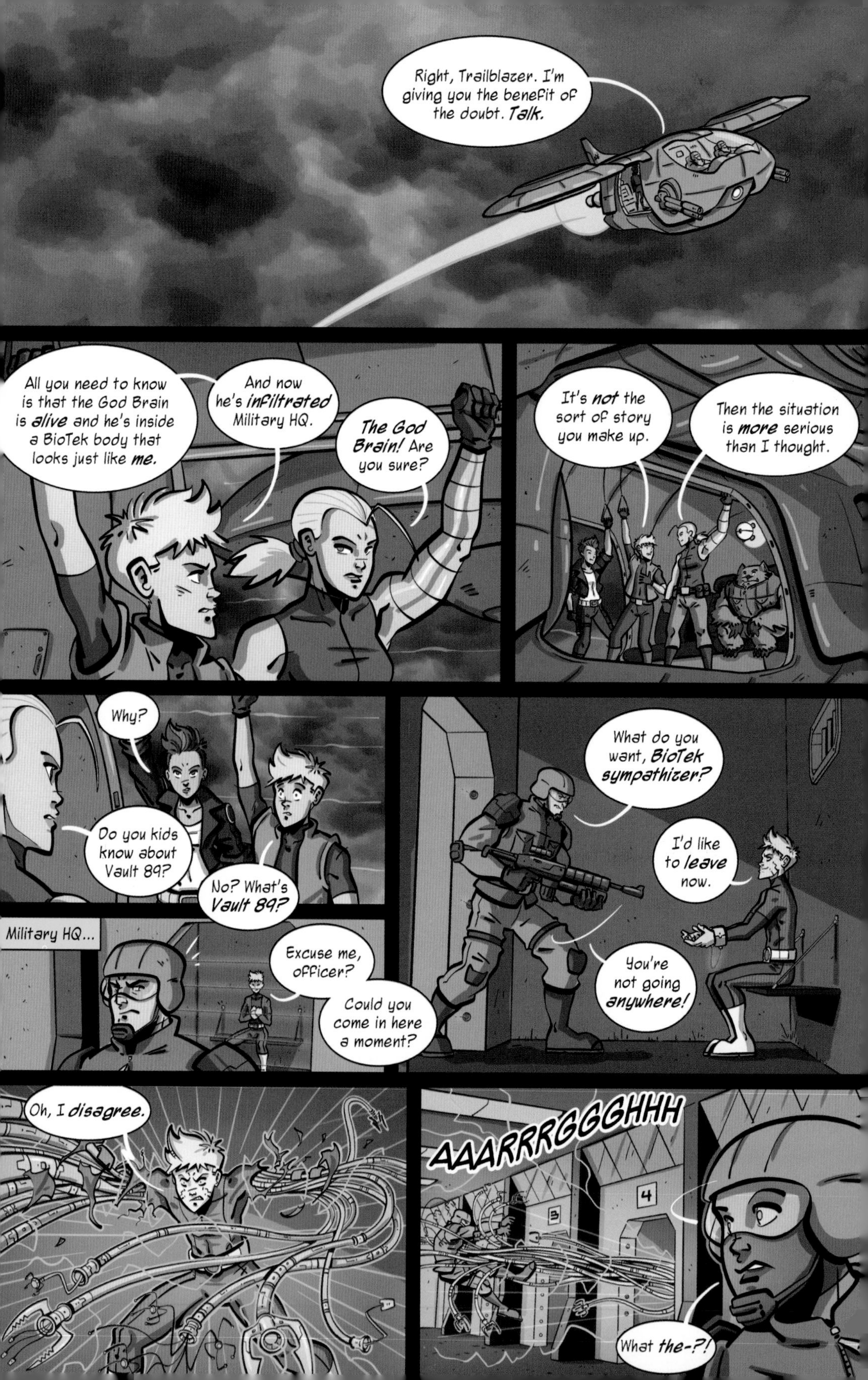
Right, Trailblazer. I'm giving you the benefit of the doubt. *Talk.*
All you need to know is that the God Brain is *alive* and he's inside a BioTek body that looks just like *me.*
And now he's *infiltrated* Military HQ.
*The God Brain!* Are you sure?
It's *not* the sort of story you make up.
Then the situation is *more* serious than I thought.
Why?
Do you kids know about Vault 89?
No? What's *Vault 89?*
Military HQ...
Excuse me, officer?
Could you come in here a moment?
What do you want, *BioTek sympathizer?*
I'd like to *leave* now.
You're not going *anywhere!*
Oh, I *disagree.*
AAARRRGGGHHH
4
3
What *the-?!*

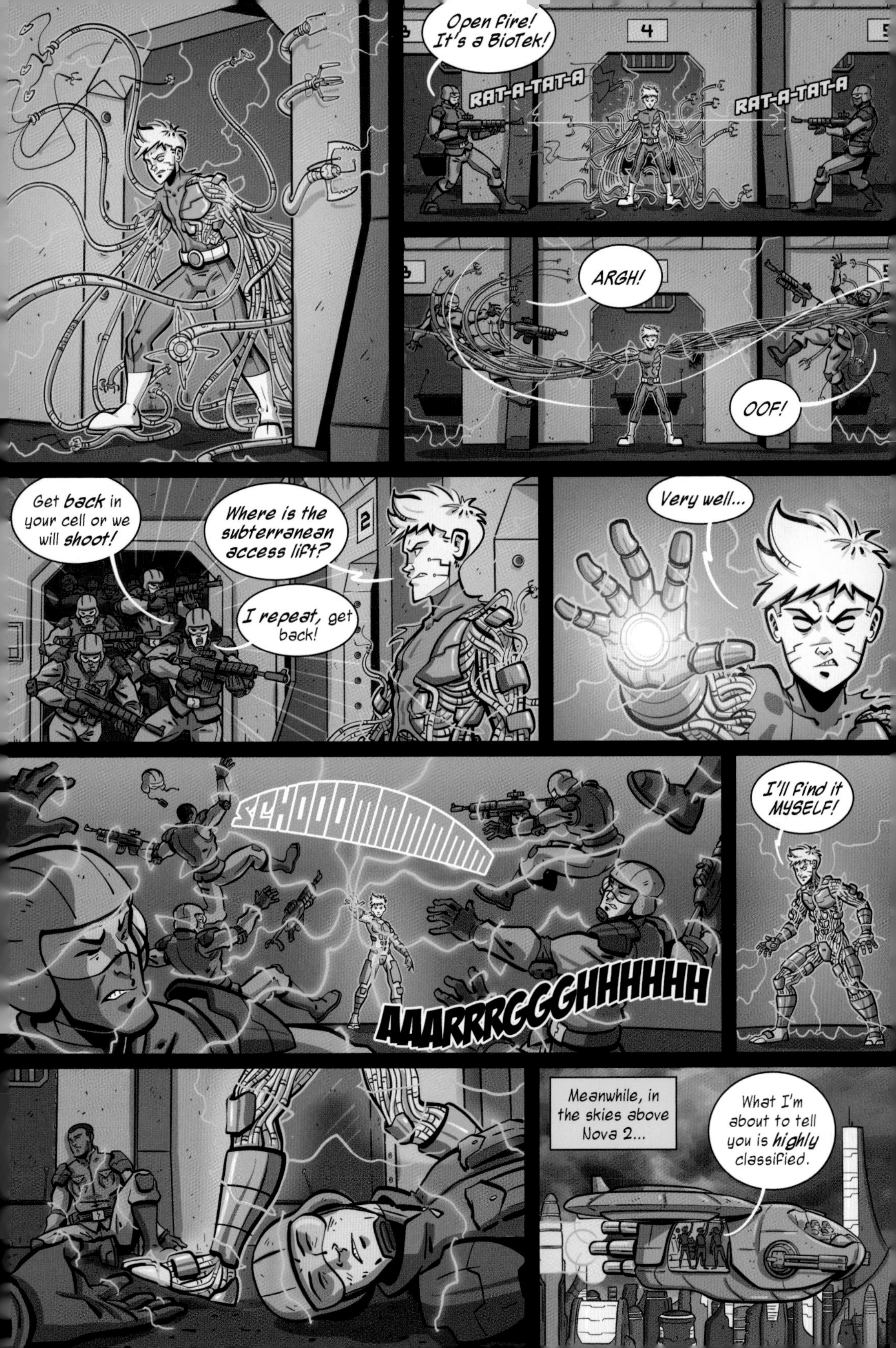
Open fire! It's a BioTek!
RAT-A-TAT-A
RAT-A-TAT-A
ARGH!
OOF!
Get back in your cell or we will shoot!
Where is the subterranean access lift?
I repeat, get back!
Very well...
SCHOOOMMMMMMM
AAARRRGGGHHHHHH
I'll find it MYSELF!
Meanwhile, in the skies above Nova 2...
What I'm about to tell you is highly classified.

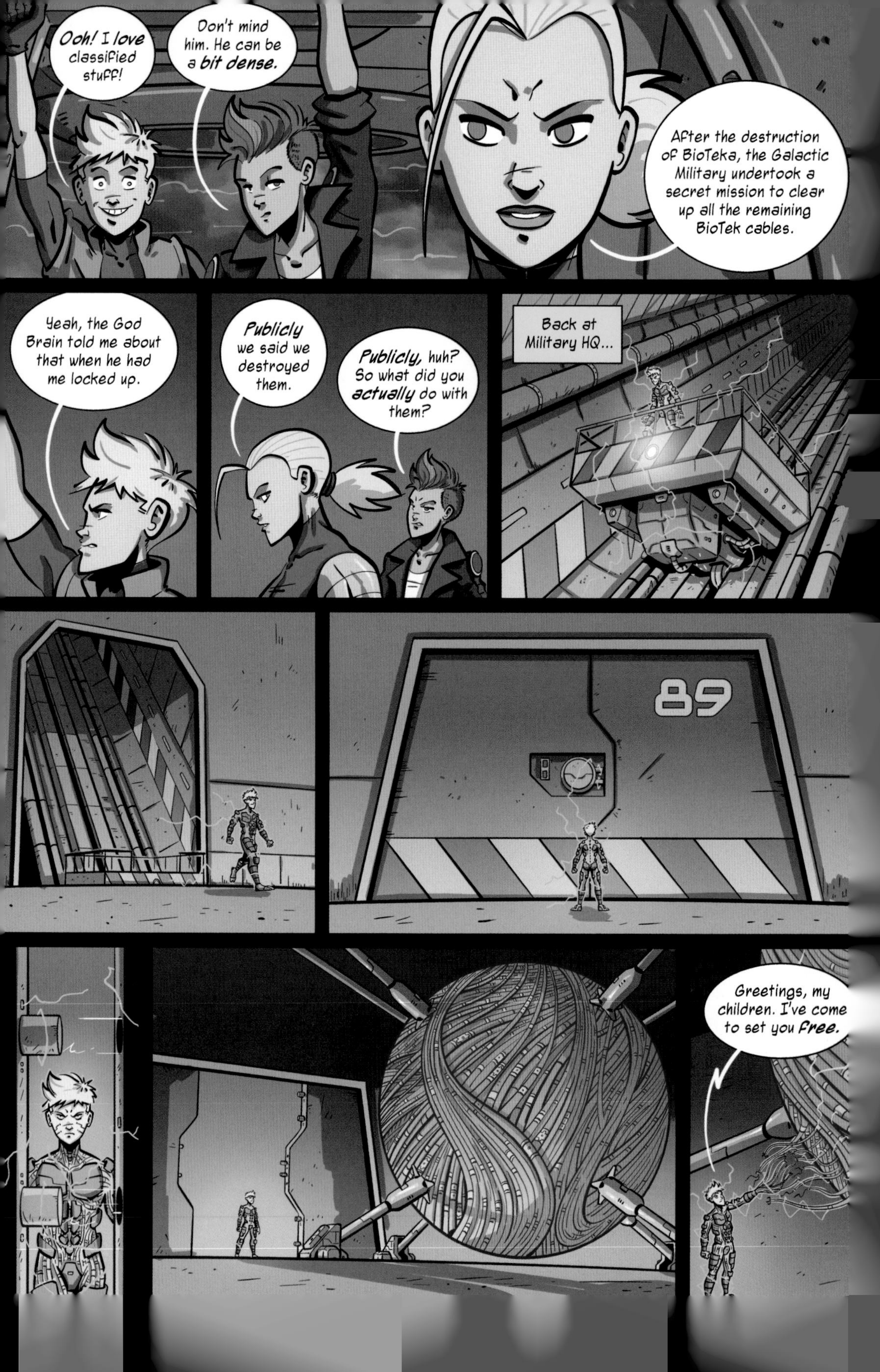
Ooh! I love classified stuff!
Don't mind him. He can be a bit dense.
After the destruction of BioTeka, the Galactic Military undertook a secret mission to clear up all the remaining BioTek cables.
Yeah, the God Brain told me about that when he had me locked up.
Publicly we said we destroyed them.
Publicly, huh? So what did you actually do with them?
Back at Military HQ...
89
Greetings, my children. I've come to set you free.

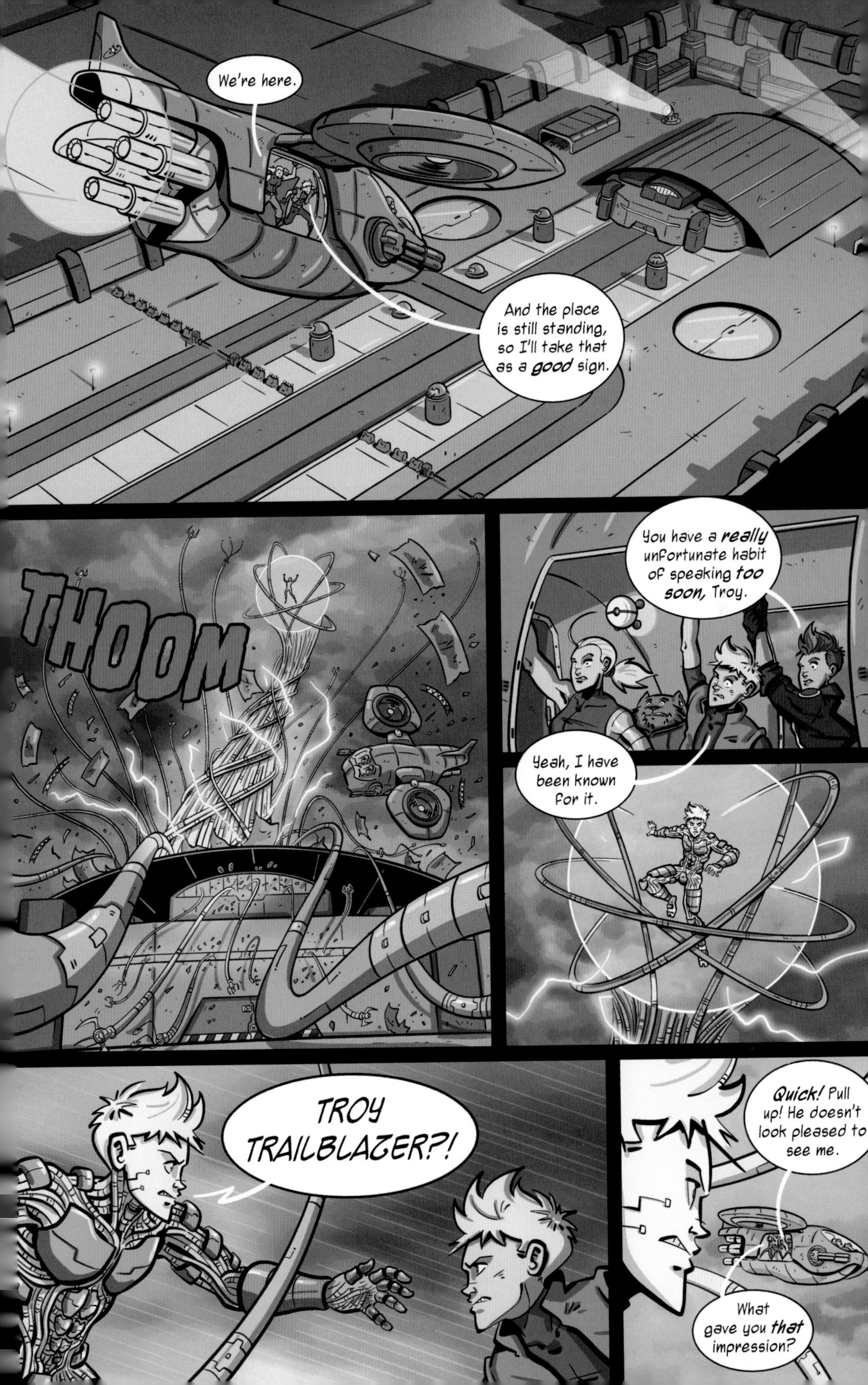
We're here.
And the place is still standing, so I'll take that as a *good* sign.
THOOM
You have a *really* unfortunate habit of speaking *too soon*, Troy.
Yeah, I have been known for it.
TROY TRAILBLAZER?!
*Quick!* Pull up! He doesn't look pleased to see me.
What gave you *that* impression?

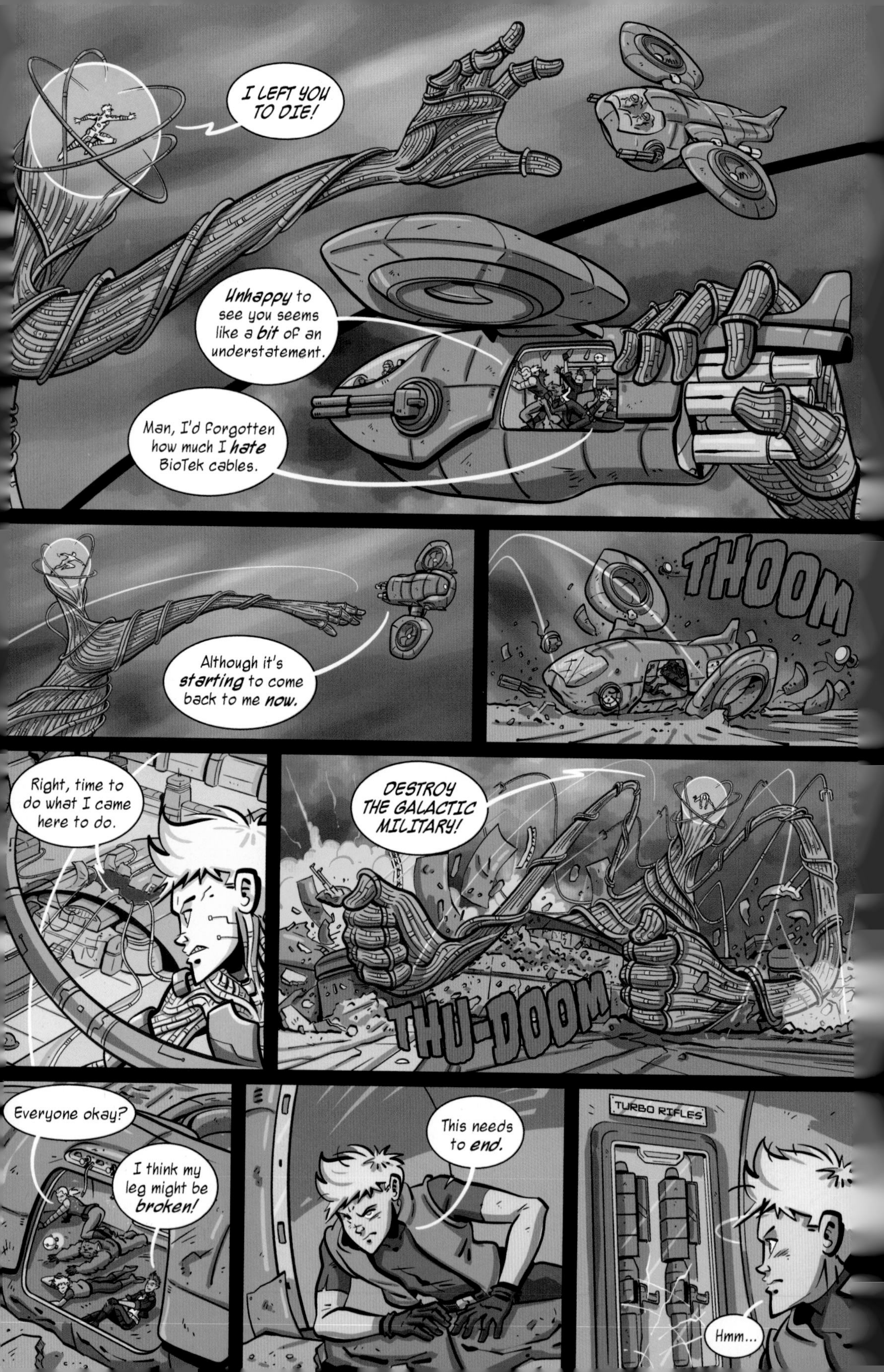

I LEFT YOU TO DIE!
Unhappy to see you seems like a bit of an understatement.
Man, I'd forgotten how much I hate BioTek cables.
Although it's starting to come back to me now.
THOOM
Right, time to do what I came here to do.
DESTROY THE GALACTIC MILITARY!
THU-DOOM
Everyone okay?
I think my leg might be broken!
This needs to end.
TURBO RIFLES
Hmm...

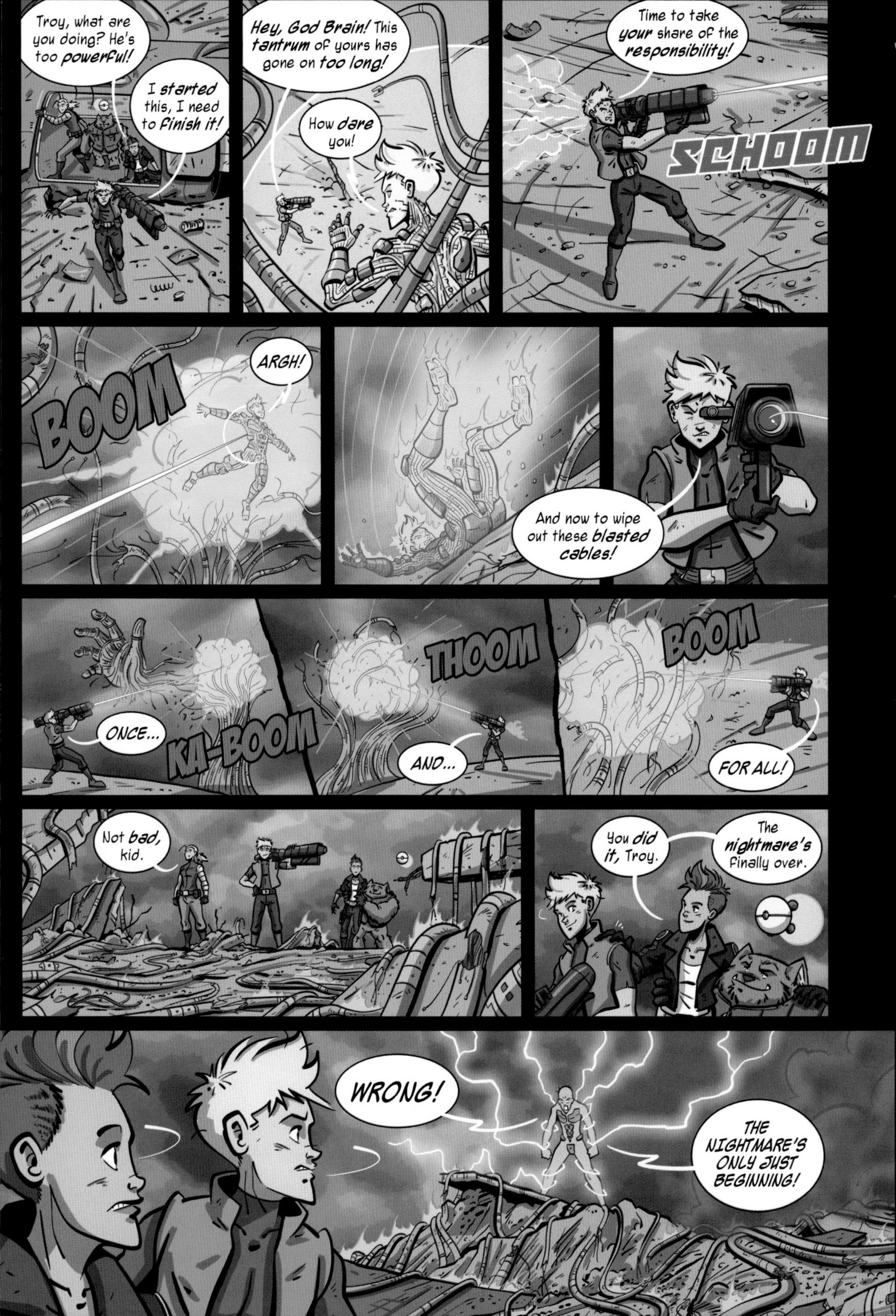
Troy, what are you doing? He's too powerful!
I started this, I need to finish it!
Hey, God Brain! This tantrum of yours has gone on too long!
How dare you!
Time to take your share of the responsibility!
SCHOOM
BOOM
ARGH!
And now to wipe out these blasted cables!
ONCE...
KA-BOOM
THOOM
AND...
BOOM
FOR ALL!
Not bad, kid.
You did it, Troy.
The nightmare's finally over.
WRONG!
THE NIGHTMARE'S ONLY JUST BEGINNING!

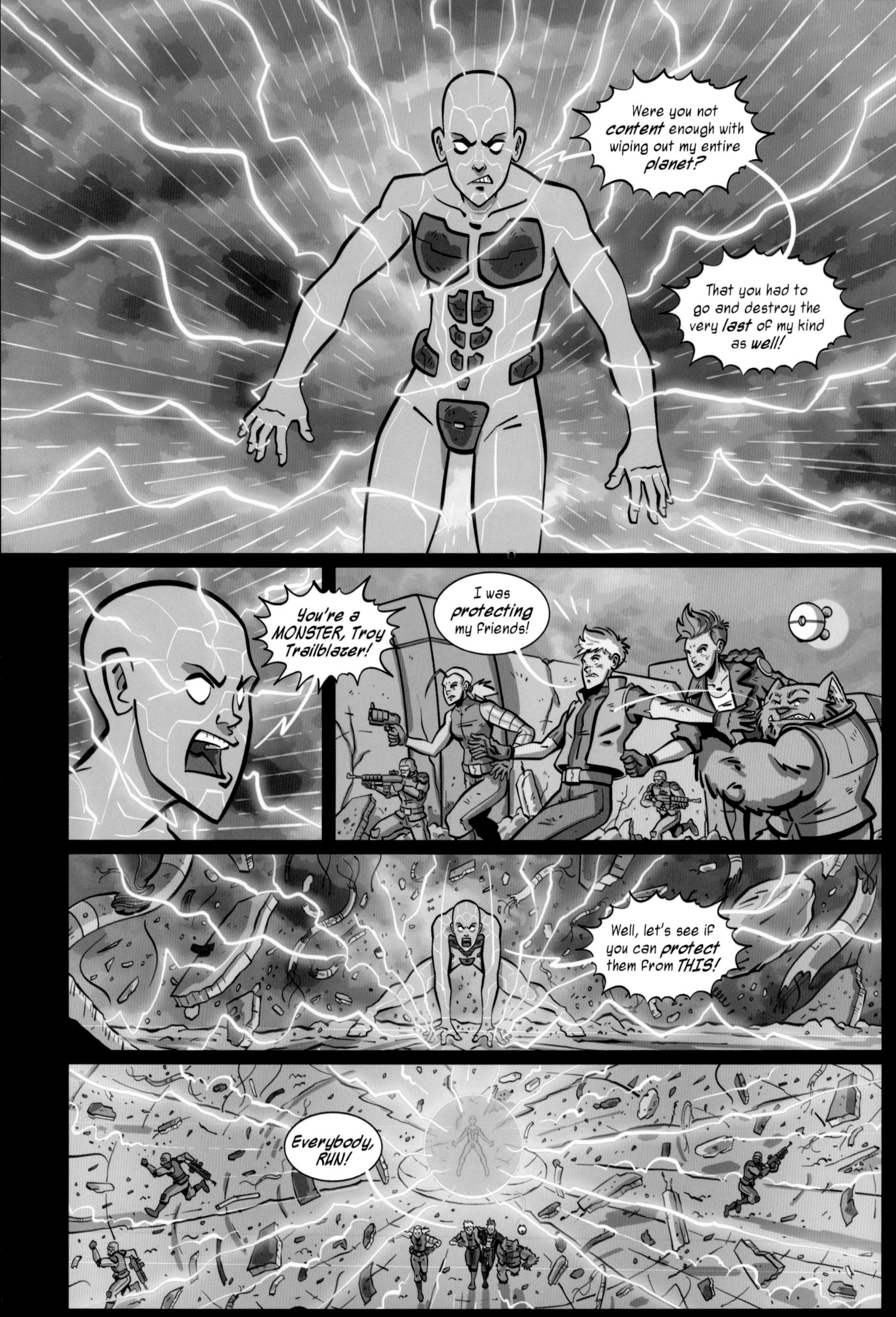

Were you not *content* enough with wiping out my entire *planet?*
That you had to go and destroy the very *last* of my kind as *well!*
You're a MONSTER, Troy Trailblazer!
I was *protecting* my friends!
Well, let's see if you can *protect* them from *THIS!*
Everybody, RUN!

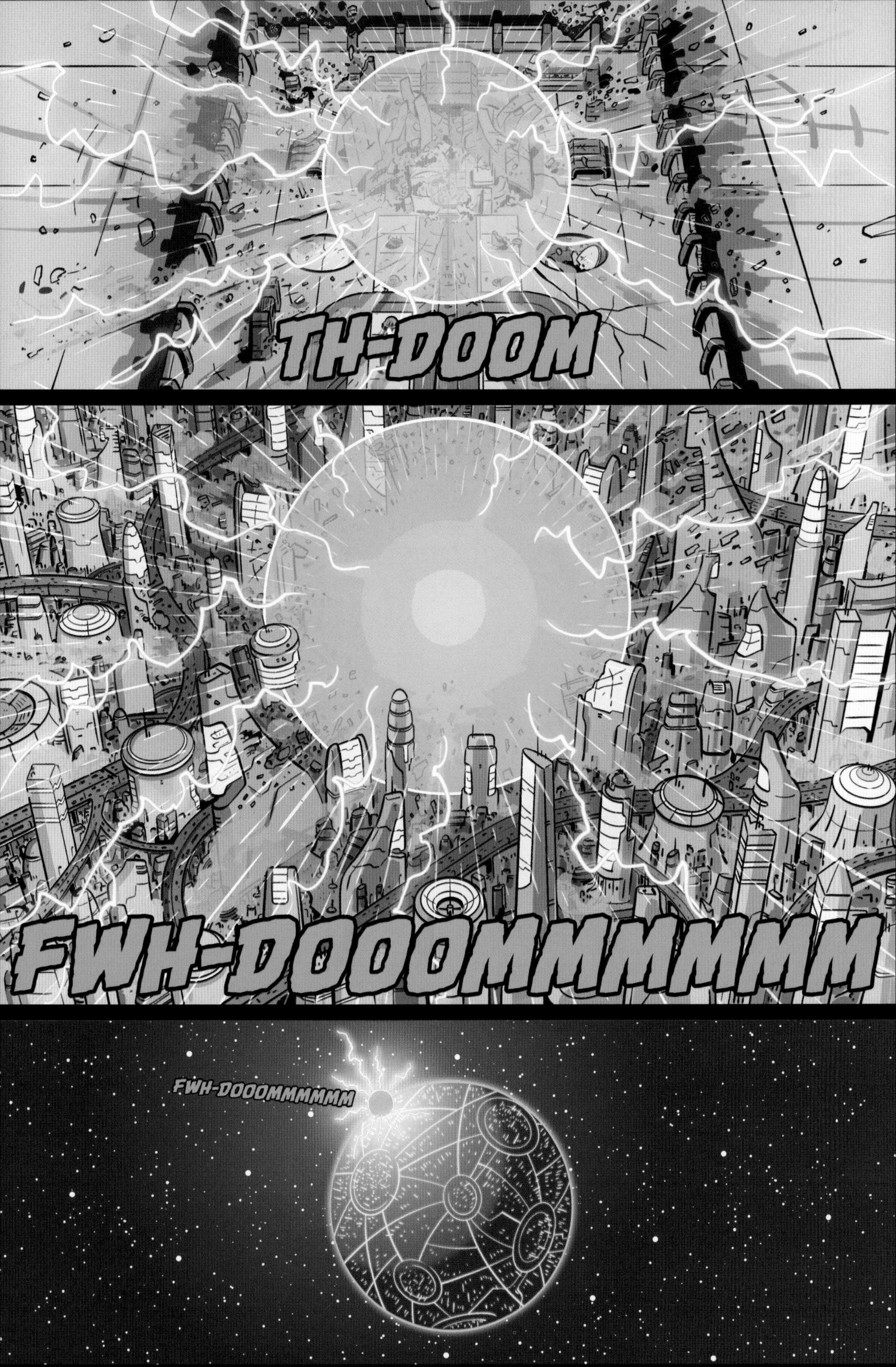
TH-DOOM
FWH-DOOOMMMMMM
FWH-DOOOMMMMMM

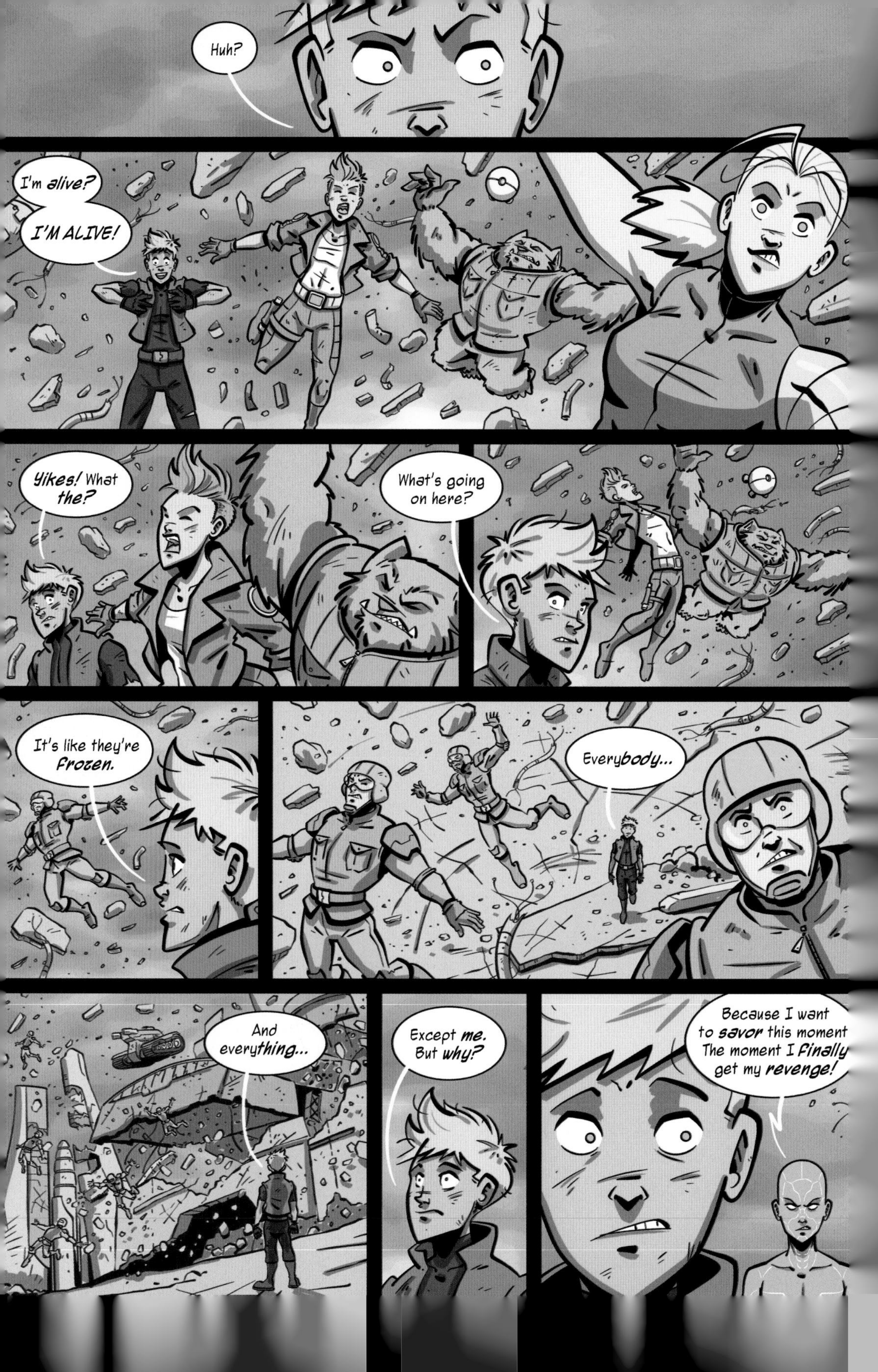
Huh?
I'm *alive?*
*I'M ALIVE!*
***Yikes!*** What ***the?***
What's going on here?
It's like they're ***frozen.***
Every***body...***
And every***thing...***
Except ***me.*** But ***why?***
Because I want to ***savor*** this moment The moment I ***finally*** get my ***revenge!***

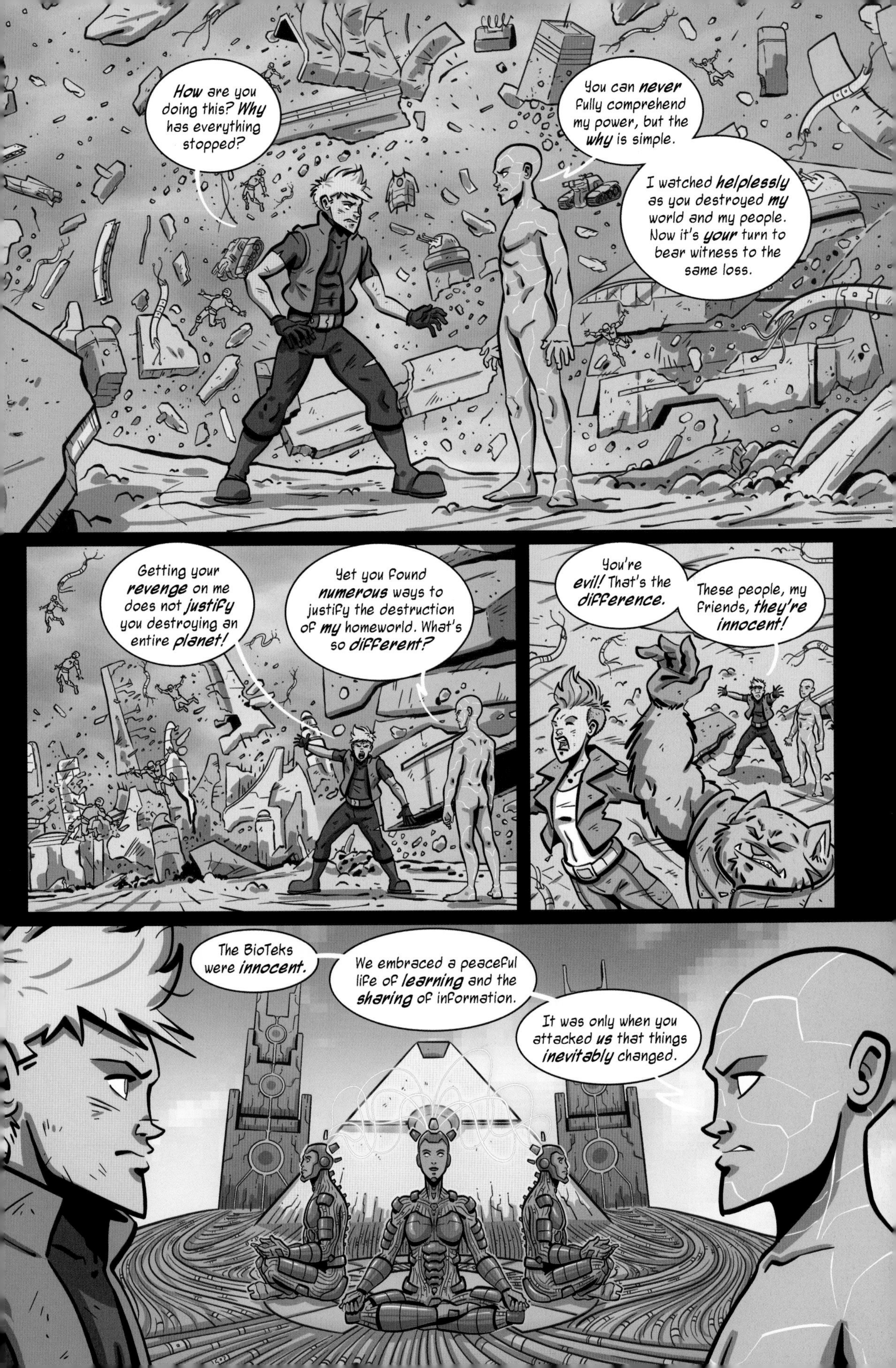

How are you doing this? Why has everything stopped?
You can never fully comprehend my power, but the why is simple.
I watched helplessly as you destroyed my world and my people. Now it's your turn to bear witness to the same loss.
Getting your revenge on me does not justify you destroying an entire planet!
Yet you found numerous ways to justify the destruction of my homeworld. What's so different?
You're evil! That's the difference.
These people, my friends, they're innocent!
The BioTeks were innocent.
We embraced a peaceful life of learning and the sharing of information.
It was only when you attacked us that things inevitably changed.

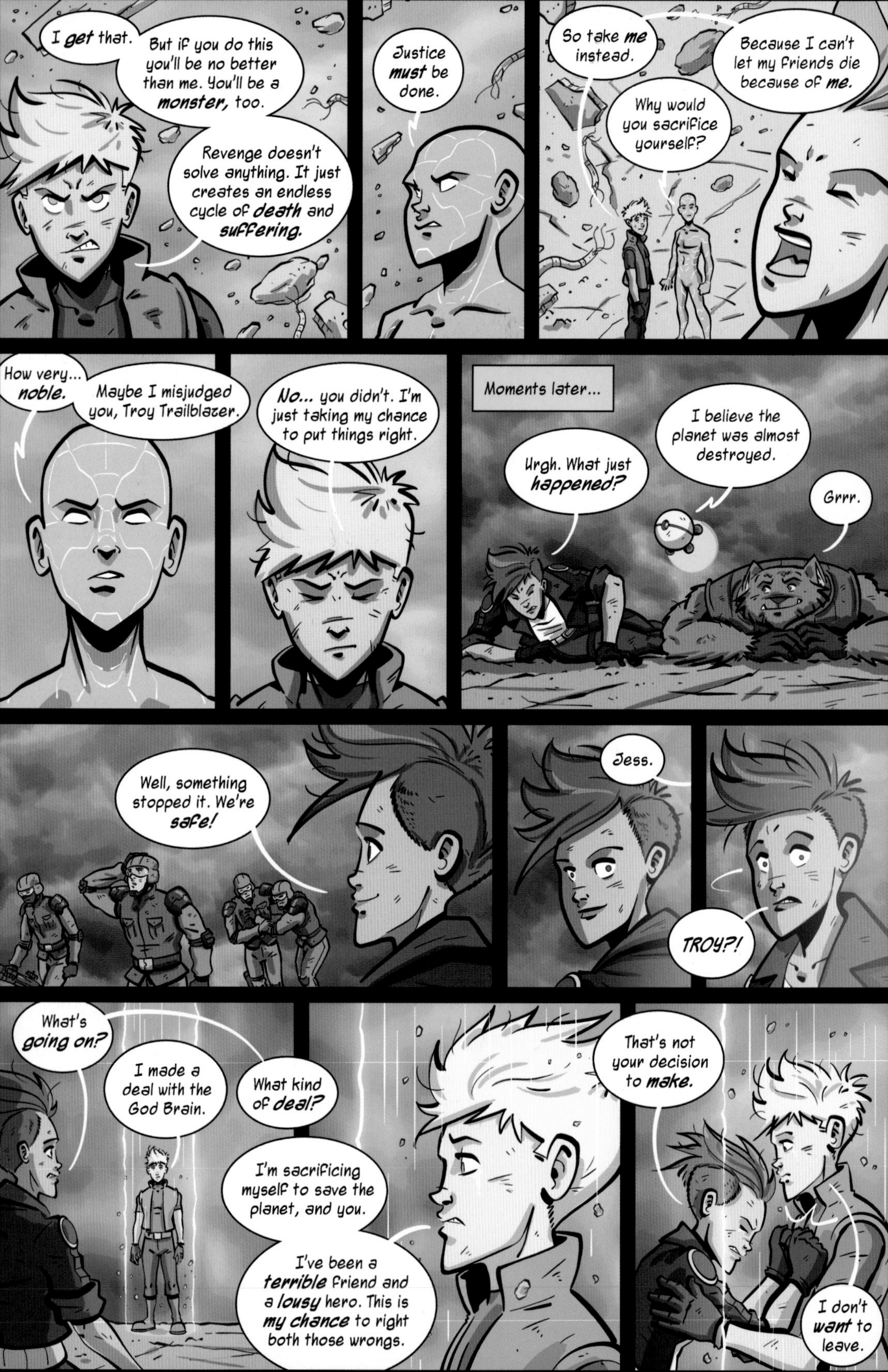

I get that.
But if you do this you'll be no better than me. You'll be a monster, too.
Revenge doesn't solve anything. It just creates an endless cycle of death and suffering.
Justice must be done.
So take me instead.
Because I can't let my friends die because of me.
Why would you sacrifice yourself?
How very... noble.
Maybe I misjudged you, Troy Trailblazer.
No... you didn't. I'm just taking my chance to put things right.
Moments later...
Urgh. What just happened?
I believe the planet was almost destroyed.
Grrr.
Well, something stopped it. We're safe!
Jess.
TROY?!
What's going on?
I made a deal with the God Brain.
What kind of deal?
I'm sacrificing myself to save the planet, and you.
I've been a terrible friend and a lousy hero. This is my chance to right both those wrongs.
That's not your decision to make.
I don't want to leave.

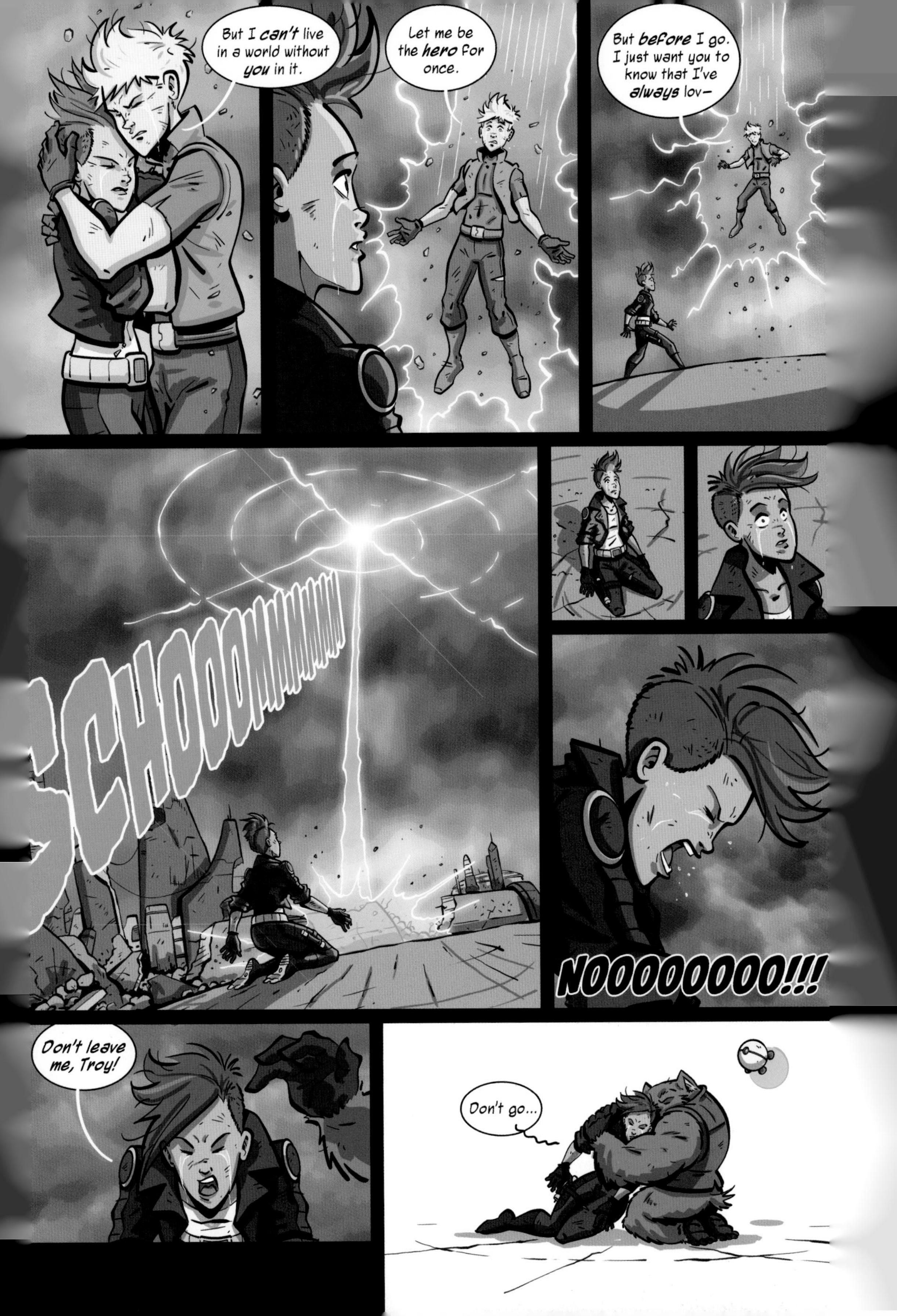

But I *can't* live in a world without *you* in it.
Let me be the *hero* for once.
But *before* I go. I just want you to know that I've *always* lov—
SCHOOMMMMMM
NOOOOOOOO!!!
Don't leave me, Troy!
Don't go...

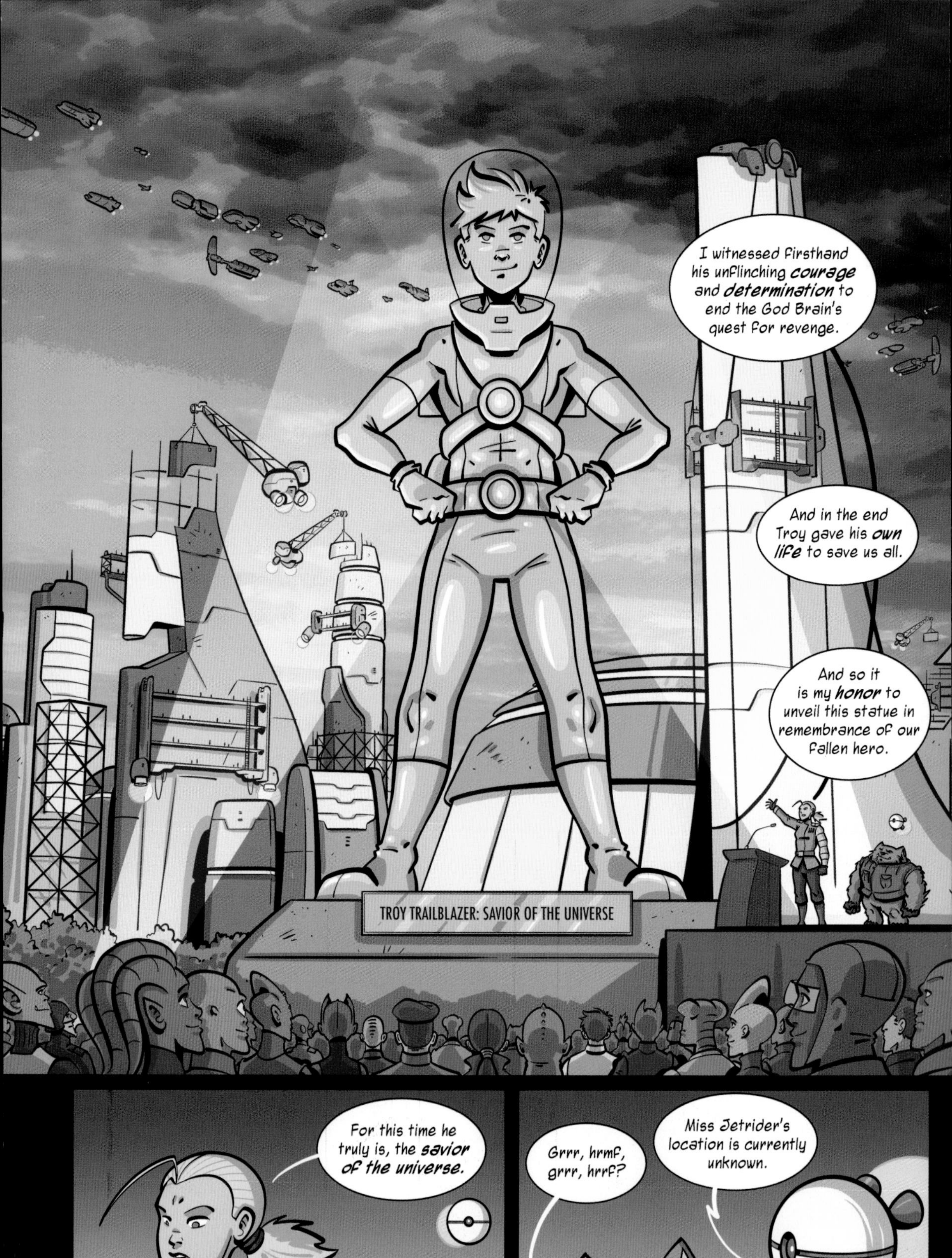
I witnessed firsthand his unflinching **courage** and **determination** to end the God Brain's quest for revenge.
And in the end Troy gave his **own life** to save us all.
And so it is my **honor** to unveil this statue in remembrance of our fallen hero.
TROY TRAILBLAZER: SAVIOR OF THE UNIVERSE

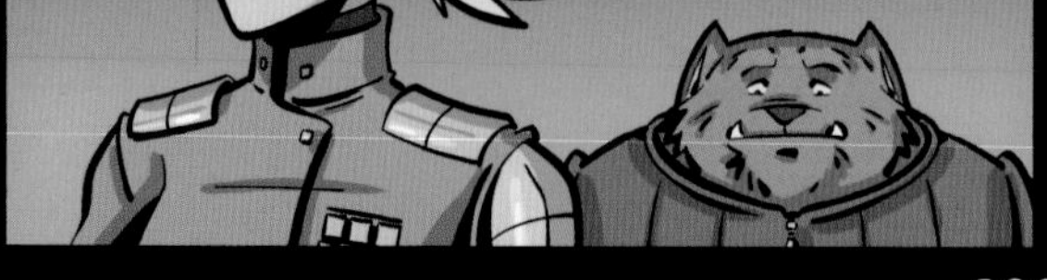
For this time he truly is, the **savior of the universe.**

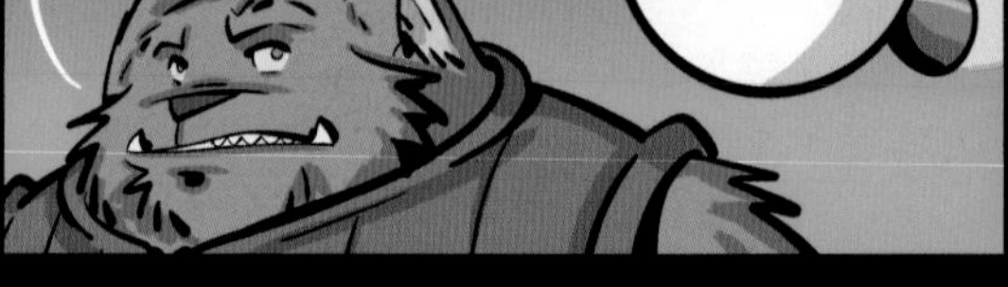
Grrr, hrmf, grrr, hrrf?
Miss Jetrider's location is currently unknown.

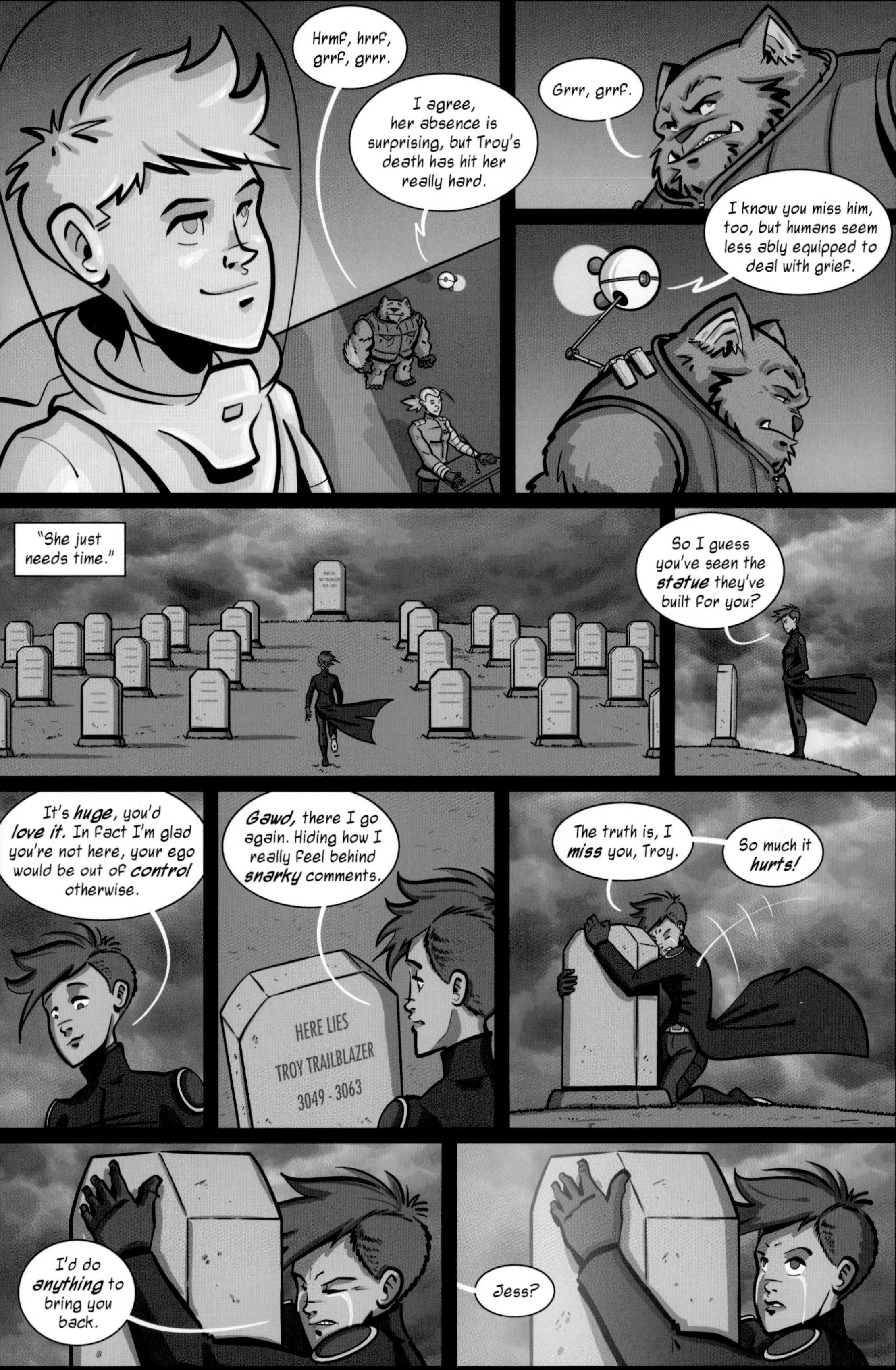
Hrmf, hrrf, grrf, grrr.
I agree, her absence is surprising, but Troy's death has hit her really hard.
Grrr, grrf.
I know you miss him, too, but humans seem less ably equipped to deal with grief.
"She just needs time."
So I guess you've seen the statue they've built for you?
It's huge, you'd love it. In fact I'm glad you're not here, your ego would be out of control otherwise.
Gawd, there I go again. Hiding how I really feel behind snarky comments.
HERE LIES
TROY TRAILBLAZER
3049 - 3063
The truth is, I miss you, Troy.
So much it hurts!
I'd do anything to bring you back.
Jess?

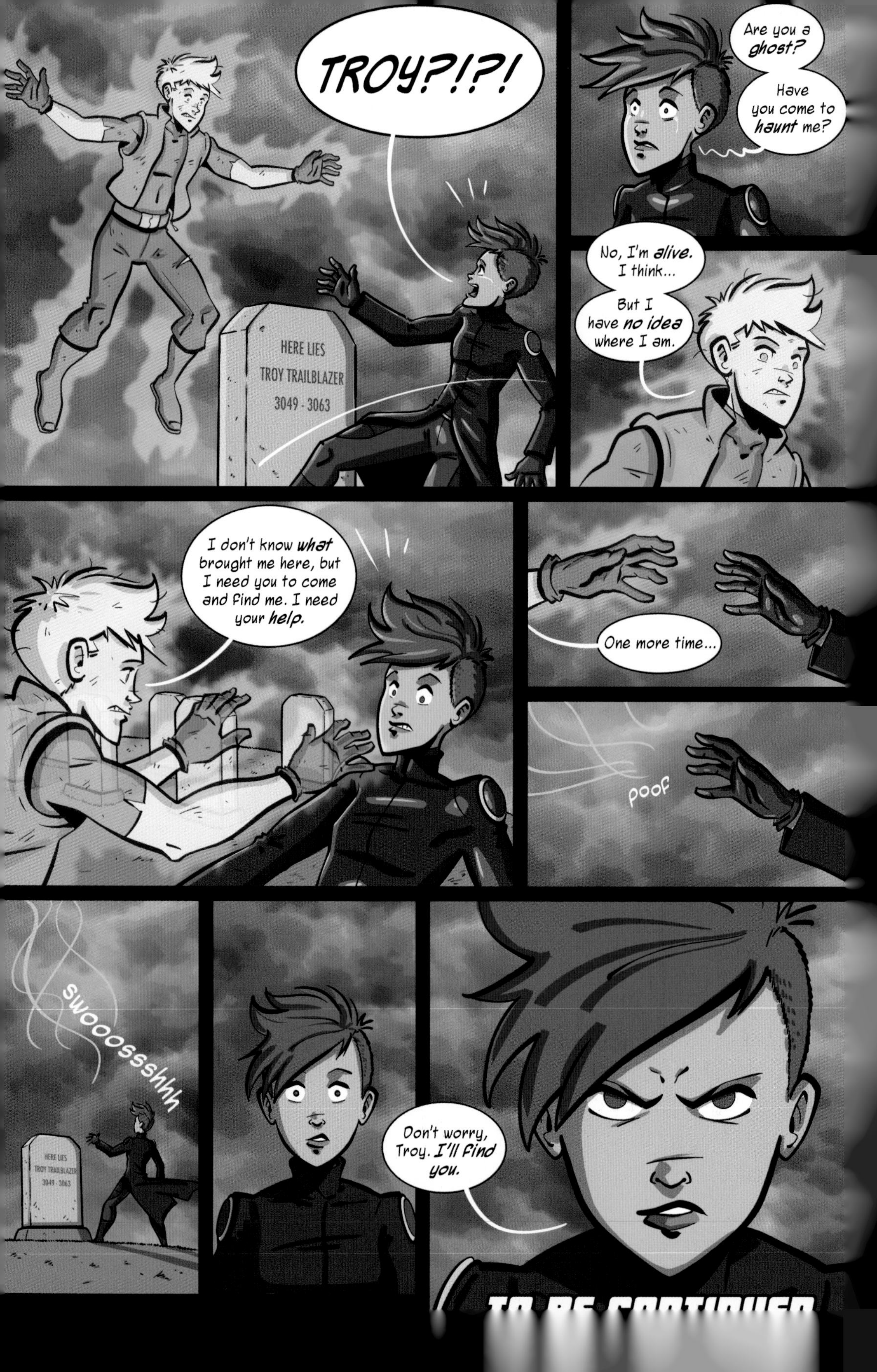
TROY?!?!
HERE LIES
TROY TRAILBLAZER
3049 - 3063
Are you a ghost?
Have you come to haunt me?
No, I'm alive. I think...
But I have no idea where I am.
I don't know what brought me here, but I need you to come and find me. I need your help.
One more time...
poof
swooossshhh
HERE LIES
TROY TRAILBLAZER
3049 - 3063
Don't worry, Troy. I'll find you.

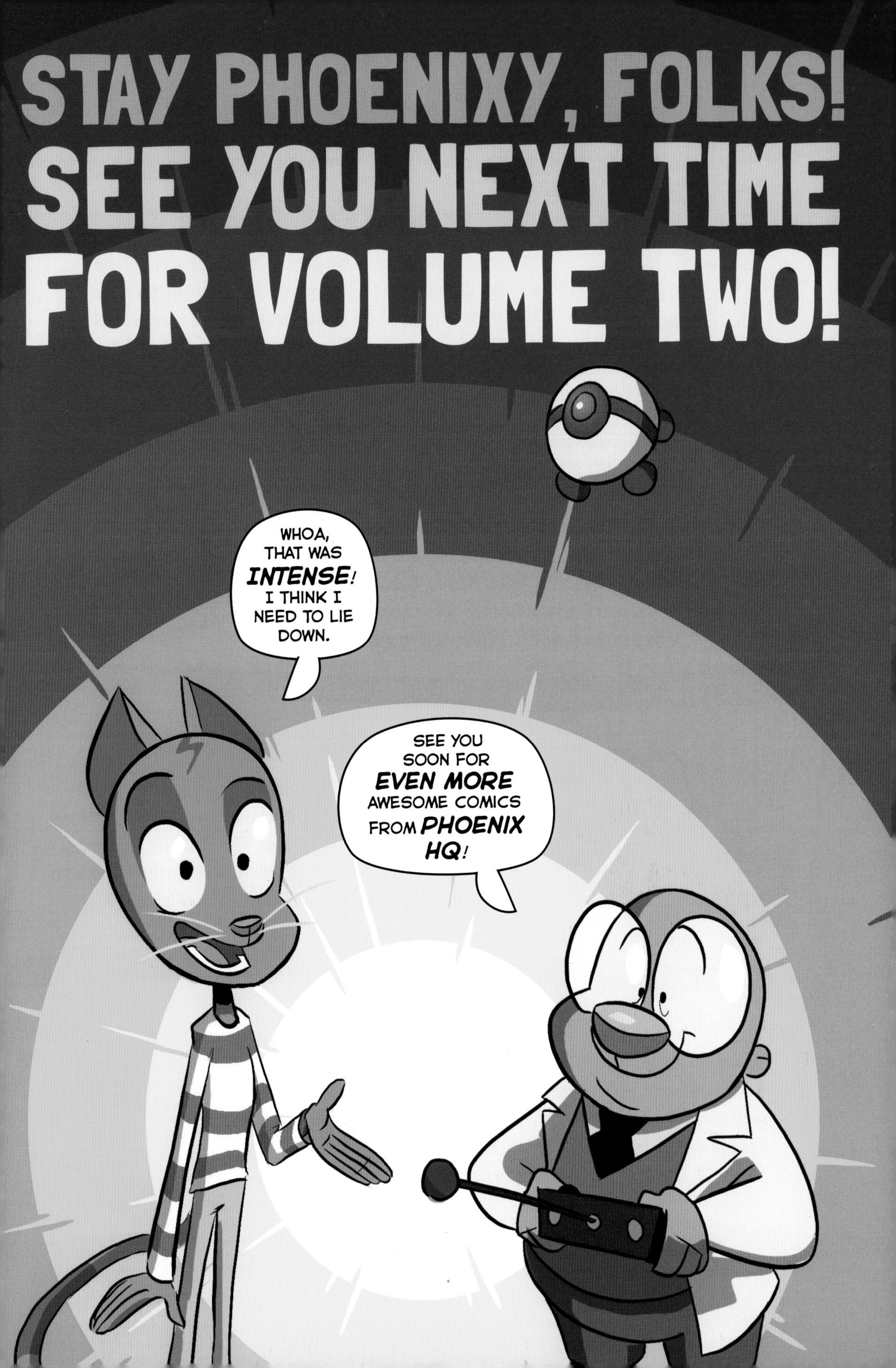
STAY PHOENIXY, FOLKS! SEE YOU NEXT TIME FOR VOLUME TWO!
WHOA, THAT WAS INTENSE! I THINK I NEED TO LIE DOWN.
SEE YOU SOON FOR EVEN MORE AWESOME COMICS FROM PHOENIX HQ!

# WHO MADE THESE

## ROBERT DEAS

is a comic artist and writer. In his early career, he worked on numerous manga adaptations of classics like *Macbeth*, and has since worked with companies such as Disney and IDW, and created his Stan Lee Excelsior Award–winning series, Trailblazers.

## JESS BRADLEY

is an illustrator and designer of cute, colorful, and quirky characters. Her clients include The Phoenix, Capstone Publishing, Igloo Books, Genki Gear, UK Greetings, and Carlton Books. She enjoys drawing, video games, and drinking too much tea.

## JAMIE SMART

has created colorful comics that have delighted children for over 20 years in the pages of publications such as *The Dandy*, *The Beano*, *The Phoenix*, and many more. He also creates children's books, including books for his ongoing multimedia project, *Find Chaffy*.

## CHRIS RIDDELL

is an illustrator and writer of children's books, and a political cartoonist for the *Observer*. His work has won numerous awards including two Kate Greenaway Medals and three Nestlé Smarties Prizes. He was the UK Children's Laureate from 2015–2017.

All the comics in this book originally appeared in the pages of THE PHOENIX comic, a weekly paper magazine published by a small a team in Oxford, England. Additional illustrations by Lee Robinson.

# AWESOME COMICS?

## MIKE SMITH

is an illustrator and comic creator. His story "Edward Hopper and the Carrot Crunch" won a Macmillan Prize, and his books include *The Hundred Decker Bus* and *Catch the Cuddle*. He also makes hilarious comic strips for *The Phoenix* under the name "Alexi Con."

## JOE LIST

is a designer and cartoonist from the north of England. He has a degree in Design: Animation and a toy protone gun signed by Ernie Hudson. He has worked with *The Phoenix*, *NME*, Hilton Hotels, M&S, Nike, Faber & Faber, DHL, and Usborne Books.

## LAURA ELLEN ANDERSON

is a children's book author and illustrator who also crafts world-domination plans for Evil Emperor Penguin. When not working, Laura enjoys doodling, baking, and making to-do lists.

## DAN BOULTWOOD

is an illustrator, comic artist, and writer. He has worked for Sony, Warner Bros., Eidos Interactive, and many other companies and publishers in the UK and US. He created Squid Squad and Haggis and Quail, and adapted Jamie Thomson's Dirk Lloyd for *The Phoenix*.

To find out more about **THE PHOENIX** comic, and maybe start reading it every week, visit our website: www.thephoenixcomic.co.uk

THIS BOOK WAS BROUGHT TO YOU BY

# Squid Bits!

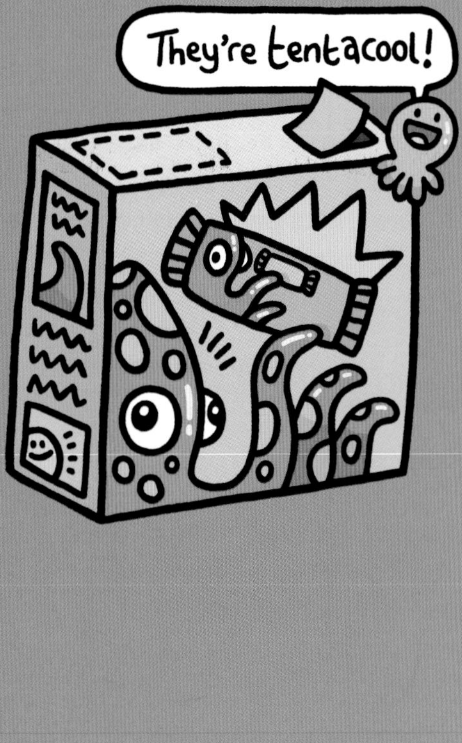
They're tentacool!

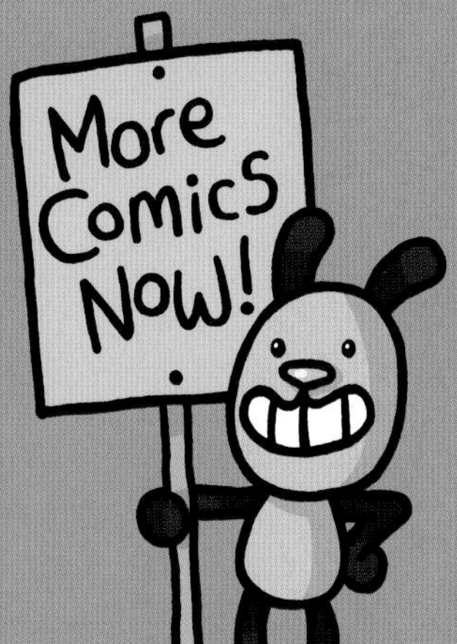
More Comics Now!

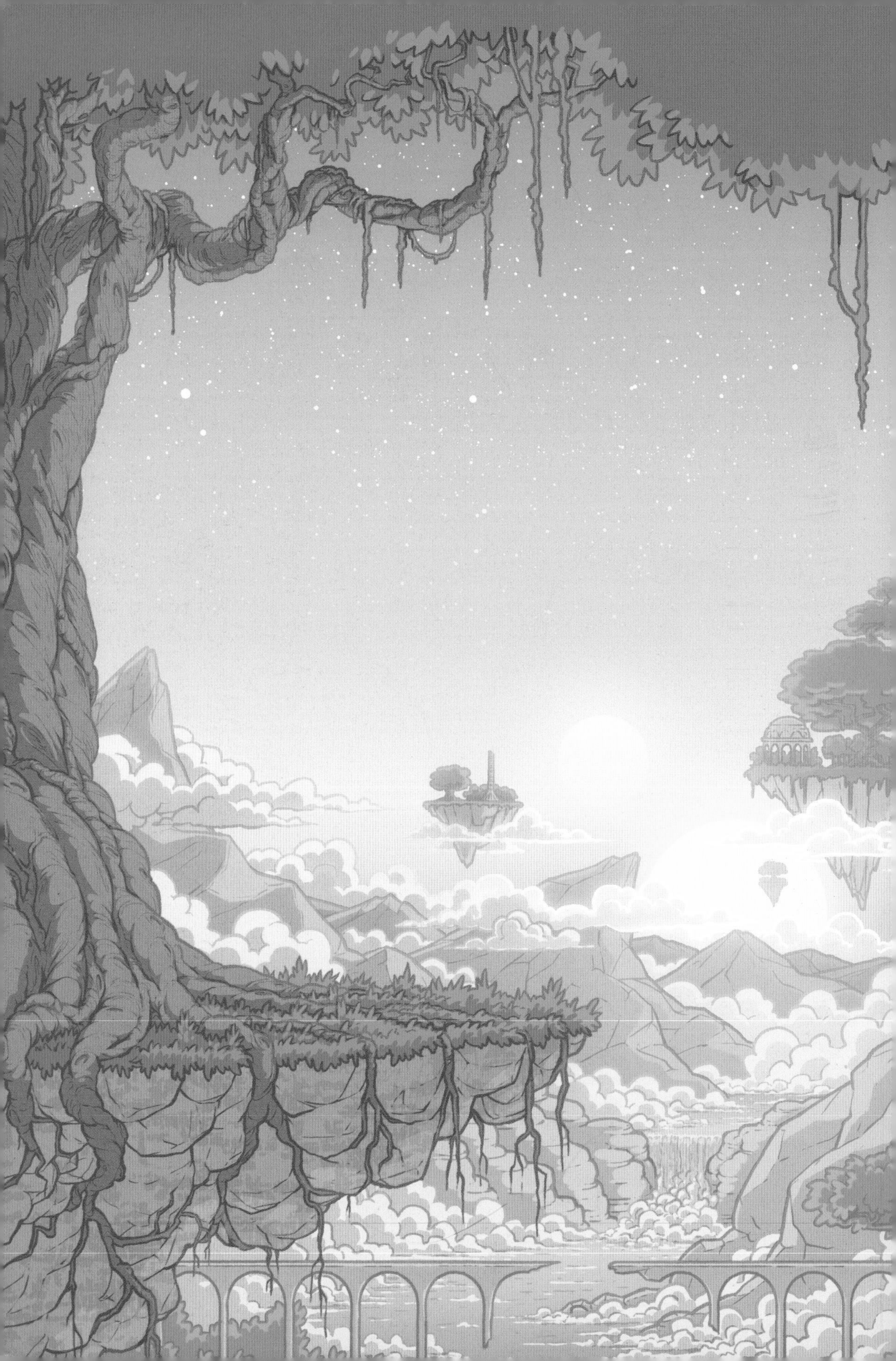